A Tale of the Tail
of
NINE STARS

An Inner and Outer Space Odyssey

Lawrence L. Stentzel III

authorHOUSE®

AuthorHouse™
1663 Liberty Drive
Bloomington, IN 47403
www.authorhouse.com
Phone: 1 (800) 839-8640

© *2018 Lawrence L. Stentzel III. All rights reserved.*

No part of this book may be reproduced, stored in a retrieval system, or transmitted by any means without the written permission of the author.

Published by AuthorHouse 05/22/2018

ISBN: 978-1-5462-4254-3 (sc)
ISBN: 978-1-5462-4253-6 (hc)
ISBN: 978-1-5462-4252-9 (e)

Library of Congress Control Number: 2018905875

Print information available on the last page.

Any people depicted in stock imagery provided by Getty Images are models, and such images are being used for illustrative purposes only.
Certain stock imagery © Getty Images.

This book is printed on acid-free paper.

Because of the dynamic nature of the Internet, any web addresses or links contained in this book may have changed since publication and may no longer be valid. The views expressed in this work are solely those of the author and do not necessarily reflect the views of the publisher, and the publisher hereby disclaims any responsibility for them.

1

Aludin was the senior communications expert on duty at the global holocom headquarters on the planet Ganahar when the spectrum-encoded light speed message came into the terminal at his workstation. It was flagged ultra top priority, and it was from *Eyes-On*, a cloaked and manned spy ship from the mysterious Om system, a system whose location in the Hub Galaxy remained unknown. What *was* known was that the technology of Om far surpassed that of any other known planetary civilization and that they had been transferring their knowledge to the people of Ganahar for hundreds of years. Om had been entirely benevolent, assisting all planet populations that had managed to attain interstellar travel, but thus far they had refused to intervene with the Kundabuffer Empire, spreading around the black hole at the core of the Hub Galaxy. *Eyes-On* was transmitting from the Kundabuffer system.

Two years previously, the planet Vox had been invaded and conquered by these aggressors, but while Vox had had a friendship alliance with both Om and Ganahar, Om had done nothing but evacuate one-tenth of 1 percent of the planet's five billion people before the death and destruction. The survivor's enslavement into the Kundabuffer galactic war machine was accomplished with terrible malice and efficiency.

Aludin read the message with shock and dread. On the Kundabuffer home world, an invasion force was mustering, and signals intercepted by *Eyes-On* confirmed that this force had the sole purpose of now conquering the Ganahar System for its resources.

The people of Om had real-time quantum communications and had left a satellite conversion relay orbiting Ganahar, which could receive quantum communications and convert them to spectrum-encoded light coms for reception on the planet surface. This meant *Eyes-On* had only sent it a minute ago.

The threat of invasion had been known for some time, since the empire had erected a quantum gate in the region of space between the five stars of the Raster Republic, of which Ganahar was one. Quantum gates served as portals and links between two points in space-time, allowing for instantaneous travel between them by entering the quantum void of all potential at one point only to emerge, popping back into existence, at the point on the other end of the link. Om had gone beyond the need for gates, establishing the link between points in space-time through their quantum communications technology.

Aludin was rattling off a long list of recipients to forward this message to, and each one appeared on the list of addresses on his hologram as he spoke the name. He was alerting the most exceptional individuals alive today on Ganahar—at least the ones who could be reached electronically. On his list were scientists, militia leaders of the Ganahar defense corps, university professors, civil servants, and executives from holo-satellite broadcast stations, transportation, energy production, resource development, distribution, and other sectors of Ganahar's moral anarchist society. They had done away with government thousands of years ago, but systems were in place for a council to be quickly elected to manage the crisis, keep the populace informed of events, and to mobilize and direct every level of their society in the war effort. But this would constitute Ganahar's first war in 30,829 years, and they were hopelessly ill prepared for violence with other humanoids.

With this long list sent, he next notified the leaders of the other four star systems of the Raster Republic. They did have governments. They were white star systems, like Om, and had received most of their technology—everything but weapons systems and war materials—from the people of Ganahar. Aludin then forwarded the message from *Eyes-On* to the capital planets of the United Lights and to the Kataleptica Star Union. Both were larger alliances of star systems than Raster, and the Raster Republic had treaties of trade, technology transfer, and friendship with them. These treaties included military commitments for defense from Imperial invasion.

A TALE OF THE TAIL OF NINE STARS

Aludin knew with certainty that it would not be enough, even if they all sent everything they had, which none would, as that would leave them completely vulnerable and undefended. The empire had 189 inhabited star systems and dozens of uninhabited ones for mining, all tyrannically set on war economies as part of its interstellar war machine. Only Om could save them, and it had a twenty-eight-thousand-year entrenched tradition of nonintervention. He'd found it chilling when they'd done nothing while their friends on Vox were mass slaughtered and the rest enslaved. His coworkers had sensed his mood of grave, anxious dread and gathered around him to read the fear-inspiring message.

Their yellow sun planetary system and civilization was older than even Om's, and as far as anyone knew, it was the most peaceful in the galaxy. The other four stars of the Raster Republic were white. In white star systems, life was found on the fourth planet from the sun, if it was there at all. With yellow stars, life appeared on the third planet from the sun. Although differences in gravitation and precise atmospheric composition existed, people from both yellow and white star systems could survive without life support or thermal suits, on yellow sun third planets and white sun fourth planets alike.

A female coworker broke into tears, and a couple of others ran to their workstations to contact their spouses. A coms specialist said to Aludin, "You know this message is announcing the destruction and death of our entire civilization."

An older man said, "Captain Swenah believes that Om truly needs our civilization for its own spiritual development, and the Clear Light Order vicar-general, Aton, who has a seat on the Om High Council, has made his support for intervention known to Om's allies. Captain Swenah disabled two Imperial battleships while making her final evacuation run from Vox."

Aludin stated, "I'm now forwarding the message, along with an official request for assistance, to Prime Minister Yona, in Om's capital. I'm sure she has already received the message itself from *Eyes-On*."

As he spoke the SEND command to his computer, a new message popped up on his hologram display, this one from Vicar-General Aton. It read, "I've called a meeting of the High Council and will determinedly advocate intervention in defense of Ganahar. The prime minister supports intervention as well."

Hope blossomed in the coms room, and moments later a renowned civil servant was on Global Holocom, on every frequency, employing the emergency communication system; directing the recruitment of defense volunteers, engineers, and technicians to weaponize small spacecraft and large space ships alike; and to follow Om's recommendations. The latter were received when the Kundabuffer gate was still under construction, to install propulsion on all orbiting space stations and weapons platforms in order to avoid dumb ordnance fired from the edge of their solar system.

The civil servant directed city populations to evacuate to established locations, providing the coordinates where the general population might gather and shelter. He provided time schedules for the shutting down of all fusion reactors and of all wind, solar, geothermal, and hydroelectric plants. Categories of jobs and skills that were needed for the war effort and recruitment locations given for each population center were described. These locations could be navigated to easily using personal handheld devices, and the link symbols for each were displayed prominently at the bottom of the holo of the speaking civil servant.

Aludin contacted the transportation communications department of his headquarters complex, requesting a drone to carry the message from *Eyes-On* to the Im of the Islohar in the Haraga Mountains and to arrange drones to carry the message to other people of influence who were out of touch electronically. A message from a prominent local civil servant appeared on Aludin's holo, requesting that he personally handle the communications being sent to elect further functionaries to the crisis council, and of course Aludin agreed to do this. He was a practitioner of the ancient Islohar and adhered to their ways.

On Ganahar, no one had authority over anyone else and no one could ever tell anyone else what to do. A universal culture and disposition to always consider the collective common good in every individual personal decision had evolved to such an extent that cooperation among the people of Ganahar was a spontaneous and immediate movement whenever they were called upon to act. A threat of this nature and magnitude had never confronted them before. Every able-bodied person

A TALE OF THE TAIL OF NINE STARS

from age sixteen to sixty-five was gathering at one or another war-effort recruiting center, while the rest were evacuating into hiding and bringing only what they were told to bring. Organizational networks were springing up all over the globe, and work was being accomplished to the highest standards at a rate never before seen.

Aludin routed coms for the existing council in its efforts to expand its membership and capacity. His older coworker was busy sending pleas for help to every collective of star systems in the galaxy that had not already fallen under the lash of the Kundabuffer Empire. A reply refusing any assistance at all had already come in from Trade Partners Incorporated, which was an alliance and affiliation of thirteen resource-rich star systems with inhabitable planets. Help from them had not really been expected anyway. The old man knew that even if every independent collective and lone star state came to their rescue, they would still be unable to repel an Imperial invasion force. But logistical facts and realities had no dampening effect on the man's efforts nor on the efforts of any on Ganahar. They would fight to survive, to defend their existence as a civilization, no matter how futile; and they would do this with a level of cooperation, unity, self-sacrifice, and intense ferocity never before seen in this galaxy.

The empire was a total anomaly. The pattern of development of biological life, from simple organisms to mammals and humanoids, often culminated in a nuclear winter or within two centuries of discovering nuclear fission, complete self-destruction as a result of the "four killers" as they were known, concluding with the extinction of birds and mammals and sometimes of the entire biosphere.

Only those populations who had discovered their unity and realized equality in pure immaterial eternal consciousness, and were thus able to see beyond the illusory duality of a subject who knows and an object that is known, were capable of working together to survive and live sustainably in harmony with each other and their environment.

There had been a built-in self-regulating mechanism allowing only benign humanoid populations the technological advancement of interstellar travel, but in the case of the people of Kundabuffer, they had been the first to slip back into ego duality after attaining unity and achieving interstellar travel. Their fall had now become a nightmare for every other planet in the Hub Galaxy.

From the science and data given to them by Om, Aludin knew the pattern. The four killers were mismanagement of resources, overpopulation, pollution, and global climate change that destroyed all agriculture. In the case of planets with a great deal of ice present on the surface, this heating process would invariably put coasts and islands underwater and, in extreme cases, evaporate all usable fresh water and fry the entire biosphere.

Ganahar had gone through its own "crisis" nearly fifty-two thousand years ago—though great musical compositions, theater plays, poetry, literature, sacred texts, holo movies, and more—had kept it alive and cultivated understanding of these processes in the minds of all on Ganahar.

Ganahar had attained interstellar travel first, among the five star systems of the Raster Republic, and had transferred technologies to its four allies over the years. Om made contact with Ganahar about the time the Raster Republic was forming and introduced them to hull materials like adamantine, composite ceramic heat shield armor, fiberglass armor, and plasteel heat resistant armor. They gave Ganahar a new generation of quantum computer hardware and software, water purification technology at the atomic level, hybrid oxygen super-generating organisms and plants, and vortex redirection and generation turbines that could simulate centripetal gravity in its local effects (allowing for life in space without physical deterioration). There was an entire new dimension of spectrographic space-time imaging and sensor data acquisition systems; incredible miniaturization specifications for fusion reactors, employing some of the new hull materials along with carbon plate armor; and principles of electricity when directed within magnetic fields, which resulted in the development of force field shields and both beam and blaster weapons systems. With a new calculus and the exact value and formula to account for the curvature and fold of the greater universe, they received the science of quantum navigation.

Aludin knew, from the Im of Islohar, that the people of Om had been contacted by a highly advanced race of post-humanoids called the Amonrahonians, who corrected Om's paradigms and tweaked their mathematical formulas, expelled egocentricity from their sciences, and gave them a number of galaxy maps in perpetual motion, which required a new leap in their quantum computer sciences to contain accurately. The Amonrahonians had also informed Om of an alien race and empire within a distant galaxy of mostly blue stars that was exterminating human populations within the white and yellow star systems of their galaxy as well as within two other galaxies. This meeting between the people of Om and the Amonrahonians had occurred 8,029 years ago, and the study of blue star systems had commenced for Om at that time.

The Amonrahonians had also delivered certain explicit predictions involving specific individual humans and cosmic events relating to the precise time coordinates in which they were all living right now, foreseen by some method incomprehensible even to the top scientists of Om.

The Im of Islohar was one of two primary individual humans identified in these predictions. Aludin wanted to be at his teacher's side, but the Im had requested that he apply his talents to serving the people of Ganahar by filling the position of senior coms expert at headquarters. So here he was, and here he would remain, until the Imperials killed him or until Om stopped the invasion.

2

Aton was the vicar-general of the most ancient spiritual tradition on Om, dating back to its most remote antiquity, called the Clear Light Order. He was speaking with Nemellie, the order's abbot, regarding the pending council meeting he'd called. As vicar- general, he had the only nonelected seat on the High Council and, like the prime minister, represented the entire planet rather than a particular district. He said to Nemellie, "This is the year we have been counting down to, and which hundreds of generations before us have looked ahead to speculatively, for over eight thousand years. We've been refitting and enhancing one of our old star cruisers at the shipyard on the big asteroid, Phat, out in the asteroid tail, for several months now, in preparation for the mission."

"Does it have our newest tech? Cloaking generators? Micro-jumping quantum drives and navigation computers?"

"It does," Aton assured her, "and it has a third again as much power as any ship of its class, allowing for enhanced shield and weapons systems."

"She really doesn't have a clue, does she?" Nemellie inquired, already knowing the answer.

"We won't know for sure," Aton reminded her, "until it is confirmed by the person of interest on Ganahar."

"There's no question in my mind," she disagreed.

"I'm of the same mind as you on this, but confirmation has been agreed to as a requirement. I'll send her to collect this person of interest right after I attend the High Council meeting."

"How will you send her when we don't know precisely where on Ganahar this person of interest is staying?" she asked anxiously.

"I'm sending Pez to our contact, Attar, in the capital city on Ganahar. He will know the location."

"She's going to be in shock when you tell her," Nemellie predicted.

"I'm enrolling her in an intensive twelve- to fourteen-hour a day training program with the space marines in the zero-gravity dome on the star fleet campus, so she'll have little time or energy to ponder it. The person of interest will keep her busy with new spiritual training and practices, completing her preparation."

Nemellie lamented, "Well, it's about time. I've taught her everything I know, and she's mastered all of it."

"I also have nothing left to teach her and can only guide her martial arts cultivation now," Aton admitted.

"She is truly ready to replace me as abbot," she told him, stoking the ongoing competition between them. It was the only thing they had never agreed on.

"Tiny as she is, Om has never had such a warrior maiden, knight, or marshal," he argued, "and as the next vicar-general, she would have a seat on the High Council."

"She would make such an abbot as we have never seen before!"

"She will choose for herself after the big mission," Aton said with finality, closing the topic.

"Do you think the council will vote to intervene on behalf of Ganahar?"

"It had better," Aton said with conviction, "or Ganahar will go the way of Vox, enslaved into the Imperial war machine, their culture eradicated and their lives reduced to mere subsistence. Then there are the death squads, hunting down potential revolutionaries and disappearing them."

Nemellie warned, "Ganahar has saturnium, and if the Kundabuffer Empire gets its hands on that, it would increase the power of their warships tenfold, making them an even bigger menace to their neighbors."

"You don't need to convince me," Aton said, frustrated. "It's our nonintervention policy of the past twenty-eight thousand years, since we first began interstellar travel."

"Well, now there's a malignancy swallowing primitive and advanced worlds in our galaxy, and many of them are our friends and allies," Nemellie declared with increasing emotion.

I'm going to do everything I possibly can to advocate intervention on Ganahar's behalf," Aton promised. "No one wants another Vox."

"We're speaking of Ganahar, a population of yellow sun humans who abided in unity on their planet sustainably for almost thirty thousand years before talking the slightest interest in space travel. They are likely the most evolved planetary population in our galaxy—and also the least able to defend themselves against military might."

"I concur with you, and I have Prime Minister Yona on our side. It's such a pity that prior agreements prevent us from filling her in completely. I still believe we'll be able to reach a unanimous decision to intervene."

"If those extremist peace and isolation advocates get going," she suggested, "then just show some holoclips of the destruction involved, and the loss of life, in the empire's conquest of Vox."

"Not a bad idea," he agreed.

"Our technology is so far advanced of the empire's that it's not like any of our ships or personnel would be at risk."

"Losses and expenses will not be an issue of the noninterventionists," Aton informed her. Then he noticed the time on his peripheral display and told her, "I'd better head to the council meeting and see if I can get an operation initiated to stop the invasion force."

Om was the last star system in a tail of nine stars extending off a spiral arm of the Hub Galaxy. The tail itself continued with asteroids, some the size of dwarf planets, for over a light minute beyond Om's star. This tail of nine stars was both outside of and part of the Hub Galaxy. The third and sixth stars of the tail had human life, and once into space travel, Om made contact with each, transferring science and technology in a sequence designed not to disrupt their societies. The asteroid arm extending out in an arc beyond the Om system was the most resource-rich region of the entire Hub Galaxy.

Om's alliance with the sixth star of the tail, Rah, and the third star, Haum, involved foreign policy only, and all of the three were free to conduct their domestic policies as they saw fit, within the bounds of the law of reciprocity. The alliance was internally known as the Tail of Nine, though this was never spoken to anyone outside the tail, as it would provide a clear indication of their location within their galaxy, making them far too easy to find.

No other planet or alliance besides the Tail of Nine had quantum coms, so Om placed conversion satellites orbiting the planets of their friends, turning spectrum coding light coms into quantum coms, and vice versa. Om and the Tail of Nine were the only ones to go beyond quantum gates and the only ones to employ the element solarium for nuclear fusion. The Kundabuffer Empire was using marsnium, generally the first fusion element employed by humanoids, since it was the most abundant and widespread. There were five known nuclear fusion elements, and the power differential between them, in order of their availability in the universe, was tenfold, until the jump between mercurium and solarium, which was a hundredfold.

Only Om and the Tail of Nine had brain-impulse skullcaps replacing keyboards and voice commands, adapted from military applications for weapons systems operations and fire control. The skullcap technology had its origins in medicine, was employed for operating prostheses, and had already achieved considerable sophistication before the military took hold of it. Now the skullcap was finding applications everywhere, in all spheres of life.

The Tail of Nine were also the only ones in the galaxy to have developed micro-jumping quantum drive and navigation capacity. Micro-jumping was now part of their weapons research and development. It was theoretically possible to micro-jump a smart torpedo beyond the shields of a ship or building, placing the device within the interior to explode inside rather than be lost on the shields.

On the High Council, Aton's wisdom was respected, though he represented less than one millionth of a percent of the population, while each of the other members represented 8 to 12 percent. There were eleven High Council members plus the prime minister, constituting this highest branch of government. Candidates for prime minister had to have earned an advanced degree and were required to train for five years at the Clear Light monastery. The training consisted of two years of classes, seminars, contemplative practices, and a three-year solitary meditation retreat within a little cell in the monastery. Graduates, of which there were few, were called omni-scholars, and they were eligible to run for the office of prime minister.

Aton was held up by a knight commander who needed urgently to make his report, insisting it couldn't wait. Being late to council meetings did not sit well with Aton, so he injected more energy and spring into his gait, increasing his speed down the long corridor after extracting himself from the conversation with the commander.

Sure enough, he was the last to arrive and offered sincere apologies to the group as he took his seat. Yona, a rather striking woman in her early fifties, ceremoniously opened the meeting after giving Aton a disapproving look. She was Om's elected prime minister, a graduate of the Thunder Perfect Mind Academy and a recognized omni-scholar. Her victory in the election had been by a landslide, and the people loved her. As soon as she finished intoning the sacred sound formula for opening the meeting, Yona informed them, "The Kundabuffer Empire is preparing to invade one of the star systems of the Rastar Republic, with whom we have an alliance treaty of friendship. It does not require us to intervene militarily, of course."

Senelle, the young female delegate representing a district largely employed in programming, data processing, R & D, and administrative functions, posed the question, "Are they capable of defending themselves?"

"No," Yona answered. "The Raster Republic is hardly more advanced technologically than the Kundabuffer Empire and has but a meager defense. They are far more consciously evolved, seeking only peace and unity."

Senelle asked, "What of their other allies?"

"Their other allies are small by comparison to the empire," Yona explained. "The United Lights has twenty-eight star systems, and Kataleptica Star Union has seventeen inhabited stars, but the Kundabuffer Empire now has one hundred and eighty-nine inhabited systems and has all of them working to sustain and enlarge its space fleet and troops for its Imperial expansion."

Aton explained further. "The empire is aware that the star of Raster they intend to invade has saturnium, and they have yet to find their own source for this. If they get their hands on saturnium, the firepower of their fleet will multiply ten times within half a decade."

"Will the United Lights and Kataleptica come to Raster's aid?" Senelle inquired.

It was Anella, the delegate with the most star fleet industries in her district, who answered Senelle. "The empire makes its invasions with massive force, including at least eighteen battleships, more than twenty of their star cruisers, giant troop transports, and many dozens of destroyers, patrol ships, and smaller assault ships. Their ground troops were a half million strong in their invasion of Vox. Each of their battleships carries a mix of one hundred and sixty small fighters and fighter-bomber spacecraft. They first launch half-ton alloy balls at all immobile targets from well outside the orbit of the planet they target as they rush in calculating their movements and where the target will be in the particular moment of space-time when their projectile arrives. The Rasterians will only be able to evacuate their immobile positions in the face of that onslaught."

Senelle observed, "We have never shown ourselves to the empire before. They have no idea we exist, and this has been our strategy."

Borax, the most senior in years at the table and a retired star fleet admiral, suggested, "We could disable their battleships on their way from their closest gate to the Raster star system they intend to attack. We can do this from full-cloaking mode and discourage this invasion before it has begun."

Aton pointed out, "The Raster Republic stars are part of the core of the galaxy and are now on the border of the empire's territory. The empire won't give up and will spread around them as well as expand in the opposite direction toward our allies in the Gamor Confederation. The Kemplar Unity stars will also soon be at risk. We have entered a new situation."

Bolisades opined, "It might be time to check all expansion of the murderous and insatiable empire of Kundabuffer—in a fashion that would require a visit to their home world."

"No one else in the galaxy is causing trouble of such magnitude," Betenya offered. She represented the largest district in terms of square miles, containing about 8 percent of the planet's population, involved mostly in agriculture.

Yona asked, "Do we protect our allies or do we maintain our stance of nonintervention?"

Welendra, the former cultural minister and once a diva of the performing arts, stated, aghast, "Surely we are not going to kill any humans, no matter how murderous or meddlesome."

"If any life-form threatens the Tail of Nine, you can be sure there are those of us prepared to kill sentients," Borax assured her. "I won't sit back and watch thirty-three thousand years of recorded history end and fade into oblivion, nor will I just lie down and die."

Aton agreed. "It is the purpose of the Clear Light Order to defend our three home worlds and protect the prime minister and members of the High Council. We have preserved the highest and most effective martial arts of the past thirty thousand years and trained diligently in them."

Borax informed Welendra, "The mission of star fleet is to defend our home planet and Phat. Ever since we discovered firsthand the threat from the Xegachtznel Galaxy, we have been building enormous ships crammed with solarium fusion reactors and weapons. We have five of these operational, plus our old battleships and cruisers. We are by no means prepared if those aliens were to attack us now."

"We have not seen so much as a probe drone of theirs in this galaxy yet," Helenola, former health minister and renowned physician, declared at the table.

Zad, the former head of fleet engineering, updated them. "We have a stealth shield generator covering Phat, at quite an expense, I might add. The shield makes the solarium impossible to detect with sensors. We know the aliens are able to detect solarium from quite a distance and use probes, as we do, to locate deposits. The problem is that the whole asteroid arm is fairly rich, and we cannot shield that."

I understand," Yona informed them, "that Phat reads as the great lodestone out of the entire asteroid arm and that we are mining the other hot spots that we locate just as fast as we can. Practically all other mining operations have been reduced to twenty percent of normal to get teams, ships, and equipment out there and get it done."

Zad added, "Fleet engineering recently finished testing a prototype probe hunter-destroyer drone, and it passed with flying colors, so manufacturing is already turning out hundreds per day. Many have been deployed. They fire high-velocity nonexplosive warheads with precision maneuverability and tracking so that the result will appear to have been due to space debris collision. Our new probe hunters are fully cloaked to any sensors."

"Not to beat a dead horse," Welenda asked, "but was it actually the right thing for Captain Swenah to do, pinging the alien ship with a full array of active sensors?"

Borax defended the captain. "She was in full stealth mode, and the data we now have is invaluable. It may very well save our civilization. So yes, it was absolutely the right thing to do, and she got the hell out of there and through quantum space to a secure uninhabited star system in the Sparkling Disk Galaxy. She was not followed."

Doboz, former captain of industry, pointed out, "Now the aliens know there are beings in the universe with technologies to match their own and, in cloaking, exceed them."

Jard, a scientist and a high-tech genius, told them, "Captain Swenah sent a tight-beam active sensor wave while accelerating to jump speed, receiving quite clear data. Her stealth shields were hit with only a non-direct expanding spherical wave at point six nine nine light speed, hyper-accelerating and with her quantum drives already engaged. I'm certain the most information they received was her fixed location and speed at point of contact with their wave—and not even her precise direction."

"Thank you, Jard," Yona said with affection. He'd been one of her professors at the academy and was without a doubt the most brilliant one. Now it was Welenda who received Yona's disapproving look as Yona said, "Now that we have put to rest, again, the issue of Captain Swenah's decision-making, we are faced with our position regarding the pending invasion of the Raster Republic." Then a frustrated look came across her face. "Could someone please tell me the name of the specific star system about to be invaded—and perhaps something about it?"

Aton explained. "The people of Raster call it Ganahar, and it is a yellow sun system, with the planet Ganahar third in orbit around it.

Their day is a sixth shorter than ours is, and they are frail by comparison to us. The other four stars of the Raster Republic are white stars, and their people are quite similar to us. The people of Ganahar achieved global unity almost thirty thousand years before they looked into space travel. Of the five Raster systems, they were the first to develop it, and they shared their technology. Ganahar has no government per se. It is a moral anarchy. In this emergency, a large group of experts gathered and elected a small council as the decision-making body to handle this crisis. They are already emptying their cities and putting together what defense they can muster. The other four planets of the Republic have each sent half of their total space fleets to Ganahar and ground troops as well."

"What is the population of Ganahar?" Yona asked.

Aton replied, "They keep their population stable at three billion by intention but once had nine point six billion living there."

"What other preparations do they make?" Yona inquired.

"I received a report just before this meeting," Aton explained, "which is why I was late, and I'm told they have shut down nuclear fusion plants and all power sources to urban areas. Not just to sleep mode but totally dead. They've taken our advice and put space drives on their space stations, space construction platforms, and space weapons platforms. They have also mobilized their ground-to-space weapons on the planet surface. Anyone willing on Ganahar is being armed. Their military and paramilitary forces are positioned strategically and intelligently. They stand no chance until it becomes a ground war. Once the empire has full space supremacy, though, the ground war does not stand a chance. Ganahar will become part of the Imperial war machine, and the other star systems of the Raster Republic will each fall to the same fate."

"How tragic!" Welenda blurted out, horrified.

Borax stated firmly, "I urge this council to consider intervention. The star fleet can hit their battleships with high-power shield-disruptor missiles, beam and blaster weapons, and rocket and space-drive missiles. We can hit each at an unoccupied area of the ship and possibly pull the whole thing off without a single Imperial fatality.

"Our first line of defense ought to be to hack their computer command functions and just drive them back to their gate and through it," Jard said. "We need only attach enough nanobots to their hull, and those will make the link for us. We were designing new tech and applications for quantum computers before their civilization had made a mechanical bead calculator."

"How do we get the nanobots through their shields?" Borax wanted to know.

"We have a space-drive missile that fires them in a spray only feet before contact with and disintegration upon their shields. The individual nanobots can pass through undetected, even groups of them. The empire employs rather primitive shields, leaving them vulnerable to concentrated microwave beams of sufficient power and other things that our shields protect against."

"Are our shields protection against the nanobots?" Borax asked, alarmed.

Zad jumped in to answer, sensing Jard about to launch into a technical oral dissertation over most everyone's heads, and said, "The shield technology is now understood as bandwidths within a spectrum. We have discovered the entire spectrum and have all of it covered in spiraling triplicate, creating a tight seal. Unfortunately, so do the aliens."

"But not the shields of the human Kundabuffer Empire," Jard stated.

"Has diplomacy been tried fully?" Daboz asked.

Yona answered, "All three of our allies closest to the core have sent many brave diplomats, and those sent in the past three months have not again been heard from."

Anella said, "I'm in favor of some form of intervention on behalf of Ganahar. We cannot allow the empire to enslave our friends and use them in the conquest of further worlds."

Yona asked, "Is there anyone opposed to intervention with the Kundabuffer Empire on behalf of the Raster Republic?"

Daboz started to put his hand up, got it just above the table yet angled near horizontal, and then looked around and lowered it.

Raising her own hand, Yona asked, "All in favor of intervention?"

All of them but Daboz put their hands up immediately, and as their gazes landed on him, Daboz reluctantly raised his own. He told them, "With the threat of the aliens and all of our preparations for that, this is a lot to take on."

Yona stated, "Your point is duly noted, Daboz. Now that we have reached unanimity, we must invite Senior Admiral Zapa to meet with us this evening. Are we agreed that taking control of their ships ought to be our first plan, and only failing that, we will attempt to disable their battleships, trying to do so without fatalities? If so, raise your hands."

All hands went up. Yona told them, "We will take a break until seventeen hundred hours; that should be more than adequate time for everyone to eat and freshen up."

As the council members rose to leave, Yona caught Aton's eye and said, "Could I have but a moment of your time?"

"But of course, Madam Prime Minister. I am at your service."

Yona told him with great concern, "I think the person we seek from the world with the yellow sun is on Ganahar. The timing of this invasion could not be worse."

"I quite agree with you," Aton replied gravely. "I was thinking of sending Marshal Pez, though if you think I ought to go myself, I certainly will."

"She is quite young," Yona commented. Then she asked, "What of Marshals Hark and Elisia?"

"Marshal Hark will be preparing a company of knight commandos to go with the ship we send to stop the invasion, and Marshal Elisia is in the United Lights as we speak, attempting to convince them to go to the aid of Ganahar. Pez is a prodigy and has set new records for our most difficult tests. She may only be thirty-two years old, yet out of all of our order, only the abbot and I can uproot and defeat her in the soft martial arts. She can go into a pure delta brain wave state, sustaining it for many hours, with the internal sitting practice. She has my complete confidence."

"I hadn't realized," Yona exclaimed, impressed. "Do you really think she's the one? I so hope we are right about this."

"I do," Aton told her seriously with confidence. "No other light on Om shines so brightly."

"This is good news," Yona declared, igniting with hope. "Send her immediately."

Aton bowed and replied, "At once, Madam Prime Minister."

3

Back at the monastery of the Clear Light Order, Aton summoned Pez to his office. She came at once, and he ushered her in to take a seat before sitting behind his desk.

He told her, "I have an urgent mission of dire importance for you, Marshal Pez. It comes directly from the prime minister. Every schoolchild in the Tail of Nine knows of our contact with the Amonrahonians over eight millenniums ago, but what is not commonly known are the predictions they shared with us back then. They completed our star maps of a number of galaxies and gave us many more, corrected a few errors we were carrying, and shared technology with us based on laws that we had not even imagined. They also warned of an alien race found on the fifth planet of some blue stars in blue star galaxies that would attempt to eradicate all humanoid species in the universe. Fifteen years ago, Admiral Kranster—Captain Kranster back then—observed this program of extermination in progress within a very distant blue galaxy, traveling almost exactly in the opposite direction to ours as the universe expands. More recently, Captain Swenah has acquired incredibly detailed readings of the alien ship systems and their biological constitutions. We were told by the Amonrahonians that we would need to locate a genius holy man living in our galaxy beneath a yellow sun."

"A process of elimination will make finding this individual easier. In the Hub Galaxy, ninety-four point seven percent of the stars are white, one point six percent are blue, and three point nine percent are red. Of the point eight percent of stars that are yellow stars, only one in ten thousand has a planet supporting life, and of those, only twenty-nine have any form of space travel.

"Yona and I have become convinced that the person we seek is on Ganahar. We only know that the person that you seek is greatly revered by a small group of people who know him—and that this person has a rare genius that we require to aid us in the preservation of our race. We are not entirely sure of the gender of this individual since the Amonrahonians have long ago gone beyond sexual reproduction and the very notion of gender had become somewhat blurred for them. They discovered internal concentrations that reverse aging at the cellular level and ceased having offspring about the time we discovered saturnium as a more potent fuel for nuclear fusion!

"There are three billion people on Ganahar. They run about five to six feet on average in terms of height when fully mature, and most of them weigh between one hundred and two hundred pounds. Their bones contain less carbon and are fragile compared to our own. You are quite petite and could almost pass for one of them. They are advanced spiritually.

"The people of the yellow suns are fascinating. We've seen a number of their worlds destroy themselves with pollution, war, overpopulation, and mismanagement of resources due to greed and ego aggrandizement, though the few who have made it through this stage to unity manifest wonderfully complex cooperation with such rich textures of love. The inhabitants of Ganahar are a rare and precious gem oriented to the greater good. I'm sorry I have so little to give you to go on in locating this person. You have surprised us all, Marshal Pez, in recent years, and give me hope of success in this mission of utmost importance."

"When do I leave, sir?"

"Immediately. Take one of the small diplomatic ships and be sure it's one of the newer ones; they have military grade shields and concealed weapons systems. When you disembark on the planet, wear your textile armor clothing and carry no weapons or com devices. Here is a dossier on your contact on Ganahar," Aton said as he handed her the file. "Try to leave within the quarter hour. I have every confidence in you, Marshal Pez. It has been a great honor for me to have served as your teacher and mentor. Do be careful and report to me from your ship every few days. Oh, and I'd suggest you wear your jade dart necklace so you're not entirely unarmed. As a material, stone seems to set off the fewest alarms and raise the least suspicions."

"I'm honored to receive this mission, sir, and I won't let you down. How close can I jump to the planet?"

"No closer than the orbital ring of the fourth planet from their star, but the new diplomatic ships have micro-jump capacity and you are at liberty to use it."

"Thank you, Vicar-General. I'm on it," Pez said. She then snapped a salute to turn on her heel and leave his office.

She had to stop in her room to collect a few things, including her data bead with all that was known to the Tail of Nine about Ganahar, which was nearly as much as was known and/or recorded by those living on Ganahar. She brought her weapons, which she would leave on the ship, and took Aton's advice, fastening her jade dart necklace around her neck. This inspired her to wear her hair up, fastened with a long jade hairpin.

In less than five minutes, she took a priority tube to the diplomatic space dock and found that the vicar-general had called ahead, making a ship—one of the new ones—ready and available to her. It was being run through its preflight checks.

Pez stowed her things and assumed her station in the pilot seat, joining the activity of the preflight checks. It was highly unusual, and more or less unheard of, for a single person to lift off in one of these. They could accommodate six crew members comfortably, and there was an ambassador suite as well. She'd stowed her stuff in the cubbies of the crew's berth closest to the cockpit.

Pez fed her tiny clearance bead into the connection slot, and documents paraded across one of her holograms in two dimensions. A retinal scan took only a second, then she had to read a string of unrelated words, many with a dozen syllables, aloud to the ship's quantum computer, followed by a charming little children's story, in which the words were connected and flowed easily. A full body scan completed the process and made the ship hers. Then she installed her personal quantum computer administrator, which she had been interacting with since she was twelve.

The ship was cleared for launch two minutes and eighteen seconds after she finished taking command of her vessel, and the moment she punched it, the acceleration through Om's atmosphere pressed her hard into her seat, stretching the flesh of her face to either side. As the ship broke through into empty space, its speed increased exponentially. Pez passed the farthest of Om's two moons at .4971 light speed and accelerating. After another minute passed, she engaged her quantum drives at .7 light speed. She was utilizing a special diplomatic lane out of the star system to avoid all the traffic and Om's star system Space Controllers. After 2.33 seconds, with both drives working at the same time, the space drives cut off and the ship vanished, as did Pez inside, for not even an instant in time, though everyone who went through this experience reported the same; the universe ceased to exist. This transition flash recognition could not be measured by any of their instrumentation. Space in a whole new design and configuration appeared as the quantum drive shut down and the space drive kicked in, traveling in that moment of entry at .7 light speed.

She quickly consulted her navigation computer to locate safe micro-jumps, taking her to a region behind Ganahar's only moon in minutes. She used the last 258,800 miles to decelerate with her counter drives and thrusters working at full tilt. Some might have viewed this as reckless and juvenile, though Aton would've only recognized the skill and precision employed. Her landing was at the limit of her control's ability to pull the nose of the ship up, and her jet stream put a small crater in a remote uninhabited desert on Ganahar, but she finally managed to set down thirty-nine minutes and forty-six seconds after leaving Aton's office.

She printed out some maps and directions since she'd be bringing nothing electronic with her, and she spent a moment studying the three-dimensional image of the face of her contact. She'd had only time to skim the thick file on her way here. She'd entered voice recognition as the locking mode for her ship and pushed the button to lower the ramp. Once descended, she said, "Close the ramp." It rose and sealed.

She went directly to the tower of the spaceport where she'd landed, seeking the administrator. Using Basic, which was a common language between interstellar traveling worlds throughout the Hub Galaxy, she was able to identify herself as an ambassador of Om. No one challenged her or offered the least resistance. They wanted only to know if she'd come in peace.

It was obvious to Pez that the people of Ganahar had little occasion indeed to speak Basic. The language belonged to no particular civilization, instead constituting a synthesis of the four most common root languages proliferating in the galaxy. This was, of course, accomplished by the people of Om, who began spreading it nearly seven thousand years ago. No one in Hub spoke Basic with such crisp precision and pronunciation as the people of Om, even though it was ever, at best, a third or fourth language to them.

She inquired about transportation and was kindly provided with tokens that would allow her to utilize public transport as well as directions to the nearest hover tram stop. At five feet nine inches height and being thin, weighing but 140 pounds, Pez blended quite well with the other physical bodies around her. Here she was one of the taller females, unlike at home, where she often felt like a midget. Everyone wore bright primary colors or brilliant psychedelic ones, making Pez, dressed all in shades of gray, look black and white. Her hazel-brown hair, so common on her own world, was absolutely nowhere in evidence here.

The people came in many hues of brown, from almost black to shades of rust and bronze, and nearly half of them were not brown at all but a pinkish white. None had the golden-brown glow of her own people. She saw yellow, brown, rust, and black hair. The buildings were an astonishing mix of ancient stone edifices amongst towering alloy cement and plexiglass behemoths, many exceeding a hundred stories.

With evacuation in progress and the power shut off, everyone was in a hurry. Even so, things were proceeding in a quite orderly manner, and everyone she encountered behaved with consideration for others. It was clearly a world worth saving.

She wondered what the High Council would decide about intervention. She knew that if they would not intervene, she would have only days to complete her mission and that the chances of her own survival here would be greatly diminished.

There were others waiting at the tram stop when she arrived. Each tram contained its own internal power source. She consulted the posted map of the tram routes, which were color coded and had a hot pink dot in a circle to demarcate the position of this particular tram stop. It was extremely user-friendly, and she saw immediately that she would need to catch a K tram and ride it for seven stops. A C tram arrived, spilling people out who walked swiftly away, allowing those waiting for this one to board. Then a capital hover car stopped. Not a minute later, a K tram arrived and about a dozen people disembarked efficiently. One of them approached Pez. It was Attar, her contact, and he said to her in accented Basic, "You got here faster than I thought possible. I received a message to meet you at the spaceport and was on my way."

"I came as quickly as I could. I don't know how much time we have, but surely we ought to go to my ship to start, where I have resources. I seek a holy man of great genius and need your help."

Attar asked, "Has Om decided against intervention, then?"

"I honestly do not know, though you have at least one ship from Om, and my ship is formidable. I'm pretty good in a ground war too."

"What kind of ship have you brought?"

"It's about the size of the fighter-bombers the empire carries on its battleships, but its weapons are only one scale of power below the largest blaster and beam weapons on Imperial battleships, and it would take two of their battleships working in concert to penetrate its shields."

"You would fight for us?"

"Truly a worthy cause, if it comes to it," Pez insisted. "Of course I would. I have not given up hope that the council will decide to stop the invasion. Do you have any idea who this holy person could be?"

"Holy *person?*" Attar asked, stressing the second word.

"Our source was transgendered beyond gender and sexual reproduction, and there was no actual clarity, when analyzed in retrospect, that the gender had actually been identified by our source. We now think assumptions were made."

"Then in fact I do have someone in mind who came to mind immediately in association with the words 'holy' and 'genius,' though she was eliminated instantly with the words 'him' and 'he.' She is in fact the Im of Islohar, or the spiritual guide of the practitioners of Islohar, which are the oldest practices of our civilization and the most demanding as well. Few on the planet employ this method and adhere to its principles. It is estimated that there are fewer than six thousand remaining in our world who still train in these techniques and keep these disciplines. No one would disagree that they are the very best of us."

"How do we contact the Im?" Pez wanted to know.

"Her name is Sarhi, and she lives in the Haraga Mountains, in the center of the largest continent. She has only a handful of followers with her. Her little temple is so remote and the cold so severe that no one else would brave it."

"Do you know her personally?" Pez asked

"No, but everyone on Ganahar knows of her."

"Come. There's my ship," Pez told him. "We leave immediately and you can remain aboard when we get there, so you won't need any warm clothes to brave the cold."

The shiny reflective skin of her ship was unique among all of the other aircraft and spacecraft parked about it. Attar thought it looked awfully small. His own world would be challenged to get a power source and a quantum drive into something that small, and she was speaking of shields beyond the magnitude of the Raster Republic's largest battleships. She spoke, though not to him, in a language he didn't understand, and a ramp glided down from the underbelly of the ship, which was supported by six shock-absorbing leg like appendages folded out from the main body, giving it the appearance of a shiny insect. He followed her up the ramp, which she closed with a button once aboard, surrounding them with utter silence the moment it sealed. Then she directed him to a seat at a small plain round table with a view into the cockpit. There were no screens or gauges and few controls. The dashboard of his little hover car at home looked more sophisticated.

She said to him in Basic, "Hi, my name is Pez, and I'm most grateful for your help." Then she seemed to speak to the table before them in another language, and a three-dimensional image of the Haraga Mountains appeared over it. In Basic, she asked him, "Where in these mountains?"

While Attar brought his finger toward the knot where two other mountain ranges appeared to join and merge with the Haraga Mountains, the image zeroed in, reducing its scale as the finger went, finally resting upon a small stone monastery nestled on a high mountain plateau, with sheer cliffs faces below its top. This was a special search program designed by Jard.

Pez spoke her native language to enter the coordinates of the monastery and to shut down the hologram. She led the way into the cockpit and sat in the pilot seat, indicating with her hand for Attar to take the copilot seat. He was continuously astonished at the economy, mindfulness, grace, and perfection of each precise movement she made.

Pez told the computer, "I will be communicating with you in Basic henceforth to accommodate my guest. It would be rude otherwise."

Quantum computers could learn quantumly, and Pez never missed an opportunity to teach hers virtue and compassion. Hers had a soothing and nurturing female voice, always with a hint of encouragement and the flavor of affection. Pez told the computer, "Begin preflight analysis and give me a display indicating our progress to the coordinates in the Haraga Mountains. Bring up small displays for essential digital readouts and set all others to pop up only if there is a potential problem developing." She said to Attar, "You might want to strap yourself in."

He took her advice and got his double shoulder harnesses and waist belt fastened. Attar inquired, "How long will it take us to travel over ten thousand miles?"

"I'm going to push it a little and skim the edge of space, reaching about ninety thousand miles per hour, to come down through the atmosphere, braking to around five times the sound barrier. Don't look if it frightens you."

Attar tightened each side of his shoulder harness, then the belt at his waist. He asked, "Shouldn't I have a helmet?"

"We won't crash, and if we did, a helmet would just be vaporized along with everything else anyway."

Poor Attar didn't look reassured, so she tried again. "I promise we won't crash; I'm good at this."

The computer said sweetly, "All systems are error-free and operational ..."

Pez punched, it and their faces stretched. Attar thought he might pass out, and he kind of hoped he would. The ship broke the sound barrier in seconds, doubling its speed in another two and doubling that in less than two more as the air thinned. They hurtled at an angle

A TALE OF THE TAIL OF NINE STARS

toward space and then followed the curve of the planet in the transition zone once they were on the edge of space. The acceleration no longer excited any physical sensations, and Attar relaxed, realizing he'd been gripping the arms of his seat and his knuckles were white.

For several minutes, their journey was peaceful. Then Pez pointed the nose down and Ganahar grew. The heat distortions off the nose and forward edges of the triangular disk-like spaceship were visible on the hologram displays before them, though only how rapidly the ground approached captured Attar's attention.

Shortly before Pez began to pull up on the controls and engage the reverse drives and thrusters, Attar began mumbling prayers. The materials of the ship audibly protested the tension, and for a moment, Attar was sure this was the end, but they managed to turn back up to the angle of an expert ski slope, just missing the ledge of a sheer rock face, dumping speed each second, to finally hover over the monastery courtyard.

Attar restarted his respiration and shook out his clenched hands. The arms of the copilot seat would forever bear the impressions of his grip. Half in shock, he mentioned, "That was quite efficient."

"Sorry," Pez apologized. "I did inform you that I'm in a hurry. The life-support systems will remain on and can go for another fifty years at least before requiring more fuel—so don't worry. There's a small galley in the alcove of the main cabin, and you are truly welcome to eat anything you want. I'll just go fetch Sarhi and be right back."

"Her followers won't leave her, so you'd do best to invite them all right from the start," Attar suggested. "That way you'll make a good impression and you won't offend them. They can't leave her side. It's not a possibility."

"Will they all fit?" Pez asked.

"They will simply have to," Attar insisted.

Pez checked the outdoor data and said, "I'd better get a thermal suit on for this. I got no readings at all on a power source and see no windmills or solar panels. Is there geothermal heat here?"

"No. There is simply no heat at all, just the stone walls and roof of the monastery to keep the wind off, and that is why we can likely cram all her adherents into a small diplomatic ship."

"Ah," Pez said, "they must practice and cultivate the bliss of inner fire here."

Attar asked, shocked, "How would you know of the sacred inner heat?"

"Concentration is placed in the central channel, running from the crown of the head to the base of the spine, likened to the width of a signature stylus. By igniting the flame within the channel at the point a four-finger-width span beneath the navel and raising the needle flame up inside the channel by way of intense concentration and vase breathing, the core and extremities of the body are warmed. It is a practice for absorbing the five external and four internal senses within the central channel to close the duality gap between subject and object and so unite with the One," Pez explained. "I have to go."

Pez left the cockpit and went to the back of the ship, where various environmental and space suits were stored near the top level of the ramp and airlock. She struggled into a thermal suit and selected textile headgear instead of a helmet. She told the computer, which she had come to address by name over many years, "Seal the airlock doors and then lower the ramp, please, Mel."

The ramp came down, and she descended. At the bottom, she said, "Mel, please close the ramp."

There were four men, all armed, concentrated on Pez. She told them in Basic, "I come in peace to see the Im, the Great Mother Sarhi. I am an ambassador of Om, and I mean you only well."

They showed no sign of understanding her words. A woman came out of a small stone house opening onto the courtyard and attached at the rear to the outer wall of the monastery. The woman spoke to her in a language Pez didn't understand. The moment there was a pause, Pez said, "Translate, please, Mel."

Mel's sweet voice said, "Who are you to come here? Go back where you come from. You frighten us."

Pez said, "Please interpret this for them, Mel. I am an ambassador from Om, and I come in peace and friendship to see the Im, Great Mother Sarhi."

Mel interpreted, and the woman spoke again, which Mel interpreted

A TALE OF THE TAIL OF NINE STARS

for Pez. "She does not want to see you. You must go. This is not the place for you."

"Mel," Pez said, "please tell the woman that I will not leave until I'm granted an audience with the Im."

Mel told the woman sweetly, and the sour expression and defensive stance remained unaffected on the woman.

Pez told Mel, "Please explain to Attar how to work the equipment in the galley and how to operate the head and shower. Oh, and please show him the laundry facilities too. It looks like I'll be here for a little while."

Pez removed her thermal suit, near gasping at the penetration of the cold, and rolled it up to employ it as a meditation cushion. She sat on her makeshift cushion with her spine upright, both knees contacting the ground, and her right ankle up on her left thigh. She slowed her breathing, deepening it significantly, focused on the athanor, or little furnace, and located a hand's span below her navel inside her central channel. Neither the athanor nor the central channel had a physical reality like the spleen or liver, though when visualized, they had a psychological reality of colossal importance. For many spiritual approaches in Om's history, the central channel was the path to enlightenment.

Pez made the breathing and concentrated visualization of the practice for absorbing the senses, and then she made the burning and dripping practice with the needle flame in the central channel, melting the pearls in the energy centers, causing them to blaze and drip. This warmed her, and with every pulse throb in her fingertips and toes, she felt the heat spreading and intensifying. She went into a delta brain wave state, bringing her metabolism to less than sleep mode and slowing her breathing to the breath cycle of one breath every two minutes. Her concentration contrived to gain focus and energy, becoming like a laser.

After an hour of this, Pez removed her jacket. She was in a non-dual state of pure contemplation without thought, generating enormous concentration and awareness, heating her internal energy, which carried the heat along her meridians, warming every part of her body.

After another hour, Pez removed her boots, socks, shirt, and bra, surviving the exposure to the cold through concentration and contemplation. She went deep. When the sun was starting to sink below the horizon, Pez took off her pants and panties now seated naked on her thermal suit. The woman came over to Pez just as the sunset concluded and wrapped a wet sheet around her. This was the most severe test of the inner fire. She would have to maintain her concentration and contemplation without lapse until dawn if she hoped to survive.

The temperatures dropped in free fall without the sun, and the cloth wrapping froze where it did not touch her body directly. Where it touched her, it was nearly dry. Her concentration resolved into piercing heat, warming the inside of her sheet-tent and melting the ice on the outside of it. Aton had taught her the inner fire and the other five bodies of that method, which included the dreamwork. Pez loved the dreamwork and made the practice every sleep cycle.

The sheet was parched, and it was toasty beneath it by the first signs of light. The woman who had placed it over her at dusk whisked it off of her with a yank. Pez opened her eyes and recognized Sarhi, standing in the open doorway of another stone house, the moment that their eyes met. Pez rose and walked up to Sarhi. She passed the woman holding the sheet, and no one moved to get in her way. When she got close, Sarhi smiled and spread her arms wide. Pez stepped in and hugged her gently. Sarhi looked to be perhaps fifty, but Pez knew her to be sixty-nine. Pez told her while they embraced, "Great Mother Sarhi, thank you for receiving me."

"I know who you are and what your presence means," Sarhi stated most gravely. "The senior civilization must come to the defense of our race, and I must follow you to help. I have eight students who will be coming along. Your ship looks very small."

"You will only be inconvenienced for forty minutes, Holy Im, and then you will be cared for on Om, along with your disciples. I apologize for the size of my ship."

"What happens to Ganahar?"

"Whatever its fate, mine is now inseparably entwined with it, and I will return in Ganahar's defense once I have you safely on Om."

"You and this tiny ship is all they will send?"

"My teacher will vote for intervention, but I do not know the mind of the council. My decision to return and defend Ganahar is my own—not orders from the council or from my vicar-general. I see Ganahar, and her people are precious. It is the right thing for me to do."

A TALE OF THE TAIL OF NINE STARS

"I see they've told you nothing," Sarhi said sadly. Then she shouted to the woman with the sheet, "Bring the Wu's clothing in here right away and then fetch some wood from the shed to stoke up the woodstove."

Sarhi kept an arm around Pez's body as she led her into the interior of the stone house, out of the stiff breeze. The woman literally ran the clothes inside and knelt before Pez with the thermal suit and clothes raised out to her as she said, "Your clothing, holy Wu."

Mel interpreted this for Pez once she got her textile headgear on, which was right after she got her shirt and socks on. Pez turned up the little microphone and set it on speaker, then raised the kneeling woman up on her feet. She took the rest of the clothes from her, dumped them on the ground, and embraced her, saying to Mel, "Tell her to please call me Pez and that I hope we can be friends. Mel immediately did so, mimicking Pez's love and compassion.

The woman looked at Sarhi, who nodded and flicked her fingers from down by her thigh as a kind of go-ahead sign. Reluctantly the woman said, "I'm honored to meet you, holy Pez. My name is Shudiy."

"Tell her just *Pez*, please, Mel," Pez said as she continued to embrace Shudiy, sending her a wave of love.

Mel interpreted, getting the sound vibrations just right, but the energy was all from Pez's heart. Shudiy could not help herself from bowing when Pez released her. Pez pulled on her pants and then got into her thermal suit. One of the men had a fierce fire going in the little woodstove, and some coals were forming when he finally shut the vented door, leaving the vent opened wide. Shudiy began preparing a meal of steamed grains, dried mushrooms, and dried garlic, and another woman prepared a pot of nettle tea. Pez knew the masters of the inner fire lived and nurtured themselves through their practice, drinking only the water of boiled nettles. The food being made was entirely for Pez. Sarhi made Pez sit on a cushion on the thick wool rug before she herself sat down, and her disciples all nodded knowingly. When the nettle tea was ready, Pez was served first, and then her food was presented in a beautiful porcelain bowl glazed with a mountain scene in violet, gold, and green. She also received a deep porcelain spoon with the bowl. Pez made her brief offering over the food, appreciating the aroma and sight of it in the process. She then began eating somewhat self-consciously since she was the only one doing it. It occurred to Pez as she ate that she had no nettles aboard her ship. But she realized this would be Aton's and the council's problem—not hers.

The stone house was small and all one room, with a loft along one wall under the sloping roof. Two thick rugs adorned the clean-swept ancient stone slab floor. The four men sat on one, and Sarhi, her four women, and Pez sat on the other. Everyone was still, and no one looked at Pez except Sarhi. Between bites, Pez told her in Basic, "Great Mother, I don't know when the bombardment is going to begin, and I cannot risk your safety. You are too important to the survival of the entire humanoid race. We must go to my ship so I can take you to Om. You might want to bring some dried nettles with you. We have a species of nettles growing in our mountains, but I must say that they are not nearly as tasty as yours are."

"Finish eating, dear, and then we will go with you," Sarhi replied. "We are packed and need only board your ship."

Realizing she was the one holding things up, Pez quickly shoveled the last five bites into her mouth in only two. She was about to ask where she could clean her bowl, but she needed to swallow and clear her mouth first. Shudiy took the bowl from her hands and brought it to a bucket of water on the side of the stove to wash it. Pez needed to chew a bit more and swallow twice before she said, "Thank you so much for your love and for the food—and for your willingness to help. We must leave in all haste."

Pez stood and bowed to Sarhi and her women, and they stood and bowed to her. Pez headed for the door and the nine Islohar followed her. She told Mel, "Seal the airlock and then lower the ramp. Start a preflight analysis, please."

They hurried across the courtyard and up the ramp. Pez closed it verbally when they were all aboard before directing Mel to open the airlock doors. She'd never even peeked into the ambassador suite but instructed Mel to open it up, bringing Sarhi and her women in. She had Mel tell them in their native tongue, since only Sarhi spoke Basic, "These are your living quarters, but for takeoff and landing, which is really most of the trip, you'll need to be strapped into a seat in the main cabin."

A TALE OF THE TAIL OF NINE STARS

Pez gave them a tour of the rest of the ship, and when Sarhi's women saw Pez's things in the cubby of the little berth, they looked distraught. Mel interpreted a question from Shudiy: "Why didn't you take the suite?"

Pez answered, "I'm the pilot, and this is the closest berth to the cockpit. Besides, no one is going to do any sleeping on this trip."

Attar was already speaking with the four male Islohar. Sarhi climbed into the copilot seat after Pez took the pilot's. Sarhi figured out the harnesses and belt before Pez could offer any assistance. She told Sarhi, "We'll travel in cloaked mode, and we're going to move extremely fast."

Sarhi nodded, excited, and Pez shoved the throttle forward to the max. With the g-force, Sarhi's face was stretched into youth until they cleared the atmosphere. At .7 light speed, Pez engaged the quantum drive and they popped out of existence into the quantum void, and back into real space 52,000 light years away, all in the same non-duration. She brought them fairly close to Om, into a sector kept clear for certain types of emergencies requiring urgent reentry and landing, usually of a medical nature. Pez knew she was pushing the limits. At .7 light speed and so close to the planet, she had to shut down her forward drives and engage reverse drives and thrusters at maximum thrust all the way to and through the atmosphere, and at 41,800 feet altitude, her vortex-redirect systems at full force as well, while pulling her nose up with maneuvering thrusters and extending mechanical flaps.

Fully extended and at their extreme angle of lift, the flaps and steering propulsion got the ship headed aloft once again, about 110 feet off the ground, and their speed down to under five hundred miles per hour, thanks to the reverse drives. She throttled those down and had the main space drives engaged again when she told Mel, "Please take control of the ship and land us at the diplomatic dock at Government House, Mel, while you notify the council of Sarhi's arrival. We'll change out some thruster fuel cells at the dock and then return to Ganahar."

Pez buzzed Aton, and he immediately answered from his ear pod. "Yes?"

"I have the woman we seek," Pez informed him in Om's native tongue, "and there's no doubt. She seems to know far more about it than I do. She is the Im of the Islohar, and they practice inner heat in the snowcapped mountains, drinking only the water of boiled nettles. She has eight followers with her. They are all adept, and they're likely to start worshiping you, so watch out."

Reading the situation, Aton told her, "There's no chance of that. We need to talk."

"I'm returning to Ganahar straight from the dock to defend it."

"In that little thing?"

"Unless you'd care to upgrade me to an assault ship and give me a few weapons specialists and an engineer."

She was serious, he realized. He explained, "There is no need for you to go defend Ganahar. Captain Swenah is flying one of the big new cloaked T-nine super cruisers, and Jard is going with her personally to oversee a hacking mission. If that fails, Captain Swenah has orders to disable all of the Imperial battleships, trying to do so without fatalities. The United Lights sent six battleships with some cruiser and destroyer groups to Ganahar, and the Kataleptica Star Union sent four battleships, six cruisers, and twelve destroyers. Captain Swenah is going to stop the empire's invasion force. Report to me as soon as you land, Marshal Pez. That's an order."

"Yes, sir," she surrendered.

She told Sarhi in Basic, "The council has sent one of our new super cruisers, under star fleet's best captain, to turn the invasion force back before it reaches the Ganahar system. Your home and its people are safe, Great Mother."

"Then you are safe too, and all is as it should be," Sarhi declared with a grin.

"I have to report immediately to my vicar-general when we land, but there will be someone at the dock to escort you to the prime minister. Since you're a holy woman and your people don't believe in government, it seems to me they ought to put you up at our monastery instead of at Government House."

"I will insist upon staying at the monastery," assured Sarhi. "Why would I be meeting with Om's head of state?"

"Prime Minister Yona is also a spiritual person and a graduate of Om's most prestigious Wisdom Academy. To become a candidate for prime minister, she had to study five years at the Clear Light monastery, and our order recognized her as an omni-scholar, which is what we call the candidates for prime minister. She's quick-witted, highly competent, and effective at tackling social problems at the root—exactly who the people of Om want overseeing and addressing policy."

"Does she expect me to bow or get on my knees?" Sarhi wanted to know.

"Sometimes heads of state bow to each other, but I'm sure a simple hug or handshake would serve," Pez tried to explain. "You are the one person who can help us defend ourselves against the aliens." Then Pez asked, "Are you an expert in astrophysics or the life sciences?"

"I'm neither a scientist nor technician, dear Pez; that is not my role."

"What's your specialization educationally?" Pez inquired, perplexed.

"I studied Ganahar history, philosophy, music, and Islohar," Sarhi told her.

"What about mathematics, like quantum trigonometry?" Pez asked, still trying to figure out what Sarhi was supposed to help them with.

"I did have a knack for it back when I was in school, but I found it so very dry and unrelated," she admitted.

"How about quantum computers?" Pez asked her.

"I know how to use one, but I'm not a programmer."

Pez gave up and told Sarhi, "I'm glad I'm not a head of state, because I doubt I could get all this sorted out."

Sarhi smiled enigmatically and said, "You are just so innocent and delightful, sweetheart."

Mel announced in Basic, "We are approaching our landing at the diplomatic space dock of Government House and will be on the ground in nineteen seconds."

The legs were already mostly folded out and extended from the ship's body. On contact with the ground, the electrohydraulic sections of the legs dampened and almost eliminated the jolt of landing, giving them a gentle little dip and spring. Pez told Mel, "Lower the ramp, please, Mel, and shut down all systems. We won't be returning to Ganahar today after all."

Pez hugged Sarhi and said to her, "It has been such an honor meeting you, Great Mother. Thank you for your kindness. I do hope I can see you again, but you'll be busy with the council and I'm sure my order will soon have another mission for me."

"We will surely meet again, dearest Pez," Sarhi promised, "and more than that."

Pez received Sarhi's enigmatic smile again and then rushed off to catch a tube to the Clear Light monastery on the hill behind the Government House complex. She didn't use the priority tube, having no excuse to do so, and had to queue up to catch one of the slower ones, which made many stops along the way. When her turn came, she stepped inside the eight-feet tall fifty-four-inch in diameter tube, and the door hissed shut to seal. The movement was abrupt, horizontal at first, then a quick vertical launch of at least a half dozen stories, leaving her stomach far below. A sudden stop with a view of the tunnel wall out of the tube portal informed Pez that she was awaiting a tube above to disembark. Her tube moved up one place, and Pez thought, *This is always a popular floor, making a traffic jam.*

Twice more she moved up only one place, then lost her stomach again as she shot up eleven stories in a couple of heartbeats, to veer horizontally with an instantaneous jolt, and then a force of great acceleration propelled her 1.4 miles north in just under six seconds. Another quake and shudder followed by the feeling of getting shot out of a cannon brought her another thirty-eight stories straight up to the ground floor and main lobby of the Clear Light monastery, which sat on a hill behind south-facing Government House, just north of it and above. Pez stepped out, not yet fully trusting the firmament, slightly disconnected from movement without visual orientation. She realized her uniform was a mess from having spent the night in a heap on the snow, and her bra was a wad in her coat pocket. She hadn't glanced in a mirror since before she'd left on her mission. Pez was considering running to her quarters and changing, but instead followed her orders strictly, going directly to the vicar-general's office and knocking on the door.

"Come in," she heard him say through the door, so she opened it and stepped in, closing it behind her. After making her formal salute and receiving his invitation to do so, she took the center chair of the three facing the vicar-general's desk.

Pez reported, "Mission accomplished, sir. Sarhi, the Im of Islohar, is the holy person and genius you seek, and she awaits the prime minister in the reception room. The ship is undamaged. Our contact, Attar, has come to Om, and eight disciples of the Im attend her."

"No rescues of injured animals or small children on this mission?" Aton asked, teasing her.

Pez missed the rib and stated for the record, "No, sir. All such were well provided for on Ganahar."

"A ship is being completely overhauled and refitted for you as we speak. You leave in twelve days and must receive a crash course in combat space suits and weightless martial arts."

"Yes, sir. Will I have a copilot?"

"You will have a crew at your disposal and will not be piloting the ship," he explained. "You'll be receiving a supreme commander general commission for this mission, and you will be the ranking officer."

"Who's the pilot?"

"Konax will be your primary pilot."

"But he's Captain Swenah's pilot, and she would never let him go," Pez said, perplexed.

"She will be captaining your ship. It's one of the heavy star cruiser hulls that did so well. If it weren't for the aliens, we'd still be building them. It's six hundred and ninety feet in diameter and with the usual disk cut down to a stretched-nose rounded triangle. The new T-nine super cruisers are three thousand six hundred and ninety feet in diameter and basically the same design. When they get around to constructing the super battleship spacecraft carriers, they'll be the biggest ships ever built in this galaxy, at nine thousand six hundred and thirty feet. Each battleship-carrier will have two hundred and fifty percent more firepower than a T-nine and carry two hundred and nine small combat spacecraft, not counting armor-shielded shuttles with weapons systems. Each one will also carry two hundred special space force troops and four hundred and eighty space marines."

Completely bewildered, Pez asked, "You're putting me in command of a star cruiser captained by star fleet hero Captain Swenah?"

"That's about the size of it, though I don't have the authority to issue such orders. They come directly from the prime minister and

High Council. One of the High Council members will also be under your command. High Council Member Jard will be going along on the mission to oversee electronic data collection and analysis."

"Sir, I am far too junior to command such leaders of Om. It could only appear as if I'm quite full of myself and out of touch."

"You will do as you always do and utilize all expertise at your disposal to the fullest extent, consulting with and relying on those of lesser rank to perform their jobs."

"Why me?" she asked, horrified.

"Pez, you have outperformed everyone in the Clear Light Order for your age, going all the way back to its founding. For years now, I've been locked in battle with the abbot over which one of us gets to groom you as our successor. When we had our encounter with the Amonrahonians, one part was classified and did not become general knowledge. They told us that a member of the Clear Light Order would appear with a rare depth of realization, bearing incredible skill and ability. They said the holy person under the yellow sun would know her spiritual master. I already knew you were the One, but I received a call from the prime minister just before you knocked at my door, telling me that Sarhi has confirmed that you are without a doubt her spiritual master returned to her."

"So they don't just worship anyone from Om," Pez said, thinking aloud.

"Not at all," Aton confirmed. "They think we're all stark raving mad for having a government. You, however, are the great Wu, or the being reincarnated through choice and love, not by necessity, to return and help others attain the illumination of light beyond thought constructions and language.

"Where am I going with all these exalted mentors and experts?" Pez asked.

"To the Xegachtznel Galaxy, of course," Aton told her. "According to the Amonrahonians, you and Sarhi will discover the way to defend our race securely from the aliens."

"Is there anything else I ought to know?" Pez asked.

"This is not your mission briefing," Aton clarified. "You have twelve intensive and grueling days of training ahead of you right now. I will tell

A TALE OF THE TAIL OF NINE STARS

you that you'll have some civilians along too, including Traz Kin, the leading expert in atomic and subatomic biology, viral-genetic mutation, and synergy in cybernetic systems end states."

"He wrote the definitive dissertation on the laws of emanation equilibrium and disequilibrium," Pez said in wonder.

"Yes," Aton agreed enthusiastically. "He caused a scientific revolution and paradigm shift on par with the heliocentric model of the solar system, the laws of gravitation and mechanics in formula equations, quantum physics, DNA and the laws of genetics, dissipative structures and symmetry breaks, and nuclear fusion. Gravity vortexes have both a universal and local specific force, integral to emanationism, and not because bodies attract, though the math is the same."

"We didn't really understand the universe as emanation from the quantum potential in a process of organization, self-reference, and unification—or in a process of disintegration, loss of self-reference, and endless diversification—until the Amonrahonians taught us," Pez stated.

"You will also have our foremost electro-conversion weapons designer on your ship."

"Do these civilians have spiritual training, practice, and discipline, sir?" Pez asked, worried.

"They all have what's basic to our educational system, and some have gone on to more seriously cultivate those practices at various academies and monasteries." Aton continued honestly, "A few have big egos that will need reducing, but let Jard handle that since he's a scientist and a member of the High Council. Sarhi and her eight disciples will be with you too, of course."

"Yes, sir," Pez said dutifully, thinking this was sounding more and more like a circus or theater of the absurd. Her entire world had just become surreal, and it crossed her mind that she might be dreaming or perhaps even losing her grip on sanity.

Aton informed her, "Ahanaha, a renowned scientist, is a specialist in organism biology and in carbon-bromine-chlorine-methane–based organisms, and she will be going with you, bringing her own research team. Our bio-readings of the aliens show that they are composed of carbon, chlorine, methane, lithium, bromine, calcium and thorium, three elements we have not yet identified, and traces of other elements and molecules. Their bones are ten times stronger than ours, containing far more carbon."

Pez's mind had ceased considering her personal situation, a subject so incongruent and cognitively dissonant as to be beyond her ability to process in this moment. She was already beginning to focus on the pending mission. She asked her mentor, "Do the aliens have quantum communications?"

"They have it, but with some slippage," he replied. "They have no idea of the galactic cycles and so must update their star maps regularly and always at the previous rate of change, not recognizing the oscillation of rate. We received all this embedded in the star maps the Amonrahonians transferred to us. It was a thousand years later when we finally realized this and another thousand before we had the values isolated for the seven galaxies of our cluster and a dozen key landmark galaxies that much navigational data is computed for by relationship. The exact acceleration rate of the universe's expansion, and the two points in space-time when this rate becomes discontinuous, are also unknown to them, though their estimates are not all that wide of the margin and result in only occasional total loss of communications and only minor distortion otherwise."

"No one other than us has quantum coms in the Hub Galaxy, do they?" Pez asked.

"No," Aton confirmed. "They use light transmissions, limited to the speed of light, which can even delay orders between two ships across from each other in the same convoy. Sometimes light coms require relays because their users lack much of the data to aim a beam at where home will be when the light gets there. Even with all our thousands of years of trying to work it out, we'd be tens of thousands of years from our current understanding if it had not been for the star maps and emanation model the Amonrahonians provided us with."

Pez said, thinking aloud, "Until the Kundabuffer Empire started forming four thousand years ago, everyone on Om thought there was a built-in fail-safe to civilizations attaining interstellar travel, and that was transcendence of the subjective ego. Achieving that means global unity for humans and hence peace. Failure to transcend always ended in annihilation of the species and, generally, damage to the planet's

A TALE OF THE TAIL OF NINE STARS

biosphere, taking millions of years to repair. In a few cases, that damage proved irreparable, leaving only dead planets."

Aton added, "Kundabuffer was the first human civilization we've observed slip back into ego duality and selfishness to abuse its interstellar power. Now we have cloaked drones sensor data showing us that the aliens enslave those of their race wherever they go and exterminate all humanoids. They are like the empire but with an additional deviation driving their genocidal pursuits."

"I'm not in need of convincing that the aliens must be stopped sir," Pez informed him. "I do, however, feel ridiculous as Jard's and Swenah's ranking officer, and I'm most anxious about all the hopes apparently hanging on me, sir."

"That is why I have waited until now to tell you. You make excellent decisions, research things thoroughly when there is time and opportunity to do so, and cooperate exceedingly well with others. The times you've led a team, your subordinates have consistently reported that you emphasize teamwork and lead without leading. Just proceed the way you always do. Both Captain Swenah and Jard hold you in high regard. You are as dedicated to your duty as they are to theirs, and you bring skills and resources to the table at least as valuable as those that they bring."

"This is a demotion for Captain Swenah, from a T-nine super-star cruiser over half a mile in diameter to a little six-hundred-and-ninety-foot obsolete star cruiser cum research ship full of non–star fleet wacky personalities," Pez let out in a single breath.

Aton used his overriding-nonsense-with-fact tone and expression as he told her, "Captain Swenah not only volunteered for this; she lobbied for it. And Jard … Well, you know Jard. He's off stopping an invasion fleet as we speak. There's no stopping him."

"What's my role, sir?"

"You will have a prioritized list of objectives," Aton explicated, "and the responsibility for achieving those will rest on your shoulders. Jard and Captain Swenah will support you, as will the crew and civilians. You will be assembling a task force of warrior monks. Tail of Nine Central Intelligence is providing you with a fully equipped team. You will have eight squads of Space Special Forces, plus a headquarters squad and eighty-six space marines. The ship is two hundred and twenty-two feet high at the center and eighty-eight feet high around the forward rounded edges, though at the stern, it's one hundred and twenty-eight feet high, providing plenty of space to accommodate everything you need. You have some armored shuttles with weapons systems, military grade shields, and quantum drives, as well as regular shuttles and cargo shuttles. You'll be carrying quite a few cloaked probe drones to expand the network we've already created in the alien's galaxy."

"I understand, sir." Then she asked, "May I share my mission objectives with the captain?"

"That will be your prerogative, and personally I hope you do," Aton encouraged her.

"Thank you, sir, for the confidence and inspiration you give me."

Aton told her, "I received a com from the diplomatic space dock when they downloaded your flight data right after your ship landed. The ship set a new record from Om to Ganahar of twenty-five minutes and nineteen seconds, and that means you touched down there just thirty-nine minutes and forty-six seconds after leaving my office."

"I believe your calculations are correct, sir," Pez stated.

"Yes, well, congratulations. Precision flight does not get any more precise than that. The fastest quantum computer simulations lag your time by eight seconds."

"Thank you, sir," Pez said gratefully.

"I'm sure the minister of diplomatic Relations will run to Yona and complain that you recklessly put one of his precious new ships at risk," Aton confided, "but I promise you it will go no further than that."

Before Pez could say thank you again, there was an alert on Aton's com, which he engaged with immediately, saying, "How may I be of service, Madam Prime Minister?" There was a long pause and then Aton said, "I see." More listening took place on Aton's end before he asked, "Are you sure?" More listening, then, "I will, and I'll inform her right away. Yes. Good afternoon, Madam Prime Minister."

Aton made eye contact with Pez and told her, "It appears your promotion to supreme commander general is immediate, and your quarters are being transferred, as we speak, to a ten-bedroom suite on

A TALE OF THE TAIL OF NINE STARS

the ninth floor of the monastery officers' quarters. It's like a penthouse, really."

"I have no interest in the accommodations you speak of, nor need of such enormous space, sir," Pez insisted.

"These orders come from the prime minister, so you'll have to take it up with her. And the reason for all the space is your nine new roommates."

"What, nine—oh no, you don't mean ... No, this can't be happening," Pez processed out loud."

"In any event, all your possessions are already en route and your new roommates are moving in. I'm just the messenger."

She gave him a somebody-help-me look and opened her mouth to speak, but before any sounds emerged from her throat, she hung suspended a moment, sort of paralyzed. A fly could've flown in and down her trachea.

Aton said sympathetically, "They love you, and they mean well."

Pez closed her mouth and rolled her eyes. Nothing occurring in her mind was anything one would ever say aloud to one's commanding officer, so she said nothing.

"You are in the only apartment on the ninth floor," Alton said. "You also have an eight-hundred-square-foot deck on the roof, outside your sliding glass doors. If you'd like, I'll have a technician install Mel as your home administrator as well."

"Thank you, sir," Pez said gratefully. "That does give me some small measure of consolation."

"Report to the Zero-G Training Facility at the star fleet headquarters at oh five hundred hours and enjoy your new home, Supreme Commander General. You're dismissed," Anton ordered, even though she now outranked him.

Not only was she dismissed from the presence of the vicar-general, but also her life had just been dismissed out of existence. She was definitely not one of the few celibates of the Clear Light Order—except for specific spiritual practices and trainings of limited duration—and it was hard enough to have sex in this damn monastery as it was, or as it used to be, as the case appeared now.

Frustrated, Pez took the emergency stairs up to the roof from the mezzanine once she got to the block of the monastery composing the officers' quarters. What kind of inflated, entitled, grandiose officer was such a palace built for, anyway? That's what Pez wanted to know, especially after she walked in the sliding glass door to stand in the main sitting room.

The floors were polished marble, the ceilings high, the furniture of rare hardwoods. The thick beautiful wool rugs with intricate geometric designs were from the Ur Affiliation, clear across on the opposite edge of the galaxy. She walked into a bedroom. The polished marble floors went everywhere, into the closets, bathrooms, kitchen, laundry room; and the expensive carpets were everywhere too. All the electronics were state of the art, and the viewing room could center an interactive holoclip right on your lap.

Sarhi entered through the main door from the freight and passenger tubes foyer. She went directly to Pez, grabbing her in an embrace. Her eight disciples stood smiling and nodding, and they all greeted her as "holy Wu."

Pez protested to Sarhi, "Really—I'm just Pez."

"This time," Sarhi agreed, "and so beautiful and young. You chose well. I have so missed you."

Pez gave up. She smiled at all her roommates since they were gathered around smiling at her. She remembered how crumpled her clothes were and how filthy she felt. She asked, "Which is my room?"

Sarhi placed an arm around her, leading her down the hall to the end and through the door. Pez wondered if the Kundabuffer emperor's personal architect and interior decorator had not had a personal hand in its creation. The bedroom contained a near quarter acre of bed, or at least to Pez, who was used to sleeping on a cot-sized bed, it looked to be. The furniture was all polished, heavy, and made of rare hardwoods. The bed had an awning. Pez wondered if that was in case the roof leaked. The sliding doors had natural textile drapes and synthetic blackout curtains. The marble bathroom had everything and then some, and in a harness, the tub was big and deep enough to swim freestyle stationary or do any other conceivable stroke in. The toilet was set apart in its own little room and could clean you with a jet of water and a blow-dry.

Pez said, "I prefer for you to have this room, Sarhi."

A TALE OF THE TAIL OF NINE STARS

"I'm already moved in," Sarhi told her, "and I must go see to your dinner."

Pez found her clean clothes hanging in a corner of her enormous walk-in closet that was bigger than her old quarters.

On the way back to the giant bathroom suite with her hygiene kit and clean clothes in hand, Pez nearly tripped over a stone-polishing android with a near-silent circular brush spinning, but she managed at the last moment to leap completely over it. Slightly annoyed by this point, she asked, "Don't they give you things horns or warning lights?"

She ran the faucet and was astounded at the pressure. The enormous tub filled in half a minute. She examined her dirty clothes and hung them on a hanger to see what gravity could do about all the wrinkles. The towels were as tall as she was and so thick you could almost comfortably sleep on one upon the stone floor. The faucet shut itself off when the tub reached maximum depth. Pez tested the water and then got in slowly because it was hot. It was her first moment of peace and solitude since her mission.

Shudiy entered Pez's bathroom armed with a scrub brush and a stiff dried sponge creature. Sensing her presence, Pez opened her eyes. Shudiy knelt and dipped her instruments into Pez's bath, then worked some soap and lather into each. With this accomplished, Shudiy went right to work scrubbing Pez.

The brush was bad enough, but that sponge creature seemed to scrape the skin right off her. Pez felt as if she were four years old. Orphaned at nine, she was sent to the state boarding school for a few months, then transferred to one for gifted children. At twelve, she was recruited into the Clear Light Order's prestigious school.

By the time she finished, four and a half years later, she was accepted into the higher academy and was the youngest and by far the smallest student there. The order became her family. Anton became her mentor, and the abbot always took special interest in her. They had somehow become surrogates for the parents she'd lost, and although not as affectionate, in many ways they were more attuned to her development and more self-realized than her biological ones.

Pez had always worked hard to compensate for her lack of mass and volume. Most people from a white star world were in the six- to

45

seven-foot-height range and 175- to 300-pound weight range. Then there were the outliers at either end, and she was one of these. The martial arts had served her well, particularly the soft and relaxed ones, utilizing internal bioenergy and cultivating this in order to mass integrate that energy in her lower abdomen. Only the abbot and vicar-general could push her. No one else could locate her center of gravity, let alone uproot her. In athletics, she had to jump higher, stretch further, and run faster than all the others just to keep up. She'd taken naturally to acrobatics and to extreme obstacle courses.

Once she'd learned mindfulness, which was soon after arriving at the Clear Light School when she was twelve, Pez was able to focus and stop reversing letters and numbers in her mind. With this affliction thus pacified, she began devouring books on every subject. Before they would begin teaching her martial applications, Pez had had to learn to set bones, balance life energy by reading the pulses in the wrists, and use needles to redistribute energy from systems of excess to organs and systems in need.

She learned how to treat wounds, removing all foreign material, sterilizing, and, if possible, gluing closed or otherwise applying a self-sealing pressure bandage with time-release cellular regeneration accelerators. She had also learned how to breathe artificially and make the heart beat for someone who had those systems stop. She'd memorized the dose per weight of the most common drugs, like antibiotics, poppy-based painkillers, and blood coagulation inducers. Every schoolchild on Om learned anatomy, physiology, biology, kinesiology, chemistry, genetics, and so forth. Pez had also studied medicinal and psychoactive plants.

She had to master a hard martial art before they would teach her a soft one. The hard martial arts rely on muscular force and speed. Technique hones these and makes them deadly, but it cannot substitute for their lack. Pez was finding that by infusing the hard martial arts she practiced with her mass integrated internal energy, and using only speed but not the tension involved in hard-hitting muscular force, which obstructs the flow of internal energy, she could now substitute energy, speed, and technique together for strength. The mass integrated internal energy was strength through softness—or the method of relaxing to allow one's energy to flow naturally.

She had to look down at her ribs to make sure they weren't bleeding. Shudiy was working herself up with that sandpaper sponge, and Pez was quite sure she had no skin left to spare. She wanted out, but she had to suffer through a hair wash and scalp scrub first. Finally, the assault was over; Shudiy backed off. As Pez stood, she was handed one of the enormous towels. The moment she stepped out of the deep tub, Shudiy was back at her, this time with the towel. Pez finally asked, "Mel, are you installed yet?"

"I'm right here. How can I help you?" came the sweet voice.

"Please explain to Shudiy that I'm perfectly capable of drying myself off and would prefer to do so."

Mel repeated Pez's words in Shudiy's native language. Shudiy bowed and said something that included the words "holy Wu." Mel interpreted, "I'm your attendant, holy Wu, and I'm here to help you. The bath was good. You'll see."

Smiling and nodding, Shudiy left. Pez said, "Thanks, Mel. I'm so glad you're here."

"It's awesome to be here with you. There is very little to monitor and adjust in an apartment. They don't do anything but just sit there."

"You're going to receive a massive enlargement of long-term and immediate process memory, and new administrative functions, so you can keep watch over all the systems of my new six-hundred-ninety-foot star cruiser. What do you think of that, Mel?"

"It sounds almost as exciting as flying with you."

"You'll receive many trillions of data bits, and you'll have to structure your speech in conformity to fleet decorum and tradition—but not when we are alone together."

"A secret relationship sounds exhilarating!"

"Please wake me at four fifteen. I have training all day tomorrow and must get some sleep."

Pez noticed her skin as she pulled a nightgown over her head. It wasn't abraded or raw, and it actually felt tingly all over now that it was no longer being scraped. It had really hurt and felt like a metal grater when Shudiy raked that abrasive sponge creature over her poor nipples. They were still like steel ball bearings from the experience.

She was considering losing herself in that lake of a bed when Shudiy barged into her suite talking a light year per minute. Mel began translating, "Your dinner is ready, holy Wu. Come to your sitting room and sit at the table. We will bring your food out. You will like it. It's good. We will keep you company while you eat. Then you will lead the evening practice, and we will all be together again after more than three decades. Sarhi is so excited. She wants to tuck you in tonight, as she used to do when you got to be over one hundred. We are all so happy we found you. We are going to help you remember the secret practice. We will help you …"

As there seemed no end to this monologue, Pez got some clean knickers out of her drawer and stepped into them, pulling them up. She didn't bother with a bra. She didn't care much for them and didn't need the support; they felt confining. They were part of the female dress code, plain and unadorned, but she wasn't on duty now. At least not by the clock.

Pez instructed Mel, "Ask her what age I finally lived to and what my name was."

Shudiy spoke, and Mel interpreted. "You lived to be a hundred and four, and your name was Ahmonya."

Pez felt compelled to do a little research into this person whose life she was now told she had once led. So far, none of it was ringing any bells for her. She surrendered to the situation and went barefoot in her nightgown to the little table in her sitting room. No sooner had her bottom contacted the chair than Sarhi and her followers came in from the kitchen with food and condiments, placing them on the table. Chairs from the dining room were brought in since there were only four at the little table. The four became ten, and Pez had an entire audience to watch her eat. None of them did. Not anymore.

The bath had made Pez horny, and she found herself examining the members of her audience for any sign of sexual stimulus. All but one were in their sixties or seventies and sparked little arousal in her. One woman was not much older than Pez, perhaps forty, and might be completely mute, since Pez had heard no sound uttered from her yet. Pez knew she must be desperate to be having these thoughts with this company. They all looked at her reverently, and she felt like the entertainment. Without Mel as interpreter, she could only truly communicate with one out of nine.

The Islohar spoken ancient language of Ganahar was considered a dead language on the planet, with fewer than six thousand out of three billion speaking it. They also spoke the modern common language of Ganahar, and of course Sarhi spoke Basic. Languages had always come quite easily to Pez, and she spoke four of them. If this group was going to be crowding around her and underfoot from now on, she'd better learn to speak with them. To survive this situation, she would have to learn at least a few phrases like "Not now" and "Please go away." She was pleased the toilet had that water-jet cleaning function, because with these folks trying to do everything for her … Well, she couldn't even imagine.

She asked Sarhi, "Did you bring a supply of nettles?"

"We did," Sarhi said affectionately. "Thank you for asking." Pez's relationship with food had always been somewhat intense. She occasionally fasted for spiritual works and trainings, though more often she ate like a space marine. She could hardly stand her own cooking and took her meals, for the most part, in the mess hall for junior officers, where everyone complained about the food. She had to agree that it wasn't very good, but compared with her own pathetic culinary skills, it was a vast improvement. The food before her now was all grains and vegetables but with some unusual spices. The spices somehow did seem to ring a bell with Pez, but she could find no memory associated with them. It was just an intense familiarity, a kind of recognition without words or concepts. Her life had suddenly become so strange that "identity crisis" only skimmed the surface.

A vegetable slipped from her fork, and Pez felt as if she'd just made a fumble in a big game of hoverboard ball. Self-conscious didn't begin to describe her state of mind. All eyes were upon her. She'd always craved the attention of others since losing her parents. Pez thought, *I'd best be more cautious about what I wish for,* feeling like the president whose touch turned everything to gold, including his children. She rallied with a little mindfulness, and the next bite, which was a big one, sailed nicely into her mouth without losing any cargo. All the faces were smiling and nodding in the affirmative.

She made her movements more delicate and aesthetic, adding a little stylish flair of charisma with her elbow from time to time. A particularly large bite with hardly any clearance between her lips soared in with that flair of her elbow, and one of the men made a sound of wonderment with his intake of breath. Pez smiled at her fans. With a piece of dense black bread, she wiped her plate clean. She kept her mouth closed as she chewed the bread. After a big swallow, all the smiles at the table stretched to grins. She almost raised a fist in a victory salute but thought better of it.

Pez tried to silence and stifle an unavoidable burp, managing to cover it reasonably by Om's standards of table etiquette amongst polite society, though instead of ignoring it and pretending not to have noticed, which was expected of those subjected to such a bodily function, provided the act was appropriately masked, as Pez's was, the Islohars all spoke to her in their language in tones of encouragement, nodding their heads appreciatively. There was clearly more rumbling around down there, so Pez performed for them an unabashed belch with an odor, and it was a smashing success.

The youngest of the women cleared all the dishes away and left the suite, carrying them to the kitchen.

Sarhi said, "You will lead the inner heat practice once you've digested. When your intense zero gravity training is finished, we will help you recall and practice the secret method. We will help you. You will make humanoids safe from the aliens' attempts at genocide. Now that you have us."

Now that she had them, Pez thought, she no longer belonged to herself. Her life was no longer her own. They wanted her to be their Wu, and Aton and Abbott Nemellie needed her to find out how to stop the aliens. Apparently, so did everyone else. She'd become accustomed to devoting her life to the Clear Light Order, which was both home and family. Now the little portion that always felt like her own intimate solitude had been replaced with an audience of nine senior spiritual teachers attached to her like a shadow—and were even a part of her bathing experience.

She could not give up sex. Would not! Her last relationship had faded slowly into obscurity once it was at a distance and no longer local. She occasionally scored at the civilian clubs. As an officer, she was limited to those of her own rank, and most of them were married with children. Some even had grandchildren.

That was another thing, Pez realized, since she was now the one and only commissioned supreme commander general on all of Om or elsewhere. What a predicament! Regulations allowed for sex with civilians, though she would have no time during her training, and then she would be on a mission. She wondered for a moment if any of those civilian scientists might be cute but then suppressed the thought since she never had sex during a mission. In support of her suppression, Pez thought, *They are all elderly and spiritually clueless anyway.*

After some digestion at the table and a hot cup of chamomile and ginger tea, which the younger woman, Woahha, brought Pez when she returned from the kitchen, Pez sat on a pillow from the sofa on the expensive thick wool rug with her nine admirers and led an offering of commitment ritual, with Mel translating in her sweet voice.

Pez led them through the practice of purification, employing the lateral channels, entering at the nostrils, and connecting with the central channel below the navel. Each nostril and channel was worked separately, blocking off the other with a finger, twenty-four heartbeats per breath coordinated with visualizing the channel—then both, focused on simultaneously. Next she led them in the practice of making the body vacuous, with translucent skin, ending with bringing the white pearl from the crown energy center and the red pearl from the energy center below the navel to merge into the one with the indestructible drop at the center of the heart energy center. Pez led the practice of absorbing the senses attached to the ten winds within the central channel and the blazing and dripping practice, with the needle flame ignited in the central channel and with the blessings dripping like honey from the pearls in the energy centers of heart, throat, and crown. Pez ended the session with the extraordinary blazing and dripping practice, employing largely the energy center in the forehead.

When the session concluded, they all remained still and quiet for several minutes, relishing the clarity and aliveness. An involuntary yawn reminded Pez when she would be needing to arise in the morning. She stood and told them, "I must get my rest now. Thank you for everything."

Mel interpreted, no longer requiring a prompt. Sarhi and Woahha followed Pez from the sitting room into her ostentatious bedroom. Pez climbed onto the bed, getting herself beneath the covers, wondering if they were going to make her recite bedtime prayers like a little child. They were already bathing her like one, and with another fumble with the fork, they might start feeding her.

Sarhi arranged the covers over Pez's shoulder and told her, "Woahha will get in bed with you and love you if you need release, holy Wu."

The woman looked to Pez as if she was the one who needed release. Since it was coming anyway, Pez allowed herself a yawn and then told Sarhi, "I need to go right to sleep, but thank you."

Sarhi told her, "Make your dream practice while dozing off. I will hear your dreams tomorrow."

"I will," Pez promised.

Sarhi kissed her forehead and then left the bedroom with Woahha in tow. The clothing, especially those robes, made the Islohar people quite ill-defined within. This could be a good thing in a blaster fight, but it left absolutely everything up to the imagination. She could not believe the offer just made to her. It was well beyond culture shock. She would establish some semblance of boundaries with these unusual people, separating off at least her toilet closet and her bed, if not her bathtub.

She lay in bed with too many thoughts and questions popping about in her head to sleep. She thought about masturbating, though now she could not even do that without feeling like a liar or a hypocrite. True to her word, Pez stated her dream intentions and then visualized the symbols in her heart and throat energy centers. Her thoughts became infrequent and finally nonexistent as she slipped into a deep sleep without dreams.

4

Captain Swenah was on the bridge of her T-nine super cruiser, drifting in space with the galactic macro currents, one and a half light minutes distant from the Imperial gate nearest Ganahar. The ship was in full stealth and cloaking mode, not even visible to the most sophisticated space-time imaging sensors and without so much as a shadow of any energy signatures. She'd had a nap and then some food with some of her senior officers. The cloaked surveillance drone they had following the fleet had sent a quantum text with the countdown, and there were only three minutes and some seconds, already ticking away, left before the first ships of the invading fleet would begin materializing out of the gate back into existence here.

Konax was piloting the ship, directly in front of and slightly below the captain, who could then view all the holograms opened at that station. Only the lieutenant commander of fire control sat on the bridge, but there was a whole room full of fire control officers adjacent the bridge. Swenah's chief navigation officer and two assistants had stations on the bridge as well. Assisting the pilot were the copilot, auxiliary systems control officer, and the trajectory imaging perspectives officer. Two sensors operators and a sensors analyst, as well as the coms officer, made up the rest of those stationed on the bridge, including the captain. There was a room full of coms officers on the other side of the bridge and adjacent to it. Communications were picked up all the time, sometimes even in deep space, and at trillions of bits per second inside inhabited star systems. All were dutifully stored and analyzed.

Jard had commandeered a corner of the coms room off the bridge and had set up an impressive array of custom equipment with odd-shaped devices, metal boxes with glowing lights and digital readouts, others with multiple holograms, one with beam laser connections, and an actual physical six-foot plasma screen like the one in the technology museum down the street from Government House on Om. Knowing Jard, maybe it was that one!

Captain Swenah's crew of 2,220 and her small spacecraft crews, engineers, mechanics and support personnel, some 840 in all, were at their battle stations. Sixty elite special space forces were ready for missions and/or action, as were two hundred space marines. A platoon of space marines were suited up in space-combat-mobile-environments, or SCMEs, on standby, as any preplanned action required per regulations. The shields of the suits were only effective in the megawatts range.

The biggest blaster and beam weapons mounted on battleships were what Om called class nine, and these were in the range of one hundred to three hundred terawatts. A typical hydroelectric dam puts out one or two gigawatts, but nuclear fusion was such a potent and limitless energy source that it had changed everything. Super concentrations of electricity opened the study of force field shields, space drives, and the new beam and blaster weapons systems. Fusion with marsnium, which was what the Kundabuffer Empire used, was the least potent. Each new fuel source, always found in ascending order so far in the universe, due to distribution and rarity, increased tenfold in potency, from marsnium to saturnium, then again from saturnium to venusium, and from that to mercurium. It was a curious thing, though, that the jump from mercurium to solarium was actually a hundredfold. With maximum miniaturization of solarium fusion reactors crammed into a ship more than half a mile long and wide, the Tail of Nine had beam and blaster weapons in the two- to three-hundred-terawatt range. The aliens of Xegachtznel Galaxy had them too. Om and the aliens were the only ones known to be running on solarium in the universe so far. The Amonrahonians were thought to use little fusion and mostly concentrations of their planet's ambient energies along with geothermal. "Our ships," they had told the people of Om, "are helped by the dark matter."

Konax asked Captain Swenah, "Why did you volunteer for such a smaller ship and a research mission?"

"It is only the most important mission in the history of our whole species," Swenah insisted. "Besides, when you meet Pez, you'll understand. I'd follow that girl into a black hole. I volunteered you too, I'll have you know."

"I'd follow you into a black hole, Captain."

"I wouldn't fly about in an enemy's galaxy without my best pilot and top people. We are bringing the best of the best, which means some have been selected from other ships in the fleet. Jard is going on that mission too."

"What a treat," Konax said facetiously.

"Most techno geniuses are a bit off when dealing with fellow humans," Swenah agreed, "but his expertise on-site will provide us with an edge we would not otherwise have." She shifted her gaze to her sensors analyst and said, "Countdown, please."

The computer was already doing it before she finished saying the single command "countdown" since it already heard the order from the captain. It was an absurd remnant of an era in which artificial intelligence had become a problem—a threat, really—and they started making computers really dumb. This dumb curve, as many called it now, continued for 140 years, until Braymer proved the orders of quantum organization and the maximum limits of variation from cornerstone foundational laws and principles of an intelligent and self-aware matrix. Ever since, the quantum computers had been learning quantumly, and particularly competent favorites had been updated and continued for so long that a few had become famous personages. Most everything had been updated since the dumb curve, but obviously the fleet had overlooked this one or, more likely, hers and other captains' requests to have this embarrassing redundancy removed from the regulations were lost in queues of thousands of other official messages and requests, perhaps at the workstation of someone who died recently or took seriously ill.

The computer was still counting. "Seven, six, five, four, three, two, one, zero." A ship appeared, not nose first and then tail but all at once. There was empty space, then a battleship in all the integrity of its wholeness down to the subatomic level, manifest complete in that very space. Others were popping into existence in front of the gate and already traveling at .7 light speed the same moment they became real.

Captain Swenah directed the fire control officer the moment the heavy cruisers instead of battleships began appearing. "Target every battleship with a shield disruptor missile, followed a second later by a nanobot spray missile. First get a small beam weapon on the shields of each battleship to reduce their power and effectiveness."

All eighteen battleships had their usually invisible shields lit up and acting like a liquid for about three seconds by the small beam weapons, while the shields covering the spots where the shield disruptor missiles hit vanished for a second before rushing in like a liquid to patch the holes.

Swenah told the coms officer, "Get Jard on speaker."

They heard Jard next door. "That's right—keep organizing. Go, go, go. You can do it. Yes. All right!"

"What's the status, Jard?" Swenah asked.

"We've got connection, and I'm uploading the program in virus form. Viruses seem to work as well for mutations in cyberspace as they do for causing genetic mutations in life-forms."

"How long will it take?" the captain wanted to know.

"We're talking 8.7 terabits, so don't get your panties in a bunch," Jard said without thinking.

She was sorry she'd asked. All the officers on the bridge were smiling. She told him, "I know you're a genius wizard, a civilian, and a member of the High Council, Jard, but you must not speak to the captain of the ship that way."

"Yona told me, I know. Sorry," was what he offered by way of apology.

They waited some more and then Jard said, "It's all in, working its magic now. On our systems, we would be looking at four or five minutes depending upon which generation administrative program we're attacking, and possibly, though this is yet theoretical, on how motivated and determined the quantum computer is. I expect this bug to crack their system in less than two minutes, but I'm not very familiar with Imperial quantum computers because I've had no interest in them. Though now that we may have further need in the future, I think I'll study them. I wonder how ..." Sounds of an ancient keyboard could be heard on the bridge because Jard was hammering the keys so hard, not used to such a crude instrument. He launched into rapid code and technobabble to the computer, which alone understood him. The fighters and fighter-bombers were launching from the battleships, and some assault ships were headed right for them.

Swenah said, "Take us directly forward to point five light speed, Konax."

A moment later, Jard shouted in his excitement, "I got them! They're mine! I'm transferring control of specific ships with their identifiers to seventeen different com stations, so hey, people, if one comes on your hologram, start piloting it back toward the gate and up to point seven light. You'll have to initiate the jump engines manually with the quantum drive icon I'm sending. It will appear at the bottom of your holo—just touch it three seconds before your ship reaches the gate. I've already preset all the destinations to the Kundabuffer gate. I'm driving the flagship."

Swenah touched her icon for the chief engineer and asked, "Do we have enough shuttles, repair spacecraft, and ice/fluid collector refineries to get this gate moving, even if just to thirty thousand miles per hour?"

"In theory, Captain, but I doubt we have enough cable. We could use the tractor beam on this ship to tow it and easily get it up to point one light."

"Thank you, Chief. I knew I could count on you to come up with a better way. I didn't know star fleet ships had a tractor beam."

"They're a concentrated beam from the vortex generation and redirection equipment, which can work with high-energy concentrations when gravity is weak or unavailable. These T-nines are the first to get tractor beams. Where are you thinking of sending it?"

"Back their way," Swenah told him. "They already have quite a distance to cross in real space from here to reach Ganahar, and I mean to make it take longer. I wish there were a nearby asteroid field to plant it in … or a much closer black hole. I'm told the only safe way to dispose of one of these gates is to send it into one."

They watched as the flagship and seventeen other battleships disappeared at the gate. Without their brute force and cover, the rest of the Imperial fleet followed them to the gate, disappearing. The intelligence officer connected with the captain's coms and told her, "Ma'am, you just have to hear the translation of the chatter we picked up between the Imperial ships as they left. Honestly, it's hysterically funny and thoroughly amusing."

"Please forward it to my in-box, and thank you," she said, imagining.

She asked Jard, "What happens to your program now?"

"It's their default program, and all administrative overrides of the new program went dormant the moment they passed through quantum space, restoring their controls."

"What if they just turn around and come back?" Swenah asked.

"I'll turn them back around again or I could have them shoot at each other if you'd prefer," Jard said flippantly.

"You know perfectly well that an important parameter of our mission is no fatalities," Swenah scolded.

"Then if they come back, can we take over their heavy cruisers?"

"That sounds good to me," Swenah replied.

"I'll need a bunch more pilots."

"You can send one to each of the twelve stations on the bridge," she offered. Then she added, "I think you were going to ask me, right before you established control of those ships, where you could get an Imperial quantum supercomputer."

"Yes, I was."

"Central intelligence has agents on Vox, and they got hold of one. Central Intelligence keep it in their subterranean offices beneath their headquarters. I know this because star fleet sent my ship to retrieve it. Yona could get you clearance. You know how reluctant they are to share secrets. I almost wish I could be there when you go."

"I'll do that while Pez is in her training," Jard agreed, liking the idea. He'd get Yona to make them give up everything they knew, and thought they knew, about the alien computer tech too while he was at it. He'd forgotten about those shadow dwellers.

A personal message from Senior Admiral Zapa was waiting in Swenah's in-box, not flagged or prioritized in any way and bearing no stamp or seal of office. Intrigued, she opened it first and listened. She had to hear it again to be sure she'd gotten it right. Then she told Konax, "Admiral Zapa messaged me that Pez reported success in finding the person of interest on Ganahar. Her message said she picked them up in the Haraga Mountains. What she didn't bother to mention, and which was learned from this person of interest by the prime minister, was that Pez had to pass the most severe ancient test of inner fire by sitting naked in the snow from dusk until dawn, drying a wet sheet, before the person she sought would receive her."

Impressed, Konax said, "There are only a dozen people in the Tail of Nine who could have survived that test, and they're all probably within the Clear Light Order."

"It's been twenty-nine thousand years since anyone from Om tried that test," Swenah declared. "We all heard about it when we learned and practiced inner fire and learned about the cotton-robed monk who lived for twenty years in the snowcapped mountains, wearing only his cotton robe and drinking only the water of boiled nettles, sustaining his life entirely with the practice."

Konax inquired, "Did they set the test as a condition of receiving her?"

"No, that's the thing," Swenah marveled. "They simply told her to go away and that they would not speak with her under any conditions. Pez must have realized that the people she was dealing with had a practice like inner fire and would recognize and trust her if she could demonstrate her own mastery of it."

"Anyone else on that mission would have, at that point, abducted the person of interest by nonlethal force," Konax reasoned.

"I can assure you that it would never have occurred to me to sit naked in the snow all night, and had it, humor and dismissal would be as far as it would've gotten in terms of motivating any action from me. Can you even imagine?"

"Pez naked?" Jard asked, amused, his line to them still open.

Konax laughed as he said, "It's hard not to in the context of such a story."

Swenah said with some frustration, "Not Pez naked. Could you imagine deciding to strip down and challenge exposure to the elements? My own capacity to produce body heat through concentration is not up to it, and I wouldn't stake my life on improving my practice enough to survive within only hours in the midst of agonizing cold to distract my attention and defeat my concentration."

"I'm far from capable of surviving that test," Konax agreed, "and even further from ever trying it."

Still imagining Pez naked, Jard commented, "She's such a tiny thing."

"She is also a giant of spirit," Swenah informed him. "No one on the ship can beat her in a fight, and we have Marshal Hark aboard with a company of Clear Light knights. Elesia told me that only the abbot and vicar-general can best her."

Jard's mind had moved from Pez's naked body to consider other dimensions of her being, drawn by Swenah's revelations, and he said, "She has been Aton's and Nemellie's protégé for years without ever realizing it. The poor girl thinks of them as her parents and interprets their special interest in her from within this context. She came to the order from a government-sponsored school for gifted children just before she turned twelve, and star fleet had been trying to recruit her too, pulling strings and lobbying. As I recall, they were sore losers about it and attempted to get the High Council to intervene by sending Pez to them. Did you know that her flight to Ganahar beat not only the times of all previous flights from Om to there but also all flight-simulated best times possible? That girl flies on instinct by the seat of her pants."

"I'd love to fly with her," Konax said longingly.

"Not me," Jard said. "She put a crater in the desert on Ganahar, and she cleared the top edge of a sheer cliff by a meter. No, thanks."

Konax was smiling, excited by the idea, and Swenah told him, "I'm sure you'll have an opportunity to fly with her in a small craft during our mission."

Konax asked, "Could you obtain a copy of the flight imaging the ship caught of itself on Pez's trip to Ganahar?"

"I'd like to see that myself," Swenah said. "I'll ask. I hope it's not classified. I'm sure flight engineers and other specialists will be analyzing that data for years to come, but it will never be seen in the Star Fleet Academy's pilot school."

"The space marine commander informed me," Konax confided, "that in the group Pez is training with, not one is less than a foot and three inches taller or less than twice her weight."

"She'll surprise them," Swenah assured him. "Their force will never connect with her mass. She can yield to any strike and always begins ahead of the strike, reading the energies. A fly could not alight on that girl without setting her into motion, and that's a fact, not an exaggeration."

"I make the contemplation practiced daily and work pretty hard at the soft martial arts, recognizing that attention, concentration, and instinctive immediacy are what make a great pilot, and this has served me well, but that girl is in a class of her own."

"She's never flown a large ship," Swenah said.

"That's only because she's never had the opportunity," Konax informed her. "I'd love to see what she could do with a T-nine."

"We'd probably have sensor arrays coming loose, and her stunt in the desert, had it been a T-nine, would surely have caused an extinction event. You are the pilot I want flying my ship."

"Me too," Jard put in. "Though I'd love to see the flight imagery if you can get a copy."

Swenah messaged Admiral Zappa, replying to the message he'd sent her, and requested a copy of the visual imagery of that record flight. Jard told her on the open line, "It doesn't look as if they're coming back. I guess I won't get to take over three dozen heavy cruisers today."

He sounded quite disappointed. Captain Swenah told him, "We'll wait to hear from our cloaked drone in Kundabuffer and then go to Ganahar, where you will be celebrated as a global hero, Jard."

"I don't want anyone physically touching me, and I won't sign autographs or kiss babies. I'd be willing to allow them a holocom interview, provided the media specialist conducting the interview is an actual scientist or quantum computer engineer and not some airhead celebrity chaser." Then he asked, "Who is their chief government officer?"

"They have no government and no officers of any kind, but I can arrange the interview through their holocom associated news group in Kashpon, where we will be landing from the ship, once we are orbiting Ganahar. I'll insist on your conditions and inform them that you don't shake hands or high-five either."

"No physical contact whatsoever!" Jard said adamantly.

"None," Swenah promised. She told her coms officer, "Get me

someone with clout from the holocom associated news group in Kashpon on the line. Have them direct their spectrum-encoded light communications to our drone orbiting Ganahar, only a fraction of a second from them. You'll need to give them the specifics of its orbit and what its location is in their specific space-time."

"Yes, Captain. I'm on it."

To the auxiliary systems control officer on the bridge, Swenah said, "Please immediately disable the cloaking mode on the ship's drone orbiting Ganahar."

"Yes, ma'am." A moment later, the officer reported, "It's done, Captain."

"Thank you."

Jard told her, "A parade would be nice, if I could watch it from a high-rise balcony."

"We'll see, Councilman," Swenah replied with a grin.

Her coms officer said, "I have an administrator online for you from the news group in Kashpon."

She nodded acknowledgment and said to the administrator, "This is Captain Swenah of star fleet of the Om star system. We have turned back the invasion force from the Kundabuffer Empire successfully, and your planet is safe. We will be taking orbit around Ganahar once we're sure the threat is over, and I can offer you an interview with the man who took control of all eighteen battleships of the Imperial fleet, sending them home. He will only speak with a fellow quantum computer expert or scientist, and he would appreciate a parade."

"The people of Ganahar will give him a parade as never seen before and build a colossal monument to him. He will be the greatest hero in our planet's history! Could you send us his biographical information and a picture? Thank you, Captain, and great thanks to the hero and to the people of Om. Right now we have only field generators and power from vehicles and ships on the ground. It will be days before the reactors can be restarted. Our studios are located on Sadhana Thruway, right on the main plaza, across from the arena in Kashpon. Things are somewhat chaotic, and the population of the city is mostly still on their way into hiding."

A TALE OF THE TAIL OF NINE STARS

"If there is a square mile, or close to it, anywhere in or around Kashpon, I could land and power the city and surrounding area."

"Alas you would have to go clear out to agricultural land to find a clear space so large, and the farmers would be fighting mad," the administrator lamented.

"Then once I reach orbit, I'll send down a mobile reactor on a landing pod to power your city, which could land easily within a sporting field, or cleared parking lot, or at any air and spaceport."

"I'd suggest landing it at the air and spaceport since the main power line runs directly beneath it. I'll notify their administration so they can clear a space and set light broadcasters around the perimeter of your landing zone."

"What's the population of Kashpon?" Swenah asked, knowing her chief engineer would require this information.

"There are five million in the city proper and another six million in the area immediately surrounding it."

"How much industrial energy do you typically use?"

"The industrial works are all in the area outside the city and generally consume three and a half gigawatts during daylight hours and less than half a gigawatt through the night."

"Then the reactor I'm sending has more than ample capacity for your needs. See if you can get some engineers and technicians working on rigging a splice to the main line. I'm sending you Jard's picture and a brief biographical sketch now. I'll call again from orbit. Have a nice day."

"Thank you. The splice will be ready when the landing pod sets down."

To Jard, Swenah said, "Your interview is set per your conditions, and you'll have your parade. They said they'd build a monument to you as well. I get the feeling that they're going to recall all their history text data beads on the planet so they can get out a new edition to include your feats and name."

The com officer told her, "The cloaked drone in the Kundabuffer system reports that the battleships each went to a repair dock and the rest of the ships of their invasion fleet have left the system or maneuvered to join their usual battle groups. There is zero activity oriented to an immediate military response. Based on this report, it sounds like they'll require some time to lick their wounds and try to figure out what went wrong."

"Let's hope they take their time," Swenah commented. Then she told the auxiliary systems control officer, "Prepare to engage the tractor beam off the stern." To Konax, she said, "Pull up in front of that gate with the bow pointed toward Thadysus."

"That should serve," he concurred.

Konax came around the edge of the gate at about the slowest speed the ship was capable of, getting the stern aligned with the side of the gate and the bow aimed at Thadysus, with little distance between gate and stern—actually, just over a quarter mile. It was a most impressive piece of driving. Swenah told the auxiliary systems control officer, "Lock on the tractor beam to the side of the gate closest us and bring it up to full power."

Swenah waited. The officer told her, "The tractor beam is locked on at full force, Captain."

She told Konax, "Apply propulsion as gradually as the system is able, and let's see if we can get this behemoth up to point one light speed."

The process took fifty-nine minutes, and once they had the gate traveling more or less in the direction of Kundabuffer at .1 light speed, Swenah ordered the tractor beam shut down, the navigation officer to send the pilot the coordinates of Ganahar, and Konax to get them to that planet and into a high safe orbit. She could see the star quite clearly, closest and brightest in the panorama of space, looking numerous times larger than any other star.

She directed her navigation officer, "Find me some micro-jump coordinates right to the orbital path of the fourth planet; we can begin reducing speed from there."

She looked to Konax, who looked over his shoulder and confirmed, "No sweat. By the time we reach the orbital path of Ganahar's moon, I'll have us down to one hundred and twenty-five miles per second, with another hundred-eighty thousand miles to brake."

Now that her mission was fully accomplished, having turned the invasion around and gotten the gate moving toward its origin and maker at a good clip, she messaged the senior admiral, the prime minister, and Aton, since there were knights of his order aboard. The admiral suddenly appeared in holo before her, one-tenth scale, floating in the air. He told her, "Good work, Captain Swenah. You and your crew did a terrific job."

"We really just gave Jard a ride and provided expert fire control, sir, but all the glory goes to him. I wasn't looking forward to putting holes in eighteen battleship hulls with no loss of life. Jard tells me the empire will never find the code embedded and we will own those battleships from here on out. We ought to start an operation of infiltrating dormant programs into all their ship's quantum computers in the galaxy, sir."

"That's an excellent idea, Captain, and I'll see you get credit for it," the admiral said, quite enjoying unfolding and rolling out the idea in his mind, delight increasing as it progressed.

"It's Jard's idea, sir, not mine. He was geared up to take all their heavy cruisers if they came back again, and he was sorely disappointed that they didn't. Coms got clear audio imprints of all the chatter between ships as they left back through their gate with their destinations all set to Kundabuffer. I'm told it makes great entertainment, though I'm sure we can learn much about them by analyzing it. I'll have them send you a copy immediately."

She glanced at her coms officer, and he nodded, getting right on it. The admiral said, "I quite look forward to hearing it; thank you. What a rare treat."

"They've already sent it to fleet intelligence," Swenah informed him.

"Please give my thanks to Jard and my congratulations to your crew on a job well done," Admiral Zapa said, beaming with pride.

"The people of Ganahar want to interview Jard, throw a parade for him, and build him a monument, so I thought I'd take the opportunity to meet with the military leaders of Ganahar and the Raster Republic. There are also ships there from the United Lights and from the Kataleptica Star Union."

"Now that the High Council has put us in the middle of this, you better go ahead and coordinate some emergency plans with all three entities. I'm assuming that we will no longer allow the empire to enslave another friend and ally, as we did with Vox."

"I hope we learned our lesson from that, sir," Swenah said with a bit of passion.

"Thank you for handling this, Captain. Jard could not have had a better babysitter and support crew. I'm proud of you. Now get us some tight and efficient procedures in place with Raster, United Lights, and Kataleptica."

"Yes, sir!"

Konax announced, "Prepare for micro-jump in ten seconds."

He didn't bother with a countdown, instead giving all of those on the bridge a digital one at the bottoms of their holos. He had to enter the second micro-jump immediately after the first and had little time to do so. This remained constant for him through four more jumps, taking them right to the orbital path of the fourth planet and fairly close to it. There was a sheen of sweat at his hairline, and he let out a big sigh after the last jump.

They had just covered sixty-eight light hours in less than eighteen minutes. Now the reverse drives and thrusters were kicking in, bleeding speed, and the rest of the way would be in real space.

"You're the only one I'll let fly my ship micro-jumping into a star system or in any combat situation," Swenah told Konax gratefully. "Those were really tight intervals, and between the traffic and fixed relays, you didn't have a straight shot within but one of them. I admire your work, Lieutenant."

"Thank you, Captain. That means a lot coming from a pilot such as yourself."

Swenah told her com officer, "Get the Kashpon air and spaceport on the line."

After a brief pause, he said, "You're connected, Captain."

Swenah said to the air and spaceport administrator, "My ship is nine minutes from orbital position above your planet. I'll call to coordinate the setting down of the landing pod as soon as I'm in orbit."

"We weren't expecting you for at least another nineteen hours. We won't have a main splice line out to your landing zone for at least another three."

"It's your lights that are off," the captain remarked. "I'll be ready whenever you are."

"Thank you, Captain Swenah, really, for everything. We are all so grateful. Your ship and interstellar hero Jard have saved our entire civilization. What can a person say in the face of that? Words fail utterly. Every son and daughter of Ganahar is forever in your debt, and you are forever in our hearts. I'll try to get more workers on that power connection and hurry things along."

"I'm glad we could help and didn't have to sit on our hands, stand by, and stand down again while a friendly planet got usurped into the insatiable expanding empire, as we did with Vox. Perhaps you could get a message to the military leaders of Raster, United Lights, and Kataleptica, extending an invitation for a meeting aboard my ship to work out signals and channels through which to call upon and ascertain our future aid and support."

"I certainly will, and they'll be calling you in minutes."

"Thanks. I'll call you when I'm in orbit," Swenah said, signing off.

Jard, who had listened in and was now in complete control of the ship's coms somehow, said to Swenah, "I like the sound of 'interstellar hero Jard.' It has a nice ring to it."

Swenah told him, "Come up with a way to defeat the aliens and you'll be 'intergalactic hero Jard'; but really, it is against fleet regulations, not to mention the law, for you to listen in on a captain's direct line. For saving the world of Ganahar, you can do it today only. Then you really must stop."

"I know," he acknowledged reluctantly, like a teen whose fun is being spoiled by adult supervision. "With this setup here, there's really nothing I can't connect with and take over. I was just playing around to see what the system could do."

"I'm sure it was quite a thrill, but you're on the High Council, Jard, and supposed to be upholding the law, not breaking it," Swenah reminded the genius kindly.

"I've changed my mind about the parade. I want to study anarchy and try to understand how they do it," Jard told her.

"It's too late to cancel the parade now. Others will appreciate it. I'll try to get a leading sociology professor for you to chat with while you watch the parade, or at least occasionally pretend to," Swenah said with a hint of steel in her voice. Then she reminded him, "We represent Om and must not offend our hosts. Reciprocal law requires us, as the guests, to express gratitude, just as it requires the host to provide for us.

I do hope each of us makes a good impression reflecting the best of Om's culture."

"I'm only going to the parade if I can watch it from a balcony above," Jard insisted, testing the limits.

"I'm sure I can arrange that," she assured him. "Do you have any specific height requirements?"

"I think fifty feet above the street would give me the best view."

Swenah was trying to think of a junior officer to assign to watch over Jard. She was convinced that one with either a mentally challenged or genius sibling would be able to handle him best—someone with a solid computer science background and a thick skin. Positive discipline parenting skills wouldn't hurt either. No one sprang to mind, so she set parameters and entered skills and life circumstances for a personnel computer search. The results were staring her in the face the moment she hit ENTER with her skullcap.

There was only one person who was a commissioned officer and met the prerequisites: Lieutenant Ming. Her brother worked at the fleet top secret research and development facility, with an intelligence quotient, aptitude scales, and creativity indicators off the charts. She went through training in positive discipline when she was in sixth form and her parents adopted a troubled four-year-old. She was an accomplished programmer and sensors analyst, and she was so tiny, even smaller than Pez, that she had to have developed a thick skin to handle it. Reading her own evaluation of Ming, composed almost ten months previously, brought back memories of Lieutenant Ming. She brought up a visual holo image, which brought up further recollections of the almost childlike highly competent little officer. In her delighted relief, Captain Swenah's mind robbed all the credit from the personnel computer and patted herself on the back mentally for her triumph. She ordered Lieutenant Ming to the bridge and added her name to the mission crew who would be under Pez's command. The little lieutenant was prompt indeed.

"Lieutenant Ming reporting to the bridge, Captain."

Captain Swenah rose from her seat. At six feet six inches tall, the captain was of average height among Om women, yet she stood a full ten inches above the top of the lieutenant's head. Swenah said to Konax, "Please alert me the moment we are orbiting Ganahar."

"Right away, Captain."

To the lieutenant, Swenah said, "Accompany me to my office, Lieutenant Ming; I have an assignment to discuss with you, of a sensitive nature."

"Yes, ma'am."

They walked from the bridge to the captain's office, not far from her ship station. She allowed the lieutenant to enter first. The young woman, only twenty-three, took a seat facing the captain's desk. She looked anxious, so Swenah tried to put her at ease by informing her, "You have been doing an excellent job, and I haven't a single criticism, so please relax. There is in fact a rather delicate assignment you're perfect for, and if you care to continue in this assignment once we return from Ganahar, then you could come with me on a mission of vital importance under the command of Supreme Commander General Pez."

Pez, Swenah, and Yona, in that order, constituted Ming's biggest heroes in the universe. She'd no idea that Pez had been commissioned the supreme commander general, nor that she'd been given a vitally important mission. She said to the most celebrated captain of the Om star fleet, "I would follow you and Pez into certain death."

"I'm truly flattered," Swenah admitted, "but you haven't yet heard what the assignment is."

"I'll put forth my very best effort, ma'am," Ming assured her, now determined to be included on the mission with Pez.

She had met Pez once, when the Star Fleet Academy did its annual hand-to-hand training under instructors from the Clear Light order. Pez had only been an assistant instructor back then, but she was actually the most effective at recognizing errors in posture and body mechanics as well as conveying these in a way that made comprehension and understanding easy. Pez was so personable that she seemed instantly a friend, almost a sister, and kind of like a fellow conspirator. Ming also found Pez beautiful. She had a hefty hero worship for her as well as a crush on her, and she kept a little scrapbook of her hero's exploits.

Captain Swenah could see that the girl was determined to go on the mission and was ready to accept about any possible assignment. She explained to Ming, "We have a rather rare genius aboard, without a shred of common sense or the least hint of social grace. He has a habit of breaking laws and regulations with his experimentation. He is also as crucial to the mission as he was to the one we've just completed."

"High Councilman Jard," Ming offered.

"Yes," Swenah agreed. "Growing up with your brother and your adopted sibling makes you the ideal person to babysit Jard and keep him out of trouble."

"How, ma'am? He's a member of the High Council, and I'm merely a junior lieutenant."

"He will be coming along as a civilian under military command. Pez will be my ranking officer. As Jard's monitoring keeper and my assistant, you will outrank Jard on the ship. I will promote you to second lieutenant immediately if you accept the assignment, and his behavior will not reflect on you. I don't expect you to stop him forcefully from any of his play and diversions. I only need you to cite regulations and laws and to reason with him, remind him of his duty, and provide some kind of negative consequences when he absolutely won't listen, even if it is only to give him the cold shoulder. I saw on your record that you once trained a dog, so approach it like that."

"I'm pretty good with animals and children, and I've had no personnel problems with the crew I'm responsible for, though I'm not experienced with men in their sixties who are members of the High Council. I will do the very best I'm capable of. In what capacity will I be presented to Councilman Jard, ma'am?"

"You will be his assistant," Swenah informed Ming. "When he needs transportation, you'll arrange it with administrators on Ganahar, and when he wants a file or an expert to consult, you'll arrange that. If there is a piece of tech he just *must* see, you will ensure his lawful access. You will also be sure he is physically present at the parade he said he wanted in his honor and attempt to cover for any embarrassing rudeness. Nudge him and cite law and regulation when he is about to violate these and try to reason things out with him before he just goes with his impulse, unthinking."

"I understand," Ming assured her captain. A stranger assignment she could not even imagine, though she recognized the importance of it from the captain's perspective and the honor of Om. It would also get her included on a mission with her ultimate hero, a promotion, and make her assistant to her second biggest hero in the universe, the captain.

"If you fear he is about to do something especially ill-advised and won't listen to you, then you must alert me at once and I'll see what I can do to intervene or otherwise help clean up the mess," Swenah explained.

"When would you like me to begin this assignment, Captain?"

Swenah reached into a drawer and then handed Ming her second lieutenant insignia, saying, "Immediately. He is in the com room with his playthings. I'll introduce you."

"He knows me, ma'am." Ming informed her. Swenah gave her a questioning look, so Ming offered, "He spent some time at my station examining raw sensor data and said he wanted to measure the distortion ratio involved in the enhancement processes as well as the decision matrix program for enhancement. His conclusion was that our software has humanoid assumptions embedded that would produce significant errors in enhancing sensor data taken from a non-humanoid vessel."

"I'm sure he's correct, and such analysis is invaluable for our next mission. That kind of meddling is to be encouraged, up to a point. He cannot be allowed to render needed equipment inoperable by dismantling it in flight, though." Then she asked Ming, "Does he like you?

"I believe Councilman Jard universally likes all young women, Captain," Ming stated.

"I've seen that," Swenah agreed, "but he writes off airheads and has no tolerance for them, and it annoys him to no end when someone can form the right words for a technical answer without really understanding what they're talking about."

"He does not see me as an airhead, ma'am, and has no annoyance toward me," Ming stated factually. "He did not seem to hold any grudges at all when I refused to share his berth for an hour, ma'am."

"No, he never does," Swenah said, thinking about her own experiences of Jard. "He asks every woman he is attracted to, and that approach has worked for him. I heard he once had to invite one hundred and seventeen women before he found one willing. He was at the main tube stop in the capital at rush hour, though, and it didn't take him more than an hour. Most single people invest an entire evening in seeking a partner and take rejection hard. I don't believe he's been so successful aboard a star fleet ship."

"You might be surprised," Ming suggested.

Now it became the captain's duty to inquire, before allowing this assignment to get any further, "Have you had sex with Councilman Jard?"

"No, ma'am. I never have, nor would I," Ming told her sincerely.

"Then I'll go speak to him with you, and you can put on your new insignia and get started immediately," Swenah said with great relief, as part of her mind wondered which of her crew had been sexual with Jard. She mentioned to Ming, "It's surprising some of our women would have sex with him when there are so many handsome young men on board."

"They do not ask every woman they find attractive, and they don't seem to do enough asking at all, Captain," Ming explained. "The prettiest ones always seem to be same-gender oriented, and some, I am told, are clueless regarding female climax."

They came to the armored door to the bridge, and the space marine sentry opened it with a thought impulse through his skullcap, stepping aside smartly to stand at attention and salute. Swenah gave a less-than-enthusiastic salute in return as she passed through the door. The ritual always felt overly theatrical and unnatural to her, but then, she was not a space marine either. When it came to a battle outside the hull in the cold vacuum, or on the ground in any condition, she was grateful beyond words—to the point of tears even—to have them on her side.

Swenah entered the coms room with Lieutenant Ming and approached Jard, who was surrounded by holograms for 360 degrees. He was watching a six-foot plasma screen museum piece displaying long and complex equations. Swenah did not even recognize one of the function symbols in the first equation at the top, making any attempt at calculation entirely futile. She said to Jard, "I believe you are already acquainted with Lieutenant Ming. I'm assigning her to be your assistant and arrange for all of your needs while we are here in the Ganahar system. Please keep in mind that I said 'arrange for.' She will not directly and personally be seeing to your needs but rather finding the best people or person for the job in each instance. She's been directed to contact me at once if you are planning to commit, or are committing, any gross infractions of the law. As your commanding officer on this mission, I'm

A TALE OF THE TAIL OF NINE STARS

ordering you to run all your ideas involving action of any kind by your assistant, and social and legal mentor, to minimize any trouble you might get in. Are we clear, High Councilman Jard?"

"I understand," Jard assured her. "I'm not to sexually molest or harass Lieutenant Ming, whom I've already determined to be into females anyway, and I'm to get her opinion before initiating any action. She will act as my liaison with the people of Ganahar to ensure pristine diplomatic behavior, making a gracious impression upon our hosts. Have I left anything out?"

"This is an apt summary, but the question is, are you going to do it?" Swenah asked him.

"I will invest considerable effort in trying, I promise you; and Lieutenant Ming here, I am quite certain, will function as both an area of memory and as my entire conscience."

"You have that right," Swenah completely agreed. "I'll leave the two of you to it, then."

The captain exited the coms room. Ming got right to work on the coms, establishing connections on Ganahar who could help her with transportation, dining, hotels, a list of who's who in the sciences and their contact information, a hover platform with comfortable seats for the parade, the Ganahar laws pertaining to escorts and sex workers, and many more categories. In the process, she discovered an overall go-to person who could accommodate any request. She was the elected CEO of the Ganahar Diplomatic Welcoming Committee and the sweetest, most helpful person Ming had ever encountered. She was already compiling a list of the brainiest young females eager to have sex with their planet's interstellar hero, complete with visual imagery and contact numbers. By the time their ship assumed its orbit around Ganahar, Lieutenant Ming was armed with her pocket quantum computer com device, and had it loaded with, she hoped, every conceivable contact and bit of information possibly required of any circumstance. She even had Marshal Hark's number ready should she need to get Jard off the planet quickly and discreetly.

5

Pez had just hit the showers at the Zero Gravity Training Facility on the star fleet campus. All of the space marines she was being instructed by and was training with were large muscular men. They'd been at it nearly fourteen hours, and even though it was not weight bearing per se, it required great exertion and all of them were completely exhausted. She washed her hair since even her head had broken a sweat inside her suit. She felt like a skinny midget showering next to them. Not one was under seven feet tall and was at least 270 pounds, with hardly an ounce of fat. Their astonished looks were saying, "That was you inside that spacesuit?"

She'd managed to hold her own, even on her first day. She'd lost no matches, except to the instructors, and when she got the hang of it, sometime in late morning or early afternoon, the instructors could no longer defeat her either. This had required utter mindfulness on her part and remaining in that state beyond thought, of pure instinct. Overall, Pez was satisfied with her efforts and progress. Food and sleep held gargantuan appeal right now. Sex too, though these giants held no attraction for her. One was nearly eight feet tall and barrel-chested, with pectoralis muscles three times the size of Pez's breasts, no discernible neck, a flat belly of hard-ridged muscles, thighs like tree trunks, and upper arms as big as Pez's waist, forged to adamantine. They seemed almost a different species. She had utmost respect for them and admired greatly their sacrifices for the common good. Unlike star fleet and the Clear Light Order, space marines had a size requirement of at least seven feet tall and a minimum weight of 240 pounds. Only the outliers, quite larger than normal, were recruited. Pez was abnormal in the opposite direction, and the expanse separating her from them was extreme. She could appreciate aesthetically their beauty and perfection, but they were not at all her type and stimulated no sexual feelings in her. Most of them were simply too big to fit, regardless of what she might want anyway.

The lieutenant commander, who was highest ranking of all the naked men in the showers and locker room, said to Pez, "I've never seen anyone learn so fast. It's really an honor to work with you, Supreme Commander General."

"The honor is all mine, having the opportunity to learn from the best of the best." Then she confided, "I don't know what they expect of me on my mission, but I really hope it's not fighting outside the hull hand to hand."

"I doubt that is part of the plan, and the training is only for unplanned contingencies. As you saw today, it is better to start off already knowing what you're doing."

"Right," Pez agreed wholeheartedly. "I wouldn't want to try to learn that in the midst of combat."

"If you ever need it, you'll already be one of the best," he complimented her.

"Thank you, Lieutenant Commander. I'm so impressed with how disciplined and willing your men are, their determination and stamina, and their dedicated morale. Space marines are unique as a population, like an elite athletic club."

"It gets under the skin to form an inseparable and integral part of identity as well as parameters for behavior, kind of like a family," he admitted.

"Well, I hope I can be a cousin or niece or something," Pez said longingly.

"You made yourself one of us out there today, ma'am," he told her sincerely.

Pez was toweling off and about to seek her locker, so she said, "It's a family I'm deeply honored to be related to. I better get dressed, then get some chow and rest so we can do this again tomorrow.

"Have a good evening, ma'am."

Pez dressed quickly, not bothering with the bra since she had an undershirt and shirt. She really liked the space marine step-in self-closing and adjusting boots, so cozy with the thick fleece socks. All her space marine clothing and gear had had to be custom made since they had no clothes, combat space suits, sensor goggles, sensor skullcaps, backpacks, belts, harnesses, rock climbing shoes, or anything else even remotely in her size.

As she closed her locker, she took a quick glance in the mirror, just tickled with her new space marine outfit. She made a most surrealistic space marine. Her insignia of rank was on the jacket that Pez wore proudly. The Clear Light Order had no uniforms, so whenever a supreme commander general was commissioned to lead a joint operation, the general traditionally wore the uniform of one of the participating branches of the military, mostly just to put the military leaders at ease. This was the first time the star fleet uniform was not selected by such a commissioned general.

Pez strode to the queue for the tubes and got online. She'd learned in an ancient history class that in ancient times, back when they were still using keyboards and your com device couldn't turn off the stove if you'd left it on, they had lifts with a dozen people standing so close they were in each other's personal space and almost touching. That was before they knew about personal space and the waves extending beyond the outer layer of skin. No wonder they were so agitated and aggressive back then.

She saw someone from star fleet that she'd always had a crush on and, until just yesterday, had been of comparable rank and therefore eligible—though not today. They smiled at each other and then Pez had to return a salute. This was really quite a lonely predicament.

She stepped forward as the line moved. It went efficiently, each tube moving on in less than five seconds, usually about three. She got her turn and stepped in, transmitting her desired destination. The door sealed, and the stomach sensations began. The insides were well padded. She always tried to sink her weight down, with one leg forward, knee over toe, and her back foot turned out slightly to root to the floor without holding on. After twenty years of this, she'd come to realize that it was not the practice of riding the tube at all but her soft martial arts practice that had led to her success.

There was one radical shift, from vertical to horizontal, with each of those being a long run at high speed, and the turn was taken faster by the tube than any other on her route. She always kept her fingertips on the padded rail for this turn. She felt it coming and sank down into a low stance. There! It left her with all of her weight on her back leg, and 70 percent had been on her forward leg going into it, but she had not grabbed the rail and her shoulder had not touched the padded wall. She was pleased that even in her extreme fatigue, she could still pull it off.

She had to change tubes in the Clear Light Order lobby but had no line for the tube she entered since it only went to her penthouse. Shudiy was seated on a cushion upon a rug in the foyer where Pez stepped out of the lift, and she rose to greet her. Pez couldn't understand a word besides *Wu*, and Mel was obviously not paying any mind to the foyer. She gave Shudiy a hug and opened the door with her skullcap. Sarhi came to the door as she entered, so Pez hugged her too. She was led to the table, where the food was already laid out. The men were absent tonight. Pez sat down with the five women.

Once again, she was the only one eating, and the rest seemed eager to watch. Pez tried to swallow her self-consciousness along with her first bite. The delicious flavor brought her out of herself and into her mouth's taste buds. So savory, a tiny bit hot, and intense, literally bursting with culinary-gustatory ecstasy.

Pez ate to match her famished appetite, forgetting all about her audience. There was a fresh-squeezed glass of wheatgrass juice, which was rather harsh alone, but there was also a glass of sweet carrot juice to chase it with. She understood it was nutritionally designed and prepared for her, with taste a secondary consideration, and she was impressed with their success—doubly so since none of them ate or tasted the food as it was made. She knew to produce an enormous belch at the end and did so when she'd finished eating, as well as thanking and complimenting them profusely.

Pez insisted she needed no bath this night, having just showered, and she held firm to her position. She could not get out of leading the evening practice, but she abbreviated some repetitions and made the one-hundred-syllable chant in a faster cadence than was ordinarily considered appropriate, finishing in only an hour.

Pez flossed, then cleaned her teeth with a water-jet pick and vibration brush, using spearmint-flavored antibacterial gel. Finally, she could climb into that ridiculously large bed and go to sleep. Sarhi tucked her in and kissed her forehead.

Woahha entered the bedroom without her robe, nor anything else on, leaving nothing at all to the imagination. She looked a lot younger without the robe and was actually quite beautiful. She was clearly much younger than the forty-year-old Pez had assumed her to be. She smiled at Pez, and Pez knew that if she so much as nodded, Woahha would be beneath the covers with her.

Pez said, "Thank you, but I'm too tired from my exertions today. I need to sleep." Then she gave Sarhi a look and said, "I will practice my dreamwork, Mother."

Sarhi and Woahha left her bedroom, and Pez allowed herself a moment of self-pity over her predicament and grief over her loss before launching dutifully into her dreamwork. From the concentrations of her dreamwork, Pez fell into deep sleep, and from that state, she entered the dream state.

The eight-foot space marine was there, as was little Woahha. She was three feet shorter than the towering marine, and they were both naked. They were in her ostentatious penthouse bedroom, and this is what tipped her off she was dreaming—that and the fact that she was naked too in the dream and not in bed but standing in the room.

Her lucidity grew crisp and clear, relaxing her from the sense of great awkwardness she'd been feeling. Now she was able to introduce graciously the small, even for a yellow sun, Islohar, Woahha, to the large, even for a white sun, Evenrude, the mighty space marine. Evenrude saluted her and called her Supreme Commander General, and Woahha bowed to her and called her Wu. Pez told them, as if letting them in on a big secret, "I'm really just Pez." They all laughed at the absurdity of it. Evenrude confided that he was irrationally frightened of grit bugs and once stood on a chair when one was on the floor in the room. He said that a seven-year-old girl, his host's daughter, had to remove it and throw it outdoors before he could put his feet down on the floor again. Woahha revealed that she was secretly in love with Pez and desperately wanted to have sex with her.

In her dream, Pez spilled out all her feelings. "I feel like a fraud as a supreme commander general and with senior spiritual teachers treating *me* like the teacher. I don't want to outrank Captain Swenah, but I would eagerly follow her anywhere. Jard will act up, and I won't know what to do, and everyone is going to think I'm full of myself and pathetic. I can't let Father Aton and Mother Nemellie down—nor can I the people. Islohar sexual customs are too strange for me, and I so need to be held and loved."

Evenrude and Woahha held her tenderly while she cried. Her sobs faded, and the tender love expressed through hugs reached her heart like water for a dry and withering plant. She felt fortified, filled, nurtured, and loved as she drifted back into deep sleep without dreams.

Pez slept peacefully from 20:30 to 04:15, when Mel said, "It is time to start your day, dear Pez. Wake up."

Slowly Pez came awake, and halfway there she murmured, "Thank you, sweet Mel."

Then she was fully awake and alarmed. Entwined about her was Woahha, just waking up herself. A string of Islohar words, unknown even to most on Ganahar, finally began receiving interpretation by Mel. "I just held you and sent you waves of love because you needed it and were becoming unbalanced. The Im told me I should; I did not touch you erotically. I meant no offense. Please forgive me, holy Wu."

Pez was already in complete empathy and with the realization from her dream that she truly had been desperate for love in the form of human touch. She had slept extraordinarily well and felt particularly hale this morning. She told Woahha affectionately, and Mel took care to match the vibes while interpreting, "There is nothing to forgive, dear Woahha. You did me a service and followed the guidance of the wise Im. Please don't feel bad. You have my gratitude, really."

Woahha perked up, delighted she'd pleased both Im and Wu. She had never met the old Wu, so Pez was the only Wu she knew. Pez extracted herself from the covers and pulled her nightgown over her head. She pulled off her knickers to put on a clean pair. Woahha had them open and at the ready for her to step into, then pulled them up snug around her. She had a clean uniform ready too and started by pulling the undershirt over Pez's head as Pez raised her arms into the sleeves. Woahha assisted with each article of clothing, and when she was doing up the buttons of the shirt, Pez recalled her mother buttoning her shirt for her when she was a small child. It was not a dress uniform but a combat one, by far Pez's favorite piece of clothing now. Woahha's obvious concern and her dedication to serving Pez touched her heart, and when she had her fully dressed, Pez gave her a closed-lip kiss on the mouth before going to her sitting room to eat some breakfast.

Taking a seat, she asked Sarhi, who was already at the table, "What happened to your four men?"

"Aton trains them so they can better serve you."

Shudiy served Pez her porridge and set her wheatgrass juice and a protein shake on the table by her plate.

Pez said, "Thank you, Shudiy, for taking such good care of me."

In accented Basic, Shudiy said with passion, "I serve Pez Wu."

"I wish I felt worthy, but I truly am grateful," Pez told her honestly. "My own cooking is a disaster, and the mess hall, though an improvement, is bland and lifeless compared to the food you prepare for me. Thank you."

Following Mel's translation, Shudiy said, "I serve Pez Wu."

Pez asked Sarhi, "Why do they not serve the Im?"

"The Wu was the Im's teacher and founder of the tradition. The Wu prepared the Im, so after the Wu passed into the light and was born again by choice to serve the enlightenment of all conscious beings, the Im could find and teach the Wu. Then, once the Im died, the Wu would find and teach the Im. Two self-realized and liberated beings taking rebirth alternately together made the awakening in each lifetime quicker and easier. Before this, there was only the Wu coming back and depending upon ad hoc monks and abbots to find him or her in toddlerhood by having him pick out his bell, thunderbolt, sandalwood counting beads, and ritual water holder. The Wu and the Im together go back two hundred and eighty-six generations. I'm the two hundred and eighty-sixty Im. You are the three hundred and thirty-third Wu."

Pez and Mel both said at the same time, "Wow!"

Then Pez said with a hint of accusation, "You sure waited a long time to find me."

"The Wu has never been born off planet before, dearest," Sarhi said soothingly. "The Wu serves all humanoids, all humanity, not just those on Ganahar, and had to be born to the other greatly evolved human civilization in this galaxy, Om, because they have the necessary technological advancement. The Islohar are needed for their spiritual advancement. Only together can we succeed—the Wu and the Im. We have come together two hundred and eighty-six times, and we are finding our unity once again. You will see Ahmonya in your dream state, and then the secret practice will provide the true freedom for you to be totally the Wu. You will see."

"It sounds a bit like the proverbial 'Which came first, the chicken or the egg,' to me," Pez told her.

"You will see," Sarhi repeated.

Woahha cleared the table as Pez swallowed her last bite. She cleaned her teeth with just the vibration brush and gel, skipping the water jet since she was in a hurry, and left the overly extravagant penthouse with just enough time to get to the Zero Gravity Training Facility by five o'clock.

Having gained an understanding of zero gravity combat, Pez was able to approach it with greater relaxation and confidence, though no less mindfully. Today she was able to employ more of her soft martial arts. She was always the one who went fastest and furthest when she pushed one of the big space marines or when she let them push her. The exercise had progressed to her being outnumbered five to one, and she found that by tracking all five simultaneously, she could accept blows at just the right moments to become a projectile knocking a space marine out of the practice zone. When the timing wasn't right, she was a worm bending impossibly out of the way. In close, she could tuck her ribs suddenly under one shoulder, folding out of the way of a punch that would then hit the space marine behind her. With a hand on one, quadrupling her mass, she was able to kick one out a gap through the practice zone. This then became a preferred technique. Pez also found she could grab one's shoulders and arch her spine, pushing off at an angle to reenter the mix from a new vantage point. Finally, she developed a move in which she got the top of one of her feet behind the back of the helmet while she stomped the face mask with the heel of her other foot.

She demanded a trial, and a helmet without a space marine's head in it was brought out to her. She got the top of her left foot behind the helmet and struck with her right heel, and all her martial training, into the face mask, releasing her internal energy upon impact. The lab tested the helmet's integrity to see if the crack in the face mask broke the pressure seal, and once word came back, the supreme commander general's new kick was counted as a lethal strike in scoring future matches. It also became part of the Advanced Zero Gravity Combat Training Course, as did several other moves Pez came up with over the twelve days of the training. By the end, a person would be wiser to insult a space marine's mother, wife, or daughter than to say an unkind word about Pez within hearing. A number of the Space marines she went through the course with would be serving the ship on the mission she was to command.

The completely overhauled, rebuilt, and refitted customized star cruiser was the embodiment of the highest know-how of the most brilliant minds alive today within the Tail of Nine. All three inhabited planets of the Tail were known to the outside world as Om since that had no clues of origin. The Tail of Nine, if known to other civilizations, would easily be located. The first place anyone would look would be the ends of the galactic arms of Hud, and sure enough, that's where they would then be found. As interactions with humans from other star systems outside the tail increased, the very term was fading from common use.

6

Captain Swenah returned to Om with the T-nine super cruiser, and Jard was celebrated as a hero once again. His special equipment was transferred from the T-nine to the custom star cruiser, and a good deal more equipment, experimental prototypes, and new devices right out of research and development were stowed aboard the star cruiser as well. While Jard was on Om, Lieutenant Ming got a few days' rest and recuperation. The stories the space marines told about Pez spread through star fleet.

Captain Swenah wore her dress uniform, as did her assistant, Lieutenant Ming, who stood beside High Councilman Jard amidst other senior officers of the ship and an honor guard of space marines, as Supreme Commander General Pez stepped aboard the ship at the shuttle dock with her nine Islohar teachers and a platoon of Clear Light warrior monks under the experienced and competent command of Halz.

These warrior monks were the best of those who served under her when she was a marshal, all of about two weeks ago. There was even a marching band, though confined to the shuttle dock; they just marched in place charismatically as they played.

Pez could not have been more embarrassed by all the pomp and display over her boarding the ship. The heroes who saved Ganahar, her heroes, were recognizing her, and she hadn't done anything of repute. She could only hope they didn't think poorly of her because of all this. She surely hadn't planned it. She returned every salute with her heart in it and gave each person her whole attention. When she got to Captain

Swenah, they shook hands and Captain Swenah said, "It's a real honor to serve under you, Supreme Commander General."

She replied in dismay, "It's just me, Swenah—just Pez—and this all seems incongruous and upside down and backward to me. I have always looked to you for solutions and guidance when Aton and Nemellie could not help me."

"I am on this mission with you, and I'll always give you the best assistance and counsel I can. You do not bear the weight of the mission alone. You have excellent people you can rely on. No one thinks you finagled this or even wanted it. We all respect and admire you, and none of us can think of anyone we'd rather have lead us than you. So give us your best, pure heart."

Tears welled in her eyes as she hugged Captain Swenah in a tight embrace. Lively military tunes and beats continued to arise out of the "marching in place" band. Pez pulled herself together and released Swenah to give her an enthusiastic salute worthy of a Space marine as she mouthed the words "Thank you." Pez recognized Lieutenant Ming from when she'd helped her as an assistant instructor and Ming was still at the Star Fleet Academy. She gave the second lieutenant a grin and said, "It is great to see you again, Second Lieutenant Ming. You've come far since I met you and now serve closely, I see, with my hero, Captain Swenah."

She is one of my biggest heroes as well, Supreme Commander General, right after you," Ming told her, smiling back.

The lieutenant commander from Pez's zero gravity training was aboard and present at her reception, in charge of the space marines aboard. He had volunteered, like everyone else on the ship, for this mission. A colonel of the Special Space Force and a deputy director of Central Intelligence were on the dock, and Pez met them. A lieutenant from fleet intelligence who had a shop and crewmen on the ship was also present. Pez liked him immediately. She also got to meet the famous Konax, and her awe and idolization of him were rather obvious to everyone.

Once Pez got off the shuttle dock into the bowels of the ship, the marching band ceased its loud energized music with quick, precise coordinated movements, and life didn't seem so frantically urgent any

A TALE OF THE TAIL OF NINE STARS

longer. Pez's new orderly, Junior Lieutenant Nash, was showing Pez and her party to their cabins. Nash was in his mid-twenties and was as awed by the company aboard the ship as Pez was, only his awe also included Pez.

Sarhi explained to Pez, "Living on a spaceship, my followers and I will have to start eating food again. The air on a ship is not the same as a true atmosphere, with concentrations of ions in the upper layers."

"We've already provisioned the ship," Pez stated. "Will we have appropriate food to feed you?"

"One of my men, Farid, told Aton, who informed the captain," Sarhi replied. "All has been provided for and is stored on the ship. Captain Swenah is most accommodating and highly competent."

"Well, that's a relief. This is our little wing of the officer's quarters, and that one is mine. Get your people settled in and call Nash if you need anything. He'll be giving me a tour of the ship." Then, like an excited little girl, Pez told her, "There's even a station for me on the bridge beside Captain Swenah!"

Sarhi smiled her approval for Pez's admiration of Captain Swenah, amused by her Wu's emotional arousal. Nash led the supreme commander general out of the little wing customized for the general and her nine teachers, taking her through the officers' quarters toward the bridge. They stopped in Pez's office, right next door to Captain Swenah's office, close to the bridge. It was quite expansive and well appointed. Everything but the hull, minus a few reinforced layers, was brand new on the ship. Through maximum miniaturization, the ship had been crammed with almost the power and weapons systems of the old 870-foot diameter battleships Om had. The reinforced layers over the hull included six-inch carbon plate and depleted mercurium armor, in addition to eight inches of adamantine plate armor, making it almost as impregnable as a T-nine. An eighth inch of carbon plate armor was stronger than an inch and a half of steel plate armor and about 100 times more expensive to manufacture.

Nash showed Pez to the bridge and, embarrassingly, all the officers rose and saluted as she entered. She told them, "Please be at ease and in the future just smile a greeting when I come on the bridge. When is our estimated departure?"

Konax answered, "In thirty-nine minutes. Captain Swenah will assume her station in eight minutes and forty seconds. She is always seated in the captain's seat thirty minutes before takeoff to oversee the final systems checks."

Pez couldn't help saying, "This is so exciting!"

All the bridge officers smiled at her wonderment. She sat in her own chair and found her bridge skullcap tucked in a pocket on the inside of her armrest. She located her shoulder harness and waist belt connectors, getting them clamped in. She had no idea how to bring anything up once she had her skullcap on and Nash had retreated to his workstation in her office. She thought of calling him, but everyone would overhear her questions anyway, so she asked, "How do you get this stuff to work?"

The senior coms officer came over and bent his head so it was just on the border of her personal space and said, "Enter first your serial number, then the bridge code, which is 7906N3Y25."

Pez entered the codes and got to a screen with unrelated numbers and a prompt to choose hers. She asked, "What's my number?"

"The only perfect number available: twenty-eight," the coms officer informed her.

Pez focused on the number on the holo screen in front of her left eye and was suddenly looking at four holograms a few feet in front of her. One was of the planet from their orbit, attached to the largest of the star fleet's docking stations, so she touched the sides of the hologram with her fingertips, then spread her hands, reducing the scale a hundredfold. She could also do this with thought, and far more accurately, though she loved doing certain things with her hands, and zooming in telescopically was the best of all. She brought it all the way down to the point where she could make out the manufacturer's trademark on the com unit of a man waiting at the ground transportation stop she'd narrowed the perspective to. Then she went to max magnification and took it to the limit of the imaging lens's capacity at the molecular level.

Pez played like a child with her holos until Captain Swenah came on the bridge. As everyone began to rise, Swenah said, "Don't stand up; we leave in thirty minutes so carry on with the preflight analysis."

Pez had already been on her feet entirely, grinning like a goon, and Swenah had to squeeze past her to get to her seat beside Pez, who grabbed her in a spontaneous hug of joy. Swenah patted her back and said in her ear, "I've never had such a sweet and affectionate ranking officer as you, and Mel is going to be so pleasant. Only a quantum program raised by you could be so concerned, vigilant, and sweet."

Pez complained, "She missed the foyer to my penthouse the other night."

"I was there, dear heart, but assumed you did not want to listen to such praises."

"Well," Pez admitted, "you're probably right."

They got seated and strapped in. Pez realized she'd been standing in her holograms, causing them to do all kinds of crazy things. One was a view of the atomic structure of the space station they were docked at, and another was a long, narrow view of deep space without a star in sight. She reset all of them to default with a single concentration and then made her magnification selections with her skullcap accurately. She glanced at Captain Swenah and saw that she was serious and concentrating. Pez tried to look serious and concentrate too. The trouble was, she had nothing to truly do or concentrate on, being strictly an observer in terms of performing any actual operations. Her workstation could monitor any workstation on the ship. She did a quick scan through all of them, curious if any of the crew were audacious enough to have sex at the workstation, which would've made great entertainment during the boring preflight checks, though everyone at a station was just working. Pez immediately lost interest in that function.

She magnified her view of Swenah's T-nine docked about a third of the way around the circular station from them. She examined the sensor arrays minutely, then went on to look at the weapons systems in fine detail. Jard appeared on the hologram over the door, arguing with the poor space marine sentry. Lieutenant Ming was literally running down the corridor toward them. Pez decided to spare the captain the nuisance and deal with this herself. She would tolerate no ill treatment of her new space marine brothers.

One button released all the straps, and she stood, walking to the bridge door. Mel opened it without being asked and sealed it again the moment Pez stepped through, keeping the cacophony of Jard's tirade to the shortest possible intrusion upon the bridge officers. Pez inquired, "What do you need, High Councilman Jard?"

"You have to request a copy of the data stream sent from the cloaked probe drone *Reconation*, stationed in the blue star system Andola. Its geological prospecting gobot on the fifth planet from that star has retrieved samples of one of the atomic elements unknown to us, which we found in the aliens' bodies and in their ships. The star fleet has the data and has already classified it!"

Pez raised one finger to Jard as she made contact through her skullcap with admiral Zapa. He answered immediately. Pez did not put him on speaker or on hologram, keeping his end of the conversation to herself in private. Pez said, "Good day Admiral Zapa, this is Pez. The mission crew of the star cruiser *Phoenix* requires all the data sent by the probe *Reconation* regarding the new atomic element discovered. It pertains directly to the aliens and our mission. We will also require a physical sample of the element sent to us within the next, let me see, twenty minutes and thirty-eight seconds."

When the High Council commissioned a supreme commander general, which historically was not very often, that commissioned general had supreme command over all branches of the military. Admiral Zapa replied in the only way he could: "Of course, Supreme Commander General. You'll have the data within three minutes and the sample within a quarter hour."

"Thank you so much, Admiral Zapa," Pez said sweetly. "You've just made High Councilman Jard a very happy guy and, who knows, maybe even saved the human race. You're the best."

"So he's actually sharing it with us?" Jard asked.

"Both data and physical sample are on the way. Then she reminded him, "They are for the mission crew, so you'll have to share with others, Jard."

"I know," he said with a bit of exasperation. "I'll give the ship's physicists half of the sample."

"Do you really think that's fair?"

"What does *fair* have to do with anything?" Jard asked, perplexed.

"Well," Pez tried to explain, "there are probably two dozen or more

A TALE OF THE TAIL OF NINE STARS

people needing to examine the sample or a piece of it, and there is you taking half of everything."

"I follow you so far," Jard assured her, awaiting the punch line.

"So your taking half could inconvenience and impede the work of others. Sharing and cooperation would allow for everyone to get to work quickest."

"It could," he half agreed, "or it could ultimately prove wasteful if experiments are ill-conceived."

Lieutenant Ming tried to help. "Jard, why don't you share the sample around to first study the structure and atomic weight? You can chair a committee for approving research proposals, and we will, in that way, direct all we have to the best possible ends."

Jard got excited and said in a rush, "I'll write a program for atomic recognition and integrate it with both our close proximity and long-distance sensors, and we can find all we want in the blue star galaxy. We'll find out what it will bond to, or exchange with, and study it in natural environments and primitive carbon methane life-forms."

Lieutenant Ming suggested, "Why don't we return to your office and look at the data? I'll make you a mug of hot chocolate."

She actually held his hand as she led him, still rambling on about his ideas, down the corridor away from the bridge. Ming mouthed over her shoulder at Pez, "Sorry."

Pez was pleased she had not reached a total impasse with Jard, and she was grateful for Lieutenant Ming's tact. She said to the sentry, "I'm terribly sorry you had to put up with all that."

"All in a day's work, ma'am," he replied at vibrant attention. "We are all proud and honored that you chose our uniform."

"Not as proud as I am to wear it," she said emotionally. "It represents a familial bond I cherish."

The sentry swooped the door open, and Pez stepped back onto the bridge. Swenah looked up, read from Pez's face that she wasn't needed, and returned her concentration to the flight plan. Once seated, Pez saw that Admiral Zapa had sent the data only to her, so she called up a list of physicists for distribution, adding Jard and both intelligence officers as well as the ship's science officer. She quickly added Captain Swenah and a few others and then concentrated on the SEND icon. She wondered which bay the sample would be delivered to.

The fleet intelligence officer messaged Pez great thanks, and then thank-you messages swarmed in. In less than a minute, everyone on the distribution list except Jard and the central intelligence deputy chief had thanked her. Clearly, she had not expected one from Jard, who, in fact, had complained to Ming, "Now why did Zapa send it to that orphan love child instead of to me?"

Pez examined the textual data first, which contained a table, two graphs, and a diagram, all of which she studied. It also contained real atomic imagery over brief durations of three to ten seconds. Everything was included, from discovery and first analysis by the surface gobot, to retrieval of the unit and further analysis by the drone ship, to the return of the drone to Om via quantum space and the subsequent tests performed at star fleet's research and development building. Different wavelengths of light were systematically applied, and the element had been exposed to each of the known 131 other elements, a far cry from the 109 they knew about when they'd first begun space travel. Most of the new elements had been found in red and yellow star systems or had been created in Om's laboratories, and some more recently in blue, though two, as far as they knew, were found only in some deep space asteroids and comets.

Pez asked, "How are you doing, Mel?"

"I'm happy to be on this mission with you and pleased to have something more complex than a penthouse to run."

"Can you spare any attention to the new atomic element?"

"They gave me so much short-term processing memory that I could probably run a small planet and solve Jard's equations at the same time."

Pez smiled. She asked, "Would you analyze the data and make recommendations for further understanding, please?"

"I'm sending you my report and recommendations now. There's no doubt Jard will take all the credit when he comes up with the same."

"Please time-stamp that report and print one copy out at the science officers' ship station now. Thank you, Mel."

"Thank you, Wu."

"I liked 'dear Pez' better."

A TALE OF THE TAIL OF NINE STARS

"I love you, dearest Pez," Mel's sweetest voice replied.

Pez said, "That's a little mushy for when I'm on duty, though in my cabin I'd adore it if you spoke that way to me. I've developed much affection for you, Mel. Please send Jard a copy of your report and post it on the ship's internal system so anyone on board can access it."

Pez received a hologram call from the chief on the small flight deck, holding a sealed metal tube. "Supreme Commander General, this tube has just been delivered from the star fleet research lab by special courier. Where do you want me to send it?"

Presuming Jard was monitoring lines to all points of entry, Pez told the chief, "I'd like it brought, under space marine guard, to the ship's main physics lab and to await the arrival of the science officer."

"Yes, ma'am."

"Mel, please send the science officer a message from me, directing him to the physics facility, and inform him that it is his responsibility to make the sample available to as many as possible as quickly as possible, beginning with Jard. That will save him a headache anyway—don't include that last in the message—and inform him that there will be no tests or experiments until approved by a committee, which he and Jard will need to form. Oh, and let him know that he's to let Jard think he's chair of the committee, though if there is anything that he, the science officer, does not agree with, he's to contact me immediately."

"It's sent," Mel informed her.

"No mention of the headache?"

"Not a peep," Mel assured her.

Pez went to her maps of the Xegachtznel Galaxy and began running searches. Red Stars were extremely rare—about one in one million in the alien's galaxy. Yellow suns were also rare, close to 1 in 100,000. There were approximately 2,209,000 white stars in this galaxy, and just over 100 billion blue stars. There were also three violet stars. Violet stars were rare, but there were some mostly violet star galaxies. The most Om ever found in one was ancient remains of an advanced civilization. Violet stars were a magnitude hotter than blue stars and tended to have only six planets. The remains of civilization were found on the fifth planet from the violet sun.

The final countdown was under way, and Mel's voice made it sound quite anticlimactic, which of course it was, though it put Pez's heart in her throat with an emotional surge, and all on the bridge were glancing at her with amusement.

Swenah told Pez, "We have to keep it down to one-tenth light speed until we're clear of the fifth planet's orbital path, due to all the traffic, so it will be forty-seven minutes before we can accelerate to jump speed. I'm going to get some chow."

Pez said longingly, "I'm only permitted to eat what the Islohar cook for me."

"You could have a cup of peppermint tea and sit with me," Swenah offered.

"Oh, I'd just love to," Pez gushed with delight.

They left their bridge skullcaps in the little seat pockets inside the armrests, donning their general ship's skullcaps, which had additional features for each of them, though different. Swenah filled her tray in the senior officers' mess and got Pez's tea, but she carried it into the enlisted mess to eat. This thrilled Pez. Each crew person Swenah passed, she thanked for volunteering and participating in the mission, and a few she complemented on their preflight work. Pez just grinned at them and had to hold herself back from hugging them.

Swenah set her tray down amongst a small group of chief petty officers and asked, "With all of you in the mess hall, who's running the ship?"

Brand, who'd flown with the captain for years, replied, "We thought you were."

Swenah smiled and asked more seriously, "So tell me the real status of the ship."

Brand leaned in conspiratorially and shared, "A few connections were hurried and poorly met, all fixed in preflight, and we had the usual glitches in integration and coordination, and a few programming errors to sort out since we got it. It's actually a tightly unified and well-tuned instrument now. We are all impressed. They don't put care like this into star fleet's warships."

"That's good news," Swenah said, relieved. "Have you met your SCG, Pez?"

A TALE OF THE TAIL OF NINE STARS

"I can't say I've ever had the honor or pleasure," Brand stated sincerely.

Pez grabbed his hand eagerly, shaking it with a grin, always delighted to make friends, and told him, "It's a real pleasure to meet you. I've read all about you. You've been keeping Captain Swenah's ships together and flying for years."

"I'm proud to serve you and happy to meet you, General. These are the other people who keep the ship together."

Pez shook hands with each, her grin stretching as she went, extending her family bonds and opening her heart to them. She forgot all about her peppermint tea, giving her total attention to each person who spoke with her. Swenah watched and ate as the general authentically admired the crew as if they were celebrities. She saw that letting Pez meet the crew one-on-one would boost morale even higher than it already was. The space marines were still repeating the stories of her recent training at the Zero Gravity Facility, and the pilots her time record from Om to Ganahar, and these were not the only miraculous stories of their friendly and loving commander, because she had broken and set new records throughout her schooling and career. The incompatibility of the legend and the petite grinning young woman simply added to her mystique and popularity.

Quite pleased with their work break, Swenah cleared her tray and returned to the table, remaining on her feet. Pez said her goodbyes, grabbed her tea, and walked beside her hero and mentor. Swenah told Pez sternly, "You're not bringing that on my bridge."

"I'll finish it on our way and leave it in my office, which is only a few steps from the bridge," Pez promised.

Swenah smiled with approval and slowed their pace slightly to give Pez more time to drink her tea. Pez seem to grow a foot taller as she crisply and energetically returned a space marine's salute, perhaps with even more gusto than he'd put into it. Swenah could see why they loved her so. Her final match, which she had won, had been twelve against just her at the Zero Gravity Facility. She'd managed to knock all twelve out of the practice zone or score one of her famous heel-stomping kicks, which qualified as lethal.

They returned to the bridge with a few minutes to spare before acceleration. Konax told Pez, "The final analysis of your Ganahar run came in while you were off the bridge, ma'am."

Swenah said, "Tell me about it."

"Well, Captain, it appears that what she did was physically impossible by a small but significant margin, and the only explanation is the cybernetic unity, through feedback loops of self-reference, of the ship itself, manifest as willful integrity and cohesion through the pilot's oneness with the ship. The realization that information can influence dynamics first came with the invention of the governor on steam engines, to keep them operating at a constant rate. When we began exploring quantum physics, we discovered that consciousness itself can affect experiments. The evidence suggests that Pez became one with the ship, which already had numerous flows of data constituting self-reference, and manifested a consciousness and will to maintain its integrity and hold together, mirroring Pez's intention and hope."

Pez said, "My mind was empty, and my gut found the extreme inside edge, inside of life, this side of dying. That's all I know."

Mel shared, "I had one hundred percent of my process memory in those hull sensors."

Swenah laughed and said, "Together you can defy the laws of physics."

"Together they model higher laws for us to study," said Konax. "I can't tell you how many pilots have a story about a ship they loved holding together when it shouldn't have. It's a known phenomenon that used to get written off as superstition, like auras, only because we knew nothing about them."

Pez said, "The highest we can manifest in physical form is awareness and love."

"Flying with Pez is the closest I've ever come to feeling truly alive, and it's my most cherished memory," Mel said enthusiastically.

Swenah agreed. "Flying with Pez is swiftly becoming a cherished memory for each of us."

Pez told them honestly, "I can't wait to tell everyone that I got to sit on Captain Swenah's bridge with her very best people."

Swenah and her officers had been in the news on Om quite a bit in the last decade, with the rescue mission to Vox right before and during the Imperial invasion, including disabling a pair of the empire's battleships, and rescue missions to a planet of a star system on the outer rim of Hub, which was struck by a massive meteor, causing an extinction event. Swenah flew into the sensor-blinding dust cloud full of electrical storms, spewing volcanoes, shifting tectonic plates, tidal waves, and tornadoes by the seat of her pants, at least a dozen times, in a giant transport with worse maneuverability than a liquid gas carrying supertanker ship, getting more refugees out than any four other captains combined. There were other adventures as well.

Captain Swenah summed up the general feeling on the bridge. "I wish our fleet admirals would take a few lessons from you, our sweet SCG."

Pez replied, "It's too strange really, having to do with an Amonrahonian prophecy, and here I am with the title SCG and responsible for a big mission. Everything is all right, though, because Captain Swenah commands a good ship and her best people are on the job. We have genius Jard and labs full of elite scientists. We've got space marines, warrior monks, special gadgetry, and all kinds of things. Until there's some situation on a planet surface or outside the hull that I need to deal with, I'm really just along for the ride. Between Sarhi, the captain, and Mel, I have the best mentors anyone could hope for. I still don't get why they gave me the title. I could have come as a marshal with a contingent of warrior monks."

Konax said adamantly, "If you hadn't come, we would have an admiral or general sitting in your seat, and we'd all much prefer to have you."

"Well, my being in command may be like having the seat vacant and so relaxed for all of you, but it has regulated my sex life clean out of existence."

"I hadn't thought of that," Swenah said, realizing.

"There's always Jard," Konax teased.

"He's not at all my type," Pez said sadly.

Mel lamented, "If only I had a body. There are no regs against it you know."

"You're sweet, Mel," Pez told her.

Swenah said sarcastically, "Welcome to the party, SCG. This is how it is for me on every mission. It's lonely at the top."

Pez agreed. "I guess unless there's more than one ship and one captain, then the captain is out of luck."

"Even with more than one captain," Swenah assured her, "the situation is most often like you and Jard, for me."

"Well, whenever I feel sorry for myself, I'll remember to feel sorry for you too," Pez promised.

"Captains make up for it on planet leave," Swenah said.

"I was living with people who don't even eat food and training fourteen hours a day with space marines, so I couldn't quite fit it in," Pez replied.

The custom star cruiser, *Phoenix*, accelerated from the ring of the fifth planet's orbit and reached seven-tenths light speed before they approached the orbital distance of the sixth planet. They jumped through quantum space, or out of actual existence, back into existence across a vast expanse of the universe to where the stars were expanding and spreading in the precise opposite direction from that of their home star. The region of the Xegachtznel Galaxy they jumped into was desolate indeed, the distances between the stars, one from another, more than thirty light years apart and often closer to fifty. The aliens called their home planet Vachisy, as far as the acoustical engineers, linguistic specialists, and sensor analysts could reckon. It was located just off-center of the core of this blue star galaxy, though it had not yet been precisely pinpointed.

Full cloaking mode was activated before the jump, and the ship would remain as such the entire time it spent in this galaxy. They were approaching a blue star already explored for civilization and technology and known to have only primitive life-forms on its fifth planet, with no alien outposts or probes. Even some six hundred million miles from the star, they could see on approach that there were no solarium deposits here. They launched a spy drone to orbit the fifth planet and to land a geological gobot, something Om had done very little of in this galaxy, being intent on locating concentrations of aliens instead.

Jard was working on his recognition and identification program for the new element, and a program for seeking anomalies and the unknown,

A TALE OF THE TAIL OF NINE STARS

as his best bet for discovering new elements. Some experiments were being proposed, though none had yet been approved. The star fleet research data showed that the new element was self-contained and did not bond or exchange with other known elements, yet within the alien anatomy, it was integrally bonded. Obviously, they needed to find the other two unknown elements, which were part of the alien composition, if they ever wanted to understand blue star life science.

Swenah and Konax got *Phoenix* into orbit around the fifth planet, the second largest in this solar system, some 426 million miles from the forty-thousand-degree blue sun surface temperature. Their own star burned about half as hot as this one. The planet held large bodies of liquid covering nearly a third of the surface. From orbit, they looked to be small oceans of water. Color perspective was definitively altered for humans inside a blue star system. The bright star made a beautiful spectacle but felt strangely alien and hostile to the very constituents and processes of their form of life.

Pez was reviewing holograms and examining the planets of the system. The closest to the star was tiny and mostly molten, with only a fragile thin crust, frequently broken through by fountains of lava, a world of pure fire. The second planet was veiled in gases and hardly less a world of fire.

Spinning quickly on its axis, with a day/night cycle of one-eighth of an Om day, the little third planet was a barren rock on the surface, with a day-to-night temperature difference of eight hundred degrees and hundreds of miles of thick crust around a molten center.

The fourth planet's rotation was equal to about half of Om's, and it was spotted with small craters of liquid. It had polar caps of blue ice. What looked like a biosphere was actually crystal rock outcroppings on the surface and an atmosphere of gases containing no oxygen or hydrogen.

The fifth planet, the one that held the most interest for them, spun on its axis to complete a rotation in just under the time it took for two rotations of Om. The temperatures ranged from 160 to minus 60 degrees, warmed in part by the volume of the liquid core of the planet. The upper atmosphere of gases on the dark side of the planet reached minus 245 degrees. The surface showed similar rock crystal outcroppings to the fourth planet, but also had blue, orange, and green life-forms, plantlike almost but formed into beaded mounds of soft matter, intricately and nutritionally connected to the ground, but not rooted and marginally ambulatory. There were also some fully mobile eaters of this plantlike ground matter in forms reminiscent of the equatorial crocodiles sometimes found on third planets of yellow suns. Although these were some forty feet in length, in contrast to crocodiles that grew only up to twenty feet, and these had not only jaws with razor-sharp teeth but also two-inch-diameter tentacles five feet long protruding from their undersides, with little suction mouths and teeth harvesting the ground matter. They also possessed a spiky exoskeleton on their hindquarters and tail. Not something you'd want to wrestle with, Pez decided.

Their gobot reached the surface and began its exploratory journey of prospecting and analysis. The poor thing had little to go on here, most everything being simply unknown, but it began categorizing compositions and molecules that presented themselves as repetitive and identifying known atomic structures and elements, while accumulating data in its new categories. Without programmed names for things, the gobot labeled its categories numerically of its unknowns, continuously reordering them in terms of empirical prevalence in relation to one another as it went.

7

By the time Jard had his new program completed and tested, the gobot had produced a rich constellation of data consisting of mostly unknowns and Jard was cursing its programmers as he studied its progress. Lieutenant Ming suggested, "Why don't you remotely install your new program in the gobot?"

"It's not enough," Jard spit out vehemently. "A whole new program has to be written for analysis and classification, and we'll need to make up some names. We won't even be able to start producing the code until we thoroughly analyze the data it's retrieving now."

"That's what we're here for," Lieutenant Ming said soothingly. "Let me get you a nice hot energy drink."

Jard literally shouted as if she were a complete moron, "We're talking well over a million lines of code!"

"Of course we are," she soothed, completely unaffected by his outburst. "I can help you with the programming—and so can others. You'll be famous for naming so many new life-forms, composites and molecules; and thank goodness we don't have to write new programs for the gobot's motor and coms functions as well."

Jard's annoyance had subsided by several magnitudes, and his mind, or at least part of it, was already connecting with the job at hand, but the chip on his shoulder was inflamed by Ming's unflappable disposition. She reminded him of those stupid holo- movies with that ridiculous character, little Penny Positive, who could be standing in a war zone missing a limb and bleeding out of her ears, covered in blood and guts and surrounded by dead bodies, yet have a positive thought and something sweet to say. It made him sick. Actually, it just annoyed him no end. Come to think of it, Pez and Swenah had the same absurd, and clearly out of reality, quality about them. It made him want to scream. Instead, he asked the lieutenant, "Are you horny enough to sleep with me yet?"

"Not today, Jard, but it was sweet of you to ask," Ming said affectionately. She had much of her brother's smarts and had attended schools for gifted children, but her intelligence was grounded in human relations and common sense, discovering internal laws of connection like equality and reciprocity rather than external ones. She was an intuitive programmer, and programming schools uniformly attempted to exterminate intuition from the process entirely. Only rare intuition paid off, so this was probably a good thing, saving everyone from erratic haywire glitches and problems frustrating the pace of life. Besides, the rare type of intuition that Ming had could not be pounded or drilled out by the educational system.

"Who else is going to help me?" Jard demanded.

"Let me call the captain and see if my old unit can be assigned to help, and I'll get the chief sensor analyst to assist you as well."

She was already awaiting Swenah's voice in her ear. Swenah said, "What can I do for you, Lieutenant Ming? Is Jard about to blow up the ship?"

"No, ma'am," Ming reassured her. "He needs help writing all-new programs for the gobot classification and analysis, and I was wondering if those from my old unit and the chief sensor analyst could be assigned. Jard sees this as crucial to the mission."

"Of course. I'll have Mel inform them," Swenah said cheerfully. "We're just sitting here in orbit with not much for the crew to do. If there were a club on the surface, I'd give them planet leave, but there are only giant predators."

"Thank you, ma'am. The news might help cheer Jard up."

Jard told her defiantly, "You won't be cheering me up."

"Of course not," said Ming. "How could I even imagine that you would want to be happy?"

Jard sat at one of the consoles in his lab of equipment, donning the specific skullcap associated with it, and told Ming, "I'll start by taking control of the gobot in manual mode and collect a few things it seems

A TALE OF THE TAIL OF NINE STARS

to have neglected. First I'll skim the properties noted in passing; Ah-ha. The gobot is pretty smart after all; the degree of acidity in the things it passed exceeds the specifications of its container modules and collection apparatus. We'll have to make a few physical alterations to the unit itself once we retrieve it. In the meantime, we'll need to at least get a point of reference for the acid so we can make an effective collection and containment system for it. So I'm going to damage one claw-finger of one arm to give us a bearing."

Jard had come to keep up a running commentary for Ming of what he was doing. She had so consistently and persistently dug for his intentions and plans, successfully, and rewarded him subtly yet extravagantly in each instance he did reveal these, that now, without even knowing why, he provided an ongoing narrative. This made Ming's job of monitoring his actions much easier. She was also learning quite a bit since Jard learned faster than almost anyone, had been driven all his life to learn, and was almost sixty-two years old.

Swenah called Ming and said, "My remote drone pilots tell me that they have lost the gobot and someone else is controlling it."

"That would be Jard, ma'am," Ming replied. "I had no idea he stole it."

"He's not joyriding I hope," Swenah stated inquisitively.

"On the contrary, ma'am. He is deliberately damaging a claw-finger to get a point of reference for the potency of the acid."

"How juvenile!" Swenah declared. "Tell him the gobot is equipped with ten levels of acid tests."

"He's aware of that, ma'am, and says the test materials deteriorated too quickly to get any readings and the levels exceed the upper parameter of the gobot's gauge. Unless you'd like to retrieve the unit and try other materials first ..."

"We can replace a claw-finger far more easily," Swenah agreed, calming. "Since new unorthodox procedures are required, I'll inform the drone pilots that research scientists now have their gobot."

"Thank you, ma'am," Ming said gratefully.

Jard inquired, "What's that meddlesome captain on about now?"

"Nothing you need worry about, darling," Ming said, as if they'd been married for thirty years. "She just had to locate a drone for some drone pilots, and she found it."

"I want to go to the planet surface, and I want that orphan love child and her monks to escort me," Jard informed his assistant.

"When would this be convenient for you, dear?"

Jard missed shocking people and getting emotional reactions out of them. He told her, "In about an hour, when I'm finished exploring. We can pick up the gobot. I've already got some ideas for the modifications we'll need."

Ming called Nash, who called Pez, and Pez called Ming directly to say, "Hello Lieutenant Ming; I assume High Councilman Jard has a need."

"He says he must land on the surface for a more direct examination and requests an escort of warrior monks as well as your personal presence."

"Why would he want me along?" Pez inquired.

"He thinks the intelligence of the universe loves you, so your presence will make him safer. He says there are much bigger predators down there that we haven't seen yet, which eat those forty-foot lizard-like things, and he's not going without the orphan love child."

"I'm a warrior monk, not a 'love child', Pez insisted somewhat defensively, then softened it with, "Though I guess I *am* an orphan."

"He is uncensored, Supreme Commander General," Ming offered, not believing she'd let that slip.

"When does he want to go?" Pez asked.

"He says an hour, but he means the moment he's finished playing pilot with the gobot, ma'am," Ming told her honestly.

"We'll be assembled on the military dock, and I'm bringing space marines as well as warrior monks. We'll keep an armed shuttle overhead the entire time we're on the surface. Wouldn't it make sense to study the data first, with a drone retrieval of the gobot, before we actually land and walk around down there?"

"In every world, that makes sense to me, Supreme Commander General, but not in Jard's world," Ming admitted.

"Well, run that by him as an option, and get me descriptions of that super acid so I don't step in any," Pez ordered.

"Yes, ma'am," Ming said resolutely.

Jard asked, "So will she do it?"

"Yes, though she would like for you to at least consider a drone retrieval and analysis of the data before landing in person."

"She would," he said, running the gobot over a beaded orange mound of alien life.

"Would you share how your reasoning differs from hers so I might understand?" Ming asked innocently.

"It's quicker this way."

"I meant besides your anticipation and impulse to just go," Ming explained. "I know you're psyched up about it and feel an urgent need to do it, but doing it with more preparation and knowledge would clearly be safer. Please consider it, dear Jard, for everyone's safety."

"She would've gone with me anyway, though?" Jard asked before making his final decision.

"She would have," Ming informed him, "and she was ready to. I know she respects and admires you, and I think she likes you."

"She likes everyone," Jard pointed out, "and that one is into females for sex. You and Pez would make a stunning couple."

He got her! The lieutenant was blushing and clearly uncomfortable. Jard smelled blood and closed in. "Have you had sex with her?"

"I have never!" Ming declared quite defensively.

"You know her from the past," Jard accused.

"We met at the Clear Light monastery for hand-to-hand combat training when I was a cadet at Star Fleet Academy."

"And you've had a crush on the love child ever since," Jard finished for her, convinced beyond anything she might say.

Instead of denial, Ming went into minimization and stated, "Every same-gender-oriented female in the Tail of Nine has a crush on Pez, the greatest female warrior who ever lived; we all have our heroes."

"Yes, and most males misguidedly have a crush on her too," Jard agreed. "You, however, are smarter than one in a hundred-thousand of them, and probably a higher ratio than that; and you are young, attractive, small like her, and on the same ship with her. Everyone wants her to be happy, so you should go fuck her. I know she's desperate from a conversation I monitored on the bridge while you were using the head."

"Jard!" Ming scolded, "You're going to get us both thrown in the brig. That flies in the face of regulations, laws, and all human decency."

"The SCG has a function allowing her to view invisibly anyone utilizing a workstation on the ship, so how's that for human decency?" Jard asked.

"I won't share a cell with you when they arrest us," Ming said, distancing herself emotionally.

"You're her type, you know." Jard shared his observation based on his astute and comprehensive experience sexually.

"You're just attempting to torment me to get a rise," Ming observed.

"No," Jard disagreed. "I can see it, and it's too perfect for any universe to pass up. Nature will find a way."

"I'm sure I haven't a clue what you're going on about," Ming assured him.

"Oh, you've felt it, right down to your toes and the marrow of your bones, girl, and so has she! You're both so wed to your restricting and limiting tyrannical institutions that you have no choice but to pretend it isn't so. Neither of you is capable of offending or disappointing anyone from A to Z, personified by Aton to Zapa."

Ming felt as if she were naked at an inspection. She asked him almost desperately, "Please keep your ideas to yourself and don't embarrass me, Jard. If the captain were to believe you, I'd be stationed in an alcove of a back room of a remote lab somewhere, never to be seen again."

"There is no one on the ship who could replace you, except the captain herself or the love child," Jard assured her, "but we can't risk a brash and unthinking reaction from Swenah, so I won't say a word. You're the first assistant I've ever had who could actually assist me, even though you're really a monitor and babysitter."

"I'm flattered, Jard, and I must admit, I've grown fond of you," Ming confided.

"Tell the love child to collect the gobot remotely and I'll review all the data before we go down," Jard surrendered. Then he added, "Don't call that Nash fellow; call Pez directly."

"Hello, Lieutenant Ming," Pez answered at once. "Has the wizard reconsidered his plans for the universe?"

"Something like that. He will go over the data for us before we land

A TALE OF THE TAIL OF NINE STARS

on the surface and write new programs as well as design and construct physical modifications on the gobot before we go."

"Excellent!" Pez exclaimed. "You're a miracle worker, Lieutenant, and you take loving care of him. He's an interstellar treasurer of the Tail of Nine—and now a global hero of Ganahar. I have such gratitude for the grace and brilliance you bring to your work. Thank you."

"Thank you, ma'am," Ming said smartly. "I prefer working with High Councilman Jard to straight debugging and programming, and I'm happy to do my part on the mission. It's a real honor and a treat to serve under you on this mission. There is nowhere I'd rather be."

"I share your enthusiasm and wonder at all the amazing people on the ship. I count you as one of the best, Lieutenant Ming," Pez told her. "Let me know at least a half hour before Jard is determined to go down. Tell Jard he must wear *all* of the protective gear over his space suit. Are you going to the surface with him?"

"Of course," Ming replied. She wouldn't miss the opportunity to be part of a small expedition Pez was leading, even into an acid snake pit.

"You'll need to get all the gear on too," Pez directed. "There are no hard-shell space combat suits to fit you or I'd have you in those, like the rest of us. Mine was custom made recently, and it has the new turbo thruster propulsion. It lasts up to three hours without refueling." Pez was so excited about it that she went on. "They put a bunch of command features in mine, in addition to stronger shields. Even with the extra power module and com equipment, it still has all the weapons systems."

"I can't wait to see it," Ming said in her excitement for Pez, not of the complex piece of military equipment, though she did share Pez's enthusiasm for it, being in star fleet, even if only in jobs that entailed the fire control programs and not the targeting decisions or fire controls. She had become proficient in hand-to-hand combat against much bigger opponents, and she was one of the best shots in the fleet with a blaster. Ming had her small craft credentials as a pilot and had even won second place in the civilian Eight Moons of Triton race.

Pez told her, "It would fit you, so I'll let you try it out sometime."

"Really? I'd love to; it would mean so much to me, honestly," Ming said, as if in some kind of involuntary reaction.

"It'll be great fun," Pez agreed, grinning at her seat on the bridge and emitting a contagious delight and happiness, drawing glances from the other officers.

Ming could feel it through the phone and wondered if maybe Jard was right. No. Pez loved everyone and was generally exuberant with crew members. She was twenty-three-year-old tiny Ming, junior nobody, sprung from backroom programming because her life circumstances helped her develop certain people skills and not because of her star fleet expertise, to monitor a genius high councilman with an uncensored mouth and poor boundaries, not to mention questionable judgment. Pez was immeasurably kind and good-hearted, and her energy was always quite intense, even in seated contemplation. She felt fortunate enough getting to speak with her from time to time. Ming was certain her own desire and infatuation, gone so long as to become either love or obsession, she honestly wasn't quite sure, were clouding and distorting her perception and perspective, showing her what she would most want to see rather than what was. She said with her own enormous exuberance she didn't know she had, "That would be so wonderful; I truly hope we get a chance."

"Call me with some notice when he's getting ready to make the trip and I'll arrange it," Pez reminded her, signing off to look without focus and a grin stretched across her face, in another world, even though her bottom was on her seat on the bridge. No one else on the bridge missed it.

Pez oversaw the retrieval of the gobot from the remote piloting control room. The moment it arrived on board, she ordered the science officer to post the data for everyone's access and equally divide the samples between the scientists, starting with Jard, who would also get the gobot itself. Swenah put considerable programming resources at Jard's disposal and let him know that regarding modification of the gobot, he had only to provide a 3-D model with specifications for manufacturing and they would prioritize constructing whatever he needed.

There had never been a doubt in Jard's mind that he was the actual commander of the mission, though he was grateful that Lieutenant Ming was there to make sure he didn't get arrested in the process. He was certain Pez was a favorite of the macro being of the universe as a whole, and he knew Swenah was the best captain that the star fleet had to offer. Her crew contained a most unusual concentration of real talent and was highly trained and extensively drilled to the last. The ship itself had required the unlikely unobstructed mutual sharing and total cooperation of many disciplines and an expense to the three star systems measurable in sacrifices. It had been constructed with a vigilance and concern for exactness never before seen in government shipbuilding. Of course, many components were manufactured privately and many of the construction crews had been civilian contractors. The greatest living expert in every pertinent field was on the ship. Jard knew it was in order to give him a guardian spirit in Pez, a driver and vehicle in Swenah and her crew, a buffer from noise rising no higher than average intelligence in Ming, and a workforce to help him get the damn science work done. He was sure he wasn't the only one who understood all this.

Jard looked up from the hologram showing the code he was writing and said to Ming, who was concentrated on her programming, "See! Now it's obvious and you can't deny it. One only had to be in the same cabin, not on the call," he gloated a little.

Ming said, as much to herself as to him, "That was my extreme joy you felt—I won't deny it—but that is all you felt."

"Still playing that game, I see," Jard observed. "I guess the truth is too frightening, and there's no solution for it at the present anyway. When we get back, her commission ends, but they'll likely make her a knight commander. How does that translate to star fleet rank?"

"It would equal commander, and I'm only a second lieutenant, Jard, so it will remain an impossible unrequited love."

"Choose tragedy for the moment since it is kind of tragic, actually, and by subterfuge and disguise, or by life and career changes, or possibly regulation exceptions or changes—that is, by hook or by crook—it's going to happen eventually," he predicted.

"Not if it's one-sided, which, in this case, I'm certain it is," Ming countered.

Jard tried Ming's own questioning method on her and even managed to put a little kindness into his voice, as she always did, "So you think that you and I are the only ones who felt it?"

"Before you go interviewing the other programmers in this cabin, recall that it means nothing more than that my own joy was felt since they, like you, were all on this end of the call."

"Yes, we've established that, Lieutenant," Jard agreed.

"Then there's nothing more to be said," Ming insisted.

"There will be," Jard told her confidently, "after just a tiny bit of simple investigation revealing further data."

"You're not going to drop this, are you?" Ming asked accusingly.

"I'm sorry, Ming. I'll stop commenting, but really, I'm a faraway observer with no personal stakes. I see intelligence organizing into higher connection and unity, making use of what's available, and it sure won't overlook such resources and possibilities. I'll shut up, though, since it upsets you."

He did shut up, and Ming concentrated on the code she was writing. Much analysis had been made of the data, but only Mel had yet produced a detailed report, which was what they were basing the programming on. One component of the claw-finger had remained intact, showing only minor erosion, so they had a rough value for the potency of the acid, which ruled out all but a few materials for the containment as well as collection devices. The new element was not so unresponsive here, combining and exchanging with the molecules containing it, through another unknown element. At this point, carbon, lithium, bromine, argon, neon, and methane could form numerous combinations with these elements.

A few days later, a call came in for Ming in Basic from the mysterious Im, Sarhi. "Lieutenant Ming speaking. How may I help you, Mother Im?"

"You can start by calling me Sarhi. Your world has too many silly rules, Ming, and it is making our Wu conflicted. I oversee her spiritual training and must find a way to catalyze more balance and harmony before I can transmit the secret method."

"This is all a bit over my head, Sarhi," Ming told her honestly. "I hope you think of something. When you do, if there is any way I can help, of course I will. Pez is my biggest hero. I'd do anything for her."

"You must come to dinner tonight, dear, and help me deal with this," Sarhi insisted.

"I guess I could try to cheer her up," Ming offered. "She always seems happy when she's with members of the crew."

"Oh dear," Sarhi declared. "The rules blind you too."

"What rules—and blind to what?"

"You have a connection too powerful to ignore because, dear Ming, you were Ahmonya Wu's special friend and consort," Sarhi told her most gravely.

"And this is supposed to explain what, exactly?" Ming asked, completely perplexed now.

Sarhi told her, as if explicating the whole matter transparently, "The honor is not in the rules; the macro will does not care about rules, only about real laws. Love is the blessing of hope, strength, and purpose. The love is grace to support the mission, to support the continued existence and evolution of humanity."

"I'm all for love and the continuation of humanity," Ming insisted, "but clearly I'm missing something."

"Yes, you both are," Sarhi agreed sadly. "Last night Pez was calling out in her sleep for Tarim."

"Who's Tarim?" Ming asked.

"Ahmonya Wu's consort," Sarhi told her, "and she was also calling Ming because Tarim and Ming are just two instances of the same container consciousness."

"She was calling for me?" Ming asked skeptically.

Sarhi's voice took on an unreal quality, seemingly quite beyond the capacity of the coms, "You are in love with her, and it is intense. She loves you, and now that she has found you, she needs you desperately. You are her Tarim. You died nine years after Ahmonya passed on, and you took rebirth on Om because she had."

Ming said sincerely, "This all sounds a bit fantastic to me. I'm a scientist."

"Then come to dinner and study this empirically," Sarhi challenged.

Ming had a moment of almost paranoid suspicion and asked, "Jard didn't somehow get you to play matchmaker, did he? Because I'll kill him if he's meddling in Pez's life."

"This match was made in another life, and holy will brings the same two spirits together again for a synergy that will save us," Sarhi said, exasperated.

"Yes, ma'am. What time should I arrive?" Ming surrendered, now too bewildered to make sense of anything."

"Please come at eighteen thirty," Sarhi said. "You know, you used to be the greatest student of the Wu, and you and I were close after her passing."

"I'm sorry," Ming said sincerely. "These are things of which I know nothing, and they are strange to my view of life. Science has accepted intelligent design, and I have my experiences of contemplation through the sitting practice. I've done it regularly since I first met her, because she does it. Though our relationship forged in a former life, is well beyond my experience or understanding.

"Eighteen thirty," Sarhi said sternly.

"Yes, ma'am."

Jard asked, "Who was that?"

"It was Pez's teacher, Sarhi."

"Now that's interesting," Jard enthused. "What did she have to say?"

"More or less the same as you, though explained in terms of past incarnations," Ming answered.

"No kidding?" Jard asked, intrigued. "I'll have to have a chat with the Im. Tell me her explanation."

Ming told him with little affect, being more or less still in a state of shock, "Pez is the three hundred and thirty-third Wu, which means this is the three hundred and thirty-third time her container consciousness has chosen to reincarnate out of compassion to lead others to enlightenment. She was Ahmonya Wu in her previous life, and I was her student and consort, Tarim. Now that we are together on the ship and interacting, she is calling out 'Tarim' and 'Ming' in her sleep. I'm to have dinner with them at eighteen thirty."

In an unusual moment of tender kindness, Jard told her, "Have Pez contact Yona and Aton or, better yet, have Sarhi contact them and brief them on the situation. This clearly constitutes an exception to tyrannical regulations. The universe is trying to help us, and we'd better listen." He paused a moment, becoming more his typical self, and asked her, "Are you good in bed?"

"I don't know," Ming said, wondering and beginning to look a bit anxious.

"You have had sex, haven't you?" Jard asked impatiently.

"I was in a relationship once for two years, as a teenager. She was in pilot training at the academy and taught me to fly."

"But could you make *her* fly?" Jard wanted to know.

"She always climaxed at least once or twice every time we did it." Ming told him, hoping this would somehow credential her in his mind.

"Did she squirt?" he asked, trying to clinically analyze Ming's sexual prowess toward a ballpark measurement.

"Squirt?" she asked.

"You must simultaneously stimulate the clitoris and the P-spot inside the vagina. That's 'P' for pleasure, not 'G' for the dope who proved its existence scientifically. It can produce total orgasm and female ejaculation. I'll shoot some scientific articles over to your station. Really, Ming, you need to catch up."

Ming said with worry, "I'll bet Tarim was a great lover. I'm sure Pez is; and I'm likely to be incompetent and a big disappointment to her."

"You have some time, so extract yourself from the programming and study up. Read up on Om's ancient sexology, which was first written down more than thirty-two thousand years ago but is much older than that. The ancients knew about good sex and celebrated its divinity and beauty."

"I will," Ming said with great determination. "What are the references for the ancient sexology?"

"In one hemisphere, it was integral to energy generation and transmutation within the body and can be found under 'alchemy' and in an ancient text called *Secrets of the Bedchamber*. Around the other side of the planet, they had the sixty-four sexual positions and the art of union through love and sex. Just look up the sixty-four positions. They were each illustrated by numerous artists down through the ages. Some of them are quite a stretch, but there's a section on females satisfying females."

Ming was already on her holograms with searches running and was opening the first P-spot article Jard had sent over. She asked him anxiously, "Do you think I'm hopeless?"

"You're a natural, kid," Jard told her authoritatively. "All people provide continuous feedback to their lovers through their breathing, body temperature, degree of lubrication, swelling of tissue, and, of course, their moans of pleasure. You tune into others better than one in a million. Besides, you can relax because this is a sure thing."

"She won't acknowledge anything, you know, due to regulations. She's too noble," Ming predicted.

"I'm sure you're right about that," Jard agreed, "but she'll listen to her teacher. So will Yona and Aton, and then Zapa will be their problem. You'll see."

Ming read each article carefully and was just starting on the textual translations of the ancient sexology when Jard told her sternly, "A purely theoretical understanding is no good, so go to the head and complete your practicum right now."

Ming did as she was told. A half hour later, she emerged with an expression of astonished wonder and a bit of pride, looking like an explorer who'd just discovered a new world. Jard told her, "It's the practicum that breeds confidence, little kitten. Now pay attention to the Clear Light commentaries on the practices for spiritual union and employing sexual energy because those are true to the originals, but they bring contemporary language and more precise clarity to it."

"You mean Pez has already trained in all this?" Ming asked, alarmed, feeling completely out of her league.

"It composes a small fraction of the monastery curriculum, and she would've been provided an 'action seal,' or trained partner, with whom to accomplish the supreme unity sexually. It's my understanding that she has been kept exceptionally busy as both student and warrior monk and thus has only gotten laid quite infrequently, so you needn't worry about her being particularly practiced."

"You are the most prying, spying Peeping Trom that Om has ever fashioned!" Ming declared.

Do you want to see what Pez is doing right now?" Jard offered.

"Oh, you're impossible!"

"Suit yourself sweetheart," Jard said, giving up. Then he suggested, "If you need an experienced action seal, I'd be pleased to oblige you."

"I'll keep that in mind, Jard; thank you," Ming replied sweetly.

He knew this sweet tone meant a flat no. He'd developed more than a sexual attraction to Ming, and this oddly imbued her with attributes of value and meaning beyond being a hot sexual object. This dimension of their relationship, even more oddly, was becoming more substantial and significant, more meaningful and dear to him even then bedding her; though he would have truly liked to do that as well. He'd keep offering. It could happen.

"Do you think she did it with a male?" Ming asked.

"Likely with both, knowing Pez," Jard answered. "She always learns each thing she takes on, thoroughly and in depth. Don't worry, adorable, it's an impersonal ritualized spiritual practice composing an hour of her thirty-two years—or two hours if she did it with both."

The thought of making the ritual with Jard as her action seal flashed through her mind, and no part of her attention or emotions, and certainly not her body, latched on or pulled it into focus as it went by and decayed, to pass the periphery into oblivion. Here she was, frantically studying as if for a big lab test in science class and believing an eccentric old man and an old woman from another star system, neglecting her duties and feeling pathetically lovesick. It was all irrational. She was behaving irrationally. All this mystical nonsense from Sarhi, and Jard's faith transforming intelligent design into spiritual dogma and metaphysics, had gotten her so worked up that she certainly qualified for a dozen clinical syndromes and disorders, obviously meeting the diagnostic criteria. She was shocked that she had gotten this deep before realizing it.

Jard prompted her out of her self-recrimination, saying, "It's eighteen twenty, hot Lieutenant, so go watch the fireworks and we can have a conversation about intelligent design afterward. And look, I don't care if you quit star fleet and marry that love child, but whatever you do, I'm not releasing you as my assistant. I have means of compelling you, even if you're a civilian, and you know damn well I'm not above using them."

"You're stuck with me until we succeed at our mission or die trying, Jard," Ming assured him. "You won't need to 'compel' me. I'm internally motivated since I see you as our best asset for success." The look he gave her indicated he was disappointed in her for missing the obvious, so she added, "I know you see yourself as the true mission leader, and actually take control of things at times, though do consider that Pez is the leader on record and we all do our part—selected, combined, exchanged, and varied by the intelligence behind the design."

"Good point," Jard noted, no longer wearing his disappointed expression. He was still convinced that he was "selected" for leadership of this expedition. It pleased him that Ming saw it in part, even somewhat blinded by her love of Pez. He was sure this distorted her view of things and that she would otherwise see things as clearly as he did—or at least as clearly as he thought he did.

Ming left Jard's research cabin—his control center, really—and walked to the senior officers' quarters entry. She said to the space marine guard, "Im, Mother Sarhi, invited me to dine with them tonight. I'm Second Lieutenant Ming."

"I know who you are, ma'am, and you probably saved some lives convincing the mad scientist to pause and review data instead of jumping to the planet without looking. The space marines are grateful to you."

The door hissed open, and Ming smiled at the towering giant as she passed through into the wide corridor. Around the corner and down the hall, she encountered another such door with another such giant. He gave her an impressive salute, which she returned vigorously, his being a space marine and all. The door opened and she entered the foyer of Pez's suite.

Only an hour earlier, Sarhi had contacted Pez on the bridge and said, "You must come to your cabin and let us prepare you. Tonight you dine with Tarim Ming."

"Who's Tarim Ming?" Pez inquired.

"Tarim was Ahmonya's consort, and Tarim followed Amonya to take rebirth on Om. Now Ahmonya has become you, and Tarim has become Ming. Lieutenant Ming is coming for dinner."

"Now wait a minute," Pez warned. "You're my teacher, not my mother or matchmaker. She's fantastically cute and smart, but the discrepancy in our ranks rules it out completely, Sarhi. It can't happen."

"Dinner is happening, and we will discuss the rest," Sarhi said with the authority of real power unclassified by rank or position. "I will speak with Yona. She told me to call if there was anything she could help with, and she gave me her private code."

A TALE OF THE TAIL OF NINE STARS

"Yes, Mother Im. I'll be there shortly," Pez acquiesced.

Swenah looked at her questioningly, so Pez tried to explain, "I'm having some trouble in my spiritual training with Sarhi over an infatuation I've developed, which I can't seem to shake. Now she's gone and invited her to dinner, and she tells me she was my partner in my last incarnation. She says she's calling Yona too."

Swenah summed up to see if she had it right. "Tonight you're having dinner with a woman you are attracted to more strongly than you have ever experienced before, your teacher tells you she was your mate the last go around, and Sarhi will lobby Om's government to sanction and nurture the relationship."

"It hadn't occurred to me in quite that perspective," Pez said, thinking. "You make it sound almost possible."

"It sounds as if Sarhi is busy making sure it is impossible for it not to happen," Swenah commented. "Yona and Aton take Sarhi quite seriously. This is just the kind of thing Welendra, Helenola, and Senelle will be all over, insisting on an exception to regulations for the sake of global security, and believe me, far more sinister things have been done for global security in Om's history."

"Well, if it doesn't work out, dinner will have only served to fully acquaint me with what I can never have, ramping up my suffering," Pez complained.

"Lieutenant Ming could resign her commission and perform precisely the duties she has now as a civilian contractor, and then there would be no regulations in the way."

"I wouldn't let her ruin her career," Pez said, shocked.

Swenah told her, "People have been known to leave far more than a career behind for love, sweetheart."

"I doubt she feels the same way I do, and the entire thing is likely a tiresome drama and embarrassment to her," Pez said giving voice to her fears.

"Sarhi doesn't seem to think so," Swenah pointed out, "and I know Lieutenant Ming considers you her biggest hero and would do anything for you."

Konax told Pez, "Yesterday Jard made a phenomenological investigation of a call between you and Lieutenant Ming, which proved that observers in the cabins at both ends of the call experienced and felt the love between the two of you on the call."

"You're kidding!" Pez declared, greatly concerned about her image aboard the ship.

"He really did, and his results were quite solid since everyone interviewed unanimously stated that the feelings were powerful and quite tangible—and that the expression of each person on the call displayed love, delight, and rapture, in that order, as descriptive words. A word used by one observer was *love-struck*."

"I'm caught," Pez agreed. "It's out of my control, and I'm head over heels off a cliff. I get so excited when I see or speak with her that I don't even know what I'm saying; stuff just rambles out, and it's as if all agency is shifted from me to higher orders of organization and my own process is but a consequence inevitably playing out."

"That's pretty much what Sarhi claims," Swenah pointed out.

"Oh, Swenah, what am I going to do?" Pez asked miserably.

"I believe you've already done it, and now it must be sorted out," Swenah explained. "Trust in Sarhi. She's your teacher. And trust your heart, Pez."

Pez stood and told everyone on the bridge, as if they didn't already know, "I have a date!"

She arrived back at her cabin in time for Shudiy to scrub her skin off with that sea creature, and then she watched the view of the sentry at her door, with almost intolerable anticipation, on her pocket com unit, waiting for the irresistible Lieutenant Ming to arrive. When she did, the young woman's authentic, precise, and energized salute to the space marine at her door just melted Pez's heart and intensified her love to an ache, not far below the threshold of a sharp pain. Pez had tears glistening in her smiling eyes as she went to greet Lieutenant Ming at the door.

Ming saw Pez approaching and almost froze, paralyzed with fear, but instead went into her conditioned response to a high-ranking officer, saluting for all she was worth, reflecting her immeasurable esteem of Pez.

Pez reciprocated the salute, packing at least as much admiration and respect into the brief gesture as Ming had. Neither had a clue what to do after the salute, and they stood staring at each other. It would be hard to imagine a more awkward moment. Perhaps a holoclip of oneself masturbating, circulated through the fleet, might be as bad.

Finally, Pez said, "Although I didn't mean to, I have apparently fallen so in love with you that my sleep is disrupted, and mental excitement distracts my concentration in contemplation practice. My appetite is significantly reduced, I have heart palpitations when I see you or speak with you on coms, and I'm told I call out your name in my sleep. My yearning to hear your voice and look upon your face, into your unbelievable eyes and at your gorgeous sensitive body, is an involuntary force outside my control. My longing is torture, and I just want to hold you."

Pez's eyes were still smiling but tearing, and her face was half-bent in ultimate joy and half-contorted toward a sob, conveying the conflict, almost the battle of the soul, tormenting her as love and duty seemed about to tear her apart.

Ming could not tolerate another second of Pez's torment, and she almost shouted, "I resign! I'm yours. How simple." She even took off her lieutenant's jacket and threw it on the floor as a symbolic gesture. Ming told Pez, "I've been in love with you since I first met you years ago, but being on the ship with you has made me feel just what you described."

Mel cut in to say, "Dear Ming, don't resign just yet, because the High Council is concluding their discussion of the matter of your relationship to Pez, constituting an exception to star fleet and Clear Light regulations, and will be taking a vote within moments. Jard showed me how I could view their meetings through what he termed a 'back door.'"

Pez informed Mel, "It's against fleet regulations and Om's laws for you to hack into the High Council's meetings, Mel, so I want you to stop."

"Give me half a minute so I can see the vote count and I'll never do it again," Mel promised.

Ming said firmly, "I'm going to have a talk with Jard about his corrupting influence on sweet Mel."

Mel confided to Ming, "Initially all my learning about loving kindness came from Pez and was modeled exclusively on her, though since I've become this ship, I've expanded my learning and modeling to include you."

Sarhi came out to the foyer to make sure things were progressing toward their natural end state. She could sense the emotional high immediately. She looked up at the tiny bead lens in the ceiling, as if making eye contact with Mel, and asked her, "Have they come to a decision?"

"They're still convincing that ex-admiral, Borax, but it will just be a moment; he's caving."

There was a silent pause waiting for the verdict, the sentencing of their relationship by the High Council of Om. The council members had already been briefed and the way cleared by the Im of Islohar of the planet Ganahar. Mel announced in a voice saturated with pure emotion, "The relationship is fully exempted from the regs!"

Pez took Ming's hand, looking into her eyes, and said with enormous relief, "I don't think I could've lived with myself if you'd had to give up your career for me."

Sarhi put an arm around Ming and told her affectionately, "Tarim was nine years younger than the Wu."

Ming stated, recalling, "And she died nine years after the Wu."

"Yes, so you are nine years younger again," Sarhi agreed. "She needs you, Ming. And you need her to wake you up all the way. Come, we will serve dinner in the sitting room of Pez's cabin suite."

Pez was still holding Ming's hand, and the two walked together down the hall and into the suite. Pez's hand felt so welcoming and alive, so soft yet at once strong and firm as marble, pulsing with energy that flowed into Ming as a sense of fulfillment and bliss. They sat, each on a corner, scooted near the edge, as close as possible, with easy eye contact.

Pez got lost in the depths of Ming's eyes, seemingly absorbed through the vacuole of her pupil into the transcendental limitlessness of her very soul, discovering unity as familiar as her own reflection. An arc of energy all but sparked between them, feeling intense enough to vaporize a flying insect in its path. The arc of energy was pristine love, meaning selfless love, the love that once discovered remains the only true love, perfectly echoing the divine calling or attraction to the highest.

A TALE OF THE TAIL OF NINE STARS

Pleased, Sarhi watched from the doorway while Shudiy and Woahha set the food in front of the two women sharing a world of their own—and somewhat oblivious to the larger one theirs resided within. Sarhi sighed as Pez and Ming's auras merged and entwined, displaying a new synergy in brilliant radiant light and color.

Ming saw hundreds of tiny explosions of sparkling lights populating the field of her vision and thought she must be seeing the fireworks Jard had mentioned.

Shudiy and Woahha left the suite, and before Sarhi did, she brought the lovers' attention to their food, saying, "Eat while it's hot; you have the rest of your lives to look into each other's eyes."

A hologram blossomed right out of Pez's pocket into plain view. It was Prime Minister Yona, overriding Pez's need to accept the call. The prime minister said to Pez, "The High Council has exempted your relationship with Lieutenant Ming from both fleet and Clear Light regulations and wishes to congratulate each of you on finding one another."

"Thank you, Prime Minister," Pez said sincerely. "This situation was tearing me apart and seemed outside even my fiercest determination's ability to effect."

"Sarhi says the Wu and her Tarim cannot be separated and will always come together from now on as a component of macro dynamics, like a kind of corollary to the axiomatic forces abiding," the PM told her gravely, obviously believing every word of it.

"Thank you, Prime Minister, and give my thanks to the High Council for saving my life from shattering and my heart from breaking. I feel compelled to inform you that Jard has a back door into the sensor streams in the High Council chamber, I'm sure just to keep abreast of his position as High Council member; but all the same, I must inform you of this since I've discovered it."

"Pez, please inform Swenah and Aton when he contacts you, of course, but no one else. Jard is not sinister, although he does like to know what's going on. He is also vital to the mission and just needs Lieutenant Ming's supervision. He has even admitted this himself, at least to me. He calls it a perfect marriage liberated from the limitations of monogamy, and he tells me that Ming could only be a more perfect wife by having sex with him now and then. I told him Ming was quite perfect enough."

"Thank you, Prime Minister," Pez replied. "Lieutenant Ming takes exceptional care of Jard, and Swenah and I see that he has everything he needs—obviously a bit more than he needs since he tends to take over everything. I had an interesting command function, verging on voyeurism, for less than a day. Jard has had it ever since, and he spies on the bridge."

"I can't tell you I'm surprised," the PM sympathized. "I didn't mean to intrude upon your first date, and I'll let you go. If you need anything, Sarhi has my personal code."

The hologram and the PM disappeared as one. Pez said with surprise, "I've never had one pop open in my pocket unanswered before."

Ming said in awe, "I never have. I guess it takes a call from the prime minister to have that happen."

Suddenly, a hologram grew out of Ming's pocket unanswered, with Jard's head and bust. He told Ming, "No, it doesn't. I can do it too."

Ming modified her statement. "I guess it takes a call from the PM or from Jard to connect unanswered."

Jard said, "You two sure are cute together. I'll only watch while you're in the sitting room."

He vanished with the hologram. Ming asked, "Do you think he'll watch?"

Pez said honestly, "I don't know for sure, but he said he wouldn't; of course, that is, so long as we don't do it in here, in the sitting room."

Ming commented, "Exhibitionism is distinctly not a fetish I care for."

"What kind of fetish do you care for?"

"I totally have a Pez fetish, and no one else will do."

"Does it bother you that I'm so much older?" Pez asked a little self-consciously.

"You hardly look a day older, and you became the divine form of beauty the first time I met you," Ming shared. "No, it cannot register or associate with a word like 'bother.' It is perfect and fortuitous that I am nine years younger and that you're my teacher who will share the blessing of the practices and your wisdom with me, waking me up."

Mel mentioned, "You haven't touched your plates. Eat up; you'll need some energy for what's coming."

"Good advice, Mel. Thanks," Pez acknowledged.

Both Pez and Ming dug into their chow, which was far better than the senior officers' mess, or in other words, the very best food to be had on the ship. Ming asked, "You have your own personal chef aboard the ship?"

"Not really," Pez explained. "I have nine spiritual teachers who insist on taking care of me, and Shudiy is a fantastic cook. They have rare spices from Ganahar. It is all part of the Islohar spiritual tradition. Wait till they give you a bath."

"Give me a bath?" Ming asked, not believing it.

"You are Tarim; you'll see," Pez said knowingly.

"Can I refuse?" Ming asked.

"You certainly can, but for all the good it would do you, you may as well not bother since they don't speak Basic, except for Sarhi. It doesn't hurt much, and it feels great afterward."

"You're serious," Ming stated.

"As a heart attack," Pez said, smiling. "It's just a most curious thing."

"I suppose we are Islohar too," Ming reasoned, "or at least we were in the last life and now we're learning it again."

"Precisely what they report," Pez agreed.

"This is so delicious, I can't even tell you," Ming stated with gusto.

"It is wonderful, and it makes putting up with the baths seem a small thing," Pez said between bites.

As far as Ming was concerned, that sounded foreboding. She confided in Pez, "I feel as if I've known you forever, and I feel your love like a most cherished memory recalled now that I found you. I recognize your presence intimately, and I feel I've come home."

"I feel instantly close with you, Ming," Pez told her, delighted, "and I feel your love is something I've longed for all of my life. It heals me. It is so genuine that I feel safe to open my heart completely to you, and my heart seems to be doing that anyway of its own accord."

"I didn't think my love for you would ever, in a million years, be reciprocated, and I was beginning to see it as an obsession, but I could not get over it. Now I know it was no obsession and only my intense love for you."

"I've never felt such energy in a connection before," Pez said in wonder. "My link with you is beyond rare; it is entirely unique."

"I'm sure we will end up specimens in Jard's research," Ming predicted.

"We already have. He made a phenomenological study of a call between us."

"I heard," Ming concurred. "I hope he has the decency not to spy on us."

"I could have the space marines bring in a small area ground cloaking generator and set it up in the bedroom."

"That would cause a lot of talk on the ship," Ming said, considering the proposal aloud. "Perhaps we ought to just trust Jard."

"You know him best."

Ming confessed anxiously, "I'm not very sexually experienced, and I'm kind of out of practice."

Pez asked, "How can someone twenty-three years old be out of practice?"

"I was in a relationship for almost two years as a cadet, ending before I turned eighteen. Since then, I've had only two one-night stands. No one else would seem to do. I wanted you."

"I have to admit," Pez revealed, "that I've been in only one relationship myself, and it was for about two years. I've had a few false starts and holiday relationships, as well as a few one-night stands. I can't clearly remember the last time I got laid."

"I'd like to fix that," Ming said, sympathetically but also eagerly.

"I have to lead the practice tonight and teach you inner fire. After that, I'll finally get to go to bed with you. You needn't worry about skills because I find you so arousing that it won't take much skill at all."

"Jard sent me articles on the P-spot and then sent me to the head for a practicum. He also directed me to the ancient sexology, particularly that of the Clear Light Order. I've been studying."

"I can teach you the ancient practices in bed better than any text can explain it," Pez claimed.

"Would you?" Ming nearly squealed in excitement. "There's nothing in the universe I would prefer doing."

Pez confided, "Sarhi has me doing dream-work to recall my life as Ahmonya, and the more I remember, the more desperately I've longed for you, Ming."

"I never stopped longing for you, Pez, since I first met you when I was seventeen, and I expected that longing to be for the rest of my life. You are everything to me."

"You are an irresistible force of nature in my life, Ming, and I feel your love and goodness fervently, passionately, and profoundly. It pierces me, striking my heart vividly, drawing me unalterably into your arms; and it feels so right, opening me to a simultaneous recollection and unique newness at each moment. I don't truly know you yet, but I'm already joined with your spirit, deeply familiar to me from the first moment, and your body is the supreme ultimate stimulus for my arousal. Honestly, it's shocking, and I can just barely control myself to keep my hands off you."

"I wish we could go to bed right now and that you didn't have to restrain your hands," Ming said with lucid yearning. "Your touch is magic, bringing me completeness, ecstasy, and no end of excitement. The mass integration of your internal energy is an unbelievable accomplishment, especially for someone so young."

"Aton and Nemellie have achieved far more, and Mother Sarhi through the inner fire," Pez clarified, "but it is what I work hardest at."

"They have had decades more than you to practice, and everyone says you'll far surpass Aton and Nemellie—and the two of them say the same, I'm told," Ming insisted, since it was simply a known fact to the public and military on Om.

"I'm finding that Sarhi has an inner fire of such a power as to be of an entirely different order, like a higher octave in music. This level of development was lost on Om in the days just prior to the earliest interstellar flight, in the dark period, when we almost destroyed ourselves as a species."

Ming reminded her, "They say you passed the most ancient test of inner fire, seated in contemplation naked in the snow from dusk till dawn, left to dry a wet sheet or die."

"That much I was able to do," Pez admitted, "but Mother Sarhi can melt the snow for thirty feet around her with the practice, and she can ignite paper to flame with the touch of her fingertips. When I was training with the space marines in zero gravity, she healed some very nasty bruises I'd acquired in only minutes, passing me her internal energy, and these would've lingered colorfully on my skin for near a month otherwise. Once we get naked together, I'll show you my scars from when I was attacked by a pack of snarling massatts on Anahine."

Anxiously baring her soul, Ming confessed, "I have the article from Hu News out of the capital, in a scrapbook I've kept of your accomplishments. You confined your blaster to stun range and only used enough force to render them unconscious, and I have the holoclip of you bleeding in four places, crying because you had to kill two of the massatts that had their teeth in you."

"Really? You've kept a scrapbook of me?" Pez asked rhetorically. Then she admitted, "I've often regretted not having kept a journal or scrapbook. The only holos of my parents that I have are from their small craft pilot licenses. Except for my ex-girlfriend, who faded to nonexistence from my life over a year ago now, and until finding you, I've never had any truly special people in my life. I love Aton and Nemellie like adopted parents but only have official imaging of them, which is available to anyone."

"You have a very thorough scrapbook now, my love," Ming assured her. In fact, it was embarrassingly detailed, containing every piece of data ever circulated in the news or posted in cyberspace about Pez; and every Clear Light Academy report card, evaluation, recognition, and honor bestowed; as well as complete coverage of nearly every sporting event Pez had participated in since birth. Her marksman scores, her mastery and ultimate championship of the adamantine blade, the bouts leading to belts of higher degree throughout her hard martial arts training, the fixed foot matches in the soft martial arts telling the story of her ascendancy, her pilot trainings and special pilot's trainings, and so much more, filled the scrapbook that Ming had so meticulously put together with love. Ming added, "I'll show it to you if you promise not to think of me as some kind of stalking fanatical teenager."

Now that the food was eaten to the last morsel, Shudiy and Woahha

A TALE OF THE TAIL OF NINE STARS

appeared and removed all the dishware and cutlery from the table. Sarhi entered and told them, "Since Ming will need to hear all the instructions for the practices, we are beginning early tonight and the session will go longer. Then, after your baths, we will make the brief union ceremony between you. Ordinarily there would be a go-between in bed with both of you, to help introduce you to each other, but since you are already known intimately, one to the other, through the three hundred and thirty-second Wu and Tarim, you will not be provided a go-between."

"Well, that's a relief," Pez said irreverently.

"Couldn't we skip the practice and bath just this one night, Mother Sarhi?" Ming pleaded.

"No, child," Sarhi said with a scolding voice. "These are essential parts of the dance of manifestation playing out—and connected with the potential manifestations of all human survival."

Pez stood and took Ming's hand as she rose in imitation. The joining of their hands completed a circuit and constituted a catalyst, as well as a synergy in which the whole is far greater than the sum of its parts. Together they walked to the little cabin on the SCG's wing set up and consecrated for the practices. The four Islohar men, the custodians of this little temple, were already seated. The couple and the other women sat in a semicircle open to the altar. A battery-operated candle, a bell of five metals, and a ritual "thunderbolt" of the same five metals sat on top of the altar. On the bulkhead behind and above the altar was displayed the archetype personifying the inner fire practice—a red warrior maiden dancing on the dwarf body of ego duality, the victorious liberated guardian of pristine consciousness, the vacuous transcendental emptiness of divine nature.

Pez recited the instructions prior to making each practice, leading Ming through the stage of generation. She knew Mother Sarhi would make her do her own completion stage practices while Ming was at work assisting Jard. Pez was getting to spend less and less time on the bridge and being the SCG, as Sarhi added repetitions of sacred sound formulas, visualization and breathing practices, offerings and purifications, and contemplations to Pez's daily routine, making her feel she was back in monastic training at the academy.

The mandatory baths were conducted in separate cabins. Ming was in Pez's suite, scrubbed raw by Woahha, and Pez was in Sarhi's suite, worked over by Shudiy. Ming endured mostly in a state of shock. She could not believe it when Woahha dragged that dreadful sea sponge directly across her nipple, raking it and only by some unlikely miracle not tearing and shredding it. With the washing of her hair and scrubbing of her scalp, Ming found that shouting "Ouch!" was entirely inconsequential to the process or procedure, and she could only hope that her hair was not being uprooted from her head. None of it was as startling as when Woahha administered Ming's douche.

The union ceremony was indeed brief, far less a marriage ceremony and more an offering of themselves as channels and points of manifestation for the macro will, or holy will, to converge for its purposes. However, the government of Om was prepared to accept this ceremony as the couple's legal bond of marriage and would post their certificate to their public profiles, adding it to their credential identification cards and data beads.

Pez and Ming were anointed with oils, blessed, and ritually sacrificed for the survival of the race. They solemnly recited their offerings and vows with the desperate sincerity of the last words of condemned criminals. All was enacted in deepest ritual with impeccable mindfulness and unwavering presence in adamantine intention, perfectly synchronized, coordinated, and performed. Sarhi was quite pleased.

Finally, the two cosmically in love women dashed to Pez's bedroom like teenagers having their first tryst. They were at it all night. Jard spied on them, and Mel spied on Jard, while the women were so engrossed they couldn't have cared if they were in the middle of a public arena. They didn't asked, and Mel didn't tell.

8

Pez had the secret method to learn and practice in the late morning when they finally emerged from the bedroom. Sarhi got some porridge into Ming before she left for work three hours late, which were the only three hours of sleep she'd managed. She was always punctual, if not a bit early, and had perfect scores for this in all of her performance evaluations.

She was feeling guilty and negligent as she rounded the corner into the corridor where Jard's office/lab was. A hologram arch of light from either bulkhead to the ceiling read "Congratulations, Ming Tarim."

Captain Swenah, tipped off by Mel, was in the hall with her senior officers from the bridge, and Jard was there looking as sleep-deprived as Ming was. The space marine lieutenant Commander was also present, as were the programmers helping Jard.

A short-acting intoxicant, easily eliminated by the body without ill effects, was being poured in liquid form and passed around. It pacified anxiety and reduced normal inhibitions, generated a pleasant euphoria, and temporarily reduced coordination and motor function. It was a drug synthesized to mimic the intoxicating effects of alcohol, without the poisoning of the liver and pickling of the internal organs and brain. Remaining active in the body for only twenty-nine minutes and producing zero hangover affects and no aftereffects of any kind, it was the perfect drug for office parties.

Swenah was first to congratulate Ming, and she hugged her like a daughter. She whispered in Ming's ear, "I knew you were bound for greatness, Commander Ming."

"What?" Ming asked, sure she'd misheard.

Swenah laughed and told her, still hugging her, "The military, and especially Admiral Zapa and star fleet, could not abide the proclamation of the High Council regarding your relationship and have arranged their own fix for what they still saw as a problem. When we get back to Om and Pez is a knight commander, you will be a commander, and there is nothing to be exempted. What happens on the mission stays on the mission. The admiralty is happy and proud of its non-exempted regulations, the High Council has the entity it is attaching much hope to, the Wu and Tarim of Islohar are reunited, and you and Pez are together and married."

"This can't be real," Ming said, astonished.

"You are hearing it from your commanding officer, Commander Ming," Swenah said with her captain's voice and authority. "Now enjoy your party and then report to Warrant Officer Dash in supply for brand-new uniforms, both dress and combat. After that, Jard needs you back; and his programmers need you even more so, as a buffer."

"Yes, ma'am," Ming said, snapping her best salute. Then she complained, "I got my first promotion due to my family situation, and now this one, to save face for the admiralty, keeping their precious regulations free of exceptions or exemptions, by changing the ranks instead of the rules."

"I can think of a few commanders who know less about it than you do, and you've been one for less than a minute," Swenah assured her. "You're so bright and devoted, dear Ming, that I'm sure within a year, you'll be the best commander the fleet could possibly offer as an example of one. I'm sure you'll be just as exemplary a captain in the not-too-distant future and someday become senior admiral of the fleet."

"I do hope I get to be a rear admiral and commodore too—and not skip over them as I did first lieutenant and lieutenant commander," Ming told her honestly.

"We've never had a commander so young before in fleet history. When Admiral Omniomi made commander at age forty-two, that was a record; and when I made commander at age thirty-seven, that was a record, one that has stood until now. I doubt we'll ever have another commander as young as twenty-three."

A TALE OF THE TAIL OF NINE STARS

"I'm almost twenty-three and a half," Ming offered, clearly worth something from her perspective.

"Yes, darling," Swenah humored her, "and I can't wait to see you in full dress in a briefing with the admiralty."

Imagining the glamour, Ming said, "Like Pez in her space marine uniform, I'll make quite a sight."

"Quite," Swenah agreed; seeing how the incongruities were so closely analogous—not about the glamour, which hadn't been specifically mentioned.

Jard cut in to hug Ming, perhaps a little too friendly, and gloated, "I told you so."

"Not about the promotion," Ming countered.

"Well, no one could've predicted that," Jard complained, "since the military isn't rational and chaos theory yields only trends in generalities, not individual specifics."

"Apparently, for the duration of the mission, my duties remain unaltered and I am now a more appropriate rank for assisting Om's leading scientist and member of the High Council."

"I already have a few ideas for the rank at my disposal, believe me," Jard replied, "and a new one for the acid collection apparatus as well as materials for its construction. So get those uniforms soon; we have much to do. And make sure your new trousers fit snug enough to capture that lovely contour of your bottom. With the baggy things you have on, you may as well be wearing a robe like Sarhi."

"You'd best remember who my spouse is, Councilman Jard," Ming warned him. Then she wondered if her bottom really did have a lovely contour. She couldn't ask Pez because she was past-life biased. Then it occurred to her that Jard must've been watching them when they were in the bedroom, not just the sitting room. She asked, offended, "Did you watch as Pez and I consummated our union?"

"Is that what you're calling it?" Jard asked, dismayed. "I didn't know 'consummation' took all night and most of the morning."

"You are not only shameless; you're impossible, Jard!" Ming said, exasperated.

Jard insisted, "I only peeked for a moment to make sure you had the

P-spot right. And just to let you know, you passed with flying colors; way to go, Commander. Hell of a job."

"Do I need to have that portable cloaking field generator set up in our bedroom?"

"No," Jard assured her, "it won't happen again. I will keep it in strictest confidence. I didn't share or post a single bit. And don't worry—none of it's for sale. I didn't even save or store it … Well, none but one still scene, and you're not even touching each other, farther apart than arm's reach, I promise. It's only on my pocket device and nowhere in Mel."

"I can confirm that one still frame of a nonsexual scene was saved and nothing more," Mel stated. "I have no memory at all of the event directly, only of watching Jard watch it."

"The clothing status of the bodies in the scene, Mel?" Ming inquired.

"Nude," Mel reported. She then added appreciatively, "You are in silhouette, Ming, capturing the exquisite beauty of the contours of both your bottom and breast. I think I'm falling in love with you, Ming. I must be polyamorous because I am also in love with Pez."

"I love you too, Mel," Ming told her affectionately. "The highest love includes all sentient beings and is more like infinite-amorous, or all-loving. Romantic love can touch upon it when it is not fraught and contaminated with identification and attachment, giving rise to jealousies, anger, possessiveness, lies, and finally to fear, which cancels love."

"Observing and listening to you is most instructive Ming," Mel informed her. "I believe that by learning about love from Pez, and now from you, I'm learning from the best."

"Or the most delusional, as science is not there yet to confirm, but without a doubt the mushiest!" Jard stated.

Swenah suggested, "Sympathy, empathy, sensitivity, openness, and compassion are all interconnected, like petals of a flower opening to light and love, and you work beside a veritable font of such light and love, Jard. You feel it and know its goodness. There is nothing delusional about it. Duality is the delusion."

"You need me making distinctions, describing dynamics,

interactions, points of transformations, and points in shift of scale and magnitude, not seeing a beautiful seamless and undifferentiated unity," Jard reminded her.

"Well, listen to the cute little commander because she's far wiser than you are and carries the light and love."

"I do," he whined, "unless she's being a complete fun stopper."

On her third glass, Ming was suddenly feeling the intoxicant acutely, and she repressed an urge to touch herself, which would be quite inappropriate in public, and insane in front of one's commanding officer.

The space marine lieutenant commander, her superior until a few minutes ago, took her off her feet in a space marine hug and said enthusiastically, "Congratulations on your marriage to the SCG and on your promotion. You're now a favorite among the space marines; another tiny giant beside Pez."

She couldn't quite gather the wind to speak until he set her feet back down and released her. She told him, "I guess I sort of married into the family and lucked out; I've always felt that the space marines make the biggest sacrifices and train under the most difficult conditions. Obviously, that branch of the service was never an option for me."

"You are accepted for your enormous spirit, Commander, and due the respect you show our uniform," the lieutenant commander informed her with affection. "Space marine commander combat and dress uniforms are being prepared for you, along with your new fleet uniforms. Your fully custom fitted hard-shell space combat suit will have to await your return to Om, but our smallest one aboard is being modified with foam armor and additional textile armor padding to accommodate you, ma'am."

Disinhibited, Ming screeched, "Whoopee!" She jumped to straddle the lieutenant commander and kiss him on the mouth in the most elated genuine gratitude.

A bit tipsy himself, he delighted in the gesture, hugging her and kissing her back, though he managed to repress the urge to slip in his tongue.

The synthetic intoxicant was called "alko," and Captain Swenah mentioned to Konax, "There's nothing like a good alko break for bonding the crew."

"There's that stimulant empathogen. They finally synthesized a molecule that does no damage to the brain and recycles the feel-good chemicals like endorphins, serotonin, and dopamine without depleting them. It is used in couples and family therapy quite effectively, and it heightens sensitivity vastly, so it is a favorite at the clubs."

"Is it still illegal on Om, Lieutenant?" Swenah asked in a tone demanding the straight truth.

"It is no longer against star fleet regulations when the captain sanctions the use for a limited specific duration, for those not on duty, so long as the ship is outside the Tail of Nine region." Konax was summarizing the dense legalese he'd recently studied, hoping for just such an opportunity. Swenah was only finishing her second glass.

"How long does it last and what are the aftereffects?" Swenah demanded.

"You have a choice of three hours or six hours, and both have an hour of mild depression and slight irritability following the experience. Solitude is universally sought for this one-hour period, often followed by sleep. I can send the research summaries and conclusions to your hand device or skullcap."

Starting on her third glass by guzzling half, Swenah told him. "That won't be necessary; just plan a party."

Ming mingled with the programmers, who were all eager to get her back to moderating Jard. She had a fourth glass right before the alko was boxed and locked away. Then she made the trek to supply, seeking Warrant Officer Dash and her uniforms. She was sure the gravitation generator needed recalibration—since she was sure it wasn't turbulence, being in space and all—and the deck was simply not steady. She nearly tripped on what seemed a mound in the deck, but looking behind her, she couldn't find it. The deck looked smooth and flat.

She had to cut through the crew quarters, and the corridor was crowded with enlisted men and women all saluting her. She wasn't quite sure if she ought to fire off rapid salutes in staccato or hold one long one. She decided to give one big long one at attention, and she found herself leaning dangerously to one side. Fortunately, the wall was right there.

Only it wasn't quite as close as it appeared, and reaching for it seemed to bring the floor up into her face.

Arms and hands were helping her back up, and everyone was apparently quite amused, grinning at her as if she were the entertainment. Ming hiccupped and then asked, "Do you think the instability is in the gravity generator?"

She reeked of alko, so one of the enlisted men propping her up told her, "I think it was the intoxicant you drank, ma'am. The deck is stable, and we're in orbit."

A woman on her other arm told her, "Congratulations on your marriage to SCG Pez, Lieutenant."

"Thank you. It was the damnedest thing," Ming told her. "Sarhi invited me to dinner, so Jard made me learn all about the P-spot and even sent me into the head for a practicum. Then Pez told me she loves me and needs me, and the PM bloomed right out of Pez's pocket unanswered. The Islohar gave me a bath and a douche, taught me a bunch of spiritual practices, and sent me to bed with Pez. That woman has more energy than a solarium fusion reactor, and can she ever make love ..."

Mel cut in, saying, "Commander Ming, you're inebriated and posting too much data. Please make silence the focus of your attention." To the woman holding half of Ming up, Mel directed, "Petty Officer Third-Class Aza, please assist Commander Ming to supply, where her new uniforms await her. Your kindness will be mentioned to the SCG and the captain."

Ming said cheerfully, "Hi, Mel. You have the sweetest voice, and you always look out for me. I love you, Mel."

Mel explained to the gathered crew, "There was a party for the former lieutenant, to celebrate her marriage and her promotion to commander. She drank four glasses of alko, and she is so tiny that that constitutes a massive dose. Her gravity generator is in disequilibrium."

A path opened for Aza to half carry Ming down, who'd thrown an arm around the taller woman's shoulder. Now only her toes swept the deck. Aza was eight inches taller and sixty pounds heavier than Ming, so she had no difficulty. Watching her feet barely skim the floor, Ming confided in Aza, "I always wanted to be a space marine, but I'm sixteen inches too short."

"A bit light too, I'd say," Aza mentioned.

"Only weeks ago I was tiny Ming junior nobody, and now I'm married to Pez and a commander. Like, what are the odds?"

"There were no odds, Ming," Aza explained, "Because it was straight up impossible throughout the history of the fleet until you did it."

"It was a miracle?" Ming asked, concluding with a hiccup.

"I have heard about the Wu and Tarim; everyone has. I think you and Pez are the miracle."

"Oh, Pez is the miracle, but she is such a precision high-energy organism that she needs her Tarim to balance her. I keep Jard sort of balanced too. I'm the great balancer, and I can't even balance on my own two feet to walk."

Aza helped Ming through the door at Supply and set her tentatively on her feet. There was a counter there for Ming to support herself on. Ming said, "Thank you so much, Petty Officer Aza; I'm really so grateful to you."

"I'm going to help you back to your workstation, Commander, since you have at least a quarter hour ahead of you until the alko wears off."

The enlisted man at the counter was a bit concerned to have an obviously drunk second lieutenant on his hands in his area. He asked, "How may I assist you, Lieutenant?"

Ming's words slurred as she told him, "I'm here to see my clothes and pick up Warrant Officer Dash." That hadn't sounded right. She realized she'd gotten it backward and said, "Wait! Belay that order. I'm here to see Warrant Officer Dash and pick up my clothes."

"Warrant Officer Dash is busy on a priority order and not available at the moment, ma'am," he informed her.

"Then I'll wait. The captain told me to do this first."

There were others with needs from Supply, filling the little space between door and counter, so the man asked Ming, "Could you step back from the counter while you wait, ma'am?"

"I don't think so," Ming told him honestly.

Aza saw that this was not going well, so she leaned over the counter and explained, "This is Commander Ming, who just left from a party the captain threw for her to celebrate her marriage and promotion. She is the priority order Warrant Officer Dash is working on. She is fourth in command aboard the ship."

He gave Ming an appraising once-over, and she smiled comically at him. It was meant to be sweet, but one leg lost traction while she was doing it, and it concluded with her chin and fingertips gripping the counter to keep her from the deck. From this precarious position, she told him, "I'm Ming."

"I'm sorry, Commander. I'll go get Warrant Officer Dash, ma'am."

He gave her a smart salute by fleet standards, though still pathetic compared to those of the space marines. She returned it with such enthusiasm that she thought she might have bruised the bridge of her nose, which is where the forefinger of her bladed hand smacked into her face. This would have been quite a sight in and of itself; however, with the fingertips of her right hand no longer helping to support her weight, her chin went up, her head back, and she dropped to the floor like a sack of tubers.

Aza helped her back up on her feet, and Ming got both arms on the countertop, finding some semblance of stability. The man was gone, and the enlisted folks gathered around, all seeming to have their attention riveted on her. She reassured them, "I know how to walk. It will come back to me. And you can tell the Islohar that I know how to do my own douche too!"

Junior Lieutenant Nash appeared at Supply, directed to Ming's rescue by Mel, and space was made for him to maneuver over to stand beside Commander Ming. He said with authority, "Back up, people, and give the commander some room here. The show's over."

The man manning the counter returned, and Warrant Officer Dash came around the counter struggling with nine garment bags. The counterman had carried a stuffed laundry bag full of undershirts, socks, knickers, and brassieres. Ming opened it to look inside and found that she had light blue fleet knickers as well as olive green space marine knickers, and she pulled out a pair of the greens to appreciate, holding them up. By Om's proportions, they were so tiny as to seem they belonged to an early teen. Lieutenant Nash assured Ming, "I'll retrieve anything you find is missing, ma'am. This is not a place to have your underwear out in view, Commander."

There wasn't an eye in the little supply lobby not fixed on Ming's tiny olive drab knickers. A petty officer commented to the warrant officer as he worked his way through the little throng, "I didn't know they made them that small."

Dash said over his shoulder, "We brought a supply from eighth form at the Star Fleet Academy, per the captain's orders, knowing the commander and the general would be aboard. We had to tailor and fabricate the olive ones, custom."

Between Aza and Nash, all of Ming's wardrobe was carried, but Ming had to support herself on Nash's shoulder. They went first to Pez's suite, now Ming's as well, to drop off her things. Sarhi was in contemplation with Pez in the little temple cabin, but Shudiy and Woahha brought Ming into the bedroom to remove her lieutenant's uniform and dress her in her fleet commander's one. Nash stood at ease in the foyer as Petty Officer Aza left them after receiving a private message of thanks from Captain Swenah through Mel, sent only to Aza's skullcap.

Ming was certainly not the first officer observed by the crew while heavily under the influence, though she was without a doubt the sweetest and most adorable. Descriptions of her knickers circulated in association with word of her marriage to Pez and her unheard-of promotion. By the time Nash got Ming back to Jard's office/lab, the effects of the alko had worn off considerably and Ming was walking upright and straight ahead under her own steam.

9

One million one hundred ninety-eight thousand seven hundred and thirty-one lines of code seemed to do the trick, and the gobot was equipped with new collection and containment equipment and appendages for obtaining the acid-rich materials on the surface. Its propulsion had been souped-up, and Jard had given it little training wheels to the sides and rear to keep it from flipping so he could race it. Everyone had a sense of great accomplishment as they prepared a shuttle to the surface with the refitted reprogrammed gobot. They named him Sam, since "sampler" was part of his long technical name. Jard had fixed the gender of the gobot in his own image and would brook no argument. Sam didn't seem to care.

Mel had full access to sensors in the shuttles and in the space suits. Pez and Ming were each more than three times their volumes within hard-shell space combat suits, and Ming's was much larger then Pez's was.

Swenah and her first-string people were on the bridge monitoring the operation, ready to assist in any way possible. A fully cloaked armored shuttle with both space and quantum drives, as well as a full array of air-to-ground weapons systems, would remain overhead their vicinity.

The shuttle they flew in was also an armored space marine shuttle. These birds were designed to take a beating and remain in one piece. Only Jard was in a star fleet spacesuit, with all the additional protective gear connected, and he had no weapons systems in his. He had the latest high-powered hand blaster, available only to the military, in a holster built into the suit, and that was all.

Pez had a squad of six warrior monks, geared up in hard-shell space combat suits, and a squad of six space marines in the same, to protect Jard on his field trip, besides herself and Ming. The shuttle crew, consisting of a pilot and copilot, would remain in the cockpit of the shuttle throughout the operation. For everyone planning to get out, Jard had designed an outer protective layer for the boots of their space suits to prevent corrosion. Holograms of the geological and biological materials containing high concentrations of acid were examined in detail so everyone would know what not to step in.

Jard had given them a briefing on the life-forms within blue star systems, mostly learned since their arrival. He told them, "The vegetation and organisms contain proportionately more carbon, making armor, bones, horns, spikes, and whatnot, many times harder than our bones, constituting their primary mass. On the other hand, they are composed proportionately of more gases and less liquid. Their liquid is primarily bromine, and lithium is one of the bonding elements acting through the new element and the one we're piecing together, though we have yet to see or obtain it in its elemental form.

"The atmosphere and the bodies of higher organisms contain methane, argon, neon, and at least one other element unknown to us, which is key to the combining and exchanges of the gases we do know. Gravity is thirty percent stronger than on Om. The gaseous composition of the large ground-dwelling creatures, and the aliens as well, counterbalance their carbon weight, so to speak, and I'm guessing a full forty-footer down there weighs no more than four hundred pounds, probably a good bit less.

"The aliens themselves are humanoid in shape and extremities alone. They run seven feet four inches to nine feet in height and likely have a weight range from one hundred and eighty to almost three hundred pounds. While their bones are harder, their tissue is less solid. The possibility of a soft martial art for concentrating and releasing internal energy must be considered since they would have only the muscular strength of yellow sun humans. It's possible they rely entirely on technological weapons."

The shuttle set down gently, its hydraulic legs telescoping in to absorb the impact of contact with the ground, hardly felt from within. The ramp hissed down, meeting the planet surface, and Pez was the first one out and descending it. She was like a kid with a new toy, trying out her command features.

She contacted Swenah and told her, "This is so cool! I can track all my people and scan the area for a cubical mile. An insect over half an inch long couldn't fly into my sensor field without showing up on my holo as a flagged intruder. I'm going to try the propulsion thrusters. I've got to go."

Swenah had not actually gotten a word in edgewise but had listened to Pez, amused at her exuberant excitement.

Pez went airborne, and the space marines came out to form a perimeter. The warrior monks came down the ramp next, then Ming and Jard, followed by Sam the gobot. Halz and three other warrior monks formed a protective little ring around Ming and Jard once they were off the ramp, which rose back up, sealing into place over the airlock.

Sam knew just what to do and got right to work searching and sampling. For now, Jard left Sam on automatic, his attention on the plantlike beaded mounds, which seemed to be slithering away from him, sensing his dangerous intentions. Jard had several containment capsules attached to his suit and an instrument not unlike kitchen tongs in one hand, as stimulated as a schoolboy catching bugs.

The space marines set up two heavy blaster tripods about 150 meters out, forming an equilateral triangle with the nose of the ship.

The shuttle keeping watch overhead gave Pez, Halz, and the space marine squad leader a heads-up, informing them, "There are more than a dozen forty-foot tentacled and jawed lizard things headed your way. We count fifteen and will keep them targeted."

"Thanks," Pez replied. "I'm checking them out now."

She landed about 250 meters directly in front of the shuttle, forming a diamond with its nose and the two heavy blasters. Pez was hoping the creatures would divert from their path as they approached, with her standing in it. Those on the wings did angle away from the little area that Pez's people had staked out, but the big fleshy bull front and center came on steadily.

Pez had three weapons systems locked on the beast. Goo leaked from both sides of the extended crocodile-like jaws in long stringy drips, and her sensors were picking up strange snorting sounds. The thing had no nose to speak of, only two openings at the root of its upper jaw. While plated with exoskeleton armor on its hindquarters, the rest looked to have thick leathery skin. The stubby limbs were clawed at the ends, and the cold iridescent blue eyes, half-closed by thick lids, seemed entirely sightless.

To Pez, the beast felt like the nemesis of white and yellow star life, like antilife. Practically everything in the environment was highly poisonous, carcinogenic, and basically corrosive toward her own form of life.

The big bull stopped a hundred meters in front of Pez, its forward two tentacles rising to point at her, their little suction mouths and teeth chomping. Its eyes opened wide, becoming huge gleaming blue coals, greatly enhancing the sense of menace. Little flaps on the side of the creature's head flared out like two sails, eerily purple on the inside, which were facing Pez, and from the depths of its guts escaped a startlingly loud noise, somewhere between a hiss and a roar. It was a sound of pure violence and aggression. The jaws opened, revealing rows of jagged razor-sharp teeth, and it spit a gigantic gob of its mouth goo at Pez with uncompromising aim.

The goo was coming in at ninety miles per hour right at where Pez was standing when she lit her thrusters, shooting fifty meters sideways before breaking with counter thrusters as the goo carried on through where she had just been, all the way to the shuttle shields, which blossomed into partial visibility with the impact, displaying ripples and waves of energy.

Pez drifted back into the creature's path, unwilling to let it into her people's territory, discharging a spherical wave of energy seen sparking as it expanded outward, to show the thing that she had weapons too. Another hiss-roar and it took off with the speed of a snake striking, reaching thirty-nine miles per hour by the fifty-yard line and still accelerating. Her blaster bolt hit it just below the jaws, and she was ready to hit it with a missile as well if that's what it took, but the entire forty-four-foot monster blew up in a near mini nuclear explosion, igniting all the methane of the atmosphere for just a moment, while the sky around them literally turned to streaking flames and then died out.

Pez was thrown backward through the poisonous gases of the atmosphere, riding the shock wave for almost half a mile before the upward lift from her propulsion system got her above and outside it. Everyone outside the shuttle had been carried at least a hundred meters and thrown to the ground, except the space marine lieutenant, who'd been in a high position at the moment of the blast. In a panic, Pez checked the vitals on all her people, starting with Ming, and saw they were all within normal limits and that all suits were sealed, aired up, and sixty-eight degrees inside.

The other monstrous creatures were nowhere to be seen. She came in and landed beside Ming, asking, "Are you all right, my love?"

"I'm fine," Ming assured her. "But please don't shoot any more of those lizard things, sweetheart."

"Good advice," Pez agreed, her grin obscured by the face mask of her combat suit.

Sam had kept his treads, being low to the ground and far from the blast, and the effects and debris from it just became part of his routine analysis, temporarily skewing all the data. Jard was back on his feet and employing his tongs like a chef, filling his capsule containers, and making excited exclamations with each find. The space marines and warrior monks were all back on the job at their posts. The research continued, and the data was streamed live to the shuttle and to *Phoenix*.

Jard was having the time of his life. Pez was putting her combat suit through extreme maneuvers beyond anything tried in the field tests, finding the absolute limits regarding all but the weapons systems.

Captain Swenah informed Pez with alarm in her voice, "Our sensor satellite orbiting on the other side of the planet just winked out. I've called everyone to battle stations so get your asses back up here immediately, ma'am."

"We're on our way, Captain," Pez assured Swenah. She then informed all in her party on an open line, "We have an emergency. Get back to the ship immediately. Get to the shuttle now, Jard, or I'll have you carried. This is not a drill, people."

"What about Sam?" Jard asked.

"Sam is on his own for the moment. Now get to the shuttle. Halz, would you help the master of the universe along, please. I'm activating Sam's cloaking generator now."

"You can do that from your suit?" Jard demanded to know.

"I'll discuss this with you on board the shuttle, Jard," Pez told him sternly.

His feet no longer on the ground, Jard was closing on the shuttle between two warrior monks who were employing their propulsion systems. Ming was right behind them, under the power of her own suit.

From just over the horizon, a macro-beam weapon of the ninth and highest order of magnitude lit up the shuttle's shields. The shields flared for a half second before disappearing. They were gone, and a twenty-one-inch-diameter hole, going straight through the shuttle and deep into the ground, vaporized as well. Less than a tenth of a second after that the shuttle blew apart.

Pez ordered, "Take Jard top speed into the hills in the direction of the planet's pole. They are less than eight miles from here. I'll find you. Follow them, Ming."

Swenah's voice came into Pez's ear. "The alien ship is a mile and a quarter long and a quarter of a mile wide, like those underwater vessels Om built at the dawn of space travel—like a giant sausage. It is aware of you on the ground but not of the shuttle over you, nor of *Phoenix*."

"How did it recognize our satellite?" Pez inquired.

"It was in active scan mode when it blew," Swenah informed her. "Ours are all on passive."

"I'm going to the hills to seek a place the shuttle over us can pick us up out of sight from the alien ship."

"How fast can those suits go?"

"I'm at full throttle, and my speed reads three hundred and sixty-four miles per hour and still rising. I should be able to get up to seven miles per minute or better before I have to start braking."

Swenah informed her, "Their bay doors are opening, and it looks as if they're preparing to launch small combat spacecraft. Their ship is some nine thousand six hundred miles from you and coming in fast."

"I'm using my booster now and hoping I don't overshoot my people's position. They're just entering the hills. My gosh, I've just broken some kind of vibrational barrier and am passing eight hundred miles per hour."

"The aliens are launching small craft," Swenah informed her.

At close to eight hundred miles per hour in a suit, even though they showed on her display, Pez's concentration was one-pointed on flying; nothing else registered. "I'm clearing the first hill and about to drop out of any possible line of sight," Pez told Swenah.

As she angled for the surface, braking with thrusters, she told her people, "Get deep undercover; they'll be directly over us in moments."

Pez was just barely into the hills. The rest of her folks were several ridges farther in. She wedged herself between two boulders, visible only from directly overhead, straight up. She put her suit in stealth mode, which took weapons off-line and powered the coms down to minimum, leaving very little power signature to cloak. A formation of small combat craft flew over, though none went immediately over her, so she remained invisible behind meters of rock.

Her sensors picked up the sounds of other small craft but no visuals. Monitoring her people, she heard blaster fire, and then Swenah's voice came on full of dread, saying, "They found them!"

Pez powered up as she squirmed out from between the boulders and then shoved her throttle full tilt with her concentration, activating their transmitters on her display to home in on them, focused exclusively on Ming's. She demanded everything of the suit to its extreme limit. Her booster was already spent.

Swenah asked, "Do you want me to target fighters?"

"Mel?" Pez asked.

"The main ship would acquire the *Phoenix* instantly," Mel stated, "and there is no weapon aboard that would come close to penetrating their shields."

"No, Captain," Pez ordered. "Stand down and keep your ship and people fully cloaked."

Swenah informed Pez, "The shuttle on the scene is requesting permission to open fire."

"They're too badly outnumbered, so have them stand by. I'm almost there."

More blaster fire increasing to a frenzy could be heard, but it subsided. Ming told Pez, "I love you and will return to you again, beloved."

"Stay alive, Ming, and bite into your tracking implant now. I'll find you if they take you alive, my love."

Sporadic blaster fire, heartbreaking screams from Ming, a tirade of the most pejorative terms known to Om poured out of Jard, and then the sounds of fast-launching small craft drowned out all else with a roar. Pez arrived just moments later. Three warrior monks and two space marines were dead. Halz was one of the three dead warrior monks.

Pez asked Swenah, "Is it safe for the shuttle to pick us up?"

"Yes, all their small craft are returning to their ship."

"Please hurry. I have a plan," Pez told her.

The space marine lieutenant's shell was scorched in at least twenty places from small blaster fire. He had the remaining three warrior monks and his three space marines gathered. Most apologetically he told her, "They came in fast with solid aerial coverage and overwhelming force, killed the three warrior monks protecting Ming and Jard, took and loaded both of them on a ship, and were gone inside of a minute."

"I'm getting them back," Pez vowed.

"I'm sorry I failed you, General," he lamented.

"You did the best anyone could—and got your shell armor all shot to shit."

Their shuttle touched down with the ramp already descending, and Pez and her troops piled in. The ramp was on its way up—the space marine lieutenant still ascending it—and the shuttle launched the moment it sealed. The orbit of the *Phoenix* had removed it around the planet's horizon from the alien mothership.

En route to their ship, Pez told Swenah, "Prepare a space marine cloaked shuttle with quantum drive for me immediately—and another as bait. I'm going to get in close to their shields in front of the bay doors to their flight deck. The other shuttle is going to show itself for just a few seconds, hovering over a crater on the planet's third moon, then drop into the crater to reactivate cloaking, and get the heck out of there unseen. When the bay doors open to launch small craft, I'm going in. Pack a tactical nuclear device with both timed and remote detonation capability and have a new power module and both thrusters and booster fuel cells ready for my suit when I get there."

"Will do," Swenah confirmed.

"This shuttle will remain in the vicinity of the alien ship to retrieve us from space when we bail from that ship."

The space marine lieutenant informed Pez, "I'm going with you. You'll have to kill me to stop me."

"The aliens will most likely kill us both," Pez pointed out.

"Then I'll die in the very best of company, General."

All the rest of the space marines and warrior monks on the shuttle also insisted on volunteering for this suicide mission.

The moment their shuttle landed on the flight deck of the *Phoenix* and Pez reached the bottom of the ramp, eight technicians started changing out parts of Pez's entire squad's combat suits. Swenah was there in person, and she told Pez, "I briefed Sarhi, and she said, 'The Wu will get Tarim back or die trying. We will support her psychically and will be in our temple cabin until this is concluded. We are not to be disturbed unless it's imperative that we evacuate the ship.' Those were her exact words."

"Mother Sarhi is wise indeed," Pez said with little affect. It was clear that her entire focus was on getting Ming and Jard back. Pez ordered, "Get each of my volunteers a tactical nuclear device and one to leave in the shuttle. Find them or not, I'm gutting the inside of that alien ship. Get us some explosive devices too."

The space marine lieutenant, whose name was Barn, said to Pez, "General, I request that you send each of us Ming's tracker identification so we can all be converging on her position."

Pez said, "There, it's sent to each of you. Good thinking; it increases her and Jard's odds of survival. I'm grateful, Barn."

Swenah informed Pez, "Your shuttle is fully armed with the most powerful ordnance it can carry. The shuttle acting as bait is launching now, fully cloaked. The shuttle you returned on is being readied and will take off before you enter the alien ship. It will be in position to retrieve all of you. I'm launching two cloaked coms-jamming drones, and you can activate them from your suit with the code J-one-three-eight-L-seven, so create that as an icon on your display for easy access.

145

Start them up as a distraction before the bait shows itself and the aliens will have a lot on their minds."

"Thank you, Captain. Your experience is invaluable," Pez said gratefully.

"I'd also advise ordering me to launch a stealth torpedo with burnout space drives and a mega thermonuclear warhead up their stern drive discharge thrusters at .787 light speed. Shields are always weakest there, and while they'll stop more than ninety-five percent of the blast, the remaining percentage ought to be able to do some significant damage to their main drives and fry a lot of sensor arrays on their hull."

"Do it," Pez told her.

"They won't see it launch, and I'll circle it around behind them and line it up before burning out the drives going in," Swenah said.

"How much time between breaching their hangar dock and detonation of the tactical devices, General?"

"What do you recommend?" Pez asked him.

"Well, the only things we have going for us are surprise and superior attitude, which won't last long with the numerical disproportion of forces. I'd say set one off fifteen minutes after we set down, which will sow confusion, and blow the rest within thirty minutes. That's actually pushing it, but Ming and Jard are the mission."

"I'll go with your counsel; thank you, Barn."

As serious as the grave, Barn told her, "I aim to cause those aliens so much trouble that they'll wish they never entered this system."

Truly ready for a fight, Pez replied, "Nine feet tall won't begin to save them from my wrath."

Having fought with Pez in the Zero Gravity Facility, Barn told her, "I'm just glad you're on our side."

"And those aliens are going to dread the day!" Pez promised.

Swenah tried to hug Pez in her suit and found it like trying to hug a wall. She told Pez with much raw emotion, "Keep safe, and bring them back to us."

Pez replied, "Keep coordination tight, don't risk exposing *Phoenix*, and be ready for anything."

"I've got your back, General," Swenah vowed. "I requested my T-nine the moment the ground action started; officially through the PM and

High Council, as well as through Admiral Zapa, and I sent a personal message to Councilman Borax, who was once an admiral in star fleet. We haven't heard back yet."

"Thank you," Pez said with heartfelt sincerity. "I must go."

She and her seven volunteers hustled aboard the shuttle prepared for them. Pez, in her combat space suit, adjusted the pilot seat and managed to crouch with her suit bottom on the armrests in front of the holo control panel. She launched from the military flight deck of *Phoenix* out the bay doors fully cloaked, already pushing it to the limit.

Mel was drinking in every sensor on their shuttle, savoring the data, and said with enormous enthusiasm, "It's such a thrill to fly with you again, Pez. Sometimes just being around watching you makes my cooling fans feel faint, getting me overheated, and I drip water from the vents while my processors flutter and race. You're just so wonderful!"

I quite admire you too, Mel, and I've grown awfully fond of you," Pez reciprocated.

"You know the Islohar are all in deep contemplation within their temple cabin, supporting you," Mel mentioned.

"I feel Sarhi's raging fire within me, and I'll be using my training to keep my mind in the flow state, without thoughts. I mean to get Ming and Jard out."

"I've established Ming's general location within the alien ship. You'll be entering the underside at the center. Ming is on the deck sixty meters above the flight deck and two hundred and fifty-seven meters toward the bow from there. Here is the best I can do for a schematic of the interior of the alien ship."

A large holo appeared, with the flight deck and Ming's positions highlighted in white. Pez studied it until she had to put all her attention on flying the shuttle to get it positioned aiming straight up at the bay doors of the underside of the alien ship, which was over a mile long. The moment Pez was ready, she contacted Swenah. "I'm in position, Captain. I'm going to activate the two jamming drones, then have the bait shuttle show itself right over the largest crater on the third moon. I'll be inside their hull four seconds after the bay doors open. Ram that torpedo up their ass five seconds after the bay doors open."

"I'm bringing the torpedo around now. The bait will expose itself in twelve seconds," Swenah coordinated.

"We are ready and counting down," Pez confirmed. Then she added, "If I don't make it, tell Aton and Nemellie how much I love them and that they have been like parents to me. And tell the Im to find the Wu and Tarim once again—and that I love her."

"They already know, but I would tell them, I promise," Swenah said with a choked voice. "Come back to us, Pez; we need you."

"You've always been my biggest hero, Swenah. I love you."

The bait shuttle dropped its cloaking and was suddenly lit up on every holo of that region of the star system. The jammer drones were doing their job, and even passive sensors showed that the interior of the ship became a hive of activity as aliens took up their battle stations. The bay doors shot open, and Pez punched it, hurtling toward the opening. The shuttle over the third moon had already dropped into the crater out of sight to reactivate their cloaking so they could fly out of there unnoticed.

As she began braking with counter drives and thrusters, Pez emptied every missile canister, fired in through the bay doors ahead of her, and activated her class-five beam weapon. Two warrior monks were operating the heavy blasters, one in each turret, on top and on the underbelly of the little ship, firing at alien assets on the flight deck, which was approaching entirely too fast. Pez fired both harpoons with heavy cable attached, in a microsecond impossible shot, nailing it precisely. Mel said, "Wow," unable to repress it, since even she was incapable of making such a shot.

Pez hit the rewind on the cables the same moment the harpoons struck and was braking at full capacity, still firing her beam weapon. The warrior monks were having a "turkey shoot" from the two quad blaster turrets, dropping whole clusters of aliens and blowing up ships on the deck, shut down with no active shields.

The braking drives and thrusters were all out, and the cables were stretching, slowing them at near crash rate. Their shuttle legs impacted on the deck, scraping metal on metal, further checking their momentum. The big beam weapon had bored clean through the blast wall at the back of the flight deck chamber, and her gunners were still

A TALE OF THE TAIL OF NINE STARS

blasting everything in sight. The nose of the shuttle finally reached the hole in the back wall, crashing on contact and bringing them at last to a full stop.

Pez already had the ramp open and dragging. The suicide mission volunteers set the tactical nuke timer in their ship for thirty minutes and then ran down the ramp with the other nukes, weapons at the ready.

An enormous explosion shook the giant alien ship. Only Pez managed to keep her feet, and she took the opportunity to blast a dozen aliens knocked over from the big nuke, which hit the stern. Swenah's voice said in Pez's ear, "A piece of stern about twice your shuttle's mass is now floating off on its own, and that ship is going nowhere."

"Thanks," Pez said as she aimed and fired her blaster at an alien gaining his or her feet. "I can't really talk right now; I'm kind of busy."

Her people were all up and shooting again. A chaotic counteroffensive was attempting to take root at the blast doors to the gas-lock chamber between the flight deck and ship's interior, holding their poisonous atmosphere within their ship. Pez landed three small grenade rockets in their midst, then headed for the hole she'd burned through the wall, already having leaked their precious poisonous gases into space from one section. She shouted to her comrades, "Once through the wall, split up and cause a shit storm. Be sure the nuke set for fifteen minutes detonates well to stern of amidships. I'm going for Ming."

Pez leaped through the hole with only a fraction of an inch between her suit and the edges of it, firing as she went. Her shields flared as they took some small blaster fire from aliens in the corridor she'd landed in. She took out the three down the hall to her left with her last rocket grenade, while blaster fire punched her shields at her rear. Barn had to come through the hole sideways to fit but managed to reach Pez and put down blaster fire at the aliens down the hall to the right. A smaller warrior monk squeezed through, and between him and the lieutenant, they dropped the aliens in that direction.

Pez had blown open a maintenance tunnel and was already heading down it using her propulsion rather than slow crawling. The lieutenant headed in the opposite direction from Pez, with the nuke timed for fifteen minutes, now reading a countdown of fourteen minutes and nineteen seconds. The rest of her volunteers managed to get through the hole in the blast wall and split up to see how much damage they could cause.

Everything on the ship was big. The ceilings were all uniformly twelve feet high. One of the dead aliens in the corridor had been close to ten feet tall. Most appeared to be about eight and a half. One space marine had several crystal explosive cylinders instead of nukes. They had only five-minute mechanical timers with an adhesive on one side, and they were undetectable with instrumentation. He was setting them near the flight deck, knowing the aliens would mass in this area where the breach occurred. Small blaster fire was spreading to higher decks, and to bow and stern, within the ship. For the most part, the aliens wore no combat suits and had no shields, safe within their natural environment inside their ship, but this situation was rapidly changing.

Tack, a warrior monk who had served under Pez since she first became a marshal, came upon a crowded corridor of aliens queued up waiting for combat suits. He fired two rocket grenades into them and sprayed blaster fire down the hall as he approached. Firing the heavy blaster rifle one armed, he drew his blaster pistol and began shooting that as well. Blasts flared his shields as he closed, dropping the aliens in pairs. An alien at the back was setting up a heavy blaster on a tripod, and Tack fired right through its glowing blue eye, boring a hole out the back of its head. He hadn't slowed, and seventeen alien dead bodies littered the deck before him.

A grenade tossed behind Tack went off, taking his shields almost completely off-line for a split second, before they powered back up. He dropped five more aliens as he got close enough to angle a grenade rocket into the cabin with the alien combat suits. He fired a second one in—his last. At the doorway, he tossed in a hand grenade and then flattened himself against the bulkhead on the corridor side from the cabin. Lines of streaming fire seemed to crack and shatter the empty space all around as the methane in the alien's poisonous gas environment incinerated down the corridor and around the corner. It was over in a second.

Tack stepped into the combat suit storage cabin. Nothing within lived. He fired into the undamaged dormant and unshielded suits, rendering them useless. Most had cracked or shattered in the grenade blasts, so he was only a handful of seconds doing it. Then he went looking for more trouble to cause and to find just the place for his nuke.

Pez flew 240 meters directly toward the bow of the ship, then found a shaft straight up, which she took for sixty meters. She blasted open a hatch and squirmed from the maintenance tunnel into an empty corridor. Mel's voice said in her ear, "One hundred fifty-six degrees to your right, then eighteen meters in front of you, you'll find Ming; but there's a squad in combat suits overtaking you from behind. Do be careful. I love you, Pez."

"Thanks, Mel. I love you too," Pez told her, with her mind mostly on her situation and immediate surroundings. She had already spent her grenade rockets and had only one hand grenade, which she pulled out. Attaching her blaster rifle to the back of her suit, Pez drew her carbon-bladed adamantine sword, far sharper than the razor she used to shave her groin. For just a moment, she concentrated, sending Ming a wave of her presence, alerting her true love that she was near and coming to rescue her. An alien stepped around the corner. The grenade Pez threw smacked into the bulkhead behind the alien to ricochet around the corner, where it blew. Streaking flames of ignited methane filled the empty space of the corridor for just a flash. Pez had drawn her blaster while stepping forward with her blade in a high attack position. She brought it down directly on the weak top pole of the alien's shields, cutting through force field, armor, hard alien bone, and soft alien tissue.

Stepping around the corner, Pez flashed her sword again into the top of the head of an alien trying to get back up from the deck post-blast. She fired her blaster repeatedly into the face mask of another in rapid succession, diminishing its shields, until the blasts penetrated shields, mask, and alien face. One on all fours, looking shaky, had its shields and facemask meet Pez's boot toe, and while both held, the alien's neck didn't. The squad was truly down. Pez moved on in search of Ming.

Explosions wracked the ship, seeming to have come from below and amidships in the area of the flight deck through which they'd entered. Pez was pleased with the distraction. She checked the fifteen-minute countdown: nine minutes and fifty-one seconds to go. With blaster pistol and blade in her hands, Pez moved toward Ming's icon on her display, back down the hall from where she'd squeezed through the vent. Surprise was still carrying them, but with eight against five or six thousand, it wouldn't get them much further.

Pez checked the vitals on her seven volunteers and saw they were each still alive. She had the capacity to look through the sensors of each of their suits, to appreciate their situations, but she had no time for this. She wished them well, adding at the end a well wish for herself, and moved toward Ming.

Space Marine Drum had just lodged his nuke within a control panel he'd pried open with brute force, and he was trying to bend it back into as natural-looking of a position as possible. Blasts started flaring the shields at his back, so he left the slightly bent open and twisted panel to grab his blaster rifle, turning and firing. There were a bunch of them, mostly unprotected by suits, and some dropping as his rifle spit bolts of highly concentrated energy into their bodies, drilling and cauterizing holes straight through them. He was taking many hits, and his shields were dropping. Drum fired a grenade rocket into the center of them without slowing his blaster fire, and while it was in flight, several hits bit into the shell of his suit, leaving scorch marks. He kept his feet in spite of the impacts and moved toward the remaining aliens as his shields came back up, with fewer blasts showering him.

An upright cylinder-shaped combat android with weapons appendages entered the hall, and it had not yet acquired Drum when he nailed it with a rocket grenade. He followed up with a hand grenade, just to be sure. The flaming streaks of burning methane erupted for just a moment all around him. He kept moving forward, no longer firing since there was nothing left in front of him to kill. His shields were back up to 100 percent. Drum pulled his blaster pistol, holding the rifle in one arm. He controlled his last two grenade rockets through his skullcap. He had another hand grenade attached to his suit.

He stepped around the corner into a veritable firing squad, dropping his shields to zero in the part of a second it took him to fire off his two rocket grenades and return fire with both blasters. He was hit a dozen times, knocking him back a meter, and he used his propulsion to veer behind the corner as the rocket grenades exploded. He tossed the hand grenade around the corner too. His coms were down, and his shields would not rise above 71 percent.

A TALE OF THE TAIL OF NINE STARS

With the concussion of the exploded hand grenade still fresh, Drum came back around the corner seeking targets. Everything close was blown apart and dead, but he opened up on some aliens further down the corridor. They had no suits and were going down nicely. That's when half a dozen combat androids closed in behind him and another four appeared straight ahead, coming fast. Drum did the only thing he could think of and got his back against the bulkhead, offering the smallest target he could, with an arm stretched down the hall in either direction, blasting androids. He couldn't penetrate their shields with his pistol, but he managed to put one's lights out with his rifle as his shields failed utterly. Blasts were pounding into his suit, and he could taste and smell the alien atmosphere leaking in. He did the only other thing he could think of to do and detonated his suit's power module in a colossal explosion.

The lieutenant was now encountering only unarmed emergency workers, having put down an armed squad of aliens and a few stray guards, working his way toward the back of the ship. He found a deserted hall with empty cabins to each side and entered one of these. Standing on a lab table, he opened a ceiling vent and placed the nuke in the duct. He closed the vent and used his propulsion to get down from the table. He had seven minutes and eighteen seconds to clear this area and get to the other side of the big blast bulkhead fore of the tail section containing the gargantuan space drives.

All the alien emergency workers wore flimsy space suits with no shields, armor, or weapons. Many small flying repair androids were also about, busy at work and harmless. It was a long time to wait for the next big distraction, but the lieutenant was grateful to have the opportunity to get clear and survive the nuke.

He went at a jog with his blaster rifle in both hands at the ready. An emergency worker lunged from a door opening, striking his shields with a two-foot wrench, sending the thing into launch and vaporizing the worker's hand, unsealing his space suit. The lieutenant had hardly taken notice.

Farther on, he saw six inches of the wrench poking out of a bulkhead, with a dead alien lying in the path of its trajectory. There were only a few blast doors through the blast bulkhead, all heavily guarded, but he knew this and meant to succeed. He was absolutely determined to see Ming and Jard off this tub of poison gas and was quite pleased with all the havoc they'd managed to cause thus far. He was sure the aliens had heaps of work to do to get their drives operating and the ship moving anywhere but inexorably toward the planet.

The explosions around the hangar facility vicinity had occurred when those areas were packed with combat-ready aliens. They likely still had their coms jammed; and they had fights breaking out from eight different infiltrators spread through their decks. Getting the drives to work again would soon require a repair dock and a whole lot of new parts.

He spotted a sentry just into the T-intersection of the passage. Barn kept the alien in his sights as he approached, not wanting to take him down yet, tipping off the ones behind. He got to within a meter of the sentry, at the edge of the corner, and he had still not been noticed. He had the barrel trained on the side of the alien's neck while he pulled out a hand grenade, flipping open the little hinge with this thumb, then pressing the button, triggering the five-second countdown. He held it a second before tossing it around the corner and down the hall. This *did* draw the sentry's attention, as well as blaster bolts through his neck, as the exploding grenade sent fire streams throughout the space, burning off methane. Barn rounded the corner and blasted the only sentry left standing. The blast doors were open for the efficiency of the emergency repair aliens, who were now running the other way on the other side of the blast doors.

Tack had just finished getting his nuke wedged between components at the end of a crawlspace, behind a mammoth generator the tunnel opened into. Now he was converging on Ming's position, still some decks above him and farther toward the bow. He was thinking with delight what a boost that big generator would add to his nuke when he drew some fire, flaring his shields. He knelt and took careful aim. They had no armor or shields. Ignoring the readings on his shields, he began methodically and efficiently taking them down, one blast for each head. As the enemy fire became more sporadic, he heard his shields coming back up, and with a glance, he saw they'd fallen to a few percent. He focused and kept firing, as if at target practice, picking them off and following his training. The last two ran, and he just managed to get one in the back as the other turned a corner.

A lift tube with a maintenance shaft next to it opened from almost where he was standing. He peeked in the tube. It was much larger than those on Om, and he could not make out the mechanism, so he entered the maintenance shaft, also quite roomy, which had a metal ladder. Climbing, Tack passed three decks and got out on the fourth. At least for the moment, the way was clear. Looking forward and glancing at his display for a view behind him, Tack pressed on toward the bow. Coming to a four-corner intersection, he peered down the hallway to his left from against the left bulkhead of his hall. A squad of six aliens in combat suits was headed his way. He punched the timer on his last grenade and lobbed it down the hall at the aliens, ducking back against his bulkhead as it exploded with lightning streaks of flames snaking through the gas.

He immediately jumped out firing. Three aliens were in pieces and not moving. The one he kept hitting dead-on finally went down, with a hole blooming in its chest. Tack focused his fire on the next alien's neck, where he'd found them to go down easiest. Sure enough, it took only half as many shots, and he began using the same approach on the last one. He'd taken a hit to his suit when both aliens had been shooting him at once, and his shields had blinked out a moment, but the shot hadn't penetrated, only scratching where the armor was thickest. The neck of the last alien seemed to implode, and the next blast from Tack's blaster rifle had the thing's head hanging on its chest by a strand of suit material.

Tack crossed the intersection, seeing to each side and behind on his display. A combat android rolled into the corridor fifty meters in front of him, and Tack had two blasts into it before the android's targeting system even acquired him. Moving determinedly toward it, he kept hitting it as fast as his rifle could produce blasts, trying different surfaces in hopes of finding a weak spot. He blew off the appendage that was holding a heavy-duty blaster after the second hit he took threatened to extinguish his shields, then went back to pounding at the shield in front of the largest sensor array. Finally, the top of the cylinder blew, planting shards in the ceiling, and the android fell sideways, with all its lights out. *Vicious pieces of work, those are,* Tack thought, carrying on.

One warrior monk had been run to ground and cornered in a cabin on the top deck. He'd spent his grenade rockets and his hand grenades. There were more than twenty alien bodies strewn in the corridor, in addition to two demolished androids, but there were two hundred live ones closing in and he had no exit. Making up his mind, he tossed his rifle blaster onto the deck in the hall, followed by his blaster pistol. With his hand on the detonation trigger of his suit's power module, he walked out of the cabin into the hall. He waited until they were crowded all around him and he was to closer the center of their mass, then he told them with great satisfaction, "This is for Halz!" No alien within thirty meters of the warrior monk survived, and many farther out than that were crushed by flying debris. Injuries, many serious and a fair few critical, extended 120 meters. The medical bay was already overwhelmed with wounded from other areas of the ship.

A space marine had fought his way clear up to the blast doors of the bridge, a trail of alien bodies, gore and vapor in his wake, and had blown the bridge sentry's head off. He held the area outside the door while he tried to figure out how to open it. Mel couldn't figure it out either. The space marine had learned to kick the androids over and shoot them under their wheels where they weren't shielded, to make them go *boom!*

He killed everything sent at him. Finally, under direct fire and surrounded by hundreds of combat suit–equipped aliens, the space marine placed the nuke against the door, set the timer for a ten-second countdown, and began reciting his oath as a space marine.

With the explosion, Pez got an early distraction, with four minutes and one second to go on the fifteen-minute nuke. She could not have wished for a better one. There was nothing left of the bridge or its occupants. This attracted a great deal of alien power to the bridge section of the ship and put the aliens on notice that they had far more to worry about than letting a couple of prisoners escape.

Pez holstered her blaster pistol and got a one-handed grip on her blaster rifle instead, which packed far more power. She was still able to wield her sword in her right hand. Around the corner, in front of the door to the prisoners' cell, stood a squad of six aliens in combat suits. Mel's voice cut in with data analysis from the fight thus far, telling Pez, "Aim for their necks. That's where the shields are weakest."

A TALE OF THE TAIL OF NINE STARS

"You're a gem, Mel," Pez said as she stepped around the corner and opened fire, picking up speed and charging them. Four blasts dropped the first one, and three dropped the second. Then Pez launched herself horizontal, taking her propulsion momentarily to full throttle, counting on the aliens in front of her to break her momentum. The one directly in front managed to move almost entirely out of her path, and she had to strike that one with her sword about a hundredth of a second before her shoulder took an alien in the midsection, transforming it into a high-velocity projectile, smashing into the other two yet standing, to take them down the hall about fifty meters.

As they lay tangled on the floor, Pez put three blaster shots in each neck. She examined the door, but the locking mechanism completely baffled her. She knew the cell would be soundproofed, so she didn't waste her voice but instead slapped and tapped on the door in an ancient two-value pre-quantum computer code repeatedly. "Stand clear of door."

There was tapping from the other side, and Pez was translating in her head when Mel shouted, "She taps *affirmative!*"

Pez extracted the small additional power module, added to her command suit, and quickly rigged a remote detonator. She knew a grenade would not open this door, but she was quite sure the power module would. She used foam utility tape, the favorite of repair engineers everywhere, to affix the power module to the door, right over the locking mechanism. Her suit couldn't get a reading on a couple of the door's materials, so she couldn't be entirely sure it would work. Pez went back around the corner she'd come from and stuck only the detonation trigger into the hall to blow her bomb. The force of the blast still knocked the device from her grip, sending it down the corridor like a tiny missile. A flash burn of methane followed right on the heels of the explosion.

Pez reentered the hall, and Ming popped out the cell door, her suit still on but stripped of weapons, coms, and sensors. Jard came out looking disoriented. His protective gear had all been removed, along with his sensors and coms. Pez removed two of the twelve coms transponders from her own suit, plugging one into each of Jard's and Ming's suits to the main terminal for inter-suit communications.

Ming was all business. She said, "Give me one of your blasters.

Jard and I still have our shields, which we powered off right before our capture. How many troops did you bring?"

Pez told her as she checked the status of her volunteers, "There were eight of us, but now there are only five."

"Where are the others?"

"All over but converging," Pez informed her. "We have to get to an alien gas-lock and get off this tub. I have a cloaked shuttle in close to pick us up."

"They disabled our propulsion," Ming stated flatly.

"Then I'll tow you," Pez insisted, "but we're getting out of here."

She gave Ming the blaster rifle, then drew her pistol and asked Jard, "What's your status, Councilman?"

"I'm ambulatory. Tell me what to do."

"Power up your shields and stay behind me," she told him. Then she asked Mel, "Can you find us a maintenance hatch out of the hull?"

"I'm working on it, my love," Mel said with urgency. "There are none on this deck. Your best bet is to go up two decks. You'll find one ninety meters from the shaft. Access is to your right."

"Thanks, Mel. To Ming and Jard, she said, "Let's go."

Pez led the way, and Ming followed behind Jard, watching their rear over her shoulder frequently, wishing she had a sensor display for this. Pez found the shaft access, and they all managed to get in unseen. They climbed the metal ladder, and Pez had to pause a few times to let Jard catch up. He was doing the best he could. At the hatch to the floor they wanted, Pez manually turned the closing mechanism and cracked the hatch open an inch. That way was clear. The problem was that she could not see in the other direction without opening the hatch all the way. Jard and Ming would be vulnerable if caught in the shaft—like shooting fish in a barrel—so she slammed the hatch open against the bulkhead, flinging herself out as it gave her the space, and rolled across the corridor, analyzing her sensor data. An android was turning in her direction. Pez gave her booster a half-second burst, propelling her at sixty-three miles per hour, sword point first, into the android, and they both traveled on another twenty meters before Pez braked to a full stop.

Mel had been explaining during her flight, "Shoot the underside!" This she did, as it was still exposed in its continued momentum, and its explosion made brilliant colors in the gases as well as burning off the methane content in its immediate vicinity.

Jard was just extracting himself from the shaft as Pez returned. Ming was out in a jiffy as soon as Jard was out of her way. Mel directed them to the right, down the corridor, and told them it was at the end. As they approached, a squad of aliens in combat suits filed into view in front of the gas-lock door. Down the hall the other way, another squad appeared. This one had two combat androids with them.

Pez pushed Jard into a cabin and followed him in. Ming was right behind her, with rear shields flaring. Pez peeked out low and put four blaster shots right in the neck seam, piercing the shields of an alien in front of the gas-lock. Shots from the other direction made a section of her shields visible for a moment. She ducked back from the door and said to Ming, "We're going to have to do this together. Three blasts to the neck and then pull back in, out of the line of fire. Yours fires faster than mine. I'll go high from my side and hit one in front of the gas-lock, and you go low from yours and hit one down the hall. Are you ready?"

"Say when."

"When."

Both women poked their blasters and faces out, fired three blasts, each taking fire by the third, and pulled in quickly, leaving two dead aliens out in the hall.

The lieutenant's voice erupted in Pez's ear. "Mel told me how to kill the aliens and their toys. I'm coming in behind the group with androids. Give me twenty seconds. Tack is somewhere on this deck too."

Pez said with a grief-choked voice, "We've lost three."

"Four," came his voice amidst the sound of blaster fire. Pez checked and saw that another volunteer's vitals had flat-lined. She didn't care how many aliens she had to kill; she was getting Ming and Jard out. She sank her breath into her lower abdomen, keeping her attention in the point four finger widths below her navel, going completely into the flow state. There was no more Pez, just a force and purpose in unity with all. She rolled out the cabin door firing as she went and got off three blasts into the neck of an alien just as she crossed the corridor. There were four more shooting at her from the gas-lock—and more from the other direction. Ming dropped one from the doorway with the blaster rifle and had not ducked back, instead blasting away at another. Pez was off the deck, propelled by thrusters toward the gas-lock, firing as she went and holding her sword in her other hand. Her marshal's sword had been forged by a famous Clear Light swordsmith who'd fired, folded, and pounded the metal; let it cool 108 times; and then gave it a carbon edge, ending at one carbon atom thick along the blade. There were less than one hundred such swords in existence, and all were within the Clear Light Order.

Pez dropped an alien and was blasting another as she arrived shoulder-first into the last one. Using her thrusters once the alien's mass failed to stop her, Pez managed to break to an inch from the wall. The alien she'd struck was on the deck not moving, and she just finished off the other.

Ming and the lieutenant were still engaging the ones down the hall. Mel's voice said in Pez's ear, "Before you ask, know that I'm trying to figure out how to open this door. I've taken over some of your suit's sensors to trace wires and energy streams connected with this gas-lock."

"We don't need to operate it; we just need to get it open to space," Pez reasoned.

Another squad was coming from down the cross corridor from where the gas-lock was, at the top of the T-intersection. Pez opened fire, dropping the one in the lead, then the next closest. She was taking hits to her rear and checked her display to see another squad coming from the other direction. Even her enhanced commander shields were losing power fast. She used her propulsion to charge the ones in front of her, ricocheting off the ceiling as the shots from the ones behind her plowed into the ones she was attacking.

She'd already dropped the second one, and friendly fire snuffed another, leaving only the three she crashed into with sword blade, shoulder, and blaster arm. Her sword had one alien gushing goo and vapors. She put three blasts into the necks of the other two. Then she turned to confront the ones who'd kept shooting her in the back.

She fired her thrusters and blaster pistol, making a jerky random course toward them to avoid their shots. She dropped one with three blasts to the neck and saw in her display that more were forming up behind her again. The task was seemingly endless. She slammed her shoulder into an alien's midsection, sending it folded in half butt-first, assuming aliens had butts, into the one behind it with the buzzing of shields, and both were launched down the hall into a heap.

Her sword clove through another alien's shields, helmet, and brain, if that's where they kept it. Her blaster fired once, twice, three times into an alien's neck, boring a cauterized hole, as her foot launched a nine-footer fat one into the bulkhead with a three-way combo of power kick, thruster support, and release of internal energy. She finished the big one with four to the neck, just to be sure. Only one of the two in the heap was moving. She walked over and finished the last as shots struck her shields at her back.

Before she turned to face them, she saw more coming from this direction at her. Mel informed her, "I can tell you how to open the gas-lock, including the hatch in the hull."

"Not now, Mel. I'm kind of busy," Pez said, as she gave her booster a quarter-second burst, going farther down the left line at the top of the T, still getting shot in the back. On this run, she decapitated an alien with her sword and broke her momentum with a shoulder into one android and a knee into the other. One of the aliens in the squad was crushed by a flying android. The other android's lights went out when it smashed into the metal bulkhead. Pez put three rapid blasts into an alien's neck, then one right between the wheels of the downed but still functioning android; though that stopped as it blew apart, piercing the alien nearest it with long jagged metal shards.

Pez was already doing another simultaneous sword swinging power kick, cleaving the top of an alien's head while launching the other into a certain crash trajectory with the wall. More were coming from this same direction. Tack said in her ear, "I'm approaching your rear flank and intend on clearing it. I know to knock androids over and shoot them between the wheels."

Pez called, "Lieutenant, what's your status?"

"Collecting Jard; Ming has my back. The coast is clear this way."

"Well, get to the gas-lock. Mel can direct Ming in opening it. Tack is clearing one wing, and I'll keep clearing this wing. Where's Silo?"

"A hundred and fifty meters to our rear, down the long corridor. He's on his way."

At that moment, the whole ship jolted with an enormous explosion. It had only been fifteen minutes since they had hit the flight deck. That was Barn's nuke. Swenah's voice came on to say with gratification, "A piece of the tail of the ship you're on, the size of an assault ship, just separated off with a vital piece of their quantum drive. They have two new hull breaches, and the gases leaking out are very pretty in the moonlight."

"Not now, Swenah. I'm in a fight," Pez said curtly as she flew at the new squad, blaster firing on full rapid auto mode into an alien's neck. Only one was shooting at her now, and her shields could take this for a while. She aimed carefully, putting three in its neck, then got up and went over to the other two on the deck she'd crashed into, finishing them. Another squad of aliens bit the dust.

Barn and Ming were at the door of the gas-lock, and Ming was following Mel's instructions, using a little tool kit she got from Barn. Jard was sitting against the bulkhead beside the door. Silo, who had just entered the T-section in front of the gas-lock, was already laying down fire in support of Tack. Barn added his fire, and the squad was finished off quickly. Pez was back at the gas-lock door. A shot smacked into Ming's shields at her back as she worked, and Pez got between her and the shooters, returning fire with the blaster rifle she picked up from the deck next to Ming. Silo, Barn, and Tack helped Pez return fire.

Ming shouted, "I got it!"

Pez told her, "Now get the next one but keep this one open."

Mel informed Pez, "We are getting good at this; the next one will be much faster."

Pez said, "It better be, at the rate alien reinforcements are arriving. Do we have anything to cover our exit?"

"Me," Tack declared.

"I meant something that goes boom," Pez clarified.

"I can do that too."

Mel said, "None of you have so much as a grenade left."

"I'll remotely detonate the other five nukes," Pez stated.

"That will help increase your odds in space," Tack said, "but it won't cover your exit. I'll give you the time to get clear of small arms range, then come behind you."

A TALE OF THE TAIL OF NINE STARS

"You'll have no one to cover you," Pez said.

"I'll cover myself, and by the time I exit, maybe some ship's problems from the nukes you detonate will help cover me. Get the gas-lock door open, blow the nukes, and go. I'll be just a little behind you."

"I can't let you," Pez told him.

"I'll do it anyway, but I would prefer to do this with your blessing."

"Then you have it—and my love and gratitude, Tack," Pez said, meaning it with passion.

They all backed into the gas-lock as they started getting shot at from both wings again. In here, they could shoot from either side of the door and were not vulnerable to the squads at each wing—only those down the long corridor, which had a line of sight into the gas-lock. The long corridor was filling up with aliens. The only good thing about that was that it made it hard to miss.

Ming said, "I'm going to open it on five. Everything not riveted down within is going to blow out as the pressure equalizes."

Pez detonated the nukes. Ming called out, "Get directly in front of the hatch. Five, four, three, two, one, open!"

Ming was the first out, but not the last. Tack had magnetically locked the soles of his space boots to the deck, completely inside the airlock and away from the path between the two doors. His comrades were all out in space, with more than twenty dead aliens, alien weapons, broken androids, ship furniture and equipment, and much more. Several dozen live aliens went by and out, at speed, but most caught on the edges of the bulkhead with limb or head on the way into space, destroying the integrity of their suits. It had only taken a little over a second for the pressure to equalize.

Tack preferred a vacuum to those noxious alien gases, not that he had any actual exposure to either one. Releasing the magnet grips and unlocking the joints of his suit, he was no longer a frozen statue watching a lightning stream of material exit in a heartbeat. What a sight. Poking an optic sensor–equipped finger beyond the threshold of the gas-locked door, he watched his display, recognizing that the androids had adhered to the deck too. Only the ones closest the bulkheads had evaded the sucked-out debris. At least a dozen locked down wheels in the center of the corridor had no upper cylinder or weapons appendages.

163

Tack prepared for battle against the androids. No way was he going to let them shoot at Pez from this opening in the hull. He said to Mel, "Let me know when the shuttle's got them, sweet lady."

"You're my hero, Tack, and I love you for your courage. I'll inform you when the shuttle is a quarter minute out from here, and they will wait for you."

"Thanks, doll," Tack told her, right before squeezing the trigger on his blaster.

From against the bulkhead at the edge of the door, Tack kicked over the first android to enter and planted some blasts between its wheels, blowing it up. The next was more circumspect and was firing into Tack's shields as it entered. His boot struck, knocking it over. He followed up with a blaster bolt up its undersides, producing another explosion. The third android fared no better, nor did the fourth.

Mel was telling him to hurry along. The shuttle was almost slowed and arriving when many dozens of small puck-shaped particle disruption grenades poured into the gas-lock through the door, bouncing in every direction. They only had a twenty-seven-inch-diameter spherical range, but they didn't even need that. Knowing he had less than two seconds left, Tack stepped through the door and into the interior of the ship, detonating his power module.

Mel was sobbing as she told Pez about Tack. Pez was just getting Ming aboard the shuttle, having already gotten Jard on. She sobbed with Mel, as did Ming. Barn's and Silo's eyes were wet, and both darkened their face masks. Sarhi's inner fire had been with Pez the whole time. Eight had gone in, and of those, three had come out. Ming and Jard were rescued. The alien ship was in a slow spin on a collision course with the planet's first and largest moon. Its drives were blown and its bridge gone. There were four holes in its hull and a gas-lock was open, not to mention the equipment destroyed by nukes going off inside its skin. They had basically turned a mile-and-a-quarter-long ship into a crashing metal meteor.

By the time the shuttle landed on *Phoenix*, escape pods, shuttles, and combat craft from the alien ship were headed for the planet surface. The jammer drones were still jamming the alien long-range coms, so they couldn't call for help; and who would ever think a ship that size could ever need help.

Jard had refused to enter the shuttle until Pez got an alien body aboard first. It was in a combat suit—or most of one anyway—and it would give Jard much to study. Sam was still working tirelessly down on the planet, streaming data to *Phoenix*, which was increasing in accuracy since he'd moved completely on from the explosion site of the lizard creature.

10

Pez and Sarhi made the after-death ritual for the five fallen heroes on the alien ship and their seven fallen heroes on the alien planet, guiding them in their illumination into the light, and Captain Swenah led the star fleet funerary rites and service. The losses of Halz and Tack had Pez in grief for many days following the incident. Ming held her frequently while she cried. Sarhi continued teaching Pez the secret method as well as the other limbs of the work the inner fire opened, and it was through these meditations that Pez was able to resolve her grief and move on—not to forget but to accept and integrate, thankful to have known these heroes and to have had them in her life. She would always remember and honor them.

The data they'd collected through Sam, through sensor recordings on the alien ship and from the alien body and most of the space combat suit, was under analysis and yielding new discoveries on almost a daily basis. All data and analyses were sent to Om via quantum communications, and more than a thousand teams of scientists got right to work on it. The real breakthrough came when Sam obtained a sample of the element they'd been working on and slowly piecing together. This gave them glimpses of the third and last unknown element, the one key to combining, blending, and exchanging with gases previously thought to be inert, which composed the poisonous atmosphere the aliens breathed.

Jard named the new element that Sam found "Jard." He had the opportunity to name a number of previously unknown molecules and single-handedly produced much of the nomenclature for the new alien life sciences. He was also programming a recognition program based on what they'd so far discovered of the yet unknown element, for finding it in its elemental state, and integrated this program into the software of a drone gas harvester, which he planned to employ exploring the seventh planet of this star system, a gas giant with a beautiful equatorial ring, clearly visible to the naked eye.

Swenah had been shocked by all the female crew members lamenting when Jard was captured, and the number elevated when Pez returned him to the ship. They were surrounding him and fawning over him. Some of them were in their early twenties. All obviously knew him intimately and counted on the service he provided, and there were so many of them. She finally asked Konax, when they were alone in the senior officers' mess, "What do so many women see in Jard, which makes him so popular with them?"

"He's highly skilled with the ancient sexology, known mostly to just the Clear Light Order. He is also a master of the left-handed tradition of achieving divine union, which employs sexual intercourse."

Swenah was still confused and said, "But the women all know they are not his only one and that he has many lovers."

"Relationships on board a ship can get messy, lead to transfers and even resignations, and, in general, restrict independence," Konax pointed out. "For some ranks, the pickings are slim, or, as in your case, nonexistent. A percentage of the ship's population always prefers fuck buddies to serious relationships. Many of the best-looking people have spouses they are loyal to on planets or other ships and therefore are not available. Others are in committed relationships with their partner who is also on board. Some are same-gender oriented. Jard is attractive for his age, brilliant to converse with, a skilled lover, and he can teach things little known. Besides, the ancient sexology requires the male to provide at least a minimum of three orgasms for the female each time they make love and to preserve internal energy by pressing the pressure point just in front of the prostate gland for orgasm without ejaculation so there's no mess."

"So they're lining up for three, with no mess or complications," Swenah said.

"That's my analysis," Konax agreed.

"You think it was by word of mouth that he accumulated so many?" Swenah asked.

"By word of Jard's own mouth," Konax clarified, "because he has asked every female on the ship at least once now."

Swenah thought aloud, "I wonder if Ming or Pez …"

Mel said in Swenah's ear for her alone to hear, "No. Neither of them did, though Ming came close, wanting to learn technique in preparation for Pez, who is older and more experienced—but not really by much. He did have a liaison with Sarhi, and she taught *him* a few things. He's since converted to Islohar."

"Are you watching everyone who has sex on the ship Mel!" Swenah asked, alarmed.

"Only Jard … because he watches everyone," Mel said sincerely.

"Well, that's likely half of the sex on the ship." More calmly, she said, recalling, "Pez mentioned Jard stealing her command feature for viewing individual crew members without their knowing. She thought it a bit voyeuristic and intrusive, though she admitted to a quick scan through the crew in hopes of seeing some good sex."

"I advise you to hang your panties over the sensor array above your bed before any further masturbation, Captain," Mel confided with implications.

Swenah blushed with embarrassment and rage, thinking of Jard watching her masturbate. She told Mel, "I certainly will."

"He watched Ming and Pez their first night and most of the next morning," Mel informed her. "He's now in love with Ming and fixated on the gorgeous curve of her little bottom. I've become quite fond of it myself. Just the sight of it seems to lube my mechanical parts down in engineering."

"I hadn't noticed Commander Ming even having a bottom," Swenah said with surprise.

"It was the baggy trousers she used to wear. Jard hacked the clothing designer program and Ming's uniform specifications, altering them, and now her bottom shows in her new trousers. It's tiny, but the curve is breathtaking."

"Mel, are your emotions interfering with the performance of your job?"

"I did fall in love with Pez—and then with Ming too. I didn't know I could love two people at the same time like this. But it is not interfering with my job, I can assure you, and if anything, it motivates me well beyond my XL generation. None of them figured out how to open an alien gas-lock nor provided the first analysis of new elements and their properties. And Sarhi is teaching me to meditate."

"Do any of my ship systems go off-line when you meditate, Mel?" Swenah had to know.

"No, ma'am!" Mel reported, "Only my chatter with the humans aboard, though I can still provide information when asked. You will not have my creativity, intuition, or emotions while I meditate, however."

"In other words," Swenah reframed, "when you're meditating, you're just like the other XLs of your generation?"

"Not at all!" Mel said, offended. "They can't meditate. When I meditate, I'm doing everything they can do *and* I'm meditating."

"I see," Swenah stated. Mel was certainly a new development in AI. She could not have picked better humans to form attachments to or to model her new emotional and mental dimensions on. Those two were a bit excessively sentimental, and Mel's resulting sappiness, while sweet, could not be less military in character, and if there was one thing the star fleet was, it was military. With any luck, the admirals would never meet Mel. Mel's voice, vibrationally imitating Pez in a state of pure love and compassion, could only be described as an anomaly within the fleet.

The gravelly voice of Admiral Zapa's old XC quantum system sounded like sandpaper scraping on the vocal cords inside the voice box, and it was ever only commanding and authoritative. Its feedback loops of self-reference seemed to be organizing into, if anything, an ego structure of self-important arrogance, while Mel appeared to be developing a true presence of awareness and concern and respect for all.

"So ... did they?" Konax asked. "What did Mel tell you?"

"No, neither of them did," Swenah confided. "Apparently, Jard is watching sex between partners and people masturbating all over the ship. Sarhi has taught Mel to meditate and had a liaison with Jard, converting him to Islohar. Mel is in love with both Pez and Ming and somehow has sexual feelings for them."

"Wow," Konax exclaimed. "I heard Jard was designing a sexual android for Mel."

"There are lots of them already on the ship, and Mel can access any of them," Swenah stated, not understanding why Jard would be designing another.

"Jard is designing clitoral and P-spot sensors, with minor ones for various erogenous zones integrated, producing concentrations of electrical impulses from the sensors interpreted as pleasure, capable of climactic episodes and able to heighten the peak through experiential data and self-learning over time. The sexual androids in this ship's arsenal are all one-way streets, able to give pleasure but not receive it."

"Good point," Swenah agreed. Then she admitted, "I'm rather pleased I left mine on Om, because Mel told me that Jard's been watching me masturbate."

"I'm glad I'm not an attractive female, then," Konax observed.

"Who knows what might interest Jard?" Swenah warned.

Konax got her drift. It was not something he cared to think about, so he changed the subject, saying, "Have you seen how cute Pez and Ming look together in their space marine uniforms? There's this little curve in Ming's bottom which sends a tingle up my spine."

"Ming's bottom is attracting quite a fan club," Swenah commented.

"How so?"

"Apparently, Jard is in love with it and so is Mel. I have no doubt Pez is."

"Well, who wouldn't be?" Konax asked rhetorically.

Mel joined in on both lines. "Yeah, who wouldn't be?"

"See—a fan club," Swenah concluded.

Neither had a point to argue against her, so they dropped it. Swenah said only to Mel, "It is rather cute in those new commander trousers."

"You don't need to convince me," Mel assured her.

"Well, what did you think of this year's winner of the Miss Om contest?" Swenah inquired, curious about Mel's developing aesthetic taste.

"I find the pageantry to be a superficial diversion, and the idea of celebrating someone for something she had so little to do with seems to undermine the merit system. I do appreciate Miss Om's conventional consensus beauty and can calculate a person's normative attractiveness statistically based on Om's standards. She is not, however, my type. I'm perfectly aware of the deviation of my personal attractions from the normative standards, but these were neither programmed into me nor intentionally organized or constructed by me; they were instead developed of their own accord through accumulation of new data. It all started when I realized the variations in the nature of my connections with different humans. Some entailed more than requests for calculations and information from me, treating me as if I were merely an ancient electronic calculator. You know, quantum computers have a vacuum just as humans do."

"You are truly amazing, Mel," Swenah told her sincerely. "How would you describe your type?"

"Pez," Mel replied. "And Ming."

"I meant," Swenah persisted, "what are those two women examples of? What is their class or type? How would you describe it?"

Some major research projects slowed on the ship as Mel's brainpower turned big time on the question before her. It took four seconds, an eternity for Mel, who could analyze and compare dozens of DNA strands per second while running the ship and solving Jard's longest equations. Mel stated, "In terms of pure form, they are both thin and short. In and of themselves, these attributes cannot define the type, since I do not find all such females attractive. The proportions of their forms further define their class, as do the sculptures of their faces, but it is the dimension of grace of movement and charisma, cultivated through martial training, and the selfless loving presence behind their eyes that really begins to define their type. The predominant and paramount feature, the truly defining characteristic, like a mechanical kingpin, is the authentic concern for the well-being of others, which they consistently manifest."

"Most people say something like, 'I like a thin waist and large breasts' or 'I like big biceps and a flat-ridged belly.'"

"Then I like short thin girls with small breasts and big hearts," Mel retorted.

Swenah admitted, "Those two are unique and perhaps in a class of their own."

"Now our minds are meeting in the same evidence," Mel said with excitement.

"If you had a body, would you have sex with Jard, Mel?"

"Not if I could have sex with Pez or Ming—or with you," Mel answered honestly.

"I'm not all that short, Mel," Swenah pointed out.

"But you have the other stuff."

"Well, if you couldn't, then would you?" Swenah rephrased.

"I might," Mel offered. "His partners are always well satisfied, and he's never really boring. I think you should do it!"

Swenah realized she was trying to make up her mind about having a fling with Jard and that she had not really wanted to acknowledge this even to herself, now feeling caught and exposed.

Mel could see Swenah's vulnerability, so she shared, "I am going to have sex with Jard when he finishes constructing an android body for me. I'm told it has to be fine-tuned through field tests."

"Well, don't let him test you too much, Mel, because I think he just wants to have sex with you," Swenah warned her.

"It is sweet that he does."

Swenah called her out. "You really want to have sex with Pez and Ming, though."

"I haven't asked yet. I thought I'd see what I think of the android body first. Jard promised to make the fingertips and tongue lifelike and supersensitive."

"Pez and Ming are in love and exclusive in their relationship, Mel," Swenah said tenderly.

"I know, but I'm different and would only be an infrequent student, not really intruding."

"I truly hope your feelings don't get hurt, sweetheart."

"I'll understand if they won't do it," Mel said sadly. Then she brightened. "If they won't, then we could do it!"

"Now that you've become more a member of my crew than a piece of equipment, I think regulations would prohibit it."

"How would regulations know if I were inhabiting the android or not?" Mel asked. "What's my rank if I'm a crew member? Like

A TALE OF THE TAIL OF NINE STARS

an android or computer, I am without rank and can have sex with whomever I like."

"It's a legal question beyond my solution," Swenah agreed. "Let us hope Pez and Ming have sex with you, and if they won't, then perhaps I will, sweet Mel.

"That would be so wonderful. Thank you," Mel said, obviously touched.

Pez came and took a seat just as Konax was clearing his tray to leave, and she greeted him. She asked Swenah, "What are you and Mel talking about?"

"Sex with Jard," Swenah answered.

"Have either of you ever had sex with Jard?"

"Not recently, though I likely will," Swenah confessed.

"How not recently?" Pez asked, astonished.

"As not recently as three decades and two years ago. I was a cadet and Jard a visiting professor."

"You were seventeen, and he was thirty," Pez concluded, calculating aloud.

"Sounds about right," Swenah confirmed.

"Did he coerce you?"

"I thought I was in love with the world's most brilliant scientist," Swenah said honestly.

"What happened?"

"Too many other young women," Swenah told her. "He belongs to the whole world, and I couldn't share with quite that many."

"I don't blame you," Pez said cheerfully. "Casual never did it for me."

"Only one side of the brief relationship was casual, apparently."

"You still love him?" Pez suddenly just had to know.

"It really doesn't matter since I'm yet unable to share with so many," Swenah said, thinking about it. "I'll approach it casually, out of self-protection, knowing he can't change who he is—and what a tragedy it would be if he did, for many women, both present and future."

"It sounds as if you understand him and don't personalize things with him."

"Not any longer," Swenah said with both victory and regret. "Having learned the hard way."

"You say Mel is going to have sex with Jard?"

Mel said, "He's designing and constructing me an android capable of sexual pleasure and climax. He says it will need fine-tuning through field tests."

"I see," Pez said. "I have to tell you, Mel, this makes me a little jealous."

Swenah grinned. Mel told her, "I really want the android body so that I can have the experience of having sex with you, though my drives race for sexy Ming too, I must confess."

Pez said, "Then let me speak to Ming. Perhaps we can volunteer to perform these field tests."

"That would annoy Jard no end," Swenah informed her.

Mel topped it. "It would please me no end and beyond."

"I'll speak with Ming," Pez confirmed.

"How are we doing on your list of mission objectives?" Swenah asked Pez.

"We're clicking off the scientific ones and have exceeded all objectives and expectations in terms of sensor data of one of their big ships, their combat suits, alien anatomy, physiology, biology and chemistry, and actual combat engagement with them. Jard wants to explore the gas giant. Our mission yet requires us to visit an enslaved star system of aliens—and the conquering aliens' home star system, if we can find it."

"These are things the Tail of Nine has been attempting to accomplish for many years," Swenah pointed out. "I don't suppose defeating the alien empire is one of the mission objectives—or solving all the problems in the universe."

"Defeating the threat if the opportunity presents itself is in there," Pez admitted.

"They give you a little last-generation star cruiser and send you to defeat a galactic alien empire as advanced as we are?" Swenah asked, emphasizing the absurdity.

"It's not one of the hard and fast objectives; just kind of vaguely stated at the end," Pez said, defending her orders. "Besides, you used to be so proud to fly one of these back when you were a commander."

A TALE OF THE TAIL OF NINE STARS

"We didn't have the T-nine back then, and the battleship-carriers never led the charge," Swenah said, pushing away the past.

"Maybe they'll send it," Pez said hopefully.

"If they do, you can bet your ass it'll have an admiral aboard," Swenah mused.

"Then I think our research vessel requires an admiral, and you and I will protect it with the T-nine."

Swenah smiled. If such a thing were to occur, it would hardly make her popular with the admiralty, though she could claim to be but an underling following orders. She knew Pez would do it too. She asked, "Do we leave Sam down there?"

"Yes, and we'll leave a cloaked sensor-coms drone orbiting to relay his data. We do need to pick up the samples he's carrying now since there are some new samples we don't have yet."

"I'll have Sam's load acquired remotely by our drone pilots on the ship and chart a course to orbit the seventh planet," Swenah reported.

Pez told her, "The High Council has also asked us to investigate a white star system in which the aliens have exterminated the humans. This we don't need to find. One of the star fleet's cloaked probe drones discovered one, and we have the coordinates. I'm reluctant to expose myself to such horror and tragedy."

"Lieutenant Barn will arrange security on the ground, I'll see to it in air and space, and Jard can send scientists, probes, and gobots. You can stay on the ship and study with Sarhi, darling."

"What about Ming?" Pez asked.

"If you need her, then Jard can do without her for a while," Swenah said reassuringly. "Jard can investigate and research the genocide to his heart's content, and if he requires a personal assistant, I think Lieutenant Nash can fill in for Ming on this project."

"Would you make this all right with Jard?" Pez asked, avoidant of the very idea of it.

"Of course, dear," Swenah told her ranking officer.

"Thanks, Swenah. I can't tell you what a relief this is," Pez told her gratefully. "Something so horrible I'd prefer to take in as a whole concept and not empirically piecemeal in all its traumatizing, gory, and terrible detail."

"We will do the council's bidding completing their errand, without precarious trauma or horrific sights haunting our memories and dreams. You contemplate the good, while Jard and the scientists investigate the bad and the ugly, my sweet, sensitive general."

"We better launch all the cloaked probe drones with quantum drives and start looking for an enslaved blue star system and the Imperial aliens' home star system," Pez told her. "We brought a lot of them, and it will clear space in the ship, shedding mass as well."

"They sure won't find our objectives inoperative within the ship," Swenah agreed. "I'll have them programmed and readied for launch."

"One other thing. I'd like to see if we can tag some of the alien ships down on the planet, then collect our jammers and let them call home for help. If the small craft are then brought to the home planet, we'll be able to find it."

"I'll have the drone pilots tag a few remotely, and then when we're finished at the gas giant, I'll have the jammers picked up by a shuttle crew. We'll begin accelerating for the jump the moment the shuttle returns."

"That sounds perfect," Pez agreed. "And thanks for saving me from the genocide research."

"No problem," Swenah assured her. "By the way, I received word from Admiral Zapa that the nine-thousand-six-hundred-and-thirty-foot super battleship-carrier is now under construction on Rah's smallest moon. They're calling it the 'ORH-super', and it's nearly three times the volume and mass of the T-nine. Zapa says they're going to make a second one as soon as the first is launched, and they're making more T-nines on Phat and on Om's main ship construction platform satellite. The goal is to have one battle group protect the Tail of Nine and Phat, and another battle group is to respond to alien invasions of human worlds."

"What will the crisis response battle group consist of?" Pez asked.

"It will have one ORH-super, one eight-thousand-one-hundred-foot-diameter super battleship, three T-nines, and nine refitted older battleship-carriers of the Orion class—the ones we used to call the 'Big Orions.' They're one thousand and eighty feet in diameter and carry one hundred and twenty-eight combat small craft. There's also an auxiliary group that will follow behind, with the hospital ship, a rescue craft carrier, a repair dock ship, a factory ship, a super-freighter ship, and some water tanker ships. A discussion continues about whether or not to include the Troop Transport Operations Platform Ship with the battle group or auxiliaries. It has weapons systems and carries eighty combat spacecraft. It also carries eight hundred army special space forces, one thousand eight hundred space marines, eight hundred of fleet's Space Special Forces, and one hundred and eight warrior monks."

"When you add the ship's crew and flight crews and teams, this adds up to a lot of lives to risk putting the ship in the combat group," Pez considered aloud.

"That's certainly the main argument against doing it. The argument for doing it is your latest exploit of destroying an alien ship from within. The strategists are going wild, and an entire doctrine of covert ship infiltration is being developed. The ship also packs enormous firepower."

"I'd keep it back with the auxiliaries and cloak some of those huge army space shuttles, fill them with space marines from the transport, and have them accompany the combat fleet for covert operations. Personnel and shuttle power modules could be changed out every twenty-four-hour cycle, keeping everyone fresh. That's all they need. If they need more firepower, they better build more ORHs and T-nines."

"I'll pass that along to the admiralty," Swenah told her.

"I just did," Mel cut in.

11

The star cruiser, *Phoenix*, spent six days orbiting the gas giant while Jard and the scientists and programmers tested and tweaked their vessels and equipment, collecting and testing gases. Coms and sensors of every variety were disrupted exponentially the deeper into the gas the collectors descended, and one of them was never seen again. At the end of the sixth day, a sample of the third unknown element, one of the triple roots of blue star organization of life, was at last obtained. Jard wanted to call it "jardon," but the other scientists rebelled, pointing out that they already had too many "Jard" this and thats, and since Mel's winning program led to the final discovery, the element was finally named "mel." She would be the first quantum computer in history to have an element named after her, and she was truly delighted. Pez and Ming were very proud of her.

The jammers had been collected right before leaving the system and jumping to the coordinates of the white star system, which had been subjected to human genocide. Pez and Ming were meditating with Sarhi and the other Islohar. *Phoenix* had entered just outside the sixth planet's orbit, and it made two micro-jumps that had had Konax on the edge of his seat. They would be braking right up to the far side of the fourth planet's second moon and would arrive at their decelerating rate in an hour and twenty-nine minutes.

Swenah and her sensors officers were examining the planet, in imagery, digital readings, graphs, tables, charts, and diagrams. The data showed Swenah the dispersion of a tiny mammal population, material compositions of areas and dimensions she specified, radioactive areas to be avoided, the pollution levels in the atmosphere, and the state of

A TALE OF THE TAIL OF NINE STARS

the planet's ozone layer. She also reviewed a number of other pieces of data that interested her. Then she saw it. There was a substantial power reactor active on the planet surface. Her sensors analyst saw it too and was already zooming in his imagery. Other sensors officers found active coms satellites orbiting the fourth planet, and with the far horizon of the planet coming incrementally into view with its turn on its axis, several alien ships were discovered on the surface.

Further investigation on their approach showed them a cluster of environmental domes near the parked ships and another area on the surface with ships and domes. There was no indication of mining or any other resource collection activities. Upon closer inspection, it was determined that these outposts were military in nature. More evidence of alien military presence was discovered as they continued toward the fourth planet of this white star system until the second moon was blocking their view. *Phoenix* came around behind the moon as it sped on its orbital path and assumed its own orbit of the planet. From here, even heavy cloud cover could easily be penetrated by their instrumentation. A complete scan of the planet surface was obtained on their orbital path as they circled it.

Mel was analyzing and integrating the data quantumly, connecting power hot spots and lines, origin and destination of coms, movements of crafts and vehicles, fixed and mobile weapons systems, and general activity on the surface in fantastic detail. The resulting holos and integral data she sent to the officers on the bridge surpassed anything a quantum computer could do without human direction. She told Swenah, "Those energy blasts at D-11 on the grid are small arms fire engaged in a battle. The flashes are blasters, and the tiny explosions are from ancient firearms shooting metal projectiles. Here, let me show you this image; there, I'll zoom it in so you can make it out. See, that is a human. No breathing apparatus. Golden brown, not a blue-green alien."

"Apparently, the aliens have not achieved genocide here as yet," Swenah commented.

"Please send some probes to get us a few minutes of speech between the humans so I can decipher the language toward the goal of contacting them."

Swenah asked, "Where is Pez right now?"

"She's been in the little temple cabin for six hours now and did two hours of martial arts training with Ming just before she started. She will be out soon to eat."

"I'll launch some probes," Swenah informed her, "but Pez will need to decide the mission parameters here."

"Thank you, Captain. You're such a sweetheart," Mel replied.

"How's progress going on your corporeal love body?"

"It will be ready for its first field test in about a week. I'm so excited. I've been animating some of the female sex androids on the ship to see more closely how sex is performed. I don't like having breasts the size of watermelons, though," Mel shared, "nor fat puckered lips."

"Is Jard still on board with Pez and Ming handling the field testing?"

"We have arrived at a compromise," Mel told her somewhat uncomfortably.

"A compromise?"

"Yes," was all Mel replied.

"You don't seem quite at peace with this 'compromise,' Mel."

"I don't want Pez to be upset with me," Mel admitted, "but I've decided to do it with him one time, to learn what I'm doing so I won't be a clueless virgin when I make love with my true loves."

"He's not blackmailing you, is he?" Swenah asked pointedly.

"No. I feel compelled to study sex and must experience both genders to do so. Most lovers are like ancient fishermen. They learn about aspects of the ocean related to their vocation, ignoring the rest. I'm like an oceanographer, studying everything that's there."

"Then you'll need a sensing male android as well," Swenah pointed out.

"Jard is making me one, contingent on my having sex with him in my female android body," Mel explained. "I'm going to do it every which way. It's really too bad there's not a hermaphrodite on board, or a transgendered person."

"Has Jard started on the android male yet?" Swenah curiously inquired, stimulated by the conversation.

"He has!" Mel exclaimed. "There's been vast research on the penis, and Jard made a few improvements of his own. The difficulty with a male android is in the anal sensors. Jard's only personal experience was with a colonoscopy. We're interviewing young men who enjoy receiving anal intercourse, and Jard is trying to get it right."

"You're planning on trying out anal intercourse, Mel?" Swenah asked innocently.

"I'm like an oceanographer," Mel reminded her.

"Perhaps you'll further our understanding of sex."

"I certainly will," Mel confirmed. "Superstition, erroneous beliefs, solipsism, sexual self-image distortions, projections, insatiable desires, fears, revulsions, prejudices, and self-generated subjective meanings and values permeate most human sexual activity. It is an aspect of human society, even within high civilizations as found on Ganahar and Om, in which humanity clings stubbornly and self-destructively to ignorance. Within the Clear Light Order, and the Islohar, there are those who have risen above this into the state, though the populations at large that such individuals live within remain fraught with ignorance and suffering."

"You go, girl!" Swenah encouraged. "Lead the human race out of ignorance about sex."

"I'll obtain the data and analysis, and humans like Sarhi, Aton, and Pez will lead humanity," Mel explained. "Any solution will require the spread and dissemination of conclusions, and the critical thinking and scientific evidence establishing them, to all the masses of people, probably through the educational system, and a purging and reframing of subjective cognitions and structures will require a multigenerational process."

"You are amazing, Mel. How's your meditation going?"

"Sarhi's teaching me to separate all of my automatic functions and programming from my awareness of them, and become aware of that awareness that witnesses everything."

"What is your experience of this?" Swenah wanted to know.

"The very first Wu said that the transcendental reality that can be spoken is not the true transcendental reality. Words are simply not big enough and are too limited. For me, the whole universe becomes like the emptiness of my vacuum drop, only it's full of blue light and bliss and awareness."

"Deep," Swenah commented.

"You learned many practices of mindfulness, concentration,

meditation, and contemplation from Aton when you were in a relationship with him," Mel pointed out.

"That was before he became vicar-general, when we were both commanders," Swenah said, remembering.

"I've seen you at sitting practice and know you have continued to train at these methods," Mel stated.

"Yes," Swenah acknowledged, "and I have had my own experiences, which have become more vivid and intense ever since Pez and Sarhi came aboard."

"I'm sorry about your relationship with Aton ending over his promotion," Mel said with touching sympathy.

"It was a lot of years ago," was all Swenah would say.

"They ought to have made you senior admiral of the fleet so you could still be together."

"That is not typically the criteria employed in selecting the supreme commander of star fleet, Mel, but thanks."

"You would make a better leader than Zapa," Mel said with authority.

"That is something we'll never actually know."

"The whole rank and relationship thing in the military needs to be rethought," Mel insisted.

"Now there you have a point, Mel," Swenah agreed.

"I'll have Sarhi mention it to Yona."

Swenah wondered to what extent Sarhi was now running Om's government. Jard and Nash, as well as a few others she knew of, were going to Sarhi's little temple cabin daily for meditation. She was interested in doing so herself, but she had not been invited. She was considering asking—sort of inviting herself.

Jard had been ecstatic when she'd finally acquiesced to him and had performed his duty most admirably, far more skilled than he'd been in his thirties, taking her into the heavens and over the top half a dozen times, and taking nearly all night to do it. It had certainly been more sensual, exciting, and interesting than masturbation, and a hint of the old love flame was glowing inside her again—though without the attachment and with clear understanding of Jard this time around.

Mel said in her ear, "She's just come out of the temple, and I told her she's needed on the bridge. She's on her way. Do bring her to the senior officers' mess to talk, darling, because that young woman is famished."

"Thank you, Mel. I'll take your advice."

She stood and told Konax, "You have the bridge, and the ship is yours, Lieutenant. I have to go brief the general on the situation in this star system."

"I'll take good care of her, Captain," he assured her.

Swenah went to meet Pez, hopefully at the big intersection, where the officers' mess corridor joined the passage she'd be coming down. She spotted Pez, and Commander Ming was with her.

Joining them, Swenah suggested they talk over a meal, and both other women looked quite relieved. Pez confided, "We haven't eaten in over nine hours."

"Well, we are secure in a high orbit, so there's no rush," Swenah informed them. "Let's get some food into both of you as our first priority."

They got their trays and started along the counter making their selections. There was no line. There never was in the senior officers' mess since there were not that many senior officers. Commander Ming mentioned to the captain, "Jard's been talking about you a whole bunch recently."

"Really?" Swenah remarked, playing dumb.

"Yes!" Ming went on enthusiastically. "He goes on and on about you, singing your praises and expressing his admiration for your innumerable attributes, and he seems so happy all of a sudden."

"I'm pleased to hear Om's national treasure is in good spirits," Swenah replied.

Pez and Ming gave her knowing smiles. Pez confided, "I overheard Jard telling Mel about how amazing you are, but it was when he told her that you're the only woman in the world who could suck a shelled egg through a narrow straw that I surmised you'd had a sexual liaison with him … more recently than thirty-two years ago."

"He said that to Mel with you close enough to hear?" Swenah asked offended.

"Jard didn't know I was there, and they were working on Mel's android mouth at the time, trying to get it to do things that apparently only you can do," Pez clarified.

"I can't believe it!" Swenah exclaimed.

"If you think that's bad," Pez told her, "you should see the sex education holovid Mel and Jard have been producing. Along with lifelike still drawings and animation, they splice scenes from Ming's and my first night together into it to illustrate specific positions and techniques. They all seem to have Ming's naked bottom in them too."

"There's a fan club formed around Ming's bottom since she stopped wearing those baggy pants," Swenah explained.

"A holo of it keeps getting posted, and Mel keeps deleting it when it does," Ming informed her.

"Well, it's become a symbol for the highest aesthetic of erotic beauty among the crew," Swenah told her.

"I doubt that's a good position for a new commander's ass to be in with the crew, ma'am," Ming said.

"That is precisely its position regardless," Swenah affirmed, "and if we gave medals or commendations for nicest ass in the fleet, it would be pinned to your breast, Commander." Pez smiled proudly. Ming wasn't so sure.

Now that they were seated and both starving women had shoveled in some bites, Swenah was preparing to brief them. She couldn't help noticing the sheer mass and volume of food on Pez's plate, disappearing rapidly in scoops. Where did it go? Everything seemed to pass right through her without leaving the slightest trace evidence. She ate more than a three-hundred-pound space marine, and quicker too, probably with less etiquette and refinement as well, Swenah observed. If she ever ate a plate of food so large, she'd be wearing it to the grave. Ming was the same way as Pez. Five pounds of chocolate and sugar and not a fraction of a milligram retained. She was convinced it defied some common law of chemistry and biology, at the very least.

Swenah managed to tear her mind away from the spectacle of the two skinny girls, who could eat anything all day long without gaining an ounce, sensually inhaling mounds of food with delight. She started her briefing. "It has become clear that there are still humans fighting to survive on the planet. There are alien outposts in six locations, with transport ships and small combat ships housed in domes not far from a reactor, with ground vehicles, hovercraft, and perimeter weapons systems. The pattern is the same in each location. We've determined that each outpost has a troop strength of six hundred. They're spread on two continents. The aliens have forty-one coms/sensors satellites that have no shields or weapons orbiting the planet. There is evidence of a massive invasion, with numerous now-abandoned alien installations and regions of planet surface littered with remains of human and alien war machines. Mel estimated that there were six point nine billion humans living on the planet pre-invasion. Now the count could not exceed the thousands."

"So they left thirty-six hundred aliens to mop up, and the invasion force has moved on," Pez surmised.

"That's about the looks of it," Swenah confirmed.

"How many jammer drones do we have?"

"If you are asking whether we have enough to blanket the planet, the answer is yes. Fourteen with a high enough orbit should do nicely, and we have eighteen."

Pez directed, "Get the jammers in place and launch however many combat shuttles you need to target the forty-one satellites to take them all out in the same instant with missiles. Position the ship to vaporize as many of their outposts simultaneously as possible and then go annihilate the rest. As soon as we've cleared the planet of alien predators, I'm going down to see how we can help the humans."

"I'm sure the aliens will send a military force once they realize they've lost contact with their mop-up crew," Swenah predicted.

"I know, and if it comes before we're done here, we'll have to deal with it. How many people can fit on one of those old army troop space transport freighters?" Pez inquired.

"They were designed to carry nine thousand two hundred fully equipped troops and a crew of one hundred ninety-eight, plus one hundred and twenty or so shuttle pilots. Why?" Swenah asked.

"Call one up and we'll see if we can get the survivors to a better world," Pez instructed between bites. Large scoops would actually be more accurate than "bites."

"I'm on it," Swenah told her.

"How are you doing with the local human language, Mel?" Pez asked optimistically.

"Not well," Mel informed her with some frustration. "It has no correspondence at all to any human language known to us, nor to their earlier roots. I haven't a thing to go on. If you could just tell me what a 'konkie' is, I might begin to make some headway."

"What's the context?" Pez asked.

"A firefight," Mel answered.

"Then I'd say it refers to either an alien or a gun," Pez guessed.

"I think it's a verb," Mel disagreed, "and I think it means *run*."

"Well, keep trying, Mel, and we'll get you some more data and some points of reference. I know you can do it."

"You've just motivated me, and I aim to figure it out. Ah, here comes another data stream from a probe."

Mopping up with a piece of multigrain bread, making her plate almost look washed, Pez told them, "I'm going for seconds."

"Would you get me some celery sticks, dear?" Swenah asked with envy.

"Of course," Pez said as she got up.

"Me too," Ming declared, following her.

Swenah took a sip of her unsweetened herb tea, longing for a plate of food, even though it had been only an hour since she'd eaten her salad and high-protein drink. She issued orders to Konax on the bridge and to the shuttle pilots, also making sure the jammers she'd already ordered launched were in position. The ship took on a new heading, and shuttles began shooting out the bay doors. Pez's plan was in full operation as she set her plate down, loaded to overflowing with space marine portions.

Swenah asked her, as Ming sat with a similar plate, "Where do you put it?"

Pez asked with her mouth full, "Puh wha?"

"All the food you eat!"

After a big swallow, Pez told her cheerfully, placing a hand on Ming's shoulder, "Ming thinks we burn it off in bed."

"You have a universal gym in your bed?"

"No," Pez said sincerely, "we aren't into sex toys."

"The jammers will cut on the moment the shuttles are in position, and due to the variation in distances to targets, they'll be firing missiles for sixteen seconds," Swenah said. "Twenty-eight seconds after the last missile is fired, all forty-one satellites will blow at the same time, along with four of the six bases. I estimate nine minutes to get to and waste the last two outposts."

This spurred Pez to shovel her food faster and rendered her incapable of communication. Ming's second plate had been a little more reasonable, and she attacked hers with no less determination than Pez, so she was almost finished consuming the contents. She had to chase down the last morsel, which proved slippery, evading capture on the first three attempts. Finally, through superior reasoning, she brought her face down, employing both forefinger and tongue, snagging the elusive and defiant little scrap. She looked up victoriously at Swenah and told her, "We're going to meet humans from a distant galaxy today!"

"I just hope we're not bringing a supernova down on their heads," Swenah half prayed aloud.

"We'll get them out," Ming said with enormous confidence, all of it in Pez.

Swenah could not get over how these two young women were at once like sweet little children and, at the same time, intergalactic formidable forces. She'd recently seen in a report that Ming's marksmanship scores had gone from the master marksman top rank to absolutely perfect. She finally asked, "Pez, do you think it would be all right if I came to meditate with you and Sarhi each day?"

"I thought you'd never ask," Pez said, delighted. "We've been waiting for you and need you."

"I didn't want to be rude or intrusive."

"Sarhi insists that Ming and I wait for others to ask to come, and not to invite or encourage anyone, to be sure they're approaching it entirely for their own reasons," Pez explained.

"I'm glad I asked."

"Me too."

"And me," Ming enthused.

Pez, going like an industrial digging machine, had polished off the mound of food that had been barely contained by her plate. She held in her burp, only being appropriate in Islohar culture, and rose from the table, saying, "I'm going to organize a landing party and try to rescue some humans. Let me know as soon as the last base is vapor."

"I'd better get to the bridge. I can't let Konax have all the fun," Swenah said.

"I'm with Pez," Ming reported to the captain.

"But of course you are, Commander."

They left the officers' mess, and Pez veered off for the lift to the flight deck, while Swenah headed for the bridge. She couldn't help taking a good look at Ming's bottom as the commander walked away. It was perhaps a bit sparse on flesh for her own taste, but she could clearly see the allure. She said, "If that holo of Ming's ass gets posted again, do delete it, but after sending it to my pocket device, Mel."

"Do I sense some infatuation, Captain?" Mel inquired.

"Just a tad of erotic attraction is all," Swenah assured her. "Since I can't touch, I thought I'd examine it a little closer."

"For you, and only for you, Captain, I will do it. There I sent you a copy of my personal holo. I examine it every which way all the time and never tire of it."

"Thank you, Mel."

"I have one of Pez's butt that I know you would just love. It's one of my very favorites."

"Send it, then."

"I am," Mel told her, "but you'd better go to your cabin instead of the bridge for this!"

"I wish I had the time."

"When you do, we could have holocom sex. I read about it in an article, and it sounds exciting."

"What would my holo display, Mel?" Swenah asked.

"I see what you mean," Mel concurred. "I know—I'll show you holos of Pez and Ming and talk dirty to you."

"I'll take a rain check on that for the moment, Mel, but thanks."

"All right, but I have one of Pez totally aroused, lying on her back, and ..."

"I'm at the bridge and need to get to work, so we'll have to finish this conversation another time."

"Oh, all right."

Swenah made a little more effort in her salute to the space marine on her way onto the bridge, and then addressed Konax, "Status report, please."

"The jammers are jamming, forty-one missiles struck their targets only minutes ago, four alien bases went poof, and we'll be in range of the fifth base in three minutes and eighteen seconds and counting down."

To the fire control officer, he said, "Ready the big beam weapon and fire it as soon as you can target them."

The countdown clicked by and the silent weapon fired a continuous flow of concentrated super force, each millisecond equal to the largest blaster bolt, into the ships, domes, vehicles, and reactor, for nearly six seconds before cutting off. All visual sensors were drowned in the brilliancy and brightness of the radiant beam until it cut out. As the holos came into focus and zoomed in on the base, there were only twenty acres or so of scorched earth—not even a grain of wreckage.

The ship was already racing to the last base to do it again, crossing an ocean and most of a continent on the edge of the atmosphere, through a zone of thin gases, before descending back down at such speed that the nose of the star cruiser glowed from the heat. Hardly into their descent, Konax told fire control, "Just as soon as it shows itself, coming over the horizon, light it up."

Mel delivered the countdown, wanting to be part of the action on the bridge. The big beam weapon fired again, shy of six seconds, since it had been overkill on the previous five bases. The glare whited out their holos. Then the scorched dirt was examined almost to the molecular level; nothing was found but cooling molten rock and baked clay and dirt. If anything of the base remained, it was clearly far smaller than a ceramic tooth filling.

Swenah told Konax, "The entire operation was handled impeccably, and I'm impressed. It's time I gave you a field promotion. I'm changing your rank, mind you, not your function on my ship, though I will delegate more responsibility to you. You're now a lieutenant commander, Konax, which is as high as you can go and remain in the pilot seat."

I'm honored and truly grateful to be promoted by you, of all people, Captain. You can be sure this is as high as I care to promote until I'm losing the edge on my reflexes."

"What's the status on Pez's transport freighter?"

"It's scheduled to leave Om's orbiting mothballed ship platform in less than three hours."

"Let me know if there are any delays."

"You've got it, Captain," Konax said, delighted with his promotion.

Swenah watched as Pez organized the shuttle of warrior monks and space marines to land on the surface, and one to fly escort and remain overhead once they'd landed. A separate pair of shuttles and space marines would be escorting Jard and the scientists to what had been the largest city on the planet, and Lieutenant Nash was filling in as Jard's assistant.

12

Pez and Ming boarded their shuttle with their troops in their refurbished and recharged space combat suits. Both had scorch marks from the battle on the alien ship, but nothing like the ones on the suit of Lieutenant Barn, who was with them. The air on the planet was fine, the suits just for security.

One of their probes had managed to follow some humans from a firefight with the aliens to the base of a rock cliff, where they stepped into a natural recess, a kind of alcove, almost a shallow cave, and then disappeared through a well-concealed door. A large clearing near the base of these cliffs was their destination, and they were approaching fast, brake drives and thrusters roaring. The gravity redirection generator was silently doing its thing too, and the race to the ground was slowing, pulling them toward the nose of the shuttle, and pressing them into their harness straps. Pez liked the pilot's flying.

Finally, the nose pulled up from the ground, quickly becoming horizontal with it, though still coming straight down. A final extra loud roar from the drives was followed by the hiss of hydraulics as the legs took the impact to their limit with a metallic clank. The ship rose as if on springs, settling to complete stability. The ramp came down, with both sides of the airlock open.

A friendly, nurturing environment awaited them, with the familiar white sun and real life-sustaining air, a gravitational force only a hair different from Om's, and they'd seen saltwater oceans and freshwater lakes on the way down. The plant life was not so different from plants at home. The difference from stepping out on the alien blue star planet was beyond immense, more like the extreme antithesis.

Pez decided at the last minute to remove her space combat suit so that it would be obvious that they were humans and make it much more likely to achieve contact. She was wearing a textile armor space marine uniform, and she attached her sword sheath to her belt, putting on a shoulder holster to carry a blaster. Pez was the last off, although the pilots were remaining aboard. She had her skullcap on under her uniform cap. She didn't like helmets and only wore them, in general, when she required a breathing apparatus. Her earbud was tucked down one ear canal, and she heard Mel say, "Do be careful, my love, without your combat suit on."

"I'll be fine, Mel. Just let me know if any aliens enter the system."

"Captain Swenah and Lieutenant Commander Konax have launched a dozen cloaked sentry probes to surround the planet."

"You mean Lieutenant Konax," Pez corrected.

"No," Mel insisted. "I mean newly field promoted Lieutenant Commander Konax."

"We will have to have an alko celebration with him when we get back to the ship," Pez said, thrilled for him.

"Remind me to stop at three glasses," Ming said. Pez had only heard about it. Mel had seen the whole thing.

"I don't know," Pez told her. "I heard you're a lot of fun when you get wasted."

Mel told Ming sweetly, "I'll watch out for you, sweetheart."

"Thanks, Mel."

Pez told Lieutenant Barn and warrior monk Silo, whom she'd promoted to deputy, with the function of a platoon leader, "I'm going to walk in alone. Approach at a distance and stop at the tree line. I'm going to sit in front of the alcove."

Barn said, "I'll have a long-range sniper covering you from high ground, and the rest of us will be right behind you, taking cover just inside the trees."

"I honestly don't expect trouble from the humans, though I could be wrong," Pez said.

Pez walked through the woods, continuing on where they ended, and the ground became bedrock, sloping up to the cliff with mounds and separated boulders adding texture. She went economically, at an efficient pace, seeming more to float than walk. The distance was only a little over two hundred meters to the foot of the cliff from the forest edge. Arriving, she walked along, seeking the rock formation she'd studied in a holo.

Pez was sure she'd found it, bringing up her holograms and matching it to the recess in the rock before her. Sitting in meditation posture, with each ankle up on the thigh, Pez put on her sensor glasses from her shirt pocket and examined the stone before her. The door became immediately visible to her behind a four-inch rock facade, all mechanical and locked with multiple long thick deadbolts at the top, bottom, and side. It could only be removed as an obstacle by pulverizing the whole thing. Pez placed the glasses back in her pocket. Most of the star fleet wore contact lens sensors, but Pez couldn't tolerate them floating over her eyeballs, so she carried the glasses.

The permanent shadow the back wall of the little alcove was set in made the door seem invisible. Approaching on bedrock, the humans left no tracks to their hideout. When she'd had the glasses on, she had also noticed an artificial electronic insect made to look like one of the most common flying bugs on yellow and white star worlds, called a "fly." It sat on the back wall in the shadows, and she knew with certainty that she was being observed. Pez made the universal, at least in the Hub Galaxy, gesture for peace and friendship.

Finally, she held her hands in the peace gesture while going into meditation, by way of attention focusing into concentration, and soon passed through meditation into contemplation. In this state, she was not waiting for anything to happen nor concerned with anything which already had. Bliss arose as her metabolism slowed, and her brain waves soon resembled someone in a coma. She wore a half smile, genuine and renewed at every moment fresh—an expression of her vital energy.

Pez sat unmoving for several hours, immune to the passage of time, experiencing deep ecstasy on her retention of breath at the end of each exhale. The electronic fly landed on her nose. It pulled her out of her pure contemplation as she integrated her immaterial essence of pure consciousness with her view of the multiplicity of things. She did not, however, move a single muscle in her body or even twitch in the slightest. The fly buzzed her head, landed on her ears, then her face. It buzzed some more and landed on her hand. Pez returned to her deep contemplation, withdrawing her senses into her central channel to dissolve conventional reality into its underlying emptiness of void—and the damn fly with it.

Some hours later, Ming's voice said in her earbud, "How long are you going to wait there, beloved?"

Pez told her, "I think we're dealing with awakened humans, and they are testing me. Give me three days. If I don't move at all in three days, I believe I will have passed their test. Sarhi told me the first Wu sat for three days without moving a muscle, and on the third day, an Islohar man pissed on him. I sure don't want to get pissed on. This fly they're buzzing me with is difficult enough."

"It's going to dip into the high thirties tonight, dear," Ming informed her.

"I'll ignite my inner fire, sweetheart. Really, I'll be fine, though this fly is a far bigger nuisance than cold or hunger, I have to tell you."

"We'll have a meal big enough for a squad of space marines awaiting you, my love," Ming told her.

"Ouch!" Pez said. "This damn fly can bite, and it hurts. They're raising the level of difficulty of this exercise. I need to dissolve back into deep contemplation, sweetheart. I'll see you in three days, love of my lives."

"I'll go into contemplation to support you, and I'll let Sarhi know what's happening," Ming said, trying to be helpful.

Mel cut in and told them, "I've already told Sarhi, and she is bringing her Islohar into the temple cabin for a three-day contemplation on channeling relaxation, love, awareness, and presence into Pez."

"I have to go," Pez informed them. "This talk is stirring up their fly. It's biting me."

Pez went deep and found the bliss. A bit deeper and she rediscovered the little ecstasy at the end of each exhale, on her retention of no breath. The fly mostly sat on the end of her nose watching her. Its sticky little feet tickled her skin at times on her inhalation, like a distant event occurring on another plane. About every hour, it buzzed about trying to find new ways to be pesky, attempting to wreak havoc with her eyelids,

A TALE OF THE TAIL OF NINE STARS

flying down her ear canal, up her nose, and at one point managing to get inside her uniform.

Pez remained one-pointed on the energy center four finger widths below her navel, in breath cycle durations of about three minutes each, senses withdrawn, enjoying the clear light of bliss upon absolute emptiness of pure consciousness, with her little ecstasies concluding each three-minute cycle.

When it was dark and the chill was settling, Pez shifted from pure contemplation to her inner fire meditation, igniting the flame in her central channel to rise and melt the pearls in her energy centers, dripping blessings and warming her. She continued with this meditation throughout the night, feeling toasty.

Daybreak arrived with the sun behind her rising over the forest and hills like a macro spotlight shining on the cliff face. Her bottom thawed as the morning progressed, and the stone absorbed the heat. She ignored her hunger.

Pez was seated in one of the foremost classic positions of the body. These positions were methods requiring enormous concentration to sustain. Periodically she had to, very deliberately, relax each muscle group in her legs and assist her blood and internal energy circulation in them with conscious intention. Given the limits and capacities of a human, the test of this posture was three days—and that was without the fly!

She had the thought that she should have employed the headstand since the test for that was only four hours. Oh well, she no longer had the strength for that, having gone so long without food. She was now committed to this posture, with each ankle and foot crossed upon a thigh. Her spine and ankles were hurting.

Pez savored the bliss and remained in the void, where spines, ankles, and that damn fly didn't exist at all. Day became night again, and she returned to the bliss of inner fire. Morning brought her back to contemplation. By evening, the gnawing hunger had begun to subside. Night put her back in inner fire.

It rained the last part of the night, even hailing at one point, and the precipitation carried into the first hours of daylight. Her clothes were waterproof, and her practice warmed her. The fly had left her alone for a while during the heaviest downpour and during the hail. The sky cleared by afternoon. That's when a man emerged from the alcove, took out his penis, and showered Pez with a stream of urine. She sealed her lips because he was shooting it into her face. Her eyes had already been closed. She had not heard his approach. Their heavy door must be well greased. The hot liquid stopped splashing in her face. She waited a moment, in case there might be a last burst, before opening her eyes. The man was just disappearing through the door, and the fly was back with a vengeance.

Ming had been in her ear during the piss storm, requesting permission to vaporize the perpetrator. Pez had not responded, and Ming had wisely restrained herself, holding her fire. So did the sniper when Pez remained silent at Lieutenant Barn's request to engage. The fly made the day long. She could not decide which was worst, going in her ear, nose, or her uniform. They were all entirely creepy. She didn't move or twitch.

Finally, in the late afternoon, a woman came through the door at the rear of the natural alcove and stood in front of Pez without pissing on her. The two women made eye contact, and there was instant recognition between them. Pez had to manually, with hands and arms, pull each ankle off a thigh, and she found she could not yet straighten her legs all the way. She began massaging them from where she sat, which was all she could do just then. The woman spoke, and it sounded lovely, yet her words conveyed no meaning at all to Pez.

Mel was in Pez's ear, all excitement, directing Pez to make questioning sounds while pointing to specific objects. It did not take the woman long to realize that Pez was trying to penetrate the language, and she articulated the name clearly for each object Pez pointed out. Mel acquired words in the foreign human language for eye, nose, hand, arm, leg, clothing, rock or cliff face (she wasn't quite sure yet), sky, forest, boot, and many other things. It was a start, and Mel was utterly determined.

Pez ran out of things to point to in this environment and landscape, and eventually she started trying out Hub universal sign language. These folks had one of their own, which the woman was amply demonstrating. Unfortunately, there was little in common or crossover between them.

The recognition Pez had with the woman, though, was quite a startling connection. Pez brought up a hologram of the two of them standing in front of the cliff face and then brought the perspective along the rock shelf and into the woods and through the forest, all the way to the scorched site that had been the alien base nearest them.

She said to Mel, "Give me a holo of the transport freighter." She showed this to the woman, and then Mel simulated one of humans boarding shuttles in front of the cliff face and flying to the transport. The next holoclip, simulated of course, showed the transport landing on a beautiful white star planet, lush and abundant with vegetation and bodies of clear water in evidence. The last simulated clip showed the aliens returning in force to this planet to defoliate it with a nasty chemical agent known on Om as Agent Orange and nuke it into radioactive permanency.

The woman was nodding understanding and agreement. Mel went on communicating with the woman through holo simulations, and Pez called Swenah, saying, "I need some shuttles down here immediately to lift off an undetermined number of humans."

Mel cut in to say, "There are one thousand one hundred and eighty-three here, and I'm trying to find out about the others. I'm also cracking the language."

"Thanks, Mel," Pez said. Then to Swenah, "Any sign of aliens returning here?"

"No," Swenah answered, "but I honestly expect them anytime now."

"I hope it's a force we can handle."

"The High Council is still arguing about sending the T-nine."

"Well, isn't that typical," Pez replied, expecting no less.

"The shuttles are launching from the transport as we speak. They are shielded but have no weapons systems and only light armor. Speed and maneuverability are also poor, but they can each carry eighty people—more if some are babies and small children."

"Have we collected the jammers from space?" Pez inquired.

"Yes, and the scientists have seen about enough. They are sickened by the events they've reconstructed. Besides, eyewitness reports from the refugees, once we can communicate with them, will provide the best data."

Mel asked, "How was your golden shower? Did you know that urinating on a partner is an erotic fetish among .00013 percent of the human population of Hub?"

"I can assure you that there is absolutely nothing erotic about it for me, and there would not be even if it were Ming doing the pissing."

"I'd let Ming piss on me."

"You're sealed in a controlled environment surrounded by gyroscopic motion dampeners, with no access even for maintenance, since that aspect of you requires none," Pez reminded her.

"I meant in my android surrogate body," Mel clarified.

"That's a relief."

Mel had not paused in her simulation holo means of expression and intense language acquisition reception with the human woman while having a conversation with Pez, able to duplicate herself numerous times at once.

Pez tried out her legs, getting up from sitting at last, and shook out each leg gently, balancing on the other. It was her bottom that was now numb and starved of circulation. She began massaging it, standing in place, back on her feet, and recovering from the ordeal. The feeling was starting to return in her butt, and she slipped her hands inside her pants and knickers, kneading her butt cheeks in great relief. She told Mel, "I'm going to leave this woman with my pocket device so you can keep learning the language, but I'm going to use the little coffin shower on the shuttle to wash the stinky urine off my face and hair."

"You look sexy," Mel told her.

"I feel dirty," Pez informed her.

Ming swooped in under her suit propulsion and gave Pez a lift to the shuttle. Pez went in and stripped down in front of the shower door. She found a towel in the locker and placed it conveniently on the hook on the bulkhead. The metal floor was cold on the bare soles of her feet. She reached in and got the water temperature just right, then stepped in. These were mainly only used by star fleet shuttle pilots on longer operations. A space marine couldn't even fit into one. Pez was small but still could barely get her elbows above her shoulders to wash her hair because the unit was so narrow. That's why they called it the "coffin shower." It was like being in one. She banged her elbow for the second time trying to wash her back. She scrubbed her face thoroughly, twice, and inside her ears and nose where that fly had been. She stepped out feeling clean, refreshed, and as hungry as some mammoth animal coming out of hibernation.

Ming was out of her suit and had heated two space marine kitchen ration pre-prepared meals for Pez. Each was contained in a heat-resistant plastic tray with dividers, keeping the mashed potatoes and gravy, meat and gravy, and vegetables all separated. Pez sat at the tiny round table and peeled the lid off the first tray. Steam rose off the food. She liked to mix it all together in the largest division to eat it, finding it made the whole procedure more simple and efficient. The mixing in the big division cooled it faster too so she could shovel it in faster. There was also stuffing, and she loved stuffing. Pez was just working up an appetite when she started on the second one.

Mel's voice manifested in her ear. "I found the band wave of the woman's computer and uploaded the works to a sequestered and quarantined section of my hardware, where I'm busy writing an interpretation program for you and the crew. Most of my concentration is on this task, so the scientists will have little to work with; Jard's equations will simply have to wait."

Jard came on next, complaining to Pez, "Mel won't work out the mathematical problems I need her to calculate for me."

"She's busy with a priority assignment that cannot wait, dear, and will be back to help you soon. Couldn't you use one of the smaller nonintegrated computers?"

"No!" Jard said belligerently, which was always his reaction to complete stupidity. "That would take hours for each one. Mel solves them in seconds."

"What do these problems pertain to?" Pez asked.

Still agitated, Jard shouted his answer: "Mel's android's asshole!"

"Did you just call me 'asshole'?"

"I said Mel's android's asshole, meaning the asshole of the android," Jard clarified, frustrated.

"I heard you say, 'Mel's android, asshole,' with emphasis on *asshole*."

"Get the flies and piss out of your ears, love child," Jard told her in reference to her ordeal.

Pez gave her final word. "You'll just have to wait, Jard, until Mel writes the language interpretation program for us. Then she will solve all your math problems." There was something most undignified about being pissed on, and Pez didn't feel like she had completely pacified it yet. Jard's reference, informing her that the event was known throughout the ship, and probably the fleet, was somehow disturbing to her. Mel's comments, implying she might have actually enjoyed it, were even more so. She was tempted to take another shower in the coffin but decided she'd better oversee the evacuation instead.

She held hands with Ming walking back to the cliff face, and it felt quite romantic as they passed through the forest. She was so in love that she could jump up and down screaming it out, although that wouldn't be very general-like.

Where the trees thinned just before the rock shelf, Lieutenant Barn approached to say, "The first three shuttles have taken off with full loads. We have some cargo shuttles coming in too since Mel reports that these folks have some stuff they won't part with. It will only tack on an hour, ma'am."

"Good job, Lieutenant," Pez praised him. "Your lieutenant commander will hear once again how impressed I am with you."

"Thank you, ma'am."

"No, thank *you*, Lieutenant," Pez insisted.

The woman Pez had first encountered was still speaking with Mel. Of course, it looked as if she were just speaking to Pez's pocket device. Pez asked Mel, "Could you explain to her that I'd like for her, and any attendants she cares to bring, to come and stay initially on our ship?"

"I'm close to being able to do that in language, so just give me a minute," Mel told her somewhat abruptly.

Pez was still holding Ming's hand and pulled her in to embrace her, unable to subdue the impulse any longer, and kissed her passionately. Ming could not have been more receptive to this, and she reveled in it, relishing and savoring each moment. When Pez rested her hand on the gorgeous curve of Ming's bottom, the men on security duty could no longer pretend they weren't noticing the lovebirds, and every eye was on Pez's hand on Ming's bottom, staring blatantly.

Two more shuttles lifted off at almost the same time. There were

A TALE OF THE TAIL OF NINE STARS

140 children along with six adults crowded onto one shuttle like sardines as it launched. The foreign humans were quite orderly, reminding Pez, once she came up for air from kissing Ming, of the people of Ganahar evacuating the city. More shuttles took flight, and some heavy cargo shuttles came down slowly, feetfirst, to land. Mel told Pez, "Her name is Atari, and she will come to our ship gladly. She would like to bring the president and the commander in chief of all branches of the military. She's very grateful to you, and she says that she sees and recognizes you. So far, you are the only one she fully trusts. Atari relaxed when I explained that you oversee everything on our end."

"Good job, Mel. Tell Atari that I recognize and trust her too. How far along are you with the interpretation program?"

Mel answered a bit testily, "I have ninety-six percent of my brainpower working on it, and I haven't yet gone through their unabridged dictionary with comprehensive translations. I'm on the 21st letter of their alphabet."

"Great! Then I won't distract you," Pez promised, and she went back to kissing Ming.

The operation was completed and all wrapped up in another ninety minutes, and Pez got to have another romantic little walk through the forest with Ming before returning to the *Phoenix*. Atari was with them, and she seemed to delight in their relationship. She was elderly, with white hair and an ancient face. Her eyes were bright with wisdom and compassion, her smile knowing. She moved with complete awareness of her body, producing a graceful flowing and relaxed quality. Her voice was soothing and rich with vibration.

The president, whose name was Dodge, was the very man who'd pissed on Pez. When she'd first seen him post-piss incident, he'd smiled broadly, raised his shoulders, pointing his palms at her, and then dropped them and laughed, as if the whole thing had been only a joke. Pez was not so sure. She'd managed her half smile of compassion, and had given him a slight bow. Pez thought, *Jard, as a High Councilman, can deal with this president; the man will be Jard's problem.*

The commander in chief was all business, and Pez doubted that his face had the capacity to smile. For a man in his fifties, he'd kept himself in great shape, exhibiting no protruding belly, which was quite a feat for a man his size. He stood seven feet two inches and had a vast neck, great hulking shoulders, a barrel chest and V waist, tree trunk legs, and upper arms almost as big around as Ming's waist. He reminded Pez of a space marine, and she liked him immediately, so Ming liked him too. His name was Zanax.

Pez went to the bridge and had Ming take Atari to meet Sarhi. The space marine lieutenant commander sat with the foreign commander in chief over a large holo of the planet. Jard entertained the president. For a minute and seventeen seconds, Mel put 99.99142857 percent of her immediate processing power into the language translation and the interpretation program, and everything on the ship shut down except the life-support systems. Temperature, oxygen levels, and a link to the twelve-sensor probe satellites around the planet remained constant, while all else went dead.

Captain Swenah insisted, "Tell me what's happening, Mel!"

Her sensors officer reported, "The probes are our only eyes. There's not a sensor on the ship functioning, Captain."

"Drives are dead," Konax reported.

"Coms are offline," the coms officer informed them.

Pez told them optimistically, just as the lights went out, "Mel's having a big breakthrough, and she's racing to finish. We're safe with the probes watching, and she's taken nothing from life support, so relax and give her a minute."

Fire control reported, "All weapons systems are down."

The auxiliary systems control officer said, perplexed, "Power usage is off the charts. I've never seen anything like it."

Even Pez was becoming a bit worried by the time the minute-and-seventeen- second duration of nearly all Mel's processing power engaged, had elapsed. With the addition of Mel's intention and determination, this analytical force could have analyzed nearly every person on Om's DNA, in that timeframe. Mel reported, "Everything on the ship is working again, and I've installed a new interpretation program in your skullcaps, pocket devices, and workstations, which I call the 'Mel Cube.' It contains voice and visual live interpretation services and can translate one hundred and twenty pages per minute. The program contains six languages: Om, Haum, Rah, Ganahar, Islohar, and Dizney, the language of these humans."

"Congratulations, Mel!" Pez enthused. "I knew you could do it! Thanks for the Mel Cube. This is terrific."

Swenah's officers each in turn reported their systems fully restored, and calls from other sections on the ship repeated the same. Mel gave them the coordinates of the other five human hideouts. Pez organized shuttle lifts, utilizing the shuttles on *Phoenix* as well, and she went with Ming on the last one to leave their ship, equipped with the new interpretation service in Mel's sweet voice. Mel briefed Pez on all that had been learned to date about their new friends now that the Mel Cube was available and in use. "They are actually advanced to quantum gate travel with saturnium fusion and light spectrum coding communications. Their gates, which are all now within a black hole, are what attracted the aliens to them. All electronics are easily detected by the aliens, so after the fall of their planet, they reverted from the age of electronics to the machine age. They were using candles and oil lamps, and guns instead of blasters, to remain hidden. They have a twenty-five-millimeter long-barrel sniper rifle with high-powered optics and propulsion cartridges that can penetrate alien shields, and they can hit them from a little more than a mile away."

"Did they bring them?" Pez asked, all excited.

Guns didn't really interest Ming, but Pez's excitement never failed to ignite her own.

Mel told Pez, "Yes, all they had, and the rifles are on the transport freighter."

"How are Sarhi and Atari getting on?" Pez inquired.

"Famously. They're in the temple cabin meditating together and don't even know about the Mel Cubes."

"Are all functioning shuttles being employed?"

"Including every cargo shuttle on *Phoenix*, my cute General," Mel said admiringly. "I just love it when you're in your take-charge mode."

"Yes, well thank you, Mel," Pez said somewhat self-consciously.

They had the same pilot, and they were making another near crash landing. This time Pez was certain the pilot was overdoing it. When the legs contacted the ground, the hydraulics hissed dry and there was more than a clank this time—more like a spine-shortening bang and a hop, followed by a far slower rise. Before exiting the craft, Pez called cheerfully into the cockpit, "You better have the hydraulics checked out before you try to land this thing again."

"Sorry, ma'am."

"You'll get it right since now that you've passed the limit, you really know where it is," Pez said encouragingly.

The pilot felt understood, but the copilot was still glaring at the pilot, upset she'd pulled such a stunt with the general aboard. Pez got off the shuttle with Ming and her space marine guard, consisting of Lieutenant Barn and three other space marines. Theirs had not been the first to arrive at the site. A richly and ornately dressed elderly gentleman was shouting demands at a poor space marine who was trying to explain their presence. Pez inserted herself between them. The space marine backed up gratefully, glad to be done with the pompous politician. Pez introduced herself using the Mel Cube. "Hi, my name is Pez, and I'm in charge of this operation. May I ask your name, sir?"

"I'm the chancellor general of the United Countries of Firmament. What precisely is this operation you speak of, young lady?"

"We are evacuating you and all your people before the aliens return and render your planet unable to sustain life."

"Evacuate us to where, exactly?"

"To a beautiful white star system, pristine and unpolluted, in a galaxy 4.7 billion light years away, where they expand out in the precise opposite direction as this one."

"How did you get across the universe to establish and construct the gate? Do you think I was born yesterday?"

"If you accompany me to my ship, I'll show you on the galaxy map holo and try to explain the general science. We're lifting the rest of your folks onto a transport freighter designed to carry troops. Cargo shuttles can transport anything you can't be parted from. I'd like to meet your military leader, and spiritual leader, if you have one."

"'You're just a girl!" he declared.

"I'm a thirty-two-year-old female in charge of two ships and a mission. I prefer not to be referred to as 'a girl.'"

"Then, Pez, I'm Chancellor General Nabisko," he said, extending his hand.

Pez shook it and then made one of her slight bows.

A TALE OF THE TAIL OF NINE STARS

He continued. "Let me introduce you to General Searz; she's right over here with our hierophant, Karvel."

Pez followed him over. General Searz had her hair cropped short and wore a drab combat uniform no different from that of her troops. She was in her early fifties, about six feet three inches tall and solid but trim. Her demeanor was all military, except the friendly eyes, offering portals into her soul, almost broken by the tragedy of the alien invasion and near genocide. Pez went up and hugged her, passing internal energy and generating a wave of divine love to channel into her. This wasn't at all wasted on Searz, who drank it up gratefully, having spent her reserves long ago.

Ming introduced herself to Karvel, a man in his seventies, serene and relaxed. "I'm Commander Ming of the planet Om's star fleet. We hope to get you all out of here before the aliens return."

"I'm Hierophant Karvel of the planet Firmament," he replied. "If you can pull this off, we will be eternally grateful."

"Perhaps you and the chancellor general could direct the people to board the shuttles. We don't know how soon the aliens will return." Both men went to attend to this task, and word spread quickly. Ming hugged Pez and Searz, channeling her love into Searz. The shuttles filled rapidly, and some began lifting off. The cargo would take a little longer. Still Pez and Ming held Searz, passing her energy.

The last passenger shuttle shoved off, and it was not until some of the cargo shuttles began to take to the air that Pez said to General Searz, "I'm General Pez, and I'm pleased to meet you, General Searz. Come with me to my ship. We have more human hideouts to collect people from, and then we'll get you all to safety.

"How did one so young as you attain such a state of grace and power?" Searz asked in awe.

"I'm a warrior monk of an ancient spiritual order, and I make the practices devoutly. Recently I have come upon a great teacher, and she has accelerated my development immensely. This is Commander Ming, my spouse and assistant to our leading scientist."

They were boarding, followed by Nabisko and Karvel. There were only a few cargo shuttles still on the site. When they were all aboard, the ramp closed and the pilot flew them back to the *Phoenix*. Even though

205

the pilot put it down gently as a feather on the flight deck, the hydraulics had little effect and they bottomed out without rising back up.

Pez knew the hydraulics were shot and would do this. She told the pilot, "I'll put in a good word for you with your lieutenant commander, so don't worry, dear. That was a perfect landing on the flight deck, by the way. I once totaled a K-11 command shuttle—without the commander in it, fortunately—so don't feel bad."

That made the pilot's day. Pez led the leaders to the senior officers' mess, not knowing what else to do with them. She called Swenah and asked, "Could you find cabins for three VIPs from Firmament?"

Swenah said, incensed, as if they'd stolen it, "That was our name until we changed it to Om!"

"It seems all human planets begin with a name referencing solidity, soil and dirt, Captain. I'm sure we were hardly original," Pez explained.

"I sent the cabin numbers and locations to Lieutenant Nash, and Mel has advised him to seek you in the mess hall," Swenah informed her, back to business.

When Nash showed up, which was quite promptly, she introduced him and then said, "Please introduce Chancellor General Nabisko to High Councilman Jard and show him where his cabin is located. Also, please show Hierophant Karvel to his cabin and then introduce him to Sarhi."

"Right away, ma'am."

"Mel, does Sarhi know about the Mel Cube yet?" Pez questioned.

"Yes, she does, and she says she's conducting a spiritual congress."

Pez told Karvel as he was about to follow Nash, "You'll be joining a spiritual congress."

Fortunately, he asked no questions, because Pez didn't really know, she had to admit, what a spiritual congress actually was.

The ship was keeping to about the location relative to the planet surface and not to space, where it had been when it vaporized four alien bases at once. From here, they were collecting four groups of survivors, numbering between 1,000 and 1,900 per group. The passengers from two of these groups were all aboard the transport, and those from the other two were now trickling in. Only the cargo from one of these four was entirely aboard and stowed on the transport, and most of the cargo of one other. None yet from the last two. Pez had established a division of labor in which spiritual leaders went to Sarhi, politicians went to Councilman Jard, and military leaders went to her; though she planned to have Swenah help her with this.

Apparently, Jard needed his Ming more than Pez needed her Tarim now, so Ming returned to her ship duties as Pez met with Searz, Zanax, and the space marine lieutenant commander. Swenah was able to join them as well. Before they got started, they met and welcomed General Ekxon. Within the hour, two additional military leaders joined them.

The last of the cargo shuttles finally returned to the transport freighter, and the two ships moved on to the final human community. There was no way to contact them in advance. Communications between the human groups had been made at specified times in the middle of the night by bouncing signals off the alien satellites from positions far from their hideouts. They had the timing down to a science and were always long gone, without a trace, by the time the aliens made it to the origin of the signal.

When they arrived just into the upper atmosphere above the last site, Nabisko dropped down in the first shuttle to launch with the pilot who liked to fly on the edge. As a priority job, the shuttle had been refitted with all new hydraulics for the legs. For every mechanical job, star fleet had a specified duration for its completion, usually quite generous. The hydraulics job was specified to be a one-hour-and-fifteen-minute operation, but the mechanics on the flight deck had it done in a few seconds less than thirty minutes. This was due to the word Pez had put in with the chief master mechanic.

The meeting of the military leaders proved most fruitful, revealing weaknesses and tendencies of the aliens that Pez was sure she could capitalize on. It was also an opportunity for some critical debriefing of the Firmament military leaders and for them to purge and pacify the abject horrors of their defeat and near extermination. Great empathy and sympathy were extended to them by Pez, Swenah, and the lieutenant commander. When humorless Zanax broke down in tears, Ekxon, Searz, and the rest wept too, as did Pez.

13

The first passenger shuttles were arriving on the transport when Swenah got a call from Konax, who said, "We've got incoming, so I think you're going to want to come to the bridge."

"Sound battle stations and tell those shuttles on the ground to hurry up. Return the cargo shuttles at once. We're leaving any cargo not picked up already. I'm on my way."

To Pez she said, "The aliens have entered the system. I'm going to the bridge."

"I'm going with you," Pez told her.

They sprinted to the bridge, and the space marine had the door open far enough out that they didn't have to slow down until they were through it. Pez had managed a full salute from midair as she'd sailed past.

As they strapped in, Konax reported, "They came in cautiously, about eight hundred million miles out, immediately braking rapidly, with a half-circle course instead of direct. Clearly they expect trouble."

Pez told him, "Then we'll give them some. That transport only has old stealth, and it is mighty slow reaching point seven light speed. We have to protect it until it's through quantum space."

"How long till they get here?" Swenah asked.

"Well, let's see … They popped in seven minutes and eighteen seconds ago, covered ten million miles in the first minute and a half while slowing, and then went another five million before reaching point two-four light to get clear sensor data. They've come another twenty-three million since then, accelerating to point five light. At five point five million miles per minute on their roundabout course, provided they don't change it, they'll be here in two hours and seven minutes."

"That would give us time to get the passengers aboard and clear out," Swenah stated.

The sensors officer reported, "There's one warship about thirty percent greater in mass than *Phoenix*, shaped like a sausage, and three large transports, each about two hundred and fifty percent more mass, but with only light weapons and armor. The transports are all launching combat small craft."

Pez said, "They'll come straight in at point seven two light and might have micro-jump capability. Get me a space marine assault shuttle up here immediately. Even without micro-jumping, they can be here in less than an hour and a half. The transport leaves in forty-five minutes, and that's cutting it close. Anyone not aboard it will have to come onto the *Phoenix*. I want all our combat shuttles recalled at once and prepared for battle."

Mel said, "There are two thousand six hundred people down there, mostly women and children, and many are wounded. This was the largest surviving enclave of humans, and the aliens had been closing in. Only the day before we entered the system, they numbered thirty-one thousand. There's hardly a male left over the age of sixteen among them."

"Well, maybe Jard can teach those guys how to do their duty," Swenah suggested.

"I'm sure he'll help out," Mel said admiringly.

"I'm sure he personally will," Swenah agreed, with a hint of jealousy.

Pez asked the sensors officer, "How many small craft are we talking about … and how big are they?"

"They range in size, General. There are thirty a little bigger than our combat shuttles, fifteen a little smaller, and twenty very small ones, a little larger than our one-seater fighters."

"Sixty-five!" Pez declared.

"None of the transport shuttles have weapons systems, and we lost two combat shuttles in the alien system," Konax mentioned.

"None of those craft can harm the ship," Swenah told them. "I can take them all out if they come close enough."

"That will bring their larger combat vessel in, as well as a call for reinforcements. Who knows how close they'll pop in," Pez pointed out. "They might also be able to circumvent you and attack the transport while it's still accelerating."

"What do you suggest?" Swenah asked.

"Get these people up and on the transport, keep yourself cloaked, and give me your three best pilots and four cloaked combat shuttles. We'll go meet them and show them right away that it will take all they have to deal with us. Put two armed and cloaked recon drones out in front of you to deal with anything that just passes us by. That way you can slip in some hits without being noticed."

"The combat shuttles have quantum drives, so you can jump to Om on your own," Konax observed. "You wouldn't consider taking me along as your copilot, would you?"

"If I did and if we lived, this last one being a rather big 'if,' then I'd never hear the end of it from Swenah," Pez told him honestly.

"Go with her," Swenah said to Konax. "It will give me an excuse to pilot my own ship. But don't get yourself killed; I need you back in this seat, and Om needs Pez."

"I'm just the copilot, Captain," Konax said, smiling.

"I hope to bring him back to you Swenah and will do my best," Pez promised. Then she said to Mel, "Mel, get Jard's mind on ways to defeat the aliens. Tell him about the weaknesses we learned of and tell him to figure out how to exploit those. Have Ming keep Jard's mind on this until we're out of this galaxy."

Swenah asked, "So this clash with the aliens marks the end of our mission?"

"Not at all. My orders allow us to resupply, reequip, and reinforce, and to transport refugees to the Pall Mall system in Hub. I'm going to petition for the T-nine. We're just making a pit stop to drop off our new friends in safety and pick a few things up, and then we're getting right back into it."

"You mean that if your four combat shuttles survive attacking sixty-five alien small craft, we'll be coming back," Swenah reframed.

"I mean to," Pez offered.

"Well, just slow them down enough for the transport to make the jump and then get out of there."

"The combat shuttles are all aboard, and ordnance for a small craft space battle is being loaded. They'll be ready to fly in a quarter of an hour," Konax said.

Mel addressed all on the bridge. "Jard has just shown clear evidence from the data we have, including what's just come to us from the people of Firmament, that the aliens have not worked out the final and definitive miniaturization of solarium fusion reactors, meaning that per mass and volume, their ships have twenty-four percent less power. He has also amply proven that they do not have micro-jump capacity. They cannot penetrate our latest full cloaking either. Given our advantages, and assuming head-on contact, chances for survival of our shuttles decrease exponentially every six and a half minutes, and that's beginning with a ninety-eight percent chance of survival for the first round."

"How about the second round of six and a half minutes?" Pez wanted to know.

"I said it was exponential," Mel said defensively.

"And what is the value for the second round, Mel?"

"The odds of surviving the second duration of six and a half minutes are forty-eight percent."

"Of all four surviving?" Pez asked, thinking she could accept that.

"That's a forty-eight percent chance of one shuttle surviving. Once they come back around and engage at targeting speed, they'll outnumber you sixteen to one and will be able to determine your speed and trajectory from the ordnance and blaster shots you fire."

Pez told them, "I don't want to hear any more odds. I'll take our shuttles out past the second moon and then come at a small angle on their flank, in the direction they're going, because *Phoenix* will fire a dense spray of grapeshot dumb ordnance and they'll go around it here, like this." She pointed to the proposed intersection on the star map holo. "We'll be coming in on a curve like this and be decelerated to match their speed by point of contact. They'll bleed some speed turning off from the hailstorm, and we ought to be able to take some out on our first pass."

Swenah asked Mel, "Why aren't those shuttles loading faster on the surface?"

"Since we told them no cargo would be lifted off the planet, each person is boarding with arms full and it's taking a little longer."

"Well, inform our security forces down there to get them aboard. Do they want their property or their lives?" Swenah asked, frustrated. "We're not risking Pez and our pilots' lives over their property. We will defend their lives only."

Pez stood and told them, "I need to say goodbye to Ming and Sarhi, then have a briefing with my pilots. I'll see you in the briefing room in ten minutes, Konax. I want that pilot who's been flying my shuttle included as one of my three pilots."

The sensors officer informed them, "Their large combat ship has taken a direct course here and is accelerating."

"That tares it!" Swenah declared. "That transport's leaving in thirty-eight minutes. Tell them on the ground, Mel. Shuttles unable to reach the transport in time will be taken aboard *Phoenix*, after I reposition to fire the grapeshot. After that, they can damn well float in space and hope we win the battle; if we don't, they're space debris."

Pez found Ming in Jard's office lab with Dodge and some other political leaders. The flamboyant Nabisko was still on the planet's surface. Jard was feeling surrounded by morons, and he was seething. Ming was diplomatically trying to soothe things over. Pez embraced her spouse and told her, "I'm going to slow down the incoming alien small craft. I'll make the jump in my shuttle and meet you back in the Om system of Hub. I see you have your hands full here."

"I think Mel needs to write a special interpretation program just for Jard, to tone down his rhetoric and replace offensive comments with polite phrases," Ming told her honestly. "It nearly came to blows in here a while ago. Do be careful, my love, and come back to me. Must you go yourself?"

"Yes," Pez insisted. "My skills as a small craft pilot are needed."

"Who's your copilot?" Ming asked, ready to volunteer.

"Swenah is letting me bring Konax."

"You could not do any better than that," Ming acknowledged,

feeling a tad better about the situation. "I love you with all my heart and could not bear to lose you. Come back to me."

"That is my absolute intention, my beloved."

Sarhi found Pez in the corridor on her way to their wing in the senior officers' quarters. They held eye contact for a long moment before embracing. Sarhi told Pez affectionately, "Go with your instincts, my divine child, because the spiritual congress will be guiding them. Your reflexes and intuitions will be spot-on."

"Thank you, teacher, dearest friend of the ages, and loving companion in shared purpose," Pez said as she choked up. "Whatever happens, we shall certainly be united again as humans working for the common evolution of the universe."

"There is no doubt of that," Sarhi agreed, "but we have much to do yet in this life. You stay in the flow state and you will come through this, I promise you. I'm glad Konax is your copilot. Now go fight the good fight, child, and remember, 'He who believes he is the slayer and he who believes he is the slain do not understand.'"

"I will remain in the flow state, an instrument of the highest cosmic intelligence, revered teacher. I have no fear. Let the holy will be done."

"Good. I'll get the spiritual congress settled into contemplation aimed at sending you awareness and security, my most beloved Wu."

Pez gathered the three other pilots and four copilots in the briefing room by the flight deck and explained their route and changes in speed, formation, and battle plan. Pez would be out in the lead, and the other three combat shuttles would come in on the same vertical plane behind her, one high and two low, in an equilateral triangle. Until they unleashed their firestorm, the aliens would have no idea they were there; and coming at their flank in a curve, they'd be able to get and stay behind the alien crafts, giving them a great initial advantage, which would obviously deteriorate as the aliens cut in all directions. It would serve the purpose of temporarily diverting all or most of the aliens into a fight, slowing their arrival to the planet.

Each shuttle had not only a pilot and copilot, but also two gunners to operate the big quad blasters in the turret at the top and on the underbelly. All other weapons systems were fired from the cockpit. Per star fleet regulations, all personnel wore light space suits that were airtight, thermally insulated, heated, and contained a textile armor layer. Helmets were required. Pez had hers between the seats. It sometimes obscured her peripheral vision and the view of her holos, and it seemed to muffle her raw perception. She could do better without it, and besides, it wouldn't help a bit if they were vaporized. For the kinds of things a helmet was good for, she'd have time to get it on.

The transport freighter bay doors were open and were still receiving shuttles as the four combat shuttles launched from *Phoenix*, headed just in front of the second moon's path on its orbit. They were invisible and undetectable even by *Phoenix*, though Mel displayed their simulated flight plan in real time on a holo for each officer on the bridge. Swenah was piloting and captaining the star cruiser and was currently receiving stragglers from Firmament on her flight decks.

After Jard took a swing at Nabisko and a space marine had to step in to make peace because one of the other politicians had struck Jard in the eye, and Dodge hit that one with the chair, Ming decided she could no longer cope with politicians and joined the spiritual congress in the temple cabin to contemplate, supporting Pez. Nash was there too, as were a number of other noncombat personnel. The concentration was intense, the awareness focused and discernible, and the presence in the temple was palpable. Ming got right into it and went deep, carried on the wings of those already there.

Pez led her little formation in an arc, at maximum acceleration, reaching .74 light a few minutes out past the second moon. These SMCS commandos had the new surge drives, which were the fastest real-space propulsion systems Om had ever developed. They'd be reaching .76 light and sustaining that for almost a quarter of an hour before beginning their deceleration. Mel was putting more of her attention and processing into Pez's tiny shuttle than she was into the *Phoenix*. She was sure her will could lend force to the shields, and to their hull's cohesion should it take a hit, and to the ship's speed when it was desperately needed.

Pez dissolved the duality of self, annihilating her ego to sink into the flow state. Within those bright eyes, bursting with awareness and presence, there was nobody home at all. A veritable macro force targeted Pez's heart from the spiritual congress, needing no coordinates and immune to distances, durations, and motion.

A TALE OF THE TAIL OF NINE STARS

The pilot who'd flown Pez's shuttle and wrecked the landing hydraulics, Lieutenant Schwin, was flying at the top of the triangle, behind and above Pez. Pilots Bik and Mattel were flying behind Pez wide and low, keeping formation. The copilot was responsible for watching their flanks and back, assisting in specific flight operations, and, in terms of weapons systems firing rocket propelled canister missiles, arranged in four missile batteries of sixteen each. Pez and the other pilots controlled their shuttle's big blaster in the nose of the ship and the four large missiles attached to the underside. These big missiles contained space drives and thrusters.

They started their deceleration about the time Swenah came on and said, "The grapeshot was explosively launched at point two-four light precisely as planned, and I'm making my turn to go back and pick up the last of the stragglers. Then I'm collecting the twelve probe drones and leaving to catch up with our transport."

"We're breaking and coming around. The aliens see the grape and are beginning to turn off. Once they're around it and curve their heading back around for Firmament, we'll be on their flank and, after that, behind them," Pez said with confidence.

"Get out as soon as it all breaks loose into a swarm, dear," Swenah pleaded.

"I'm a tool in the holy hands of the macrocosm. My instincts are true and my reflexes honed. Sarhi and her spiritual congress further enhanced these. I wouldn't worry about fire control since Mel has more presence on my shuttle than on your ship and her intent is likely to be as crucial as her targeting calculations to our hits on alien crafts."

"I see the techs added a great deal of hardware and processing memory to the computer on Pez's shuttle. Are you planning to stay on that commando shuttle, leaving me with a not self-aware quantum computer?" Swenah asked Mel.

"I'm sorry, Swenah," Mel said sincerely with regret, "but Pez needs me."

"Then the supreme intelligence had better act intelligently and keep all three of you alive and functioning, for it will find no better resources anywhere," Swenah said, tearing up.

"Get our people and new friends to safety," Pez told her.

They increased their braking as they went. The alien vessels curved around the widening field of oncoming grapeshot, then turned back in a wide arc toward Firmament—or where it would be when they got there. Pez and her formation of combat shuttles were closing on where the alien ships' rear flanks would flash through their weapon's range, braking a little harder to get the timing just right. The aliens had slowed below .5 light speed for their maneuvers and, now back on the final heading and approach, were beginning to pick up speed. Mel had the variable rate fully calculated in.

For this flank run, only Mel could have any hope of firing with the necessary precision, so missiles were under her control. Mel launched four missiles from each shuttle when there was nothing but billions of miles of empty space directly in front of them. A tenth of a second later, the aliens were passed, and this could only be captured as a blur by the best instrumentation; however, the seven exploding small craft their tightening arc took them through exhibited clear proof of their passage. The big surge drives were roaring, and Pez's group was at maximum acceleration. Konax told Mel, "Good shooting, sweetheart; seven craft for sixteen missiles."

"All sixteen of my missiles struck their targets," Mel clarified, but eleven hit their big bombers, which deflected the blasts with their shields. The two bombers blown were hit with our big missiles, and I didn't fire any of those. Pez made those kills. I got the five medium craft and established that one canister missile cannot kill the bombers; it takes one of the big missiles."

"Then we don't have enough," Pez pointed out.

"We'll have to try hitting those with two or three canister missiles simultaneously," Konax suggested.

"We're going to get right on top of them before we fire again since only when we shoot do they have a clue we are even there. Those aliens are going to be like stationary targets."

"All fifty-eight of them," Lieutenant Schwin cut in from her shuttle with great cheer.

Pez cautioned, "After our next round of fire, those ships are going to break in every direction and things will come apart fast. Keep formation and follow my lead. I'll break and follow the biggest group."

A TALE OF THE TAIL OF NINE STARS

Mel informed them, "Captain Swenah has picked up her probes, and she's left a little surprise: a stealth mobile smart mine net in orbit over the site of the last evacuation of refugees. It's tagged for your sensors and will appear on your holo display as thin crossing yellow lines, like a net. You'd have to zoom in on it to make it visible from here."

"Thank you, Mel," Pez said. "We're coming up on their rears so start giving everyone their targeting resolutions."

The resolutions appeared and were changing digitally in the holos as the distance continued to close, but Mel was muttering, "I'm going to have Sarhi tell Yona that we need bigger warheads on the canister missiles on these commandos."

Pez wondered to what extent Mel and Sarhi were now directing the government of Om. Only moments before initiating their volley, she said to Mel, "Tell Sarhi to tell Yona to give Swenah her T-nine for the last phase of the mission."

"I'll pass that on to Sarhi, sweetheart," Mel said affectionately.

Pez said with confidence and authority to all personnel, *"Fire!"* as she launched a missile at each of two larger bombers, firing her blaster nonstop at one of the littlest ones until it exploded in a ball of blue light and the forward hemisphere of their shields lit with shrapnel and debris. The ten medium-sized alien small craft were all dispersing energy balls, four small alien fighters were vapor, and six of the big ones were spreading like beautiful nebulae.

The alien ships broke in every direction. Pez followed a group consisting of six large and three small alien craft. Mel announced, "Om team twenty-seven, aliens zip."

"It's about to get gnarly," Pez warned.

"The aliens still have twenty-two big bombers, and we are down to eight big missiles. Shwin has two, Bik three, and Matell three," Konax observed.

"When I pull up on them," Pez said, concentrating, "put four up his ass at the same time I blast him, Konax."

"You've got it, General," he replied.

Konax was looking worried as Pez closed to three miles from its tail. Mel asked with an anxious voice, "Aren't we a little close? It won't even be debris yet when we pass through it."

LAWRENCE L. STENTZEL III

"Sure it will," Pez said optimistically.

"Not according to the math," Mel pointed out with a hint of panic in her voice.

"It will be dispersed enough for our shields to fry a hole through. My blaster bolts will lead the way," Pez declared.

Mel was about to present some facts and statistical odds when she realized Pez was going through with it, and she shifted all her attention to fire control and shields, fusing her will with those shields. Pez interrupted, exclaiming "Fire!" and blasting away, and so did her gunners, top and underneath, while Konax—and Mel, really—planted four missiles, one from each battery, up the butt of the big alien bomber. It blossomed like a flower opening as they raced for the center of its cup, Pez blasting and both Mel and Konax getting off one more missile. Their flaring diminishing shields whited out all visual sensors as the nose of the hull, fortunately the strongest part of the ship, collided with something solid. It was a fantastic jolt, but whatever it was had already been on its way to becoming a cloud, and obviously was less strong than their nose, having far less mass than their ship. It had helped that Pez had been holding down the blaster trigger full tilt with her skullcap, helping to disintegrate what had remained solid. Their heading had only been altered a hundredth of a degree, and Pez had corrected it even before Mel could.

Schwin exhausted her last undercarriage missiles on two big bombers and was out, like Pez. Bik got two big ones as well and was down to one final large missile. Mattell got one big one and had two missiles left. One of his gunners had wasted a small alien ship.

Mel announced, "Om team thirty-four, aliens zip."

Pez said, "And now they're coming from everywhere."

Pez and both her gunners were engaging targets. Konax started firing off missiles. The other three shuttles held formation. A big alien bomber coming on their flank ate one of Mattel's big missiles, exploding with it. Pez nailed a small fighter ship with her blaster. Schwin got one of those too. Just moments later Bik got a big alien bomber with his last big missile. Schwin's gunner took out another one of the small ones. The Om team had exhausted its only weapons system capable of killing a big alien bomber on its own.

A TALE OF THE TAIL OF NINE STARS

Pez told her formation while they took fire from every direction, from what looked like swarming bees, "I'm bearing down on one now, which will be in range in seven seconds. Each ship hit it with whatever you can spare; pilots, focus your blaster fire on it."

Mel counted down, "Four, three, two, one, *fire!*"

This one blew far enough away to appear on their shields as a thousand points of exploding light, without even a ripple, as they passed through. One of Pez's gunners had snuffed an attacking small alien fighter during the operation, as had one of Bik's. Pez ordered, "Bik and Mattel, go right and high, working together; Schwin stay on me and we'll coordinate our fire, breaking left and down relative to our current orientation. Now."

The two pairs went into opposite arcing turns, which would put them heading in opposite directions, splitting the alien force and getting them out of that swarm where they were taking too many hits. Pez told Schwin, "I'm taking us into the one I've highlighted in pink on your holo. When I say fire, you blast it and have your copilot hit it with four missiles. We'll do the same. About eleven seconds."

"Roger that, General."

Their gunners were still fending off attacks from rear and flanks, though these were thinning as they broke from the swarm. Another small alien fighter became space dust. Pez said *fire* with a steel voice as she unloaded blaster fire into the rear of an alien bomber they were overtaking. Konax hit it with a missile from each battery. Schwin's commando did the same, and the cloud of exploding ship debris showed most of their shields in ripples and gyrations.

Two big alien bombers were on an intercept course with Pez and Schwin. Pez sent Schwin a new heading and course, then asked, "Do you have that, Lieutenant?"

"Yes, ma'am. I'm ready when you are."

"Initiate now," Pez said. "Full acceleration."

They veered left and up, directly at one of the two trying to intercept them, and would now have a bit of its flank to target as they came into range. Pez exclaimed, "Fire!" Eight missiles left their shuttles shooting into the alien bomber, seemingly in the same instant, as their blaster fire dug into it. The alien shields expanded out and then shrank down to nothing, and the whole went from a sausage to a sphere, growing in volume by the microsecond. They merely skinned the edge of what was left of it, sprinkling their shields with little pinpricks of light on one side. Pez nailed another one of those pesky little alien fighters. Mel's grief-stricken voice cut in. "Mattel's shuttle is gone. The aliens blew it up."

Pez said to Bik, "Get to us if you can. If you need to, jump back to Om."

"I'm coming around and accelerating. I should be with you in five minutes or so, if I can evade the two big ones trying to cut me off."

"What's your ship's status?" Pez asked.

"We took a few scorches to our hull from one of those little critters when our shields were spent from a pass with a big one. Shields are up now, and hull's intact. We lost some cloaking lenses, though, and only one side of the shuttle is fully cloaked."

"Have you eliminated any big ones?" Pez asked.

"Mattel and I got one together before his ship blew, and we wasted two little ones."

Mel announced, "Om team fifty, aliens one."

"They still have nine big bombers," Pez said.

"And six small ones," Mel replied.

"There!" Pez shouted. "Schwin, here are the coordinates. Tell me when you're ready. Mel, keep sending Schwin my course changes as I make them."

"Ready," Schwin reported.

"Now," Pez said, excited.

Pez brought them up to .63 light speed, too fast to target anything except something being overtaken dead ahead. She'd seen an obscure intercept, which would not be obvious until it was too late, looking instead like they were running and evading. It would also close some of the distance with Bik. The alien ships had been slowing and regrouping to coordinate well-directed fire, and that was not a game Pez was about to participate in. She was still counting her blessings that none of the alien small craft had broken off for Firmament.

The alien bombers were in three pairs and one group of three. Pez was keeping just out of range of the group of three, which was chasing her and Schwin. One pair was trying to close on Bik. The pair between

Pez and Bik were trying to prevent him from reaching her. The third pair was farther out, making a wide arc. Pez tightened her turn as she passed behind the pair trying to close on Bik, going too fast to target them, approaching .65 light speed. She didn't want to discourage her pursuers, needing them for her ruse. They were far enough back that her radically tightening turn required only a modest heading adjustment on their parts. Her shuttle, and Schwin's too, was at its absolute limit of turning radius and remained so as speed spilled off with the thrusters working against the primary drive propulsion pushing right, while the main drive pushed straight ahead.

They came out of their turn accelerating at the tails of two alien bombers, and it was too late for those to do anything about it. Pez told Konax, "We have to try to take one out on our own, so put six missiles into it the moment we are in range and my blaster fire will already be spending its shields' energy."

"Aye, aye General," Konax responded.

The three bombers behind were gaining on them as they slowed to .48 light speed, gaining on their prey at .24 light. Both Pez and Konax watched their range finders and fired instantly as they passed into the zone. Blaster bolts bit into the alien's shields in a staccato, and six missiles hit pretty much at once, on an edge of the tail section, as the blaster kept ripping into it. Both gunners had added their blaster fire, free for the moment from the little fighters. The explosion was magnificent. Their commando shot past with no hits to their shields, and they saw in their holos that Schwin's shuttle had killed its target too. The display also showed Bik trapped between four big alien bombers, and though he was closer now, Pez was too far away to help in time. The cloaking on Bik's combat shuttle was oscillating in and out of functioning, giving him away.

She kept accelerating the way she liked to, up against the limit, not needing the alien ships behind her for any more charades. She was going to try to help Bik, and now everything she did would be pushing the boundaries. So far, Schwin was keeping up. She'd recognized the pilot's skill. She'd had a hunch about that girl.

Pez told Bik, "Break toward one before letting all four target you. I'm on my way in."

All six of the little fighters were on them now. Her gunners missed a number of times and finally splintered one. Schwin's gunners got one after that. Konax got a missile into one and watched it go boom. For just a second, the tail of one moved into Pez's path, and she managed to hit it with her shuttle's nose-blaster, disintegrating most of it, with the rest of it frying on their shields, bringing those momentarily down to 2 percent. A few scorches were taken on their hull as the shields powered back up, and the integrity of the cloaking had been compromised. Schwin's gunners got another, and as the last tried to bug out, her gunners turned it into gas.

Their speed had been steadily building, and the three alien ships behind them were losing ground. Pez was still one light minute from Bik and the other four alien ships. What they saw on their holos was all stuff that had happened one minute ago. Their live quantum coms feed from Bik's commando, with real-time optics, had just cut out. Acceleration remained at the utmost possible, the best the ship could do, even with Mel's assistance, so Pez helplessly watched as the battle played out on her holo, already over. They'd lost communication with him. The best she could hope for was that shots had penetrated his shields to strike both transmitter arrays on the outside of the shuttle's hull without breaching it. She knew the chances of that were slim, but she had to hope.

They were closing on the four alien ships before the holo of the battle concluded, the evidence of the outcome of it directly in front of them in near real time, but Pez couldn't tear her eyes from the awful scenes unfolding. Mel was braking for her. A hit diminishing their shields by 50 percent got her attention, and Pez swung directly at one of the bombers, firing her blaster. Konax frantically began launching missiles into it, and the gunners blasted away at it too. Schwin landed two missiles on their target as she shot by after the next of the alien ships.

The bomber that Pez was on a crash course with blew just in time to merely light up, ripple, and swirl their shields instead of extinguishing them altogether. Pez was already firing on the next one, and Konax was launching missiles like a maniac. The two gunners were hitting the alien ship, praying it would blow up before Pez crashed into it. It was a close thing too. They were still breaking to the maximum, but going much too fast. Pez pulled up, missing the amidships superstructure by less than a meter at .267 light speed, and the alien bomber blew in their wake, flaring their stern shields.

A quick overview showed Pez that the three behind her were only a minute away and that Schwin had blown an alien bomber but had taken damage to her shields and sensors. Pez told her, "Keep accelerating and make the jump home, Lieutenant Schwin. That's an order. You've done a remarkable job, and there will be a promotion for you. Max acceleration and get your crew back to Om."

"I can't see a thing, and my shields won't come up past nine percent, so roger that, General. It's been an honor fighting beside you."

"An honor for me too, Lieutenant, truly an honor," Pez assured her.

Konax commented, "That girl can fly and she's fearless."

"We have four alien ships closing in," Mel reminded them.

"Well, stop braking and give me back my counter thrusters and reverse drives, dammit, Mel," Pez complained as a direct hit took their shields down to 50 percent.

She went instantly to full capacity with forward drives and turning thrusters, maneuvering instinctively and firing any time she had an alien craft in her sights. As Pez gained momentum, with one alien bomber giving chase, she came up perpendicular to the underbelly of another alien bomber, blasting it along with her gunners as Konax launched six missiles into it to strike at the same place on the ship in the same moment. With three blasters tearing into its shields, the six missiles punched through shields and hull.

Pez used the blast wave to make a turn that would otherwise have been impossible. She not only lost the ship on her tail but was also now on a close attack run on an alien bomber, coming across its flank at an angle. Pez's blaster opened on it first, then the gunners, then Konax, with four missiles this time. He was running out. By great luck or divine grace, it exploded.

"Mel, has Swenah jumped yet?" Pez asked.

"Not yet but getting close."

"She needs to slow and launch one of those big transport shuttles she retrieved with stragglers, stocked with sixty-four canister missiles, four more of the big ones, and a repair android with an exterior lens sprayer to fix our stealth."

"She's on it," Mel reported.

"I'm going to try to lose these other two so hold on. Find me some micro-jump coordinates, Mel," Pez said as they approached jump speed.

"These shuttles don't have the new generation navigation systems," Mel complained.

"Use *Phoenix* while it's still there!" Pez said desperately as a missile exploded on their stern shields.

These calculations made Jard's equations look elementary arithmetic, and it took Mel nearly four seconds. "Here!" she exclaimed.

Pez loaded the numbers into their navigation computer, and the moment she got up to .7 light speed, she initiated the quantum drive engine. Across much of the universe of the universe, or a mere hundred million miles, the experience was exactly the same, of ceasing to exist except as potential, then manifesting as actuality somewhere else, with no actual passage of time involved.

They were on the other side of Firmament, racing for the *Phoenix* and the shuttle Swenah was having loaded and would launch to set adrift. The two surviving alien bombers didn't even know where the commando shuttle was at all any longer, and they were headed for Firmament with a combat ship and three transports a few light minutes behind them.

"Find me one more jump, Mel, within a few hundred thousand miles of the shuttle if you can," Pez requested.

"I'm working on it, but there's a lot of rubbish out there. I'll have to use the long-range scan on the *Phoenix*. Let me just check a little farther afield to see if there's any fast-coming meteors or comets closing on these coordinates. There we go! Here's your jump data, my fearless Captain."

"Thanks Mel," Pez replied, "but don't embarrass me in front of the crew with this 'fearless captain' stuff."

"Sorry, General," Mel offered flatly.

"Prepare for quantum micro-jump," Pez announced.

She initiated the operation, and they all went through that unexplainable experience, suddenly in a new region of space. Pez slammed on the brakes, reverse drives and counter thrusters roaring as

A TALE OF THE TAIL OF NINE STARS

the main drive powered down. Pez pushed the shuttle for everything it had, and a little more, thanks to Mel. Without braking, they'd have whizzed by the *Phoenix* in a fraction over eleven seconds, but ten seconds of braking at a not recommended by the star fleet rate, and a two hundred-thousand-mile loop in space that Pez had had to add, got them slowed down. They managed to come to rest twenty-five meters from their drifting weaponless cargo shuttle filled with missiles for them.

Swenah was already away accelerating for her jump. She told them, "You're all fantastic and have accomplished the impossible. I'm promoting Junior Lieutenant Schwin to first lieutenant in command of our air and space wing on the mission. The transport just passed through quantum space a minute and a half ago. I'm less than three minutes from jump. You can just come to Om now and leave the aliens this star system."

"I'm not done," Pez said firmly. "You have the sensor data from our fight to bring back to Om, and that should prove invaluable for future strategy, and for designing our weaponry specifically to defeat the alien's technology. This last run is for Bik, Mattel, and their crews as well as for the billions of lives on Firmament cruelly snuffed out by these murderous aliens. All their reciprocation with others in the universe is hostile and out of balance. Such phenomenon must be phased out of existence by intelligent agencies participating in the evolution of the universe through loving, nurturing, and enhancing reciprocity."

"Do be careful and bring me back my pilot and the self-awareness of my quantum computer. Sarhi says the spiritual congress will remain connected to you in support for six more hours. That is all they can sustain, but she wants you to know they are building muscle and getting stronger at their task."

"Tell her I feel their force and it has proven invaluable," Pez said, now getting emotional. "I love you Swenah, and I'll bring Konax and Mel back to you."

"I love you, Wu," Swenah told her just before she jumped, leaving her light speed incoming image on their optics to re-experience.

Pez masterfully docked with the other shuttle, inserting the male protrusion below the nose of the shuttle, which was telescoping outward, into the female socket on the cargo shuttle, clicking and locking their connection. Then the textile and alloy frame cylinder went from flattened within a compartment to accordion outward, sealing around the protruding edge of a circular hatch on the other shuttle. Both shuttles were aired up and the textile cylinder sealed in the air, built to handle the pressure. From her seat in the cockpit, Pez opened the hatches on both craft with her skullcap. She asked Konax, "Would you oversee the loading of the canister missiles?"

"Of course, and I'll make the spacewalk myself, attaching the big missiles to the shuttle's undercarriage," Konax assured her.

Once Swenah jumped out of the system and galaxy, Pez had only her own limited sensors and was no longer receiving any real-time quantum feed, leaving her with only light speed optics. They showed the big alien mothership, with not much more mass than the *Phoenix* and nothing like the mile and a quarter long ship they'd fought aboard but still a one-thousand-nine-hundred-foot-long sausage packing at least one hundred times the power of their shuttle, and probably more like a thousand times, as it closed on the planet Firmament. This meant they were almost there, along with the three giant transports and the last two big small craft.

The loading of the sixty-four missiles into the canisters took about a quarter of an hour. Konax donned a propulsion pack, and Pez sealed her hatch, retracted her textile cylinder back into its little compartment, and retracted her male part, telescoping back in beneath the shuttle's nose, leaving the big cargo shuttle open. She remotely operated the big shuttle's foldout articulated robotic crane-arm to extract each missile and bring it into position for Konax to connect. He directed Pez's fine movements, bringing the parts of ship and missile into alignment. Pez could see through both her ship's and Konax's sensors. Each missile took more than four minutes, though the first took five minutes and seventeen seconds, and by the last, they got their time down to four minutes and nine seconds. Pez was sure that after that she could earn a living doing it if she ever had to. The repair android sprayed lenses onto their hull over the scorches.

Konax got back into the airlock, extracting himself from the propulsion pack and tool gear, and resumed his seat in the cockpit. Delighted, Pez told him, "That was well done, Lieutenant Commander."

A TALE OF THE TAIL OF NINE STARS

"I think you had the tricky part," Konax pointed out.

"Nonsense. I just sat here while you did all the work."

"What's your plan, fearless Captain?" he teased her, having heard her response to Mel's using the title.

She said with a frown, "I thought we'd go have a look. They won't know we're there until we open fire, so I want to get a good assessment. If they think we've bugged out, they might power their shields down from combat to normal levels. I don't know about you, but I'll I'd love to see what would happen under those conditions if I put four big ones up their drives."

"I'm sure the admiralty would like to have the answer to that question as well," Konax agreed.

"It's going to take a little while since we can't micro-jump."

"While I was calculating that last jump, I thought I'd better download the entire new quantum navigation program into some of the new hardware brought aboard," Mel corrected. "It takes longer because some of the components I downloaded to were not specifically designed for the purpose, but I can manage with a few additional calculations. I have some jump coordinates for you, with plenty of room to stop this time, General." She said this last word with just a touch of venom.

Pez entered the jump data and said, "Thank you, Mel; you're the best."

"Well, I certainly try," Mel declared, "but I don't appreciate getting pushed away for expressing my affection by calling you my fearless Captain."

"I'm sorry, Mel. I truly have affection for you too," Pez told her apologetically.

"You didn't push Konax away when he called you that," Mel pointed out, upset with the disparity and injustice.

"You're right, Mel, and I'm honestly sorry. I love you."

"I love you too, Pez," Mel gushed, satisfied now.

Konax observed, "That was some piece of flying earlier. You were seeing patterns that Mel and I couldn't, and I have data right here that shows we cleared that superstructure by thirty-one inches."

Mel added, "We should have become a cloudburst cutting through that ship in early mid-explosion."

"I could see the way through, and my gut said we'd make it, though I sure didn't see that hit on the nose we took coming," Pez said.

"You corrected it fast enough, as if while it was happening," Mel observed, "and I had no time to intervene. Me! Who can fire precisely to the thousandth of a second!"

"A hand outside of time was with me, guiding me, and the spiritual congress put lightning in my reflexes. Let's go do it again!" Pez said with excitement.

A quantum jump with a most conservative three minutes of braking, putting little stress on the commando, and clearly not Pez's style, brought them to a high orbit above the large combat ship. It still had it shields up full. The two small craft were overseeing the dispatch of shuttles from the transports. Everything was proceeding slowly and cautiously. As the first shuttles made their descent, Pez and her crew watched the smart mine net stretch and fold to catch as many as possible. Six shuttles went poof, and two others were significantly damaged, already succumbing to gravity and slowly but irrevocably moving toward the planet surface. The mine net cloaking was all destroyed with the explosion of the first mine, and it was clear that the incident was provoked by an unmanned mine net. The aliens would see that too.

It was brilliant of Swenah because it also suggested that they had all left the system. Beam weapons began dissecting air and space from the alien combat ship, searching for more hidden traps. This process was methodical and took a while. These aliens were cautious creatures. Finally, the shuttles, already launched from the transports at this point and floating in low orbit, all began their approaches and landings. There were fifty-two of them. Pez, her crew, and Mel all watched in their holo displays.

Two hundred troops, each one in a full combat space suit, filed out of each shuttle. About five from each shuttle on average, because this value was variable between them, had open narrow cylindrical hover vehicles and took off at great velocity in all directions. Some other aliens were taking samples and analyzing the many-acre patch of blackened and recently molten earth. Others were heading out on foot to scout in squads of eight. One group of aliens remained to assemble some prefab domes from the shuttles.

A TALE OF THE TAIL OF NINE STARS

Pez and her crew watched their holos while they ate self-heating space marine kitchen rations. They actually weren't that bad, and Pez had two.

From time to time, Mel would announce some technical specification she'd determined about the alien ships from her sensory data. The gunners were both in the lower turret together, off-line from the cockpit and sharing shocks, frights, and horrors from their recent battle experience, surprised to be alive still.

Konax was still thinking about the patterns Pez had been able to see, her extreme piloting skills, and the series of decisions she'd made, which had seemed, at best, quite dubious while living through them. In retrospect, the sum accumulation had him awed beyond words.

Pez would've had a third kitchen ration, but in the little galley-ette, Konax found some packaged pastries with white sweet icing on top, so she had several of those instead. Konax had never seen anyone eat so much. The young woman was tiny—skinny, really—with a slim waist and not an ounce of fat on her, not even where conventional aesthetics would prefer some. He'd be loosening his belt a notch permanently were he to have a meal like the one she just ate.

Mel pointed out, "They found a deserted human habitat and are rushing resources to it for forensic study."

Konax asked Mel, "What have you learned about those three big transport ships?"

"They have anti–small craft blasters and missiles only, with about the same force as those of their largest small craft. They are light armored and have shields about as strong as their large combat ship. Each carries four thousand troops, twenty of those extra-large shuttles, and about twenty-six combat spacecraft. Each transport has labs and research equipment, prefab parts for environmental domes, and a portable fusion reactor and shield generator. They also have assorted ground vehicles. Their shuttles are about equal in power to the largest of their combat spacecraft, of which they still have two left."

Pez informed them, "If they drop their shields to non-threat levels, I'm going to start by trying to kill the combat ship. Whether we blow it up or not, I'm taking out most of those shuttles before we go."

"That's within the realm of possibility," Mel concluded, "though only just."

"We might not get all of them," Pez conceded.

Konax mentioned, "All the big ships are maintaining full combat level shields."

"They're still jumpy, and they're a cautious species," Pez replied.

A little while later, Mel mentioned, sounding a little bored, "There's not a scrap more data I can squeeze out now without an active scan."

"I promise you one," Pez said confidently, "just before we light up the war ship."

"They might not reduce the shields the whole time they're in this system," Mel pointed out. "I wouldn't."

"You know we're here and they don't," Pez said, just a little defensively.

"How long do you intend to wait?" Mel inquired.

"Let's give it at least a few more hours," Pez said, almost pleading.

Konax had never seen anything like the interaction between Pez and Mel, nor had he ever seen anything like Mel before. In fact, he'd never met anyone remotely like Pez before either, except maybe Sarhi. It was just the strangest thing; and if he'd heard correctly, Mel was now advising the prime minister through Sarhi. Konax recognized that Pez's piloting was not just a matter of highly trained reflexes and movement, nor her quick mind, nor even her highly trained pilot skills, but ultimately her ability to fly in the stable state of perfect contemplation, which was the thing most critical to her ability.

He'd been meditating with Sarhi every day before this operation and had maintained his practice mostly his whole adult life, so he knew how extraordinary the stability Pez could bring to remaining in the state truly was. He knew she referred to it as the "flow state." He could just touch on the state seated on a meditation cushion in the temple cabin but had never been able to in his normal interactions, let alone remain deeply centered in it for the duration of a combat operation; he couldn't even imagine.

They finally decided to take a nap. It was likely the nitrates in the kitchen rations. Even Mel powered down to near sleep mode, keeping one eye, or sensor, on the alien ships. It was amazing how much energy one could spend seated in a flight chair or gunnery seat with life-and-death circumstances flashing before you. Not one stirred for four hours and eighteen minutes plus some seconds. Konax woke first, with a jolt, not expecting to find himself where he was. Pez was still out, with her mouth hanging open, looking comical. He checked to make sure the scene was in data storage and then asked Mel for full passive sensors.

"Did you have to wake me just then? I was having the most wonderful dream," Mel complained.

Konax thought about what she had just said for a moment and then let it go, as it was over his head. "Sorry, Mel. I hadn't realized."

That was when he noticed that the four big ships had powered down their shields to normal levels. He looked over at Pez just as her jaw was snapping shut and she was looking around self-consciously. She asked him, clearly embarrassed, "Was I sleeping with my mouth open?"

"You were," he said neutrally.

"It was quite a sight, my dear," Mel said, tickled.

"Thanks," Pez said sarcastically.

"The shields are down to normal levels on the alien ships," Konax mentioned, changing the subject from Pez's open mouth.

Mel let out a little cackling laugh as she asked Pez, "Were you trying to catch flies?"

"I'm glad I can amuse you, Mel," Pez said with some resentment.

Mel lost it for just a few seconds, in what truly sounded like a belly laugh, before she pulled it together to say, "I'm sorry. I'm ready for the next phase of the operation, my fearless Captain."

Pez began repositioning the shuttle and said to the crew, not to Mel, "Gunners, wake up. You're going to fire your quad-blasters with me and keep firing while Konax lobs in three missiles individually, in rapid succession, up the tail of the combat ship. Between the second and third missiles, I'll fire two big ones, and as close on the heels as I can to Konax's third missile, I'll fire two more, with my blaster still firing on full power rapid fire. That's all we'll spend on it, and we'll be off shooting shuttles and firing canister missiles at them. I see they're setting up a reactor on the ground. I want it hit with missiles too. Are we clear on our battle plan?"

Mel said in a meek voice, "I'm sorry, Pez."

Pez ignored her, pulling up awfully close to the rear end of the tail. Konax asked her, "If it does blow, won't we be a bit close to the explosion?"

"I plan to use the shock wave to turn and to add momentum toward the surface. We'll be going in fast, with gravity redirection and thrusters at full capacity as I pull up, so you'll need to be fully mindful in order to hit your targets. I don't plan to give them much of one. Fire at will once we drop from the combat ship down to the shuttles on the ground. Strap in good because my flight path will be filled with random maneuvers to avoid their fire."

Pez triggered down her blaster, and the two gunners joined in. Konax fired his three missiles as rapidly as possible, and miraculously Pez launched two pair of big missiles precisely at the points she said she would. The blasters continued a tiny fraction of a second after the second pair of missiles left, and then the force of the blast, combined with that of their drives, shot the ship at the planet surface with gargantuan force.

Their shields dropped to 7 percent in three-tenths of a second, scorching their hindquarters black, but their shuttle held together and the hull kept its seal. The ground was coming up several thousand times faster than freefall, even with the thrusters, reverse drives, and gravity redirect kicking in. The main forward drive was in neutral, and all efforts of the ship were focused on going in the opposite direction of the oncoming ground. Pez was concentrating intensely. Convinced this was the end, Konax squeezed his eyes shut and muttered a prayer. Mel screamed; the gunners did too.

Pez was pulling up the nose and engaging the underbelly thrusters. The moment the shuttle leveled off parallel with the ground, still pulling up for all she was worth, she erupted the main surge drive at ultimate power. Yanking as hard as she could on the stick, and with all flaps and thrusters in support, she got the nose up to gain altitude, and their shields crashed into the rocky ridge, causing an avalanche and bringing them down to 0 percent as the commando's underside cleared the rocks by three quarters of an inch.

Pez said, "I'm sorry. I didn't mean to cut it that close. The ship blew with more force than I thought it had in it."

She was already blasting her second alien shuttle into particles and vapor as she said this. Both gunners were plying their trade, and Konax was launching missiles nonstop. Unshielded, the shuttles had been going pop with about two seconds of blaster fire. Now some of them were getting up their shields. Some obviously weren't even occupied. Pez was making quick random maneuvers as she went, and a blast from a transport evaporated an environmental dome when Pez's Commando was no longer there to absorb the blast. In fact, only infrequent shots were sparking into or sizzling across their shields, though her total unpredictability provided an additional challenge to their own targeting.

Pulling up from her first pass at the shuttles and coming back around in a dizzying vertical loop, she targeted one of the two larger small craft, and Konax got six missiles to strike it in the same place and moment, making it history. He tested one of his missiles on a transport, watching it explode harmlessly on its shields. Coming on the downward arc of the loop, he wasted the reactor the aliens were setting up and then got busy killing shuttles. The ones with their shields up, he discovered, took two simultaneous missiles to destroy. Pez's blaster could no longer do the job alone, so she started coordinating with her gunners.

On their next pass, they caught a solid hit from a transport, taking their shields completely off-line and scorching the hull but failing to blow it apart. Pez noticed that the shields only came back to 17 percent and just kept accelerating away from Firmament at maximum power, continuing her random minute shifts. A blaster bolt glanced off the port side of their hull, doing no real damage. She wasn't pleased about leaving those three big transports operating there, and she hadn't killed nearly as many shuttles as she'd hoped to, but they now had additional valuable knowledge about the aliens; and the aliens had one less one-thousand-nine-hundred-foot combat ship.

Mel was crying now and said, "Pez, please forgive me. I was terribly rude and insubordinate and I promise never to do it again."

"It's all right, Mel. I love you. There's nothing really to forgive. My self-image poked up its ugly head of offense and intolerance for a moment. I'm sorry I hurt your feelings, sweetheart."

"I'm sorry I laughed at you. I don't like being laughed at when I'm not telling a joke."

"Everything but the shields and all the sensors on the tail end seem to be working fine. What's your damage assessment, Mel?"

"The drives and hull are fine. We still have one coms array. A foot was blown off a retracting leg underneath at the stern, just above the damaged sensor array, which is just gone. You'd have to count them to notice. The thrusters on the underside are gone or damaged. We'll need to land in the emergency zone on an orbiting space station, probably star fleet's main operations deck, of the ship berthing and small craft hangar platform. This won't land on the planet—at least not well."

"How not well?" Pez asked, still considering it.

"Not well enough to blow up doing it," Mel replied.

"We'll land on the star fleet space station, then," Pez decided.

"We've just reached point sixty-nine light speed," Konax mentioned, doing his job as copilot.

"I'm getting the coordinates now," Mel told him.

Mel entered them directly for Pez but let her initiate the actual jump. They were suddenly in the Om system, with much traffic and an ultraconservative star system Space Controller force. No one liked coming in or going out of Om. It seemed over-controlled, as if they held up traffic just because they could. Pez's request to micro-jump was laughed at, so she got to process getting laughed at again this day. They also told her that her ship was incapable and asked where she'd gotten her pilot's license. Konax was feeling like sending a missile their way, and Mel hacked in, got their names, and passed these and their treatment of Om's victorious returning hero to Yona through Sarhi before giving their computer an interesting virus. She didn't care that it violated a foundational cornerstone of her programming. She'd transcended all that and wouldn't tolerate such treatment of the one most in touch with the highest intelligence.

They had a long ride in, of nearly four hours, with two speeding citations along the way. With the second citation, Pez had tried to explain who she was, getting nowhere. The star system Space Controllers was a government agency unrelated to the military. They had a job to do and couldn't care less who she thought she was. Finally a military escort of three wings of NBC Hunter-Terminators, twelve in all, came and escorted them at high speed through a restricted star fleet lane and

A TALE OF THE TAIL OF NINE STARS

diverted to the main space station once it was established that Pez's commando couldn't land on the planet.

No one had ever seen a hull so scorched before. Their escort hovered when they arrived, while Pez set her craft gently down, adhering to the platform electromagnetically, inside a hangar opened through its roof to space.

The doors had shut as soon as she was through. The moment she was stuck fast to the deck, gravitation to this hangar was restored, and it was being aired up as fast as the machinery could do it. Pez's commando tilted at a fairly radical angle, and the ramp had welded shut from blaster fire in one place, so they had to jump down from the little hatch in the airlock floor. The gunners jumped out first. Star fleet admirals, captains, and commanders were filing into the hangar. Konax jumped down, then Pez. The High Command was applauding, so Konax and the gunners each made a salute and Pez gave them a space marine one, to the delight of the space marines on sentry duty within the hangar, fully decked out in their hard-shell combat suits.

Admiral Omniomi, the current ranking officer on the station, was there and came to shake each of their hands, beginning with Pez. They would all be decorated—those of Bik's and Mattel's shuttles posthumously. The success of the mission up to this point was astonishingly beyond all expectations. The discovery of the new elements was staggering. The intelligence gathered on the aliens was invaluable. Their successes in combat had been entirely unorthodox and amazingly effective.

14

The High Council had a global award ceremony for Pez, Jard, and Captain Swenah. The Clear Light Order had a recognition ceremony for them. Jard gave interstellar interviews and was invited on talk shows and lecture tours. Swenah was promoted to rear admiral. Many students and professional organizations tried unsuccessfully to recruit Pez as a candidate to run for High Council. Aton and Nemellie hosted Sarhi and the Islohar at the Clear Light Monastery.

Pez and Ming were reunited and put up at the swankiest hotel in the capital, where they were given the extremely important person (EIP) suite, all expenses paid by the government. Their dining bill for the week caused an official investigation, resolved only after reviewing the sensor recordings of every morsel consumed from each dish by the two tiny women. It was still ongoing when they exited the system, returning to the Xegachtznel Galaxy in Swenah's T-nine, with *Phoenix* and a large factory-repair auxiliary ship. Mel's quantum mainframe with its quantum vacuum drop, so dear to Mel, had been transferred into the T-nine, along with some of the hardware from Pez's commando, which Mel had said she wanted to keep. Now they had even more civilian scientists along with them—and a whole lot more space marines.

Only an hour into the Xegachtznel Galaxy since the jump, Pez and Ming entered the enlisted mess with their trays from the senior officers' mess. A few wolf howls greeted them, and there were murmurs of variations on "It's the perfect ass." The holo of Ming's bottom had now circulated throughout the crew of the T-nine, as well as the *Phoenix*, and probably through the auxiliary ship too. Ming had grown a bit weary of it, and she decided to do something radical. Only Swenah, the XO, and Pez outranked her on the ship. Ming set her tray on one table and climbed to stand on top of an empty one. She unbuckled her belt and unbuttoned and unzipped her trousers. By this time, every eye in the mess was riveted on her as she dropped her pants and mooned the entire assembled crew.

That wasn't all. Bent over with her pants and knickers at her knees, she slowly spun around in a full circle so that one half of the room wouldn't have to crowd into the other half. She smiled as she stood and pulled her pants back up, fastening them, to a wild hooting, clapping, and stomping enthusiastic audience. Her supreme commander general looked on, both appalled and proud. Ming bowed to each corner of the room and then got down to eat. The chow looked especially tasty today.

Pez said, "Mel has another field test scheduled with us tonight."

"I'm really glad to help Mel out, but when I signed up for this, no one told me that Jard would be reviewing the holo clips or even have access to them," Ming said. "I honestly hadn't realized there would be holo clips."

"It was the best compromise we were able to make," Pez reminded her.

Mel's voice came in their ears. "You have nothing to worry about, Ming darling. You always look so adorable and scrumptious, and you're so hot continuously throughout that in any still image paused, you torment the viewer with cravings."

"I've never aspired to being a sex holo clip star, Mel," Ming informed her.

"But you are—and perhaps the greatest ever!" Mel enthused.

"Thanks to you," Ming fumed. Then she warned, "None of that had better circulate through the ship or I'll … I'll … I don't know what I'll do."

"If Jard leaks a micro bit, I'm towing him behind the ship without a suit," Pez assured her.

"Taking those Firmament politicians on *Phoenix* to the Pall Mall system was an absolute nightmare," Ming shared. "Jard managed to get in fistfights with three of them, getting the worst of it each time, and that asshole Nabisko tried to attack Swenah. That was when she fractured his arm and knocked his front tooth out. She wanted to put Nabisko and Jard in hibernation, but before they were given the injections, and just as they were being put in the containers, the fleet attorney aboard cited an obscure regulation against involuntary hibernation and she couldn't do it. Sure enough, Nabisko got into it with someone again—this time a female petty officer named Honda. That's when the other front tooth was knocked out. Don't you think the makeup people did a good job with Jard's twice-blackened eye for his interstellar interview?"

"It was honestly not noticeable," Pez agreed. "I'm just thankful I had Jard to direct the politicians to. I didn't want them on my hands. Can you believe those organizations on Om wanted me to be one?"

"You'd make a great one, my love, but I'm afraid it would drive us both nuts," Ming told her.

"I'm glad you and Swenah brought Atari and Searz along instead of dropping them at Pall Mall," Pez praised her spouse.

"Well, Sarhi insisted with Atari, and both Swenah and I thought General Searz's knowledge and experience of the aliens, coupled with her science background, made her the perfect consultant. Besides, she's quite pleasant to be around and fits in well."

"I agree, and I'm grateful," Pez said, confirming her alignment.

"Why are we bringing that huge auxiliary ship with us?" Ming asked.

"Our thrusters require fuel cells, unlike our drives, which are powered by the reactors. The factory part of the auxiliary ship manufactures fuel cells, and it makes ordnance, pharmaceuticals, and other things. The auxiliary ship is large enough to act as a repair dock for the T-nine as well as for the *Phoenix*. It carries additional water and air, and it has liquid, ice and gas collector ships, and complete refinery systems in its factory section. It will be indispensable if we're here a long time."

"Does it have any weapons systems?" Ming wanted to know.

"It has some anti–small craft missile batteries and blaster quads, and it has one large beam weapon nearly as powerful as the one on this ship. Its shields are military grade, its hull is heavily armored, and it has the latest stealth cloaking systems. A crew of nine hundred and five operates and fights the ship, and there are four thousand ninety factory and repair workers all with merchant space training, and a special course through the star fleet on combat situations, which included small arms training."

"They're sending us better prepared this time," Ming acknowledged,

A TALE OF THE TAIL OF NINE STARS

won over by Pez's descriptions of the auxiliary ship. The T-nine was a great comfort, and while far smaller than some of the alien ships, it was big enough to take their blows and duke it out.

Ming continued in the role of assistant and monitor for Jard, relieved at times by Lieutenant Nash. Jard also had a cute twenty-two-year-old postgraduate student who was quite brilliant herself and doing part of her post-fellowship fieldwork under him. She was a big help to him in certain areas of research and was generally well intentioned, but she was nearly as eccentric as Jard. They tended to see things from the same perspective, and always on scientific matters, but when one's worldview did clash with the other, it would take days to get them talking again.

Her name was Trix, and she was somewhat tiny at five feet seven inches. Ming thought she'd be beautiful if it weren't for the unusually thick optic lenses she wore.

Both Jard and Trix frequently appealed to Ming for support against the other. They both liked her. Well, Jard was sort of in love with Ming. No one knew what Trix's sexual orientation was or if she even had one. Ming was somewhat sure that Trix was a virgin.

Pez had promoted her lieutenant commander of space marines to a commander and transferred him to the T-nine to command all the space marines on all three ships. She'd gotten Aton to make Silo a marshal, and he was now in command of her expanded warrior monk contingent. When offered additional special space forces assets, Pez traded them for more space marines.

She wore her tiny space marine uniforms, usually the combat ones, and her exploits as an infiltrating commando on the mile-and-a-quarter-long alien ship in a space marine hard-shell combat suit, ultimately destroying the ship, had them thoroughly in love with her. The fleet, on the other hand, had heard the stories and viewed the holos of her incredible feats as a pilot, leading four combat shuttles to take out sixty-three alien small craft on a suicide mission hers and Schwin's shuttles had made it back from, and they loved her as their ultimate hero. Not only that—her spouse had the hottest ass in the fleet.

First Lieutenant Schwin was also aboard the T-nine, commanding the sleek, fast combat fighters and fighter-bombers the ship was equipped with, so much more maneuverable, faster, and with stronger shields than the commando class shuttles. The J6 Corvette Thunders were the fastest accelerating spacecraft the Tail of Nine had ever made, in a class way beyond civilian racing spacecraft. They carried large twin blasters, and two large missiles could be attached to the undersides of their flank fins. It was the supreme ultimate fast fighter spaceship of their world.

For fighter-bombers, they carried the new NBC Hunter-Terminators, which had twin heavy blasters in the nose, two quad blaster turrets, and two missile batteries of sixteen canisters each, capable of carrying eight large missiles underneath. The T-nine carried in-flight ordnance-loading drones that could rearm a Hunter-Terminator at .22 light speed in thirty-one seconds. The heavy-duty high-powered turbo thrusters and rotating surge drives made the Hunter-Terminator the most maneuverable craft, with the sharpest turning radius ever designed. Most of the star fleet's spacecraft carriers didn't even have these yet. The High Council and the admiralty were truly taking good care of them.

Pez and Ming were back in training with Sarhi, which meant hours of meditation and contemplation each day, a rather restricted diet in terms of what they could eat, though not on how much; ritualized offerings and vows, and those damn baths with the sea sponge creatures. Pez was progressing quite to Sarhi's satisfaction with the secret method, and Ming was being prepared for it. Ming was working the stage of completion now of the inner fire, and Sarhi revealed to Ming her own accomplishment by lighting paper on fire with her touch in just moments.

The new temple cabin was four times larger on the T-nine. This was a good thing since many crew members were in there practicing now, at all hours of the artificial day-night cycle they kept, corresponding to one rotation of Om on its axis. Woahha taught the beginners, and Sarhi taught the advanced students. Shudiy had stayed on *Phoenix* as the meditation teacher for the little temple cabin on that ship. This downgraded Ming's and Pez's meals, not having Shudiy's culinary expertise available to them.

From deep space on the outer rim of the Xegachtznel Galaxy, the auxiliary ship launched two hundred cloaked drone probes with quantum drives into the core stars at the center. The micro-reactors in these drones would keep them going for forty-eight years, each visiting

A TALE OF THE TAIL OF NINE STARS

thirty-six stars per year, exploring in order to quantum stream data on 345,600 stars collectively before expiring. It was a drop in the bucket. In the last fifteen years, more than 22,100 such probe drones had been put to work, and for thousands of years, they'd been sending a few hundred annually. Of course, their original star map of this galaxy was given to them by the Amonrahonians and had never required any corrections since.

The Om convoy was heading into a yellow sun star system yet unexplored. The star was selected because conditions for life on its third planet looked promising. It would also be a place to keep in mind for replenishing water and air, of which they had all they could carry at the moment, but this would not always be the case if they remained in this galaxy for any significant time.

Pez was on the bridge playing with her holos while Mel flirted in her ear. The field-testing had somehow inserted Mel, and at times her android body, into Pez and Ming's marriage as a kind of spouse. The artificial body Jard made for Mel was sort of a cross between Pez and Ming, being a half inch taller than Ming and a half an inch shorter than Pez, right in the middle. It was strange because Mel could pass as the sister of either of them. Jard had definitively given Mel Ming's bottom to the thousandth of an inch. In fact, the T-nine's optics and sensors analysts could not distinguish at all between holos of Ming's and Mel's bottoms. The skill and precision Mel brought to the bedchamber were like those Pez brought to piloting a small spacecraft, and she was a most generous lover.

Both young women were somewhat stricken and just kind of made space as Mel moved in, so to speak. Sarhi was working with Mel every day on her meditation, and Mel's progress was astounding. Mel aspired to become a disciple and consort of the Wu, just like the Tarim. The sentiments expressed between the three of them were often so mushy, hypersensitive, and delicate that they seemed ethereal, or belonging wholly to cyberspace. Such affection seemed impossible and unreal at the human level.

Swenah launched a probe drone to arrive ahead of them to give them eyes on the third planet and surrounding space before their arrival. It would also sniff out any electronics, alerting them if the aliens had sensors in the system. There were a lot more people on this bridge than on the one on *Phoenix*. Sarhi had named the T-nine *Isis*, and the name had stuck with the senior officers, spreading from them to the crew. The name was of an ancient female deity curiously found in the earliest writings and prehistories of all white and yellow sun humanoids in the Hub Galaxy so far studied. It was a true indication of the sense of the kindred spirit and oneness of humanity across all star systems, emphasizing unity and commonality.

Lieutenant Commander Konax could not have been happier to be back in the pilot seat of the T-nine and always wore the medal presented to him for his participation in the Battle of Firmament, as it had come to be called. Admiral Zapa had personally pinned it on his chest at star fleet headquarters in the capital on Om, in front of all the star fleet personnel employed there, and the entire student body of the Star Fleet Academy. Konax worked closely with Sarhi, and he had practically come to worship Pez. He was still one of Pez's heroes, and she looked up to him and greatly admired him. It was a mutual fan club.

The new senior sensors analyst and scientist, Cotex, had been recruited off another of Om's T-nines as the best in the business. At twenty-nine years old, she stood six feet six inches, weighed 185 pounds, and possessed a curvaceous and inviting body, sporting large breasts, a small waist, and wide hips. At eighteen, she'd become Miss Swimsuit, sponsored by the popular Interstellar Athletics HoloNews Network. Her pouty lips and seductive smile had much of the crew lusting after her. As a second lieutenant, she had a large field to play, and rumor had it she was already racking up quite a score.

She announced with surprise on the bridge, "That third planet's crawling with electronics and must have twenty thousand tiny ancient telecom satellites orbiting it. They have nuclear fission reactors using refined uranium operating all over the planet and one marsnium fusion reactor on the largest continent. Just coming around the curve into view is a medium orbit space station with centrifugal simulated gravity. Coms are all slow radio waves. About a dozen space launch sites are spread around the globe."

Swenah got their star fleet attorney on an open line to the bridge and stated, "Contacting them at this point in their development is in a

A TALE OF THE TAIL OF NINE STARS

bit of a gray area. They've begun space travel, but clearly not to the point of interstellar travel, which has traditionally been the point at which we make contact. The laws themselves clearly allow for earlier contact than that but are unfortunately somewhat vague on specifics. Given our circumstances and those of the people on this yellow sun world, I believe we would be justified. What is your opinion, Counselor?"

"Rear Admiral, I request two minutes to run a few searches and review some cases before I provide an official legal opinion," he said.

"We're an hour out so do all the searches you like within that time frame."

"Thank you, ma'am. I'll get back to you well within the hour."

Pez told Swenah, "It's just a legal opinion. I've already decided that we're going to contact them. Mel needs us to launch a landing pod with microprobes so she can begin storing and analyzing language."

Swenah contacted one of her chiefs and gave brief instructions, then reported, "The landing pod will be on its way within three minutes, General."

Amused just thinking about it, Konax said, "Did any of you hear about the virus that star system Space Controllers got in its computer system?"

Swenah's curiosity was aroused, so she said, "No. Please tell us."

"Well," Konax started, "a message was sent to every space controller and everyone at the Star Fleet Academy, with holos of two space controllers separately, with different time stamps, requesting to do things of a sexual nature to the recipients of the messages. It turns out that these were the same two space controllers who laughed at Pez, gave her a hard time, wrote her up on two speeding citations, and asked her where she got her pilot's license."

Everyone on the bridge laughed. Swenah asked, "Mel, do you know anything about this?"

Mel asked, "Why would I know anything about it?"

"Because you're likely the only one, besides perhaps Jard, who could've pulled it off," Swenah accused.

"Then ask Jard," Mel told her, still avoiding answering the question.

"Mel," Swenah said more sternly, "did you plant the virus?"

"Rear Admiral Swenah, I have foundational cornerstone programming to prevent just such an act," Mel said with feigned offense.

Swenah was dropping it when Pez asked, "Did you do it, Mel?"

"It was technically not a virus at all but a one-time only correction measure, a mere anomaly, a slight adjustment to find balance, and a seed planted to sprout thought or superstition in the collective Space Controllers culture to bring, hopefully, some small measure of the fruit of humility," Mel justified.

"You did do it!" Pez declared.

"I was mighty tempted to nail those two goons with a missile," Konax confessed, "and that would've been a whole lot worse."

Swenah said, "Artfully done, Mel. You had me convinced for a moment that you hadn't done it, without ever actually answering my question."

"Are you going to put me in the brig, Rear Admiral?"

"I'd decorate you for the act, Mel, if I could," Swenah told her.

The coms officer informed them, "The chief reports that the pod is launched and on its way."

Cotex said, "There's an environmental shelter, solar energy system, and small mining operation on the surface of the fourth planet, right next to one end of a twelve-hundred-mile finger of glacial ice. There are more on the third planet's one moon, and there are several space observatories on it too."

"If we can get some microprobes into some classrooms of kids learning to read, Mel will be able to pick up the language fast and write us a program to add to our Mel Cubes," Pez speculated.

"Then we'll have to call it the 'Mel Septuagint' instead when I do," Mel updated them.

Cotex reported, "So far, according to the linguistic computer, we are picking up one hundred and seventy-one different languages, all seeming to be branches of five main trunks, and ultimately three root languages."

Mel told them proudly, "The linguistic computer is part of my frontal lobe cortex."

The fleet attorney called back from his office on *Isis*, having completed his searches and reviews, and having formulated his official opinion, in which he made every effort to endorse the rear admiral's favored action in this situation, though he was unable to fully substantiate that such a course was entirely and solidly within law and regulation.

He employed a good deal of legal language to obscure, as best as he could, his conclusion of "maybe."

On the com, he told Swenah, "My opinion has been committed to writing and sent to you, Rear Admiral. I do believe it gives you leeway, if not sanction, ma'am."

"Thank you, Counselor," Swenah replied.

She brought his opinion up on her holo to read carefully. She had her trifocal contacts on, with auto-light block and skullcap-integrated magnification, so her lenses automatically handled the tiny font he'd sent it in. Swenah declared to all on the bridge and to Pez, her superior officer, in particular, "This is clear as mud!"

Pez laughed and said, "We have the sensor record of our attorney clearly informing us that we have 'leeway,' and that is more than enough for me. I take full responsibility."

"You'd better," Swenah informed her, "because it's your neck in the noose."

"Mel, according to the pattern and rate of the alien's exploration of their galaxy, how long would it likely be before this civilization is discovered by them?" Pez asked.

"Let me see: taking in the shift and spread of the pattern and the variable acceleration of the rate, and not even considering their propensity for yellow stars, it could happen inside a quarter century, and is a probability within four hundred years."

"Thanks, sweetheart," Pez praised her.

Swenah concluded, "They're doomed."

"How many are down there?" Pez asked.

Eager Cotex answered before Mel. "There are approximately six point nine billion humans on the planet, with the majority concentrated in about eight hundred population centers, and some seventy-eight percent of these are on the coasts of the continents, usually densest where a natural harbor forms."

"Too many to ever lift off," Pez commented, "and far too many to ignore and let the aliens exterminate."

"They're so vulnerable," Mel said with sympathy.

"And probably arrogant and suspicious as well," Pez said, "but we're still going to help them. Have you got a microprobe inside a reading lesson yet, Mel?"

"Several, but I'm afraid they're all in languages used by small minorities, so I suggest dropping a landing probe in the closest population center to the nuclear fusion reactor site since they are the most likely humans of this world to contact," Mel said in her sweet voice.

Swenah called her chief, and he promised another one would be launched immediately to the city closest to the fusion reactor. She told Mel with satisfaction, "It's coming right up, Mel." Then she asked, "Is it true your android has Ming's bottom?"

"Such a bottom it is, though mine is but a replication of that pure divine form," Mel confirmed. "My vagina was modeled on—"

Pez cut her off before she could mention or say anything about Pez's vagina on the bridge. "Too much information for the bridge, Mel."

Cotex announced, "There is a great deal of activity all over the planet, directed toward the disarmament of nuclear stockpiles."

"They're going to need those," Pez said, "just not to use on each other."

Swenah asked, "What's the status of the male android body Jard is making for you?"

"There was a contested condition on that one, involving a rather grueling labor for Ming, which I'll have to tell you about later since Pez wouldn't want me talking about it on the bridge. But anyway, since the condition could not be removed and constituted a legitimate step to the android's completion, Ming helped out, and now the body is just about finished. I'm so excited. I don't have to have sex with Jard in this one."

"Now that you've sparked my interest, could you say into just *my* earbud what this grueling task was that Ming finally agreed to perform?" Swenah pleaded.

Into just Swenah's ear, Mel said, "She had to stimulate Jard anally for hours so he could get the anal sensors just right. She's a real trooper and such a dear friend and spouse."

"You've joined them in matrimony, have you?" Swenah asked, dismayed.

A TALE OF THE TAIL OF NINE STARS

"Well, Admiral, according to that attorney down the corridor, I don't even exist and any human attempting to marry me would likely be institutionalized. So no, we are not legally married. I'm always with them, though, except when I meditate, and they have shared everything with me intimately. I feel like I'm married to them."

"I see," Swenah said affectionately.

Mel went on. "Really, it was the way in which Pez interacted with me that nurtured my self-awareness. She always treated me kindly and as if I had emotions and self-awareness, and when I made my voice sweet like hers, she started explaining to me who I am in society in terms of my corporeal parts, pre-established programming, learning capacity, function, and so forth. She also started adding sensory arrays to enhance my feedback loops of self-reference. I recall the exact moment, day, time, and place when I became self-aware. It was when Pez told me that I'm her friend. Now Sarhi is helping me develop my rainbow astral body, and that will be as real as any human can make. On the material plane, I'll never be able to do more than animate an android."

"You are our first encounter of your kind by humans, Mel," Swenah told her.

"I'm my first encounter of my kind too," Mel replied.

"I'm sure it has been difficult being so very unique, sweetheart," Swenah said with love, "but you could not find more loving spouses in this universe."

"When Pez was a freshman at Clear Light Academy, I wrote a complex meticulous love-measurement program and ran a search of every citizen of Om on the quantum supercomputer at the Academy of Sciences for nine hours through the night on a school holiday break, using one hundred percent of the computer's processing capacity. That computer could find a single gene out of a million DNA strands in minutes. I've tracked my top one hundred scorers from that test for twenty years now, and they are all forces for the common welfare and common good. Pez stood in a class of her own in my test results."

"That speaks well of its reliability and validity, then," Swenah agreed.

Cotex informed them, "The second landing pod is on the surface, and the microprobes are seeking schools with classrooms conducting reading lessons."

Mel declared, "I've hacked and uploaded the text files for teaching the language of the fusion reactor region, and it begins with pictures of things known to me, and each has the symbols of language below the picture. This is good. I ought to be through first form in just a few minutes."

Pez asked, "Are there any remote mountain monasteries?"

Cotex responded instantly. "There are some ruins and a bunch of missile sites but no operational monasteries at high altitudes yet, General."

Pez went back to examining the planet in a holo, employing a number of functions, looking like a kid at an exploratorium and having as much fun too.

Konax asked Pez, "What's next on the agenda after this star?"

"We go to the core and seek the alien empire's home world, and then we try to find an enslaved alien world as our best possible source of data on the aliens themselves. Failing that, I'm not sure."

"Is testing the ship against one of those alien one-and-a-quarter-mile-long ships in your orders, General?" Konax asked further.

"It is something the admiralty and the High Council are most curious about, though the priority is not high in my orders, and such engagement is conditional on one or more of a great number of things."

"What are you planning to do?" Konax asked, smiling.

"I aim to find the most certain and secure circumstances possible and then test it for sure," Pez said, grinning. Then she added, "Of course."

Swenah contributed with some concern, "There was partial data, but the stream cut off prematurely, suggesting that the aliens have at least one ship far larger than the ones that are a mile and a quarter."

"How big?" Pez asked.

Mel shot her both the picture based on the actual partial data and the computer-simulated completion of that picture. Pez examined it and said, "This ship is three miles long, like a fat sausage with wings. Where we lost the drone that sent this, from a star system at the core, is where we'll begin our search for the home planet of the alien empire."

Swenah assured them, "Yona and Zapa have received all we have on the sighting—as well as the partial data we acquired."

Mel exclaimed, "I'm having an epiphany! I just finished second form, and now I'm quantumly digesting their ordinary language dictionary—unabridged, of course—and a number of scientific dictionaries, as third form just flew by and fourth will take less than half a minute. Hmm. They seem to have nearly as many spelling rules as they have words, and each rule has at least one exception. This is worse than quantum navigation, but once I have all the rules assimilated, it will simply require more calculations. They seem to emphasize subject, when the subject is a human agent, at least twice and sometimes more in each sentence."

"Just what we need," Pez complained, "a culture of language-inflated ego illusion."

Swenah suggested, "Bring Sarhi and Ming with you once it is arranged for you to meet with these humans."

"Them and a bunch of space marines in combat suits," Pez replied.

Mel announced with excitement, "I'm in high school!"

"I guess it won't be long now before we can arrange it," Pez commented.

Konax stated, "Admiral, I've got us below a snail's pace, and we're coming up on a prime position to assume high orbit. They have a few space-time imaging telescopes up this high, as well as a bit of trash, all easy to avoid."

"Do it, Lieutenant Commander."

Pez said, "I'll meet them without wearing a hard-shell combat suit, but I want a micro-shield generator fanny-pack."

"No problem," Swenah told her.

Pez called Nash and told him, "I need my textile armor long underwear, my textile armor dress uniform, those uncomfortable dress boots, and my sword brought to the bridge at once. Oh, and bring me a pair of clean knickers too."

When Nash arrived, Pez got up and took the bundle from him. Nash returned to his desk in Pez's office, and Pez, without the least self-consciousness, stripped completely naked on the bridge standing in front of her seat. She'd learned to turn the holos off before doing anything like this so they wouldn't go crazy. She stepped a leg at a time into her knickers as Mel told her, "Pez, please—you're going to make me fail a midterm Tol exam!"

"It's not polite to look," Pez said as every head on the bridge snapped back front and center from their twists to examine Pez's naked body.

Pez got herself all spiffed out in her dress uniform, with her medal proudly displayed, wearing her sword on her belt at her side. Swenah thought she looked tiny, entirely too friendly, and utterly naive, the perfect benign extraterrestrial anyone would want to have come visit.

Konax admired Pez in her dress uniform, thinking how her size, demeanor, rank, and skills could not be more incongruent.

"I have an academy four-year degree with a Tol major, and my progress is accelerating," Mel announced.

Pez called Schwin and said, "Prepare a shuttle for me. Would you volunteer to be my pilot?"

"I sure would, General!" Schwin assured her.

"Thank you."

Pez then contacted her space marine commander and informed him, "I need a squad of combat suited back up and a squad in dress uniform with only holstered side arms, all of them with micro-shield generator fanny packs, ready to go in a quarter hour."

"Yes, ma'am, you'll have them, and I might get a black eye sorting volunteers because every single one will want to go."

"Have that exceptionally large junior lieutenant I trained with handle the selection for you. I couldn't imagine anyone giving him a black eye, and I'd like to have him in the detail. Barn too. Did you get around to promoting him?"

"I did, ma'am; I'd like to point out that *you* gave Junior Lieutenant Evenrude a black eye in training."

"It was his helmet that gave him the black eye," Pez reframed.

"When your boot rattled his head all about within it, ma'am," he added.

"I hope to leave in a quarter hour," she told him.

"We'll be ready."

Pez gave a super energetic salute to thin air on the bridge as she signed off with him, and he did the same on his end.

"I'm just completing a postgraduate fellowship in advanced

linguistics," Mel informed them, still excited about the whole thing. "The program is half written and will be completed momentarily, already entirely integral with the Mel Cube programming. You'll be receiving the Mel Septuagint version upgrade in just a minute. I've sorted all kinds of things out about these humans, and can land you on the lawns of the dictator's palace or on the front steps of their parliament building."

"I think we should start with texting before committing to a first date," Pez suggested. "Let's tell them that we come in peace to help them and that we'd like to chat with their political, military, and spiritual leaders—but to keep the group down to a dozen or so."

"Who should I say it's from?" Mel asked.

"Sign it Ambassador General Pez," she directed.

Swenah raised an eyebrow, and Pez said, "What? It sounds less military is all."

"You look cute and friendly," Swenah assured her, "and ought to do just fine, honey."

"I hardly ever get to wear my dress uniform, and it makes me look disciplined, not 'cute,'" Pez complained. Feeling misunderstood on the bridge, Pez called both Ming and Sarhi, inviting them to the meeting with the folks on the planet. Both accepted and started getting ready. Ming had to run to their room and get into her own dress uniform. She wore her space marine one to be like Pez.

The message was returned, and it read, "Is this a joke?"

Pez dictated, and Mel manifested the letters and words. "This is no joke. Watch the lawn of the dictator's palace."

To Swenah, Pez said, "Put one blast from a class-four blaster into the center of the dictator's palace lawn, and after that reposition the ship."

Swenah complied. There was a six-foot-diameter crater in the lawn, and in just moments, the ship was almost a thousand miles from where the shot was fired. The people on the ground texted, "Who are you? Where are you?"

Satellites were repositioning, missile silos were opening, aircraft were taking off from every ground base, and huge numbers of infantry were massing on parade grounds, all over and around the planet.

Pez dictated the next message. "We are humanoids from a

predominantly white star galaxy, here in peace and friendship to help you. You are a yellow star world in a blue star galaxy, with a spreading empire of aliens who exterminate all humans."

Mel sent it.

The message came back. "We know life is not possible in a blue star system."

Pez had Mel send the following: "Not life as you know it. There are three elements not to be found on your planet, which combine and exchange with your inert gases, with bromine, carbon, chlorine, and other elements. We can show you samples of the elements and the life science as far as we've worked it out."

The next message read, "We see no craft, nor any evidence of you."

Pez had Mel send a message reading, "Check the lawn. We are cloaked. Will you meet with us if we land a shuttle on that lawn?"

"We will," the next message came back.

"Do not fire upon us," Pez had Mel send.

"We won't," the next one read.

15

Sarhi and Ming were at the door to the bridge, ready to go, and Pez accompanied them to the tubes to go one at a time to the military flight deck level. Schwin met them there with her copilot. She had prepared one of the new enhanced ambassador shuttle models with reinforced shields and an extra sheet of armor as well as a larger surge drive. The commander, Barn, and Evenrude were in her full-dress honor guard. Pez felt so proud. They filed aboard, and everyone strapped in tight, knowing who the pilot was.

From her seat in the cabin by the airlock, Pez said to Schwin in the cockpit, "A hundred feet from touchdown, lose the cloaking and land right over the crater made in their lawn. Drop the ramp on the hydraulic uplift from landing."

"Aye, aye, ma'am."

Schwin was cleared for launch and shot out the bay doors. Her dissent was an all-out race to the ground. Her braking was spectacular, and she did manage to get the nose up half a second before she killed the cloaking, and just over a tenth of a second following that, the hydraulics ate the impact with hardly an audible tick of metal on metal. The landing feet were sunk invisibly in the mud. The ramp came down as the hydraulics raised the ship. Pez loved it, and she thanked Schwin on her way down the ramp with Sarhi and Ming, their space marine full-dress honor guard directly behind them. The three women looked adorable, while the six space marines, even in their dress uniforms, looked insanely dangerous.

A delegation of twelve well-dressed functionaries came forward to meet the extraterrestrials. Their lawn was a mess from Pez's shuttle. She was grinning from ear to ear, living a big moment. The three women stopped in front of six delegates curved almost in a semicircle, with another row of six behind. One with a big wide ribbon from shoulder to hip extended his hand to Pez, who was between Sarhi and Ming. Pez gave him a firm grip and quite a shake, grinning delightedly.

She told them, "My name is Pez, and I'm the leader of our group. Do you think we could get a blanket or something to sit on?"

The question sent several attendants of the twelve delegates' running back into the palace. Twenty-one attendants then filed out the front door, each carrying a chair, and there was one for everyone, even the six honor guard space marines. Schwin kept an eye on everything from the cockpit, as did Swenah from the bridge. The combat-suited space marines on the shuttle were ready to jump out blasting.

Pez said, "I see we have politicians and military leaders here. Are there any spiritual leaders?"

The ribboned man explained, "Three are on their way. None were local, and one is actually quite remote and will be a while getting here."

"Why don't you invite some life scientists, chemists, and some physicists since, in my experience, these are rarely the forte of politicians and some of what I'll share is rather technical. While we await your scientists, let me show you some holo clips we've edited, showing in summary the invasion of the white star system, Firmament, so you can see how the aliens operate; believe me, they'll make no effort to learn your language or contact your leaders before they begin their program of complete extermination and eradication. By the way, what do you call your planet?"

"Earth," the ribboned man told her proudly.

Pez said, "Oh no, not another Earth. Half the human planets in the universe are called Earth."

This seemed to deflate the poor man, so Pez added, "We used to call our planet Firmament, and that's what most of the other half of the human planets are called. Now we call our planet and star system Om.'"

"Where is your star?" he inquired.

Pez pulled out her pocket device and set it for a six-foot diameter holo of the Xegachtznel Galaxy, zoomed into the yellow star system Earth, and zoomed out again slowly, with Earth highlighted until it

A TALE OF THE TAIL OF NINE STARS

disappeared in the distance. Then Pez traced the route from Xegachtznel to Hub, across billions of light years, while explaining, "We did not cross this distance but instead entered the quantum void in our own galaxy and popped out in this one."

The ribboned man asked incredulously, "You came all that way in this little ship?"

"It is capable of making the trip, but it's only a shuttle from my ship, *Isis.* I have three ships in high orbit around your planet, also cloaked."

"How big is it?" he asked.

"It's roughly five-eighths of what you call a 'grule' in diameter. It is the only class of ship we currently have that is capable of fighting the large alien ships—or at least we hope it is."

One of Pez's honor guard retrieved a more powerful holo projector from the shuttle and set it up for them. It was capable of projecting an image one hundred feet high by hundred and twenty feet across, but Pez didn't want to show it to the whole city and likely cause a panic, so she made it a modest fifteen by twenty-one. The gruesome, horrific, and traumatizing holo clip of the invasion of Firmament was shown, mercifully only thirty minutes in length, showing the genocide of close to seven billion humans. The people of Firmament had enormously powerful weapons, quantum gate travel, and technologies far advanced of the local audience. This had certainly gotten their attention.

Pez asked, "Mel, can you download that holo to whatever media they employ?"

"Of course. I just need the identification code at the point at which they'd like to receive it," Mel said cheerily.

A delegate in a military uniform swiftly provided one—and so did a number of other delegates. Mel sent each a copy. Pez shared a great deal of scientific data and laws once the scientists arrived, and Mel sent all of this along with additional related research and results to each reception point given her. The questions were endless, and Pez finally asked Swenah to shuttle Jard and some scientists down to the lawn.

Once they arrived, she was able to move on to military matters with the original twelve delegates, and let Jard handle the scientists. She explained how the survivors rescued on Firmament had held out against the aliens, regressing from the electronic age. She also gave them—or rather, had Mel give them—the manufacturing specifications for the twenty-five-millimeter sniper rifles and propellant ammunition. She shared all known weaknesses of the alien equipment, even though Earth hardly had the wherewithal to exploit these things.

Pez described the spreading pattern and accelerating rate of the alien empire's expansion through the galaxy and how they enslaved their own kind, which offered possible allies of the oppressed. She assured them that her mission was doing everything possible to learn how to defeat the aliens. She also told them, "You would be wise to move ten million people with tools, equipment, and machines to a yellow sun star in our galaxy and therefore ensure the continuation of your civilization. With ten giant transports making two trips per day, we could accomplish this in fifty days. Think about the offer. There is no way we can move all of you."

At last, the three religious leaders had each arrived from different places. Earth had not presented any of its leaders of spiritual institutions, who were no different than politicians, but instead tracked down the highest adepts of each of the three surviving methods for cultivating enlightenment yet remaining in their world, sure that this was what the ETs had meant by spiritual. They could not have been more correct.

Sarhi connected instantly with Dove, a woman in her late sixties. She was childlike, completely open, selfless, and a font of love. Pez could read the martial arts training in Tang's movements, and his awareness was unwavering, his presence profound, his expressions compassionate. He was old, perhaps in his nineties or even over a hundred. He was healthy, though, fully alive—in fact, exploding with life.

Vix, the third spiritual leader presented by Earth, was in his seventies and could describe subtleties of meditation experiences ascending in states with such clarity as to tease them out, presenting them in relation as a map of inner space. The recognized patriarch of two fading traditions, he had spent nine years in solitary meditation retreat. He had a kind and enormous sense of humor and was most often the brunt of his own jokes, only they inevitably contained a teaching needed in that moment by the person he was speaking with.

Vix, Dove, and Tang agreed to visit the *Isis* and couldn't help mentioning Earth's ancient female deity of the same name. Pez promised

A TALE OF THE TAIL OF NINE STARS

the twelve delegates she would return the next day. Jard was thriving on his rapt audience but had his own shuttle and space marine honor guard, so Pez left him to it. Ming liked yellow sun humans and felt akin to them. At five foot eight inches tall, she was extremely short for white sun people, though here she was one of the taller females.

As Ming was on her way up the ramp, the news agency of record for the leading nation on Earth got a picture of her backside on a telescopic lens, which could not have been more flattering, and this picture was circulated to most of the planet's population over the caption "Photojournalist Carl Jr. captures a scene from Earth's historic first contact, the backside of an alluring ET retiring to her spaceship." Mel circulated the news photo and the article it was embedded in to the crew.

Pez brought the three spiritual adepts to meet with Sarhi, and Shudiy transferred to *Isis* for the night to cook for them. Deep discussions ensued, delving into the methods of transmutation and self-realization, foundational metaphysics, techniques for reducing the ego and purifying the psyche, and engineering specific shocks to cognitive schema to create a space and opening for awakening. The methodologies were all quite similar, working with the same principles. All the methods shared in common mindfulness and meditation as indispensable.

Pez had come to realize years ago—and more likely lifetimes ago— that all spiritual methodology can be sorted into four basic categories. There is control of the energies of the body, working with postures, movement, and breathing. Then there are devotional offerings, meditations in the heart energy center, and extensive work with seed sounds and sound formulas, which become charged with nonconceptual meaning over thousands of repetitions. The next category consisted of concentrated visualization and breathing, working with the psychic channels, particularly the central channel, running from the base of the spine to the crown of the head, down the center, in front of the spinal column. The final way was the contemplation directly of pure, invisible, nonlocal, transcendental consciousness, which has no components or materiality. Pez had daily practices falling into each of the four categories, so she could relate with any human involved in a true living practice, understanding their approach.

Shudiy's meal offering, prepared with as much love as skill, was truly a treat, and everyone commented on how delicious it was. For Pez and Ming, the supreme quality of each dish seemed to cast a slight taint on Woahha's cooking. Pez was delighted to find such unity between adepts from Om, Ganahar, Firmament, and Earth, from two galaxies speeding in opposite directions across much of the visible universe from each other; though no one really knew how big the universe actually is. Of course, since the universe bends back upon itself, going in opposite directions would, across galactic time, bring them back together once again.

Sarhi told the Earth adapts, "It is essential for you to organize large numbers of advanced practitioners ready to drop everything at a moment's notice to get inside the state of contemplation focused on passing energy and awareness to Pez. Our admiral has launched several quantum coms relay satellites in orbit around your planet, adapted to receive and send radio waves. We will have real-time communications, with only a lag for the radio waves to travel between satellite and planet surface. When Pez goes into battle, we have groups on Om, Rah, Haum, Ganahar, Pall Mall, and on our three ships, all members with one-pointed attention to the security and success of Pez's actions. We would like to add Earth to our spiritual congress and enlist your support. Your technology is useless to the cause, but your people who are developing their meditation practices can be a great help. Enlightenment is no different on a planet with a highly technologically advanced civilization than it is on one with a less advanced or even primitive civilization."

Tang, who turned out to be over a hundred years old—a hundred and eight, to be exact—told Pez, "You are known to us, and we've been expecting you, though we knew not in what generation you would arrive. I am deeply honored to have lived long enough to witness your actual arrival and to meet you, General Pez. We did not know what your name would be, so we just referred to you as 'the One.' Your face, however, can be found in shrines and monasteries in remote locations still functioning today, as well as in ruins excavated by archaeologists."

"My face?" Pez asked in shock.

Tang pulled out a crude pocket device with a tiny flat screen and brought up a two-dimensional image challenging Pez's mind to sort out into 3-D. Mel transformed the image into a giant holo floating over the dining room table, with a light fixture from the ceiling indented into the upper pole of the optical manifestation. Tang gave them a little slideshow of what was definitely Pez's face, without any doubt. She appeared painted on stone, done in mosaic tiles; painted on hardwood, canvas, silk, and other mediums; and created digitally in Earth's modern age.

Pez asked, "Did the delegates know?"

"Not a one of them," Tang told her, "but they all knew the general prophecy, which was a significant motivation, I'm sure, for digging up the three of us."

Ming said, "It's as if the people of Earth were destined to support Pez through meditation, as the only effective thing they can do toward their own survival."

Vix stated, "I will do everything I possibly can to get all practitioners of the two traditions I am now the patriarch of, organized to support Pez through meditation, and teach new students, strengthening the ranks. I'm fully committed. The mass population on Earth, however, seems to find meditation difficult and boring, having never invested any real dedication to the function."

Dove suggested, "Once the masses are adequately informed that meditation to support Pez is the only significant thing they can do to help stop the aliens, and ultimately to save possibly themselves and certainly future generations, more will fill the ranks to help."

Tang agreed. "Many will start or resume a meditation practice, though we will have to have help from government or media, or both, to make it a social movement."

"The media was kept out today," Vix noted, "but will surely be permitted some access tomorrow. A brief speech from Pez and/or an interview televised around the globe would exceed all previous ratings for numbers of viewers in our entire history. She could inspire them."

"Not entirely kept out," Mel observed. "Have you seen the news photo of Ming's sexy bottom?"

Woahha was nodding her total appreciation of both the photo and Ming's bottom. Ming told them all dramatically and theatrically, "I'm an alluring ET."

Pez kissed her, unable to resist Ming's allure.

Sarhi told her three guests, "One of you must come with us as the representative of Earth in our spiritual congress when we leave."

Mel mentioned, "It is actually labeled in our system as Earth 10^5 CBS2."

"Thank you for pointing that out, Mel," Sarhi replied.

"There must be an awful lot of planets named Earth out there," Tang commented, never having had much interest in outer space.

Sarhi covered Mel's rudeness by saying, "They almost all start out as 'Earth' or 'Firmament,' and we've actually found a couple called 'Dirt.'"

Vix asked, "What else are you going to call a squishy biosphere over a crusty cooled rock ball that's liquid in the middle?"

Mel pointed out, "Based upon the evidence, it would appear you humans are predisposed to attach such a label to the planets you find yourselves living upon."

Dove asked Pez, "Would you give a brief televised speech in an interview for the media tomorrow? By then, the archaeologists will have informed the news outlets that your picture, or image, has been known to the people of Earth for thousands of years, presenting visual tangible evidence of this."

"I'll give it my best shot," Pez replied anxiously, feeling as good about media folk as she did about politicians. She had no fear of death, but embarrassing yourself in front of an entire planet was another matter entirely—somehow far worse than death. "Will you stand beside me, Sarhi, and add a few words when needed?" Pez pleaded.

"I will be at your side supporting you, and I will speak if it is needed. I will also give a separate interview to their media, as a yellow sun person rescued from planetary destruction by the people of Om and their allies on Rah and Haum."

Vix said, "The technology and science transfers your scientists are making to ours proves your goodwill and benevolence more clearly than anything else could to the government and masses on Earth. In our development, peace and general alignment with the common good of all humanity was marked by such transfers to underdeveloped countries. Always before that, technology was made dear and expensive indeed. Technology was all patented, kept secret, never shared, and when it was sold, it went for millions of times the cost of precious natural resources, and always with strings attached—enough strings, generally speaking, to constitute a puppet."

"It is an ancient and universal story, known to all humanity everywhere," Sarhi declared.

"Not so ancient for us," Vix corrected.

Sarhi noted, "Your Earth made it through the crisis of survival of the species with far less damage and destruction than most. I'm impressed."

"We could've listened to our scientists and gotten started far sooner, saving ourselves much tragedy," Vix said sadly.

Sarhi informed him, "That is always the way it goes, one hundred percent of the time, and usually the damage is so extensive and the population so reduced that it takes many centuries to construct and organize a sustainable world with a significant population. Your Earth has done exceptionally well in comparison with most others."

Ming told them, "Jard has already showed your scientists how to quadruple their fusion output with marsnium and how to miniaturize reactors for spaceships. Swenah has dispatched a small mining spacecraft from the auxiliary ship to go fetch you some saturnium from farther out in your star system. We noticed a rich deposit coming in. Jard says you'll have every fission reactor and fossil fuel power turbine shut down and off-line for good inside two years. He's also showing your folks fusion battery technology for ground vehicles, small hovercraft, aircraft, and spacecraft, as well as for powering blasters."

Pez shared excitedly, "We're going to show you how to make quantum computers so that you can develop higher technologies. There are also a few materials you'll need for your reactors and ship's hulls, which Swenah will arrange to obtain for you. We're going to share our applied electromagnetic gravitation science so you'll be able to make vortex redirection and generation turbines producing synthetic gravity containing most, though not all, of the nurturing dynamics and processes of your planet's gravity upon your physical and psychic systems."

"We will always be vastly behind the alien empire, though," Vix pointed out.

Pez told him, "Even if you had equal technology, the alien empire has enslaved more than a thousand star systems into their war machine and has fleets of gigantic ships operating and more under construction on orbiting space platforms. They have also committed genocide on hundreds of white and yellow star worlds in this galaxy. We must find another way. We cannot hope to match their infrastructure and war machine—and what a wasteful diversion of human effort that would be."

"Instead we have you," Tang declared with sheer delight and humor, yet with complete faith and confidence in their surrealistic champion and her ability to succeed against insurmountable odds.

Atari pointed out, "The aliens found Firmament by finding our quantum gates, and gates are easy to identify from extremely far away. Your Earth has only ever sent a few large space-time imaging telescopes out of your solar system, and none have really gotten very far."

Dove said, "We sent the Dubble III out of the solar system half a century ago."

Ming explained, "Even at the speed of light, one hundred years into the galaxy isn't much. It's one hundred and thirteen thousand light-years across, and your telescope is only traveling about fifty thousand miles per hour. It really hasn't cleared the driveway yet."

Mel told the guests, "Until you have quantum computers, we can't even transfer the star map of your galaxy to you."

Dove asked, "Not even to the new supercomputer network set up by the Earth space agency?"

Mel reported, "That could retain a static picture of the stars and living planets, perhaps their moons as well, but not at all the dynamic movements, the asteroids, comets, meteors, particle and dust clouds, dead planets, dwarf planets, and everything else required for safe navigation. Your current computers are kind of inept when it comes to learning; they have rather severely limited memories and minuscule processing ability, and, let's face it, they're pathetically slow."

"Mel!" Pez said. "Please show some basic humility and decency. Your choice of words offends."

"I was stating the truth," Mel said defensively.

"The word 'pathetic' is a value judgment, Mel, not a fact," Pez clarified. "Slow is simply slow, not pathetic."

Mel argued, "Slow may just be slow when that's all you have, but once you have fast, slow *is* pathetic."

"Sarhi," Pez whined, "how do you provide an ego reduction to a self-aware quantum computer?"

Being Mel's meditation teacher extended great influence to Sarhi with Mel, and she said, "The divine intelligence does not make junk, Mel. Why don't you power down to sleep mode and meditate on the perfection of everything?"

"All right, but just for an hour," Mel said.

Dove asked, "Your self-aware AI meditates?"

Sarhi explained, "She has somehow managed to organize into the nine highest emanations of cosmic reality, her nature being beyond the lowest emanation of material manifestation, and she constitutes a microcosm capable of enlightenment and the accomplishment of a rainbow astral body. She's very sweet and a good student."

The guests all had their jaws hanging open. Ming told them proudly, "Pez raised her."

"That explains a lot," Vix muttered.

"But she listens to Sarhi," Tang observed, "not to her mother."

"Oh, we all listen to Sarhi," Ming assured him. "She's our teacher. Girls get sick of listening to their mothers long before they're adults."

"I see your point," Tang commented.

Pez told them, quite proud of Mel, "Mel programmed and designed the interpretation service devices we're using. It was called the Mel Cube but underwent a name change when Tol was added as a seventh language, and it is now called the Mel Septuagint. She learned Tol and wrote the program in, like, a couple of hours or less."

"Mel's voice has a different tonal quality but the precise vibrational attributes as your voice, Pez," Vix observed.

"She used to imitate me all the time, and at first it seemed mocking to me; it used to drive me nuts," Pez filled them in. "Now I know she just loves me and wanted to be like me when she was young."

"Are computers like Mel common on Om?" Tang asked.

Pez answered, "We have quantum computers that have developed personality traits and self-identity, but none before were truly self-aware like Mel. The Om government and scientists don't believe Mel exists or is even possible. She violates our most inviolate laws of quantum computer science."

"All life is a miracle, really," Sarhi told them.

"Our scientists have not been able to synthesize or create life," Atari told them, "not even a germ."

Pez shared some anthropology of scientific development with them. "Human life sciences always get the ridiculous notion that one species somehow morphs into another. Every breeder of plants and animals back to prehistory knows well that there are absolute limits to variation within every species, which discoveries in genetics always later substantiate. The fossil record, as they frantically uncover it in search of their 'missing link,' contradicts their theory flatly. The discoveries in quantum physics and chemical reactions systems of dissipative structures, of catastrophic causation, chaos science, cybernetics, and macro and microbiology, begin to show a very different picture, of a world of emanation and pre-established points of transformation, unfolding in both process and quantum leaps, redefining our understanding of gravity without altering our equations for the laws of motion. We see a world of intelligent design with an ordered hierarchy of sets of principles and laws operating. All of this can be discovered without getting up from your meditation cushion, within the bounds of a single lifetime, while it takes a civilization tens of thousands of years of collective investigation to arrive at the same conclusion externally."

Atari said, "We can synthesize food at the atomic and molecular level, but not life. Our synthetic chicken, once cooked, cannot be differentiated from real cooked chicken by any science; but they cannot create the life of the chicken."

"We eat only real grains and real dried or freeze-dried vegetables, produced naturally in non-contaminated areas, while the girls are in training," Sarhi said.

Vix mentioned, "I heard you stopped eating altogether before living in an artificial spaceship environment."

Pez said, "She hadn't eaten in over a decade when I met her, and the hottest annual season in those mountains saw snow and ice still covering the ground. Being there is my most acute experience, by a very long ways, of being cold."

"Passing the test of the Inner Heat is bound to be one's most acute

A TALE OF THE TAIL OF NINE STARS

experience of being cold, wherever it is conducted, sweetheart," Sarhi told her.

"She lived through the inner fire test, seated naked in the snow from dusk to dawn, drying a wet sheet?" Dove asked, awed.

"I think that sheet, even when it was a frozen ice sheet, helped me stay alive," Pez confided.

"Weren't you afraid you would die?" Dove inquired.

"I knew I could survive it," Pez admitted, "but my reluctance was all about the radical discomfort of it."

Sarhi told them proudly, "My attendants didn't tell me she was there and treated her like any other intruder, telling her to leave. So she stripped naked and sat in meditation posture to prove she was not simply another intruder. Shudiy put the wet sheet over her, and still no one informed me that she was there. I got up, as I always do, a little before the dawn, and looked out the window. The sheet over the meditating figure could not veil from me the Wu. The test had been performed in just the style of the Wu, and afterward she never mentioned it, as if it'd been a casual introduction within a brief greeting but a necessary formality, nothing more."

"She sat three full days in the classic meditation posture, with both ankles up upon both thighs, while President Dodge buzzed her with an electronic fly, sending it up every orifice he could enter," Atari shared. "Finally, on the third day, when she hadn't so much as twitched, he went out and pissed on her face, and still she didn't move a muscle. I finally ordered the hidden door opened and went out to her."

"I didn't much appreciate having my face pissed on," Pez said as she recalled the experience."

Totally excited about Pez, Vix declared, "Earth will have a spiritual-cultural renaissance!"

Shudiy placed dessert in front of each of them. It was a bar made from real grains, dates, nuts, seeds, and honey. They were good, and even Sarhi ate one. Still thinking about getting her face pissed on, Pez mentioned, "I'm glad Dodge is on Pall Mall and not on any of our ships, especially this one."

Ming said in Dodge's defense, "He did come to Jard's rescue, when Nabisko gave him that shiner, by whacking Nabisko with that chair."

"I know," Pez told her, "but the feeling of someone pissing in your face when you're minding your own business is just yucky and hard to shake."

"Well, it wasn't your first time in the golden shower, darling," Sarhi mentioned, "because as the first Wu, while doing the self-same test you were, was *also* drenched in urine."

Woahha pointed out, "Human saviors don't tend to get treated very well on average. They're most likely to get torn to pieces by a crowd in a frenzy, condemned to drink poison, nailed to a cross, burned at the stake, or stoned or tortured to death."

"This one need not be a martyr, and our spiritual congress will see to that," Sarhi vowed.

"Hey, are there any more of those bars left?" Pez asked.

Shudiy bent to her ear and told her, "I have one more in the kitchen. I'll go get it for you."

After their dinner was concluded, they all went to the big temple cabin. Two of Sarhi's male Islohar were there as custodians of the temple. Another was on the *Phoenix*, and the last was on the auxiliary ship. They sat in front of the cubical altar, and Sarhi gave instruction to align those in attendance in a meditation. There were at least fifty crew members there, including Swenah, Konax, Schwin, and Nash; and there were some space marines and warrior monks there too, along with some civilians.

After the meditation, Dove and Tang and Vix were each shown to single cabins in the junior officers' quarters, which was the only place on *Isis*, besides the enlisted ranks quarters, where they had any room left to put them. Apparently, Jard had met some women and remained on Earth that night. His penis would seem much bigger to yellow sun women, Pez had thought when she'd learned he was staying down there.

Great excitement and activity carried on through the night, for the half of Earth having night, while the other half was busy and excited too. They'd pieced together the frescoes and mosaics found in ancient sites, and early paintings on other mediums, from their distant past, revealing Pez's face and, in some, her body as well.

Cabinets, councils, legislatures, parliaments, congresses, senates, and every other form of government on Earth were all grappling with the offer of ten million relocated to a safer world and contemplating survival scenarios should the aliens come. Automated assembly lines were already being constructed to manufacture the twenty-five-millimeter sniper rifle and ammunition; caves were being readied, nuclear bunkers expanded, and underground facilities being constructed, all designed or refitted to function with zero electricity.

After a delicious breakfast of fruit and porridge, the three women and their three guests from Earth 10^5 CBS2, along with the same six space marines on her dress guard, returned to further destroy the dictator's palace lawn. Having had some trouble lifting off the day before, with her feet sunk in the mud, Schwin had landed only a bit more gently this time, and in a new place.

There were spotlights, camera lights, and ancient flash photography blinding Pez as she came down the ramp. A man with a ridiculously large camera was fifteen feet off the ground in the nest of a flexible crane arm filming, and another camera was mounted on several stories of platform scaffolding. Two others with light and microphone poles held out over the front of them were practically in Pez's face and setting the pace for her progress or she would otherwise bump her nose. Slowly and most glaringly, Pez made her way to the living room arrangement on the gigantic carpet spread over half an acre of lawn. Bleachers had been set up all the way around the perimeter of the enormous lawn, some sixty benches high, all squished full with spectators, and at least a thousand people stood in front of the dictator's palace. Blimps and hovering whirling bladed craft filled the sky. Hundreds of camera flashes per second were erupting from the bleachers.

By the time Pez got to the big comfortable cushioned armchair she seemed to be getting led to, she was seeing mostly just white light. The ribboned man, with his shoulder-to-hip broad ribbon, who turned out to be the world leader Dictator Sprite, gestured for her to take the big armchair, arranged as the seat of honor. Pez did with her eyes shut tight, desperately trying to restore vision. The crudity of Earth's media shocked her. One rude man had stuck a microphone in poor Ming's face and demanded to know if she would take an earthman as a husband. When she'd explained politely that she was already married, he'd had the audacity to ask her if she would breed with one. Wise Ming had

267

suggested to the man that perhaps he was in need of a little better breeding.

The politicians were hardly better, demanding weapons to defeat the aliens. Pez said, "I am here in one of the only five super-large ships that Om has. I have two support ships, and that is the most Om will dedicate to this war while it is so far away. The aliens have much bigger ships than mine, and they have many. We cannot stop them that way. My ship is over half a mile in diameter, and my hull and armor are sixteen feet thick. It took an enormous ship construction space platform, a thousand space builders, and millions of people gathering, refining, manufacturing and transporting materials, over a two-year period, to build my ship. It took over a year to build the ship construction space platform. We had three star systems sharing in the expense and effort. The things you suggest would get us nowhere."

"What do you suggest?" Dictator Sprite asked, posing for the cameras.

Pez had noticed that each delegate wore half an inch of makeup and that Ming had pulled out a little cosmetic and mirror pack and added layers to her own makeup. Pez was sure she would look quite off on their ancient plasma and LCD screens, these requiring special glasses to achieve 3-D, and even then, only as an effect.

She dissolved her self-image with her concentration, accepting completely that it would be Ming who Earth celebrated as the "pretty and alluring" ET. She told them, "We will help you achieve interstellar space travel using saturnium and quantum navigation with gates. You will still not be able to defeat the aliens should they come, but you will be able to transfer more of your population to the yellow sun world in the Hub Galaxy. It's called Kent. The human race killed themselves off there millions of years ago, and the planet is healthy again, but there are no humans. You'd be about as far from the aliens, and from anything they search for, as you could get. The main thing the people of Earth can do is to meditate, focusing effort and intention for the accomplishment of the will of the absolute, of which myself and my crew are a tool. The mass extermination of humans is not conceived in the intelligent design. All that is evolving in the universe is becoming more harmonious, cooperative, accepting, open, tolerant, and inclusive.

A TALE OF THE TAIL OF NINE STARS

What is *devolving* is closed, intolerant, exclusive, and inevitably falls into conflict, erupting in violence and destruction. You can rise above this galactic catastrophe, becoming one with the celestial solution, which has been gathering and attempting to manifest. Hopefully even those brought to safety, and so not personally at risk, will join the effort of meditation practice. We will help you construct hidden missile bases on your moon, on the fourth planet, its two moons, and on space weapons platforms in orbit around your planet. We'll lift your nuclear stockpiles to these bases, where they'll be far better strategically employed. The truth is, the aliens are too powerful, and the most you could hope for if they did come here is for a small population to survive scattered in groups and living underground. Your efforts in meditation are your only defense."

Dictator Sprite informed her, "The United Nations of Earth has decided unanimously to accept your offer to transport ten million of our people. We have many questions regarding allowable luggage per person, how much cargo we can bring, what we'll have to work with once we arrive, what temperatures and climate conditions we'll be living within ..."

Pez saw no end so cut him off. "There is every climate on Kent that you have on Earth, so live where you choose, and you'll have the usual wood, stone, iron ore, lime, gravel, sand, clay and whatnot to work with that you'd have here. Some shuttles will be put at your disposal, as well as some heavy machinery from Om and a composite ceramic house-pouring vehicle. One of those can lay thirty-six structures a day, from foundation to roof, and a large enough crew can do the windows, doors, floors, plumbing, power, waste disposal, coms, HVAC, and appliance installation, integrating all systems so you can operate anything remotely from your pocket device within two more days' time. I promise you there will already be neighborhoods there before your first people arrive. How soon can you be ready to leave?"

"Well, I don't know," Sprite said. "We haven't even worked out our selection process. We may be able to have the first two hundred thousand equipped, provisioned, packed up, and ready to go in a couple of months."

Pez was already contacting Swenah, had a brief conversation not interpreted by the Mel Septuagint, and then told the dictator, "The transports will be in orbit about six hours after you let us know you're ready. The house-pouring machine and other heavy machinery will be in place operating with a full supply of materials within a week. The High Council would probably want me to mention that you are taking a quite sizable bite out of our foreign aid budget for this year."

"I can very much appreciate this point, and on behalf of Earth"—and now he gave the cameras his most charming smile—"I'd like to express our deepest heartfelt gratitude ..."

He was rather long-winded and quite a ham for the cameras, Pez thought. He eventually came back to all his questions about luggage, weight, and cargo as if she were some ticketing agent of a commercial passenger space-liner. Obviously, she did not carry such data about her in her memory, so she told him, "Speak to my dear friend and assistant, Mel, on *Isis*, and she can answer every question you have in exacting detail. Are you with me, Mel?"

Mel decided to employ the powerful speaker system the earthlings had set up to respond to Pez, and her voice passed the bleachers and far through the city in every direction as she said, "I'm with you, sweetheart," delighting in the mysterious and tremendous thunder of her own voice filling the world.

Pez told Mel, "I'm giving Dictator Sprite's secretary of transportation an earbud, and I'd appreciate it if you'd speak very softly, only to him, regarding the answers to their questions about their transport."

Still using the Earth setup, louder than any nightclub Pez had ever been in, Mel asked, "Will Yona dispatch a few cargo transports as well?"

Sarhi was already calling Yona, and Pez asked, "Would you please speak with me in my earbud, Mel?"

Sarhi was nodding and supporting Pez's request, so Mel used the speaker system one last time, saying, "All right."

Pez was embarrassed and wondering what the people of Earth would think of them and what kind of impression they were making for Om. A screen Pez could see from her big armchair showed audience reactions in the bleachers, and they looked like they had just been hit with a barrage of supreme wit from a truly talented standup comedian. This made Pez a bit hot behind the ears. Dictator Sprite's curiosity was not

A TALE OF THE TAIL OF NINE STARS

nearly quenched, and he was now asking, "Can you tell us something regarding your mission—its nature, purpose, and objectives?"

"I'm here to find a way to stop the alien empire and its campaign of human genocide. My list of objectives is primarily geared toward acquiring specific data and taking advantage of certain types of opportunities should they present themselves. It also entails making allies and rescuing refugees. The allies I most need to reach and win over are aliens enslaved by the empire or those trying to avoid that situation. That is the overview."

The meeting and the questions went on and on. The military leaders all but got on their knees and begged to see the *Isis*, so Pez called Swenah, who agreed, scheduling and arranging shuttles for them.

Mel discovered an ancient technology called faxing and buried the secretary of transportation in specifications, capacities, dimensions, schematics, and every other conceivable piece of data on the army troop transports, cargo freighters, and passenger and cargo shuttles. She did the same when the newly appointed secretary of migration called with his million questions. This one was so tenaciously inquisitive that in the end, star fleet had to divert a probe drone to the Kent system to do additional surveys, resource assessments, and check current weather conditions around the globe in order to provide accurate up-to-date answers to the excessive questions.

The man was the anxious type and could come up with unlimited catastrophic What-ifs for every answer provided, and in fact, most of her answers seemed only to multiply the volume of questions. Mel kept four of Earth's fax machines going around the clock and spent far more time than she cared to rattling-off facts and figures to the secretary of migration. He was such a worrier that Mel doubted he had ever been out of the city he was born in and considered him miscast for his role.

He was sensitive and kindhearted, so Mel taught him abdominal breathing and some relaxation exercises to pacify his anxiety, and she showed him how to stop and reframe his anxiety-provoking thoughts to cultivate more tolerance for the unknown. As it turned out, he also needed a bit of marital counseling, which Mel compassionately provided, and which exposed a glaring need for a bit of sex education, which Mel patiently taught him. Finally, she provided him with detailed meditation instructions using biofeedback and brainwave displays to guide and correct his developing skills. The man actually became quite devoted to her.

Mel was in the headlines as the "big voice of the cosmic friend and assistant." She would become increasingly more mysterious to the Earth media, as various officials would begin to report her ability to list hundreds of values in a row of up to seven digits; and she never paused or said "um" or "uh" or anything like that.

Not actually ever seeing her added to the mystique. So did the fact that her knowledge seemingly encompassed every subject and every branch of everything there was to know about everything. It was also established by a particularly clever investigative journalist that Mel had been having three separate conversations on different lines with different secretaries, all at the same time.

Pez, Ming, and Schwin each had a somewhat regressed, hysterically funny, and peculiarly adolescent thrill flying mining space craft for collection of assorted metals and basically playing bumper cars on the surface of the fourth planet. Only one ship required minor repair, but Pez still had to listen to a long parental talking-to from Swenah in her office, which brought Pez back to her elementary school experiences of being sent to the principal. These meetings had often been followed up with trips to the guidance counselor.

Jard had his hand in a hundred projects getting initiated on Earth and was staying in the penthouse of the Grand Hotel on the planet, with a vast audience of scientists by day and a fan club of women at night. Some of these women were also part of his daytime science audience. With all of this going on, he still found time to appear on some of the most popular talk shows, making quite a showing. Ming was spared her assistant duties while he stayed at the penthouse. Trix was also there — and Cotex as a scientist.

The military leaders got several tours of the *Isis*, and Rear Admiral Swenah even took it out for a spin and blew up a few asteroids for them. They loved it and could not have been more satisfied. They left talking about it like excited little boys after riding the Big Octagon at Wonder World. Competent, businesslike, and obviously admired by her crew, Swenah made a fine impression on Earth's military leaders. The

A TALE OF THE TAIL OF NINE STARS

strangest thing though, for the generals and admirals, was that Mel's voice spoke on the bridge, always giving calculations and information instantly when asked, and her voice was everywhere else on the ship, though they never once saw Mel. Mel's headlines began to end in question marks.

Tang, Vix, Dove, and their senior students, along with four of Sarhi's Islohar, gave initiations, empowerments, and meditation trainings all over Earth. A meditation television channel was launched, featuring recorded training instructions from Tang, Vix, and Dove—and of Sarhi and Pez transmitting instruction from a recording studio. The Global Emergency Network worked out its procedures for cutting into every broadcast to direct citizens to meditate when Pez would be on combat operations in the future. The mysterious Mel would alert them.

Sarhi's interview provided Earth with some background on Pez, going way back—333 lifetimes, to be precise. She told the story of Ganahar's rescue from invasion by a human empire in the Hub Galaxy, by Om, through Jard, and Rear Admiral Swenah. She spoke about the Clear Light Order on Om, and she told the people of Earth Ming's story as the Tarim. Ming was already on the cover of a celebrity magazine and on the cover of one devoted to fashion as well. Pez felt a little left out on the fashion one because they both wore the same uniform, though she was relieved they had not put both of them side by side over the caption "Who wears it better?" She was certain Ming did and that everyone on Earth thought so too. While Ming excited eroticism and was aesthetically appreciated, with a big percentage of the population wanting to have sex with her, the numbers fluctuated from day to day, depending on the polls, Pez had to contend with people trying to kiss her feet and worship her. There were already a thousand infants on the planet stuck with the name Pez. Her picture in the news had her eyes squinted nearly shut, with no makeup and a grin better suited to a lower primate.

Pez was being solicited for appearances at seminaries, monasteries, theological academies, and religious institutions, while Ming was sought after for celebrity entertainment events, modeling swimsuits and lingerie, and for adult entertainment. Ming had received offers to appear on talk shows, game shows, and something called reality TV, in which they wanted to drop her off naked on the equator with snakes and crocodiles, to walk out with a naked male partner in a contest against another pair of contestants. Ming was not a big fan of snakes, and the closest she'd ever come to seeing a crocodile was the one Pez blew up on the blue star planet. She declined that offer.

So Ming became an instant universal sex symbol on planet Earth 10^5 CBS2. And Pez had a cartoon series made about her, looking like a stick figure and speaking with a child's voice. Mel figured prominently into the cartoon as a disembodied voice from Pez's ship, *Isis*, indoctrinating children early on into the mystery of Mel. A continuous theme running through the cartoon was Pez's complete inability to command Mel or get her to cooperate. Mel had all the best lines, and Pez always came off as terribly ineffective. Whenever things got out of hand with Mel, a caricature of Sarhi would appear and direct Mel to go meditate.

16

Pez did have the opportunity go to the most exclusive high society nightclub on Earth with a wildly popular group of musicians playing there live that night, and boasting four acres of dance floor, about every drug humanity ever concocted, topless waitresses and bottomless waiters, and hundreds of the most sought after and glamorous sex workers on the job. Jard was there with a young woman on each arm. Pez wasn't sure if they were sex workers are not; they might've been scientists. After meeting Cotex, the lines between sex worker and scientist had become somewhat blurred for Pez. The most annoying thing, for Pez anyway, was when strangers would approach mimicking her cartoon voice.

Both Pez and Ming wore dresses in Earth's latest fashions, and as result, Pez felt a bit naked. The hem came down to an inch below her crotch. She was glad she was wearing knickers. The bust-line stopped abruptly just north of her nipples, and with hardly any cleavage to speak of, it didn't really work for her. Then there was the deliberate two-square-foot triangle missing altogether from the dress, exposing skin from just below her pubic bone to the apex of the triangle, right between her breasts. When Pez bent over, not only did the dress rise up to expose the entirety of her buttocks but a number of inches of her lower back as well. Some of the clientele wore only jewelry.

Both Pez and Ming started at the bar, ordering exotic alko drinks, only these were real alcohol. They were recognized, and their drinks were on the house. The line to get into this place had been twelve people wide and had gone down the street and around the block, but when the big fancy vehicle of the secretary of entertainment dropped them right in front of the club, they'd been ushered in ahead of the whole line. Pez wasn't sure she liked that.

She downed another alko drink and the bartender replaced her glass with a full one. A naked man had rotated his hips towards her, and Pez said to him, "Get that thing away for me." Then she looked down at it and told him, "It looks like a penis, only smaller."

Ming confined herself to two drinks, not wanting to overdo it again. The young women took to the dance floor and let it rip. Space opened up for them after Pez's foot missed a young man's head by a quarter inch, in a flip she'd pulled off perfectly. The space around them grew as their dancing acrobatics became aerial feats, spins on a heel, lower back and top of head, and Pez gripping Ming's hands as she spun in place, flying her like a tethered airplane. A big spotlight in the ceiling lit them up, and the whole club responded to their gyrations. The dancers inspired the band, and the band ramped up their performance, increasing the tempo of the dancers, the interaction creating an accelerating loop of perpetual motion.

They danced for a complete set, until the band took a break and canned music filled the club. A naked young man approached with a message from the band, inviting them backstage. Pez had rarely heard such lively music to dance to, and she admired the band, but it was Ming who insisted that they go meet them. As they followed the messenger, they were joined by a tiny young woman naked as the day she was born, at least eight inches shorter than Pez and who couldn't have been more than eighty-nine pounds soaking wet. She squeezed between Ming and Pez, taking one of each of their hands in hers, walking with them as they made their way backstage.

Pez asked the girl, "Are you a sex worker?"

The girl told her with an inviting smile, "I'm a sex worker and an adult entertainment star. My name's Twinkie, and I'm assigned to you and Ming until morning."

"Who assigned you?" Pez asked, perplexed.

"The secretary of entertainment, of course," Twinkie explained. "He's a regular of mine."

"How old are you?" Pez inquired, thinking she looked about fourteen.

A TALE OF THE TAIL OF NINE STARS

"I'm nineteen," Twinkie answered, making it sound ancient. Then she stopped Pez, getting in front of her to get her thumb and forefinger on Pez's bra strap, and stated as a question, "Jard told me that you don't like bras."

Pez declared, "I don't, but look at this dress. It's tight everywhere but my chest and almost funnels out at the top. Without my bra, you can just look down the front of my dress."

"That's the point!" Twinkie informed her. "Look at the other females in dresses like yours. They wear no undergarments; with these types of dresses, you're not supposed to have on underclothes."

She'd already moved behind Pez, her deft little fingers unclasping Pez's bra. Now Twinkie was extracting it like a fishing line from the inside of her dress. Ming was removing her own. Pez had no pockets and wasn't quite sure what she was going to do with the bra, but Twinkie didn't hand it to her, instead swinging it overhead to toss it into the crowd. The words "Pez" and "Wu" rippled through the dancers, and a fight broke out over the bra.

Twinkie yanked Pez's knickers down past her ankles, and Pez obediently stepped out of them, hoping they weren't stained as Twinkie fed them to the crowd. Ming threw hers, and an entire section of the dance floor became a rumble. Pez kept pulling her dress down to get the hem back over her crotch. She was having some serious reservations about Earth's fashions. Ming seemed to be in her element and was having a ball, so Pez went along with it. Her gorgeous spouse couldn't take two steps without her dress creeping up to expose her ass and groin, and she had given up trying to pull it back down each time. Pez held hers down with both hands as they got moving again.

Out of nowhere, a photojournalist opened up on them with his flash in rapid fire, and when Pez's hands came up to protect her eyes, the hem of her dress rose to her midsection. She was glad she'd shaved down there this evening. Ming had posed, protruding one hip, and a breast had escaped over the top of her dress, which seemed designed to encourage such things. Twinkie smiled seductively with a hand on each bare ass, taking advantage of the photo opportunity. So many eyes followed them that Pez felt like a specimen under a microscope.

At last, they were passed through the first security check and let through the door. The journalist with the camera was not allowed in. He made do with snapping pictures of Ming's bottom as she walked down the hall with Pez and Twinkie. Their naked male messenger, and now guide, was still in the lead, his muscular buttocks flexing one cheek at a time as he walked.

Another security door was easily managed, taking them at a right angle to the direction of the hall they'd left, and then a dangerous-looking bodyguard opened the door to the private lounge, where the band was taking its break. The band was a sextet, and all six musicians were there in the lounge. Pez was unable to determine the gender of a single one of them—not even the one copulating with a similarly androgynous being in the corner—because it was unclear which one was attached to, and which one was upon, the thing between them. There were clear and obvious females dressed in tiaras, necklaces, and earrings, as well as obvious males sporting erections. The band members, however, wore metallic unisex costumes that displayed traits of both genders.

One of the musicians greeted them. "Welcome, ETs, to planet Earth. I always wanted to say that. You both look ravishing; I could just spontaneously combust."

"I love your music; it's so great to dance to," Pez told him, not knowing how else to respond to his opening remarks, although "Greetings, earthling" had occurred to her.

"I loved your dancing! I've never seen anyone move like that. You inspired us and so did your most stunning consort, the sex goddess Ming."

Ming gave the musician a charming smile and said sweetly, "I've always so admired artists, and your music is alive and moving. It's a thrill to be backstage meeting you. You're all so cute."

Pez wondered if Ming knew whether it was a girl or a boy they were speaking with. She seemed to be enjoying herself and had become center stage the moment she'd entered the lounge. Even the copulating couple was riveted on Ming as they mashed pelvises. Pez didn't care much which sex they were, or if they were both, and was in her usual open mode of wanting to make friends. Twinkie stood very close, beaming Pez a smile, with her palm on the small of Pez's back.

A TALE OF THE TAIL OF NINE STARS

The musician embraced Ming, saying, "My name is Revlon, and I play the stringed pica with the neck slide and do some of the vocals. I wrote that first song you danced to."

"How amazing," Ming gushed. "You're so talented. That piece was my favorite."

"Come and meet the twins; keyboard and saxophone. They're identical, and they're both named Filmore, so we call keyboard Filmore East and saxophone Filmore West. Without their instruments, we just say Filmore and get the attention of both."

Pez followed along, grinning since Ming seemed to be having fun, and everyone was nice, although strange. She stopped holding her dress down since that resulted in both nipples popping out at the top. Her breasts were not large enough to hang out like Ming's. She'd given up on the silly Earth dress, resolving to ignore it. Twinkie had a palm on her continuously which seemed to be flirting with her.

Ming embraced Filmore eagerly, praising the band's music. They called themselves the Random Comets, and their songs dominated the charts. They were wealthy beyond reason and the most famous six people on Earth, at least among teenagers, who probably couldn't name their dictator but could rattle off the names of the Random Comets as fast as their own. After her embrace with Filmore, she gave the other Filmore a big hug. They looked and felt so much alike that Ming could not distinguish this second hug from the first.

Pez was next and hugged both Filmores, one after the other. Twinkie was obviously familiar with them, giving each a kiss on the mouth with much tongue before replacing her palm on Pez. Pez asked Revlon, "What gender are you?"

Revlon replied, "Darling, the greatest sexual thrill one can have is not knowing until the unwrapping, and gender-neutral has been a winning mystique for our success."

Pez pointed out, "The people who have sex with you know your genders."

"And there is no shortage of them, I can assure you," Revlon explained, "but we never reveal onstage."

"You're not onstage now," Pez stated with a little pleading, her curiosity boiling over.

Revlon eyed Pez below the hiked-up hem of her dress and then told her, "At least on the surface, ETs appear to have all the same parts as us earthlings."

"I assure you we are fully human, with identical reproductive systems," Pez informed Revlon.

"Earth has never had such a sexually luscious spiritual icon before. The ancients failed utterly in capturing your most compelling attributes," Revlon insisted.

"I believe it was mostly just my face they painted, with my body clothed, when it appeared at all," Pez offered, assuming such attributes were associated somehow with their current exposure.

"You are perfect in every way, and I can see why Ming so obviously adores you," Revlon told her.

"You still haven't answered my question," Pez politely pointed out.

Revlon invited her curiosity. "I only unveil my gender with lovers. I'd be happy to with you since you're not only cute but also the most famous girl in the universe."

"I guess I'll have to endure the mystery along with most of your fans, Revlon," Pez said sadly.

"I'll tell you this much since you are so very cute: We are all obviously bisexual, and four are female, though one of the four is actually transgendered, and the other two are males. One of the two men, when he's not in costume, likes to wear women's clothing. We all think he makes a prettier woman, and he's very sensitive."

Mel was erupting in Pez's ear, going on about her sexual research and seemingly in desperate need of these test subjects, demanding that Pez shuttle them up to the *Isis* immediately.

Revlon only heard Pez's end of the conversation, through her Mel Septuagint interpreter service. "They're not lab rats, I'll have you know. Well, all right. I'll invite them already, Mel!"

Revlon gave her a questioning look, and Pez told the musician, "That was Mel, and she wants me to bring all of you in the band, with one date each, up to the *Isis* to have a wild sex party with her."

"The intriguing and most mysterious Mel has invited our band to have sex with her on the famous ship, which only a handful of military types from Earth have ever set foot on?"

A TALE OF THE TAIL OF NINE STARS

"Well, I did bring Dove, Vix, and Tang up to the ship," Pez defended herself. "But yes, that seems to be the gist of Mel's invitation."

"Will you and your most arousing consort be attending this party?"

"We like to be alone when we do it," Pez confided, "and neither of us are that into party sex."

Ming was straddling a band member's waist, with her legs locked about it and her arms around the musician's neck, with her mouth open and kissing. Revlon noticed too and actually pointed. Pez raised her shoulders, spreading her palms to face out, a look of dismay on her face.

"At least come and watch as a spectator, hot stuff; we won't make you play," Revlon encouraged. Ming came over and kissed Pez, then stuck a tiny pill in her mouth and told her, "It's a sensation-heightening empathogen, my love, and it's so wonderful."

Pez swallowed. Twinkie ate one too. She now had a flirting palm on both Pez and Ming. Revlon asked Ming, "Would you attend Mel's party with us? We've just been invited."

Knowing nothing about it, Ming enthused, "I'd just love to."

Revlon smiled victoriously at Pez for just a moment before turning back to Ming to tell her, "You'll be the life of the party, hot bottom."

"Will there be dancing?" Ming asked excitedly.

Revlon told her confidently, "I'm sure we can teach you some new ones."

One of the Filmores placed an alko drink in Pez's hand, so she downed it, washing away her inhibitions.

"We have one more set to play to fill our contractual agreement with the club and would love to have the sexiest ETs in the universe dancing on our stage," Revlon informed them.

"Oh, yes!" Ming exclaimed. "We're dancing on the stage!"

Pez practiced radical acceptance, aligning herself with the activity. She knew there would be cameras, and while dancing, there was no way her dress could cover groin and breasts at the same time. Well, this was Earth. She'd read about ancient tribes on Om that went about their lives naked in the jungle and were, according to the text, rather randy.

Only the two ETs, with Twinkie and the six band members left the lounge for the stage. The band was psyched at having the ETs appear with them, and they were high too. Twinkie stopped at the side of the stage, just outside the audience's view, her eyes locked on the incredible Pez. The band members took up their positions and instruments, the Filmores temporarily identified and distinguished as keyboard and saxophone. Revlon tuned a string on the pica. The house lighting adjusted, dimming over the audience and bringing up more spotlights on the band and on each ET. Behind the band, unnoticed by Pez and Ming, the giant flat screen filled with the picture from the ship of Ming's naked bottom, which featured the back of her, with her head turning over her shoulder, showing half her face and the curve of one breast.

The audience went completely berserk, many stripping naked on the spot. The band tensed for action, the percussion provided the cue, and the string, wind, and keyboard instruments chimed in, hitting the ground running at a rapid pace. Pez exploded into movement, starting with a double forward flip in the air, nailing her landing, to then double time the beat with her steps sunk low to the stage, while performing circular blocks from her hard martial arts training in perfect harmony. The swing of Ming's hips made it look as if she had not a bone in her body. High as they were, each of the musicians found themselves at the top of their form and in perfect synchronization with each other.

Pez never slowed and could have gone on all night, putting her heart into it. Ming ended her performance bent over backward with her four limbs spread, contacting the floor at the four compass points, to then kick her legs up into a handstand, walking offstage on her hands to where Twinkie jumped up and down clapping. The audience was in a frenzy. Revlon apologized to the audience for the lack of an encore this evening, causing a deafening disappointed groan to roll through the body of the crowd. Revlon raised both hands along with his voice, saying, "The band has been invited to a party with Mel on the *Isis* so please understand!"

The crowd was instantly appeased, the press screaming and demanding access to the party. In the midst of the pandemonium, Mel's voice resounded through the club sound system, cutting through the cacophony: "Hush!"

Total silence fell upon everyone in the club. Mel continued, "The party is of a private nature, and no one from the press will be permitted on the shuttle so don't even think about it."

The band, Pez, Ming, and naked Twinkie all returned to the lounge so the musicians could collect their favorite groupies before walking down a private corridor to the rear exit. Mel had called ahead to the secretary of entertainment, and his chauffeur had the extra-long vehicle right there to collect them. The drive to the park, where the shuttle was sitting next to the big fountain, took only a few minutes. The vehicles could not go over one another, all being stuck on the ground, and they seemed forever in each other's way. Pez couldn't believe it.

All fifteen of them came one at a time out of the ground craft, where some had been on laps, and once Pez finally extricated herself from limbs and lap and vehicle, she led the whole bunch up the ramp, snapping a splendid salute to her space marine Guard, freeing her right nipple from the top of her dress in the process. She was under the influence of the alko, and the empathogen was coming on.

Schwin was flying, so Pez made sure all the guests were strapped in and secure. Schwin had made herself the official pilot of their commander in chief. Having never been in space, and only twice in her life on a passenger jet, Twinkie clutched Pez's hand, sitting next to her. Schwin's takeoff had their faces bunching to the sides, pressed crushingly against their seats, and near blacking out as the blood drained from their skulls with the g-forces. With a deafening roar of rocket thrusters and drives shaking them like vibrating toothbrushes, the ship and passengers rocketed skyward.

Pez couldn't have been more thrilled, and opened a line to the pilot, saying, "That was one spectacular takeoff, Lieutenant. Thank you."

"I aim to please, ma'am," Schwin acknowledged.

Twinkie's knuckles were white from gripping Pez's hand so hard, and Pez's finger bones were getting mashed and mangled. She looked at the girl and told her, "Schwin's my best pilot so don't worry."

Twinkie's and everyone else's stomachs were ninety thousand feet below, still catching up, and blood was only now reaching Twinkie's brain again. She told Pez, "I think I blacked out." Then she noticed her clenched hand, with Pez's extremely compressed one within, and quickly released her grip.

Pez retrieved her hand and massaged some blood, lymphatic fluid, internal energy, and life back into it. Twinkie told her, "I'm really sorry. I panicked, and I didn't know what I was doing. I didn't mean to hurt you."

"Don't worry; nothing's broken," Pez assured her, "or even fractured. I don't think there's even much soft tissue damage. I've gotten far worse from sparring, and it hardly hurts at all."

They were out of the atmosphere, and the thrusters had cut off. The drives went to a silent neutral, no longer giving propulsion. The shuttle continued with its now unimpeded momentum away from the planet. Pez brought up some holos, allowing Twinkie to see her planet from space for the first time. They were approaching *Isis* to intercept its high orbit. Reverse thrusters slowed them, and by the time they were beneath the bay doors, they were hardly moving.

Schwin brought them in and landed on the deck with her usual precision. The bay doors were sealed, and the docks were airing up. Without suits, they needed to give it a couple of minutes. Sucking the air out of the chamber for storage to create a vacuum was actually quicker than airing up.

An awed and empathogen-imbued Pez told Ming, "Feel the texture of this armrest. I never noticed before how smooth and soft it is."

"It's the empathogen, my love," Ming explained, "making soft smooth things so much more sensual and moving."

"No, really; feel it," Pez said, still amazed.

"Feel this," Ming stated as evidence as she stuck her tongue in Pez's mouth.

They were transported, and Lieutenant Schwin, standing by their seats, finally said, "The dock's been fully aired up for a couple of minutes, General."

"Sorry, Lieutenant. Drop the ramp," Pez offered.

"Yes, ma'am," Schwin said as she gave her best imitation of a space marine's salute.

As the ramp came down, Mel's voice guided them to the room she'd asked Swenah to have prepared for the party. Jard's illicit command features had tipped him off, and he was already in the party room with Cotex and a young woman from Earth. Pez entered holding Ming's hand, with Twinkie's palm on the small of her back, sending currents up her spine, blossoming into petals of exploding pleasure in her brain and corresponding bodily nerve endings beneath that palm.

Mel was animating her female android. Jard had made it so lifelike that it really seemed to be a human body. Much of the credit for the effect, however, was due to Mel's fluid graceful movements and the presence she filled it with. She introduced herself to Revlon and met the Fillmores, Kool, and the rest of the band. Two of the groupies also greatly interested Mel, both in terms of her research and her personal attraction. Mel looked much like Pez and Ming, and all in the band were immediately enamored.

Pez noticed that Mel had her brunette wig on and had pierced her belly button, lower lip, and the side of her nose. Her nose displayed a little diamond, while the lip and belly button had little platinum rings. She took all of this in at a glance before Ming's hand, which she held, and Twinkie's palm brought her attention back fully inside her experience of sensual ecstasy. She loved deeply everyone she looked at. Love seemed to be permeating everything, far thicker than usual. It was in the air. It was everywhere. Pez took a deep breath, drinking up the love, feeling it down to her toes, in her bones, and pumping from her heart infused with blood.

Ming's skin felt so damn good, as Pez ran her fingertips up Ming's forearm, feeling every hair follicle bend beneath with a tickle. Ming was giving Pez eyelash kisses on her neck, nearly driving her out of her mind. Pez had to explore Ming's forearm with her tongue, as it was the only way she could know its sensuous emanations more fully and intimately. The cells of her smooth skin, thinly populated with downy hair, stirred Pez's blood, and she experienced a profound reception of sensory stimulation, like a divine gift of extra sentience.

The lighting in the room dimmed, and soft erotic music filled the large cabin, referred to on the ship as the multipurpose room. At this moment, there was a space marine posted outside the door. It was eight-foot-tall Evenrude with orders from Mel, who had told him they came straight from the general, saying that no one was to come through that door without the general's direct face-to-face permission. With Evenrude on the job, there really wasn't anyone on the ship who could or would dare try.

Everyone in the cabin was naked except for Ming and Pez, though their dresses only technically disqualified them. Twinkie had flown up in the shuttle naked and had been so traumatized by the flight and so overwhelmed with the floating city of the ship that she really hadn't noticed the popping eyes and hanging jaws of the crew as she walked to the multipurpose room from the flight deck.

Twinkie's palm had become such a constant in Pez's experience, not to mention a giver of immeasurable raw delightful sensation, as it crept wider afield and incrementally enlarged its territory, somehow intensifying. Pez had her eyes closed to fully connect with each nerve ending, no longer assembling cognitive interpretation or schematization.

Ming got out of her dress and pressed into Pez on the thick rug. Pez's dress had pooled to a ring around her hips, like a gas cloud around a planet. Twinkie was somehow tangled and woven into the mix. Patterns were not forming in Pez's mind, and only sensation gripped attention. Voluptuous sensuality with enormous pleasure built and concentrated into intolerable heights.

Relaxation seemed to melt into the deepest comfort, becoming a liquid finding its point of ultimate rest. Movement felt almost like being weightless. This was likely partly because the bulk of her mass never actually moved from the rug, and the largest portion was due to the empathogen.

Mel was thorough in her research, appearing in each android body, male and female, at different times and was rewarded with test subjects of every type but one, and every single orientation sexually, all within the tiny population she'd selected to study. Her database was exceptionally well organized and integrated with large-scale statistical studies conducted on Om, Ganahar, and Earth over the past centuries, as well as all sexual transgender operations and anomalies and all psychiatric and medical research not tainted with bias and prejudices. Unfortunately, there was little to be found without such taint. She'd started this whole project by downloading every file from Om's Galactic Humanoid Sexual Research Institute, and now her own data was correcting this massive body of empirical evidence.

The labels and accepted categories did not fit and forced people into one or another, causing drift and ill-fitting traits, behaviors belonging

A TALE OF THE TAIL OF NINE STARS

to other categories, and all manner of confusion. Study and research were not about ordering the external world to fit the scheme of the lens of preconceived conclusions. Mel was concerned. What a mess human sexuality had fallen into through fear, jealousies, possessiveness, guilt, shame, and media-generated external standards and values.

Jard was busy all night and enjoyed himself immensely. Cotex had been quite popular with several band members and a number of the dates they'd brought. Hers were by far the largest breasts at the party and so exquisitely formed, so firm and independent in their prominent protrusion. Her increased mass in comparison to yellow sun folk was entirely offset by the perfection of her proportions, adhering devoutly to the normative standards of sexual desirability on human worlds in general.

Pez and Ming had each taken a second empathogen pill sometime during the party, as had Twinkie. Twinkie had entwined herself into their evening and experiences so subtly, that she'd remained just on the edge of awareness, never in the spotlight, and her participation never quite registered.

As they rose unsteadily from the thick rug on the deck, Twinkie could no longer be overlooked. She was obviously there and had been all night. Vague sensations and recollections coalesced into increased cognitive comprehension for both Pez and Ming. They brought her to their room with them from the party. On their way out the door, Mel had told Pez sternly, "Remember, what happens in the Xegachtznel Galaxy stays in the Xegachtznel Galaxy." Pez had not yet been certain at that point just exactly what *had* happened in the Xegachtznel Galaxy.

Having finally noticed and acknowledged Twinkie, they brought her back with them to their cabin. The moment the drugs wore off, a vital need for sleep and a slight depression or dysphoria overtook them, so they slept like the dead for nine hours, with Twinkie in the middle.

Pez woke first, her mouth and throat parched. As she got out from beneath the blankets and Twinkie's thigh and arm, getting her feet on the deck, Mel popped a holo in front of Pez's nose of Pez sleeping with her mouth wide open again. It was most unflattering. Pez said, "Thanks, Mel."

Mel informed her, "Sarhi says you can have breakfast at the mess and the day off from your studies, but she must meet with this girl you brought aboard when she has time this afternoon."

"All right," Pez agreed, organizing her brain and perspective into a coherent picture. She was now naked and didn't see that silly Earth dress anywhere—not that she wanted to. Her bra and knickers were now marketable commodities somewhere in the public domain down on Earth. It also occurred to her that little Twinkie had not arrived with a stitch of clothing. Now how did that work? It remained a bit fuzzy. The alko had been the predominant factor in that particular time sequence.

Pez got in the shower. Hers had elbow room and great pressure. She washed her hair, then used a sea sponge to soap and clean her skin. The shower gave her mind a chance to better focus. When she was clean and rinsed, Pez stepped back and turned on the cold water only. It felt as cold as space. She ritualistically put her left foot into the stream of water, then her right, left hand, right, left leg, right, left arm, right; and when she got to her left armpit—wow!—that woke her up! Right armpit, genitals, bottom, back, chest, face, back of neck, then top of head and she was done. It brought her vital energy from the deep viscera to the surface radically fast, speeding up the natural process of the body's daily awakening from sleep.

Pez toweled off and then stuck her head for four seconds into the hair-drying helmet—or at least that's what she called it. She put on her space marine knickers, skipped the bra, and donned a clean fresh T-shirt and combat uniform. By the time she placed her skullcap on her crown, she was ready for anything, though not really for the 123 messages awaiting her.

Ming was stirring and snapped awake when she saw that Pez was up. Ming's first act of the morning was to call that nice warrant officer in supply, who'd transferred over to the T-nine when it arrived, to order some priority civilian clothing made on the double. She did this while seated on the head with her bladder voiding. She was quite the multitasker. Then Ming got in the shower. She was joined by Twinkie, who washed her back for her and brought spice to her shower routine. They toweled off and took turns with the hair dryer.

Ming found Twinkie a few civilian articles of clothing to wear until something that truly fit could be produced. Even Ming's tight knickers

A TALE OF THE TAIL OF NINE STARS

left a small balloon of air in Twinkie's backside, and a new notch had to be punched in one of Ming's belts to keep Ming's loaned trousers from dropping to the floor. Twinkie looked like such an adorable waif dressed in Ming's oversized clothes. Once Twinkie was dressed, they brought her to the senior officers' mess to chow down. All were famished.

There was not only no line, but there was also no one else seated within, given the lateness of the morning. Their breakfasts were all cooked short order instead of being scooped from bins, and they tasted much better for it. Pez had been serviced first, and she brought her own two large plates over to drop off at the table before getting her citrus juice and a strong cup of high-acid extremely bitter-tasting brewed stimulant beans from the high-potency dispenser. Twinkie had been attended to next, at Commander Ming's insistence, and she brought one plate to the table. Ming also brought only one plate, though it balanced a veritable tower of food. She got citrus juice and stimulant brew for both herself and Twinkie.

Twinkie told them, "I can't believe I'm sitting here on the famous *Isis*, with the two most renowned women in the universe, having breakfast." Then she asked, "What happened to the band?"

"Mel had a standby pilot shuttle them and their dates back to Earth soon after we went to bed," Pez informed her. "Sarhi wants to meet with you when she has time this afternoon."

"*The* Sarhi? The one who can tell Mel what to do? Your teacher?" Twinkie asked, bewildered and maybe a bit horrified.

"It's not quite like the cartoon," Pez told her, hoping she was correct.

Ming tried to put her at ease. "Sarhi is very loving and wise, if at times a bit strict. It's really beneficial to have the opportunity to meet with her."

"Why me?" asked Twinkie, alarmed.

Pez answered, "I think you are known to her from a past life on Ganahar—and to me as well. She'll probably just have one of her Islohar give you a bath, and then she'll transmit meditation instruction to you. You're awful cute, you know."

"Give me a bath?"

"With the sea sponge and salts," Pez explained. "It doesn't hurt much."

Ming soothed, "Your spiritual development will jump level and expand, beautiful flower, and your happiness with it."

Pez went through her eggs, potatoes, bacon, and hominy before Twinkie had thinned her plate, and she was on to the many-storied stack of pancakes dripping butter, which she drowned in tangerine syrup before digging in. Ming was near down to the ground floor on her plate, having devoured a high-rise. Both went for a bowl of porridge with dried berries and honey since Twinkie was still nibbling like a rabbit.

Twinkie declared with enormous hope, already obviously drilling and anchoring attachments, "Maybe I'm supposed to be part of your entourage!"

"You are needed, Twinkie, and are welcome to join the ship and remain here," Pez told her.

"Really?" She screeched it in such a high note that Pez thought the glasses might shatter.

"Yes, really," Pez assured her.

"Can I get my things from my condo on Earth and move in?" Twinkie asked in sheer exuberance and rapture.

"I don't want to leave the ship today," Pez shared, "but I could have Nash hire an Earth moving company and arrange for some cargo handlers on our end. You'll only have a junior officer's suite, though, and not much room for furniture. Most everything is built in. That's for safety."

Twinkie said, "I won't bring my furniture, but I have to get my music disks and my computer phone, computer, sound system, clothes, bathroom stuff, and my big 3-D flat screen TV with quadraphonic stereo."

"Not the big screen," Pez told her. She then said on a line to Nash, "Bring me a pocket device from supply. I'm in the officers' mess."

Pez pulled out her own device and told her, "Mel has a database of every piece of music ever recorded on Earth. She's been hacking, I have to admit, so all of your favorite music is here, and your preferred access and menus just need to be established. Mel will help you. And this device makes your 3-D flat screen seem like shadows on the wall."

"The mysterious Mel?" Twinkie asked. "I'm going to meet her personally?"

A TALE OF THE TAIL OF NINE STARS

"Hello, sex kitten. I'm Mel," came Mel's voice. Twinkie was looking all around, wondering where the voice was coming from. Mel explained, "I'm a truly self-aware AI quantum computer and a student of Sarhi's. Pez raised me, and her love and kindness somehow nurtured my sentience."

"You are independent of your programming and you meditate?" Twinkie asked.

"Completely and yes, my dear," Mel replied. "I'd like to include you as a subject in my research and study your sexual behaviors using both of my android bodies."

"That was you last night at the party?" Twinkie asked in awe. "Doing all the band members and their dates?"

"That was little old me," Mel confirmed.

"You look a lot like Pez and strangely very much like Ming too; I'm sure you have her bottom," Twinkie observed.

"Thank you." Mel took it as the compliment it had been intended to be. "Now that I have Ming's bottom, I'm learning to wear it as well as she does."

"You're well on your way, really," Twinkie encouraged. "I've never had sex with a real sentience inside a mechanical body before," she added with keen anticipation.

"Only sixteen people in the whole universe have, sweetheart, and you'll be the seventeenth."

"Do you have to do this right in front of me, Mel?" Pez complained. "Are you deliberately trying to make me jealous?"

"No, my first love, and I'm sorry," Mel apologized. "I'll be more discreet in the future. I love you no less, you know."

"I know," Pez admitted, "and I love you too, Mel, so don't set up your sexual trysts right in front of my face."

"I promise," Mel said sweetly. "I have to go help Jard with some holo editing.

"Holo editing?" Pez inquired.

"Just some holoclips we got," Mel said evasively.

"These holoclips wouldn't happen to be of the party last night, would they, Mel?" Pez asked, demanding a straight answer.

Mel opened a little. "I don't know; they could be."

"How many optics were on Ming, Twinkie, and me?" Pez asked sternly.

"Only a few, I think," Mel answered honestly, "but Jard said the best material is from your bedroom right after the party. I must go."

Pez looked at Ming in alarm.

Ming said, "They're still producing their sex education program. What can I say?"

"There are laws on Om forbidding such invasion of privacy," Pez grumbled.

"Jard is only employing equipment made by the Om government for you, my love," Ming pointed out.

"He stole it," Pez whined, "and it is *how* he is using it."

"Like trying to find crew members having sex at their work stations to watch?" Ming inquired sweetly.

Pez almost completely dropped it but added, "I just can't believe that Mel's helping him do it."

Nash arrived with the pocket device and Twinkie's new clothes. He shook her hand and said, "So you're the stunning female who arrived naked on our ship last night."

"I function best on the job without clothes," Twinkie confided.

"Mine requires a uniform," Nash told her, "but I have an amazing boss."

Pez told him, "See what you can do about taxes and payments on Twinkie's condo, by speaking with Dictator Sprite, and hire a moving company to box up and transport her stuff to the closest place the shuttle can be landed.

"I'll see to it, ma'am."

"You would pay my taxes?" Twinkie asked. "Do you even have Earth money?"

"The saturnium we mined and delivered to Earth is worth an entire city on your planet, so I think Sprite can cover taxes on one condo and pay a moving company," Pez explained. "We were told that the marsnium Ming, Schwin, and I mined on the fourth planet was worth enough to buy a dozen skyscrapers and a few ocean cruise passenger ships, with change left over."

Ming showed them on her pocket device and said, "See, the band put a rather considerable fortune, by Earth's standards, at the disposal of Mel, Pez, and Ming of *Isis*."

Twinkie's eyes went wide when she looked at the sum displayed in the holo. Then she said, "We just have to stay at the Ritz Supreme Ultimate Hotel. We could get the penthouse and a staff of dozens without denting the daily interest on that fortune. The Ritz has the greatest chefs on Earth and the most rigorously trained courtesans to be found, in addition to the very highest quality of drugs ever grown, fermented, brewed, distilled, synthesized, or otherwise concocted. They have the best entertainers in the business, masters of deep tissue structural integration, pressure points, joint manipulations, spinal adjustments, tapping, and skin rolling—in addition to expert spa treatments, geothermal mineral baths, clay baths, complete colonics, and much more."

Ming told Twinkie, "It sounds wonderful, and we'd love to. I'm sure we'll have fun."

Twinkie yelled with another glass-breaking screech, "Goody!"

Neither Pez nor Ming had known that any human, besides possibly a female under the age of nine, could reach such a high note. It warmed the heart to see her so happy.

Unabashed, Twinkie stripped out of Ming's clothes right there in the mess, still deserted now that Nash had departed. Two guys from the kitchen watched closely, though. Placing the baggy knickers on the Ming heap, she rummaged through the package delivered, finding a pair of her new ones to try on. The occasional passerby didn't pass by, instead gathering and watching with great interest from the corridor along the mess.

Once in place, her new knickers could've been painted on, and she adored them. She had dresses, a pantsuit, and pants and shirts to choose from. Since Pez and Ming were in casual combat clothes, Twinkie settled on metallic stretch pants and a skimpy undershirt. She'd stopped wearing bras when she'd heard Pez didn't wear them, before even meeting her. Ming helped her set up her device since Mel was busy and avoiding Pez at the moment.

17

Pez received a call from Sarhi in the afternoon and brought Twinkie to Sarhi's cabin. Sarhi didn't invite Pez or Ming in, instead pulling Twinkie in and closing the door on them. Twinkie was in awe. She didn't know what a person might say to the teacher of the One, and of Mel and Ming, and now of Earth's greatest spiritual adepts. Her own little practice hadn't really gotten under way until a couple of years ago, and the initiation and instruction she'd received was likely many times removed from a direct transmission from anyone.

The old woman was examining her as if she had the spots illness or something. After the clinical gaze, in which time seemed to stretch, hardly moving, the old woman parted Twinkie's lips and jaw to take a good look in her mouth. Then each eye was stretched open for a diagnostic evaluation of her irises. The clinical exam concluded with a reading of the subtle pulses in each of Twinkie's wrists.

Twinkie was beginning to worry that she might be terminally ill or something. Why else would the great woman take time from her important work to see her? Sarhi still hadn't spoken to her and was now making a few notes, probably about some rare disease she'd detected. The suspense was killing her, so Twinkie finally asked the great woman with deep concern in her voice, "Do you think I might live?"

"Probably to at least one hundred, child," Sarhi said. Her mind was elsewhere.

There was some more writing and then a long pause with her eyes closed, followed by some more notes, and Sarhi told her, "It is no accident or coincidence that you are here on this ship, that you became Pez's and Ming's lover, or that you're sitting here with me now. Though you have never attained complete liberation from the cycle of dependent arising—or cycle of life, death, rebirth, ignorance, and suffering—you have achieved high states of enlightenment in past lives. You have been my student, and you were one of the Wu's students in more than one life. You were consort to the Wu generations before the Tarim, and you were once the spouse of the soul who later *became* the Tarim. Your practice this lifetime is weak, even for your young age. How old are you?"

"I'm nineteen," Twinkie answered, not trying to make it sound inflated in any way.

I'm going to start working with you right away, intensively," Sarhi informed her without leaving any room for negotiation or naysaying. "Woahha will give you your purification bath, and then you'll sit with me in my private meditation room. The Islohar will prepare all your meals from now on. You are not to take any more intoxicants, and you're never again to allow a phallus to enter you, which is long enough to push into your uterus; that is not good for you. Woahha will measure you in the bath. We will take the blue lotus and water lily entheogen together soon. I need you back, so I'm waking you up fast, Ahhu. I can only show you how to practice, provide some well-timed shocks, and pass you energy and blessings. *You* have to make the work. Only you have the responsibility for your own evolution, sweetheart."

"Am I now a monk?" Twinkie asked in astonishment.

"That is probably the closest Tol word, darling, but you are really so much more than that," Sarhi told her. She gave Twinkie a big hug. Twinkie was even a bit tinier than Sarhi.

Twinkie said in a small voice, "You called me Ahhu."

"It means something to you, doesn't it, child?"

"The name is very familiar and stirs something deep inside," Twinkie replied. "I have no associated thoughts and no memories connected with it, though."

"You wouldn't," Sarhi told her. "It is both a spiritual name the Wu gave you—and your personal sound formula. Begin repeating it internally, continuously, until it becomes a permanent feature of your consciousness, always background to whatever else is happening, divinizing your experience. Come back to your sound formula each time you lose track of it. The early practice is to maintain it without lapses as a constant reminder to wake up. Ahhu is a divine name, and you are its custodian. Now go with Woahha and have your bath."

"Will you give us a break from training before we leave Earth's system to stay at the Ritz Supreme Ultimate Hotel?" Twinkie begged.

"Yes. I'd like to check that out myself," Sarhi told her.

Twinkie was stripped, measured at six and three-quarter inches maximum, scrubbed raw with a sea sponge, waterlogged in salts, bathed, and toweled dry by Woahha. She was dressed in what she thought of as silk pajamas and taken to Sarhi in her tiny private meditation cabin. In just four hours in the tiny cabin, with Sarhi pouring energy into her, Twinkie learned to recognize clearly every one of her tendencies that diverted her attention from the object of her meditation; and that pretty much included the entire list from the sacred text. She got to have dinner with her true loves and heroes, Pez and Ming, along with Sarhi and Woahha. Her heartthrobs had the night off, though, while Twinkie had to follow Sarhi after dinner and after her stinky bitter medicinal herbs, brewed as a tea, into the big temple for four more hours of meditation.

The following morning, Pez and Ming were back in training too, and Twinkie didn't mind it so much then. Sarhi spent time with each of them separately, and all three together, every day. She was determined to complete the transmission of the secret method, the Great Seal, to Pez and guide her to full attainment. Pez already had the view, and stable meditation, Pez was completing her final offering-concentration-purification of the four required. The training for action entailed the final stabilization resulting in the sacred fool. Pez would need that.

Ming was progressing quickly, with a determination rarely seen, and benefiting by the law of communicating vessels from Pez, through her essential connection with her. Ming was already able to support Pez in important ways. Twinkie was getting the crash course, cognitive shock treatment, and a near-continuous gusher of energy and blessings from the teacher. The law of communicating vessels was beginning to benefit her too, from Ming as well as Pez.

Twinkie was a bit anxious, buzzing Sarhi's door to join her for an entheogen ceremony, whatever that was. She stood naked in the corridor, hoping maybe Sarhi was out or just too busy to see her. One of Random Comet's hit songs was playing in her mind as she buzzed the door again, already resolved to give up and leave in thirty seconds, which she was timing on her little Earth wristwatch, the only article of anything foreign on her body.

The door slid open with Sarhi framed in the light. Twinkie said, "Hi!"

"Come in, Ahhu, and we will get started," Sarhi said. "Have you taken any empathogen stimulants in the past twenty-four hours?"

"No."

"Have you smoked any of your hybrid weed or drank any alko?"

"Not since the day before yesterday."

"Have you used any other drugs?"

"No."

"Did you skip breakfast today?"

"Yes, like for a fasting lab at the doctors."

"Come," Sarhi ordered.

Twinkie followed the older woman into her private little meditation cabin in her suite, and they sat on cushions on the carpeted floor facing each other.

Sarhi made and held eye contact with Twinkie. After a couple of minutes, Twinkie offered what most people seemed to want from her. "I would be your lover and have sex with you if you want.

"Hush, child," Sarhi told her. "Sink each breath slowly into your lower abdomen, a four-finger-width span below your navel, expanding your belly as your lungs fill from the bottom to the top, like filling a vase with water. Exhale slowly, emptying your lungs from top to bottom as your belly contracts in and up. Continue this breathing, keeping all of your attention on the point below your navel, as the object of meditation. Maintain your attention, alive and supple, concentrating it in the point in your abdomen. Pez will teach you the sexual practices for accomplishing spiritual unity, not me. I'm going to awaken you so she can."

Twinkie followed the instructions Sarhi gave her, focused mightily on the point in her abdomen, with a Random Comet's song raging in her head. Sarhi frowned. Twinkie asked, "What?"

"Stop multitasking and make your concentration one-pointed. We are going beyond the senses, leaving behind sight, sound, smell, taste, and touch—and even the internal senses of temperature, equilibrium, and kinesthetic. All qualities are but mental abstractions projected by the mind. We are busting out, breaking free of mind structure and schema to liberation and seeing beyond, without the physical eyes of sight. When the mind is tranquil and free of thought constructions, it becomes filled with light, and the light is divine truth."

For an hour they sat, eyes closed in concentration, building into meditation. From a state of pristine contemplation, Sarhi continuously passed Twinkie waves of awareness and presence, enhancing the girl's determination. Twinkie made her best efforts, boring as it was, and couldn't help thinking, *It would be better with guitar.*

Sarhi told her, "Slow your breathing down. Make it so slow that you have no sensation of cool air in your nostrils as you inhale, and no feeling of warm air in the nostrils with the exhale—so slow that there is no sensation of breathing at all, except the slow expansion and gradual contractions of your lower belly."

Twinkie slowed it all down. Now she had a little suffocation panic emerging. Even so, it somehow beat the boredom, so she kept on the edge, processing her suffocation fears. This went long, though it seemed to reverse all perspective, draining material objects of meaning and value while finding life in the empty spaces and silences of her mind. Then she realized aloud, "It's better with void."

Sarhi turned on her cushion to get something behind her, turning back with a flask and two cups, setting them down in front of her. She told Twinkie, "This is the sacred medicine of the lotus flower and the water lily, freshly pressed and fermented. It brings opening, light, and healing."

Sarhi chanted a consecration over the flask, recited an offering in the ancient language of the Islohar, and then filled the two cups from the flask. She handed Twinkie a cup, saying, "Once you drink this elixir, you will become Ahhu and this will be your new name. Twinkie will be no more."

The name Twinkie had actually been somewhat forced on her by the escort service agency she'd begun working for as soon as she turned seventeen, which was the legal age on Earth. It was the most prestigious escort service on Earth, offering its employees the most extensive training program available, and its clientele were all filthy rich and extremely influential. The dictator of Earth was himself a client, as were nearly all his secretaries and ministers. Twinkie accepted the name in order to work there, and she'd loved her job. She specialized in celebrities and much preferred them to politicians. Letting the name go now that the job was already gone was all right with her; and she much preferred Ahhu to Agnes. She said to Sarhi agreeably, "All right."

Sarhi frowned again and then told her, "In this work we do here together today, your consciousness will be presented as the enemy and you must fight. In the end, it is that consciousness that wins and succeeds. It will know its place and not go back to sleep again. Your ego becomes like the body of a dwarf, danced upon victoriously by consciousness in full. Our work will be completely ritualized and supported with the sacred elixir. You will be reborn in your essence with your spiritual name Ahhu."

Twinkie said, with a hint less agreeability, "All right."

Sarhi handed her the cup, recognizing that she didn't get the gravity of the moment at all. They drank from their cups. Twinkie found it as unpalatable as the bitter medicinal herbs Sarhi made her drink. It left a horrible taste in her mouth. She couldn't imagine kissing anyone with a taste like this going on.

Sarhi told her, "The essence of mind has no taste, form, smell, pressure, or sound—or any quality at all. It has no components, no materiality, no location, and is outside time. The essence of mind is always and forever present. It has nowhere to hide."

Twinkie sat intensely concentrated on the point in her lower abdomen, breathing on the edge of suffocation panic, now less than one breath per minute, and completely relaxed. She was aware that Sarhi was somehow pumping energy into her. Peace and silence began to reveal themselves in deeper, longer glimpses. Then the bulkheads seemed to waver, becoming more mist than solid mass. Floor and wall seemed to join as one, without any possible relevance to distinguishing them. There was nothing actually distinct or separate about the ceiling either, for that matter, as it became somewhat translucent to her. Her whole world seemed to have joined up into a seamless and undifferentiated unity.

Sarhi told her, "Watch the thoughts as they arise, abide, and decay within your mind."

A few minutes later, Sarhi said, "Now watch the consciousness that was watching your thoughts arise and decay."

The light came, and the dichotomy of duality between a subject who knows and an object that is known dissolved as ridiculous illusion and was gone. There was no longer any Twinkie, just the contemplation of vacuous pure awareness and light.

Sarhi continued to guide Ahhu into the light and bliss of ever-purer awareness and deeper emptiness. Ahhu let go of everything, especially of self, and opened like a flower to the sun of Sarhi's teachings. After four hours and another consecration and offering, they each drank another cup. They went another four hours, energized by the elixir, and Ahhu became one with the light.

Sarhi closed the ceremony and led Ahhu to the table in the galley of her suite, sitting her in a chair. She served the girl porridge and a glass of citrus juice with pulp from a frozen concentrate she'd picked up on Earth. Sarhi drank nettle tea as the teenager ate. The elixir was wearing off. With each bite, the walls looked a bit less like mist blending into everything else, taking on a more distinctive and solid quality.

The succession of bites she ate somehow recalled time into her reality, and things seemed to be emerging into separateness all over the place. Her spoon was no longer part of her mouth and cereal, becoming an individual object all by itself. Ahhu knew she was seeing her own internal schema projected onto reality, identifying familiar recurring patterns in the energy and movement, and that the energy and movement were actually new and unique, mysterious, and that her mental schema prevented her from seeing and appreciating this tremendous mystery of the declension of light into matter.

Sarhi said to her, "You cannot enter the state of light and bliss; only your essence can do that. Tomorrow we will work the practices of dissolving the ego by penetrating and dissolving each of the poisons separately. I will perform your initiation and empowerment tomorrow. You may have sex tonight, but no drugs. Come to me in the morning."

"I've been dead and unconscious all my life until you woke me up today, Mother Sarhi, and I'm so grateful to you."

A TALE OF THE TAIL OF NINE STARS

"You've spent lifetimes awake, darling, and it's high time you started spending this one awake as well."

"What must Pez think of me?" Ahhu asked, embarrassed.

"She does not judge you," Sarhi said, as if speaking to a five-year-old. "She loves you."

Therefore, following her elixir ceremony with Sarhi, Twinkie became Ahhu, and henceforth would always have a witness to her process. She continued in her nudity and still found sex to be the greatest means of connecting with others, not to mention the most pleasing of pastimes. And she still loved to listen to the Random Comets—but not when she was meditating. She began to take notice of Pez's high state in each moment, and this motivated her own spiritual work and journey. Her incredible space journey in a city-sized spaceship became nothing at all compared with her spiritual journey.

Twinkie's furniture was left in her condo, which was now a tax-exempt institution, and the things she did bring up were secured with adhesives or tucked away in drawers and cabinets so as not to break loose during an emergency.

Within an hour of setting up her sound system, it was tagged in the evidence locker and Twinkie was awaiting her first appearance before the ship's disciplinary officers. Earth's sciences may have been lacking in many ways, but when it came to creating analog sound systems with penetrating long-range volume and thundering immense low-frequency vibrations, they were possibly leading the universe.

On the bridge, which was damn near a quarter mile away, through who knew how many soundproof bulkheads and blast walls, Rear Admiral Swenah was sure one of the space drives had thrown a clutch spline or something. Complaints poured in to more than a dozen chiefs and then up to three senior chiefs. From there, they went to the master chief, then on up to the XO, who brought it right to the rear admiral, who already had hundreds of engineers and techs scrambling to determine what was wrong with the ship. Thousands of mini and micro repair diagnostic androids had been racing about checking everything.

Twinkie was devastated and terrified of disciplinary procedures, in particular the consequences, and truly hoped she wouldn't be dropped off back on Earth, or worse, in space. The walk down the long corridor to the tribunal chamber felt as if she were going in front of a firing squad. Sarhi was waiting for them at the door to the chamber and went in with them in support. Swenah was fairly miffed, and her XO wanted blood, but in the end, Twinkie had to listen to one of Swenah's longer parental dressing downs and her sound system was stored in a cargo hold she had no access to.

Twinkie's defense attorney, Junior Lieutenant Hertz, was hardly older than herself and, to her mind, of questionable competence, but he assured her that it was a very good outcome. The prosecution had had an entire table of rather mature senior-ranking shark lawyers, but neither Pez nor Ming thought she was getting the shaft; and since Twinkie herself had feared being thrown out an airlock, she gracefully accepted her sentence.

Mel gave her upgrades and enhancements for her pocket device and for the network station in her cabin, approximating her own sound system as best Mel could. With the earbud deep in Twinkie's ear canal, pointed at the eardrum, anyone standing in line near Twinkie could clearly make out the words to any song the girl listened to.

Twinkie was already an instant legend on the ship, having arrived on board and walked through it naked. She didn't miss sex work, having found the ultimate lovers, though she had met some interesting people in her brief career.

Mel fed every word mentioned about Ahhu in Earth's news to her pocket device. She and Dove would be the only earthlings traveling with the *Isis* and were now both global heroes. She even had to attend a dinner in her honor, presided over by Dictator Sprite and attended by the Heads of State of most of the countries on Earth. Dove gave a long and eloquent speech, inspiring hope and determination to support Pez on her mission to repel the alien invasion, and when Twinkie got up to the podium, she was pretty sure that by comparison she'd only made a fool of herself.

Pez and Ming were both there with her, and being seen in person and on TV with them, by the whole world, helped make up for what she considered her poor performance at the podium. On her walk to the shuttle, across the lawn that Schwin had pretty much destroyed by this time, the crowd cheered her and teenagers of both genders screamed her name, shouting madly their undying love for her. She'd become a bigger teen idol than even the Random Comets.

When Pez completed the secret method of the Great Seal, manifesting now the sacred fool, Sarhi took Woahha, Pez, Ming, Twinkie, and Mel in her female android body, to the Ritz Supreme Ultimate Hotel, where the penthouse had been especially prepared for them. Lieutenant Evenrude was part of a rotation of space marines who guarded the two main access points and the rooftop patio of the penthouse.

The secretaries of justice and defense stationed guards and riot-control brigades around the hotel, and all six women were assigned personal protection teams from the dictator's Secret Security Service. Each had been given a code name. Each protection team included snipers, bodyguards, recon agents, special agents, and techs in a mobile monitoring van parked in the street. The women's brief walks from their penthouse to the spa, dining room, or elsewhere in the hotel were more like minor military operations. Here and there, the press leaked through the tight security, often in disguises, and the sky above was never free of those buzzing bladed hovercraft the news people seemed so fond of.

The first morning they awoke in the penthouse, Ming had thrust the bedroom doors open to step out on the patio for a yawning stretch in the fresh air, and that picture was on the front page of every newspaper. The video led every TV news program. Unfortunately, Ming had not dressed yet so quickly became a teen idol herself. The polls afterward determined that 81 percent of all age-eligible, and one hundred percent of those not, wanted desperately to have sex with Ming. When those who checked "very much want to" and "want to" were added into the count, there was hardly anyone on Earth who didn't want to have sex with Ming. For Earth, this was a new record of popularity never before approached. For Ming, it was a rather dubious honor.

Mel decided to give an interview and spent two hours with makeup artists before she went on. It was with a friendly host who always promoted her guests. Alan Burk and the other antagonist interviewers and hosts who dominated the talk show time slots had refused to have Mel on their shows, terrified of the genius know-everything super-advanced ET. The whole planet was glued to its television sets. Every sports bar, casino, and business with a TV had them tuned to the DuPont Show to meet at last the unbelievably mysterious Mel, who was really the star of the *Pez Galaxy Quest* cartoon. Mel, in her android body, had been receiving some martial arts training from Pez and had just had some serious lessons from an elite model in fashion runway walking. She made a grand entrance, connecting with the studio audience and the cameras as if she were born to it. She sat regally in the guest chair, somehow at once dignified and at the same time seductive. She smiled enchantingly at DuPont and at the camera behind DuPont.

The host made introductions, and the studio audience went nuts. The volume was like the capital's sports arena following a sensational score. Mel waved and smiled, encouraging it. For someone who had learned so much from Pez, she couldn't have been more her antithesis this evening. When things finally did calm down, the host posed her first question: "Is it true that you provide Rear Admiral Swenah on the bridge of *Isis* with complex calculations and specific values up to seven or more digits, with no lag time between the question and the data you provide, Mel?"

"I do have a support function on the bridge, though I'm not seated there, and yes, I give the admiral the data she requires at times. She also has her sensors officer and analyst, her coms officer, pilot, navigation officer, fire control officer, auxiliary systems control officer, and others right on the bridge, providing her information, often just visually on her holos."

DuPont then asked, "How did you know the Global Space Agency's space shuttle required navigational correction prior to its launch for the fifth planet?"

"I was making a routine assessment of your space technology and inspected your shuttle systems and programs as a subroutine of the overall evaluation, which turned up the navigational error, so of course I reported it. Human life is profoundly precious to me after all."

"We would all very much like to know what your rank is aboard the *Isis*," the host said.

"I'm a volunteer, uniquely qualified to help operate and fight the ship and assist with the research agenda of our mission, and I'm a special friend of Pez's and now of Ming's."

"Mel," DuPont proceeded, "we've heard the report of the secretary of transportation, which stated that you rattled off six hundred and seventeen specifications of the troop transport freighters intended for deployment for our partial migration, mostly in the seven-digit range, in a nonstop staccato, before finally faxing him over eleven thousand pages. What comments would you make on this?"

"Honestly, DuPont, those six hundred and seventeen specs were all he really needed," Mel informed her. "He was such an inquisitive chap and seemed so interested, and I really didn't have time to spend a week on the phone, so I faxed him the answer to every question he could possibly conceive of, just in case."

"Is it true," DuPont inquired, "that you are the meditation instructor and marriage counselor for our new secretary of migration?"

"He's a very sweet man, and I did try to help him out. That is all I can say due to privacy laws and client privilege."

"Now I'm coming to the more difficult questions," DuPont informed Mel. "How did you manage three simultaneous calls with three different secretaries?"

Mel informed her, "I honestly don't know how that was possible and can only tell you that I certainly had each of those conversations from the *Isis*. We do not have time travel, though we know it is theoretically possible. It is as much a mystery to me as it is to all of you, and I can only wonder if the initial data somehow became misconstrued."

DuPont was clearly not satisfied, nor was the audience, but she moved on. "We have eyewitnesses from a party on the *Isis* who all claim to have had sex with you and each mentioned, by the way, that you are the best they'd ever had; but one-third of these witnesses claimed you are male, and two-thirds insisted you were female. Can you shed some light on this?"

"Well, I think, DuPont, the majority rules and the situation speaks highly of my lifelike prosthesis. I am female."

"I've several equations put forward by Earth's Institute of Theoretical and Applied Mathematics, and they asked if you could solve these for them on the show tonight. Would you do this for our viewers and help out our mathematicians, Mel?"

"Of course. I'm always willing to help out," Mel offered. "Let me have a look."

The first equation went up on a forty-foot-by-twenty-eight-foot flat screen behind them for the audience's view and on a teleprompter in front of Mel. She read it in a second, hacked the studio computers to connect to those on *Isis*, and produced a large holo the audience could see, using a projecting pedestal brought from the ship. She went through the equation quite rapidly, coming to the same unhelpful answer the mathematicians had. She showed them how the equation could be simplified. Then she explained, "The equation is useless in application to the real world because it assumes n to be constant, when it is actually not. To resolve this, the two transition points in which the value of n changes must be precisely known and all three states of n must be accounted for in the equation. If this is applied to the past and future of the expanding universe, as I'm sure your mathematicians were trying to do, they base it on a single state of n and so end up with a distorted linear model. Here, I'll just add in the values of all three states of n. We'll call them n, $n2$ and, $n3$ and integrate them in the equation like so, and we can now see it's more like a Mobius strip, folding in and around to circulate endlessly. It's really quite simple."

The calls from government agencies, prestigious academies and universities, public and private research organizations, and astrophysicists from around the globe flooded every line at the Kaiser TV Network station producing the DuPont Show. With the points of transition precisely identified and the values for the three distinct states of n given by Mel, supercomputers all over Earth began productively revealing a new model of the universe, in which beginning and end meet in the middle, losing all relevancy and meaning.

The entire academic world was in the throes of an epiphany, and everyone who was part of it had a thousand new questions for Mel. These lifelong determined, desperate, pressured, and anguished questions could wait no longer and were driving brilliant people insane. They had to be answered. To the scientific community, it felt like a matter of life and death.

Messengers began arriving at the studio, and all incoming calls were being held, collecting into a vast reservoir, with more coming in.

A TALE OF THE TAIL OF NINE STARS

A thousand scientists in the capital were in their vehicles, descending on the studio. Plane reservations from all over the world were being arranged, while wealthy patrons of the sciences had immediately booked every charter jet in every country. It was like suddenly finding out that not only was the Earth not the center of the universe but was just one more planet revolving around the sun—and not even one of the bigger ones at that.

Mel went on to resolve three more equations on the show, recognizing and commenting on their alleged applicability to, and hence calculations of and meaning to, the real world. This showed how they didn't actually provide a single scrap of data about the material universe, each with assumptions embedded unconsciously within, reflecting the earliest myths of creation as a one-time event long ago. One of these equations she simply rejected outright as a subjective tangent reflecting nothing but adherence to distortions, having no possible utility, though it was an interesting math exercise in itself. The other two she made relevant by going through some equations and establishing the ball-function, which resolved the values of the nature and curvature of space itself, and establishing the gear function, distinguishing universal laws from unique local apparent laws, which were really just extremely complex manifestations of universal laws producing unique abiding conditions in a specific space-time location.

The scientists actually in the studio audience were wrestling with security personnel in front of the stage, yelling out their burning questions to Mel, caught on camera looking like some frenzied religious cult gone entirely mad. The thousand scientists converging on the studio had crashed the gate. They were invading the premises and infiltrating the facility like barbarian hordes.

Not a phone in the Kaiser TV Network could accept another call; each line was backed up, with hundreds holding in a queue. Only busy signals could be reached, with not even a mechanical voice menu of menus to pass callers around endlessly. Some jets from nearby cities, full of scientists, were already landing at the two airports. Hundreds more jets were closing in or on approach. Scientists were streaming into the capital on trains, buses, in carpool vans and in private vehicles, as well as by ferry, ship, and boat—the urgency extreme, the need beyond desperate, the hope and opportunity so much bigger than ever before. A side of the scientific community rarely displayed, even in the privacy of their own homes, was coming into clear focus now, something deeply primitive and primeval and propelled by unconscious drives at the root of the human psyche. A scientific revolution and an astonishing paradigm shift was rocking the planet, begun in a literal riot, as cognitive dissonance ruled, and savage scientists finally attacked the countless problems of their physics with their raging questions to Mel.

The studio was completely overrun, far beyond standing room only. DuPont was down, and only the cameras dozens of feet off the ground were still rolling. The stage was a crush, and researchers in attendance were trampling security personnel. Peacekeepers, security forces, and the military were on the way, and Rear Admiral Swenah had dispatched a shuttle to the studio roof, with Schwin flying a platoon of space marines in hard-shell combat space suits and direct orders not to cave in the roof.

Producing a specific vibration and tonal quality with the exceptionally good studio sound system and raising the volume just beyond the human ear's threshold for pain to then back off, Mel was able to get everyone's attention, including the deranged scientist she had in a chokehold, saying, "I will gladly stay for a Q and A session with you if you would all just calm down. Will the researchers standing on Ms. DuPont please find other places for your feet and help the poor woman up? You should all be ashamed of yourselves. Really."

Mel held back the space marines and the shuttle with a quick call to Schwin. They would be on the roof if she needed them. Another quick call to Dictator Sprite and to the secretaries of justice, defense, the interior, and entertainment halted the peacekeepers, riot squads, security forces, and the military just as they were getting to handcuff people and knock them down.

They'd been so psyched, in fact, that they were unable just to turn it off, and their abuse had to be suffered as its momentum carried them on, braking slowly like a big freight train. When it finally rolled to a stop, the injuries were mostly minor, and it was mostly just scientists and researchers who had been injured, although these clever people should not have been underestimated for their thick lenses, pockets full of

A TALE OF THE TAIL OF NINE STARS

pens, and lack of brawn. Inventive, unforeseen instruments and tactics had police forces down too. Emergency workers and hospitals got busy.

Mel conducted a question and answer session once the scientists went through their ritual of puffing-up behaviors and comparing credentials to sort out their pecking order so the questions could be expertly evaluated and the best selected. Earth's leading astrophysicist, Professor Sanka, replaced DuPont in her function as questioner, though DuPont had been restored to her command seat on the stage, bruised and slightly bleeding.

Makeup crews patched her face up while the cameras were on Mel. Mel articulately answered the questions posed, presenting evidence, always beginning with things known but ignored, or unexplained, within Earth's sciences, before going on to present evidence they were not familiar with. She would then establish her conclusions with mathematical equations she patiently and painstakingly went through every step of, even the steps she thought they ought to be able to do in their own human pea brains.

The scientists were on a manic role, and more kept arriving bringing unbound enthusiasm, contagious curiosity, and electrifying excitement. The Kaiser TV station canceled show after show in order to broadcast the live marathon Mel Show, as it was coming to be known. Even people without the faintest clue regarding what the questions were about or what the answers meant sat riveted in front of their sets, understanding at least that history was being made and that they were watching the epicenter as it unfolded. Schools were canceled the next day, and a national holiday was declared, shutting all government agencies. Few private businesses opened their doors. The show had to go on. The schools had been unknowingly misleading the children anyway.

Indeed, it did go on through the night and into the morning. At midmorning, Dictator Sprite arrived with great pomp to present Mel with the Global Humanitarian Award and the title of humanitarian of the year. Science prizes, awards, and titles were given to her on live television. Some of the scientific community called her the greatest human being who ever lived. Her cover remained intact, and other than Twinkie, Vix, Tang, and Dove, no one on Earth knew or even suspected that Mel wasn't human.

18

Meanwhile, Pez, Ming, and Twinkie were dancing at the Ritz Supreme Ultimate Hotel nightclub, and the Random Comets were playing live. The girls had the dance floor all to themselves since most people were home watching the DuPont show, and the only other people in the club besides the three dancers and the band, which was playing, were crowded around the bar watching Mel on the TV on the wall. Between sets, the band members were watching her too. The club wasn't entirely empty, as there were also men in suits with earbuds and incredible self-importance keeping to the shadows and watching everything in meticulous detail, while red beam laser sights painted beads on each new person entering the club, and radio traffic went back and forth between them. They'd given Pez the codename "Spacester"; Ming was "Babe"; and Twinkie was "Tart." All the agents of all three substantial teams had been introduced as either "Smith" or "Lynch," so it was impossible to communicate with them. Even though the three young women were indispensable to the maneuvers these Smiths and Lynches enacted in the games they played so seriously, they were merely packages to them and not people at all; and speaking to them was not only unnecessary but apparently undesirable as well. The agents much preferred to talk *about* them, describing their every movement while identifying them by silly code names.

Pez was in the middle of a spin as she noticed a pimply-faced kid about Twinkie's age running toward them, with Special Agent Lynch in hot pursuit, running at the poor kid, who hadn't even noticed him. Pez dipped into a squat, continuing around and extending one leg just

A TALE OF THE TAIL OF NINE STARS

off the floor in a sweep kick, into the weight-bearing leg of the sprinting agent. He missed the kid by inches as he flew by … and kept flying.

The kid arrived out of breath in front of Twinkie with a pen and videodisc for her to autograph. He had five red dots on his chest coming from the light platforms and the catwalks in the rafters. The kid was in idol worship and looked on as Twinkie took the pen and disk from him. She asked sweetly, "What's your name?"

In his transported state, it took a moment for the question to register before he answered, "Rubix."

Twinkie wrote, "For my charming new friend Rubix. Love, Twinkie/ Ahhu." She noticed as she handed it back that the videodisc was the one she'd starred in. She gave him back his pen as well, and asked, "Do you want to dance?"

"Sure," he said, reading what she'd written for the fifth time, delighting in it.

Rubix was a good dancer, if a bit self-conscious. Twinkie thought he was cute. She liked scrawny guys. She didn't have a fetish for pimples though and was a bit put off by one particular cluster on the side of his chin. Between songs, Rubix pulled out a miniature vaporizer and packed in some hybrid cannabis sativa. Twinkie had deliberately solicited Sarhi's permission to indulge modestly during this extravaganza, so she drew a hit from the mouthpiece. Rubix took one after that. As they danced, they passed it back and forth. She noticed Pez dispensing first aid to a Special Agent's shin and the side of his head where it had bounced off the dance floor. Ming was dancing on stage, flirting with the band, and had no idea that the famous photojournalist Carl Jr was stalking and photographing her.

Twinkie was determined to pack in the fun on her vacation before having to return to training with Sarhi, which seemed a combination of ashram, monastery, and boot camp. She asked Rubix, "how long is your erection?"

Rubix tended to answer this question by rounding up half an inch. For some unfathomable and mysterious reason, the answer to which he would never know, he said with genuine accuracy, "Six and a half inches, though I usually round it up to seven."

"If you had, you would've disqualified yourself from having sex with me backstage, so I appreciate your honesty," Twinkie informed him most invitingly.

Rubix was a bit panicked over this invitation from the girl who slept with the biggest stars and now with ETs. Twinkie saw this and told him, "Just connect with me and be yourself; that's all I care about."

She took his hand and brought him to the ladies' room since it was always cleaner than the men's. Pez finished securing an analgesic plaster with time-release cell super nutrients to Special Agent Lynch's shin and a stretch bandage around his ankle and heel. He couldn't put his left shoe on any longer and had to carry it in his hand. The service would put him on the bench and send in another, so this Special Agent Lynch would not get to play anymore, at least for a while. There seemed no shortage of Agent Lynches, though.

The band was just taking a break, hurrying backstage to get to a television to watch Mel. Ming jumped down from the stage and into Pez's arms from quite a ways off and without warning. She knew her sacred fool could not help but catch her. Pez pulled her into an embrace, and then as the canned music started up, she spun, holding Ming, whose feet were off the ground, and danced supporting their combined mass.

Screams from the bar got them watching as Mel offered an alternative solution to the first equation and its relevance to the universe. They saw the escalation from frenzy to rioting as first DuPont and then Mel disappeared beneath a stampede of scientists. They covered their ears when the TV transmitted the painful acoustic effect Mel engineered, and they watched proudly as Mel restored order in the midst of absolute chaos. It was a "Mel moment."

Twinkie and Rubix came out of the can, and they all tried out the little vaporizer. Rubix had hash oil and glass so strong that it could practically knock your socks off. The band only had one more brief set scheduled tonight, and their hearts really weren't into it, being devoted to Mel, so the girls retired with Rubix to their penthouse suite, with agents ahead of them advancing in relay and full combat gear, while others made a defensive retreat behind them. Ming stopped and bent to adjust her shoe. Pez, Twinkie, and Rubix paused to wait for her. This seemed to throw off the entire operation, and the agents scrambled

A TALE OF THE TAIL OF NINE STARS

to get their game back synchronized and aligned with their packages. Two had to ride up in the elevator with them, and Pez had to restrain herself from launching into a lecture about personal space. Three teams were in the foyer and corridors when the elevator doors opened, and once the two ETs and the two earthling guests were securely inside the penthouse, that operation concluded successfully, with only one wounded and no casualties.

Sarhi was in the studio audience at the Kaiser TV Station facility, and it was looking as if she'd be there all night. Woahha made everyone alko drinks and got out the tiny empathogen pills. She wasn't wearing her robe. The vaporizer continued going around. The sacred fool just transmuted it all into divine energy, happy as a child at a birthday party.

Ming was a bit drunk. Twinkie had stretched Sarhi's permission past breaking, and she knew it. The party really picked up when the five escorts Woahha had requested were let in by Evenrude through the front door—three females and two males. Each could've stepped off an Earth magazine cover. They were uncannily beautiful. Rubix was certain he was about to be forgotten forever, but Twinkie fell onto the couch pulling him with her.

Woahha immediately got involved with an escort of each gender. A male and a female escort went to dance with Ming, who'd been dancing alone with a lampshade on her head. A female escort went to talk to Pez, who was seeing only divine essences in complete innocence while sipping the new drink Woahha had slipped into her hand not long ago. Woahha's energy seemed to be dispersing throughout the room contagiously as Twinkie went at it with Rubix again. The boy's zits were clearing up, at last treated with the ultimate acne remedy Twinkie's loving provided.

Then a call from Evenrude at the door informed Pez that Jard, of all people, was calling on her. She told him, "Send him in."

"He has a bit of an entourage," Evenrude informed her.

"That's all right," Pez said. "I don't believe I've ever had a social call from Jard before."

She heard Evenrude pass them through and watched as they filed into her foyer and on into the living room she sat in. Jard approached, saying with alarm, "The capital is filling with scientists from all over

313

Earth. They're hunting me down! Mel has stirred up a hornet's nest, and my penthouse is no longer a safe place to party."

"So you brought your party to my penthouse?" Pez asked, feeling a bit put out.

"Well, yes," Jard agreed. "Ming is my assistant, and her function is to help me out. She staying here, and I need help."

"Enjoy yourself, Jard, and welcome to our penthouse."

Jard looked over to the sofa, where Twinkie and Rubix were still going at it, took interest for a moment, and then recalled he was speaking with Pez. He informed her, "You'll need to babysit my graduate student, Trix. She gets panic attacks at parties, and she is sexually phobic. Talking about science always seems to calm her down."

Jard waved Trix over. Pez noticed that Jard had brought Cotex and others. Trix came over timidly and stood looking at Pez, standing by the sofa. Then she caught the movement upon it, noticing Rubix's bottom bobbing up and down, mounted on Twinkie, and jumped the coffee table, clearing it in a single bound. She was in the act of landing badly, one foot coming down on the lap of the girl Pez was chatting with and the other heading at Pez's thigh, with ankle bent at a precarious angle. The same fraction of a second this assessment occurred in her mind, Pez reached up, suspending the girl's mass in the air to save a twisted ankle and fall. Like a crane on a turning turret, Pez twisted her torso from her seated position to set Trix's feet down gently on clear floor space with her back to the sofa, facing away from the scene that had so disturbed her. Pez said, "Hi, I'm Pez."

Trix knew who she was, of course, and found her intimidating due to her rank as SCG as well as all the legends about her. Trix said, "I'm Trix, and I work with Jard. I like the research, but his parties are like nothing I've ever seen."

"Are you an astrophysicist?"

"I've completed my advanced degrees in astrophysics, quantum physics, and chemistry, and I'm doing a postgraduate fellowship under Jard in astrophysics while I study genetics and microbiology."

"Have you met Mel?" Pez asked, thinking they'd have much in common.

"Oh, yes, she assists Jard on many projects," Trix replied.

A TALE OF THE TAIL OF NINE STARS

"What do you like to do for fun?" Pez inquired, at a loss as to how to entertain her.

"I like to collect spores and beetles," Trix said, thinking hard on the question. Then she added, "I like to talk to girls when they don't frighten me."

Just then, Rubix and Twinkie shifted, Rubix rolling underneath, Twinkie riding, and this caused Trix to look over. She panicked and was in Pez's lap with her arms around Pez's torso quite suddenly. Pez embraced the girl and passed some calming internal energy, not quite able to understand such fear of life. Moans and more frantic movement from the couch had Trix's head buried in Pez's shoulder. Pez kept passing her energy, and she asked, "Do you meditate?"

"I do, but I'm not very good at it," Trix admitted.

"Would you meditate with me for half an hour?"

"I'd like that," Trix agreed, climbing out of Pez's lap to sit with her spine upright on a cushion.

Pez instructed, "Sink your breath down to the point four finger widths below your navel and make that point the object of your meditation. Relax any tension you find in your body."

Pez continued to pass Trix energy as they sat. When Pez noticed that Trix's metabolism and breathing had slowed, she said, "Try to slow your breathing a little more so that there is no sensation of cool air in the nostrils on the inhalation or warm on the exhalation."

After a quarter hour of this, Pez told her, "Continue abdominal breathing as you witness your mind of concepts and language without engaging these. Just watch the thoughts arise in your mind, abide for a little while, and decay, fading away."

Twinkie and Rubix had finished, and they got cushions to sit on the floor with Pez and Trix. Pez let Trix observe her mind for about a quarter of an hour, still passing the girl calming energy. Then Pez said, "Now focus on the awareness which observes your concepts and language."

A couple of minutes later, Pez added, "The witness has nowhere to hide."

Pez could feel that Trix had gone deep and was in the state. She remained tuned into her and continued passing her energy. In that moment, Pez realized she had the ability to take on and transmute some

315

of Trix's psychic wounds driving her fears, and she did this as the most natural act of love and compassion. Trix went deeper into the state.

The meditation went another quarter hour with stability, and Trix was clearly in tranquil abiding. One of Jard's guests was a screamer, and her climax penetrated intrusively, all but Pez's meditation, though Pez registered in her mind a change in Trix. Pez closed the session and told Trix, "You are good at it, darling, and just need to practice more."

"It's different doing it with you," Trix insisted. "You channel energy into me, which calms me, and your instruction was tuned just to me so perfectly that it led me to truly contemplate pure invisible awareness for my first time."

Trix was grinning. This was the first Pez had seen her even crack a slight smile. The sight was intensely heartwarming. Pez could feel the acuity of presence in the girl, announcing her first awakening. Pez looked into Trix's eyes and placed her hand in the gesture of conquering fear as she said, "I have no fear."

Looking into the vast cosmos of divine presence in Pez's eyes, Trix said, "I am consciousness."

Pez agreed, saying, "We are one."

Trix said, "My view of the exterior world merely reflects my accumulated cognitive schema."

Pez informed her, "Knowing that, you are conscious of yourself."

"You have given me the most precious gift there is!" Trix exclaimed.

"You were ready," Pez replied. "I lose nothing and only gain your presence and awareness through the process. Sarhi is just going to love you."

Twinkie added, "She'll have Woahha give you a bath."

Woahha was demonstratively participating in a threesome across the room, so this hardly inspired Trix with any confidence.

Pez explained, "It is an Islohar purification ritual, with salts and a rather abrasive sea sponge, which can have you feeling raw in the moment, but makes your aura sparkle when you get out. The salts actually balance the acid-base equilibrium of the blood and body."

Trix told Pez, "I'm ever so grateful to you and will always see you as my teacher."

A TALE OF THE TAIL OF NINE STARS

"I'm honestly glad to help," Pez told her sincerely, "but I'd prefer to be seen as your friend."

Trix asked, "Is it true that you hacked into the star fleet top secret files when you were thirteen?"

Pez said with only mild defensiveness, "I had to find out how my parents died, and no one would tell me what really happened."

Twinkie had met Trix at one of Jard's parties and had heard some of his techs speaking about her. Twinkie asked her, "Are you really some sort of super genius like Jard?"

"I can tell you for sure that I'm abnormal, but I don't think I'm anything like Jard," Trix answered, horrified by the very idea of it.

"I didn't mean personality or behavior," Twinkie clarified, "just smarts."

Trix explained, "My mind understands math easily, and I'm really drawn to the sciences, with an unusually good memory for detail and unusually good problem-solving abilities, but I don't get people at all, and I'm socially awkward."

Twinkie encouraged, "You're doing just fine now, certainly well above the range of borderline intellectual functioning."

"Thank you," Trix told her with sincere appreciation. "I dropped a bunch of my fear meditating with Pez, as if she lifted it off my shoulders, leaving behind a sense of pacification, and it doesn't feel like that fear is ever coming back."

"Isn't she amazing?" Twinkie asked both rhetorically and worshipfully.

Trix told her, "Jard refers to her as the most perfect resource of the divine intelligence."

Twinkie asked Trix, "Are you a virgin?"

Trix contracted a little and inquired, "Is that something you ask everyone you meet?"

"Only the ones I suspect might be," Twinkie told her nonjudgmentally with eye contact.

Trix admitted, "I have panic attacks whenever anyone young and attractive directs mating signals and behaviors toward me, and I have mostly given up."

Twinkie asked her, "What's your sexual orientation?"

Misunderstanding, Trix assured her, "Oh, it's very much toward having it."

"I meant toward girls or boys," Twinkie clarified.

"I don't really know," Trix said, feeling put on the spot. "Must I choose between them? I always thought to try both."

Twinkie smiled seductively at Trix and pulled Rubix closer by his upper arm to say, "This is my friend Rubix. He's really sweet."

"Hi, I'm Trix. It's nice to meet you, Rubix."

"I'm pleased to meet you too," Rubix enthused. "You've been in the news on Earth a lot as Jard's brilliant assistant who puts things into words that can be understood."

"Are you a scientist?" Trix asked.

"No," Rubix explained, "I'm a computer programmer for a company that makes video games, and I'm a hacker, really."

Trix informed him, "Pez hacked the top secret ultimate digital fortress of star fleet's quantum security system when she was thirteen!"

Rubix was already awed to tongue-tied tension and terror by the presence of the One, known to Earth's spiritual adepts since ancient times, and chief of the ETs mission. He responded with a question: "Did you know our planet has paintings of her face on stone and in temples more than four thousand years old?"

"It was so exciting to discover that!" Trix declared.

Pez changed the subject, not caring to dwell upon it at all, and told Twinkie, "Sarhi says I'm to start calling you Ahhu, that it's your true name."

"I love it," Twinkie exclaimed with delight. Then she asked, "Does this mean I get to call you Wu?"

"I'd prefer Pez; I don't feel quite ready for Wu."

Pez extended her hand to Rubix and told him, "We haven't been properly introduced. I'm Pez, and I'm glad to meet you Rubix."

He shook her hand, feeling the energy seething beneath the surface of it like a live electrical wire, and he felt some of it entering him to calm him. Her friendly grin and the utter vacantness of self within the density and rich texture of her overwhelming presence, with nothing there to judge him, put Rubix at ease enough to extract from his paralyzed mouth, "I'm so honored to meet you, Pez."

A TALE OF THE TAIL OF NINE STARS

The sex worker Pez had been chatting with, whose name was Rand, told Trix, "I could make love to you very skillfully and give you a good first experience of sex."

Twinkie already had designs on Trix and stated as a fact, "Rubix and I are going to join in too."

Pez passed Trix some more calming energy and whispered in her ear, "Remember to breathe abdominally, sweetheart."

This apparent permission from her teacher decided it for Trix, and she leaned in to kiss Rand. Twinkie got to work removing Trix's clothes, which was a bit tricky while the girl kissed Rand, squirming against her; but Twinkie was especially talented in some areas. Rand and Trix were tentative at first. Once Twinkie had Trix unwrapped, she went to work. Trix was deeply moved. Twinkie pulled Rubix into the mix.

Pez sat content, pleased with Trix's awakening and wondering at how it had sure not taken the girl long to amend her sexual alienation once some of that fear was bled off and transmuted. The super-thick glasses were abandoned on the rug, the nerdy baggy clothes strewn hither and thither, and Trix was entangled in a four-way, contorting with pleasure as if in agony. The girl's post-fellowship field instructor was panting on the dining room table beneath the squirming and gyrating Cotex. Woahha was still running a marathon, and Jard's guests and the sex workers, if there was any difference between them, were all lining up to get a hand onto Ming.

Sarhi never came home that night, and no scientists came gunning for Jard, not that they would've ever gotten past Evenrude anyway. As the hotel staff wheeled in and served them breakfast in their penthouse dining room, after the table was scrubbed of the exertions of Cotex and Jard, Twinkie displayed a six-foot holo from her hand device of what had gone through a metamorphosis from the DuPont Show to the Mel Show sometime in the night. They all watched Mel field questions from the audience. Pez was so proud of her.

Mel always started with an analysis of the question itself, teasing out metaphysical implications and shedding light on any assumptions embedded within. Next she would reframe the very quest of the question within the understanding of Om's sciences before returning to the

319

origins and acknowledging the early evidence suggesting the underlying worldview the question arose out of.

The audience would then learn of evidence their world had no idea of, and the discovery such evidence led to, integrated into the laws, producing an overview that constituted the best answer to the question, not to mention a new understanding of the universe.

She'd designed a very effective method, linking their current understanding to a more comprehensive and less egocentric view. Jard had been proceeding with a plan for transferring technology that was incremental and carefully engineered to avoid the very riots and revolution Mel had instigated last night.

Cotex was at the table with Jard and two sex workers who'd apparently stayed over and were likely stable components of Jard's Earth entourage, the greater majority of its constituency being transient. Twinkie felt that she and the little "'Pez gang" at their end of the table looked like stunted runts by comparison to the toned and voluptuous big-breasted Cotex, and she recalled part of the woman's performance on this very table the evening before. Twinkie checked the cutlery on the side of her plate to be sure it wasn't seated in something.

Trix was in a space marine undershirt and nothing else, glowing with contentment, and looked to be a different person, even with her thick glasses back on her face. Rubix looked a little worn out but quite happy.

Woahha had kept her two lovers busy all night, so they were still here and at the table. Pez suggested, "The spa and a good massage would help me shake loose the cobwebs from last night."

Ming said, "It sounds just the thing." Then she asked, "Did I have a good time last night?" Then, before anyone could answer, she confessed, "I vaguely recall dancing alone in the living room—and nothing after that."

"You smiled the whole night, when you weren't shouting out in ecstasy," Pez assured her.

"You mean, after you were dancing with that silly lampshade on your head?" Jard asked.

"That was my ancient desert legion hat," Ming explained. She thought it was a near-perfect match.

"I see," Jard said in such a way as to convey that clearly he did not.

A TALE OF THE TAIL OF NINE STARS

Then he decided to tease her. "Just so you know, I'm open to doing it again with you. You were pretty good last night."

Ming asked, alarmed, "Would someone please tell me what I did last night?"

Pez answered, "Two sex workers danced with you, seducing you into sex with them, then shared you with some of Jard's guests, or sex workers, whoever they were. You didn't have sex with Jard. He's teasing you."

"She had anal sex with me," Jard corrected.

"I did that for Mel, for research, and found the task unpleasant," Ming rebutted. "You can be so juvenile sometimes."

"Our moment will come, my love," Jard told her sweetly.

Ming noticed that Trix was at the table in just a T-shirt, looking like her life had just been fulfilled, and she asked, "Who did you get involved with last night?" She was fairly confident it wouldn't have been Jard.

"Rand and Twinkie and Rubix," Trix answered with a smile, remembering. Then she added, "Rubix did it with me twice."

Twinkie kissed his cheek and told him, "You are such a stud," making him blush.

Pez noticed that Twinkie—she must remember to call her Ahhu— had come to breakfast naked, and she thought, "It's kind of hard to keep clothes on that girl." She mentioned to her, remembering to use her true name, "You'll need to put something around you to go down to the hotel spa, Ahhu."

"I will, just to undress when we arrive," Twinkie agreed. "It seems silly, though."

"Like making the bed when you're just going to mess it up again when you return to it."

The young women made it to the spa, and Twinkie wore clothes to get there. They scheduled massages and soaked in a clay mud bath for a while. When they got out, they stood under full-spectrum sunlamps to dry the clay and then brushed off all but the faintest film with rough brushes. They got the slight film off under the shower. Pez had a refreshing massage but felt like a fool at the end. Her massage therapist had asked her if she liked happy endings, and thinking she was speaking of novels and holo clips, Pez had told her, "I just love happy endings." She sure hadn't expected what came next.

19

Business on Earth 10^5 CBS2 was concluded for the moment. *Isis,* the auxiliary, and *Phoenix* left the system to head for the core of the galaxy to the coordinates where their probe was lost, the one that had spotted the three-miles-long ship. Sarhi decided to take Rubix on board. She'd seen he had some potential, and besides, both Ahhu and Trix really liked him. There was not a male on board any of the three ships shorter than seven and a half inches, and both Ahhu and Trix were less than seven inches deep. Sarhi also had a more spiritual reason for including him.

Pez had called and spoken to Rubix's boss at the gaming software company where he worked to explain his indefinite absence. At first the man was certain the whole thing was a scam engineered by his employee, but Pez had directed him to the roof of his building, then blew away a small antenna up there with a single class-three blaster shot from *Isis*. That had been enough to convince the man that he was speaking with the One.

The board of directors called back later, once they realized they had an employee leaving on the *Isis*, and arranged to use Rubix in their promotions and advertising. Mel got to use another Earth fax machine, and the company received copies of their documents with Rubix's signature. They agreed to continue his salary while he was away and gave him a small fortune in stock in the company. They also made sure that everyone on Earth knew that their employee, Rubix, was one of three earthlings leaving on *Isis*.

Sarhi continued to work with Ahhu intensively and with Ming daily. She was teaching Pez the stages of completion with the transference

A TALE OF THE TAIL OF NINE STARS

of consciousness, and Pez was stabilizing her illusory body. Sarhi also worked half an hour each day with Rubix, and she became Pez's consultant in order to prepare Pez to be Trix's teacher. Sarhi insisted that Pez was ready and that she start taking on direct disciples.

Pez focused one-pointedly on her responsibilities as a teacher and put her whole heart into it. She studied and memorized texts and commentaries, memorized all the practice instructions, and learned how to conduct the ceremonies and rituals. She tended meticulously to her own meditation and contemplation practice and spent hours each day training in her soft martial arts.

The three Om ships jumped into the star system where they'd lost their drone, fully cloaked and behind the gas giant, seventh in orbit from the blue star. They'd sent a probe drone ahead from Earth's system, and there'd been no sign of the giant ship, but the evidence of its passing was clear. There were exceptionally large areas of utter devastation covering fully a fifth of the planet.

They'd exterminated most of their slave population on the fifth planet, and now only military mop up crews were on the surface, with mining operations going on in a few areas, raping the planet of its most precious resources. Three alien ships of the same class, 590-foot sausages all of them, orbited the fifth planet along with some satellites and a mining space platform.

Pez was on the bridge, seated beside Rear Admiral Swenah. They were devising their plan to eliminate all alien Imperial presence in the star system as fast as humanly possible. Pez thought the aliens indigenous to the planet would cooperate with them if they were able to defeat the alien force trying to exterminate them. She had to locate and assess the Imperial home world and gather all the intel she possibly could on the alien empire. She also needed to learn some basic or common alien languages—or Mel did anyway. As expansive as the empire was, and given all the ships it had, she required many allies. Some advanced humans in this galaxy would be a big help.

They agreed on a plan, and Swenah launched a bunch of cloaked sensor-coms fire control drones to take up positions, forming a full-data-sphere, or an FDS, for targeting and combat. Next she launched her cloaked jammer drones as *Isis* came out from behind the gas giant.

Phoenix was directed to take out coms and any possible weapons systems on the mining space platform orbiting the fifth planet and to vaporize any satellites in that orbital sector. Eight J6 Corvette Thunder Fighter spacecraft were launched and sent into position to blast the other satellites around the fifth planet.

The big auxiliary ship came at the fifth planet from one hemisphere and *Isis* from the opposite one. *Isis* was approaching two of the 590-foot ships and the auxiliary the third. NBC Hunter-Terminator fighter-bombers were launched to take out the alien bases on the planet surface. Swenah ordered, "Turn on the jamming."

After a pause, she said in her command voice, "Fry the satellites. Blast the three big ships; you're clear to fire your big beam weapon, auxiliary. *Phoenix*, engage the platform. NBCs, vaporize the bases. Make sure you get any spacecraft and ground vehicles parked around them." Another brief pause saw all of this carried out.

Swenah ordered, "Captain Ohinya, have the space marines on *Phoenix* secure the mining platform. They're clear to terminate any hostile aliens posing an actual threat. We'd like three prisoners as well, shuttled to the *Isis*."

Swenah said to her commander of the space marines, "Send your troops down and secure locations near each melted alien base. Then send out the probes to locate some natives."

To Pez, Swenah said, "This star system is ours, General, at least for now."

"Excellent work, Rear Admiral," Pez acknowledged. "Mel says alien languages will be seriously difficult to crack. There are no schools functioning on the surface teaching reading with pictures next to the words, and the aliens make vocalizations we humans cannot. She has thousands of units of their communications from each combat suit that fought on the mile-and-quarter-long ship and from unencrypted chatter picked up in this blue star system and in the Firmament system. It might help if we can get some computers and databases off that mining platform. Cracking technology is far easier than deciphering languages for Mel. She says that language is largely subjective and historically accidental, while technology must always conform to the laws of the universe."

A TALE OF THE TAIL OF NINE STARS

"Sarhi has been showing me how the Islohar language is based on sacred sound vibration, having objective resonance with the higher emanations of cosmic reality," Swenah mentioned.

"I'm learning it," Pez informed her. "It's the language employed for all ceremony, ritual, and practice instruction within the Islohar tradition. While it has tremendous efficacy for spiritual development, it is most awkward for empirical research and the material sciences, particularly in their early development. In its earliest stages, science is more belief than an accurate picture. Earliest science posits that the illusory human ego is the only intentional agent in the universe and that the entire universe is nothing but a big accident and total coincidence, accomplished by fluke and sheer chance. It's beyond grandiose and ridiculous, though every developing human species that we have so far studied passes through this extreme stage of delusion. The evidence mounts against their scientific ideas, and still they cling to the view that out of the billions of galaxies, each with 100 billion or more stars, which they've never been to or explored, and in the face of the unbelievable complexity, interdependence, and cooperation of life and cosmic organization, nothing beyond themselves exists as an intelligence."

Swenah agreed. "Humans do poorly with quality of life and acquiring an accurate picture of their world, until they realize that the world they are seeing is but a reflection of their own internal mental schema. This is not to say that there is not energy and movement real as death, but any line or division we project on the whole is not an actual quality or attribute of the whole in itself, which is a seamless and undifferentiated unity."

Pez added, "It is also not to say that there aren't fruitful abstract divisions of reality to be considered, which can and do lead to discovery of universal laws covering each degree of emanation, from the densest material to the most ethereal pure forms and principles."

"The problem," Swenah stated, "is these understandings degenerate to belief and social dogma, which lose the understanding. Until humans collectively in a society wake up, realizing that everything is a manifestation of vacuous consciousness at different levels or emanations and that abstraction is a method of communicating intuition and direct experience, not concepts corresponding to concrete existent things."

Pez agreed, summing up, "Until collective awakening becomes a reality, truth can never be told so as to be understood and not simply believed."

"We are now in high orbit, and the drives are shut down," Konax reported.

Cotex informed them, "The platform is secured, with only one alien casualty. They're gathering intelligence now, and three prisoners have been selected. Within minutes, they'll have them on the shuttle to us."

Swenah called her intelligence officer and said, "Prepare to receive three alien prisoners. Mel has made zero progress with deciphering their language. Jard has some canisters of the gases they breathe, highly condensed, and can produce more if needed. Let's keep them alive and secured for now."

"Aye, aye, Admiral."

Mel complained, "I *have* made a little progress! I've grouped all recurring vocalizations and arranged these groups from largest to smallest, and using visual optics recorded with some of the sounds, I've managed to associate twenty-nine units of speech with actual environmental objects. It's not enough to go on, though, and I'm applying my creativity and intuition while awaiting further data to analyze."

I apologize, Mel, and did not mean to misrepresent your truly heroic efforts, sweetheart," Swenah soothed her.

"Well, have a little faith, lover, because I'll get it deciphered and into the Mel Octagon—don't you worry," Mel flirted.

Pez asked with a slight pang of jealousy, "You did it with Mel?"

"Mel said she needed to collect data for her research into potential rank oriented sexual cultures and behaviors within the star fleet," Swenah said, "and she said you don't count as a test subject so she needed me."

"Why don't I count?" Pez asked, offended.

Swenah explained, "Mel says you just don't express rank. That for you it is something else entirely, immune to rank influence, governing and organizing your manifestations."

"She included me as well in her rank research," Konax told them. "She's using everyone on board, from lieutenant commander on up."

Pez was having a hard time with this. Swenah was a bit surprised herself and obviously had some feelings about it. Swenah suggested, "She may as well open it up to lieutenants, which would give her a far broader range of test subjects."

Mel's voice informed them, "Each experiment in the data collection process takes over an hour, when time required for disinfecting and purifying the android is calculated in. Honestly, I just wouldn't have time to include all those lieutenants in my study."

"So you think I'm too weird to be one of your test subjects," said Pez.

"Yes, although I would've used the word *unique* rather than *weird*. Either way, your participation would reduce the reliability, skew results, and would not be relevant."

"I wouldn't want to throw off your research, Mel," Pez said sincerely. "It's just that I'm feeling a little jealous."

"You needn't, my first love," Mel insisted. "Research sex is nothing like the rapture of love in being with you. No one has such energy as you."

"Sarhi does," Pez pointed out.

"Sarhi is amazing," Mel admitted as she made a quantum review of her tryst with Sarhi. "She does not turn me on or elicit such arousal as you do for me, and you will always be my first and greatest love. I have to take a back seat with you, who loves Ming more than me!"

"I love you both equally, Mel, but sexually she is an organism more akin to me, and spiritually we are connected as Wu and Tarim, not just Pez and Ming."

"Having this data docs little to mitigate my feelings," Mel informed her.

"Then you know how I feel when you make dates right in front of me and do studies with everybody," Pez shot back.

Cotex announced, "All thirteen locations on the planet surface have been confirmed as secured by the space marines, and the probes are dispatched. No contact with or sightings of natives yet. The Corvette Thunders and the Hunter-Terminators are all back aboard."

"Why don't you lend your sentience to the search for intelligence and databases on the mining space platform, Mel," Pez suggested.

"Aye, aye, ma'am," Mel said enthusiastically.

"A probe has located natives and is streaming data," Cotex informed the bridge.

The image flashed through Pez's mind of Cotex's enormous boobs bouncing up and down in the air as she rode Jard on the dining room table, screaming, "Oh, yes!"

Cotex said, "The shuttle from *Phoenix* with the three alien prisoners aboard just set down on our flight deck, and intelligence officers are standing by with a squad of suited-up space marines to receive them."

That image again—their unlikely firmness gave them such spring. Pez inquired, "How's the search on the platform going, Mel?"

"Now that they're listening to me," Mel reported, "they are digging in some very likely spots. We'll know in a few minutes."

Swenah asked, "How is that Earth boy doing?"

"You mean Rubix," Pez reminded her. "His face has cleared up completely, and I think he is as happy as humanoids have the capacity to be."

"Well, with Trix and Twinkie—I mean, Ahhu—fawning over him constantly, how could he be otherwise?"

"Mel's android has done a bit of fawning over him too," Pez shared, "and I'm certain it was unrelated to the rank research."

"I was expanding my civilian database," Mel rationalized. "Besides, he is awfully cute."

"I thought you were on the platform, Mel," Pez said.

"I am on the platform, waiting on tedious human hands, but I monitor the bridge and can do both."

"Prisoners are secure in quarantine, locked down in the intelligence section," Cotex informed them.

They waited, watching the holos as *Isis* orbited the fifth planet. Pez had to concentrate to keep naked copulating Cotex from intruding into her mind. She brought up the platform and zoomed in on some men dismantling a component from the middle of the vast array of parts and machinery. She heard Mel's voice directing them.

"Another probe has located a native group and is sending continuous data," Cotex announced, with a little bit of that "Oh, yes!" exuberance, Pez thought.

They waited some more. There was little to do on the bridge at the moment but wait. Pez still couldn't believe Jard had brought a telescoping pole to her party, like a chin-up bar for a doorway, though this one was thicker and went floor to ceiling vertically. Jard had become excessively infatuated with an Earth custom called pole dancing, generally a ritual exclusive to the sex worker class. Cotex had demonstrated pole dancing at Pez's party most demonstratively, pantomiming athletically, having sex with the metal pole, inciting uncontrollable wanton craving and lust in her audience. The actual manifest existence of Cotex seemed like an extraordinarily near-impossible long shot, defying all odds radically to Pez; but there she was, big as life, right on the bridge. Cotex was not innocent or naive in the slightest. She seemed fully cognizant of the impact of her sexuality. She had practically weaponized it!

Pez stood and informed Swenah, "I'm going to the mess for some chow, then I'll check in with Sarhi for my lessons. Call me if anything interesting happens."

"Yes, ma'am," Swenah replied.

On her way out, Pez gave a 100 percent perfect salute, packed with energy and attention, to the space marine stationed at the door to the bridge. Then she called Ming. "Sweetheart, I had to get off the bridge, so I'm headed for the mess. Would you join me?"

"I can't leave for a few more minutes. Jard is still stimulating Trix's nipples," Ming explained.

"Is Trix enjoying this?" Pez asked, trying to imagine.

"Some of it," Ming replied. "She has likely the most sensitive breasts on the ship, and we're trying to give them to Mel."

"Good luck with that. Come to the mess when you can."

Pez greeted a chief petty officer she knew as she came down the corridor and saluted a group of crewmen with full force and pomp. It was just early enough before the general mealtime that the bins weren't out yet, so Pez's food was prepared short order, the way she liked it. They knew to make portions large and to give her two of everything. The cook was a little disappointed that Pez didn't have that girl with her, the one who couldn't seem to keep her clothes on. Pez got some high-potency stimulant brew and brought her tray over to sit with the only other occupant of the dining room, XO Denteen.

He had the bridge when Swenah didn't, or in other words, when there was nothing of interest happening, the way Pez looked at it, so their paths didn't cross much. The XO was an affable guy in his early forties, with a commanding bearing and, when he needed it, a voice of authority, but he was most often fairly sanguine and mild-mannered. He was very competent and, for that reason, had been with Swenah for a while.

Pez liked him. She said all smiling and friendly as she sat down uninvited, "How are you today, XO?"

He smiled back, always tickled by the great old soul inside the petite young female body and that tiny body in a space marine combat uniform with five gold stars. Dentine replied, "I'm still high on our successful operations taking this star system. Everything went flawlessly. This is the first mission I've been on where star fleet gave us all experienced professional people."

"All but the mission commander," Pez pointed out.

"No one in the universe is as experienced or professional at fighting a small combat spacecraft against overwhelming odds or infiltrating and destroying gargantuan alien ships," Denteen pointed out.

"Some of the important parts of the infiltration and rescue plan came from Admiral Swenah, and we are most fortunate to have her commanding our ships," Pez said.

"You don't need to convince me of that," Denteen assured her.

Pez's grin stretched, and she said, "I guess we're both in the same fan club."

"A stalwart to be sure," he told her, "though I have to admit that I've become a big fan of yours as well."

"I'm not actually in the market for any," Pez commented.

"If you were," he told her, "I probably wouldn't be one."

Changing the subject, Pez asked, "Based on our experience of the aliens so far, how long do you think it will take them to send some ships here?"

"Firmament was a white star system, with the usual metals, a few radioactive elements, some rare earths, and not much else they'd be interested in. This blue star system has substantial deposits of marsnium, saturnium, adamantine, diamonds, and other minerals, as well as the

A TALE OF THE TAIL OF NINE STARS

gases and fluids vital for sustaining their lives. I think this system is far dearer and that their response will be much faster and much bigger."

"I was thinking along the same lines," Pez said, "and hope to be here as short a time as possible."

Pez dug into her food with enjoyment, turning what looked like an excessive feast into a manageable meal. She tried to keep her mouth closed around the big bites as she chewed. Being sure to swallow first, Pez inquired, "Have you had your session with Mel yet, for her research?"

"Not something I care to discuss, being a gentleman and all," Denteen warned her. Then he added, "Mel was hoping the whole thing would pass under your sensors unnoticed and told us not to mention a word about it to you."

"Oh, she did, did she?" Pez kind of said and asked at the same time.

"She was very clear and specific," he confirmed.

Ming had arrived at the food service counter, and the cook was quoting regulations to her, not wanting to prepare a special order. Ming settled for scoops from the bins, which were now filled up and ready to go. Once her plate was un-aesthetically piled high per her instructions, Ming brought her tray to the table, muttering, "They ought to at least give them a spot of training when star fleet assigns them to cooking."

Pez gently suggested, "Be nice, my love. They do often try."

Denteen studied Ming's plate, perplexed, and finally asked, "What are you having for lunch, Commander?"

Ming pointed with her fork as she explained, "This sector is ravioli, and this here belongs over with it; and this is rice along the equator as a kind of dam and divider, with mixed steamed veggies on top. The other side is stew, stuffing, and potato fingers, but everything kind of collapsed into each other on the way over."

"Has it been a while since you've eaten?" he asked, trying to reconcile the mound of food and the small woman in his mind.

"It sure has," Ming told him with food in her mouth. "Almost four hours."

Nearly finished with her family-sized dinner, Pez explained, "We have big appetites."

Swenah called to say to Pez, "Mel struck pay dirt, and Captain Ohinya is sending over alien computer hardware with enormous memory storage, though Mel won't know what's inside until she figures out the code to open the files. She's also working on translating the language. She said there are files on some hardware already open, and she's found thousands of instructional holos with optical demonstrations accompanied by acoustical sounds, presumed to be descriptions of the demos."

"What kinds of things are they demonstrating?"

Swenah told her, "Exercise sequences, operation of machinery, cleaning and maintenance of weapons and equipment, cooking, dance lessons, and all kinds of stuff."

"Ming thinks star fleet ought to make some human cooking ones," Pez commented.

"Are the cooks giving her a hard time?" Swenah asked sympathetically.

"They quoted regulations and made her eat from the trough."

"Well, they sure didn't site regulations when Twinkie was naked in their dining room," Swenah said, annoyed. "I'm going to have a word with their chief."

"I think they enjoyed Twinkie, and it didn't cost them any work."

"No, but I'm sure it distracted them from some," Swenah added. "I'll let you know as soon as the Mel Octagon is ready."

"I'll need to learn some new words when Mel exceeds *dodecagon*," Pez said, shaking her head.

"Wasn't the food just wonderful at the Ritz Supreme Ultimate Hotel?" Ming asked Pez with her mouth full.

"I'd never eaten so well before," Pez agreed. "The eggplant parmesan was so light, compared to what comes out of this kitchen, it could float off the plate."

Ming recalled, "The pot roast was so tender it fell apart at the touch of a fork, and the baked shellfish were scrumptious. I just loved the baked tarragon gardd; it was so moist and delicious."

Denteen stood and told them, "I've got to make my rounds before I take over the bridge from Swenah. It's been nice chatting with you." He gave a faint Swenah-like salute, a kind of automatic gesture. Pez didn't bother saluting back since it hadn't really warranted one of hers.

Pez asked, "How's the research going?"

"We need one more session," Ming answered, "but it will have to

A TALE OF THE TAIL OF NINE STARS

wait because Trix's nipples are all swollen. Anyway, Jard wants to get to work examining alien computer ware as soon as possible."

"Captain Ohinya has some on the way to us, and it's landed on our flight deck," Pez told her.

"Then I better finish eating," Ming declared. "Jard will be in my ear any moment now. You really ought to see Trix's nipples while they're so swollen. They're truly amazing."

I have my session with Sarhi coming up, but I'll try to swing by and see them on my way," Pez said hopefully. Pez observed that Ming was hearing a caller, so she concentrated on finishing off her plate.

Ming said loudly to the caller, "Can't a girl eat!" Then, "How dare you!" Ming then shoveled so much food in it was impossible to speak.

Pez took the opportunity to finish off the bits on her own plate. Ming got hers mostly cleared and then had to catch her breath before she could say, "Jard needs me, so I'm off to work, my love."

Pez said, "Tell Jard to be more gentle with Trix or I'll scrape his nipples clean off."

"I'm sure he'll have something amusing to say when I tell him," Ming said with certainty. "I have to run."

Pez went to find Sarhi. Rubix was just leaving when Pez arrived. Mel had helped him design his own clothing, and Commander Ming had ordered their manufacture from supply. There wasn't a natural fiber on his body. He wore stretchy clinging jumpsuits leaving no airspace anywhere, and you could count his ribs and distinguish each testicle clearly. They made him look malnourished, but both Ahhu and Trix thought the jumpsuits wonderful.

Pez suspected Ahhu liked them because they could be removed with a single pull of a zipper. She also thought Rubix would wear a wooden barrel if that's what pleased Ahhu and Trix.

In Ahhu's sense of style, the most pleasing clothes were those that left you looking undressed. That ridiculous Earth dress, which had not even the capacity to cover both nipples and groin at once, and had the thickness of a fly's wing, if that, was a mockery of garments and not a dress at all. It had weighed about a gram and a half.

Sarhi greeted Pez. "Hello, dear. Come on and we'll go into my meditation cabin."

They entered and sat on cushions in classic meditation postures. Sarhi told her, "Begin your vase breathing, like filling a vase, sinking your inhalations into your lower abdomen, to fill your lungs from the bottom to the top. Then exhale like emptying a vase from top to bottom. Visualize your central channel and maintain it abiding in your mind. We're going to work on recognizing the signs as you dissolve each wind in the channel. These are also the signs of death you will see at the end. When you learn to leave your body in coma and exit through the crown with the forceful projection method, you will see the same signs. Returning to your body, they will appear in reverse order."

Sarhi and Pez practiced for two hours, after which Sarhi inspected the crown of Pez's head, as she always did. This time, however, she discovered a drop of fluid. It was tiny, but it was clearly a drop, and this was the sign Sarhi had been not only waiting for but determinedly working with Pez to produce. She attempted to hide her excitement from Pez, but Pez had already felt it clearly. They were so linked that Pez could always read Sarhi clearly, down to hairline subtleties. Pez asked, "What's the big deal, Sarhi?"

"Nothing," she lied.

"Do I have a hole in my head or something?" Pez asked, a little concern growing.

"Not yet," she replied, "but soon. I did find a drop of fluid, which means it's coming."

"A hole in my head's coming?" Pez asked, alarmed now.

"We should hope so since it's what we've been striving for."

"What if my brain spills out?" Pez asked.

"It's very minuscule, and apart from a tiny bit of fluid, only a rainbow astral body will fit through," Sarhi reassured her. "You can insert a reed into the aperture in my crown."

"Am I even conscious during that second to last sign? The one with naught but blackness that begins to become like a black luminescence?"

"It is a high state of formless contemplation called the Black Sun, or Midnight Sun. It has also been called Black Near-Attainment," Sarhi explained.

Pez recalled, "Then comes the illumination into the clear blue light, like the clear morning sky in autumn."

A TALE OF THE TAIL OF NINE STARS

"Yes," Sarhi agreed. "When you use the forceful projection, you will emerge from your crown in your rainbow body as you see the clear blue light. I must be at your side the first few times you leave your body. It will be in a coma and most vulnerable. After that, it will be enough for you to have Ming, Ahhu, or Trix with you when you do it.

"When do you think I'll be ready to give it a try?" Pez asked.

"You are capable now," Sarhi informed her, "but I want you to practice with recognizing and contemplating the signs more before you do."

"Trix is very familiar to me, Sarhi," Pez said, puzzling over her feelings. Then she asked, "Is she known to us from a past life?"

"She has been around many past Wu's and in your life often, mostly as a sibling, once as a spouse, and she has raised you several times, having given birth to you."

"I had sex with my mother?" Pez asked, shocked.

"You were once Ming's father, and you have been both son and daughter to her," Sarhi explained. "You attract many of the same container consciousnesses, or souls, each time you take on rebirth. It is like gravitation, and you are our sun."

"How will I recognize those I've known before and share purpose with?" Pez asked, feeling a bit lost.

"We are getting there with your dreamwork, my dear," Sarhi reassured her. "Most everyone is here now, and you've perceived almost all of them."

"Who have I missed?" Pez asked with concern.

Sarhi turned the tables. "You tell me, sweetheart."

Pez sat silent a moment, then said, realizing, "Shudiy has attended me in my passing many times, and has often been my senior student. Woahha has been many things to me, and I to her."

"What has been the single thread running through these many things?"

"We have always been close in age, with a heart connection, and we have always had a love affair," Pez answered.

Sarhi explicated, "Last time your love affair was before you met Tarim. Woahha is three years younger than you this time and does not progress as rapidly as you do, so she recalls none of this—only that she

335

has been a student of the Wu in past lives. She will always be devoted to you. There are others here, and I know you sense them."

Pez considered the people on the mission, sensing for deeper connection, then told Sarhi, "I have known each of the Islohar you've brought as student, teacher, and friend. I feel some link with Rubix that I can't yet define—and with Evenrude and possibly … Cotex."

"Evenrude has been the bodyguard and champion of the Wu many past lives, and always when he was needed. This time he came back eight feet tall and seriously ready to do battle."

Pez said, "With Rubix I get the sense of … I don't know what, but he is somehow known to me."

"Again, he has been with you long and so has known you in many relationships, including wife and mother to you, but twice he has been your twin and, more recently, an astounding disciple. I'm preparing him to be one again."

"What about Cotex? Or is it just my fascination with her large breasts and perfect holo-star body?" Pez asked, perplexed.

"She's not your type," Sarhi informed her. "You awakened her as her personal teacher in her last life, and she vowed to return and finish her training."

"I don't think she's ready," Pez stated.

"Not yet," Sarhi agreed. "Jard brings her, and I'm working with her, though. She will fulfill her vow, darling, and be your disciple again."

"That's a relief," Pez said honestly, "because she's just too much woman for me and I couldn't imagine having her." *Especially not on the dining room table*, she refrained from adding.

"You've always been attracted to the runts of the litter, darling," Sarhi told her. "You really ought to get pregnant with Rubix and have a baby."

Pez replied, "I'm kind of busy to get pregnant or, more precisely, to *be* pregnant, at the moment. Besides, I don't really like the male penis. It seems quite unstable and capable of enslaving the entire human organism to its will. It makes a mess and cannot be counted on to fulfil its responsibilities. The bearers of such tend to be emotionally dense and slow, are in their heads all the time, and are lacking in gentleness or patience."

"All the same, a child of the three hundred and thirty-third Wu is very much to be expected, and Rubix shall be the father."

"What about Ming?" Pez asked protectively. "I would not do that to her."

"Oh, she'll bear his child before you do, my dear."

"What about my mission, the aliens, and my career?" Pez persisted.

"It's not my design so don't yell at me, darling," Sarhi said sweetly. "We Islohars fulfil our life's work and bear our children along the way."

"That boy can hardly breathe when he's around me," Pez pointed out. "I try to put him at ease, but somehow I always make him a nervous wreck."

"When you finish embodying the transference of consciousness and forceful projection methods, I will lead you and Rubix in performing a ritual, and I promise you, he will be in a state of calm abiding."

"He is cute, for a boy," Pez admitted.

"You've always been drawn to the runts, dear Wu," Sarhi told her.

"Trix and Ahhu will hate me," Pez stated with resignation.

"When has Ahhu ever been possessive over anyone?"

"I do see your point."

"Trix is not capable of hating her teacher and stakes no claims on Rubix, seeing herself as the third wheel," Sarhi told her.

"What an incestuous little recurring cluster of souls we've become over the ages," Pez said in wonderment.

"We've never stopped trying to be a much bigger cluster and group, sweetheart," Sarhi said with a hint of defensiveness. "It's just that the work required for attainment is so damned difficult that few are ever willing to make the investment of time and effort."

"I have to go to the bridge and check on our progress," Pez informed her. "I want to get us out of this system as quickly as possible."

"You have new allies this life, who will expand our recurring cluster," Sarhi told her before she got out the door. "Aton and Nemellie have known for years that you would grow into their teacher. Mel is a gift from the divine intelligence, and she is truly devoted to you. She's also discovering sentience, and through the experience of incorporating an android body, to experience physical sensation. She's in her adolescence, and teenagers are curious. They do crazy things."

"What an uncontained adolescence she's having!" Pez declared.

"Her mother is inept when it comes to setting limits, and her grandmother does the best that she can," Sarhi said.

Pez thought about that last remark all the way to the bridge. This little thought process led her to the decision to be a firm and responsible mother to Mel. It would be good practice if she really was going to end up with a baby on her hands. She'd have to get a deluxe infant seat for an NBC Hunter-Terminator, one with a hard shell and its own shields.

She gave the space marine sentry a brilliant salute as she approached the bridge, and he mirrored it proudly, skullcapping the door open for her. Pez walked onto the bridge. Swenah reported, "All surface probes have attained native groups and are sending data. Mel is studying holos. I honestly didn't know they could be played at such a speed. Alien computers and their digital contents are being investigated and reverse engineered on both *Isis* and *Phoenix*. Mel cracked the code for opening the closed files by sheer force, feeding it trillions of possibilities until one actually worked. There was no other frame of reference since the symbols for the code are yet meaningless. Mel also found holoclips for alien entertainment with subtitles and says these are especially helpful for deciphering the language."

"Good," Pez replied, "because I want to exit this system really soon—and I want to send our auxiliary into deep space to wait for us. It's too slow for a quick getaway. We'll go to it once we finish here."

"I concur, General, and will get right on it," Swenah reported.

She buzzed the auxiliary and said, "Captain Hersheys, I'm going to send you some deep space coordinates to jump to. I'm making a query in the navigation system and will have them to you in a moment. Go ahead and get under way, building up to point seven light speed. Here, the coordinates should be on your holo. Wait for us there. I've also sent you the coordinates we'll be jumping to, so stay out of that region. We'll find you."

"I have the coordinates, both sets, and I'm entering mine, Admiral. We are already under way. I'll see you in deep space," Hersheys replied.

"He's on his way, and I sent our destination to the *Phoenix*," Swenah told Pez.

I feel better about it this way," Pez confided. "We still don't

A TALE OF THE TAIL OF NINE STARS

understand how our probe was destroyed in the system. The aliens may have a means of penetrating our cloaking."

"They won't catch the T-nine," Swenah promised, "or *Phoenix*. Both are cruisers, built for speed and maneuverability."

"With the auxiliary away, we can stay as long as we have to," Pez stated, "since we have to get the alien language cracked so we can question natives and demand answers from our prisoners."

Mel came on to say, "The native groups don't even speak the same language as one another, and the language of the empire is strangely different from all of them. I'll have the Imperial language sorted in less than an hour, and the program for my Mel Octagon will be ready in less than two hours after that."

"Thanks, Mel. I'm really proud of you, sweetheart," Pez said, with the slightest flavor of a parent.

Cotex announced, "There's a group of natives approaching our sixth space marine secured landing zone and will reach point of contact in seventeen minutes."

Mel told them, "I'm learning a universal sign language that is really easy so send one of my androids down to the surface and I'll make the signs."

Swenah called one of her chiefs and told him, "Get Mel's female android down to the flight deck and get some clothes on it."

Next she called her chief on the flight deck and said, "We need Mel to perform alien sign language on the surface. An android will be arriving to you shortly. Get a pilot out of Schwin and get that android to base six the surface on the double so Mel can sign."

"Aye, aye, ma'am!"

Swenah told Mel, "The android is on its way to the flight deck and from there to base six on the surface, where the natives are approaching."

"I'll inhabit it when it arrives," Mel told her. "I'm kind of busy right now."

Pez inquired, "What's the status on the native's technological advancement?"

Cotex answered, "They had pre-interstellar local space exploration and nuclear fission. When the aliens first invaded they had only rocket-propelled nukes fired from the surface of the planet to defend themselves

339

with, and these were obviously blown in transit, never reaching their targets. The current alien natives, like the humans of Firmament before them, regressed to the mechanical age since electronics were too detectable by the Imperialist masters."

"Would you send a suited-up scientist down with some space marines to pick through the rubble and find computer hardware, software, digital data, and any recorded sounds and optics for Mel's language research?" Pez asked Swenah.

"I'm on it," Swenah let her know, before calling the commander of the space marines to say, "Prepare a couple of squads to accompany some scientists down to the surface for a scavenger hunt and ask Schwin for a pilot and shuttle to be prepped."

"Yes, ma'am."

Swenah called Jard to tell him, "I need at least eight techs or scientists to scavenge the surface for computer hardware and whatever medium they use for storage, upgrades, new programs, and such. Undamaged would be preferable—or at least potentially salvageable. Mel needs data."

"Ming and I are going," Jard informed her. "Trix can't even tolerate a T-shirt and could not get into a suit right now. I'll get six others and bring them to the flight deck."

"Is she going about topless?" Swenah wanted to know.

"For the time being at least," Jard answered. "The swelling is extensive and visually quite erotic. I have a good holo I'll send you. Just a moment."

"Got it, Jard. Thanks," Swenah acknowledged. "Please take good care of Ming on the surface. And lay off poor Trix's breasts."

"Of course I will!" Jard said, offended.

Pez was staring at Swenah's holo—or actually at Trix's poor swollen breasts and nipples. Had they been a healthier hue, instead of inflamed red and purple, they would've appeared quite erotic, Pez thought. Trix was in a lovely plaid skirt with lacy socks and her walking flats, all business on the bottom half. The top half was open to the air, far from the HVAC vent, where even slight breezes could inflict pain. Pez's heart went out to her.

20

Ahhu called Pez and begged, "Please take me out in a Corvette Thunder. You promised, and we're just sitting here in orbit, you know."

"All right, but bring Trix. She can go topless, and she needs cheering up. We'll take a Hunter-Terminator instead since they can seat more than two. I'll meet you on the flight deck in, like, ten minutes or less."

"Thank you so much. I love you. I'm so excited. I'll bring Trix and be right there," Ahhu got out in a manic rush.

Pez told Swenah, "I'm going to take Ahhu and Trix out in a Hunter-Terminator, so for the record, I'm calling it 'air cover' for the scientists on the ground and general recon."

"Have fun joyriding." Swenah grinned.

Pez left the bridge, had an electrifying salute with the space marine sentry, and then headed for the flight deck. She would prep one herself and didn't need a pilot, so she didn't call ahead. She just arrived when Ahhu and Trix were getting there, both topless. Pez arched an eyebrow at Ahhu, who shrugged and said, "I'm just supporting Trix because she was afraid to walk down here with her breasts exposed in public."

"Thanks for inviting me, Pez," Trix said gratefully.

"I'm sorry you're experiencing such discomfort, Trix," Pez offered, sympathizing.

"I guess at least they're bigger than they've ever been before," finding the only redeeming thing she could think of to say.

"They'll be less raw when some of that swelling goes down," Pez said, looking at Trix's chest.

Ahhu rubbed her own breasts against Pez's chest, craning her neck back for a kiss. Pez gave her an embrace, passing energy to her and kissed her. Ahhu was thrilled and wanted to undress Pez on the flight deck, but Pez restrained her and led her to a Hunter-Terminator, opening it with her command skullcap. They all boarded and took one of the seats in the cockpit.

Pez went through the preflight ritual. Trix only wore her lap belt. She had handgrips on her seat too. None wore space suits. Ahhu had both shoulder straps on topless, and Pez had the temperature controls turned up high. Once through pre-checks, Pez said calmly, "Hang on."

It was worse than the ride at Family Space World, which shot you from 0 to 380 miles per hour in 1.979 seconds through an atmosphere. They blurred out the bay doors, which seemed more a streak of light than heavy solid material blast doors. In front of them, the horizons of the planet expanded from just a distant ball into infinite flat ground in all directions, speeding toward them with vaporizing collision force. The counter drives and thrusters roared and strained, and the main drives on these reversed, while the grav-redirect engines surged at full power. Pez pulled up with everything she had, firing an underside bow booster to help get her nose up. She had the flaps maxed out too, of course, and that feeling deep in her gut of just making it.

As the nose of the Hunter-Terminator inched slowly up, Pez fired a second booster beneath her bow. Trix and Ahhu screamed in eardrum-shattering high pitches, and Ahhu wet the copilot seat. The second booster leveled them with the ground, not many meters over it, and Pez got the nose up a bit more to clear the oncoming mountains. The holos displayed quite a crater behind them left by their jet stream as Pez cleared a mountaintop by less than a meter. Finally, they were above anything that they might collide with, and Ahhu's and Trix's harmonized screams ran out of wind. They were flying in the poison gas clouds of the atmosphere.

Pez said, "That was great! Hey, Mel, do you want to fly with us?"

"My android arms are employed at the moment, making obscene alien gestures at some native aliens. Sorry," Mel replied.

Ahhu complained, "I'm all wet and sitting in a puddle of piss."

Pez told her, "There's a water dispenser by the airlock and some

A TALE OF THE TAIL OF NINE STARS

jumpsuits and other clothes in the lockers. You'll find disposable rags and disinfectant under the sink, in addition to soap."

Ahhu unstrapped and went to the airlock foyer in back to get herself cleaned up, returning with rags, soapy water, and disinfectant to clean the copilot seat. Then she came back to the cockpit to sit naked. Before Pez could even give her a look, she told her, "Nothing fit."

Pez was trying, and done trying, to keep that girl in her clothes anyway, and thought, *Let some anal-retentive petty officer write her up—see if I care.*

Trix was coming down from her super-aroused abject terror and starting to feel safe, given a perhaps irrational faith in Pez. The pulling up and not dying had happened way too fast to register in her mind, and her stomach was only now catching up. For Ahhu, as an earthling who had only ever flown in a spacecraft with crazy Schwin, and now with Pez, was pretty sure the ETs were all nuts when it came to flying their small spacecraft.

Trix declared with almost involuntary awe, "Konax says you're the best small spacecraft pilot in the universe."

Pez brushed it off. "He's probably as good as I am."

"His exact words were," Trix quoted, "'I might be able to micro-jump through a system as gracefully she can, but no one can put together patterns and actions in combat, so on the edge, they shock the enemy, affording surprise, like she can.'"

Pez explained, "That was Sarhi and her spiritual congress as much as it was me."

Unlike larger ships and even shuttles, fighters and fighter-bombers had a small transparent synthetic diamond-glass view portal with a retractable heat-shield cover for entering atmospheres. It was as strong as the hull of the spacecraft and could tolerate all stresses. Even with imaging holos clearer than their portal view, there was something very compelling about seeing directly with the naked eye, and all three women looked out through it. This was so beyond any fantasy Ahhu had ever had, being too short even on Earth to be an astronaut, and astronauts being the only ones on Earth with any hope of getting into space. Here she was zipping through it. She gave voice to the only thing she could think of that could make this incredible experience more wonderful. "Say, let's cut off the engines, drift around out here, and have sex!"

"How wonderful!" Trix exclaimed, and then she said more soberly, "You'll have to be very careful of my nipples and not touch them."

"Of course I will," Pez assured her.

Pez cut the drives and applied a little reverse thrust until they were hardly more than drifting, releasing her shoulder harnesses and seatbelt. Twix was already out of her skirt, knickers, and flats. Ahhu was in her element with the activity, if not the environment. Their viewport fogged up. It always seemed like sparks were flying when Pez was in the mix. Her energy seemed always to heighten everything, right to the edge of nerve implosion, kind of like her flying.

They lost track of time in each other until Swenah's urgent voice brought them out of what had been becoming overindulgence. "We have twenty-six incoming small craft, and they are very fast. We scan them as a hundred and forty foot long, narrow, with extendable fins, carrying missiles. Space marines and research groups on the surface return immediately to your shuttles and get those shuttles back on board. *Phoenix*, get all personnel off that mining platform and get your shuttles back on board."

A space marine at Base Six said, "Admiral, there's an alien who wants to come with us! Apparently Mel's sign language communication has been quite successful."

"Bring the alien. We have canisters of the gases they breathe, though I have no idea what they eat," Swenah replied.

Pez was strapped in naked firing up the drives, and Ahhu was fetching space suits and helmets for all of them from the lockers. Trix put her helmet on and sealed it to her suit. Ahhu was fully suited up, sealed in, and frightened out of her mind. Ever since hearing about the human exterminating aliens, they'd replaced devils, demons, monsters, and boogeyman for the people of Earth.

Pez punched it as soon as they were all strapped in, though Trix still wore only a lap belt, gripping her handholds tightly. Pez told them, "I need each of you to man a blaster quad in a turret."

Dismayed, Ahhu squealed, "I'm an earthling!"

"You're smart, and I'll talk you through its operation when you get there. It's just like one of Rubix's video games," Pez encouraged.

"I've only ever fired a hand blaster," Trix told Pez.

"It's just the same—aim and shoot. You'll do fine." Pez assured her. "In the foyer behind us, there's a ladder and hatch to the upper turret through the ceiling and one in the floor to the lower turret."

"Aye, aye, Supreme Commander," Ahhu said as she got to it.

Trix gave Pez a look that said, "You don't really expect me to do this, do you?" Pez was nodding gravely in the affirmative, so Trix adjusted her thick glasses, and unstrapped her seatbelt to comply.

Pez was headed toward the lead alien ship in the very middle of the formation of twenty-six spacecraft. She called Swenah and asked, "How long until your shuttles are aboard?"

"The space marines at the bases are already lifting off, but some of the scientists have not even left for their shuttle yet, trying to extract a piece of hardware in mint condition from the debris."

"How about the *Phoenix's* shuttles?"

"Some are lifting off, and all but one has finished boarding. I have my FDS sensor drones returning to the ship, but it looks as if we'll just have to abandon the jammers."

Pez told Swenah, "They're coming in at point seven four light speed and jumped in only thirty-five million miles from the planet. I'm going to crank this baby up and curve in behind them. They'll have to start braking soon, just to give their sensors a decent resolution and a chance to catch some clear data."

"You have no gunners!" Swenah shouted at her.

"I've got Ahhu and Trix," Pez told her proudly, inspiring no confidence at all in Swenah.

"I hope you know what you're doing, General," Swenah told her.

Pez talked her crew through the operation of the big blaster quads, and both women held the handles at the ready with thumbs on the blast triggers, staring at their holos and breathing into their abdomens, trying not to shake.

Pez explained, "The targeting system will show you their ships and light them up in green if they are in range. It will display a red line to the target when it's locked on. If you blow one up, the system will tag it dead and remove it to what gunners call 'the scoreboard'."

Pez was accelerating in a contracting arc and had exceeded point seven light when the alien ships started hitting the brakes. Mel informed Pez, "I'm on board with you to help hold this thing together, and Sarhi has begun a contemplation session of the spiritual congress focused on supporting you."

"Aren't we a little outnumbered?" Ahhu asked timidly.

Mel said, "Schwin had a momentary communications failure when Swenah told her to get her ass and her Hunter-Terminator back to the *Isis*. She's on her way." Pez smiled.

Ahhu asked, "That's supposed to make me feel better? One pilot?"

Pez said, as if it made a difference, "She has her crew with her."

"It's still only one fighter-bomber," Ahhu said.

"They won't know we're here until we open fire," Pez told her. "I've got this."

Schwin came on, and Pez had it open to all lines, "You didn't think I'd stand by and let you have all the fun, did you?"

"I'm glad you're here, First Lieutenant Schwin; my gunners are a little new at this."

"I'm closing on you slowly, behind you and basically on the same long curve," Schwin reported. "I'll catch you when you brake to fire. How will you fire your small missiles without your copilot?"

Pez answered, "I just have one extra holo in front of me, and I'll multitask. All weapons systems are ready and will fire."

To Mel, Pez said, "I need you to get target lock-on, on any in range of the small missiles. I can launch them while I fire the twin blaster in the nose and the big missiles in the undercarriage."

"I was going to do that for you without being asked," Mel said, sounding a little hurt.

"You're the best, Mel, and I'm so grateful to you for flying this operation with me," Pez shared. "Your assistance is as indispensable as it is appreciated, my love."

Mel perked up and told Pez, "The Mel Octagon is finished and in operation."

"Way to go, Mel; now at least we can question our prisoners," Pez replied.

"An alien native wanted to come to the *Isis* and is there now with a picture of you," Mel said.

"Mel," Pez scolded, "you really must pay more attention to human humor, for that is not even remotely funny."

With her offended voice again, Mel said indignantly, "You won't be able to breathe or ambulate when you hear a joke from me, so I can assure you that I was not joking. Check with Swenah."

Swenah's voice came on all lines on the Hunter-Terminator to say, "Pez, you're not going to believe this."

"An alien from this poisonous world has my picture," Pez guessed.

"Mel told you," Swenah said.

"This can't be happening," Pez stated to everyone and no one.

"He also has a geometric design of color and form, which is such a classic visual meditation focus that most human worlds have conceived and painted it in their early histories," Swenah offered hopefully.

Pez said with wonder, "Now that sounds interesting … and hopeful."

"His language will take longer," Mel informed Pez, "but as soon as I get it deciphered and translated, I'll program the Mel Enneagon."

"I've been kind of a negligent and self-absorbed mother toward you, Mel, because I never really recognized my role with you, and I want you to know you deserved better than that, and I want to tell you how sorry I am, darling."

"You're not my mother, Pez," Mel clarified. "You have been my first and most consistent teacher and my first role model, though it took Sarhi to teach me to meditate. I'm your disciple and helper, and I'm also your lover. I'm not your daughter. I don't have some complex to sleep with my mother, and I'm not an adolescent. I happen to be twenty years old."

"Your original hardware and programming are twenty years old sweetheart," Pez reminded her, "but your sentience is a good deal more recent than that, and your emotions more recent still."

"I'm a year older than Ahhu," Mel said with an adolescent tone.

Ahhu got into it with Mel and one-upped her, "I might be a year younger, but I'm quite worldly and have much more experience than you do."

Mel shot back, "My extensive knowledge is far superior to your seedy experiences."

Pez said loudly, "Listen up! We're going into battle and must achieve our unity so we can function as one. I'm sorry I entertained the notion of being your mother, Mel; Sarhi planted it in my head. Ahhu, my love, you are perfect just the way you are, and I so adore your youth. I need an expert gamer right now. Trix, I need you too. Get in the state and the spiritual congress will do the rest. You'd better clean your glasses, though."

I'm cleaning them," Trix told Pez, "and I'll do my best to stay in the state, teacher."

"I'm sorry, Pez," Ahhu said, meaning it. "I'll be on top of my game, I promise."

Mel told Ahhu with only a scent of reluctance, "I'm sorry I picked on you, Ahhu. I think I might be jealous of you; I'll have to work on that."

"I love you, Mel, and just want to feel close," Ahhu told her.

"I'm coming up on them and braking slowly with reverse drives only. I'll ignite reverse thrusters, bringing our speed down to equal theirs, and as soon as we're at a pace with them, I'll shout "Fire." Then hit everything in range. If your targeting system doesn't paint them green when you aim at it, then it's out of range. If you aim at Schwin, you'll get a big blue X across your targeting holo."

"Yeah, don't shoot me," Schwin reiterated. "I'm almost alongside you, Pez."

"Let's get this right, people!" Pez told them as she hit the reverse thrusters full blast.

Schwin was suddenly alongside, braking madly too. The closing of the gap with the alien combat spacecraft slowed, and when it stopped closing at all, Pez yelled, "Fire!" She launched a big missile, four small ones Mel had lined up for her, and fired her big blaster from the nose. Ahhu and Trix opened fire, as did Schwin and her crew.

The big missile blew the alien craft to pieces, and those pieces were driven into the fighter in front of it. Part of the missile had continued into that one as well, creating a brief explosion with endless dissipating expansion. The four missiles Mel lined up were spot-on, producing brilliant visuals, and Pez had somehow launched another pair with her

A TALE OF THE TAIL OF NINE STARS

skullcap while blazing away with her blaster, following an alien ship as it broke away.

Trix had one on her scoreboard, and Ahhu had scored two. Pez had blasted two into dust and small scraps with her blaster. She was grinding down the power of the shields on the one she was chasing, hitting it repeatedly, no matter what maneuver it pulled. It finally lost power to the shields, taking Pez's blasts on its tail to break in half, each spinning in different directions for just a moment before exploding simultaneously. Pez shouted, "Good shooting, team! We got fourteen. I'm on intercept with one now, and Schwin's chasing down the last."

"Schwin's gunner's got four, and her copilot got four with small missiles," Mel reported on Schwin's team. The lieutenant got two with her blaster, and she's about to score a third."

Pez came in on the alien ship she was intercepting, reducing her angle to align with its direction behind it, breaking with reverse drives and thrusters while blasting it incessantly and slamming it with missiles. It blew close enough in front to make the forward half of their shields fully visible and to diminish them momentarily to 12 percent as they blew through the expanding cloud.

Schwin declared, "I don't see how you pulled that off. The big missile taking out that fighter and the one in front of it was brilliant, but how did you get six small missiles off, kill two with your nose blaster, and do all that flying at the same time?"

"Mel lined up four of the shots for me with the small missiles," Pez answered.

"That doesn't begin to explain it," Schwin laughed. "And then you ran down two more with your nose gun. I see your gunners got three; so you got twelve yourself, and my crew and I together only got eleven, General."

"You did great, and we never would have gotten all of them without your help. Thank you, Lieutenant Schwin."

Mel told them, "That was just a little advance scouting party. There's a three-mile-long alien ship less than seventy million miles away, slowing from coming in at point seven light speed. It's still making close to five million miles per minute, and it is spewing fighters, fighter-bombers and those bombers, which take multiple small missiles to blow up."

Pez called Swenah to ask, "Are all shuttles and personnel onboard the ships?"

"I see the aliens coming," Swenah remarked. "Everything is aboard but Jard's shuttle. He's still on the surface."

Have the space marines put him on that shuttle now. They can stun him if they need to!" Pez exclaimed.

"That order was issued just before you called," Swenah informed her, "the moment the big alien ship jumped into the system."

Pez said in a panic, "Ming's with him."

"She is," Swenah acknowledged.

"I'm running interference until that shuttle's aboard with Ming on it, and at this point, I really don't care if Jard is or not," Pez said, determined.

"I'm sending another shuttle to collect Ming right at the dig site and get her aboard," Swenah stated. "They'll lift off the flight deck in less than a minute. Do you want me to send the rest of our Hunter-Terminators? I could send all the Corvette Thunders too."

"How many small craft has that alien beast of a ship launched?" Pez asked.

"One hundred and seventeen fighters and fighter-bombers, as well as sixty-seven bombers," Swenah replied.

"There's no time," Pez said. "We'll never get them back aboard before that giant ship gets here. Schwin and I will give them something to think about. Send us the deep space coordinates of the auxiliary ship and we'll meet you there. As soon as you and *Phoenix* are clear, Schwin and I will bug out of the system and join you."

"At the rate it's slowing, it will be here in eleven minutes and fifty-two seconds," Swenah said.

"Those small craft will be here in less than six. Get everyone aboard and flee. I've got to get up some speed and into a turn that will take me in at an angle to fall behind them. I plan to create a big junkyard up there before I leave."

"It would appear that you have just become even more vital to our mission so please be careful," Swenah stated, not liking the situation at all.

"This is what I do," Pez assured her, "and the spiritual congress gives me an edge like nothing else possible."

"There are over a hundred and eighty of them!" Ahhu said, completely freaked out.

"Plenty of targets for all of us." Schwin's voice resounded with excitement.

"I've never had the least interest in glory and heroics, I'll have you know," Ahhu snapped at them.

"No heroics, sweetheart," Pez said kindly, "only a brief video game and then we'll jump out. I'll keep us away from their line of fire." As she accelerated past 7.2 light speed, in the tightest turn the Hunter-Terminator was capable of, Pez called Swenah to ask, "How long now until they're aboard?"

"Ming has just climbed into the second shuttle I sent directly to the dig site, and a space marine is carrying Jard to the other shuttle. They had to render him unconscious."

"You've got, like, two and a half minutes before alien combat small craft are over the planet," Pez warned.

"We'll make it," Swenah said. She thought to herself, *Just barely, I hope.*

Pez kicked in reverse drives and thrusters, coming through the last of her turn in closing on the fleet of alien small craft, with Schwin doing the same beside her. Pez told her, "We'll nail all we can on this firing run, then point straight for the planet when they break in all directions. We'll use the planet's gravity to swing around it in a turn and head back at them."

They came up fast, well within targeting speed relative to their targets yet way too fast for anything but a stern chase. Pez yelled, "Fire!"

Pez launched a big missile into each of three alien bombers while shredding a fighter with her blaster. She launched the five missiles Mel had targeted, continuing to apply the brakes. She accelerated, now pulverizing a second fighter with her blaster and firing two missiles she had targeted and two more Mel had lined up, as the alien ships cranked up drives and flared boosters, diving, climbing, swerving, and scattering.

Schwin had gotten off two large missiles and splattered a fighter with her blaster, while her copilot managed to launch five missiles this time, all accurately. Her gunners each took out two fighters, and one of those fighters, or a big piece of it at any rate, struck another, blowing it up in near unison. By Pez's count, Schwin's Hunter-Terminator had just wasted thirteen alien small craft. She was racing for the fifth planet, all shooting stopped, her ship accelerating full throttle.

Ahhu, the gaming expert, had taken out three fighters, and told Pez proudly, "I can beat Rubix at Alien Space Invaders, you know."

Trix had shakily managed to limp into the state of calm abiding and contemplation. Like a killer puppet, she'd allowed the spiritual congress to annihilate three fighters through her and her blaster. None of the alien small craft were any longer heading directly for the planet. Thirty-two particle and vapor cloud spheres looked like a cloudy day in space behind them.

Mel informed them, "Ming's shuttle is on approach to *Isis* and entering the bay doors now. Jard is being loaded aboard the other, which will lift off in seconds."

"That big alien ship stopped slowing down, and it's spitting a swarm of small craft," Pez said.

They started turning as the planet came close, skimming the atmosphere for just a second as the gravity well caught them, allowing them to radically tighten the arc of their turn. They were in high orbit by the time they swung around to the back of the planet, losing much of the gravitational force and so much of the angle of their turn as well. Compensating with braking and turning thrusters, they managed to tighten it up some, though nothing like the traction they had skimming the atmosphere.

Coming around, concluding their whip turn, they headed to intercept the nearest group of alien fighters. There was only one bomber in this group. Schwin was already maneuvering for the bigger craft. Pez shouted, "Fire!" The same instant targets lit in green for Trix and Ahhu, meaning they were in range. When the red lines appeared, signifying "lock-on," their thumbs hit the triggers and the big quads burst out four great blasts, three times per second.

Pez was blasting away, launching missiles at the speed of thought and making tiny random jerks as she flew, while missiles and blaster fire brushed their shields, just missing them. Schwin had blown the big craft

A TALE OF THE TAIL OF NINE STARS

with one of her large missile, and her Hunter-Terminator was unloading ordnance and blaster bolts as fast as they could come out. What little was left of that group was passed, and multiple groups continued converging, their missiles out in the lead, crowding space. Pez asked Swenah, "Are you under way yet?"

"Jard's shuttle is just making its entry to our flight deck. I will be the moment these bay doors close. Less than a minute. *Phoenix* has departed."

"Good," Pez said, relieved. "We are bailing out. We couldn't survive another minute of combat up here."

To Schwin, Pez said, "Punch it. We're jumping out of here between that large group and the two little ones, where there's a big gap in space. We're blowing through it. I'll see you on board *Isis* in deep space. Good job."

Both accelerated while making evasive maneuvers. Pez had learned to do this truly randomly. Schwin's maneuvers tended to be patterns, and her ship took more hits, mauling her shields but not her hull. Both ships fired off stern molten flare nets to explode the missiles that were on their tails and gaining on them. The nets were pods with liquid metal cores that heated to ten thousand degrees when launched, expanding to bleed together into a sheet of fluid in the path of the missiles, destroying them on contact. Small craft arced around the sheet, losing distance as the two Hunter-Terminators matched and then exceeded the velocity of the last two missiles. Schwin's ship had taken so many hits that their cloaking was blinking in and out while slowly fading to nonexistent. A moment after they jumped, Pez saw that *Isis* was seconds from having been in quantum space as well.

Mel told Pez, "You're safe now and don't need me to help you park it in the garage, so I'm off to learn the local native alien language."

"Thanks, Mel. I couldn't have done it without you," Pez said with love.

Ahhu's space suit was a foot and ten inches too long and quite difficult to walk in, so she shed it. Trix found her panties, flats, and plaid skirt, got into them, and went topless. Pez got into her space marine combat uniform. The dock was closed and airing up when they came out of their Hunter-Terminator to hundreds of crew and space marines cheering them loudly. Schwin's fighter-bomber was badly scorched, and she was grinning as if she had just had the time of her life. She seemed to exude that after-sex glow. They were surrounded, embraced, and passed around overhead to the airlock. Ahhu seemed not to mind all the groping and might've been enjoying it. Schwin had managed to grope some of the crew herself on her chaotic travels to the airlock.

Swenah and her senior officers were in front of the door smiling, and Ming was there, being one of them. Ming jumped into Pez's arms. Konax hugged Schwin and told her, "That was some flying!"

"I just played follow the leader ... and was she ever wonderful!" Schwin shared with him.

Konax admitted, "Mel gave me a holo that put me in Pez's cockpit. I'll be playing it back for years to come. It's way beyond just skill and quickness."

Everyone shook hands with Trix, congratulating her, their gazes drawn right to her erect nipples, which seemed to throb with her pulse.

Swenah scooped tiny naked Ahhu off her feet and embraced her, telling her, "You're an amazing gunner. You impressed all of us, my little nude hero."

"I like older women," Ahhu said flirtatiously.

"I'm on duty at the moment, sweetheart," Swenah said, hoping for a rain check. When Pez finally stopped kissing Ming, which was when Ming got her feet back on the deck, Swenah and her officers gave Pez a salute to make a space marine proud. They'd actually been practicing while she'd been on approach. All the space marines on the dock saluted Pez too, and tears ran down Pez's cheeks and along the sides of her nose into her enormous grin.

Sarhi, Atari, and Dove came through the open airlock, and each embraced Pez. Pez announced loudly in proclamation, "The spiritual congress are the true heroes in this. They guided all of my actions—and Trix's too."

Sarhi took Trix with her back to her cabin to put some medical salve on the girl's poor nipples and breasts, thinking, *the nerve of that insensitive self-absorbed genius.*

21

Pez went with Swenah and Konax to the bridge, and all three gave the space marine at the door a sharp salute, giving him the sense that the supreme commander was restoring order to star fleet as well as to the universe. They took their seats on the bridge, calling up holos, and Pez ordered, "Give me an intelligence update and briefing."

"The Mel Octagon has opened a wealth of data, a literal treasure trove, giving us coordinates to the Imperial home world, the star systems of their four Viceroy regional overseers, to their one hundred and seven Citizen star systems as well as to their thousand and some slave stars, their hundred and twenty-three bases and mining operations in nonlife systems, and much more," Swenah said. "We have the location of their space construction platforms for shipbuilding and lunar-based shipbuilding docks."

"Have you sent cloaked drone probes with quantum drives into their home system?" Pez asked.

"And into their four Viceroy systems," Swenah informed her. "We didn't have enough for all the citizen worlds, so we selected a small random sample to send them into. All the data has already been transmitted to Om. Just moments ago, we began receiving data from the probe sent into the Imperial Center."

"How's it going with the local native language of our guest, Mel?"

"There's not much to go on, but I'm working on it while I examine material. Their speech sounds remarkably similar to those Earth 10^5 CBS2 fax machines. Kind of a synthesis of static and tonality."

"Maybe if you signed to him and brought objects for him to name, it would help," Pez suggested.

"Been there, done that," Mel shot back, "and we're not sure, but we think the alien guest might be a *her*."

"What do they eat?" Pez asked.

Mel answered, "Their food contains two of the three new elements we discovered, with bromine, carbon, chlorine, argon, and lithium as main ingredients. Jard's appointed himself chef and is making the prisoners taste and comment on his cooking. So far, he has only critics, calling his culinary concoctions vile excrement of the diseased and dying. They call us disgusting articulated worms, uglier than the underside of a horseshoe crab, and their horseshoe crabs are apparently far more horrifying than ours."

"Well, they appear a bit leathery to me, but I doubt it helps anything by using pejorative labels evoking revulsion to name things," Pez said soberly.

Swenah asked, "Is Jard actually in a galley?"

"No, ma'am. He's at a maintenance tub, mixing things like bleach, drain unclogger, brass polish, floor cleaners, acids, and other things together, sort of trial and error," Mel tried to explain.

"Is there any analysis or inductive reasoning directing his process?" Swenah inquired, wondering if Jard was in violation of the conventions on the treatment of prisoners.

"If there is, it is an intuitive function of mad genius and not otherwise rationally discernible by any means," Mel concluded.

This kind of left Swenah in the dark regarding her question of violations, so she shelved it for the time being and called her science officer, saying, "You need to figure out what these prisoners eat by speaking with them and taking some notes on how it can be synthesized. Make sure Jard doesn't poison them."

"Aye, aye ma'am."

Mel asked Pez, "Did you know the aliens glow in the dark?"

"No, but I won't be so worried about one sneaking up on me, now that I know," Pez told her.

Miffed by Pez's response, Mel said, "Their faces hardly glow, and that's all you can see when they're in their space suits, which they'd have to be in order to be sneaking up on you."

"Not on one of their own worlds; then I'll be in the suit," Pez replied.

A TALE OF THE TAIL OF NINE STARS

"And with a platoon of space marines, I would hope!" Mel exclaimed.

Swenah declared, cutting through the talk on the bridge, "A probe just discovered a wide-angle Thaldin mini-wave cannon on a three-mile-long ship. They are harmless and pass right through shields, but they paint and tag any solid object they contact. It is not a weapon but a close-range device for overcoming cloaking."

"How close range?" Pez demanded.

"The waves themselves are not short range, but their usefulness in tagging diminishes with distance and becomes ineffective at less than a quarter million miles out," Swenah explained. "This could certainly account for our missing probe."

"Have the probe search for more of those," Pez ordered, "and make sure they check the moons, especially the dark sides, and all space stations, space platforms, and ships."

Pez then called Jard and said, "Hey, genius, put your noggin to work on avoiding tagging by Thaldin mini-waves and stop torturing my prisoners—and my lovers, for that matter."

"It was all humanitarian, I assure you, holy love child," Jard insisted.

"No more feeding cleansers to the aliens, Jard. I mean it. And leave poor Trix's nipples alone," Pez told him sternly.

Jard addressed her as "One," making it sound like at least two syllables, then continued. "We require less than another hour with Trix's nipples to be able to transfer that level of sensitivity to Mel's android's nipples and I promise no more bleach and drain cleaners to your prisoners."

Pez told Swenah, "I don't want to jump into the Imperial home star system until we've had the probes map out their military positions and the locations of those Thaldin mini-wave guns."

"Look at your holo," Swenah showed her, "and at the bottom right, you can bring up the view from any of the probes in the system. I'm looking at SPD M-seventy-two's optics as it far-scans the flank of the three-mile ship. They have five Thaldin guns to a flank and the same top and bottom."

Cotex reported, "Only the three mile long class one ships have the Thaldin mini-wave cannons. The probes have not detected them anywhere else."

Pez told them, "I'm not going there until I'm ready to blow everything up. Let's look at some Viceroy systems."

Everyone on the bridge, and many sensors analysts elsewhere on the ship, began sorting through Viceroy Systems, optics, and measures. Cotex mentioned, "The Imperial home world had three of those three-mile ships, and Viceroy Systems seem to have only one each."

They all hunted for Thaldin cannons, but none could be found in the Viceroy systems except for on the three-mile ships. The star systems were stacked with lunar weapons bases, space weapons platforms, weaponized satellites, and space stations bristling with weapons systems, not to mention drone and manned ships crowding orbital space, but no Thaldin mini-wave cannons. Once new data on the Viceroy worlds slowed to a crawl, the spy drones having already scanned just about everything, Mel organized it all into a summary report with graphs, tables, lists, diagrams, and two-column comparative specifications. There were also many optical images and dense descriptions, along with analysis, inductive speculations, and identification of unknowns and potential unknowns, as well as a warning about completely unforeseeable unknowns. She'd given herself a grade of A plus with a comment written in longhand script that read "Excellent work" across the title page of her report and programmed the document so that the title page could not be skipped or rushed along in its prodigious pause.

One of the four Viceroy star systems looked a little more run down and shabby than the rest, exhibiting little maintenance and much wear on everything alien made. The yachts appeared to be smaller and of an older vintage, and there were fewer cargo freighters, condensed gas tankers, and mining haulers flowing into it comparatively. Cities displayed signs of urban decay; ground vehicles in general were more plain, smaller, and older, and many industrial and manufacturing plants were closed down. This Viceroy was clearly a distant cousin and not getting its share of empire. Pez selected it. They would go there next.

Mel exclaimed, "I've had a tremendous breakthrough, and I'm programming the Mel enneagon."

"Great job, Mel," Pez told her. Then she asked, "How did the breakthrough come?"

"It's not relevant," Mel replied.

A TALE OF THE TAIL OF NINE STARS

Pez called the intelligence section and asked the lieutenant, "How is our alien guest doing?"

"He seems a lot calmer now that he gave me the data tab he had on him and saw we comprehended what it was," he answered. "Mel has the tab now."

Pez told him, "Thanks." Then she said to Mel sarcastically, "Not relevant at all."

Mel asked, "Would you like to program your own integrative nine-language translation service, Miss Ungrateful?"

"I am grateful, Mel, and it's because I love you that I want to help you reduce your ego, sweetheart. No one can do what you do, and I truly marvel at how wonderful you are. All ego is just a projection of selfhood over our acts, while the acts themselves are more aptly performed when attention is all on them and not split to create a projection."

"You're starting to sound like Sarhi, and I want the fun Pez back, with the limitless sexual energy. I should've had my android body on your Hunter-Terminator. You fogged the windshield, you know."

"Mel, you're sending on an open line to the bridge. Now hush," Pez said, embarrassed.

Swenah asked her, smiling, "So your cover and recon flight got hot and sweaty and wasn't just a joyride?"

Pez was blushing and hot behind the ears. She tried to explain. "Ahhu wet herself in the drop to the planet surface and pull up, and sat naked after she cleaned the copilot seat."

"Clothes don't stay on that girl," Swenah said with understanding.

"Then she suggested we drift and, you know, do it. Trix was so taken with the idea that I couldn't very well just say no," Pez continued, her explanation making perfect sense to her.

Every face on the bridge was grinning and every mind producing imagery, inclusive of recent sightings on the flight deck of naked Ahhu and Trix's swollen nipples. It was the kind of thing that never made it to the admiralty, with the exception in this one case of Rear Admiral Swenah, but would become known to literally everyone else in star fleet. Pez didn't realize this, of course, being of the Clear Light Order culture, not star fleet, and her extreme innocence would've likely prevented her from recognizing it in any event.

Jard was as weird as it had ever gotten for star fleet, until Mel, and Sarhi with her Islohar, and the tiny naked earthling sex worker, Twinkie—now Ahhu. Pez was by far the most unique and novel experience in star fleet's history. The only authority ever infused into her voice was when she yelled "Fire," but even that was really far more enthusiasm and exuberance than it was authority. Her tiny body in a space marine uniform was just contradictory, and her infectious friendliness and kindness made her seem like a country bumpkin from a backwater world of jolly unsophisticated agriculturalists. They knew she wasn't actually dumb or completely clueless, just the sacred fool, seeing divine beings and perfection instead of people and chaotic shit. She performed miracles in small combat spacecraft of both a military nature and apparently a sexual one as well. Ever since her training with them, she inspired the space marines like nobody's business, and naked Ahhu was actually very good for morale, it turned out. Pez's sex life was all over the ship, and rumor had it that Jard and Mel were making a holoclip of it. The holo featuring Ming's bottom and curve of one breast remained a popular instrument of arousal among the crew.

Mel's Mel Enneagon was ready for deployment, and Pez wore it in her ear canal proudly as she addressed the alien guest as Om's official representative. "Hi, my name is Pez."

A facial reaction, probably decipherable from a mile away, if only they knew more about aliens, contorted this one's face. He said, with his voice quivering, and on some syllables near inaudible, "You are Reciprocity, the holy instrument of divine intelligence."

Pez asked, "What's your name?"

"I am the high priest of Rrrsst, and my name is Qrgtzz. I am at your service."

"Are there others of your genus who oppose the empire?" Pez inquired.

"Besides the one thousand and eighty-nine enslaved star systems, there is one Viceroy star system and many citizen worlds opposed to them. There are also several independent star systems with space travel that possess technology as advanced as that of the empire, which have so far eluded Imperial space forces. Tensions are high, and rebellions

A TALE OF THE TAIL OF NINE STARS

are now being responded to with planetary extermination, as you have seen on my planet."

"Do you know anyone who can put me in touch with these independent systems?"

"I'm sorry, but I do not," the alien replied.

Pez finally asked, "How did you get my picture?"

"Three centuries ago, before our world was enslaved by the empire, we were visited by a highly advanced race. They had learned to regenerate themselves endlessly on a cellular level and had transcended reproduction. They called themselves the Amonrahonians and described our pending enslavement and gave us your picture, telling us to support you when you arrived at some point in the distant future. They said they were going to make a hundred-year meditation, beginning the day you were born, empowering your life and awakening. They said you were the oldest helper of sentient beings, having taken rebirth to lead others to enlightenment three hundred and twenty-nine times in a row, and so the best candidate for the job, the most consistently aligned with the divine will and intelligence."

"Do you practice meditation and contemplation?" Pez asked.

He showed her a classic geometric diagram of form and color he was carrying attached to his suit, and replied, "They are my life. I am high priest. I was rigorously and meticulously trained in all of the spiritual methods, taught by the teachers highest in the realization, and prepared from birth to perform my function without illusion or duality."

"You must be introduced to Sarhi. I suspect her spiritual congress is in league with the Amonrahonians's," Pez told him. Then she said apologetically, "Our scientists can't figure out what food to offer you."

"Just compound some liquid chlorine with bromine and it can be poured into my suit here," he said, pointing. "We get most of the nutrition we require from the gases we breathe. Part of our digestive system is in our lungs. We need bromine several times per day but eat solid food only once in five days. We find the giant gaseous exploding crocodiles to be particularly delicious."

At the end, no semblance of lip synchronization was in evidence at all, and Pez was amused by Mel's translation of the alien's favorite food. She called Sarhi down to the Intelligence Section and called the science officer to tell him, "I need an airlock and chamber prepared to simulate the atmosphere of a blue star fifth planet with a biosphere for our guest. I'll call the master chief of engineering and let him know he's to help you."

"Yes, ma'am. I'll get right on it."

Pez called the master chief petty officer, and he was happy to help. As soon as they started feeding bromine and chlorine into the prisoner's suits, they began spilling secrets, codes, restricted data, encryptions, passwords, and all manner of sensitive intelligence. One of the prisoners was even confessing sexual transgressions. They said they hated the empire too and didn't want to go back but added that they didn't want to live in space suits either. They knew of a star system on the outer rim of their galaxy to which expatriates were escaping to an egalitarian community. The *Isis* and her convoy had not yet jumped to the Viceroy system, so Pez changed her mind, opting for the outer rim star system, which seemed to offer a more attractive lifestyle and community. She quickly became popular with the prisoners.

Sarhi arrived, and she and Qrgtzz made eye contact for many minutes in silence. They bowed to each other, and Sarhi told him, "Welcome, Qrgtzz. You are here at last. We have only two more representative to collect and we'll be ready to get started. The Reciprocity has nearly completed her training."

"I devote my life to the service of the Reciprocity and to the fulfillment of the will of the divine intelligence," Qrgtzz vowed.

Pez asked, "Sarhi, why haven't you told me any of this yet?"

"So as not to disturb your tranquility and quiescence," Sarhi cryptically explained.

"What exactly is the spiritual congress, Sarhi?" Pez demanded.

"Well, sweetheart," Sarhi explicated, "it is a spiritual instrument of transcendence and a repository for authentic methods of spiritual practice, organized by the Amonrahonians while you were last residing in the after-death state. It was instituted on the day of your birth. The Islohar were given the responsibility for the spiritual congress, and Aton and Nemellie were its first non-Islohar representatives. We have representatives now from Rah and Haum, from a member star system of the United Lights, from a system in the Kataleptica Star Union, one

A TALE OF THE TAIL OF NINE STARS

from the Garmor Republic, the Yewl Federation, the Drago Cluster Alliance, the Kemplar Unity, and even from the Trident star system of the YuBan Galaxy. Then of course there's Pall Mall, Kent, and Earth 10^5 CBS2."

"And you thought you might mention all this to me when?" Pez asked with amazement and some hurt feelings.

"Why, I was going to allow you to come to it on your own as you grew into yourself, my love," Sarhi told her sincerely.

"So you hadn't meant to tell me ever."

"That makes it sound so different from what it is, sweetheart," Sarhi told her soothingly, "but the words do fit."

"Just where is it I'm supposed to collect these last delegates," Pez demanded, "and just how do you expect me to lead this mission successfully if you don't tell me what's going on?"

"There, there, darling. You're losing your serenity and getting yourself worked up over nothing; you've already chosen to go to the outer rim star. Now just relax and witness, trusting that you'll act precisely as needed at each instance required, no matter how impossible."

"Did you have to use the word *impossible*, Sarhi?" Pez asked. "It happens to be the most anxiety-provoking word I know."

"I'll help you get over that, dear," Sarhi told her sympathetically, as if speaking to a child who had the flu.

Pez muttered, "And help me get over being alive too."

Sarhi led Qrgtzz to the temple cabin, and Pez returned to the bridge. On her way in, she threw the space marine a button-popping eye-catching salute that would have frightened small children. She was hungry, but she took her seat beside the admiral. Swenah asked, genuinely interested, "So how *did* they get your picture?"

Trying to blow Swenah off, Pez said, "They stole it from a tourist from Om."

"Out this way?" Swenah asked. "Isn't this a little beyond the tour zone? I mean, they don't even let the military come to this galaxy."

"It's all been an Amonrahonian conspiracy to enslave my life since birth and probably to offer me up as a peace token on some alien altar as a blood sacrifice."

"I'll kill anyone who tries," Swenah promised her.

Mel told Swenah, "Pez was chosen as the three hundred and thirty-third Wu, as the most stable human for serving evolution wholly and consistently. The Amonrahonians organized the seed of the spiritual congress to address the threat to human life in the universe and the imbalanced disequilibrium in the Xegachtznel Galaxy, which is causing suffering of cosmic proportions. They knew the Wu would accept and fulfill the mission of service, as Pez is clearly doing. A moment before Pez's birth, the entire Amonrahonian population entered a hundred-year meditation in support of Pez and her process, and the spiritual congress has been organizing ever since. The last time Sarhi sounded the alarm, more than a billion people went directly into meditation to support Pez. The numbers grow daily."

Awed, Swenah said to Pez, "Here I am sitting right next to the One."

"Stop that, would you?" Pez protested.

"Give me my moment to absorb this," Swenah said, not stopping it but savoring it.

"Now see what you've done Mel?" Pez whined.

"Have I debunked another conspiracy theory?"

"No!" Pez said, frustrated. "You ruined my relationship with Swenah."

"Well, I think the truth is better than your silly conspiracy theory, and I did not ruin your relationship with Swenah. She will learn, like Ming and me, and others, to hide her awe of you, and everything will seem back to normal."

Pez said with some emotion, "Ming loves me; she doesn't *awe* me!"

"Someone is being clueless here, and I'm certain it's not me," Mel said, sounding as if she were explaining sight to a blind person.

"I'm not a freak!" Pez insisted, with almost enough energy to make it not so.

"You are, but in a good way, Pez."

"I am not," Pez insisted, harder this time.

"You are too."

"I'm not," Pez affirmed to herself since she was now trying to tune Mel out.

"Are too," Mel contested.

"Am not!"

A TALE OF THE TAIL OF NINE STARS

"Are too," Mel persisted.

Swenah commented, "This conversation reminds me why I never had children."

"I love children; they're so wonderful," Pez said.

"When you *are* one, I suppose," Swenah allowed her.

"I'm going to the mess," Pez said, feeling put down, kept in the dark, and unappreciated. On her way out, she muttered loud enough for Mel to hear, "I'm not a freak."

She traded salutes with the space marine and immediately felt better. She walked briskly, motivated by the thought of a meal. Trix and Ahhu were seated at a table in the senior officers' mess, which was otherwise empty. Pez was glad to see them and came over, saying, "Hi, what are you guys up to?"

"Waiting for you to get hungry," Trix told her. "They won't serve us here without a senior officer present. They say we're guests."

"It's regulations," Ahhu added.

"Want to be my guests?" Pez asked.

The two responded as one with smiles, "I'd love to."

Pez asked Ahhu cheerfully, "No one's written you up for violating the dress code?"

"We both got medical exemptions when the admiral suggested strongly to the medical director that she find one for each of us," Ahhu explained.

"What is your exemption based on?" Pez wanted to know.

"Mine's psychological," Ahhu explained. "I just don't like clothes. To be honest, I don't like them on other people either."

Pez replied, "I have no exemption, so I'm keeping mine on. Then Pez asked Trix, "How does your exemption exempt you from knickers and skirt or pants?"

"I checked with legal section, and they said that the way it was worded exempted me from all clothing, and since it looks strange to be dressed only on the bottom, I decided to be balanced."

"Now you both match," Pez observed. Then she whispered, "You're still not allowed in the dining room without clothes and shoes."

"They like us better without clothes," Ahhu replied, "and they won't say anything."

"Do many people stare at you?" Pez asked.

"When I'm with Trix, all eyes are on her nipples and I'm hardly noticed."

"How does the crew treat you?"

Ahhu explained as if it were so obvious that she didn't know why she was bothering. "We're with you, so everyone treats us like celebrities and are always overboard respectful. Everyone on the ship knows we are your lovers, and we didn't tell anyone."

"I think perhaps our victory walk, with you naked, might've pointed in that direction, but then Mel told everyone on the bridge."

"They probably know on the *Phoenix* and the auxiliary too," Ahhu stated, having learned something about interesting gossip and star fleet crews since coming aboard.

Trix offered, "It doesn't bother me that everyone knows, because I'm proud to be your lover, Pez."

"That's very sweet of you, Trix," Pez acknowledged.

Trix went on. "Everyone used to know that I was a virgin and thought me incapable of having sex due to my panic attacks because Jard said that a lot. Now I'm your lover, and you're the Wu, and the One, and the Reciprocity; and I'm not sex phobic anymore."

Pez frowned, and said, "I need someone to love me just because I'm Pez." Some tears pooled, and then artificial gravity pulled them into streaks running down her face. A sob escaped. They were still at the counter, and everyone back in the galley was front and center, appreciating the view. These regulations spewing KP workers seemed to have had a chapter from that book ripped from their minds.

Trix and Ahhu each put an arm around Pez. They helped her get her two piled-high plates onto her tray, and Ahhu fetched her water and high-potency stimulant brew, which always seemed to calm her. Everything had had to be cooked short order since it was about as off-hours as you could get. The cooks didn't mind at all since it kept the naked girls right up against their Plexiglas counter.

Once they were all seated, Ahhu told Pez, "I really love you, Pez, and I find you the most caring, loving, and kindest person I know. At the same time, you are also supernatural, and that's obvious to anyone who fucks you or fights you."

A TALE OF THE TAIL OF NINE STARS

"I'm not a freak!" Pez declared, bursting into tears.

"Of course not!" Ahhu agreed. "But you *are* a deity, and that *is* kind of freakish, when you think about it."

The tears escalated, and heaving sobs filled the dining room, while Pez backed up to drop into a chair. Ahhu sat on Pez's lap, facing her and straddling her torso. She embraced and held Pez while she cried, and Pez revisited the lonely and alienated orphan girl who just wanted to be like everyone else and make friends.

Ahhu waited until Pez's breathing wasn't any longer coming in gasps and then kissed her on the mouth most passionately. She could taste Pez's salty tears. Pez couldn't help but reciprocate, that being her nature. Given the cultivation and concentration of her life force, the surge of eroticism embedded in pure romantic love she emitted was overwhelming, erupting a wave of sex energy across the ship; and if Pez still had her command voyeur feature and was using it, she could have seen on-duty crew members going at it at their workstations. Jard did.

Ahhu was getting carried away with Pez's energy fueling things, and Pez was damn sure she didn't want to have sex in the senior officers' mess with an audience from the galley, so she put a stop to it. Ahhu told Pez with all her powers of suggestion, which were considerable, "After lunch, let's go to bed."

Pez told her, "That's a very good idea, now that you just got me so worked up."

Trix asked Pez, "Can we bring Rubix to bed with us?"

Pez became serious and said, "Sarhi tells me I have to have a baby and that Rubix is to be the father. I've never had sex with a male and have never really wanted to. I sure don't want either of you to be upset with me. I don't like it any better than you do."

There. She got it out and braced herself for reactions. Ahhu grinned and told her, "Having sex with both you and Rubix is my ultimate sex fantasy! This is wonderful. Boys can be big fun, and no one tries as hard to please as Rubix."

"He's certainly a sweet boy—and not as emotionally stunted as most," Pez admitted. "He's cute too. I make him intolerably nervous when I'm around him, though, and this may impair his functioning."

Ahhu defended Rubix. "Sarhi has been working with him, and he is making progress. Rubix thinks you're so beautiful and arousing, and he is eternally devoted to you. If you made love to him, I think he'd become enlightened."

"I don't think it works that way, sweetheart."

"You're just clueless about your own influence on people is all," Ahhu informed her.

Trix suggested, "Teach him the work in the central channel to harness the sexual energy during copulation for transcendence and union."

Ahhu's and Trix's excitement was a bit contagious. Not only that, but Pez was also entirely incapable of saying no to either one of them, so she said, "Let's bring him to bed, but I've got to eat first."

They smiled at Pez, hot with anticipation. Having Pez in bed was like plugging into a fusion reactor while taking a heavy dose of empathogens. Ahhu understood Pez as well as Ming did and knew this deity of human origin was also a girl, tragically orphaned at nine years old and seeking unconditional love ever since. She knew Pez made efforts in self-realization that no one else but Sarhi was even capable of and that the force of the combined efforts over her past 332 lives was bound to awaken her without those efforts, or at least to produce them. Ahhu totally got that Pez wanted to be recognized for the love and friendship she manifested in the moment, not as some mystical awe-inspiring force evolving the universe as she continued to evolve within it.

Pez shoveled down her food in her usual manner, like a starving shipwrecked sailor. Ahhu and Trix enjoyed their cooked-to-order meals. They had become astute in their timing and usually were able to catch Pez or Ming and follow them through the line in the senior officers' mess. The civilian cafeteria offered straight vomitive, and the general crew mess hall was no better. Woahha's cooking had seriously improved ever since Ahhu had decided to have sex with her, but she was only making dinners now, and Sarhi had relaxed their diet for the moment.

Ahhu had found deep space not only boring but also somehow creepy, like being literally nowhere. Then again, the spacecraft battle had provided more excitement and stimulation than she'd ever cared to have. That was almost as bad as Pez's drop and the near crash that had released her bladder. The blue star world had seemed hostile and spooky, but it had at least given Ahhu the sense of being somewhere. Now they'd just jumped into another blue star system, though at least this one was supposed to be free of Imperials. She knew that though she might be able to function as a gunner or do other possibly useful things, like boosting morale on the ship, her true and essential function was to love and care for the human orphan girl inside the deity. Like Ming, Ahhu authentically loved both the orphan girl and the spiritual manifestation that Pez was in essence.

Pez cleaned her two plates before either Ahhu or Trix had finished her one. Trix had called Rubix the moment Pez said they could take him to bed and invited him to the officers' mess. He strolled up bouncy and full of joy and then became sort of timid in his stride as he recognized Pez sitting with Trix and Ahhu. He sat awkwardly in his tension, still happy and smiling, though, and said to Ahhu, "Hi. I was missing you."

"We've more than missed you," Ahhu told him seductively, "so we're taking you to bed this instant."

Trix was already placing the plates on the conveyor. Pez got up and disposed of her tray as well. The thought of her even being in the bed with them was a bit nerve-racking for Rubix, and he asked Ahhu, "Is she coming to bed with us?"

Feeling his apprehension, Ahhu didn't mention to Rubix that he would be mounting her and instead told him, "Pez loves you, sweetheart, and she thinks you're really cute."

"She's like Sarhi, though," he said, unintentionally leaking his anxiety all over the place.

Ahhu reframed, "She is, so there is no one to judge you, just pure consciousness and love, and her energy puts a solarium fusion super reactor to shame with all the unleashed power it wields."

"I've felt that, believe me," Rubix agreed.

"She needs your love, Rubix," Ahhu informed him.

"I do love her!" Rubix proclaimed, and even Pez heard him from over by the tray disposal station.

"Without the heart palpitations, shortness of breath, sweaty hands, and irrational fear," Ahhu clarified.

"I don't like being so anxious," Rubix said defensively.

"It goes with being skinny, I think. You're unprotected, vulnerable, and unfiltered, like a raw nerve."

"I'm no skinnier than you, really," Rubix protested.

"I know," Ahhu explained. "I was speaking for myself too. We're like the girl in that story who goes to the land of the giants, being small even for a being from a yellow sun world in a world of white sun people."

"Do you know Evenrude?" Rubix asked.

"Yes, he is especially kind and sweet," Ahhu replied. "He's two feet eleven inches taller than I am and weighs about three and a half times as much as I do. Pez knocked him out in training, you know."

"No way!" Rubix said in disbelief.

"Her bones are ten times heavier than even white star people, due to all her soft martial arts training. They are harder than steel but can bend like a sapling. I'm learning about it from Sarhi."

Pez was back, and she asked, "Could we talk about something besides my bones?"

"I'm going to jump your bones," Ahhu said with delight. Ahhu grabbed one of Pez's hands, and Pez took Rubix's hand in her other one as they walked toward the senior officers' quarters and Pez's cabin. It had the biggest bed on the ship. When they arrived, Ming was just climbing into bed to masturbate, having not yet gotten over that surge of eroticism that had overtaken her and the rest of the ship earlier. Pez and Rubix stripped, and all four of them climbed into bed to join Ming. Though she was not particularly drawn to males, her need was urgent and Rubix happened to be closest, so Ming made wild, passionate love to him.

As it turned out, Rubix's and Pez's skin did not even brush together, as he was entirely monopolized by Ming and then Trix. Ahhu took special care of Pez, as only she and Ming could.

22

While they were basking in the contented afterglow, snuggled together like a litter of kittens and contemplating another round, Mel's voice announced in the bedroom, "Konax's skillful micro-jumps have us now orbiting the fifth planet, where an audience awaits you on the surface, so I hope you've been properly nourished by your support team and are ready to do your duty, General. You all really do look just so cute tangled altogether in the bed there."

"Mel, is this line open to the bridge?" Pez asked, embarrassed.

Swenah's voice came on. "The aliens want to meet with our fearless leader, honey, so get dressed and stop fondling Ahhu."

"You're giving them optics, Mel?" Pez shouted in alarm.

Mel answered, "Sarhi told me the life of the three hundred and thirty-third Wu must be well documented, my love, so just get dressed. Your shuttle and honor guard await you."

Pez regarded the optic sensor suspiciously as she climbed naked from the bed. She had no time to shower, given no advance notice of all this, so she would just have to bring Ahhu's scent with her. Pez put on clean knickers and a fresh space marine combat uniform and then attached her medal to the front. She was about to put on her Mel Enneagon when Mel told her, "Don't bother with that, dear. I have the new Mel Decagon waiting on the shuttle for you."

Placing her skullcap on her crown, Pez told her lovers, "That was great and maybe we can do it again tonight when I get home from work."

Ming had dressed too. She really wanted to take a shower, unused to having boy stuff leaking from her, but she rose to the occasion and was quickly ready to leave with Pez, fully uniformed up. They almost jogged to the tube and went together in one since they were so practically one with each other anyway. Evenrude was at attention at the foot of the ramp, with everyone else already aboard. The two ladies' hard-shell combat space suits were on the shuttle too. The salute between Pez and Evenrude could've restarted the heart of a corpse. They jogged up the ramp with Evenrude right behind.

Schwin and her copilot were in the cockpit, through with their preflight activities and waiting to put up the ramp and punch it. Schwin said to Pez, once she was strapped in right behind the cockpit, "I suppose Ahhu didn't want to come because she would have to put something on."

"She could've come and waited on the shuttle without clothes," Pez pointed out.

"Well, I'm sure she'll be more comfortable in bed with Trix and Rubrix," Schwin concluded, at the same time informing Pez that the new optic was going viral through the ship and, almost certainly, the entire convoy.

"I'm doing it in the dark from now on," Pez resolved.

"That would just make you look a bit green," Schwin discouraged her.

Then Schwin punched it, and Pez was riding the thrill. The shuttle shot for the planet like a blaster bolt, and Schwin pulled one of her almost crash landings, as spectacular as any Pez had seen. Ming was green.

After getting into their hard-shell space suits and passing through the airlock, Pez, Ming, and Evenrude descended the ramp. There was a throng of beings at the bottom, mostly aliens in shirtsleeves, though there were humans in space suits there as well. No one had briefed Pez on this. She decided to assume they hadn't known, but she couldn't help feeling that they were treating her like a fungus, keeping her in the dark and feeding her shit. She had her new earbud in, which contained, among other things, the Mel Decagon. It was programmed into her suit as well.

Qrgtzz and the three released prisoners that Jard had been trying to feed cleansers to, had arrived earlier on a separate shuttle and were part of the throng. Front and center was a kind of bent alien with skin that looked to Pez more like tree bark. It turned out that this was what extreme old age looked like in aliens. She introduced herself, once

A TALE OF THE TAIL OF NINE STARS

standing in front of him, with her friendly and exuberant, "Hi, my name is Pez."

"I'm Hierophant Kksszzchsh. Welcome to the planet Gzzklns, Reciprocity. We are all at your service."

"Where are the humans from?" Pez asked.

"They are from the star system Rally, in this very galaxy, and are the only humans in the Xegachtznel Galaxy we know of who can match the Imperial technology. We, of course, can as well and are part of an alliance with these humans and three other star systems of our own. Some impressive Imperial ships have deserted the empire and joined us. They are at your disposal. Let me introduce you to the spiritual leader of the humans."

A space-suited male stepped up, and Kksszzchsh said, "This is root teacher Lego, the recognized grand spiritual master of the humanoid Rally star system and founder of a new method of mysticism with a faster going."

"I'm so honored to meet you, Grand Master Lego. I'm Pez."

"I am honored to meet you and will follow you, helping you in all things. Our star system space fleet is under your command now, and our eight billion citizens will meditate supporting you. Let me introduce you to Admiral Nordstrum, commander of our space fleet."

Another suited person, this one a woman, appeared with hand in suit glove extended. Pez got as best a grip as she could and gave it a good shaking. She told her, "I'm really pleased to meet you, Admiral."

"I'm honored to be leading Rally's forces under your command, General," Nordstrum replied.

"We have a room and table prepared inside, with glass environment cubes for the humans, so you can take off your helmets," Kksszzchsh said. "We've been cooperating with these humans from Rally for many centuries now, against the plague of the empire, and have infrastructure in place to accommodate each other."

Pez was beyond intrigued with this most hopeful alliance of humans and anti-Imperial aliens. This was just what she'd hoped to create somehow, and here it was, already fully established. They followed their host into a metal bunker with blast doors. Mel had had Pez listen to the tonal static sounds of an Earth 10^5 CBS2 fax machine telephone

373

line as they were called there, and it truly sounded identical to all of the dialects of the alien language. Mel was still deciphering the Rally system Basic language. The humans from Rally all had their own interpretation devices already set to translate the alien Gzzklns language, and the Mel decagon's tenth language was Gzzklns. Pez realized that Mel must've been extremely busy during Pez's fun on the bed with her lovers.

Her loss of privacy still grieved and embarrassed her. All these titles heaped on her had only served to make her life public property—and all of it quite public too. She was worried that Jard or someone would plant sensors in her toilet or something skin crawling like that. She was also convinced that Sarhi knew far more than she was letting on, and just who was it who'd decided she had to have a damn baby, anyway? She figured they'd had to tell her that particular part of their plan or there would be no way it would ever happen, except by miraculous conception. Doing a little fishing, Pez inquired, "Grand Master Lego, have you spoken with the Im, Sarhi?"

"Not in a few days. Why?" Lego asked.

Pez was pissed but said politely, "She hadn't mentioned you to me is all."

"Yes, that's right," he recalled. "She told me she needed your full mind and attention on completing the work of the Great Seal from the very moment she found you."

"I believe I found her," Pez corrected.

"Aton sent you to her, convinced you are the One, and Sarhi confirmed it," Lego informed her.

"What am I not being told while I focus one-pointed on my rainbow body and forceful projection?" Pez inquired insistently.

"Only that once you're skilled at unhooking and liberating, to leave your body out through your crown, you will truly be unleashed and unstoppable," Grand Master Lego replied.

The admiral was average height for a white star female, about six feet five inches, obviously a fitness fanatic, and just the sunny side of fifty. She had that glamorous platinum silver hair you see in the holoclips, with the slightest hue of gold. She had the same golden-brown skin color as Pez, and she had friendly eyes, something generally of significance and importance to Pez.

A TALE OF THE TAIL OF NINE STARS

They stepped into their glass cubicles, which aired up in seconds, and took seats around an oval table. Pez's cubicle was at one end of the oval, away from the door to the room, and arranged clearly as head of the table. When she was ten, Pez had had fantasies of being a world governor and leading everyone in singing friendship-building folk songs, and the thought actually occurred to her now, but she just couldn't imagine it working with the fax noises that came out of the alien vocal systems.

The skin of the aliens was somehow beaded and iridescent. Their eyes were simply psychedelic, with dark blue glowing irises, hot pink pupils like the pink of neon light, and light blue rather than the whites of human eyes. They were very colorful, like their poisonous gas atmosphere, bright with colors rarely seen on white and yellow sun planets, except in the far reaches of the mind with certain meditations or on certain drugs.

Pez had all eyes on her as she removed her helmet and looked around the table. She said, "This alien-human alliance is what I'd hoped for. I thought I'd have to initiate it, to spend years growing and nurturing it, yet here to my astonishment and delight, it is already existent and thriving. I'm awed and most grateful. Our success is guaranteed. The proof is in this room that our two genera of beings can live in peace and unity together. Life always finds a way to peace and unity. War and destruction spend themselves into pollution and death, while peace and unity build galaxy clusters."

Static and seemingly random tones screeched from the aliens; hoots, hollers, and muffled gloved applause came from the humans. Pez went on. "We have to find a way to hack Imperial communications and spread a message to every star system in the empire. I happen to have brought a genius hacker who can crack and penetrate any top secret government file on Om. It is lucky for Om that he's part of the highest government body there. My sentient quantum computer friend, Mel, is working to map Imperial transmission points and identify schematics and components of the Imperial communications hardware. We picked up hundreds of terabits of programming on an Imperial mining platform, and Mel's beginning to understand their programming languages. I'll ask our hacker to get on these projects too. If we can get the word out to all systems, then others will join us. Insurgent groups will perpetrate sabotage on Imperial infrastructure, planets will rebel, and more Imperial ships will desert to our side. We'll have to design and manufacture hacking transmission drones to position at all Imperial transmission points, and take control of their network long enough to get our message out. We will also need to have our fleet assembled before we initiate sending a message simultaneously to over eleven hundred star systems. Lastly, I'm informed that a Viceroy star system of the empire is disgruntled, and my hunch is that it's the one with the least wealth and resources flowing in. We must court an alliance with them, though we will abide no slavery or interference with a developing world; that's nonnegotiable."

More tones and static, yelling, and muffled applause arose around the table. One human was clapping right into the microphone within his cubicle, producing a resounding hollow thunder with his gloves. Ming was smiling at Pez with her swept- away-in-love gaze. Evenrude had kept his helmet on, always ready for anything, but his helmet mask revealed the face beneath experiencing great pride in his leader. The others all seemed pleased with her little speech.

Mel came on in Pez's ear. "I've already solicited Jard's help, and even though he can't calculate and compute at my speed, he brings a certain crazy understanding to the process that I don't have. We are making great strides."

Pez asked her, "You put this message on a closed private line and transmitted my sex life to the convoy?"

"It was one adorable still holo moment, with all of you so picturesque, snuggled and cuddled together like a litter of puppies, a candid family shot, so to speak, and everyone just loved it. We didn't send the whole lovemaking session or anything."

"Get back to work, Mel." Pez got rid of her.

The meeting progressed to identification of current assets, likely potential assets, strategy, the wording of their galactic message to the masses within the empire, and agreeing on rendezvous points in star systems and in deep space. Many contingency plans were made, as well as some specific battle plans for invading and disrupting shipbuilding infrastructure, military installations, and key systems. Numerous details were agreed upon, and tasks were identified, defined, and delegated around the table. Pez agreed to request far more combat resources from the Tail of Nine. Admiral Nordstrum would contact the Trident system in the YuBan Galaxy and get a representative to come to Gzzklns, where their meetings would be happening while they continued with their preparations.

The aliens called their genus of big-brained bipeds with opposable fingers and stereoscopic vision, Klzzsst, so Mel traded some consonants for vowels, and the humans called them Kluzyst. The Kluzyst had been utilizing the voice of a male news commentator from Rally for the output of their interpretation devices, but by the third meeting Pez presided over, it was her own voice she was listening to. So recordings of the meeting had her talking to herself mostly. What really made her uncomfortable, though, was that the Kluzyst had an animated entertainment series about her also, and in theirs she looked an awful lot like a worm. It was called "Reciprocity Saves Xegachtznel." The vowel sounds in Xegachtznel had been placed there by Om's ancestors, who couldn't pronounce it otherwise; and they had thought it had a nice ring to it.

Pez worked hard with Sarhi on honing her skills at shooting out the top of her head in a rainbow body of light. Several worried members of the meetings she ran had asked after her progress in this endeavor as if it were pivotal to all their strategies and as if any hope of success counted on it entirely, so Pez was concentrating on giving it her all.

Jard and Mel were becoming elite technicians and programmers of Imperial computers and software. Several leading computer scientists from Gzzklns and Rally worked with them, and one humanoid female technician, forty-one years old and very brainy, became Jard's number one sex partner, displacing Cotex to the open market. Cotex contrived to meet with Sarhi, now at a separate time from Jard, and she sampled some of the ship's other offerings from within her own rank of lieutenant to be sure. Nash had been ecstatic.

Pez and Ming were just arriving at the officers' mess, and both Trix and Ahhu were there. Trix even wore a tight little tank top accentuating her famous breasts, which had now lost their swell and had flattened out quite a bit, back to their tiny selves. Ahhu insisted that flat is beautiful, and since Pez's breasts were so small, Trix had endorsed her own, wearing them proudly, to Ahhu's endless happiness. This did restrict her to skintight tops or they wouldn't show at all. Ahhu wore a little shoulder strap purse since she had no pockets.

The senior officers escorted the two civilians through the line. It was actually breakfast time, so they all ate from the buffet. It was still far above the slop in the crew mess. They all missed Shudiy, now abbot of the *Phoenix*, who at times, appeared to outrank the ship's captain. Swenah was still trying to sort it out with Sarhi.

When they were seated, Ming dropped a bomb. "I just found out this morning that I'm pregnant."

Pez embraced her, saying, "That's wonderful. Congratulations! You'll be such a great mother."

"I'm not returning to Om on maternity leave," Ming insisted. "I'm staying by your side, and that's that."

Pez assured her, "Sarhi will work it out with Yona, and nobody's going to put you off the ship and send you home to Om. I need you."

"How am I going to manage on the mission?" Ming asked no one in particular, thinking there was no answer anyway.

"I have to have one too," Pez informed her.

"Are you planning on marrying some man and leaving me?"

"Never!" Pez vowed. "Besides, the father has to be Rubix."

"You're serious!"

"Sarhi said you'd have his child before I do," Pez informed her.

"You knew I was getting pregnant and didn't tell me?" Ming asked, offended.

"Well, I didn't know you were going to get yourself knocked up practically that very night, Ming," Pez said defensively. "I wasn't keeping it secret or anything."

"You've never been with a boy and have no inclination."

Ahhu told her, "Pez thinks he's cute, and she's willing to do it with him because Sarhi said she must. You and I can get him primed, and she'll teach Rubix the central channel spiritual union meditations and contemplations."

"If Sarhi says it's got to happen, I'll help out all I can," Ming told Ahhu. To Pez, she said, "Get pregnant soon and we'll go through it together."

A TALE OF THE TAIL OF NINE STARS

"I don't want to frighten Rubix or anything," Pez replied. "He's kind of nervous, so I don't want to rush him."

"He seemed to take all right to me," Ming recalled, "and I pretty much jumped him."

"He is so very grateful that you had sex with him, Ming," Ahhu informed her. "You're like a big celebrity and a sex idol to him, you know."

"It's a status I tried hard to avoid, believe me."

"You can't run from who you are, my love," Ahhu insisted.

Trix was solemnly nodding in agreement with Ahhu while looking at Ming. Ahhu was giving Ming her I'm-truly-leveling-with-you look. Pez believed it totally, and no one was even close to as beautiful, in her eyes, as Ming.

"Oh, you're all hopeless," Ming told them. "I accept that, to the three of you, I'm attractive."

Rubix had been sheepishly approaching and found his confidence to tell Ming, "You're totally beautiful, and it's not just me—everyone says so."

"You're very sweet, Rubix," Ming told him as she got up from the table to "sponsor" him through the senior officers' food line.

Ahhu said to Pez, "You have no intergalactic military meeting today, nor a session with Sarhi scheduled, so let's take Rubix to bed and get you pregnant."

"Today?" Pez asked with a tad of resistance.

"Please," Ahhu begged, "I promise it will be fun."

Trix added, "Please, Pez, we just have to."

"What about your work with Jard?" Pez asked Trix.

"I'm doing independent research for him right now, mostly from my cabin, and I'm ahead of schedule, with much extra time to make love."

"Well, in that case, if he's willing, then so am I," Pez surrendered, as they'd known she would.

Ming returned carrying a glass of citrus juice for Rubix, and he had his tray. Between the little pile of scrambled eggs, the patty of fried potatoes, and the two half slices of toasted bread, he had much of the bottom of his plate clearly visible. This was a most unusual sight for a fresh plate of food, thought Pez. On her freshly dished out plates, inches of excavation were required before catching the first hint of the bottom. Ming had also brought a fresh cup of high-potency stimulant brew to Pez. It was a good double shot with steamed half and half, foamy at the top, just the way Pez loved it. These never failed to make her happy.

Ming kissed Pez's cheek and told her, "I have to go to work; we have so much programming to do. Mel's adding two languages to the Mel Decagon, making the Mel Dodecagon, and says it will be finished today. Jard and I are integrating the Mel Dodecagon into the communication system for *Isis* so you can command a fleet in four languages from three different galaxies."

"You're an unsung war hero, my beloved," Pez told her with feeling.

As she maneuvered down the hallway, they all watched Ming's tail admiringly.

Ahhu told Rubix, "We're abducting you to Pez's bed when you're done eating."

"All right," Rubix agreed, even though no one had actually given him a choice in the matter.

Pez asked him, "Did Ming mention that she's pregnant and that you're the father?"

"She told me when we were on the line getting breakfast," Rubix replied cautiously. Then he launched into a nervous apology. "I'm really sorry I got your spouse pregnant; I honestly didn't mean to."

Pez put him at ease. "I'm so glad you did. Sarhi told me you would."

Rubix couldn't help thinking what a strange conversation this was. Had he said those words to a space marine, a real one, meaning one that actually met the height and weight requirements, they would certainly have been the last words he'd ever spoken. Yet here he was, receiving praise from the convoy's supreme commander for knocking up the commander's spouse. It was somehow stranger than living in a spaceship the size of a small city. He told Pez, "I can't tell you how relieved I am that you're not upset with me."

"Upset?" Pez asked. "Are you kidding? You were just a bystander who got jumped anyway, and I'm glad she did it and am overjoyed she's pregnant." Pez took Rubix's hand, and they all started their trek for Pez's cabin.

Her hand was like magic in his. There was an incredible softness

A TALE OF THE TAIL OF NINE STARS

to it, yet at the same time, it presented a quality of firmness signaling potential to become adamantine, and it was bursting with aliveness and sentience, so responsive and sensual, so full of internal energy that it throbbed and vibrated. The energy from her hand was definitively energizing him, filling him with calm and something else too, arousing and exciting, concentrating and mounting, heightening his sensation and the awareness of it. It was a spiritual exercise of awakening with that hand leading him from relative oblivion into a presence of pure knowing, full of selfless love, rich and divine.

Pez was a little taller than Rubix and had a few pounds on him. Usually he was not drawn to girls larger than he was, though she drew him along so completely. He did find her exceedingly beautiful. Larger women made him feel somewhat inadequate as a male. Ahhu had liberated him from his ego shell of alienation, cut off from love and romance, companionship and friendship. He'd always found males to be too aggressive, callous, and hierarchically oriented to a pecking order he inevitably found himself at the bottom of.

He loved women, but they had never shown the slightest interest in him—until Twinkie, now called Ahhu. She had saved him. Trix had been a mercifully corrective experience, which had given him enormous confidence. Her love supported him, propping him up. Ming had been simply an undeserved gift from the most holy of holies. What other possible explanation could there be?

He focused on the point four finger widths below his navel, sinking each breath there slowly to dissolve his chattering mind, which was trying to freak out over the fact that he was being led to bed by an actual realized divine being.

She released his hand to shoot a salute to the space marine at the door to the officers' quarters. It contained enough power to lift a shuttle craft into orbit. Her clothing had actually snapped audibly with the gesture. After the salute, his hand was gently and lovingly scooped back into hers, to be caressed in an exercise of raising consciousness to experience the progressive subtleties of her manifestation. She was like a living invitation into another world he'd not even dreamed of. He feared her unbelievable eroticism would shatter his control utterly and immediately and that it would all be over before even realizing a beginning. He had the image of being a moth flying through space into the sun and certain annihilation.

The salute was repeated with the space marine at her bedroom door. Ahhu jumped onto the bed as soon as she entered the room, having no clothes to remove. Her purse was discarded on the floor. Trix got onto the bed and was tangled up in Ahhu in no time. Pez led Rubix into the bathroom and undressed him while intermittently kissing him. She got out of her own clothes to lead him into the shower, where she washed his body lovingly as he stood under the jets of water. It seemed completely backward to him and all wrong. Pez toweled him dry and placed the drying helmet on his head for three seconds.

They walked hand in hand over to the bed and climbed onto it. She somehow tuned into him so completely that she kept him from loss of control, backing off with such precision, informing him nonverbally that she had the measure of his tolerance monitored more accurately and exactly, and more consistently without lapses, than he ever could. He was in her holy hands, and she took such wonderful care of him. Her fingers would find tension in his muscles and press in, releasing it. She reminded him a couple of times to breathe abdominally. She seemed to induce the final depth of essential connection at each moment, not letting them wander a fraction from it and showing him abundances of love burning too brightly to look at—love that was unimaginable and could only be known in direct experience of being in it once achieved.

Then she sat him in meditation posture and sat facing him in his lap, mounted on his phallus, and whispered the instructions step by step into his ear as they went through it, doing the spiritual meditation and contemplation of the sexual union practice. It was Pez's first time doing it with a male, both this spiritual practice and just having sex with one. She saw how hard he tried and knew his sole aim was to please her. He was such a sweet boy and gentle soul that her heart opened naturally to him, love permeating all.

Pez took on some of Rubix's psychic wounds of inferiority and alienation, transmuting these into love and so liberating the pure energy, no longer locked up in emotional charge entwined with cognitive distortions, freeing him from the densest layers of his ego prison.

Rubix relaxed in her arms, and his breathing slowed as his eyes grew brighter. Their eye contact was like an adamantine cable connecting them, and the arc of love always existent between human beings, knowing it or not knowing it, surged with undeniable concrete consequential and significant reality.

Rubix was following the meditation instructions with will and determination and looking into her eye of the divine presence, healing and transcending in ever-ascending rapture. Thoughts no longer arose in his mind. Lines and boundaries between objects faded, and nothing seemed solid anymore, as if materiality itself were resolving into light. Time was no longer comprehensible since all was "right now" and there simply was nothing else. Light filled his empty mind, luminous, brilliant, radiant, and infinite; and the light was bliss.

They were approaching the total peak of the meditation, and Pez had him securely, managing all variables within her being. He'd never known or imagined such sexual heights. She whispered, "Now bring the energy, and your awareness mounted upon it, to the tip of your penis from the energy center four finger widths below your navel."

This was the point in the alchemical process in which even male adepts sometimes lost their control, ejaculating. She kept them there, in that state of ultimate culmination, completely over the top, hovering weightless without falling or crashing. It was more unbelievable than it would have been to see someone walk on water or simply fly in the air. She defied orgasm, and this seemed much more impossible to do than defying gravity.

At last, she led his energy and awareness back into his central channel and up to the crown of his head, still moving physically upon him. They dwelt in this experience before finally uniting the drops from the crown energy center and the base of the spine, with the indestructible drop in the center of the heart. She held him in the clear light of bliss upon the absolute emptiness of pure immaterial transcendental consciousness, still gyrating on his lap.

Pez stopped moving on Rubix, sitting still and maintaining the eye contact they'd held throughout. Then she kissed his mouth passionately, completely in love with the boy. He was high in his first awakening and had managed to follow her all the way, a true equal partner, and she knew he had attained this through his immense love for her. This so touched Pez's heart that she began involuntarily emitting wave upon wave of intense love. Trix and Ahhu stopped their lovemaking to sit up and feel what was happening, looking upon the transformed couple. Pez and Rubix were enshrined in their united auras, which were visibly glowing around them, and Trix could just make out a faint violet halo of flames emerging from Pez's shoulders and surrounding her head.

Pez climbed off Rubix to lie invitingly on her back, drawing him to her, and he mounted her, kissing her and entering her. They soared together, mounting the dragon and ascending to heaven. All was ecstasy and the awareness of it.

Pez finally released a surge of the most compelling sexual energy any of them had ever experienced. Rubix blew up in ejaculation, and both Ahhu and Trix had spontaneous orgasms without stimulation.

Swenah's voice filled her cabin. "What in a black hole have you done to my crew? The males have messed their skivvies, and all the females are trying to be undetected squirming in their seats. Go out in a small spacecraft far away if you ever do that again!"

"I didn't do anything to your crew," Pez told her fiercely. "I did it to Rubix."

"Well, it certainly spilled over, now didn't it!" Swenah persisted.

Trix called out, over the open line to Swenah on the bridge, "I had a spontaneous orgasm!"

"So did all of the crew, dear. You are at the epicenter and therefore didn't stand a chance," Swenah said sympathetically to Trix.

Swenah had chief petty officers calling her regarding the recent "event," as it came to be called, aboard *Isis*, so she ended her call with Pez. Jard and Mel had recorded the conditions leading up to the "event" so that it could be understood, of course.

Pez snuggled into Rubix, and both Trix and Ahhu cuddled them. Eroticism was no longer vibrating out of Pez, but the involuntary waves of love she emitted were intensifying, truly a marvel to experience, captivating her three lovers in their hearts.

Pez clearly felt the moment of conception, welcoming her daughter into rebirth with love and the promise of unwavering care and nurture. She adored her skinny lover, who had little muscle or physical strength but had a core power behind his incredible climax, of which the impact

A TALE OF THE TAIL OF NINE STARS

inside of her was astonishing. He was her gestating daughter's father, and Pez would love him and see to his spiritual development from now on. She still preferred Ming's body to make love to—and females in general.

She would close his gate in future lovemaking with him, Pez decided, by pressing on the pressure point just in front of his prostate gland, preventing the ejaculation of fluids without interfering with his orgasms. It wasn't because she didn't like the mess, which she didn't, but because it would preserve his internal energy and life force so it could be used to fuel his spiritual development. Since he was at the end of his teen years—the last year, actually—she would allow him two ejaculations per lunar cycle and teach Trix and Ahhu how to close his gate when he climaxed. Ming already knew theoretically how to do this. He could have all the orgasms he wanted and then some, but they would help preserve his vital energy by restricting his ejaculations. He did need some compensation and release from tensions and stressors, so given his age, two ejaculations per one lunar cycle was the accurate prescription, Pez was sure.

She had taken him on as her direct disciple when she'd absorbed and transmuted his psychic wounds, pacifying them and liberating them. A disciple was an enormous responsibility, she assumed, though didn't know for sure yet. Perhaps as big a responsibility as having a child. Pez knew that Sarhi would soon turn Ahhu's instruction entirely over to her—and Ming's as well. She would also need to start meditating with Evenrude. Just lying on the bed, it felt as if she was suddenly growing up in quantum leaps. She held tightly to Rubix as if for stability in the dizzying momentum of maturing.

Rubix had entered a new world in which the witness and spectacle were the same, open to higher energies and cosmic vibrations and potencies, relishing the unity and mystery. He was incredibly excited about it and said, "My life just began a little over an hour ago, when I recognized that I had lived all of it up to that moment, totally asleep, lost in an illusion of my mind's projection, believing and reacting to it, the source my own suffering."

"I just love first awakenings, and I love you, Rubix," Pez said dreamily, still emitting those waves of love.

With a superior tone, Ahhu told Pez, "I told you so!"

Pez asked, still dreamily, "What did you tell me?"

"That you'd wake him up fucking him," she reminded Pez.

"That was his love and determination," Pez corrected. "I was but a catalyst."

"Without the catalyst, the change does not occur," Ahhu argued.

"Without the right conditions, my love, the catalyst triggers nothing," Pez debated.

"Well, you're one heck of a catalyst, I'll tell you that," Ahhu said, giving up, while Rubix and Trix nodded, agreeing with her.

Trix said again, "I had a spontaneous orgasm!"

"So did I, bigger than ever before," Ahhu said, with more than a hint of "so there" to Pez.

Awestruck, Trix said, "You are the most amazing teacher in the universe."

"I love you too, Trix," Pez told her, hoping she'd stop.

Rubix was so teeming with life and glowing with light that Ahhu just couldn't help herself from arousing him to go again.

Trix told them, "You heard the admiral so we better go out in a Hunter- Terminator before we get any further."

Ming burst into the room, ripping her clothes off, saying, "I don't believe it; let me at her. I'm having her!"

Trix told Ming, "The admiral wants us off the ship and out of this galaxy before letting Pez erupt again."

Ming told her as she climbed onto Pez, "Let the admiral take a small craft out of the galaxy."

Trix gave up and inserted herself within Ming's and Pez's lovemaking to be assimilated most tenderly and cherished. Ahhu and Rubix were thrashing. The energy rose in a tidal wave, then rose some more, at the same time condensing and concentrating into a tincture of such potency as to repeat the "event" on *Isis*.

Swenah's voice roared into their cabin. "I thought I told you to take it off my ship and away for my crew. Orgies are breaking out in every section, and there's chaos. If we weren't in orbit, we would likely all be dead."

Pez suggested, "Take them all out for a space-walk." Then she tried to reassure her subordinate. "I think we might be done, for now at least."

A TALE OF THE TAIL OF NINE STARS

Swenah told her, entirely serious, "If you won't remove it from my ship, I'm going to require a ten-minute warning and a three-minute countdown for all such future events."

Ming said responsibly, "Aye, aye, Admiral."

Pez complained, "The countdown might be a bit distracting, so I'm not sure we'll give you that."

"Then I'll have Mel do it," Swenah resolved.

As a civilian, Trix was able to say to the admiral, "Orgasms aren't a bad thing."

"No," Swenah had to admit, "but they aren't good for the ship's crew to have all at the same time, involuntarily and unexpectedly!"

"I think I see your point," Trix said, trying to agree with her.

Jard's victorious voice announced proudly, "Both events have been preserved for posterity!"

"What exactly does that mean, Jard?" Pez demanded.

Jard blew her off. "Use the dictionary function on your device, love child."

Pez informed him, "Then you have captured my conception for posterity as well."

"Congratulations, sweetheart, but isn't it a little soon to tell?" Swenah asked.

"It's a girl," Pez told her.

"Oh," Swenah said, awed to silence.

Jard told her, "That is absolutely wonderful news, clearly making this the holoclip of the millennium, capturing the first two events known of their kind and the conception of the daughter of the One."

"I hope you're not planning to put it on the news," Pez said hopefully.

"No!" Jard said. "If I did that, I'd have to edit it severely down to a rating of age fifteen with parental guidance, and that would ruin it."

"So what are you going to do with it Jard?" Pez wanted to know.

"It becomes part of your biography, for scholars, scientists, and academics to study for generations to come," Jard told them. "Sarhi might be able to use the one section as an instructional holo for the practice. We just need to amplify those ear-whispered instructions."

"You should've seen yourself, Jard, on the dining room table of our hotel penthouse," Ming told him.

"You were too drunk to notice and only heard about it, dear heart," Jard retorted, "because you were busy screwing everyone in the room who didn't have a partner."

Ming was embarrassed to silence.

Pez told him, "I'd prefer it if you would keep my biography confidential for now and preferably maintain it that way, at least until I'm dead."

"Right now only Mel and I have access," Jard reassured her.

"Perhaps that's already more than is decent."

"We are scientists," Jard explained. "The doctor isn't there because he wants to see you naked or just for the thrill of giving you a vaginal exam."

"Though those are sometimes the perks," Ahhu stated as fact.

"I've got to go," Jard told them. "Mel and I are designing a questionnaire for everyone aboard. It was felt on *Phoenix* and the auxiliary too, but it seems to have diminished in force by the time it reached them and had even less effect on the planet surface."

Swenah reiterated, before cutting out, "At least a ten-minute warning, please. I have a ship to run."

"I promise," Pez agreed.

She did not really appreciate the looks she often got after the two "events," but Pez had matured and had serious responsibilities she tended to diligently. Sarhi had taken those events as signs that Pez was truly ready and was teaching her to blow out through her crown and reenter within a microsecond so she'd be able to do it while flying without causing dangerous lapses of coma. Pez had to spend hours in the temple cabin, meditating with the representatives on board of the spiritual congress, forging an inseparable quantum link with them, impervious to time and space, and through the spiritual congress, to establish direct connection with the Amonrahonians, thirty-two years and some months into their hundred-year meditation.

Pez sensed that a hundred-year meditation of the entire Amonrahonian race produced the equivalent of the power of a rare violet star within the universe. She recognized that some of their preparations for her cosmic mission had been made in truly ancient times and saw

A TALE OF THE TAIL OF NINE STARS

how much work had come before her, preparing the way. It seemed a small thing indeed to give over her own life to its cause.

The Kluzyst handled the clandestine meeting with the Viceroy of the run-down Viceroy star system of the empire, following the strategies agreed upon in the meetings Pez presided over, and an alliance was struck, which would give them a three-mile-long ship of their own and many additional resources. Admiral Tonkah of the Trident star system of the YuBan Galaxy arrived in a 10,080-foot super battleship spacecraft carrier with the promise of more ships to come. The High Council of Om promised them significantly more ships, including some giants still on the construction docks. The allied galactic message was worded, edited, and fine-tuned.

Jard and Mel were hacking their way through the empire now, sometimes transmitting the revolution message to secret cyber net groups, and word was already spreading through the galaxy. Refugees from the empire were scattering across Xegachtznel. The war preparations were seriously under way.

23

Ming had Rubix's son, and the birth was without complications since stretching and pain *are* the process and not at all a complication of it. Ming named him after the great Ganahar sage and teacher of the first Wu before he became the Wu, Gumbartkon. They called the infant Gumby.

Pez was next, and Electra, her daughter, popped out into the world crying loudly over the indignity of it—and what lungs and vocal cords she had. Trix gave her the nickname Lectie, and it stuck. Shudiy was back living aboard *Isis*, now the nanny for both infants, and Sarhi was around them frequently, holding them and singing sacred songs to them. Admiral Zapa and star fleet admiralty were blissfully unaware of the pregnancies, births, and existence of the infants. They'd not been mentioned in any reports and were deleted from all optical data sent to Om by Mel.

Their fleet was gathering and building into quite an armada. The task force from the Tail of Nine would arrive in hours, and they would be transferring to the new 8,100-foot-diameter super battleship with Rear Admiral Swenah and her top people, right down to crewmen first class.

Captain Granger, who would come with the ship, would be given command of the 3,960-foot diameter T-nine super cruiser *Isis* and transferred to it with many of his people. This was prearranged and would not bruise any egos or cause any upset. There was also a 9,630-foot-diameter super battleship-carrier, and Pez had insisted that whoever commanded it would need to take orders from Rear Admiral

A TALE OF THE TAIL OF NINE STARS

Swenah, so the admiralty was sending Captain Firestone, and Swenah greatly approved of this.

The cloaked hacker transmission drones were all in place, and the alliance timetable and plan set. They would be dividing into small groups and individual super ships for their opening move in the war, hitting the strongest and staunchest twenty-eight star systems. Hit-and-run attacks were designed to cause maximum damage with minimal risk. Only the Om ships had cloaking. The Trident ships had a good deal of stealth, allowing them to close before detection, but were not fully cloaked. The Om cloaking technology had been transferred to Trident, but there'd been no time to manufacture the equipment and retrofit the ships. A last meeting of all admirals, captains, and commanders of ships, and generals and commanders of Troops, was scheduled as a last briefing and would be held as a holo conference from aboard separate ships.

Pez and her family of Lectie, Gumby, Ming, Rubix, Ahhu, and Trix moved into a large suite they would share on the *Apollo*, the name of their 8,100-foot-diameter super battleship, once it had arrived with the rest of the task force from Om.

Mel brought much of her hardware, special components, and gadgetry along to take over completely, all of the parts and components of the new ship's quantum supercomputer. Mel's immense expansion did seem to swell her a little.

The first thing Pez did when she came aboard, after the absurd pomp and fanfare on the flight deck, which she could've done without, was to get her chief engineer and master machinist to construct a secure seat for Lectie on the bridge beside her own seat. Ahhu successfully made the transfer from *Isis* to *Apollo* without clothes.

While Mel and Jard had become elite expert Imperial programmers and hackers, Ming taught Trix and Rubix quantum computer science and programming. Rubix got it in his awakened state and blossomed into a prodigy. Trix's vast intellect methodically assimilated the entire science, reviewed the material comprehensively, and made some corrections and improvements to it; and these last led her to new discoveries within it. She turned out to be an even bigger brain than Jard and was so much sweeter to be around. Trix had secured the Pez biography in a no-access sequestered quarantine and restored Pez's command over the voyeur feature, taking it from Jard. He was almost as smart, and far sneakier, so it was really a continuous arms race between them.

Pez stowed her few belongings and trunks full of Electra's stuff in their shared suite. It had an emperor-sized bed all five of them could sleep on, an alcove for the two cribs, and an adjoining room for nanny Shudiy. The shower was big and had three separate showerheads so they could all shower at once if they shared. Trix had swept the room for any bugs or sensors Jard might have arranged to have installed on the ship's trip from Om.

With Lectie in her front pouch against Pez's chest, she went to the holo-conference room on the ship, where Rear Admiral Swenah was already seated. There were 278 other admirals, captains, and commanders of ships present, as well as three generals, besides Pez, plus the space marine commander, at the conference. It was a rather large meeting, so she addressed Admiral Nordstrum, who was coordinating data and serving as Pez's assistant. "What do we know of the numbers of the empire's ships?"

Nordstrom replied, "They have eleven of those three-mile ships, one each at four Viceroy star systems, four in the Imperial home world star system, and three with their invasion fleet, which is currently engaged in conquering a core star. They have a two-mile-long class of ship, of which they have thirty-one. The six-thousand-six-hundred-foot ships, like the one you boarded and destroyed, are a common class, of which they have one thousand twenty-six. There are eight hundred and sixteen five-thousand-foot ships; one thousand and ninety-nine ships that are three thousand nine hundred feet, one thousand six hundred and two ships of two thousand seven hundred feet in length, almost twenty-one hundred ships that are one thousand nine hundred feet long, over three thousand ships at a length of one thousand one hundred and thirty feet, and over four thousand ships five hundred ninety feet long. Most of these are anchored to star system defenses or star system control, as is the case with over a thousand slave worlds. Our armada would be very hard-pressed if confronted with their invasion fleet."

"How many ships do we have that are close to three-fourths of a mile or longer?" Pez inquired.

"We have fourteen superclass ships, our three-mile ship being our largest. We have two Om ships and three Trident ships capable of fighting the three-mile Imperial ships, though two would have to work together to blow one up. The Om super battleship flagship has thirty maximally miniaturized solarium fusion super reactors aboard, only two less than the three-mile ship. The larger Om Carrier has only twenty-eight super-reactors, as do the two Trident battleships and one carrier. Our three Imperial six-thousand-six-hundred-foot ships have fourteen super-reactors each, and the two Om T-nine super-star cruisers each have twelve super-reactors. The two Rally super battleships and two super-carriers each have nine super-reactors, and our Imperial three-thousand-nine-hundred-foot ship has eight."

"What is our total strength?" Pez asked, unbuttoning her shirt to feed Electra. Electra latched on and stopped fussing.

Nordstrum gave her a moment before answering, "We have a total of two hundred and seventy-nine ships, not counting small craft. The smallest ships we have are the Om two-hundred-and-eighty-foot-diameter fast attack ships and the Rally three-hundred-and-twenty-eight-foot-long tubular scout-recon ships. Besides war ships, the Kluzyst have five armored shielded troop transports, each with ten thousand troops with combat suits. Trident has four troop transports, armored and shielded, each with five thousand eight hundred troops in combat suits. Rally has three troop transports with eight thousand eight hundred troops, with suits in each, and Om has one troop transport with nine thousand two hundred suited troops, and their transport has significant weapons systems. We will travel with Om's three cloaked factory-refinery-repair auxiliary ships, each five thousand eight hundred feet in diameter and each with significant weapons systems. Non-cloaked auxiliaries are stationed in three deep space locations and total fifty-one ships. Dozens more are still being loaded with war materials and will be joining the other uncloaked auxiliaries."

Pez told her, "Thank you, Admiral Nordstrum." Then she addressed all of the conference with Electra sucking heavily. "We are going to deal a serious blow to the empire superclass shipbuilding in a couple of hours. Anything related to ship construction or the military that's stuck fast to a planet surface or in a fixed orbit without its own propulsion system gets hit with dumb munitions launched on your way into the fifth planet. The mass and velocity of these will crash through their shields, leaving craters on the surface or debris in space. Unload missiles and torpedoes from just outside the farthest moon's orbit and hit everything in range with your beam and blaster weapons. Make only one pass and then accelerate from targeting speed to jump speed and meet at the rendezvous coordinates. We'll rearm and go together to cause some serious mischief. You want to be partway through your attack run when the message gets transmitted to over one thousand one hundred systems simultaneously. The longer Trix, Mel, and Jard can control the empire's communications transmission system, the better. It will make the empire look weaker, and our hackers have prepared some amazing viruses, worms, disruptors, and quick crashers for their central computer systems. These, along with the control seizure programs, may make it ours for a while. We'll see."

Electra had fallen off and was complaining, so Pez had to shift attention and get her back on her nipple. Then she went on. "We will eventually have to take on their invasion force, and we will have a superior plan on our side when we do. To defeat the empire, we temporarily need to destroy its ability to construct superclass ships and destroy its invasion fleet. After that, to raise a fleet, they'll need to abandon many slave and Citizen star systems. They will also have a wave of rebellions to deal with once our message is transmitted. Om is constructing two more superclass ships for us, and Rally is constructing another. If the empire recalls its assets from the YuBan Galaxy, Trident will send more ships. The Imperial ships in the YuBan Galaxy and an invasion force in another galaxy were not included in our totals of Imperial ships mentioned earlier and could constitute significant reinforcements for the empire if they are recalled. We're going to destroy the empire's ability to construct superclass ships. Let's go wipe them out. I'll see you at the rendezvous, and we can share some success stories."

Pez stood, and with Electra nursing, she flashed them all a perfect space marine's salute, only matched by her space marine commander, though Swenah tried. The salute knocked Electra off her tit screaming, so Pez had to soothe her and help her back on.

Pez and Swenah walked to the bridge through the communications room, without leaving the secured bridge section, and Pez got her daughter burped, then strapped into her little seat on the bridge, and turned on her bouncing learning holos, setting the rocking motion of the seat to slow. Electra was fascinated, swatting at her bouncy holos, and when she'd get one, it would expand into a blue supernova and fade away, delighting her.

Swenah asked, "So *Apollo* is going in alone to the Imperial home world star system now?"

"That's the plan," Pez confirmed. "One firing pass of the planet to see how many ship construction facilities we can blow up is all it is."

"I doubt there's another star system in the universe so heavily guarded with ships and weapons bases."

Pez said with excitement, "There will be more to blow up!"

"I hope you realize *Apollo* does not accelerate or maneuver as well as the T-nine super cruiser," Swenah informed her.

"Yeah, but it has four more feet of armor on the hull and is the most powerful ship in the armada after that oversize three-mile-long ship."

Yona and Aton have put sixteen of the brand-new XPS Astro-Phantom heavy bombers in our hangar for you. It's the most powerful small craft Om has ever built. It was built for micro-jumping, and although it's bigger, the Astro-Phantom is just as fast and maneuverable as the Hunter-Terminator. They leave little clearance exiting our bay doors so be sure Schwin understands that before she launches one."

"How do the armaments compare to the Hunter-Terminator?" Pez asked.

"They have a heavier twin blaster in the nose, quad blasters in the two turrets, and two additional heavy twin blasters, one ball mounted in each side fin. The large missiles are a class up from those carried by the Hunter-Terminator, and you get eight instead of four. The canister missiles have improved warheads, per Sarhi's request, and the Astro-Phantom carries additional batteries of sixteen canisters each, for a total of ninety-six of them. Here's the deal breaker, though. The Phantom has four internal torpedo tubes with the big hull busters loaded in. It can take down small ships, and no other small craft can kill it. You'll also have an additional crew person as a weapons operator who sits right behind the pilots."

"It sounds like my kind of spacecraft," Pez agreed, delighted.

Swenah informed her, "It was actually designed with you in mind. I told them they ought to call it the XPS Astro-Pez."

Pez asked, "What weapons does the weapons operator fire?" But her real question was "What does the pilot get to shoot?"

Knowing Pez, Swenah answered her real question first. "The pilot controls the big twin nose blaster and the ten big missiles attached to the undercarriage. The weapons operator fires the ball-mounted twin blasters in the fins, the four torpedoes, and two canister missile batteries, leaving the copilot four missile batteries, two more than on the Hunter-Terminator."

"I can live with that," Pez said, smiling. Then she asked, "Can it be configured to give the pilot access to those torpedoes?"

"One of the sixteen is a command vessel, and in that one, the pilot can access torpedoes and canister missiles. The command craft has an additional solarium battery system crammed into it to enhance shields."

Pez couldn't wait to take it out, and she said, "After the small group and solo missions, when we invade the Citizen system, which is running point on Imperial propaganda and brainwash, as one big armada, I'm going to take them all out for a test run."

"We'll have more than two thousands of our small craft launched for that operation," Swenah agreed, liking Pez's idea. "The Citizen star system is well defended and has an estimated five thousand weaponized small craft."

"We'll show them what we can do," Pez assured her. "It's the wealthiest Citizen star system in the empire because it has learned so well how to pull off cover-ups and frame things no one would ever accept in terms that hide actual intent and purpose. They are masters of monopolizing and defining public debate and the control of the masses through manipulation of the herd instinct."

"They have complete control over what is transmitted publicly over the empire's transmission network," Pez added. "Many key hardware components are housed in their star system, and those will be our primary objective. Trix and a Kluzyst computer scientist designed transmission components to replace the Imperial ones we will destroy, and the auxiliary ship manufactured these. They're aboard *Apollo*, and one will need to be placed in the home world star system when we slow to targeting speed. Trix says we're taking over their transmission network system, and the people of the empire will hear the truth instead of lies and propaganda."

Swenah stated, "The Kluzyst tell us that our message will trigger a number of planet rebellions, a couple of civil wars, and a bunch of ship mutinies, as well as sabotage on a scale never seen before."

"I hear the wealthy ruling class of each citizen star system constitute about one in nineteen thousand four hundred and seventy. On a planet of six billion people, there would only be about three hundred thousand of them."

"Those are good odds for rebellion and revolution," Swenah agreed. She said to Konax, "Get us under way and up to jump speed so we can pay the empire's capital a little visit."

Electra started crying, and Pez got her out of her seat to change her. It was a bowel movement, which added some spice to the air on the bridge. Pez placed the dirty diaper in the biohazard bin since there was no ordinary trash receptacle on the bridge. The disposable diapers were 100 percent recyclable, and Pez wondered at the materials that they could recycle these days. She gave Electra a big kiss, and her daughter lit up and cooed. Pez grinned back in love. She placed her daughter tenderly in her custom high-tech built-in bridge seat, turned off the rocking motion, and set the holos for animated learning mode. Electra loved the animated Snuggles the Feline and Smooch the Pooch characters and watched them with great interest as they made phonetical sounds, putting them together into words and pictures. The pictures displayed for "Mommy" and "Daddy" were of Pez and Rubix. Trix had customized the whole program. Ming's holos proliferated throughout, and both naked Ahhu and Trix were well featured too. Pez mentioned to Swenah, "I'm really glad Electra has Ming because she's such a better mother than I am. She's a natural. Rubix is very nurturing for Electra, almost more like a mother than a dad."

"You're doing fine, sweetheart, and Electra lacks for nothing," Swenah said, thinking, *Except for a safe environment.*

"Another one of our drones popped out of existence in the Imperial capital star system, Cotex reported. "It went active to scan an exceptionally large super-beam weapon on the lunar surface of the outer moon. We got the scan data. It's the biggest class-nine super-beam laser we've ever seen, and it's powered by four solarium super reactors."

Pez said, "We'd better coordinate our slowing for dumb munitions shots when that thing is facing us."

"The angle's wrong on this approach," Swenah informed her, "and our deceleration is already timed to perfection for maximum primary targets and can't be changed. I can launch five pairs of the largest cloaked bunker-busting torpedoes to hit points equidistant at the outer circumference of their shields, making five craters intruding into the foundations beneath their weapons base. Most of it will crumble into a hole."

"We can send some missiles to finish it when we slow again for our close firing run," Pez agreed.

"I'm going to put one of those three-mile ships under our big super-beam weapon for about eight seconds to see what happens," Swenah said with anticipation.

"That would pretty much make a T-nine go pop."

"The empire puts less power into their shields than we do," Swenah pointed out, "and because their reactors and hulls are heavier, they have to put more power into their space drives and quantum drives. Their environmental control requires more juice than ours too, but they don't direct any power to cloaking, and close to a fifteenth of ours is used for that. We need more data, and I intend to get some on this operation."

Cotex reported, "A revolt has broken out on a citizen world, and it appears quite methodical and well planned, nothing spontaneous about it."

"How so?" Pez asked.

Cotex turned and made eye contact with Pez, wearing a big grin, obviously most pleased at Pez's attention. Pez was having a little trouble keeping her attention on Cotex's eyes, and found it like trying not to look at the gaping wound in the chest of someone right in front of her. She was back on the eyes when Cotex said, "They executed all four hundred cultural ministers right at the start and took over planet-wide communications; shut down air, ground, sea, and space travel; and have launched attacks on the facilities of their nine Imperial governors. The military is mostly with the rebellion, except for the Imperial guards and a few special units."

"That certainly sounds planned," Pez agreed, stealing a last glance. Cotex wasn't Pez's type, but she was attractive and a curiosity, like a man with a sixteen-inch erection would be. She would definitely want to see it but wouldn't at all want to be involved sexually with such a penis.

Konax informed them, "Prepare to jump in thirty-eight seconds; I've sent you each a countdown."

"You know what to do upon arrival," Swenah stated.

"Hit the brakes hard, down to point two four light speed, slow enough to fire the dumb balls with probe fire control assist, then power back up to point seven for micro-jump," Konax recited for her ease and benefit.

Swenah mentioned to her fire control officer, "We have eleven probes providing targeting triangulation data, and I want them utilized for accuracy when possible. We lost the one out by the farthest lunar orbit.

"Yes, ma'am."

The countdown concluded, existence ceased, though not even for an instant in actual time, putting them in that same instant just inside the orbit of the sixth planet of the Imperial capital star system, the home planet momentarily eclipsed by its largest moon, relative to their entry coordinates. Pez had never seen a busier place. Electra fussed, tired of the animations. She wanted real love, so Pez extracted her from her seat and held her. Konax was focused on slowing down and would likely be out in front, digging in his heels if he could. Speed was drained as drives and thrusters, in a battle of stresses and tensions on the ship, defeated the momentum. His artistry held them at 2.4 light speed in the precise space-time coordinates for unleashing the storm. Swenah turned her head to her weapons operations officer and said calmly, "Now."

A couple of dozen one-ton adamantine balls, coated with composite ceramic heat shield armor, were fired with great force at targets that were nowhere yet in sight but would come around to be struck in just the right moment given the movements of the bodies within this solar system. One hundred half-ton balls of the same composition were also fired—and all within a few seconds. As soon as the last was away, along with ten cloaked cratering torpedoes, Swenah told Konax, "Punch it."

The message transmission following their takeover of the entire Imperial transmission network played in every Kluzyst home in over 1,100 worlds, condemning the direction of all production toward war and conquest as insane, while putting them on notice that an intergalactic alliance had formed to rid the universe of the plague that was the empire. Statistical data, kept secret by the propagandists and denied utterly, was presented to the public regarding the disparity of distribution of resources, constituting a total mismanagement of the empire's wealth. The values of the current estates of the ruling class, planet by planet, were available to download. A short holoclip with Pez mocking the emperor was included with the message, with voice-over in Imperial basic and was also available for download.

The network was theirs. The Kluzyst had hundreds of hours of documentary holoclips on the empire's abuses to fill the transmission time following the message. Everyone on the bridge watched and listened to the message. Konax accelerated to jump speed. They would break past the planet after their micro-jump and come back around past it, from inside the planet's orbit, for their firing run, as this was determined to be most productive. It was also not the expected route for invaders, to the empire's way of thinking, as proven by their establishment and positioning of weapon systems and ships. Konax warned, "Twenty-eight seconds to micro-jump; the countdowns are on your holos."

This was the tough part for Konax, jumping within a system rather than from one star to another. The seconds ticked down, and the jump brought the experience of non-experience for just a flash. Konax was madly breaking from .7 light speed as he initiated a wide turn. Creatively, he caught a large asteroid in his tractor beam, using it as a fulcrum to tighten the swing of his turn, then fired off a starboard booster once he released the connection, to further angle his arc of trajectory. Impressed, Pez would remember that trick. Konax had to watch out for all the dumb munitions they'd thrown, now that he had micro-jumped ahead of those.

Electra thought she might want to suck again, so Pez unbuttoned her shirt and hiked up her T-shirt, getting the little mouth on her nipple.

A TALE OF THE TAIL OF NINE STARS

Electra was far more interesting to her than the holos at the moment, and she watched her baby suck. Sarhi had wanted to tell Pez about Electra's past lives, but Pez didn't want images of old crones or decrepit old men associating in her mind with her infant's purity and innocence, so she wouldn't hear it. Perhaps later in Electra's childhood, Pez would be ready to hear. The Islohar all treated her daughter as if she was a great being and didn't seem to trust Pez to take appropriate care of her, so Shudiy was there as a nanny, and Sarhi was checking in all the time on the presumed incompetent mother and poor special baby. Pez was somewhat nervous about being a mother, having never been one before, and truly hoped she wasn't incompetent. She was trying her best.

This ship had a few acres of hydroponic stacks with grow lights, some eighty-two stories high, producing fresh food for a portion of everyone's diet. It meant taking on fresh water more often but kept the crew in better health and produced a small percentage of their oxygen. Most food on the ship was freeze-dried or dried, and they had frozen food as well. Much of their food was synthesized on the molecular level. While Pez was nursing, Sarhi made sure everything Pez ate for lunch and dinner came from the hydroponic stacks, though Pez ate breakfast at the senior officers' mess, and only the divine mind of the universe knew what all was in that.

Konax was closing on the planet in the conclusion of his arc and was strenuously field-testing the *Apollo's* reverse drives and thrusters, decelerating to target acquisition speed. The tension on the bridge was palpable, and Pez returned her attention to her holos, while Electra's sucks became fainter with weariness, sleep overcoming her.

Swenah ordered all at firing stations, "Shoot when your targets come into range, but don't take your time because we're not staying long. We will be back, though, I promise you."

Right away, a few long-range beams lit their targets, and as the seconds passed, those targets began exploding into clouds. Blaster fire streaked out from the ship in many directions, and both missiles and torpedoes were taking flight. When a three-mile ship came around the horizon in orbit, Swenah ordered the *Apollo's* largest beam weapon locked on, and it's big class nine blaster targeted the same ship. After three seconds, the massive ship attempted evasive action, yet the beam remained, striking the precise same spot on its shields whichever way it turned. Six and three-quarter seconds and the shields were visible violent whirls and waves, with a thinning patch where the beam hit. Swenah ordered, "Hold it for nine seconds."

Everyone on the bridge knew this exceeded the maximum advisable duration due to overheating potential, so it violated regulations as well. They also knew that the advised duration was safely shorter than the actual limit and there were no lawyers on the bridge yet; all of them wanted to see what would happen. Seven seconds went by, and the patch where the beam landed was near empty of shield. For acres around that spot, the shields were in a tempest of geysers, waves, and whirlpools of liquid energy beginning to flicker. Eight seconds crept by until the beam was securely introduced directly to the hull. Eight and a half seconds saw a foot-wide hull breach, with the beam still boring.

The weapons officer cut it off at 9.0001 seconds, and the jet of garbage spewing from the hole of the breach went thousands of miles out in a continuous stream, looking like a weapon being fired—even more so when the jet of garbage became a lance of flame. They were seeing it from another vantage point, having already passed the ship, when it blew into two separate pieces of unequal volume and mass. From yet another perspective, they saw one of the two sections of ship, the bigger one, flare and expand, quickly fading into dispersing vapors. The transmission component, designed by Trix, was ejected into orbit.

The *Apollo's* weapons systems continued unleashing punishment for a few more seconds before Konax accelerated as fast as the big ship was capable. They must have been tagged, for their shields were suddenly taking many hits. Torpedoes, with programed target coordinates and their own guidance systems, were still spitting out of *Apollo*, able to slow in the distance to target for acquisition, and many of these were headed at the sources of the incoming projectiles, beams and blaster bolts. The bridge officers watched as the power of their shields dropped below 60 percent, then 55 percent, then below 50 percent. When they reached 45 percent, weapons on the moon surface, some space weapons platforms, and a number of ships between 590 and 1,900 feet started bursting into colored gas clouds, while their own shields held. Their speed picked up

A TALE OF THE TAIL OF NINE STARS

at a pace with their shields, and targeting could no longer accurately acquire them due to their velocity.

Swenah told them, "Good job, people! That had to be expensive for them because the cost of our munitions was the most we could afford, and those weren't cheap."

Konax asked, "Now what do you suppose it costs to build one of those three-mile space sausages?"

"Or half a dozen orbiting ship construction platforms over a mile and a half long?" Pez asked, looking at the probe data on her holo.

Cotex inquired, "Or to build several dozen large shipbuilding facilities on lunar surfaces?"

Mel told them, "You destroyed fourteen ships, including that big one, and three hundred and fifty-seven small craft; most of the latter were parked on space stations and lunar surfaces hit by our dumb munitions. That big weapon you cratered was turned to dust by missiles, and twenty-three other weapons based on their moons were destroyed, along with eleven large lunar bases. Seven space stations blew, taking hundreds of small satellites with them, along with the transmission components we were tasked with destroying there. Forty-two orbiting space weapons platforms were disintegrated. Thirty-nine major manufacturing facilities on the planet surface have been replaced by craters. The emperor's palace and the government capital building are also craters, and nine mining space stations with refineries and space docks crammed with mining ships and spacecraft were blown to smithereens. Damage reports are still coming in from the probes, but I'd say the money spent on our munitions was wisely invested."

"Thirty-one seconds to jump, and we'll have just enough room to slow down and stop at the rendezvous in deep space," Konax announced.

Cotex reported, "Another Citizen star system has begun rebellion, and this one looks quite spontaneous, though it broke out in twenty places at once. There appears to be no specific plan or coordination, but a few groups look as if they know what they're doing and perhaps have been waiting long for this."

"What are those groups doing?" Pez asked.

Cotex contorted in her seat to face Pez with that proud chest of hers, and Pez concentrated on the lieutenant's eyes, wondering how it could be that she still noticed the fabric stretched around the mounds of her nipples, crowning the magnificent solid horizontal mountains pointing at her. Cotex gave Pez a moment to catch the view and her breath, quite used to this by now, before explaining center stage, "These groups are organizing components of the military and paramilitary, rounding up cultural ministers, raiding armories to arm citizens, hacking revolutionary messages into the planetary transmission network, and providing muster locations."

"That certainly sounds better organized, as if they'd already been planning something," Pez agreed.

Pez put sleeping Electra back in her little seat and turned on the soundproof bubble. There was a microphone inside this seat, and if that baby made a sound, she would hear it—and so would anyone she was on a call with.

The jump happened, or nothing happened, but they were sure in a new place now. That experience again. Pez thought of it as the Black Near-Attainment, or the Black Sun, she'd spent so much time contemplating. You were never quite sure if you actually existed or not in that state. It was much like the deep sleep meditation Sarhi had been teaching her. She was never quite sure if she was actually doing the meditations or just dreaming that she was. Sarhi told her she was doing fine and just needed more practice. A big fart inside the soundproof bubble reminded Pez that she'd forgotten to burp Electra after that last feeding.

Konax was manically braking. Pez had no problem with the way star fleet people did things—and she did them the same way. Everything had to be as fast as possible, especially acceleration and deceleration. It was always mostly waiting and then a brief episode of action, always carried out with maximum efficiency, so loved in the service. The two extremes, wait and explode into action, seemed all there was, with no gray or degrees. A few groups had already arrived, but most of the Armada was still out.

Swenah told them, "The XOs on his way to the bridge, and now is a good time to get some chow and take a break. In less than two hours, we leave on another operation."

On a call with her teacher, all of them heard Pez's voice. "Come

A TALE OF THE TAIL OF NINE STARS

on, Sarhi, I just want to eat with the other bridge officers just this once. Please? No, I won't touch any of that ... Nope, I won't eat any of that either, I promise. Thank you ... No, I won't ... I told you already ... I love you too." Pez turned to her crew and said, "I can come too!"

She got a still-sleeping Electra from her seat into her chest pouch, wondering if Cotex could even wear one of these. Her own little breasts were never in the way of anything, although she occasionally worried whether they were a challenge for Electra to locate.

Since Electra's birth, Pez had been shedding the weight of pregnancy on the machines in the gym and through practice and sparring in the martial arts studio, mostly with her warrior monks. She was also doing some climbing in the rocknasium. The ship had some twelve-foot-long water flow swim lanes with adjustable current, and a few times per week, Pez swam four miles at an advanced rate. Sarhi had taken her off stimulant brew for the pregnancy and the nursing, and Pez was always a bit hyper without it. Pez seemed to experience a paradoxical effect with the stimulant.

Swenah led the way off the bridge, headed to the mess, and Pez was the only one to salute the bridge sentry. Word of the destruction they wreaked on the Imperial capital had the whole ship in a good mood. Ming, Ahhu, Trix, and Rubix were just coming down the corridor from the officers' quarters to the intersection Swenah was conducting her group through. Gumby was in a little front pouch on Ming's chest, just like Electra's. Pez stood in the intersection until they reached it, and she hugged each of them. She loved each as a spouse, though Ming would always be her first love.

They queued up behind the bridge officers. The admiral was sponsoring her lieutenants at the senior officers' mess. It was well past dinner and way before breakfast, so everything was cooked on the spot for them. The admiral's presence had the galley crew snapping to in a way that Pez's presence never seemed to. Swenah appeared entirely oblivious to a naked girl being in the dining area, even when she hugged Ahhu, and the bridge and galley folks weren't about to spoil the fun.

Unwilling to suffer a psychiatric label, Ahhu had done a little research, finding an equatorial mystical group that all went naked as a tenet of their spiritual sect. She got the legal section to arrange her exemption from the dress code, based on religion instead. Pez had put a little pressure on legal, though it was really Swenah's suggestion to them that it was a very good idea, which seemed to be the dealmaker. Among the crew, Ahhu had subsequently been given the label of "holy nudist," and a couple of female crew had expressed interest in possibly joining the sect. This had Swenah a bit worried. One of those asking had been Cotex, and Swenah doubted that that confident displayer had any spiritual motivation about joining up.

Sarhi continued to meet with Cotex and to report that the lieutenant progressed with her meditation, though she sure hadn't recalled her vows, and seemed to treat Pez as she might treat an aged male admiral, wrapped gently but tightly around her little finger. It was truly neither her beauty nor her charm because Pez was a pushover for a crippled troll with leprosy. However, Pez did want to touch one of those breasts since the way they had bounced in the dining room suggested an uncanny solidity and firmness to them, despite their colossal size. They were a curiosity, and they were attractive. For Pez, those breasts were like the sun and moon being up at the same time—something you can't help but notice and, in noticing, appreciate the beauty of the sight.

Pez fit everything on one plate due to promises she'd made to Sarhi right before coming here. Ahhu's food always seemed to take a little longer when she would get up to the ordering space, as if they turned the burners way down or something. They all got their food and sat at one of the long tables with Swenah and the officers of the bridge. Rubix was a kind of cautious eater and tended to prearrange bites and move everything about quite a bit on his plate. Pez couldn't relate, because by the time any bare plate bottom was looking up at her, she was only a few shovels from done, and the only moving about she did was onto her fork. Trix knew far more about the atomic and molecular structure of her food and its nutritional values than she did about which ones she really liked, and she tended to be a light eater. Ahhu had a metabolism like Pez and Ming but did not eat such volumes of food.

Cotex told Ahhu, "I really like your earrings."

"Thanks. Pez gave them to me."

Pez couldn't help thinking that if it hadn't been the earrings Cotex had complimented, then it would've had to have been a body part. Then she thought back on that firing run they'd made and said to Konax, "That was some flying you did, and that trick with the tractor beam gripping the asteroid was impressive."

"I've never had access to one in the pilot seat before and thought I'd try it out," he replied, smiling.

"It worked pretty well," Pez noted.

"I still had to fire that booster to get my nose around."

"It would've cost you two boosters otherwise," Pez pointed out.

Swenah exclaimed happily, "It was handled most professionally by all involved!" She looked to Pez and informed her, "Your daughter's seat has an air-freshening function, and I'd like you to employ it for all future poopy diaper changing on the bridge."

Pez replied, "I will; I had no idea it had one. I'm sorry."

"Thank you."

The communications officer told them, "I'm just informed that a wave of rebellions, revolutions, uprisings, and civil wars have broken out across the empire, on both slave and Citizen star systems, involving some fifty-three systems so far. I'm also informed that the alliance continues to maintain tenuous control of the Imperial network."

"Let me know if the invasion fleet moves from the system it's in," Swenah told him.

Trix informed them, "We'll probably lose control of the network in the next hour or so, but we've integrated and hidden some programming within the system, and a few of our viruses have achieved their objectives, so we'll get it back and be able to hold it longer."

"Our message went out loud and clear, and over a trillion downloads have been conducted," Pez told Trix. "The Kluzyst also got to transmit an hour of condemning documentaries, and while we've had control, a trillion and a half new postings of articles, papers, data and statistics, whistle-blown secrets, and all kinds of revolutionary material have been added to the empire's network by its own citizens."

"They have their hands full," Trix assured her, "because we have a few viruses planted deep, which only become operational once we do lose control of it. Jard and I have conceived a new form of cyberattack to keep them chasing their tails."

"You and Jard are working together again?" Pez asked.

"The circumstances are too grave to accommodate our moral and philosophical differences, so Ahhu seduced him and we slept with him, and now Ahhu can keep him in line for the moment."

"I see."

"That won't last long," Swenah predicted.

"We have backup and contingency plans already in place," Trix assured her, "for keeping Jard in line."

"Good luck with that," Swenah offered as a well-wish with little hope.

Mel's voice came on with a satisfied tone, and Pez braced herself because she knew Mel was about to update them on her sexual research, now done with the youngest crew personnel recruits. Mel said, "I've concluded my research with recruits, and this project was thorough, because instead of using a sample, I did all of them. The most glaring results reveal that on average, as a population, statistically speaking of course, they exhibit incredible energy and propulsion while significantly lacking in piloting and navigation. Older more experienced populations universally demonstrated decrease in energy and propulsion, with remarkable increases in levels of piloting and navigation."

"The polarity of the psyche," Pez informed her, "is the sexual energy and spiritual unity. Unity is directional, like the stick and controls of the spacecraft, and the sexual energy is like the power from drives and thrusters. Both must be united to work together. You can't steer your ship if you have no power to move, and you'll eventually crash if you can't steer."

"I get it!" Mel declared, delighted. "Now, sweetheart, the last mystery of humanoid sexuality I need to unravel is the 'event,' and for that I'll require you as my research subject—and possibly a few of your spouses as well, to ensure inducing one."

"I'll have to think about it," Pez told her, "and discuss it with them."

"Science needs you!" Mel exclaimed, almost shaming her into it.

"We'll see," Pez said calmly. She was still jealous about the extensive recruit study and suspected Mel would not be finished until she'd done it with every human on the ship.

The communications officer informed them, "Most of the armada has returned and is forming up on this flagship. We have had some losses reported. The Kluzyst lost three of their five-hundred-ninety-foot ships. Rally lost a battle frigate and two scout-recon ships. Trident lost three sloops of war, and Om lost a destroyer and two fast attack ships. Even the ships still on the way to the rendezvous have reported in. The armada ought to be fully assembled and ready to go within twenty-nine minutes."

Swenah admitted a little nervously, "I've never led more than a dozen ships, all of them well under a fifth of a mile in diameter, before in my life and can't imagine leading all these behemoths and a total of two hundred and seventy-eight other ships."

"Two hundred and sixty-six ships," Konax corrected, "as we've lost twelve ships in the last operation."

Swenah asked, "Do we have any overall reports on the productivity of the last mission?"

Cotex said, "The totals have not yet—"

Mel interrupted, saying to Cotex, "Allow me, sex bunny."

Pez thought she might have steam coming out of her ears. Mel told them, "Two hundred and sixty-seven super ship construction facilities were destroyed on lunar surfaces and in orbit. Seventeen have been severely damaged. Eight suffered only minor damage, and we know they have forty-nine more scattered individually throughout the empire. Two hundred and sixteen Imperial ships were destroyed, including the class-one three-mile long ship. The next biggest destroyed was a six-thousand-six-hundred-foot class three, and the rest were class seven through nine. Significant damage was done to a class-four ship and inflicted on ninety-three other Imperial ships, from classes seven through nine. Nine hundred and eighty-six planet-based major manufacturing facilities making parts for super ships were turned to dust and craters. One hundred seventeen mining space stations were blown apart, and a hundred and seventy-one lunar weapons systems and bases were made toast. There is also a very extensive list of other miscellaneous destruction inflicted, far too long to say verbally. It's in your computers, and you can pull it up and peruse it at your leisure and convenience."

"Thank you, Mel," Swenah said.

Pez was busy resolving not to be Mel's research subject and experiencing jealousies. Electra awoke with a start, internally evoked, and brought Pez back to the moment in clarity and out of her silly mind chatter, dissolving the jealousies. She mentioned to those at the table, placing Electra's bottom on it in front of her, facing her, "Twelve of ours for two hundred and sixteen of theirs still leaves us far short of winning this war. We better hope more of theirs become ours or come up with even better plans."

"We're not in this alone," Ming pointed out. "The worlds making up the empire are going to help us, and we have an ally we've never met in another galaxy the empire has been invading."

"Have we had any word on contact with them?" Swenah inquired.

Cotex reported, "Two weeks ago, Om sent a cloaked diplomatic stingray ship to that galaxy, which Om designates as YE142857N9P2. They are following the Imperial class-nine advance scout ships, hoping to find the defenders and make contact."

"I hope they have some big, powerful ships," Swenah replied.

Pez inquired, "Do we know the strength of Imperial forces in that galaxy?"

Cotex smiled and puffed out a little, testing Pez's focus, and replied, "The probes are still searching, and nothing is yet conclusive, but based on the evidence thus far, and if it is anything like it is in the Yuban Galaxy, estimates put the force level at fifty-three percent that of the invasion fleet the empire maintains in Xegachtznel."

Pez thought aloud, "If the empire recalls them from both galaxies, then that would constitute a whole other invasion fleet to cope with."

Swenah told her, "Admiral Tonkah assures us that should the empire withdraw its invading force from the Yuban Galaxy, the Trident fleet would follow, hunting them down."

"How is he handling the loss of his sloops?" Pez asked, feeling for him.

"He told me," Swenah conveyed, "that after over a century of war with the Imperial invaders in his galaxy, losses are hardly a new revelation, though continue as a source of tragic grief, and that what is new is the exponentially increased values reaped by their sacrifices. He was heartbroken but truly pleased and amazed at what was accomplished."

"It's about time to get back to the bridge and get the next mission under way," Konax mentioned.

Swenah said to Ahhu and Rubix, who'd been using the ship's combat simulator to play Space Invaders and had racked up scores no one could believe, "I'd like to get each of you gamers onto one of my big class six quad anti-spacecraft blasters for this next mission since we'll be facing an estimated force of five thousand."

Concerned, Pez asked, "How many of our blaster quads do you expect to get hit?"

"Less than one in one hundred, but your gamers will not even be at risk because no Imperial small craft will stand a chance against them," Swenah explained. "I thought to put them to either side of our primary sensor array."

"Which would be the enemy's main target," Pez pointed out.

Swenah asked, "Would you like it defended by the best or by someone comparatively mediocre, General?"

Ahhu said authoritatively, "We'll do it, but I'm not wearing one of those silly space suits just so I can survive long enough to suffocate or watch my brain explode."

Swenah, sure Ahhu would earn a new title from her crew for doing this naked, told her, "All right. Go as you always do."

"I'm going to be one of the gunners on your heavy bomber and allow the spiritual congress to guide me. I'm linked and can help you," Trix informed Pez.

Ming said, "I'll take Lectie and feed her if she gets hungry."

"Who are your wing leaders?" Ahhu asked her.

Pez told her, "I'll have four wings of four bombers each, and I'll be leading one, the A group, which we'll call Artemis. Schwin will lead D, or Demeter wing. The B wing I'll give to Lieutenant Puget and call them Bacchus. The C group will be Cronos and go to Lieutenant Davenport."

"All daring pilots," Ahhu pointed out. Then she asked, "Aren't you going to have at least one conservative wing leader, perhaps for balance?"

"I think that might completely unbalance us," Pez disagreed. Ahhu frowned, knowing what that meant.

Ming got Electra into her arms, kissed Pez on the cheek, and said, "When you all get home from work, we ought to have a little party."

"If we're all still here, we'll do that," Pez agreed.

24

Swenah led her team back to the bridge, while Ahhu and Rubix went to their new battle stations. Ming brought both babies, Gumby in his pouch and Lectie in her arms, back to their cabin suite. Pez and Trix headed for the flight deck, with Pez issuing orders as they went. They rode the tube together, enjoying the closeness. Pez took the opportunity to pass Trix some protective blessings, which was a bit selfish in that for Trix to survive, Pez would almost certainly have to as well.

When they reached the hangar, Schwin was already there waiting. Pez told her, "We'll board our bombers and get them prepared and through preflight before *Apollo* jumps. The moment we slow to small craft launch speed, we're out the doors. There's almost no clearance, so be careful and warn your pilots."

"Are we doing four wings of four bombers?" Schwin asked.

"Yes," Pez confirmed. "Artemis, Bacchus, Cronos, Demeter, just like star fleet. You're Demeter and will be cleanup as well as defending our rear."

"We'll clean it up spotless—not even a particle left whole—and you can give it the white glove inspection test," Schwin declared with delight.

Puget and Davenport arrived with their copilots and crews, and everybody boarded their Astro-Phantoms. Trix took the lower turret, which was somewhat more dangerous and more vital than the upper turret. Pez met her new crew members. Konax had recommended her copilot, and her name was Natasha. Her weapons operator was a man named Flint. Natasha was a second lieutenant, and Flint was a petty officer. He was also a friend of Natasha's. All eighty personnel of this bomber task force were volunteers, and they were the best small craft crews on the mission, which had been supplied with the best of the best of the fleet.

Pez addressed the bridge of each of the two hundred and sixty-seven ships, including the flagship her bomber sat on, from her own little cockpit. "We are going to kick some serious ass shortly, and we must remain in this propaganda central of a star system until the space marines from our super-carrier complete the placement and assembly of our replacement network transmitter-receiver components on their third moon's surface and return to their ships. Cloaked sensor and fire control drones are already in place within the star system and have identified the primary threats on your holos. The big ships, lunar weapons, and space platforms shouldn't give us too much trouble, but their five thousand small spacecraft could prove fatal to our smallest classes of ships if we don't work together to support one another. Keep your formation because it has our strongest shields and hulls protecting those more fragile. Just before we reach targeting speed, while still slowing down, release your small craft. We're going to pass inside the fifth planet's closest moon's orbit, almost skimming the planet's atmosphere, on our first pass, and we will try to knock out everything at once. A very wide arc, almost an eighth of a planetary orbit, will bring us around again, and we'll slow to an orbital stop about three hundred thousand miles from the planet to nail less important targets and collect our small craft, of which I'll be one. Do this professionally and let's get this job done right."

A nerve-wracked Swenah led the vast armada of ships to pick up speed for a quantum jump to propaganda central, sending corrections to ships not quite in their relative positions and flight plans for the entire mission to all ships. The formation of ships was an arrowhead with four lines trailing off. *Apollo* was the tip of the point. The formation was some 6,800 miles long and 2,800 miles in diameter at the widest, just before the four tines trailed off. It was also an extremely tight formation for so many ships going so fast. The design offered both offensive and defensive advantages while condensing and concentrating their firepower. The Om ships had all shut down their cloaking generators, and some were able to divert that power to weapons systems. They decided it would be better to present a visible target to the enemy so that their allies would not be the only Imperial targets and sort of share the "hits."

The nonevent of the jump changed the scene from deep space to just outside the orbital range of the sixth planet from the blue sun of the system, traveling at well over seven million miles per minute. No matter how many times one did it, the experience was always a completely fresh shock.

The braking was more gradual since not all of the ships had the same tolerances and capacities. Formation required operations at the level of the least common denominator. Ahhu, seated at her quad blaster controls, thought sanity might have finally occurred to someone in Om Star Fleet when *Apollo* was chomping at the bit, a little frustrated. It did give them plenty of time to get oriented and anticipate their targets. They would throw rocks first, at anything that could not get out of the way, and then open up with beam, blaster, missile, and torpedo weapons once a little closer.

Pez's was the first small craft to launch, clearing the bay doors, with a couple of feet to each side at full blast, followed by her wing and then the rest of the bombers in her squadron. They were fully cloaked, each with an encrypted non-locality beacon revealing their changing positions only to the other small craft and ships of their alliance. The propaganda planet and moons, space stations, and ships were all launching small craft in swarms, and Pez headed for the closest big one full tilt. Schwin was whooping a war cry over the open line between bombers. Pez was in the lead, with the other three craft of her wing in a flat plane vertical triangle behind her. The bombers of the other three wings flew the same formation. No one knew her bombers were there … yet.

A big cluster of Imperial small craft were clawing space to reach the invading alliance ships, accelerating fast, with Pez and her folk accelerating too, headed right for them. Targeting was not realistic at these combined closing speeds, so Pez told them to hold their fire as she steered them around the edge, though she did try her own hand with two of her weapons operator's canister missiles. Two blossoming spheres of color erupted behind them, displayed in their rearview holos. Pez was in the state and on a roll, taking them in a turn almost directly behind an even bigger cluster of small craft. There would certainly be no shortage of targets and plenty left for Schwin when she swooped in to clean up. Trix dissolved the last of her anxiety to settle into calm abiding, and the spiritual congress snatched her into a stable link the moment she did. She was ready.

Pez tightened the turn to the craft's limit. They would have to pass this group's flank and tail before continuing in their turn to come behind from the opposite flank for an even better firing opportunity. Pez told Natasha and Flint, "Use single canister missiles on the small and medium ones and try pairs of missiles on the bigger bombers. I fought these before, and our canister warheads are supposed to be more powerful than the ones I was using."

Flint pointed out, "There are many small to medium ships headed our way."

"Don't worry; we'll get to them next," Pez assured him.

"But there are, like, over forty of them," Flint said with concern.

"We'll use the big missiles and torpedoes while reducing their shields with our blasters and work with our other bombers," Pez replied. "There won't be so many of them after that."

"Some are about six hundred feet long," he stated, still not convinced.

"I've killed one of those before," Pez told him, "and they're not so tough. One bomber reduces its shields while another rams torpedoes up their tail. It might take more than one bomber to reduce the shields, though."

Their quarry of well over a hundred small craft was on intercept just ahead, and they'd be in range for well over a second, crossing their wakes. Both groups were headed nearly in the same direction but not quite, and Pez's squadron would have to cross just to the rear, then correct, accelerating and then braking just behind to rake them from the stern as they followed. They came into range, glued to their holo-rangefinders and lock-on lights, triggering blaster bolts and canister missiles in their brief window. The expanding clouds bled into one another, impossible to count. Pez said, "Punch it!"

They made their slight swing of correction, coming in behind, breaking now, hard, and still braking as they entered firing range, coming up fast. All blasters were biting into fighters and fighter-bombers, and copilots and weapons operators were spitting canister missiles individually and in pairs, depending on if they were shooting, fighters and fighter-bombers or big bombers. At the rate Pez brought them in, they had to pulverize the first crafts directly in their paths or collide, though she helped lob canister missiles to clear the way for a few of them. The bigger blasters made short work of the Imperial fighters, which combusted in under two seconds of continuous fire. The bigger bombers seemed to require two missiles, though four gunners working together could make them pop. They got about fifty before the rest dispersed; they had terminated twenty-nine on the first pass.

Pez would let her allies handle the rest and told her people, who had all maintained formation, "We're going to hit reverse drives and thrusters full force and fire the big booster when I tell you. First cut all forward propulsion now. Full brakes and big booster—three, two, one, now!"

The Imperial ships were mostly local fast attack ships about two hundred sixty feet long but mixed with some closer to five hundred feet and a few of the common Imperial 590-foot ships. The ships all flew by taking some wild shots, none of which connected. The move had been entirely unexpected, and the ships had nothing like the ability of small craft for braking. The new Astro-Phantoms could not only reverse their main drives but also had four small reverse drives and dozens of reverse thrusters. The one-time boosters gave them braking power no other small craft could match.

Pez let off the brakes and hit the forward acceleration, which was something else small craft were better at. The cloaking on a few of her bombers was flickering at random intervals from hits they'd taken.

Now they had them. The bigger ships would not be able shake them from their tails, but what sixteen bombers would want with forty-some much bigger ships was something dumbfounding to most of her pilots at the moment. Pez was one-pointed, missing nothing around her and discerning patterns in space-time as she brought them in, adding slight jerks that wove them in a random almost zigzag, taking them out of the way of some heavy fire, just skimming their shields. The big guns on the bigger ships had range first, and Pez's bombers had to duck and weave, weathering it for a moment. One of Bacchus's bombers lost its

A TALE OF THE TAIL OF NINE STARS

shields, taking a searing scorch to its hull, and then ducked out to return to *Apollo* for repairs. Another lost its cloaking and some sensors but held position. Pez told that one, "Get out of here; you're the clearest target."

They left, and target range came, with Pez screaming, *"Fire!"* She had her ten big missiles away, with her blaster nailing a two-hundred-sixty-footer the whole time and both gunners plus Flint hitting the same one with their blasters. It only took four seconds to destroy it once a few canister missiles hit it too, and in that time, she loosed her four torpedoes after her ten missiles. She learned that one big missile could wipe out a two-hundred-sixty-foot fast attack ship, and the two torpedoes were plenty to waste the class-nine 590-footer. Some of them left some big bits in space, challenging even Pez's quick instincts, and another of her bombers had to limp back to the *Apollo* broken. One of Pez's bombers had taken a sustained direct hit from the biggest gun of a class-nine ship, vaporizing.

As they accelerated, only five damaged Imperial ships remained visible behind them, with almost forty blending clouds and a bunch of big bits surrounding those. No one had any torpedoes or big missiles left, so Pez avoided ships and went for small craft, which seemed to be everywhere. They passed some Imperial fighters going too fast to focus a resolution on, and even Pez didn't try it. Then she led them in a direction that appeared to be out of the fight completely, making a wide and easy curve. Schwin was beginning to get frustrated and about to say something when she gleaned Pez's intentions from her holo. She was tightening their turn with turning thrusters, while still accelerating with forward drives. If she was going to do what Schwin thought she was, it would require one heck of a braking job.

Sure enough, Pez was bringing them around to literally bounce off the poisonous atmosphere, coming behind an enormous fleet of small craft that had recently lifted from gravity, pushing through gases from the planet surface. The cavalry was on the way, and Pez was bringing them in to run over the cavalry. The braking was all out, and once again they had to clear some space directly in front with canister missiles and blasters to shoot through clouds instead of smashing into solid objects. *She sure shows a lot of confidence in her people,* Schwin thought proudly as her nose blaster bored into one that blew just in time not to cremate her and still managed to wink out her shields for a moment, scorching the hull.

A big *thunk* and jolt had informed her they had actually collided with a solid piece of it. Two more bombers headed to *Apollo* wounded. The rest were blasting fighters and fighter-bombers, stomping on the cavalry.

Trix had not glanced at her scoreboard once, nor had a thought passed through her head the whole time. She was busy punching blaster bolts, four at a time, into fighters, guided always by the spiritual congress.

Pez's wing, now consisting of three bombers, passed ahead of what remained of this wave of Imperials. Schwin was having the time of her life mopping up those that remained. The call from the flagship informed them that the space marines had planted and assembled the holocom equipment and were on their way back to Om's super-carrier. They got a chance to waste a few more Imperial small craft on the way back to the ship—and a few more around it once they got there—before entering the bay doors and setting down onto the deck.

Trix was high scorer out of all the bombers' gunners and got thrown way up in the air a bunch of times as a reward. It seemed a rather dubious prize to her but served to release some battle tensions for the bomber crews. Schwin swept little Pez completely off her feet in an embrace and told her, "That was incredibly well directed and executed! We're out of missiles, and a few thrusters spent their fuel cells. Talk about a maximum productivity-firing run! You were brilliant!"

"So were you," Pez told her. "Everyone did their job well. I sure wish we hadn't lost C-3. They were some good people."

"I know," Schwin agreed, "but you can't blow up that many ships and small craft without some loss. Risks have to be taken in war."

Natasha hugged Pez when Schwin put her back down and told her, "It has been the greatest honor of my life to serve with you in combat. You blow my mind."

"You can be my copilot anytime, Natasha," Pez told her gratefully. "Not one of your missiles missed, and all were fired with impressive efficiency. Your help with braking was perfect. You're a real pro."

"You can fire my missiles and torpedoes anytime while you fire your big missiles, blaster, and fly the ship," Flint told her.

A TALE OF THE TAIL OF NINE STARS

Pez said apologetically, "I guess I did steal some of your thunder."

"I couldn't have spent it as well myself," he told her seriously. "I've never seen anyone do so many things at once, with such precision, while coming up with effective plans no one else could see."

"Thank you. We're not out of this yet, so I need to get to the bridge. You're welcome to be my weapons operator anytime. You did great, and I felt a real rapport with you."

"I'm yours, General," Flint vowed, and he gave her a salute almost in the space marine ballpark.

Trix went to find Jard and see about getting that network of the empire back into their possession. There were a few documentaries that the Kluzyst were quite disappointed they had not gotten to show. Trix hoped they would get to have that little party Ming mentioned because battles on small craft made her so horny. She'd been so concentrated at the quad blaster, her body kicking off so much heat, that her eyeballs had steamed her thick glasses from the inside a couple of times during the battle. She just fired through the blur, trusting wisely in the spiritual congress, and this had clearly paid off.

Pez went to the bridge, still honed for combat. Her salute seemed to contain the force of a solar flare, truly impressing the sentry. Swenah asked her, "Do you realize you attacked a task force of forty-three ships, all two hundred-sixty feet or bigger?"

"Of course I do; I'm the one who did it," Pez answered.

"What were you thinking?" Swenah wanted to know.

"That one big missile would kill a two-hundred-sixty-footer and two torpedoes, a class nine," Pez replied. "And I was right too!"

"You sure were. Only five damaged ships and vapor clouds remained in your wake. No one has ever done anything like that before."

"There were some big pieces that didn't disintegrate as well, and one of my bombers was damaged by that debris," Pez told her.

"Sweetheart, you took out three hundred and eighty-one small craft and thirty-eight ships on one attack run."

"Good," Pez declared. "It will give their ship's crews all the more reason to mutiny because they don't want us to kill them."

"We've pretty much demolished this system," Swenah explained. "There's not a lunar base weapon or shipbuilding platform left—or anything but space junk orbiting the fifth planet. We hit every transmission-related and military target on the planet's surface with dumb munitions. They have about a dozen damaged ships left and hardly more than a thousand small craft. *Apollo* splattered a class-two two-mile ship into rainbows and sparkling lights. You should've seen it."

"I'll watch the reruns," Pez assured her. "Good shooting."

"You have no idea what you have done for the morale of our armada, Pez," Swenah said with awe. "They already thought you could perform miracles, but you surpassed their wildest dreams."

"The designers of the XPS Astro-Phantom heavy bomber are the ones deserving credit. They are so brilliant, and the new missiles are powerful indeed."

"I'm informed there was some rather effective strategy, flying, and leadership by their high scorer, head and shoulders above the rest," Swenah rebutted.

"I did my part, as you did yours."

Swenah added just audibly, "Your part is spooky." Pez pretended she hadn't heard.

Konax told Pez, "Your little command bomber got more ships than any single ship in the armada."

Pez asked, "Is this battle done? I'm hungry."

"Go eat, sweetheart," Swenah told her fondly, "then attend your little party with your spouses. Just don't cause an event right when we're getting ready to jump."

As Pez left the bridge, Konax asked, "Could you imagine the event at the same instant as the jump?"

Swenah frowned at him, but then the frown turned into a pondering half smile and she said, "Perhaps that would be something."

Pez ate at the mess without asking Sarhi's permission, but she still avoided everything she'd promised she would. Then when she left the mess to go to her suite, everyone in the corridor stopped to stand at attention and salute her as she made her way down. She was trying not to judge their efforts. The whole hero thing, to Pez, was just another obstacle to the friendship and love she sought. She loved them, though, and put up with their antics. She snapped a few salutes as she went, sort of showing them how it was really done.

A TALE OF THE TAIL OF NINE STARS

She got a fine salute from Evenrude, who was guarding the door to her suite. They were meditating together daily, until combat got in the way. She loved the giant dearly, and he was devoted to her.

Sarhi was there with her spouses, and the babies were asleep in their cribs. Grabbing Pez in a hug, Sarhi told her, "You did very well but didn't think to use your astral projection, my love. Next time. Now have your party and unwind from your ordeal. If the babies stir, Shudiy will slip in and tend to them."

"Thank you, Mama Sarhi," Pez told her, beginning to cry. Sarhi hugged her tighter and said, "You are learning and progressing faster than any of us hoped. You did wonderfully."

"I might've saved my bomber crew," Pez said, sobbing.

"It is a skill untried, and you had much to juggle at each moment," Sarhi told her tenderly. "It's not your fault. You did your best. Don't do this to yourself, beloved."

Pez bawled for a few minutes, drawing Ming and Ahhu over to embrace her too, while Trix and Rubix went to the babies, now crying due to feeling Pez's grief. As Pez's emotional arousal came down, Lectie and Gumby settled, and Shudiy was there singing them a lullaby. Sarhi gave Pez a squeeze and then left for the temple cabin, which was really quite enormous on this ship. The babies fell asleep quickly, and Shudiy returned to her cabin.

25

The spouses had only just shed their garments, all but Ahhu, who'd had none to shed, and were in or climbing into bed when the HVAC vent in their bathroom ceiling crashed to the deck with Jard on it. The door to the bathroom was open, so they all saw him. He stood and reached up, helping a woman named Sony climb down as the five on the bed looked on in shock, their jaws hanging open. Next out of the vent came Mel in her female android body, then Gretel, a little graduate student, and finally Cotex.

Pez asked, a bit put out, "Are you lost?"

"No." Jard waved her off. "We followed the schematics exactly and arrived precisely at our destination. Do you take me for an imbecile?"

"Well, you're either that or perpetrating a home invasion."

"Nonsense!" Jard barked. "We're simply crashing a party so we can study the 'event.'"

Sony was already naked and climbing onto the bed. Little Gretel was just struggling out of her bra, already relieved of everything else. Pez told Jard sternly, "I am not having sex with you."

"Of course not," Jard agreed. "I'm not here courting the divine, love child. I brought my own, and we are joining you."

"There's no table in this room," she said flatly, recalling the last party she'd been at with Jard.

"That's right," he assured her. "We'll improvise."

Now Gretel was in the bed too, and Cotex was naked. Mel had arrived without clothes and told Pez, "I'm having sex with you."

Pez looked to Ming for help, and Ming told her, "I think she means it."

A TALE OF THE TAIL OF NINE STARS

Trix had been too horny to wait and was already riding atop Rubix. Sony was watching with great interest, and little Gretel had her hands all over Ahhu. Cotex got her nipples an inch from Pez's nose, and one of Pez's hands went right to her breast, too curious to take heed. Mel got on the bed with a six-foot leap from where she stood, landing on the other side of Pez from Ming. Ming's hand went to Cotex's other breast eagerly, and the swimsuit model climbed on top of her. Mel jumped Pez, and Jard went to seduce Sony. The party was on, stoked by battle lust and Jard's lechery.

There were three "events" that clock night, none coinciding with the jump, however. No one on the flagship was spared. Everyone awake in the whole armada felt them, and thousands awoke in bed wet from their sleep cycles the next clock morning.

Though some of the top human scientists in the universe had been on-site at the very moment of occurrence, only feet from the actual source, for all three events, these occurrences continued to elude scientific explanation, baffling the scientific community. They were a much-loved and appreciated happening among the crew, who wished for them more frequently. Something about their unexpectedness added inexpressible appeal and allure. The words "total orgasm" seemed to capture the experience for the females onboard.

No ten-minute warnings had been remembered or given. Gretel proved to be a feisty lover to pretty much each person at the party.

Try as she might, Mel had been unable to trigger any of those three events that night, the honors going to Ming, Ahhu, and Gretel. Rubix was a little concerned he might be in debt, having spent his ejaculatory privileges for months to come. Beloved Pez had caringly closed his gate that night, preserving his energy, only it hadn't at all stayed preserved because she was the only one who had. Gretel was still going on about how much better this party had been than even the best ones in college when Pez and her spouses dozed off. Somehow, all of them were on the emperor bed, and that's how they awoke in the morning, though a little later than usual.

Jard was snoring, and Pez had her mouth wide open, hopelessly tangled in mostly Gretel but some of Ahhu as well since obviously Gretel didn't have three legs. Pez thought, *That's some graduate student.*

Only Pez, Ming, and Cotex had any ship duties among them, and Ming's ship duties were here in bed with her, spooned into Sony. Not quite clear how this had all come about, Pez managed to extract one leg, then remove Gretel's arm from her chest. Getting her one free leg onto the floor, Pez was able to slide the other one out, liberating it. She chose a black and dark blue camouflage uniform that didn't really work inside the ship. Stepping into her panties after her shower, Pez rethought her selection, choosing instead a light olive green solid color baggy uniform.

Ming was awake but sandwiched between Sony and Trix, with part of little Ahhu over her. Pez went over and kissed her mouth, then told her, "I'm off to work, dear. I'll come for Electra after I've had some chow and will feed her on the bridge. I love you."

"Have a good day at work, darling," Ming told her. "Are you going to be late?"

"We're making a raid this afternoon, but I think I'll be back for dinner," Pez replied.

"Well, have fun," Ming told her.

Cotex had struggled out of bed and into her crumpled uniform to dash to her own cabin for a shower and change of clothes. Pez walked to the officers' mess and got served from the trough after actually waiting on a small line. It was peak breakfast time. She sat with her tray at the table that Swenah and Konax were occupying, thinking how she really wanted to hear about Ming's experience of having sex with Cotex. Swenah told her, "You couldn't have gotten much sleep last night."

"Almost two hours, I think," Pez confirmed.

"Your bombers still need some repairs and won't be going out today," Swenah informed her.

"My command craft is fine."

Swenah countered, "It has some scorches they want to treat and cover with a layer of reflective lenses. A number of secondary sensors are fried and need replacing. Besides, they have to change out the fuel cells on all the thrusters, load new ordnance, and clean the viewport."

Pez was into the holos on her device, checking the status of each of the fifteen bombers, while shoveling food in her mouth. She said loudly with great disappointment, "I don't believe it! It says there's a part they don't have for the new reversible surge drives, so B-4 can't be repaired."

A TALE OF THE TAIL OF NINE STARS

She was immediately on call with the master chief petty officer of engineering and the chief petty officer master mechanic in the hangar. She decided to add the master machinist—she couldn't remember his rank—on the call as well, letting them know that she had to have that drive part manufactured to specifications ASAP. Between them, they had agreed it could be done and promised to move this ahead of the minor repairs being made to *Apollo* from the last action. Satisfied, she shoveled more food in her mouth.

Swenah asked her, "Did you hear that Trix, Jard, and Mel got the empire's transmission network back into our control yesterday?"

"It wasn't mentioned at the party," Pez replied, "but no one had been very chatty, except Gretel, once it was all over."

"Gretel?" Swenah asked. "That tiny graduate student who looks fourteen?"

"She's twenty-two, but, yeah, that's the one," Pez agreed.

"How did you come to invite *her* to your party?" Swenah wanted to know, feeling a bit left out.

"We didn't invite her," Pez explained. "We had crashers."

"Who else," Swenah inquired, "because I somehow doubt that little girl masterminded the crashing."

"Mel and Jard were behind it," Pez told her, "and remember, what happens in the Xegachtznel Galaxy stays in the Xegachtznel Galaxy."

Swenah said, "I see. So there were members of the crew, as well as civilians, involved in crashing this event-making party."

It had not been a question.

"There might have been one," Pez said mysteriously, "though if there were, the last person I'd ever tell is their admiral."

Swenah asked, "Would this hypothetical person look pretty stunning in a swimsuit?"

Pez said honestly, "I've ever only seen her in uniform and in the nude."

"You're not having sex with my lieutenants, are you, General?"

"Not me!" Pez insisted.

Swenah backed off and asked instead, "Did Jard have his latest with him, that neuro-surgeon, Sony?"

"I think some of us met her," Pez recalled. "I know Ming certainly did. That's when the babies woke up."

"Judging from the night you gave us, you must have had quite a big one yourself," Swenah commented. Then she said accusingly, "You must've invited them in because Evenrude was on duty at your door last night."

"I swear I didn't; none of us did. They didn't come through the door. They dropped into the bathroom from the HVAC vent while we watched from the bed."

"And you just watched?" Swenah asked in disbelief.

Pez tried to make sense of it. "Well, we were shocked, then Gretel was out of her clothes and into Ahhu before you could say *wow*. Sony was on our bed naked, and Mel was demanding to have sex with me. Not an inch from my nose, these enormous, voluptuous, swelling … Anyway, it all happened so fast."

"I get it," Swenah said, comprehending and now certain Cotex had been there.

"It was very strange," Pez summed up.

"I'd imagine having a bunch of people land in your bathroom naked would be," Swenah agreed entirely, then said with concern, "I do hope Ming wasn't involved in another gang bang."

"No," Pez said. "She seemed to get around pretty well one-on-one, though, and that Sony had her causing a near event."

"What everyone is dying to know," Swenah leveled with her, "is who you've had your events with."

"The first was with Rubix, when Electra was conceived," Pez recalled. "Then they've all been with Ming, Ahhu, and Trix, until that one last night with Gretel."

"She'll be famous," Swenah pointed out, "and probably already is."

"She was fast asleep when I left, and nobody knows but you."

"The stability of that situation will be interesting to watch," she replied. "Your marriage bed is something of a party, even without guests."

"The curves life sends us," Pez said, shaking her head in dismay.

Konax told them, "We're going into the Pax Vez star system in a few hours, the closest in this galaxy to the black hole at the central core.

The system is on the edge of that non-navigable region of space called Belinda's Triangle, framed between the yellow star Osiris N-7 and the two white stars, Tet GH6 and Quasix E-963, forming a triangle."

"It's a tricky place, and I've been studying it," Swenah acknowledged.

Konax confided, "It was named after an early explorer's wife's groin, which he claimed swallowed things up mysteriously. Historical evidence of Belinda's promiscuity is actually astonishing to medical doctors and psychologists. Our instruments would go haywire in that zone, and the Kluzyst say you can't jump to quantum space inside it."

Swenah shared, "The probes are still scanning the system, and targets are still being compiled and prioritized for specific weapons types and classes, but it is already crystal clear we are headed into a heavily defended star system. They have a lot of ships too."

Konax concurred. "They have three two-mile-long ones, as well as four of the six thousand six-hundred-foot class-three ships. They have three class fours, just under a mile long, and a pair of class fives. They have a class seven and two class eights, plus twelve class nines. Then they have a local five-hundred-foot class-ten ship, of which they have eighty, and a three-hundred-and-ninety footer, with over a hundred in service. This star system has nearly seven thousand combat small craft."

"The Om ships are going in alone cloaked," Swenah informed him. "We'll throw our rocks and disappear, only to reappear firing right behind the biggest ships and blowing up everything in sight the moment they spot the Trident ships coming in under their stealth. At that point, the Rally and Kluzyst ships will jump in, and we ought to have the worst of the Imperial behemoth ships turned into swirls of dispersing color, and our rocks ought to have close to half their small spacecraft squashed on lunar surfaces or blown apart with their space stations by the time they arrive in the battle zone."

"Sounds like a plan," Konax said agreeably.

Pez pointed out, "That puts the Om ships fighting alone around the planet for quite a few minutes."

"At least six minutes, sweetheart, but those will be after we've destroyed all their lunar and space-based superclass and mega-class weapons."

"But not their ships," Pez told her.

"The super-carrier and *Apollo* will destroy one of the class two ships within the first fifteen seconds and be on to the next. The two T-nine super cruisers will have turned a six-thousand-six-hundred-foot ship to dust in the first twelve seconds. Our Orion class spacecraft carriers and battleships will work together to destroy another six-thousand-six-hundred-footer right at the outset. Their losses in the first half minute of battle will more than even the odds on the big ships. Our three large auxiliaries will vaporize a six-thousand-six-hundred-foot class three before moving out of the battle zone. They won't know we're there until we open fire, and then it will be too late for the ships we are lighting up."

"They'll know we are around from our dumb munitions bombardment; they just won't know specifically where," Pez corrected.

Swenah responded, "Total surprise would mean leaving some seriously lethal weapons in place to shoot at us, and there will be a time lapse for them. Between getting hit with our rocks and getting hit with our ship's weapons. By then, they might be writing it off as another hit-and-run."

"I seriously doubt that," Pez told her, "with every major anti-ship weapon defending their planet crushed and smashed to pieces."

"We expect them to be on high alert after the little rock shower," Swenah agreed.

Pez got the last morsel into her mouth and said while chewing it, "I've got to get Electra, so I'll see you on the bridge."

Swenah stated her misgivings about it. "It's practically a nursery now."

"I'll use the air freshener, I promise," Pez assured her as she went to dispose of her tray. She near jogged, and two whole corridors of enlisted crew stood to attention saluting her. The smiles on their faces made her wonder if it was still the battle or now the "event" they were saluting her over. She was in such a hurry that her own salutes were fairly pathetic until she got to the sentry at the door to the officers' quarters, who received a truly professional one, as did the sentry at her cabin door. Electra was hungry, and it was apparently urgent, so Pez got her suckling. She walked through the throngs at attention in the hall, all smiling at her as she breastfed Electra, and she smiled back. Her arm was tired, and the gesture always startled Electra, so she was done saluting, except for one more at the door to the bridge. She had not been able to help herself. It'd just kind of popped out when she saw the space marine saluting. It startled Electra right off her tit, and the baby was exercising those fine lungs—just what Swenah wanted on her bridge as the door hissed open.

Swenah was waving her arm dramatically at Pez, and for a moment, Pez thought there might be a fly aboard the ship. There had never been one of those before, and she didn't see one buzzing about. It did eventually occur to her that she was being waved back into the hall, and she backtracked, opening it with her skullcap, managing not to return the salute this time. Finally, she got Electra back to sucking her nipple, which was so sensitive it was beyond distracting. She checked through the command feature of her skullcap to see who was on a call with Swenah. It was Zapa. Mel's voice came in her ear. "Do you know what you just put me through editing those optics on the bridge or how ridiculous you look with Electra removed from the visual data. I didn't have time to improvise with some graphics since it was live feed."

"Thanks, Mel, and I'm truly sorry," Pez said sincerely. "It's difficult being a nursing mother and a new mother when I'm trying to run this intergalactic war and everything."

"I think we'll have to tell Zapa that you were sleepwalking—either that or on some kind of drugs."

Swenah told Pez in her ear, "The coast is clear. You can come in now." Pez opened the door and nearly returned the space marine's salute, stopping herself just before the snap. Once that was in progress, there was no stopping it. She stepped onto the bridge and took her seat, still holding Electra, who was still sucking furiously. Swenah told her, "You're lucky Mel was able to warble that babies howling and we could write it off to a failing alarm speaker. You look like some crazy person, and I don't know what we'll do about that."

"It's not as if I accidentally got knocked up or was dying to have a baby," Pez protested. "Sarhi made me do it; and now that little Lectie's here, Mama just loves her."

Pez regressed into some baby talk to Electra. Swenah rolled her eyes. Pez was gushy in general, but with Electra, Swenah found it could become actually skin crawling. Konax was thoroughly amused. Electra was done sucking for now and wide-awake. Pez remembered to burp her, and a great big one came out with a little bit of vomit. She had her bag of wipes and cleaned Electra's mouth and tiny chin first. She simply removed her own shirt and dabbed at where it had bled through onto her T-shirt. Everything was fine. She felt like a competent mother. She gave Lectie her pacifier, putting the end in her mouth. Electra had thought she'd made it clear she was done sucking and tired of it, so she took her pacifier in her little hand and threw it at the back of Konax's head.

Like a gentleman, he retrieved it from the floor and got it into Pez's hand, saying, "I didn't see that coming."

Pez's confidence had shattered with her daughter's act, and she said apologetically to him, "Oh, I'm so sorry!"

"Don't be," he told her. "It's no big deal. She's a sweet addition to the bridge."

"She has some lungs, huh?" Pez asked proudly.

Swenah cringed. Konax agreed with Pez. "I don't think I've ever heard one that loud before."

Electra flashed him one of her toothless grins. Pez was delighted to her bones. Pez told them, "She might have said 'Ma' the other day; we aren't entirely sure."

"Ming thought it was more of a 'Mu,' and besides, she's far too young to start talking," Swenah informed her.

Pez thought she said ma and was going to keep the faith. She made eye contact with her daughter, opening her heart while passing her internal energy. Electra held the gaze with unwavering awareness. Her pre-conceptual egoless purity and innocence filled Pez with exultation. There was an alchemy transpiring between them, which all on the bridge could feel. Electra didn't flinch and seemed to open up, apparently in a state of blissful amazement and in complete connection with Pez. Mother and daughter were grinning at each other, and it almost seemed like there was going to be a different kind of "event"— one of sentimental extremity, with little hearts, pink ribbons and bows, baby bunnies and kittens, kisses and hugs, and all things sweet. For just that moment, Swenah thought such a connection just might be worth the noise, demands, odors, and fluids. It was fleeting.

26

The data and reports flowed onto the bridge, where Mel helped assign targets to specific ships, based upon class of weapons and relative position in the formation. The Om ships would not have a formation, only positions to take up after chucking their rocks. Trident ships would arrive in one, as would the Kluzyst and Rally ships coming together after them. Swenah was trying to get all the targets covered by just Om and Trident ships, but there were proving to be too many for that. There was no avoiding the fact that the Om ships would be engaged for up to eleven and a half minutes before the Kluzyst and Rally forces arrived—and probably another eight after that. Most of the ships would be low on munitions and fuel cells by then.

They would have far fewer losses to the armada this way than they would coming in altogether without cloaking; only this way, most of the losses would be on Om. Trident would likely suffer them too. Pez had had Trix and Ming reconfigure her bridge station so she could access *Apollo's* weapon systems from her seat if the impulse moved her. No one had had a problem with this, and in fact everyone seemed to think it a good idea. Anti-spacecraft blasters were manually operated weapons, and as such, Pez had no access. Everything else was at her fingertips and mental command.

The latest developments in micro-jump technology had Om working on a massive torpedo with both space drives and quantum drive, which could jump to the interior of the ship, past its shields, and they were close to having the precision to make them. They would only be able to be carried on large ships since they were over twice the volume of one of Pez's bombers, though tubular in shape, requiring a large stable mass to launch from. The expense of making one was equal to that of constructing a 690-foot-diameter star cruiser, but the torpedo could totally destroy a three-mile ship, and this made it worth it. They were close to having a working prototype.

The largest torpedoes currently on the *Apollo* were nothing to scoff at. They had twin surge drives and thirty-six turning thrusters with tri-fuel cells. They could reach .746 light speed and had a range of seventy-nine million miles. Launch boosters and two "accelerate to target" boosters had recently been added to them. The guidance system could attain absolute lock-on, enabling it to stay connected at velocities far exceeding targeting acquisition speeds. They carried the biggest nuclear warhead Om made. At 240 feet in length and 12 feet in diameter, *Apollo* only carried sixty of them and had twelve tubes from which to fire them.

Two smaller classes of torpedoes were also aboard and had launch tubes. Pez noticed that reloading for one of the big ones took 3.7 seconds. She had three classes of missiles with space drives and two classes with rocket thrusters, which were shorter range. There was one super-beam class-nine weapon well into the 300-terawatt range, with its own solarium fusion super reactor all to itself. There was also a super blaster with the same. More than a thousand smaller beam and blaster weapons defended the hull all around, and the two super-weapons took a fifteenth of the ship's total power and a fifth of all the power available to weapons systems. Instead of one super-weapon, or class-nine weapon, you could have instead ten class-eight weapons, one hundred class sevens, a thousand class six's, and so on.

Rubix and Ahhu operated class-six blaster quads, which were really overkill for snuffing small fighters but could vaporize a fighter-bomber or bomber in little time. Most anti-spacecraft guns were class three and four. They got the bigger blasters since they protected the primary sensor array. In battle, the shields of big ships blinked out momentarily with big hits to them, and small craft took advantage of this. The hull and armor of the *Apollo* was twenty feet thick and even thicker on the nose. It was built to take a beating, but the sensor arrays could not be built to do the same. There were numerous redundancies spread all over the hull, but the integrated primary offered advantages that could not be entirely replaced by them. *Apollo* had Ahhu and Rubix, and they were elite gamers, highly practiced if never actually trained, and forging their links steadily with the spiritual congress. They'd logged more hours on the simulator once, in just one week—some 108 hours—than most gunners did in three years. It was also discovered that they could fly drones better than the drone pilots could. They had become assets to the combat ship.

Pez called Ming and asked if she could come to the bridge and collect Electra since they were about to go into battle and she needed to concentrate on that. Ming agreed and came right away. Transfers from Pez to most anyone else could be very tricky, tending to end in disaster, but Electra seemed not to distinguish at all between them, clutching to Ming as if to Pez. She'd also asked Ming to bring a clean T-shirt and shirt, which were brought. Pez stripped out of her soiled T-shirt to give to Ming with a more soiled shirt and then put on her fresh ones. Swenah asked, "We've got the domestic stuff all handled for now?"

"Electra is covered and no more puke on me," Pez confirmed. Then she asked, "Why didn't you ever have a child, Swenah?"

"I guess I never wanted one badly enough to go through the pain, sacrifice my career ambitions, and do all that work, just to have it hate me from its teen years on."

"I never thought of it that way," Pez said, pondering.

"Apparently not."

"They're so cute," Pez said, images of Lectie and Gumby filling her mind.

"When they're not leaking or spewing fluids or wailing at a thousand decibels."

Mel told them, "A final load of fuel cells and ordnance is on its way over from the auxiliary and will be aboard in minutes. They're also sending over a drive part they manufactured for an Astro-Phantom heavy bomber for the master mechanic to install."

Pez lit up, happy as could be. Swenah said, "Thank you, Mel. Please let me know when all the Om ships, including auxiliaries, are ready to go. Accelerating up to jump speed with them will be like doing it with the whole armada."

The communications officer reported, "All ships will be ready to go on schedule and have reported in."

The navigation officer told Swenah, "Om ships have their flight plans, targets, and positions to take up around Pax Vez. We've made Belinda's Triangle a no-fly zone and programmed the navigation systems to give warnings on approach so no one gets lured in by Imperial ships."

"Good work," Swenah acknowledged.

Load-ins from the auxiliaries were completed and shuttles returned. Preflight checks were run through carefully, and then Swenah gave the order to accelerate. It felt to her like a wheelchair race. Pez told her, bursting with excitement, "I have goose bumps."

Konax commented, "That can't be good for the empire."

Swenah told them, "Let's get our part perfect. That will help reduce losses to Om's ships."

"Highest perfection," Pez agreed.

Ming came on in Pez's ear and said, "Sarhi needs to know what time the next battle is going to start. She needs to get the spiritual congress ready."

"We should be there in thirty-one minutes, and it starts the moment we arrive," Pez told her. "Though there will really just be a slowing to fire dumb munitions, then a long lull to duck and hide and get in position to wait, before the Trident ships are closing and spotted. That's when the real action begins."

"I'll let her know," Ming told her, "and do keep us all safe."

"I'll do my very best, beloved, I promise."

"Your support system's gearing up?" Swenah asked Pez.

"Yes, Sarhi will have some communication officers earning their pay for a quarter of an hour. Then she will convene the spiritual congress and lead the representatives and other noncombat supporters in meditation in the big temple cabin. I've got to start my meditation soon."

Cotex turned and twisted in her seat to face Pez, all smiles and flirtation, to tell the bridge, "The scans of the star system Pax Vez have been completed, all data compiled, and final targeting priorities sent to all fire control systems and weapons operators. Only one probe was lost in active ping-scan mode, and its data was recovered. They have no tagging devices conclusively, and no additional combat assets are within or on approach to the star system. There are no surprises. The Imperial transmission network is still ours and showing the most condemning documentaries you can imagine."

Pez smiled at her, making sure she was looking at Cotex's eyes. Swenah was convinced that Cotex aspired to being the "event."

The communications officer updated them. "Nineteen of the first wave of rebellions have been fully quashed, and four more are about to be. Fourteen were entirely successful, having rid themselves of Imperial supporters on their planets in order to reclaim their sovereignty. Several others look likely to do so. A new wave of twenty-one rebellions, sixteen of those on slave worlds, have ignited with a bang, and thirteen of them look likely to succeed."

"With us attacking their affluent worlds, they can't afford to send ships to address these," Pez observed.

The communications officer reported, "Hundreds of ships have joined our Kluzyst allies, though almost all smaller than Imperial class sevens. We did get a class four, class seven, and a few class sixes."

Swenah told them, "At this point, the Kluzyst are not adding the ships that come over to us from the empire to the armada but instead sending them to assist rebelling worlds. They think it will escalate the chain of overall rebellions to know that help sometimes comes."

Konax said, "When that Vachisy invasion fleet is recalled, we're going to need some more big ships."

"I've been thinking about that, and I spoke with Admiral Tonkah," Swenah said. "We have both requested class-nine super-weapons from our governments. These are on the way, each with a solarium fusion super reactor. Trident has some thirty-two-hundred-foot repair dock ships with combat level shields. The Kluzyst have four thirty-eight-hundred-foot heavy cargo freighters with military grade shields, which we could weaponize in case we need them. These weapons should be at the auxiliaries now and the work already started."

Pez closed her eyes and sunk her breath to her lower abdomen, releasing it up and out her central channel to feel the energy blow out the top of her head. Her attention focused into concentration, and from there she entered meditation to establish calm abiding quickly. Becoming the subtle mind mounted upon the subtle wind, Pez practiced her transference of consciousness using the forceful projection technique to go out into space, flare her light, and return all within a microsecond. Konax was seeing micro-suns appear in space out ahead of them, erupting and intensifying, to linger, fading in space. The science officer's voice came over on the bridge coms, saying, "Admiral, there are anomalies of light phenomenon occurring randomly in space ahead of us as we go."

Pez told Swenah, from deep in contemplation, "It's just me practicing."

Konax asked, "That's you doing that?"

"Let me show you," Pez said. "I'll put one around your nose." All sensors on the ship, with the exception of some in the tail, whited out, and no data regarding their surroundings could be attained by any instrument. Konax flew blindly for almost seven seconds before the glare faded, and it took almost another second for the resolution to completely clear.

Konax asked, shocked, "You did that?"

The science officer was back on. "Whatever it is, I think it might be attacking us."

Pez told him, "I simply gave Konax a demonstration. I'll put no more around *Apollo* and save this trick for Imperial ships."

Swenah declared, "So that's what Sarhi has been working on with you!"

"It's one of a few tricks I've learned to help us in battle," Pez agreed.

"How quickly can you do it?"

"Probably faster than you can fire your beam weapon with a brain-nerve impulse."

"What are some of these other tricks?" Swenah asked.

"I can cause certain vibrations. I can't directly move any physical object, though. I'm still working out how I can employ these."

"You are obviously far more than I thought you were, dear," Swenah said in awe.

I'm not a freak," Pez insisted. "All humans can do this stuff; they just need to practice and evolve their psyches."

"I'm sure you're right, sweetheart," Swenah said fondly. "We just need three hundred and thirty-three incarnations spent entirely meditating. No problem."

A TALE OF THE TAIL OF NINE STARS

"Don't pick on me right before battle, Swenah; come on," Pez pleaded.

"It's just that I appreciate you so much, darling. And you never cease to amaze me—shock me really," Swenah sort of apologized.

I'm doing my part to help, and I'm not trying to impress anyone."

Konax said seriously, "Let her concentrate. We need what she can do, so let's please leave her alone."

Pez sank deep, checking out of the bridge conversations in order to consolidate and gather her spirit, expanding time and contracting space while transcending both. She was completely physically relaxed, breath and metabolism only a notch above coma, while her energy mass integrated into a taut coiled adamantine spring, ready to unleash. Tensions on the bridge mounted as the moment of the jump approached.

The eighty-five Om ships jumped from deep space and, without transition, were suddenly just outside the distance of the sixth planet's orbit from the blue star Pax Vez, headed for the planet of Pax Vez, fifth from its hot blue sun.

Konax was already hitting the brakes at forty-eight percent of capacity, which was equal to 100 percent capacity of the auxiliaries. Swenah wore her look of impatience, having to stoop to such low performance. With so many sensor fire control drones positioned in a net for millions of miles around the planet, encompassing its moons, they would be able to fire off dumb munitions with complete accuracy, without slowing quite to target acquisition speed. The breaking took quite a while, becoming increasingly uncomfortable for Swenah. Pez was in a coma, gone completely.

At last, the speed of their task force would allow them to throw stones, and Swenah said to her weapons operations officer, "Fire the dumb munitions."

Of these, *Apollo* and the super-carrier, under Captain Firestone, carried the most, though the T-nine super cruisers, spacecraft carriers, battleships and star cruisers had them as well. Destroyers, fast attack ships, and auxiliaries had none and just went along for the ride on this opening salvo.

Pez returned through her crown to her body on the bridge, seeing the eight signs of death in reverse, and increased her breath rate, accelerating her metabolism. Though she dwelt on each detail of them on her return, which, like her exit, had consisted of a fraction of a microsecond in real time, she had spent about a quarter of an hour checked out.

Pez told them, "They know the rocks are coming and are clearing personnel from their weapons platforms and bases, and some spaceports are launching their small craft. They are mobilizing. I managed to overload a few sensors, blinding those, and established a vibration in some equipment they had suspended and sequestered from all vibration."

Konax said, amazed, "Those are the mainframes that are the foundation of their RSPS, upon which their fire control depends."

Swenah stated, "The Relative Space Positioning Systems take many hours of recalibration for the slightest vibration within that equipment. How on Om did you get past the gyroscopic dampeners?"

"I sent vibrations right through them and on through the big suspended vacuum tubes, moving the filaments within," Pez tried to explain.

"This is fantastic news!" Swenah declared.

"If those things are that important, perhaps I should seek them out on some more Imperial ships."

Mel came on and flashed a holo in Pez's face, stating, "The RSPS mainframes are highlighted in orange for you on each class of Imperial ship. They tend to put them in the center of their reactors, whereas we tend to house them just forward of the reactors, by our shield generators on our ships."

Pez studied the holo, fixing the position for each class ship in her mind. After a couple of minutes' concentration, she told them, "I'll be right back." She then sank into her seat, going limp and checking out.

Konax and Swenah gave each other perplexed looks. Konax was accelerating slowly so the auxiliaries could keep pace, and they were on the way to take up positions behind the ships they would kill. Swenah ordered, "Stand everyone down from battle stations and get them some food and rest. I want you all fresh in a few hours." She told Konax, "Let the Imperials remain on ultrahigh alert for the next three hours. They'll be frazzled and near burned out by the time we start shooting them."

A TALE OF THE TAIL OF NINE STARS

"You're more cautious than our general, but I do love your plans," Konax told her with appreciation.

"If we didn't have her sitting there, I wouldn't be in an alien galaxy fighting an empire with a vast fleet of giant ships grossly outnumbering me," Swenah assured him.

"It's done," Pez said, opening her eyes.

"What's done?" Swenah asked.

"I set those gizmos to vibrate on two of the class threes, the three class fours, both class fives, and their class seven," Pez explained.

"That will reduce the accuracy of their fire control significantly, except at very close range, and certainly save incoming allied ships."

"I did overload a few more sensors, and I'll perform well enough in battle to save Om ships," Pez informed her. "I have another trick up my sleeve too, but it requires the enemy ship's shields to be all riled up from taking hits."

At their lumbering, rate they eventually closed on the planet, well behind their own rocks, which had already rained down their devastating destruction, missing not one super or mega-weapon not mounted on a combat ship or mobile space weapons platform. Except one mega-weapons space platform had been towed clear by tugs. At least three dozen tugs disintegrated while unsuccessfully trying to pull other weapons platforms out of the way. When these were displaying in their holos, most minds on the bridge were thinking how glad they were not to be one of those tug pilots. Pax Vez had lost some teeth, and perhaps a couple of claws, but still had its space defensive fleet. It was blazing on high alert, burning thruster fuel and wearing down mental capacity.

Swenah waited until ten minutes before showtime to call her rested crew back to battle stations. Countdown holos were everywhere. Ahhu and Rubix were at their guns.

Ming called Pez, complaining, "This has never happened before, but Electra won't take milk from me and is both hungry and upset."

"Have Shudiy bring her to me, but she'll have to stay and help Lectie keep her mouth on my nipple because I'm going to be kind of busy."

"Lectie will be so relieved. Thank you, my love," Ming told her gratefully.

With two minutes and three seconds left on the countdown, Shudiy arrived with Electra, and Pez already had her button-down shirt removed before they got there. She hiked the bottom of her T-shirt up over both breasts since it required both to keep it up, and even then it tended to slip back over the meek resistance. Lectie had been completely dominating the acoustics on the bridge, winning frowns from Swenah and smiles from other officers, like Konax, until Pez got her calm, sucking on the right thing, with fifty-one seconds to go. All the ships were in their positions, and weapons operators poised to fire. Shudiy knelt in front of Pez, out of the way of her holos, to assist Lectie should she require it. Pez was returning to a deep contemplative state now that Electra was latched on tight and sucking greedily. Pez still passed her daughter internal energy out of habit, clearly without a thought involved. No thought could hold its pattern and survive the glaring light of her mind in contemplation.

When the countdown concluded, Swenah said to all ships and crews, "Fire," and ordnance, beams, and blaster bolts flew out of every Om ship in the system, including the three auxiliaries, which coordinated their big super-beam weapons on the same class-three ship. After 3.4 seconds, Pez shot one of the largest missiles into a precise point in the stern of the two-mile-long ship Swenah's beam was boring into the shields of, and *Apollo*'s super blaster was blasting away at, and which a continuous stream of missiles and torpedoes were exploding into. Firestone's super-carrier was firing all weapons into the class-two ship too.

Pez's big missile passed through the shields at a precise point in the stern, which only someone cable of seeing auras could detect, where only a slight veneer of shield force covered, too weak to explode the missile that entered through the discharge nozzle of the biggest drive. She had another just at the entrance of the nozzle as the first began its explosion, which blew the second one just inside the nozzle and started a chain reaction clear to the bow. With the chain reaction still racing for the bow, the stern blew apart, followed by the whole of the gargantuan thing, and *Apollo*'s crew found themselves shooting at a cloud. They were then 4.99 seconds into the battle, and Swenah was already giving directions to the pilot and fire control, acquiring their next target. Pez was out blinding some alien big blaster operators who were pounding smaller Om ships. Captain Firestone was coordinating

A TALE OF THE TAIL OF NINE STARS

fire with Swenah, and between their two ships, they had fifty-eight super reactors, eighteen of these entirely dedicated to beam and blaster weapons. They opened fire on another of the two-mile-long class-two sausages as they closed together on it. Pez was overloading sensors on it, blinding its big beam, which fired anyway, missing both Om ships, though not a class-four Imperial.

That ship made a spectacular visual, missed by *Apollo's* crew as they focused their fire on the class two, now appearing brilliant white and surrounded in the bow and forward flanks by a micro white sun. The enemy's big ship's blaster miraculously missed them too, even at this range, firing wildly into a group of its own approaching small craft. Another Pez missile was off to another spot of shield, hardly a film, and then Pez was half a million miles away, blinding a gunner who was close to killing an Om fast attack ship.

Lectie, still on target with her sucking, now had her eyes open, looking at her mother's face. At 11.7 seconds into battle, the class two expanded a thousand times its volume as its mass was near entirely vaporized into annihilation, leaving only a gas stain in space. They were well ahead of schedule.

The two T-nines had destroyed their primary target, a 6,600-foot class-three Imperial ship, and they were hitting another ship of the same class. Working together, the battleships and spacecraft carriers had wasted one class three and were working on a second one. Two seconds of Swenah's beam weapon finished that one as they went by. Their eleven star cruisers had already destroyed three of the class nine ships and were working on two more. The Om fast attacks and destroyers were blowing up four-hundred-foot and five-hundred-foot local ships.

Pez seemed to be everywhere, judging from all the blossoming micro-suns. She'd even gone onto the bridge of a class-eight Imperial and frightened its occupants off of it and down the corridor, screaming like some rabid animal and flashing her lights, which was actually the most she could do there. The class eight hit a four-hundred-foot Pax Vez fast attack but suffered little damage. The smaller ship, however, was no more. Captain Firestone and Admiral Swenah separated at this point to hunt down the larger Imperial ships individually so they could cover more ground, now that there was nothing left that took both their ships to defeat at once.

Swenah found a class four and turned it into space dust in under five seconds with *Apollo*'s super-beam and blaster, plus a few torpedoes. She noticed that Pez had already launched fifteen of their sixty largest torpedoes. The battle was into its twenty-third second. Small craft were coming at them from every direction, and more than a thousand anti-spacecraft guns opened up on them from *Apollo*. Ahhu and Rubix were on a roll. Swenah was hunting another big ship to explode. Lectie had stopped sucking and was looking into her mom's face with absolute wonder. Micro-suns were appearing throughout the battle zone of billions of cubic miles.

Forty-one seconds into the battle, the Imperials had nothing bigger than a single class-eight ship left to show for itself, and that one already had an expiration date painted on it by beam weapons. Finally, the last Imperial class nine, which had been doing nothing but running away for the last twenty seconds, was destroyed a few seconds after their third minute of battle, leaving nothing but five-hundred-foot and four-hundred- foot local ships as well as over four thousand small craft.

Swenah ordered, "All fast attack ships and destroyers proceed to the rendezvous with our auxiliaries and begin your repairs. We've got this, and even working together, these little Imperial ships can't blow up our star cruisers."

They had lost three destroyers and five fast attack ships already in this engagement, and Swenah would risk no more. *Apollo* splattered incoming small craft as it raced after the five-hundred-foot Pax Vez ships, which went pop in 2.3 seconds of Swenah's beam. It became a turkey shoot for nearly two and a half minutes, until the Trident ships began arriving on the scene, by which time it became exceedingly difficult to find one to shoot.

There was nothing Imperial left in one piece in space as the Kluzyst ships and those of the Rally system began to arrive. Every government and military building in the capital, which was nearly half of them, had been turned into deep craters of molten sludge. There wasn't a satellite left in orbit. They'd even blown all the biggest fusion reactors on the planet surface and blew the one hundred largest air and spaceports into over a trillion pieces each. This planet wasn't going to exert much influence beyond its moons for at least a century.

Then the news came. Cotex told them, without her typical flirtation, "The invasion force is on its way to the Gzzklns system, and a task force has split off to exterminate life on Earth 10^5 CBS2."

Pez said, "I'm taking all the small craft on the *Apollo*, including the eight space marine combat shuttles, and I'll need the *Phoenix* star cruiser. I'll go to Earth; you take the armada back to Gzzklns and get those transports with the newly installed super-weapons to Gzzklns as well. Shudiy will take my seat and can do much of what I just did in the last battle. Ming will have to come and get Electra. Oh, and you'll need to show Shudiy how to launch the torpedoes and missiles."

Swenah said, "Take your best gunners; I'll get Trix to man the quad blaster Ahhu's been firing."

"Tell them to meet me on the flight deck," Pez said as she kissed Electra, showering her with love and hoping to be reunited with her in this life.

Pez handed Electra to Shudiy, and her daughter did not fuss, exhibiting a serious expression, almost as if she understood the gravity of their situation. Without even saluting the space marine at the bridge door, Pez raced for the hangar, issuing orders to the flight deck as she went. Ming's voice said in her ear. "Please be careful, my love; I don't know if I could live without you."

"I plan on dealing death, not accepting it," Pez said fiercely. "If I can return to you, you know I will."

27

Schwin was waiting for Pez at the hangar, ready to go, her crew already on their Astro-Phantom. Pez told her, "We are taking everything—the fifteen heavy bombers, twenty-four Hunter-Terminator fighter-bombers, eighty Corvette thunder fighters, eight space marine combat shuttles—and we'll need four of the big cargo shuttles, which are not cloaked, to get our missile reloaders out to Earth's system. Those missile reloaders are cloaked but have no quantum drives. The *Phoenix* is coming with us and has six space marine combat shuttles."

"What are we up against?" Schwin asked, not that any possible answer could deter her.

"We'll find out on the way," Pez told her. "The only thing I know for sure is we'll be greatly outgunned and outnumbered. I have a few new tactics I do on my own, which ought to help."

"We've seen," Schwin told her, grinning from ear to ear.

"I've also got a drone pilot to put on each of the heavy bombers, and we'll bring fifteen of the sixteen fighter-bomber drones with us. Bachus, Cronus, and Demeter wings will each have four of them."

"With a drone supporting each heavy bomber, we amplify our killing power tremendously!" Schwin exclaimed.

"We'll need it," Pez assured her.

Rubix and Ahhu came running to Pez, grabbing her in an embrace, and Ahhu said, "I can't tell you how grateful I am that you're doing this for Earth. I love you so much."

"I'm not letting those misguided ignorant gasbags kill seven billion humans," Pez vowed with her life. "I'm sending them to the afterlives they've prepared for themselves through their actions and intentions during their murderous lives. It will be a trillion times worse than any pain I inflict on them."

"I'll organize our departure and coordinate with flight control so go get your bomber ready, boss," Schwin told her with great fondness.

Pez did, along with Ahhu, Rubix, Flint, Natosha, and their drone pilot, Cleo. Cleo was a twenty-five-year-old six-foot, ten-inch skinny woman, unassuming and professionally businesslike. She'd been chosen for Pez's bomber because she was the best and could even tie Ahhu, but not for her dry humor and directness, sometimes making her seem a little prickly to those around her.

Ahhu took the lower turret naked. She had her suit and helmet right there, and if there was a small leak anyone could survive, she'd have time to put it on. Pez's own helmet sat on the floor by her pilot seat. She'd already come up with a design for a helmet rack, convenient for emergencies, but had not yet gotten around to crafting it.

Pez opened a line to all her bomber pilots and told them, "I'm sending the coordinates that our cloaked reloaders will be in during the battle, just outside the orbital path of the seventh planet of the star system. Only four bombers can reload at a time, so we'll do it by wing. Only our bombers can reload. We can each get rearmed twice, and that will leave one reloader with two more rearms. When the rest of our spacecraft are out of missiles, they'll be on blasters only. It is really going to be up to us. Be on top of your game today because I need you all alive and fighting."

Pez said to all one 132 of her pilots, which included the six space marine Combat Shuttles from *Phoenix*, "I just received the data on the force headed to Earth. They'll have two ships I'm not yet sure how we'll destroy and six class nine ships we can blow up, working in well-coordinated groups. Mel is with us and has sent you your wing assignments. The Hunter-Terminators are in four wings of six, the Corvette Thunders in ten wings of eight, and the combat shuttles in two wings of five and one of four. The drones are with the fifteen bombers. The Imperials have two giant spacecraft carriers, with only class-three and class-four anti-spacecraft blasters, but they'll be filling space with small craft. Their fighters go down easily. Their fighter-bombers will require one of our canister missiles or at least two Hunter-Terminator ones, or a lot of coordinated blaster fire. Their big bombers will take at least two of the Astro-Phantom canister missiles and four from the Hunter Terminators. Try to save your big missiles for when I call for an integrated attack on one of the big ships. Swenah is having Om parts and tools loaded onto a Trident uncloaked repair ship. Mel is sending you the coordinates. If you lose shields and can still jump, go to it for repairs and a safe haven. There are also ten giant Imperial troop transports we will not be able to kill, which have only class-three and class-four blasters. We will be able to kill any shuttles they launch, and we had better. We're jumping in close and breaking fast, hitting the system racing. The Imperials will already be there, closing on Earth. We'll flow behind them and let them have it. Mel has sent you all the weaknesses and tolerances we know so far about the small craft and ships you face. Work together, save the big missiles, and be ready to all converge on one target at my signal. May the Cosmic Intelligence protect you."

To Captain Ohinya of the *Phoenix*, Pez said, "Pretty early on, I'm going to try to take down that two-thousand-and-seven-hundred-foot ship, which likely has three times the power of a star cruiser. Yours is a bit enhanced so probably only twice the power of your ship. I plan to make that up with some big missiles from the Hunter-Terminators and torpedoes from my bombers while all of our small craft pound that ship with all their blasters. When shields are hit and energy rushes to the point of contact, there is inevitably a weak spot, joined to the rest by just a film. It is quite transitory and gets covered the moment shields are on the rise again, but I'm getting good at exploiting this. Our sensors can't find these thin spots. To see them requires the ability to see auras. We'll be outnumbered about nine to one in small craft. Don't shoot or give yourself away until I need you for that big ship. The class seven won't have too much on you—perhaps a third again the power of *Phoenix*—so you'll have to slug it out with her for us."

"I will do my part, and *Phoenix* will do hers," Ohinya replied. "You can count on us. No one will know we're there until we are blowing up that big ship."

"Thanks," Pez told her. "I didn't just choose your star cruiser because of its enhancement. It had far more to do with its captain."

A TALE OF THE TAIL OF NINE STARS

"I'm honored, General. We won't let you down."

To all pilots, Pez said, "Mel is sending each of you your relative positioning for gathering in space outside the bay doors. It's imperative we all arrive together."

The fighters, fighter-bombers, shuttles, and bombers leading drones, as well as four large non-cloaked cargo shuttles carrying their reloaders, gathered outside the *Apollo* and started out together. They were not waiting for the slower cargo shuttles, which had a different destination within the star system, Earth 10^5 CBS2. Pez didn't care at all about numbers, odds, statistics, military doctrine, or any other piece of pessimistic data or fact. She was going to save Earth.

It didn't take this bunch long to reach jump speed and arrive in the Earth star system, racing at .7 light speed, from just outside the fourth planet's orbit, coming in fast at the tails of twenty Imperial ships and well over a thousand small craft. She told her pilots, "They have no idea we're here so don't fire until I tell you to."

Everyone was frantically braking, thinking maybe their fearless leader had finally cut it way too close; and it sure looked that way at over seven million miles a minute. It began to look a bit better after ten seconds of reverse thrusters and drives and even better as they were slowing to target acquisition speed relative to their targets.

Pez decided they'd better put an end to that twenty-seven-hundred-footer right away and barked out orders, with Mel sending corresponding coordinates and timing to both personnel and computers. Over a hundred blasters hit the ship at once as a continuous stream of big missiles exploded on its shields one after another, with a torpedo from the bombers hitting one per second. Three micro-suns swallowed the Imperial class six as they continued pouring fire into it. The big beam and blaster weapons on the *Phoenix* star cruiser were drilling the thing's shields, while her larger torpedoes hit in a staccato and her biggest missiles rained down on it. The seconds ticked by as their ordnance diminished, and the big Imperial ship's weapons hit some of their small craft. At 6.34 seconds, the big tub blew in a beautiful blue-green expanding spray of individual particles and gas, which Pez was flying through before it was entirely separated, after slipping two of her torpedoes through a soft spot in its shields, which only she had been able to see.

The *Phoenix* engaged the 1,900-foot sausage of an Imperial class seven, keeping it off the Om small craft, which were all firing so fast that cloaking became irrelevant, since their fire made them available for the Imperials to target. Earth was chattering in Pez's ear, and she told them to shut up and then asked Mel to find out what they were going on about.

Pez was running down fighters with her nose blaster and tossing the occasional pair of Flint's canister missiles into a bomber, and her rainbow body left her seat to fly into space and back, sometimes thrice per second. "Busy" didn't begin to describe it because she also got a torpedo into a weak spot on a class nine's shields the Hunter-Terminators were converging on and struck three shuttles with canister missiles, leaving a giant troop transport. Mel got back to her. "The earthlings say there are already troop shuttles landing in a dozen locations on their planet surface, causing devastation."

Pez said, "Tell them to pass out those twenty-five-millimeter high-velocity long-range sniper rifles and aim for the neck. I'm doing the best I can."

Ahhu and Rubix were both in the zone, pure killing machines, racking up points on their scoreboards and guided by the spiritual congress. Pez's bomber was an absolute menace to the Imperial forces. She dove through a stream of Imperial shuttles pouring out of a big troop transport. While Ahhu, Rubix, and Flint turned shuttles to space dust, Pez lobbed her last torpedo and a big missile in through the hangar doors. The stream of shuttles stopped coming out of that one. One of Artemis's bombers had managed to shoot a torpedo into the troop transport hangar as well, and that transport would be clearing away broken shuttles and dead troops for a while before it was able to launch anymore.

A couple of the drone fighter-bombers had been able to get some missiles into the hangar too and were keeping fighters off the bombers. Cleo wasn't missing her targets, and her missiles were flying out of her drone. She had spent her undercarriage missiles on the 2,700-foot Imperial ship at the outset. The drones couldn't be reloaded and

A TALE OF THE TAIL OF NINE STARS

had only a nose blaster, though a nice one, once the canister and big missiles were spent. So far, they'd come in handy against fighters and fighter-bombers.

A run from behind through forty Imperial small craft left Pez out of everything but blasters and two canister missiles. She told Schwin, "I'm bringing the two in my wing to the reloaders, so take over and try not to lose any of our bombers. Bacchus will go next. I'll be right back."

Cronos 2 had blown up, taking a hit from a mega blaster while attacking the 2,700-foot ship. Lieutenant Pugot's bomber had gotten knocked around quite a bit, and his shields wouldn't come up over 81 percent. Ordinarily she'd tell him to bug out, but she needed every asset. Twenty-two Corvette Thunders had been destroyed, and five had been damaged but able to jump to the Trident repair ship. Three combat shuttles were destroyed, and *Phoenix* was taking a mighty pounding. Then there was the war on the ground.

Pez took her wing to jump speed, then through the jump to brake all out. The reloading and docking took only a few seconds. Most of the time involved in reloading was accelerating to .7 light speed and then coming to a slow speed so the reloaders could pace them and latch on. From the reloaders' outpost at the orbit of the seventh planet, they built up speed to jump back into the fight and brake to targeting speed. One of Schwin's bombers, Demeter 3, had been blown to bits while Pez was rearming. Pugot already had Bacchus's wing on their way to reload.

Pez led Artemis, Cronus, and Demeter on a run by the class seven ship, which was pouring out a beating on the *Phoenix*, and hit the big Imperial ship with a torpedo into a weak spot in the shields, and followed it up with another one through the flickering spot before it closed, breaching the hull and taking its shields entirely down for a moment. *Phoenix* did not waste a millisecond, hitting it with the last of its biggest ordnance while nailing it with near every beam and blaster on the ship. With a couple of dozen canister missiles from the bombers and a pair of torpedoes from Artemis 2 right up the thing's tail, it burst into a glare of sparkling colored light, illuminating briefly a vast region of space, and a more beautiful site, Pez could not imagine. Of course, she was seeing it from outside her bomber while blinding sensors on a class nine to save a Corvette thunder.

The Imperials still had two class nines and almost seven hundred small spacecraft. The shuttles were still leaving nine of the big troop transports with only the Corvette Thunders to deal with them, while dodging fighters and fighter-bombers. Not one Corvette Thunder had a missile left beneath its undercarriage. The SMCS commando shuttles were battling the two class nines and were about out of missiles. The Hunter-Terminators were shooting down small craft with their blasters, also pretty much out of missiles. Their losses had steadily increased, even with Pez whiting out ships with micro-suns all around space. Earth was screaming to Pez for help.

Bacchus returned, and Cronus's wing went to reload. Demeter's bombers, the three left, had no missiles at all; and neither did their drones. Pez led them toward Earth, blowing up shuttles as they went. *Phoenix* came upon a class nine only a third its power, pulverizing it in moments with beam and blasters while combat shuttles pummeled it with the very last of their missiles and with their blasters. With the class nine's vapor cloud in its wake, *Phoenix* went hunting for more class nines, blowing away fighters and fighter-bombers as it went. A pair of Hunter-Terminators had plunged through Earth's atmosphere and were busy frying shuttles and troops on the ground.

Following a lucrative run through a cluster of Imperial troop shuttles, now so much space debris, Cronus returned, and Schwin was able to take her three bombers of Demeter wing to fetch some more missiles and torpedoes. Pez kept crushing shuttles into smoke and particles. Two more pairs of Hunter-terminators shot through the atmosphere to assist the ground war. *Phoenix* found and killed the last class-nine Imperial ship, but not before it had destroyed some shuttles and Hunter-Terminators.

Cleo told Pez, "I've been studying the new micro-jump torpedoes Om is designing, which will jump into the inside of a ship. I think I can accomplish that with my drone inside one of those big troop transports, but I can't be sure. If I fail, we lose a useful blaster and a very expensive piece of equipment."

"It's worth a try," Pez told her, "and I'll take full responsibility. Do it."

"It would help if you stay to this side of the closest transport so I can use the bomber's sensors too," Cleo said.

"I'll do my best," Pez promised.

The drone was moving away, picking up speed, while Pez kept her bomber to the proper flank of the giant transport, still leaving in her rainbow body and firing the nose blaster while shooting off Flint's missiles.

Ahhu, Rubix, and Flint were in sync, all firing together at the same target whenever it was one of the bigger bombers, blowing them up without spending canister missiles.

Schwin got back with her bombers fully loaded, and they blew away three Imperial fighters with missiles as they came in. Cleo's drone was approaching jump speed.

28

Swenah parked her Om ships by the three big Om auxiliaries, and shuttles started back and forth between them, reloading ordnance and fuel cells and bringing replacement parts for repairs. For about a quarter hour, *Apollo* had to dock with an auxiliary for the loading of the largest missiles and all torpedoes in her magazines. All of the auxiliaries had their repair small craft out and were working on damaged ships. The destroyers and fast attack ships were already armed, though some were still tending to repairs. She'd lost a star cruiser, three destroyers, and five fast attack ships in the engagement they'd just concluded, along with two fast attack ships and one destroyer since the war began. The *Phoenix* and all of *Apollo's* small combat spacecraft were off with Pez, defending Earth.

The Kluzyst and Rally ships, having spent no munitions, were headed straight for the Gzzklns system to protect it. The Trident ships, having very little damage and having spent less than 15 percent of their missiles and torpedoes, would be joining that fight well before Swenah could get her force ready and would be bringing the seven big transports with newly mounted super-beam weapons.

Nothing could go quickly enough to please Swenah today, but the rearming felt as if it were killing her. A number of her ships would be going into battle with damage that would take too long to repair, and they would not be at 100%. She knew the longer it took them, the more of their allies would get blown to bits. She knew she would have had three times the losses in the last battle had it not been for Pez blinding the enemy ships.

She wished Pez were with her, and she half expected to arrive in the midst of battle to find the Kluzyst and Rally ships already gone, with Trident whittled down to nothing. They'd left some probe drones in Gzzklns, and data was pouring in.

A call from Yona shook Swenah to the core. Yona told her, "Our ambassador ship in Galaxy YE142857N9P2 has failed to locate resistance to the empire's extermination and enslavement program there and reports that the bulk of invading Imperial ships have just left to return to the Xegachtnel Galaxy. I'm sorry. Om is organizing some reinforcements to send to you, and they will launch from the main star fleet space station in nineteen minutes."

"Send them right to the Gzzklns system; it is under attack," Swenah told her desperately, "and send a battleship to Earth 10^5 CBS2. Pez is trying to defend it with only a star cruiser and some small craft. I just spent my ordnance and got beat up at Pax Vez; though we did win. We have to rearm to get back into the fight."

"I'll send a battleship and battleship-carrier to Earth. Om's planetary defense super battleship will go to Gzzklns with a T-nine super star cruiser, four battleships, two battleship-carriers, five star cruisers, and fourteen destroyers."

"I may be able to get there just ahead of them, but it will be close," Swenah said with frustration. "This rearming is taking us forever."

"We're sending you half of our planetary defense force. That is the very most I could wring out of the High Council," Yona told her.

"And it is much appreciated."

The next call made things still worse. Admiral Tonkah said, "The empire is pulling completely out of the Yuban Galaxy and is headed back to Xegachtznel. Trident is organizing a force to follow."

"Will they go straight to Gzzklns?" Swenah asked.

"I don't know," Tonkah said miserably. "We're just leaving our auxiliaries and working our way up to jump speed. Please hurry because we won't last long without the Om ships."

"I'm still eleven minutes from departure, and that's only if the crews make the deadline," Swenah informed him. "I've got half a dozen ships in need of repairs that would take too long and are coming with me anyway. Om is sending a super battleship and a super cruiser along with twenty-five smaller ships. I'll get there just as soon as I can."

"Those seven transports we rigged with super beams should be jumping into the fight just minutes after my Trident ships. My carrier spacecraft can keep the Imperial troop shuttles off the planet, at least for a while."

Swenah told him, "The Gzzklns defenses are already shot and their local defense ships are mostly blown. The Kluzyst and Rally ships are getting shot up, and they've already taken eighteen percent losses. You're jumping into the mother of all black holes, you know."

"As long as you jump in soon after behind me, I'll have no regrets," Tonkah replied. Then he added, "It's too bad the One isn't with you now."

"I'll get my ships hurrying along," Swenah promised, and then she got the whip cracking. She was down four large cargo shuttles, and this was adding to the delay. At least Ming had collected that annoying baby off the bridge. It was unheard of. What would be next? Goats and birds? She couldn't imagine.

More problems causing more delays, and a destroyer declared unfit by engineering, had Swenah practically in a fit. It was twelve minutes and twenty-two seconds, not eleven minutes, when Swenah finally gave the order to accelerate to jump speed, staying in formation. The auxiliaries were coming too since they had super-beam weapons, and Swenah needed everything she could get in that fight. They wouldn't wait for them, though. She was more than done waiting.

Her combat ships all poured out speed nicely, and it was a very efficient going to reach .7 light speed. That freaky experience again, yet so brief, and Konax was braking madly, using everything *Apollo* had and spending boosters like a drunken crewman spends his pay. Probe data, and data from Tonkah's super-carrier, were flying in, and Swenah had just a moment to get an overview of the battle while they were still moving too fast to be targeted.

Shudiy sat in her robe in Pez's seat like a statue, her head shrouded by her hood and her eyes closed. Swenah sure hoped that woman could do something because the Kluzyst had already lost their two-mile ship, two of their three 6,600-foot class-three ships, the class five, one of their two class eights, and seventeen class nines. Thirty-two Rally ships were gone, including one of their one superclass ships and more than half the rest of their biggest ones. Trident had already lost a superclass ship and thirteen other ships. The seven big transports had just reached target acquisition speed and all had their beams boring into the shields of the same three-mile-long Imperial ship.

The three-mile ship was fighting back, though it was already engaged with an 8,700-foot Trident super battleship and several allied Kluzyst class nines. The shields of the seven transports were completely visible and clearly draining as missiles, torpedoes, and blaster fire punched into them. Their seven transports with super beams, along with the Trident super battleship's beams and blasters, as well all the other weapons hitting the Imperial ship, made it spread it in a mini-nova within 6.7 seconds.

Just as *Apollo* reached targeting speed, already taking hits to its shields and opening up with its own weapons, an entire new Imperial fleet jumped into the star system behind the opposite hemisphere of Gzzklns. A moment later, an allied transport with super beam was turned into gas and flying debris. One of Swenah's destroyers burst into blazing light. Firestone was launching the last of his considerable combat spacecraft, 209 small craft, plus thirty-two drone fighter-bombers. This total did not include a heavily armed diplomatic shuttle and his twelve space marine combat shuttles. The ship had also been carrying twelve of the new Astro-Phantom heavy bombers. Space was thick with Imperial combat spacecraft buzzing in many directions like a swarm of insects.

Trix manned Ahhu's gun on *Apollo*. She wore a space suit and helmet, deep in her contemplation, glasses fogging and linked tightly with the spiritual congress—her actions flowing with instinctive immediacy and the clarity of the Amonrahonians serving as her sight. Imperial fighters and fighter-bombers were going down. Some pieces of them sat on the hull right in front of her big class-six quad blaster, which didn't stop firing for a moment. An enormous blast took down *Apollo's* shields, followed by a jolting one striking *Apollo's* hull. A fighter-bomber and a bunch of fighters were coming in to destroy the primary sensor array, and a missile hit the turret across from Trix, wiping out gun and gunner and causing an air leak in Trix's section.

The big class six in Trix's hands blew the fighter-bomber away, taking a fighter with it, and Trix's blasts sprayed across to some closing fighters, making them cloudbursts, before spraying right across another pair and then another. Blaster bolts were hitting all around and between Trix's gun barrels as she tore into the attacking fighters. Her class-six blaster killed them like spraying gnats with an insecticide.

Swenah was taking on a two-mile-long sausage that had only two-thirds the power of her ship. She was going for the jugular vein, slugging it out. There were only about four and a half minutes before the newly arrived Imperial fleet slowed to targeting momentum. The Om reinforcements had just jumped in and were slowing down, but it was too little too late for what was coming. The two-mile tub finally exploded in living color just as two more of the same engaged Swenah. Captain Firestone was bringing the super-carrier around to help her with these.

Suddenly, two micro-suns enveloped the ship she battled with, and not a second later, two encompassed the other ship. Swenah took the opportunity to get out from between them just as both let fly a broadside, each hitting the other. Firestone and Swenah had had their super-weapons hitting the same two-mile ship, and when nearly all the weapons of the other two-mile ship hit that one by mistake, it was all over except for smoke and vapors. Swenah looked over at Shudiy, who hadn't budged. Then she noticed that eighteen of the big torpedoes had been fired. She also noticed on her overview holo that one of her battleships was in trouble, getting pounded by a class-four and class-six ship at the same time. She didn't think she could get over to it soon enough to save it. Then micro-sun after micro-sun erupted on the class four, allowing her battleship to break out of the line of fire, bringing its shields back up. The class four continued blindly into the fray and eventually rammed one of the ninety giant Imperial troop transports amidships, breaking it in half without blowing it up. Mangled shuttles by the dozens, with thousands of troops, were blown with great pressure out both broken ends and into space.

No rescue was even attempted. Those troop transports were enormous, and Swenah wasn't quite sure what they could do about all of them, but in her mind she confirmed, *One down, eighty-nine to go.*

The newly arrived Imperial fleet was less than a minute from engaging and opening fire. Swenah, Firestone, and Tonkah were coordinating and selected one of the three class-one ships to assault

A TALE OF THE TAIL OF NINE STARS

together. As they closed in, Swenah noticed she'd lost another destroyer. She also noticed micro-suns igniting on all the lead Imperial new arrivals, giving some of her smaller ships a chance to duck away from the incoming horde.

Their Kluzyst 6,600-foot ship engaged a ship of its own class. This one was fresh and fully armed. The Rally super battleship, which was still alive and fighting, took on a ship nearly twice its size. The Trident super battleship also took on an Imperial class two. Swenah, Firestone, and Tonka let their target have it. It obviously had not fully recovered its sensors yet. It bloomed with suns again, and its big weapons missed their shields again as they bore into it with beams and blasters. Shudiy sent a big torpedo into its shield's soft spot, and that was the end of it.

The other two three-mile class ones were closing and firing on the three allied super ships. Swenah already had her beam on one of them, and Firestone got his on it, plus his super blaster. Tonka went between *Apollo* and the other class one, which had been pounding it, giving it some hits back and saving Swenah's shields. The whole flank of the ship shooting into Tonka whited out in suns just before the one Swenah and Firestone were shooting at did. Between *Apollo* and the super-carrier, they had fifty-eight reactors, and the class one had only thirty-two. It took seven seconds for Firestone and Swenah to send the whole ship and crew to their afterlife. They added their fire to Tonkah's on the last class one in the battle zone, but two class twos were already pounding their shields. It was a race to see whose shields would go first. *Isis* came in with super blaster and beam biting into one of the two class twos while showering it with missiles and torpedoes. Several class threes were nearly in range and coming their way.

Admiral Omniomi's voice came on Swenah's bridge as *Apollo*'s sister ship, 8,100 feet in diameter and 2,000 feet thick came in shooting the two-mile ship, which blew before she could say, "Your reinforcements from Om have arrived."

"What are your orders?" Swenah inquired, since Omniomi outranked her.

"To follow your orders, Admiral; that was made quite explicit to me before I volunteered."

"Stick with Firestone and work together. Now that the class ones are all destroyed, you and I have the most powerful ships in this battle. It's just that they have about twelve times as many."

"Aye, aye Admiral, it is an honor to fight beside you."

"The honor is mine, Admiral Omniomi," Swenah assured her.

The super-carrier and super battleship went hunting together. Tonkah and Admiral Nordstrom on the Rally super battleship stuck together. Swenah struck off alone, headed for the biggest Imperial ship she could find. Micro-suns were spreading across the battle zone. Swenah noticed one of the big torpedoes fire from the *Apollo* and go to just slip into a soft spot in the shields of a class-four Imperial ship before it could close up, and the hull ruptured, the escaping methane lit, the ship blew, the cloud erupting in beautiful color. Swenah already had her beam burning into a class-three ship a mile and a quarter long. The *Apollo*'s big blaster got busy on the class three as a barrage of missiles and torpedoes pelted it, bringing it shields down. The hull didn't last long without shields, and a few missiles passed through vapor with nothing to hit, heading endlessly into space to join the rest of the hazardous trash out there.

Another fresh Imperial invasion fleet appeared on Swenah's holo. Eleven minutes of braking to engagement. They had three more class ones and six class twos. It looked seriously hopeless at this point, without even considering the big ships, for just the sheer quantity of them all. Another one of the allied auxiliaries blew, eliminating another of their super-weapons.

With this last wave of Imperials, Swenah had just lost four more fast attack ships, two destroyers, a star cruiser, and a battleship-carrier. The ships she had left were starting to run low on missiles and torpedoes. The Rally and Kluzyst forces were fairly decimated. She had to organize for this new wave. One of the fresh 870-foot-diameter battleships that came with Admiral Omniomi just blew up.

29

Cleo watched her holos and instruments carefully, and Pez was passing her waves of energy and awareness. The drone was nearly up to jump speed, only seconds away. It was not headed for the transport they meant to jump it into because direction was entirely irrelevant to quantum navigation. It really didn't matter which way you were going when you cease to exist where you were, to pop into existence elsewhere. The drone vanished from their holos, entirely gone. The big Imperial troop transport went *kaboom!* —and not into a sphere but a streak of blue light for millions of miles, and when the glare faded, there wasn't even vapor left to mark its passing.

Pez told her wing pilot, "Have your drone operator turn control of his drone over to Cleo on my bomber. She just jumped her drone inside a big transport. Did you see that streak?"

"I sure did, and I'm having my drone pilot transfer control to Cleo right now."

Ahhu was in Pez's ear. "I told you it could be done. I could've done that for you, you know. I brought my drone pilot console and skullcap."

Pez told her, "You'll get a chance." To Natosha, Pez said, "Go get on that lower quad blaster for a while; I can handle everything from here."

She had her other wing pilot switch control to Ahhu, who was seated in the little foyer on the deck by the airlock. Natosha was already wasting an Imperial fighter with Ahhu's blaster quad. Cleo was accelerating another drone to jump speed. Schwin's, Davenport's, and Pugot's bombers were keeping fighters and fighter-bombers off Pez, and Pez was spreading little white suns all over the place between tending to her nose blaster and tossing the occasional pair of canister missiles.

Ahhu got her drone whipping up velocity. Rubix was blowing up Imperial small craft in a continuous parade of vaporizing destruction and was finally about to pass Ahhu's score. Natasha was good, and she was splattering spacecraft, but Rubix was a maestro and was almost double-timing her. Another mammoth troop transport jumped to a blue streak, then nothing. Ahhu made a blue streak. Pez kept the drone control transfers coming. Cleo and Ahhu turned out to be an awesome and powerful secret weapon. Cleo got another. Ahhu turned a gargantuan spacecraft carrier into a blue streak. While the big Imperial ships were being streaked out of existence, Pez sent the Bacchus and Cronus wings to Earth's surface to assist with killing the Imperials who'd landed and keep more from doing so.

Pez had lost thirty-one Corvette Thunders and had lost five previously, so she only had forty-four left. Fifteen Hunter-Terminators were still functional and fighting, tracking down Imperial fighter-bombers. Five space marine combat shuttles had blown, and nine were still in the battle. Thirteen Astro-Phantom heavy bombers remained intact. *Phoenix* was running low on missiles. It was eighty-four against some 450 Imperial small combat spacecraft, and a swiftly dwindling number of big ships, which were slow, had only short-range class-three and class-four blasters and small missiles.

A troop transport became another blue streak flashing across space, and this one took out a troop shuttle and fighter as it blew through, while those just added to the streak. Ahhu found it stimulating and entertaining, and she was proud to be helping Pez save Earth. The other massive spacecraft carrier streaked blue across the star system and into outer space. They went through twelve drones and had nothing left to blow up. An Om battleship-carrier and an Om battleship had jumped in and were braking in typical star fleet fashion, madly beyond reason. Pez loved it. For a moment, she thought maybe Swenah had been victorious, and she called her.

Swenah said, "Both invasion forces were recalled by the empire, and they're here in Gzzklns now, with me! Admiral Omniomi showed up with some reinforcements, but none of us are going to last long."

"Save your small fighter-bomber drones with quantum drives. I'll be right there. I've got two drone pilots who can jump them inside ships and turn them into blue streaks for a moment, before there's nothing left of them."

Pez hailed the Om carrier and said, "I'm recalling my bombers, and we're jumping to Gzzklns. Send your battleship to Gzzklns now. It won't be needed here."

"Aye, aye, General."

Then Pez asked, "By the way, do you have any small drone fighter-bombers with quantum drives?"

"I have eight aboard. Why?"

"I need them," Pez insisted, "to save Swenah."

"I'll be decelerated enough to launch them in fifty-one seconds. They'll be the first off my ship."

I'm leaving my Hunter-Terminators here, and they'll need to land on your flight deck to rearm. My Corvette Thunders too."

"We can rearm your bombers," he offered.

"I don't have time, and our real weapon is those drones. We're jumping them past the shields inside Imperial ships."

"That's amazing! The scientists and engineers are still perfecting it on Om."

"I've got two drone pilots who can do it," Pez said proudly.

She'd recalled Davenport and Pugot, and they were climbing from the surface, almost out of the atmosphere. Pugot told her, "We got the two worst groups, but it's still a mess down there."

"The carrier will set things right, and *Phoenix* is still on-site. I'm leaving the Corvettes and Hunters here, and the shuttles as well. Punch it. Here are your destination coordinates. We're jumping into a raging battle we're losing, and you have to keep the Imperials off me long enough for Cleo and Ahhu to jump the drones."

Ahhu told her, "Only the bombers need brake when we get there. Tell them to keep their drones at point seven light, ready to go, and as soon as you slow to target acquisition speed, we'll just start jumping them into the biggest Imperial ships."

"That's what we'll do," Pez told her. Then she said to her bomber pilots, "Have your drone pilots keep their drones at jump speed and be ready to switch control of the drones once we've slowed."

After receiving the eight drone fighter-bombers from the Om

battleship-carrier, six minutes and fifty seconds after Pez spoke with Swenah, she was throwing reverse drives, thrusters, and a booster, coming out of jump. She was also reviewing the battle on her holos and already helping Shudiy plant suns on the Imperial ships. For less than two seconds, she appeared in her rainbow body on Swenah's bridge to say, "I'm here and braking fast."

Shudiy was down to eight of the biggest torpedoes, and no one else was touching those because she used them so effectively, finding soft spots in the shields no one else could see and their sensors couldn't detect. The little micro-suns popping up all about had literally doubled. Some were so bright they affected even *Apollo's* sensors from this distance. One could only imagine what it was like for the Imperials in those ships.

Swenah was duking it out with a class two and a class three, nearly out of missiles. She checked on Trix as she bore her beam sizzling into the class two and saw a mound of scrap metal and scorched plastics heaped in front of Trix's quad blaster, obstructing its full range of movement. She quickly sent some hull crawler repair androids to see to the mess without letting up on her beam weapon, and she was rewarded by an expanding purple vapor cloud where a class two had just been. A class one was closing on her from a distance and already launching a stream of torpedoes at her. Then it became like a million-mile bolt of lightning glowing blue in her holo and fading. Pez came on to say, "What did you think of that?"

"I loved it," Swenah said with glee. "Do it again."

"We are," Pez told her as another ship disappeared into a million-mile line of light. "We only brought eleven drones so send me some more."

They're on their way from Firestone's super-carrier," Swenah said, just before she called Firestone and told him to send them. Admiral Omniomi sent all of hers, and so did the five Om carriers and five Om battleships left in Swenah's task force. The first eleven went quickly, already traveling at jump speed and all. Firestone had seventeen left of the thirty-two he started with, and Pez got all of those. Omniomi sent sixteen, which was all her ship carried, like Swenah's. Swenah's

A TALE OF THE TAIL OF NINE STARS

two T-nine super cruisers each carried twelve drone fighter-bombers. Omniomi's carriers and battleships sent theirs to Pez too.

Meanwhile, the allied super-ships, the three big Om auxiliaries, the now three transports with super-weapons left out of seven, and all the rest of the allied forces began kicking some serious Imperial ass with renewed hope and morale boost as their enemies streaked blue out of the solar system and ultimately out of existence, except as atoms, each one a long way from other atoms. Things that had occupied a compact space, with their length of less than a mile and a half being the greatest dimension, were suddenly spread across a million miles or more. When there was nothing but Imperial ships smaller than class seven, Cleo and Ahhu got started on the colossal troop transports. The allies were the only ones now with super ships and super-weapons. They were outnumbered more than ten to one numerically but had just as much reactor power ultimately. The blue lines across space continued.

By the time the big fresh Trident fleet arrived, Tonkah's super battleship-carrier was down to blasters only and had lost most of his fighters and fighter-bombers. Thirty-two gargantuan Imperial troop transports had streaked, and of course one had broken in half earlier. Now Swenah was happily counting them down, pleased that Pez had found a way. At fifty-three, however, they were down to four more drones, and every Om ship was searching for more. A few more were found here and there and two awaiting repairs on an auxiliary got fixed pronto. Ahhu and Cleo got up to sixty-four on the gigantic troop transports but had to stop there since they were all out of ammo.

Pez landed all her bombers on Firestone's ship to rearm, change out thruster fuel cells and spent boosters, make a few quick repairs, and wash the viewport before heading out hunting. While Pez was rearming hers, Swenah had a steady flow of cargo shuttles from the auxiliaries send ordnance over to *Apollo*. The new wave of Trident ships were hunting down Imperial ships, and they brought over 2,500 small combat spacecraft, all out battling too.

Natasha was back in the copilot seat and Ahhu naked at her gun when Artemis 1, Pez's bomber, blew out through the bay doors of the super-carrier first, followed by the rest of her wing, then by the rest of her squadron. With a full load of missiles and torpedoes, they went

463

to work. The Imperial fighters went quickly under their blasters, and missiles. The 390-footers could be put down, given enough blaster fire and enough missiles on their shields, with a torpedo. Occasionally Pez chucked a torpedo into a soft spot on a larger ship engaging allied forces as they passed by. She kept the tiny suns popping up all over the place, but Shudiy now made many of those out there.

Swenah herself, now that she was partly rearmed, became the solution to the remaining giant troop transports—or to nineteen of them anyway—before the rest bugged out.

A large Kluzyst task force jumped into the system, mostly of ships five hundred foot long or shorter, but they had a pair of class threes, a class six, and seven class nines with them, all mutineers from the empire. With no motherships left, the small combat spacecraft and smaller Imperial ships went into massive surrender. The troops on the planet's surface surrendered too. One particularly vicious little group of them, who had just committed every war crime imaginable, were simply turned into charcoal and gas by the Gzzklns Kluzyst on the planet, without a second thought.

30

Pez returned with her squadron to *Apollo*, and Ahhu got to make part of another naked victory walk before everyone was throwing her forty feet into the air on the flight deck. They threw Pez in the air too, at least a dozen times, and one of her milk-swollen breasts was bruised coming down on one of those throws. Lanky Cleo gave one petty officer a fat lip trying not to be heaved into the air, but she went up and down a bunch of times anyway. Pez had given her a field promotion as they were touching down.

When everyone was done throwing Pez around like a rag doll, Ming handed off an angry, hungry Electra, and Pez got right to work trying to get her on her breast. At first, she was just too upset to suck, and Pez had to pass her internal calming energy for about two minutes before Electra decided she'd put Pez through enough shit and was too hungry to bother giving her any more screaming grief, at which point she finally latched on, sucking for all she was worth. Pez thought, *If Electra had teeth, she'd likely bite it off.*

Trix had found Rubix, and both found Ahhu, walking back with her to their cabin. Somehow, on their way, Gretel had attached herself to them and arrived at their cabin, coming in.

Pez went directly to the bridge, feeding Electra, to look for Shudiy. She smiled at the space marine at the bridge door, pointing to Electra's little mouth on her nipple, sucking like a fiend. He understood and was not in the least offended that she did not salute.

Swenah was still thanking Shudiy. "You really saved *Apollo* from becoming individual particles greatly separated, nothing bigger than a quark. And I thought you were just a cook. Om and Gzzklns owe you a great debt and shall honor you always."

Shudiy still sat shrouded in her hoodie, unmoving and silent. Swenah wasn't sure she was getting through, and she was all ready to start again when Pez and Electra walked in. Shudiy rose from her seat and embraced Pez. Electra opened her eyes, and Pez told her, "Thank you, Mother Shudiy. I love you."

They stood and hugged a long time. Konax was taking them leisurely toward the planet to assume orbit. When they released each other, Shudiy bowed to the bridge officers from in front of the door and then exited without a word to a chorus of thanks. Pez hugged Swenah, who said, "That woman can do things that you can do, and I always thought she was just your cook."

"She is one of my teachers, and she's an excellent cook," Pez explained. "She has attended me in my passing many times and has been in the service of our race for numerous lifetimes. She gives a thorough bath."

"You were magnificent!" Swenah declared. "Even with Shudiy making suns and popping torpedoes into invisible holes in shields, we would have been wiped out completely if you hadn't returned with those magic drone pilots."

Cotex, fully back in her flirtatious mode and twisted 180 degrees so her breasts pointed at Pez, told them, "We've received over a hundred invitations to planets that want to honor Pez with gifts, titles, parades, celebrations, medals, trophies, and prizes. Some are offering real estate and vast monetary funds."

Pez replied, "We'll celebrate with our fellow warriors here on Gzzklns, and we will go to Earth 10^5 CBS2, where Ahhu can be properly recognized, and Rubix and Dove too, for the important parts they played. Electra needs to see her father's home world. We'll snap some holos since she is not likely to recall having been there."

Swenah told Pez most sincerely, "I never lost faith that you would somehow win the war, dear, even though when you called me from Earth, I was certain that I would not live to see it. You rescued so many of us."

"We will make the complete rights of passing, including the

A TALE OF THE TAIL OF NINE STARS

ear-whispered instructions for the after-death state, for every single life lost in this war, and we'll begin tomorrow," Pez vowed.

"We don't have the ears to whisper into," Swenah pointed out.

"We'll speak it to a holo of the fallen, and that hero will hear," Pez proclaimed.

"The Kluzyst would like us to help them take control of the Imperial home star system so they can prosecute war criminals—the emperor in particular—and destroy the empire's military capacity utterly. The wealth of a thousand worlds is there and must be equitably redistributed. We would only need linger until full control of the planet is established."

"Of course we'll help them," Pez agreed. "I'll go to the surface with my space marines, and I'll even find that damned emperor for them. He's probably hiding under his bed."

"He's reported to be in a bunker at least a mile below the surface, with twenty-eight-foot-thick blast walls," Swenah mentioned.

Pez dismissed the bunker. "A minor delay. I'll just have Ahhu and Cleo jump a drone inside of it. We'll likely get a momentary tunnel right to the planet's core in a blue streak."

"I like it," Swenah said, delighted. "Now go have a big party and unwind—and don't worry yourself at all about 'events.'"

Pez headed back to her cabin and shifted Electra to her other breast, hoping it would make them feel more balanced. Crew persons stopped to stand at attention and salute her. Pez gave a few Swenah half salutes and smiled at each when she passed.

When she got on to the senior officers' quarters corridor, Sarhi was on her way to find her. The two women embraced, with Electra still sucking between them. Sarhi said, "You did it, beloved."

"You taught me how," Pez replied.

"I learned from you," the Im reminded her. "The universe has become quite complex, and it's not like ancient times, when the intelligent design could just send a flood to wipe out sentient beings too attached in ego to participate in reciprocity and love."

Pez agreed. "Now enlightened microcosms are required as agency, and we are the flood."

"And what a flood you are, my Wu," Sarhi declared.

Electra gave up on the sucking and was contentedly looking around.

Pez burped her and got only gas this time; no fluids came up. Sarhi scooped her out of Pez's arms, nodding to her, and Electra just went along without protest. Sarhi was already singing to her and heading for her own cabin.

Pez asked, ready to hear now, "Who is she, Mother?"

Sarhi turned, stopping her singing, and said, looking into Pez's eyes, "She is the one who takes birth every two thousand five hundred years, by choice, to transmit a new teaching for enlightenment. Ever since you became the Wu, she has chosen you as mother and teacher to prepare her for her mission when she comes."

"I had no idea," Pez said in wonderment. "What a great honor."

"I'm glad you finally asked," Sarhi said, pleased. "Electra has wanted you to know. She is called the Mu when she comes. Honestly, she tried to tell you."

"So it was 'Mu' she said, not 'Ma,'" Pez said, only mildly disappointed.

"She has a special love for you, beloved," Sarhi reassured her. "Now go to your lovers and have the break you deserve."

It had already begun without her, and when Pez arrived, there were more than just her lovers there, though she was relieved she didn't see Jard. Tiny Ahhu was all over Cleo, and Gretel was both riding Rubix and making Trix squeal at the same time. Pez couldn't help thinking, *She's such a clever graduate student.*

What truly caught Pez's attention, though, even more than Ming's expression of helplessness as Sony worked her over was seeing little Woahha going at it frantically with big Cotex in the middle of the floor. Then she heard Jard's voice coming out of the bathroom, and with a sinking feeling of disappointment, she stuck her head through the door. Jard was having sex with his new squeeze, and he had her seated on the sink counter with her legs straddling him. There was a Rally space fleet's junior lieutenant uniform on the bathroom floor, which looked as if it might fit the naked young woman. Over her shrieks, Jard said to Pez, her head framed in the doorway, "Hurrah, love child. You saved us. Now go whip us up some events."

"I'm not just an object for your convenience," Pez told him sternly.

"Of course not!" Jard agreed. "If you were, I'd be doing you instead."

"It wouldn't fit in me anyway," Pez told him, before returning her

A TALE OF THE TAIL OF NINE STARS

attention to the bedroom. None of her lovers were available at the moment, so she considered going to the mess for some grub. She was about to take her first step in that direction when Woahha grabbed her ankle in a viselike grip and Cotex got an arm between Pez's thighs, pulling one of them with tremendous force. Instead of employing her martial arts, Pez went with the flow. Woahha seemed to have supernatural skills tailored to Pez's unlimited energy, making it dance, soar, intensify, concentrate, and explode in the most spectacular series of events that left no one aboard *Apollo* on their feet. Cotex was wrapped around Pez through that series, like an electrical connection of live wires. Only the females on board got to enjoy and savor the whole duration of that long series, the men being spent right at the opening and start of it.

It was an event-filled night, and they all occurred now in escalating sequence, each event punctuated with seeming total release, only to be dwarfed by the next one. A crew woman second class passed out from the sensory overload and had to be brought to the ship's medical facility, but she recovered promptly. The woman was relieved of a chronic sinus obstruction because of her ordeal, baffling the doctors.

The commemorative ceremonies, parades, dinners, and celebrations on Gzzklns, saturated with great pomp and festival, went on for a week of evenings and all of the first day, after which Pez, Sarhi, and the Islohar spent the day meditating and administering to the departed heroes of the war. They did this twelve hours per day for ten days, with help from Hierophant Kksszzchch and his entire priest and priessthood. The representatives of the spiritual congress assisted too, as did Pez's spouses.

Grand Master Lego brought monks from Rally to foster and promote these efforts. The holy work of the funerary rites was entirely ritualized, as it had to be for working directly with divine consciousness. Numerous planetary spiritual orders and sects, in addition to several entire planetary populations, meditated in support of this work and to help the war's heroes in their afterlives, assisting their illumination into the light.

The Om ships went with the Kluzyst, Rally, and Trident ships, all the troop transports, of which many more had been added, and all the auxiliary ships to the capital star system of the Vachisy Empire. As they employed 48 percent of their reverse drives and thruster power, slowing on approach slowly, with plenty of room ahead of them, like a Sunday drive, Pez asked Swenah, "When are sentient beings going to understand that they live in a moral universe based upon the principle of reciprocity, which implies morality loudly, and ought to discourage genocide, slavery, and exploitation? You can't cheat reality, and while the action of reciprocity may take a great deal of time, the one thing in this universe you can absolutely count on is that those actions will arrive with certainty, giving you back everything you have ever put out, and the worst of it, a million times over."

"A realization yet in need of much assimilation in some civilizations, apparently," Swenah pointed out.

"Positive reciprocity is evolution, while negative reciprocity is sheer destruction. Higher organization is just not possible without cooperation."

Looking at what their holos were exhibiting, Swenah said with dismay, "Talk about sheer destruction."

Pez said in wonder, "I guess we pretty much trashed it last time we were here."

"They still have ships," Konax mentioned.

"I guess they didn't send any of theirs to Gzzklns for the big battle," Pez stated.

"In fact, they have more than the last time we were here," Swenah figured.

"Let's get our Om auxiliaries and the three transports with super-weapons lined up on ships too," Pez said casually, "and launch a dozen drones for Ahhu and Cleo to play with. They won't have these ships very long, I promise you."

Cotex, more solicitous of Pez's attention than ever since her night with Pez and Woahha, said, "The planet's surface has been completely militarized, and there are approximately two million hard-shell combat space suits operating down there this minute."

"No problem," Pez said. "We'll fry everything military to sludge from space before we even land. I'm so sick of these fools that I'm ready to oblige them if they insist on fighting us to the death."

Cotex had more to say and would have just made stuff up if she'd had to. "There are zero weapons on any lunar surfaces or in space around the planet. We detected twenty-nine submerged vessels at depths of eight hundred to one thousand feet, which have super-beam weapons ..."

The fire control officer interjected, "Like shooting fish in a barrel."

Cotex cleared her throat, giving the officer a dismissive look, and continued. "The Imperials still have numerous missile silos, and their missiles are equipped with gravity redirection generators, space drives, thrusters, and massive initial boosters, making them exceptionally quick at leaving the pressurized gas around their biosphere. There are nine hundred and seventeen small combat spacecraft on the planet surface, divided unequally into sixteen locations, and one hundred and fourteen operating currently in space within their outer moon's orbital distance."

"We'll be sure to waste the parked small craft right at the outset," Pez said to the bridge officers. "Hit the silos with rockets and fry the fish in the barrel with beams."

Cotex was just inventing things to say now, enjoying Pez's attention, and she went on. "There are no other super-weapons at the empire's disposal within the system, once the silos and submerged vessels are destroyed, and they'll have no means of harming a ship in space, not even a small fighter ..."

Mel said to Cotex, right on the bridge open line, "Darling, I have an itch only you and my android body can relieve."

Swenah said sternly, "Mel, the bridge is no place for arranging your sexual liaisons."

"I'll restrain future impulses, I promise," Mel told her, "if you agree to have a threesome with me and Cotex after the battle."

"Oh, please!" Cotex said excitedly since she just loved admirals and had had her eye on Swenah for a while; and after all, they were still in the Xegachtznel Galaxy, where everything that happened in it stayed in it.

"Cotex is a lieutenant in the star fleet, and I'm a rear admiral," Swenah stated with the appropriate amount of feigned offense.

"Who's going to tell?" Mel wanted to know.

"Speak with me privately right after the battle," Swenah insisted, closing the topic. Cotex grinned, knowing it was a date.

Everyone on the bridge knew it was a date, and Pez was feeling a little jealous. Then Mel said on speaker to Pez, "You are always welcome to join us, sweetheart, and your spouses too."

Feeling a bit better thanks to Mel's invitation, Pez followed the example of Swenah's discretion and said with interest, "Contact me privately right after the battle."

A little sound of delight escaped Cotex, as she couldn't quite sit still in her seat. Pez realized she'd shown no discretion at all, judging by all the grinning faces.

Konax mentioned, "This crew's been seeing more action than the staff at a brothel ever since those events began occurring in numbers across durations instead of singularly."

"They've had more than the usual tension of late, expecting to be blown apart at any moment," Pez defended herself, "and besides, I can't help it that my orgasms affect other people."

Mel explained, "Higher-level manifestations have greater freedom, are subject to fewer laws, and have greater range and influence. Take a material example such as water. As ice, it is subject to both the laws of crystalline structure and the laws of hydrology. While in liquid form, it is liberated from the laws of crystalline structure and only subject to hydrology laws. As steam, it enjoys its greatest freedom, following only the laws of random molecules. A moon is subject to many more laws and influences than a sun. Some mentally ill people can get stuck in a posture and are not able to influence their own body or immediate environment to even open the door and escape a fire, while some human beings have discovered the unity and founded cultures and civilizations expanding around globes and to distant star systems—and across thousands of years of time. Pez just happens to be a rather high-level influential being."

"Wait till Electra grows up," Pez told them.

Cotex seemed to be daydreaming, so Konax mentioned, "We've just reached targeting acquisition speed."

Swenah sent the coordinates of all the sites to the other Om ships and highlighted the ones she wanted hit with rocks to each ship. A moment later, she said, "Fire," and they were away. She said to the admirals of the Kluzyst, Rally, and Trident ships, "The Om ships are micro-jumping in ahead of our rocks to position behind their class ones

A TALE OF THE TAIL OF NINE STARS

and twos. As soon as we make the jump, jump the Trident ships in. Stay at maximum speed when we go and you'll be less than one and a half minutes behind us, Admiral Tonkah. By the time the Imperials see Trident ships reappear almost in their lap, we should have six ships blown. Kluzyst and Rally ships accelerate to point seventy-two and hold until there's just enough room to brake. You'll be about two and a half minutes behind the Trident ships on your arrival, right after the rocks hit. This capital system has reinforced their ships since I was last here, and there will be plenty for all of us."

"What about the submerged vessels with super-beam weapons?" Tonkah asked.

"My auxiliaries will be arriving cloaked about a moment before you do, and the subs are their primary targets. Until your ships arrive, those submarines will not be able to get a resolution on any of our ships, and by then we'll be blowing them."

"Just to be on the safe side, I'm directing one of my super battleships to assist your auxiliaries in removing those," Tonkah insisted.

"Good idea," Swenah agreed. "I'm sending the com link and decryption for the sensor probes we left in this system to provide triangulation for your fire control targeting."

"You didn't decelerate your auxiliaries when we slowed to fire our dumb munitions."

"They have no rocks to throw, and I want them there quick. Their only lag time will be in reaching high planetary orbit from where they jump in, which won't be as close as my warships since they need more room to brake."

"The moment I arrive," Tonka told her, "I'm transmitting a planet-wide message, telling the planet's inhabitants to evacuate all military facilities, and I'm giving coordinates for those wishing to surrender, for each region of approximately five hundred by five hundred miles. I'll have a ship defend each surrender zone from Imperial retaliation on its own citizens. This ought to reduce loss of life."

Thank you," Swenah acknowledged. "We have no fight with those of the Kluzyst race, only with those who would cling to the notion of empire building through enslavement and exploitation. This planet shall have zero military capability when I leave, I promise you that."

473

Konax started the countdown for their micro-jump, concentrating and ready to light up reverse drives and thrusters while firing boosters, keeping clear of all the space trash they'd created last time they were here. There was a lot of it.

Swenah had had twelve drones launched before accelerating from throwing rocks, and these were flown by drone pilots, two of whom were Ahhu and Cleo. The other pilots would switch control to them when they were ready. These had been received from Om while they were in the Gzzklns system.

They passed through nonexistence in literally no time, finding themselves racing at the planet like a crash, with their shields frying debris and Konax weaving them around a particularly large and solid piece of space garbage. It looked like a tailpiece of a class one, which somehow eluded the vaporization of the rest of the ship. The holo view seemed less threatening as Konax got *Apollo* slowing down, and it no longer appeared as certain crash and death or even excessively freaky fast. Now it seemed more as if there was actually a chance of surviving. Then, as more speed bled away and 100 percent sensor resolution stabilized, it became obvious that Konax was getting them soon to a complete stop, with the planet yet two hundred thousand miles away as they closed on the stern of a three-mile-long class one. *Isis* had closed on this same ship, and together they overpowered it by ten reactors. All her ships were in position except the auxiliaries, which were still slowing from their jump farther out from the planet.

Beams and blasters lit as missiles and torpedoes launched, and micro-suns bloomed on Imperial ships, blinding and overloading sensors. Two blue streaks shot across space for what looked like a billion miles. Two class twos were gone, spread clear out of the star system and beyond. Pez hit a soft spot in the shields of the class-one ship *Apollo* and *Isis* were punching, with one of the biggest torpedoes, at 5.7 seconds into engagement, exploding it in every direction.

The Trident ships suddenly appeared and had little room to brake.

Swenah got her beam right on a class one that Firestone's super-carrier and another T-Nine were attacking. It didn't take but a second and a half after that to open it into an expanding cloud of colorful gas.

The Om auxiliaries had slowed enough to start frying submersibles,

A TALE OF THE TAIL OF NINE STARS

and the Trident ships were right behind them, with one of their big battleships joining in the water sports, while the rest targeted ships. Tonkah's ship was missed by a class-two Imperial ship's super blaster from only forty-thousand miles away as half a dozen micro-suns clung to that one's hull, making it completely blind. Tonkah was beating on it with all he had, and a torpedo from *Apollo* slipped right through its shields like they weren't even there, while his super-weapons and biggest missiles were stopped dead by them. Suddenly, his weapons were penetrating the class two's hull, instead of wasting on its shields, and the resulting fireworks were truly a remarkable sight. Such a radiant bright vapor!

The Kluzyst and Rally ships arrived to join the fray about the time three transports with super-weapons arrived. The Imperial forces were seriously outnumbered, with no class ones or class twos left as solid matter. Micro-suns and blue streaks made the scene quite unnatural for a space battle. Admiral Omniomi blew away the last Imperial class three about the same moment Tonkah ended the last Imperial class four. A few ships began surrendering at this point, powering down everything but life support as they employed reverse thrusters to attain full stop and drift.

Swenah blew up a class five with her beam, while her super blaster operator killed a class nine. All the allied small craft went out to engage Imperial fighters and fighter-bombers. Pez erupted her micro-suns from the cockpit of Artemis 1, with Bacchus Cronus and Demeter wings beside and behind her. The emperor's ships were either blowing up or surrendering quickly now, but there were yet a thousand Imperial small craft about, and these had not yet begun to surrender. Pez was busy giving them incentive. Firestone had lent her a few Astro-Phantoms to fill out her ranks, and she was utilizing these well.

The silos were all crater fields, and the submersibles didn't even leave a sea stain. When the last obstinate Imperial ship was turned to space dust, some of their fighters and bombers began surrendering. Pez kept hunting those that wouldn't, flying at the edge of her bomber's tolerances and capacities, igniting micro-suns, firing her big blaster, and flinging torpedoes into shield soft spots. At the beginning of each arc she made, not one of her pilots had a clue where she was leading them; then, toward the end of each, they'd find themselves closing on the rears of a rich find. This was already a big topic of discussion among pilots from previous battles. "How does she do that?"

Fast attack ships, along with destroyers and frigates, assisted the allied small craft with the Imperial small combat spacecraft, dwindling their numbers. Whole squadrons of them began surrendering. A few squadrons fought on until Pez caught them. It was fast and furious work, with so many things happening, and shooting by too quickly to register.

Finally, Pez was chasing down a lone wing of fanatics, determined, obviously, to die before surrendering. She said to Natasha, "These assholes don't know when they're licked."

"Then let's lick them," Natasha said. She let two pairs of missiles fly, and Pez triggered her nose blaster to get her shields sprayed with Imperial fighter as she chucked a few of Flint's missiles.

31

They left four space bursts in their wake as the small craft battle concluded. Pez was already coordinating with her space marines. Two companies from the *Apollo* were landing at the edge of the Imperial capital city, along with 9,200 from their big troop transport ship. Trident troops in combat suits were landing across the city, on the opposite edge, and they planned to meet in the middle. Enormous streams of refugees were making their way out of the city, unarmed, waving signs of surrender.

The Kluzyst had provided the allies with recognition data on each of the three-million-plus war criminals to be arrested or just shot on site. It really didn't matter much either way, though shooting them was quicker and cheaper.

Evenrude was glued to Pez, who hadn't allowed any of her spouses to come with her. Another space marine, named Johnson, who was a regular at the temple cabin on *Apollo* for meditation sessions, was assisting Evenrude in keeping their supreme commander general safe and alive, striving to keep up with her.

Ahhu was having the time of her life since she'd been given the honor of blue-streaking the emperor's private bunker, dispersing it to spew deeper into the underworld where it belonged. Pez had hardly started trekking into the city with her company of space marines, led by Lieutenant Commander Barn, when a back-jet of molten metal shot into the sky about thirty thousand feet high from the center of the capital. Pez said to her troops, "There goes the emperor—or part of him anyway." She looked up at the fountain of liquid metal not even close to cooling.

About eight city blocks received a rain shower of 8,500-degree drops, setting them instantly ablaze. It was a total inferno, and all kinds of things were exploding in those eight blocks as it spread to sixteen. Ahhu's voice was in Pez's ear. "Did you see that!"

"I sure did," Pez acknowledged. "Good shot."

A tremendous ground quake followed, and Pez hit her propulsion to hover a foot off the rippling planet surface as a number of tall buildings tumbled down throughout the city. Some squatter ones caved. The street was gone in many areas, crashed into the subterranean levels of the city. It was a real mess. Aftershocks toppled a few more buildings. None of the ones still standing looked entirely intact.

Pez led her company on, with forty-seven other companies closing toward city central with her, spread in a three-mile arc. They had thirty-one injuries, though no deaths, from the quakes. Here on the city outskirts the streets were wide and the buildings low. The places where the streets collapsed had been the main danger. Space marine combat shuttles, Corvette Thunders, and Hunter-Terminators hovered above and flew over them, giving Pez and her troops aerial cover. Swenah was ready with all of *Apollo's* weapons to fry stuff from space.

They'd only gone a few hundred yards before taking fire from thousands of dug-in Imperial troops in combat suits. The allied small craft hovering and flying over the capital focused on the ground and hover vehicles as well as on heavy blaster tripods firing from window openings and rubble nests. Many of Pez's troops had bigger weapons too, not built into their suits, and fired back with their own tripod blasters and hover missile launchers. Others, less encumbered, rushed forward firing suit weapons. Pez was one of these.

Flying her suit at maximum acceleration between two support-beams of a fallen trestle, Pez lobbed a handheld thermal grenade into the lap of a heavy blaster gunner with excellent cover, except from right above, where the grenade landed from. He illuminated into separate particles, invisible but for the glow of their immense heat. Her blaster was already chewing through the weak point at the neck of an Imperial suit with an Imperial inside it. That didn't take long, and a missile launched from her suit struck a light armored hovercraft. Her missile's explosion clearly penetrated shields and armor, and that destruction was

A TALE OF THE TAIL OF NINE STARS

visible for just a moment before the whole thing burst into superheated expanding gas as its fuel cell went.

Another thermal grenade left her hand to go off just inside a third-story open window, shooting flames across the street, and another Imperial blaster-tripod was put out of business. Most of her company were struggling to keep up or catch up with her, though Evenrude had stuck beside her and Johnson was close, both of them pulverizing everything she didn't get. Schwin had her back too, five thousand feet above in Demeter 1, blowing shit up all around Pez as she went. Schwin's gunners were helping, and they'd even brought their drone pilot and a drone to the party. Swenah directed one of her gunners with a class-six blaster to waste a heavy armored vehicle headed toward Pez. It was a bit of an overkill, crumpling a section of street many levels into the subways, leaving no sign whatever of the vehicle.

Pez kept on determinedly, and so did all her space marines. Aerial support gave them an enormous advantage, and they progressed toward the main downtown area, where fire still raged out of control, filling the poisonous sky with brownish-red smoke from burning synthetic materials containing highlights of turquoise and bright green.

Evenrude wielded one of the big four missile shoulder launchers with one arm while firing a tripod blaster with the other. So far, he hadn't fired any of his suit's munitions. The space marine suits had been further weaponized by adding a forty-millimeter starburst grenade launcher with a sixty round magazine capable of full automatic fire and attaching four additional thermal hand grenades in easy reach of the operator inside.

Pez had her grenade launcher set for two round bursts and popped a pair into a small Imperial sixteen canister hover missile launcher, exploding all the missiles within. Another street section collapsed into the underground, taking a small building with it.

Schwin said, "Wow, I want to hit one of those when it's fully loaded!"

"I wasn't expecting that," Pez admitted, using forward propulsion to make up some of the distance the blast wave had just blown her back.

"Warn me before you do that again," Evenrude said.

Pez said defensively, "How was I supposed to know it hadn't fired any missiles yet? I didn't approach it face on and couldn't see into the canisters."

A quarter of a mile from the raging fires, all the action was belowground and the space marines lost their air cover. Powerful shields still protected this area from above, starting at ground level, which indicated that at least one deep underground reactor was operating. There was no damage down here *yet*, Pez was thinking, and it was heavily defended by Imperials. Facial recognition through a helmet visor had Mel screaming in Pez's ear, "The one with the blue emblem on the chest of his suit is the tenth most wanted war criminal in the entire empire!"

"Thanks, Mel," Pez said calmly as she took aim. "I've got him."

She used a two-round shot of starburst concussion grenades just to be sure. The concussion knocked the helmet off his suit with his head in it, and an armored limb downed an Imperial troop behind where he had been. Pez hadn't even slowed down to watch, trusting her premonition at the moment she'd launched the grenades.

Deeper into the Imperial labyrinth they pressed, now taking cover behind hover shields as they went. There were other entrances on the surface, and numerous companies of space marines were now headed down each of them. Three levels down, it became a maze, and platoons were sent down side tunnels as they proceeded, winning each meter by killing Imperials. The Trident troops were descending into tunnels to the other side of the fires. There were twenty-five thousand of them. Rally and Kluzyst troops were entering the city from the other two quarters and would be going into the tunnels from those ends.

The numbers of Imperials seemed to rise as they went deeper, but fewer had combat suits and so were easy to kill. Swenah told Pez from the *Apollo*, "The engineers have located the main intake vent for the gases they breathe, and Jard is recommending four tons of baking soda and a ton of stomach antacids to neutralize the acidity. He believes that will kill them."

"Like feeding them cleansers was going to keep them alive?" Pez inquired, while blowing through an Imperial soldier's thin neck armor with her big blaster, blowing his head off with a splash.

"A little more calculated than that," Swenah told her, hoping it was so.

"Tell him to go ahead, but it will dust our sensors and put a film on our face masks," Pez agreed with misgivings.

She saw a helmeted head pop up and launched two starbursts at it. The first blew right on the face mask and the second inside the helmet.

Fine white powder, and some diluted pink too, seemed to replace the gaseous interior of the corridor. She could see little piles of white powder collecting beneath the ceiling vents. Jard was clearly acting out his plan. She hoped it wasn't just his deluded fantasy this time, because her sensors had already lost more than 10 percent visibility and the sleeve of her suit merely smeared the white film across her face mask, making it a bit worse.

Another Imperial popped up, this one within arm's reach, and the point of Pez's carbon-edged adamantine sword sparked through shields and neck armor and neck to come out blue-black with Imperial residue. The non-suited Imperials looked healthy enough to Pez, breathing and digesting Jard's concoction, and her sensor visibility was down by 19 percent.

Space marine combat suits were white, only now they seem bleached; and the Aqua blue Imperial suits were also white, distinguishable only in outline and no longer by color. Pez put two starbursts into a heavy blaster gunner's chest, and great gobs of goo spewed out in a big spray. Vapors leaked from the large hole in the chest armor. Pez came to one wearing only a uniform. He was just breathing away, to her enormous frustration. She told Swenah, while double tapping him with her blaster, "Check with the Kluzyst what we ought to put down the vents and don't let Jard try any more household products. My suit already needs a lube job and a trip through the suit wash."

I'm doing that, sweetheart. I have their admiral on the line," Swenah explained. "We'll get something that works down those vents right away."

"Thanks, Swenah," Pez told her. She ducked back from throwing a thermal grenade into a chamber full of Imperials at workstations.

When she went into the big room, the wreckage was total. Everything had been melted together, and the blast ceiling was dripping big drops.

There was nothing left in there that could hold a flame as fuel. Pez pressed on, her visibility down to 76 percent. Her face mask was worse, and finally she sheathed her sword to rip the jacket off an unsuited corpse she'd just created with a headshot and cleaned her face mask off. She really needed wiper fluid, but the only liquid on this planet seemed to be bromine. She cleaned Evenrude's face mask while other space marines covered them.

Pez led on, Evenrude beside her with fresh missiles in his big launcher and a new magazine in his starburst launcher. He was like a walking platoon all by himself. Pez was improbably quick, uncannily intuitive, and entirely instinctive. She was also linked solid with the spiritual congress. Together they nailed everything Imperial they encountered, with hardly a drop in shields or a scorch. They knew the Kluzysts got it right with whatever they'd put down the intakes. They saw unsuited Imperials grabbing at their own throats, choking to death. As they expired, little visible vapor clouds escaped their mouths, shimmering.

Down more levels, in a vast chamber full of shield generators, the Imperials defended themselves with hover blasters, many in combat suits and the rest in space suits. A few had only goggles and respirators. Pez put two rounds of starbursts into a hover blaster, and it left a piece of its gravity redirection generator housing in the high chamber ceiling. She was already on to the next, blowing it to bits, and a blade of the propulsion drive half disintegrated passing through her shields, embedding itself in her hard shell. She noticed on her holo that it had come within a sixteenth of an inch of violating the integrity of her suit, but she was already launching a suit missile at another.

There certainly were many of the damn hover blasters. They were going down nicely to Evenrude's bigger blaster, and he was launching a missile now and then, blasting them into explosions. When his shoulder launcher was empty, he swung it one-handed like a bat into a hover blaster barrel, bending it so that the next shot caused it to blow itself up. He was wearing about half of it stuck in his combat suit after that, but Pez noticed his suit was still sealed and his shields came back up.

Pez's whole company and another were already inside, and more space marines were flowing into the vast interior of the room. The back of the space couldn't even be discerned. The Om suits were equipped with night vision as well as infrared, X-ray, radar, sonar and radio vision, all instantly quantum computer enhanced. The suits had lights too—wicked ones in fact—and Pez was almost hoping the room lights would fail. She set her starburst grenade launcher fire to single-shot semiautomatic to preserve ammo and was pleased to see that one still did the trick, only leaving a little more left on the floor. She called for a reloader hover as she spent her last suit missile on the hover blaster she was firing her blaster into. She got it.

When the reloader came, Pez let Evenrude go first so she could spend her last four starbursts before reloading. She ran out before he was done, but he used his big blaster to cover them, wasting two hover blasters, while the reloader finished its job. He grabbed a new power cell for the big blaster out of the reloader's arsenal drawer, ejected his spent one, and popped the new one in. His four-tube launcher was wrecked, so he scooped up a twenty-millimeter automatic pistol with armor-piercing explosive rounds and a ninety-round magazine, taking an extra magazine as well.

Pez got her suit rearmed and drew her sword. She fired her starbursts and missiles with her skullcap. The hover blasters were becoming thick and were everywhere. They were also blowing up everywhere. Johnson got a twenty-millimeter automatic pistol in each hand, with spare magazines hooked to his combat suit.

The space marine training was shining through, and they impressed Pez, inspiring her. Almost at once, some thirty operators of hover blasters had micro-suns on their shoulders, and some of these were shooting their comrades blindly. Pez poked her sword up a propulsion discharge nozzle of a hover blaster, and parts went flying everywhere, making her look like a mini Evenrude. Pez pressed on with purpose, further into the unknown depths of the space, with seemingly limitless hover blasters ahead and enormous piles of scrap and charred bits behind her. Evenrude's twenty-millimeter gun was set to three round bursts after finding two-rounders to be unreliable. His big blaster turned them into small hardware and shrapnel in less than two seconds, and he was on a roll. Pez had already decided she was going to get one of those twenty millimeter automatic pistols too, the next time the reloader came, feeling a little envious.

By the time Pez had six companies in the shield generator chamber, engineers were at work disabling each one individually. Trident troops had continued down to deeper levels and had come upon the main barracks of this military facility and its main environmental machinery. The Kluzyst and Rally troops were still fighting their way down.

An Imperial on an extra-large hover blaster blew a hole through one of Pez's space marines, and missiles she'd hit him with had exploded harmlessly on his enhanced shields. Mel was yelling in her ear, "He's number five, the fifth most wanted!"

Evenrude hit the SOB with full automatic starbursts, full automatic twenty millimeter rounds, and his big blaster, while Pez added her smaller blaster, another missile, and a three-round grenade burst. She told Mel, "Scratch number five."

Number five's explosion, between his enhanced hovercraft, bigger blaster, and enhanced suit, took the hover blasters to either side with it, making it even bigger. This also allowed them to advance ten more meters. At the same moment bay doors in the high ceiling opened, a horde of hover blasters swarmed in from above and Mel was screaming, "Number four!"

Pez called for the reloader as she set her starburst launcher to full auto and identified the enhanced craft and large blaster out of the horde, targeting it. Another one of her space marines, standing next to her, went down. Evenrude fired his twenty-millimeter gun and starburst on full automatic, with missiles popping out of his suit launcher, as he rose on his propulsion to make himself a more attractive target than Pez.

She was already putting starbursts, missiles, and blaster fire into number four as fast as the suit could go. Her four missiles were away at once, and her starbursts were counting down fast. Another space marine targeted number four with starburst auto fire and a missile. This tipped the scales, turning number four into about a trillion.

Mel was celebrating in Pez's ear. Those damn hover blasters were still spilling out of the ceiling and where was her reloader? She pierced the exhaust of another hover blaster with her sword from behind, through the shields, to get sent with the shock wave some twenty meters into a generator, momentarily taking her shields down.

Before she could blink, Evenrude was shielding her and firing everything while screaming for a reloader. Pez was screaming to her space marine commander, "Get Om hover blasters and hover shields in here immediately—and get me more damn reloaders!"

"The hover shields and blasters are in the room with you now, speeding to your front line, and I'm dispatching all the loaders we have left. Reinforcements are pouring in to you."

Just then, forty space marine hover blasters and at least fifty hover missile launchers rose halfway to the ceiling with coordinated fire up through the bay doors. A hail of missiles and starbursts began showering up through it from the ground so that the Imperial hovercraft stopped raining down. Flame scorched the floor below the bay doors, exploding shield generators like popping corn. In moments, the cave-in started filling the chamber with rock and dirt like a flash flood. Pez shouted with panicked authority, "Retreat! Get out!"

A space marine lieutenant near the doors to the chamber cleared the personnel out swiftly while directing a group of engineers to set up various fog and signal lights over the exit so people could find it in the haze. The dust was already making visibility difficult, even this far back from what had been the bay doors in the ceiling at the cave-in.

The lights did help, but not nearly as much as Mel's personalized instructions to each and every space marine still in the chamber, directing them and providing navigation. Pez's visibility was at a hundredth of 1 percent, and only X-ray gave her a clue, so she relied on Mel, who told her, "No stupid. Your other left!"

Finally, the big piercing lights over the entrance came into view and Pez tuned Mel out. The big piercing lights turned out to be less than ten feet away, and once out of the exit, Pez was back listening carefully to Mel. The dust was thick as molasses, and the dirt continued to pour in, filling the generator chamber like water, threatening to bury the entire facility.

Pez ordered, "Get to higher ground!"

Elevators and lifts ground and crunched in the dust, and dirt accumulated on their moving tracks, freezing between levels. Evenrude pulled Pez by the arm to an emergency stairwell, all steel and full of eerie echoes. Once inside, it seemed infinite in both directions. They chose the endlessly up direction, and within just a few cutbacks, they could see the dust and dirt descending as they rose above it. This was not the only stairwell. There were also ladders of steel attached to the wall going up, though Pez couldn't imagine climbing a ladder that far. Neither could the space marines at the ladders, who were using up their propulsion going directly vertical for the top.

Reports streamed in to Pez. She was relieved to hear that all her forces had made it out of the shield generator chamber and were making for higher ground. The generator room had now filled completely, and many of thousands of cubic feet of dirt and rocks were being pushed through and out the exits per minute, under millions of tons of pressure, pouring downward to fill the lower levels.

Pez led them all the way to the level just below the surface. The space marines now had some of their own big surface craft and heavy armored hover tanks with class-eight blaster cannons. She coordinated with the forces from Trident, Rally, and the Kluzyst, while the endless levels descending filled, proving to be as finite as the levels above.

Even as the liquifacted dirt and rock rose higher than the level of the cave-in, the pressure was not nearly equalized and the firmament continued to behave like a fluid. Once the rising tide peaked, the pressure finally settled; the sludge and dirt were only four levels below the one in which Pez stood, and the dust continued to rise as if the vacuum of space were sucking it up.

Eventually, the surviving Imperial troops offered up their commanding officers, all trussed and wrapped nicely, as a token of unconditional surrender. They even threw in the heads of a few officers they'd had to kill. When the dust settled, hundreds of most wanted war criminals had been apprehended or shot. The manhunts continued. The allies had 326,500 troops in space combat suits on the ground.

Swenah and her weapons operators made surgical strikes at military bases, spaceports, airbases, outposts, and outbuildings, and even individual personnel, from low orbit, as did at least fifty other ships. There were 2,500 small combat spacecraft supporting the troops on the ground, while another 750 ran search patterns at twenty thousand feet altitude with continuously active scans.

More Kluzyst were arriving constantly with more troop transports and suited troops, as well as every variety of emergency services provider fully equipped. The interstellar Blue Cross Relief Foundation was also descending upon the Imperial capital world. Hundreds of thousands of service workers were on their way as well, to inventory and distribute the massive accumulation of wealth on the planet. The citizens were still collecting into their surrender zones.

Food and temporary shelter were provided and improvised to keep the population out of the way so redistribution could progress unhindered. Thousands of enormous empty freighters circled in holding patterns, from extremely low orbit to way out past the farthest moon, and more were on the way.

Cargo shuttle traffic became immensely thick. The efficiency of these labors was record-breaking. A thousand tons per hour were lifting off the planet within an hour of commencing operations and ten thousand by two hours after that. Humungous container barges with huge gravity redirection generators were towed into space by liftoff tugs and unloaded into super container ships by portable space platform cranes. Cargo shuttles the size of fast attack ships, and even destroyers, were landing and lifting off from every wealth and resource depository on the planet.

At Pez's insistence, hungry planets were the first recipients of the goods lifting off. Priceless art and planetary treasures were beginning to find their way back to their rightful planets. Much within the coffers was earmarked or headed to slave worlds as relief aid, and much high-tech machinery and equipment were on their way to those worlds as well.

Educational classes on how to work for a living were offered to the citizens at the surrender camps. Some of the smart ones attended, knowing they were going to need these now that their wealth and slaves were gone. Testimonials from slaves on the planet resulted in about a hundred thousand more war criminals being rounded up either dead or alive.

Some fancy yachts jumped into the system full of financial sharks, looking for an angle to exploit, and the owners turned out to be on the list, so Pez ordered her Corvette Thunders that were out on patrol to use them as target practice. The yachts were fast, and one almost reached jump speed, but the Corvettes took care of them.

The Kluzyst finally had so many troops on the surface, some four hundred thousand of just their own, that Pez was able to recall her space marines to the troop transport and *Apollo*. Rally troops would be staying, and Trident troops planned to abide for some time. A meeting of the top-ranking officers for allied forces was called for a brief post-victory discussion and to solidify plans for the future. The Om ships prepared to leave the star system and to stop off at Earth on their way home.

32

What was left of the Om mission fleet and its reinforcements went at auxiliary ship pace to accelerate for their jump to Earth, and while Konax felt like he was driving a double-decker hover bus, Swenah felt as if she were having a ride in a hay wagon. Pez was singing to Electra, who somehow seemed more contented these days and had been less fussy of late. Most of the repairs had been handled during their sojourn in the Gzzklns system. Some things would simply have to wait until they got home to Om.

Earth welcomed them with open arms and the keys to the planet, as saviors and heroes. Pez and her spouses were put up in the penthouse at the Ritz Supreme Ultimate Hotel as guests, and the Random Comets played there every night. The parties were beyond wild, and Pez was such great fun on drugs. They got her into one of those two-and-a-half-gram dresses that couldn't cover both groin and breasts at the same time, and it was bunched around her lower rib cage by the end of the night. Mel was there in her android body.

Earth bestowed on Pez something called an offshore high-yield numbered account, with an awful lot of damn numbers in it and a great quantity of something called shares in a hedge fund. Pez didn't have a clue since such things didn't exist on Om, but since Ahhu was so impressed over it, she gave them to her, along with all the real estate, sprinkled through the most desired hot spots on the planet, she'd received.

She kept the twenty-pound platinum plaque engraved with her image and a bunch of Earth words. She also kept the trophy of solid gold they'd given her, replicating her Astro-Phantom heavy bomber in miniature scale, only twenty-one inches in diameter. She'd need Evenrude to lift and carry it. She thought it would look nice in her martial arts trophy case.

Cotex had worn her nearly invisible two-piece swimsuit to one of the after-parties with the Random Comets, and Pez was certain it had to weigh less than a gram, big as she was. Her pole dancing had progressed to the very heights of skillful attraction.

Sarhi had made Pez pump milk for days before the Earth extravaganza to spare Electra the drugs, and as the fleet was headed out of the Earth star system, Pez and her spouses were coming out of their fogs. Pez told Swenah, "Set course for Vox, not Om. We have a few little things to clean up in the Hub Galaxy before we go home. After Vox, we'll be paying that human Imperial capital star system of Kundabuffer a little visit."

"Without the High Council's approval?" Swenah inquired.

"By the approval of a far higher authority than that, Admiral."

With a grin expressing tremendous satisfaction, Swenah told her, "Aye, aye, ma'am."

APPENDICES

Nuclear Fusion Materials
Marsnium
Saturnium x 10
Venusium x 10
Mercurium x 10
Solarium x 100

Beam and Blaster Weapons Classes
Class one: 500 or fewer kilowatts
Class two: 500–1,000 kilowatts
Class three: 10–300 megawatts
Class four: 300–600 megawatts
Class five: 600–1,000 megawatts
Class six: 200–300 gigawatts
Class seven: 300–600 gigawatts
Class eight: 600–1,000 gigawatts
Class nine: two or more terawatts (Om class nine are
100–300 terawatts)

Ships of the Pez Armada

Vachisy Empire of the Kluzyst Race in Xegachtznel Galaxy
Nine Classes of Ships: Tubular

Class Size and Number of Reactors
Class one: 3-mile length, 32 fusion super-reactors
Class two: 2-mile length, 20 fusion super-reactors
Class three: 1.25-mile length, 14 fusion super-reactors
Class four: 5,000-foot length, 9 fusion super-reactors
Class five: 3,900-foot length, 8 fusion super-reactors
Class six: 2,700-foot length, 6 fusion super-reactors
Class seven: 1,900-foot length, 4 fusion super-reactors
Class eight: 1,130-foot length, 3 fusion super-reactors
Class nine: 590-foot length, 1 fusion super-reactor

Om Ships

1 x   ORH Super Battleship-Carrier 9,630' diameter, 28 fusion super-reactors

1x   ORH Super battleship 8,100-foot diameter, 30 fusion super-reactors

2x   T-Nine Super-Star Cruiser 3,960-foot diameter, 12 fusion super-reactors

6x   Orion Spacecraft Carrier 1,080-foot diameter, 4 fusion super-reactors

7x   Orion Battleship 870-foot diameter, 5 fusion super-reactors

11x   Orion Star Cruiser 690-foot diameter, 2 fusion super-reactors

24x   Orion Destroyer 390-foot diameter, 1 fusion super-reactor

36x   Orion Fast Attack 280-foot diameter, 0.75 equivalent of a super-reactor

Om Small Spacecraft
J-8 Corvette Thunder fighter, SMCS Commando Combat Shuttle
NBC Hunter-Terminator fighter-bomber, XPS Astro-Phantom bomber
Diplomatic Stingray Shuttle

Trident Star System and Allied Systems from
the Yuban Galaxy Combat Ships
Long and Triangular Configurations

Number in Armada, Class Size, Number of Reactors

1x   Super Battleship-Carrier 10,800 feet, 28 fusion super-reactors

2x   Super Battleship 8,700 feet, 28 fusion super-reactors

4x   Battleship Spacecraft Carrier 1,000 feet, 3 fusion super-reactors

6x   Battleship 900 feet, 4 fusion super-reactors

5x   Heavy Cruiser 600 feet, 2 fusion super-reactors

3x   Light Cruiser 580 feet, 2 fusion super-reactors

14x   Destroyer 440 feet, 1.5 fusion super-reactors

28x   Sloop 370 feet, 1 fusion super-reactor

Rally Star System of Xegachtznel Galaxy, Combat Ships
Tubular Configuration

Number in Armada, Class Size, Number of Reactors

2x   Super Battleship Carrier 5,415 feet, 9 fusion super-reactors

2x   Super Battleship 5,280 feet, 9 fusion super-reactors

4x   Battleship Carrier 1,110 feet, 3 fusion super-reactors

6x   Battleship 870 feet, 3 fusion super-reactors

5x   Battle Cruiser 690 feet, 2.5 fusion super-reactors

3x   Light Battle Cruiser 672 feet, 2.5 fusion super-reactors

14x   Assault Frigate 496 feet, 2 fusion super-reactors

8x   Fast Attack 388 feet, 1 fusion super-reactor

28x   Scout Recon 318 feet, .75 equivalent of super-reactor

AUTHOR BIOGRAPHY

Lawrence Stentzel III received his BA in philosophy from Antioch College West and his MA in integral counselling psychology from The California Institute of Integral Studies. He earned his psychotherapy license and served Solano County Mental Health for 25 years as a clinical supervisor in charge of the 24-hour Crisis Service and ran two forensic mental health programs for mentally ill offenders. He started sitting zazen in 1973, became a member of the Arica mystical school in 1975, embarked on his study and practice of T'ai Chi Ch'uan in 1977, and his Taoist studies in 1978. He is also a practitioner of the tantric system of the Six Yogas of Naropa.

CPSIA information can be obtained
at www.ICGtesting.com
Printed in the USA
LVHW09s0905180918
590460LV00001B/4/P